THE
Regency
BRIDES
COLLECTION

Seven Romances Set in England During the Early Nineteenth Century

THE
Regency
BRIDES
COLLECTION

Michelle Griep, Nancy Moser,
Erica Vetsch, MaryLu Tyndall,
Amanda Barratt, Angela Bell, Susanne Dietze

BARBOUR BOOKS
An Imprint of Barbour Publishing, Inc.

Print ISBN 978-1-68322-371-9

eBook Editions:
Adobe Digital Edition (.epub) 978-1-68322-373-3
Kindle and MobiPocket Edition (.prc) 978-1-68322-372-6

Published by Barbour Books, an imprint of Barbour Publishing, Inc., P.O. Box 719, Uhrichsville, Ohio 44683, www.barbourbooks.com.

Our mission is to publish and distribute inspirational products offering exceptional value and biblical encouragement to the masses.

ecpa Member of the
Evangelical Christian
Publishers Association

Printed in Canada.

Contents

First Comes Marriage by Amanda Barratt 7
Masquerade Melody by Angela Bell 75
Three Little Matchmakers by Susanne Dietze 135
The Gentleman Smuggler's Lady by Michelle Griep. 197
When I Saw His Face by Nancy Moser. 259
The Highwayman's Bargain by MaryLu Tyndall. 337
Jamie Ever After by Erica Vetsch 391

First Comes Marriage

by Amanda Barratt

Dedication

To the incomparable Jane Austen and Charlotte Brontë
for penning captivating and romantic novels
that have fueled my own British-set stories.

And to Jesus—who forgives, loves, and always redeems.

Chapter One

June 1811
London

A lady never sallied forth unchaperoned. Least of all to a place with the reputation of Vauxhall Gardens.

For most of her seventeen years, Charity Stanwood had considered herself a lady. Yet the term could carry with it a most inconvenient mantle. Ladies sat in the parlor beside their mamas, embroidering or talking of new ball gowns. Ladies did not court scandal, venturing out by way of bedroom windows to seek the company of gentlemen with less than spotless reputations.

But then, no young lady of her acquaintance—that she knew of, anyway—had ever found herself under the spell of Percy Browne.

Clutching his arm, moving through the elegantly—and not so elegantly—dressed crowd, Charity's nerves fairly sizzled with the excitement of it all.

"It's wonderful, Percy!" She lifted a hand to ascertain that the diamond comb securing her hair remained in place.

"We've only just begun to taste the delights tonight has to offer." Resplendent in regimentals, Percy cut a figure handsome enough to flutter the heart of even the most demure female. He leaned toward her, overwhelming her with the scent of mandarin.

Thank goodness Charity had ceased thinking of herself as demure. The barest inhale was enough to send scorching heat eddying through her body. And they hadn't even begun to sample the arrack punch, a beverage known to make even the stodgiest matron giddy as a schoolgirl.

A giggle leaked out as she playfully disengaged her arm from his and sidestepped away. "Oh, Percy. You say the most shocking things."

He reached out and captured her waist. "I do apologize. Vauxhall always addles my brain. Must be something in the air."

In the novels she furtively read when no one was watching, many a passage described the way a gentleman's eyes smoldered as he gazed upon the object of his affections. Charity drew in a breathless gasp. At that moment, looking down at her, Percy's eyes utterly and undoubtedly smoldered.

"'Tis only the air that affects you so?" She dipped her chin and fluttered her lashes—another novel-learned tactic. Novels were really all she had to rely upon for advice on how to attract a man. Other than her secret meetings with Percy, her knowledge of the male species was limited to dancing a quadrille while chaperones looked on or allowing herself to be escorted into dinner by some potential suitor handpicked by her papa.

"Little minx." The warmth of his hands seared through the scanty muslin of her gown. "You know full well the power you have over me."

Power. What a delicious word. And he'd admitted it. She, debutante, held power over Percy Browne, soldier and well-known rogue!

"Do I indeed?" Her voice emerged as a breathy whisper, her heart beating in time with the jaunty music coming from the direction of the pavilion. No gothic novelist could have written a better beginning to a proposal. For surely such words as his could only be followed with a declaration.

If her mind wasn't so muddled by his intense gaze, she'd have turned it to deciding which young ladies of her acquaintance would make the best bridesmaids.

"Shall I prove it to you?" Without waiting for her answer, he maneuvered her away from the brightly lit pavilion. Lamps hanging from stands and on trees lit the air with shadows, and the lapping of the River Thames lent magic to the balmy summer night.

Excitement thudded in her chest as they turned down one of the secluded paths, placed in convenient isolation for those wishing to find privacy amidst the cacophony of fellow guests. She clung to his arm, hurrying to keep up with his strides. Her eyes widened as they passed other couples in the throes of behavior sure to elicit a fainting spell should the redoubtable matrons of London discover their newest debutantes' whereabouts.

Did people really do such things in public? Here she'd thought that simply accompanying Percy to such a place reached a dizzying height of scandal.

A hint of trepidation snaked through her. Perhaps there were some bounds when it came to propriety. But despite Percy's reputation, he was a gentleman at heart. She was sure of it.

Yet why would a gentleman take her here?

He stopped. Fireworks exploded overhead, sending a shower of stars cascading across the night sky. Charity's breath caught at the brilliant display—golds and reds and blues melding together in shimmering arcs of color.

She glanced at Percy, her back bumping up against a row of tall bushes. He didn't seem at all enamored by the celestial show, his gaze riveted on her.

Sweet victory. What were trifling hesitations and simpleminded proprieties when this man looked at her with such ardor? Nonsense. Errant nonsense, that's what. A tempting smile found purchase on her lips. The sizzling heat of his pursuit far exceeded that of any simpering milksop found at the side of her fellow debutantes.

"I do declare. Vauxhall is certainly a—"

Her next words were cut off as his lips descended upon hers, just as another explosion suffused the sky. A gasp escaped as his hands skimmed down her shoulders, settling on her waist.

She might be a master when it came to flirtatious glances and coy words. But in this, he possessed the experience, and she was far out of her depth. His kisses bred fire within her, evoking sensations as delicious as they were foreign. Head tilted back, she surrendered to his caresses, senses swimming as his hand moved to the collar of her gown—

"Charity Stanwood?"

The voice produced a jolt similar to a tub full of ice water being tossed upon a drunkard. Percy spun 'round. Charity's gaze snapped up.

And landed upon disaster in human form. Lady Drucilla Blackthorne stood, rooted to the spot, a jeweled lorgnette held up to one squinting eye.

"Lady Blackthorne." As if by rote, Charity's knees dipped into a curtsy. When she stood again at her full height, she scanned the darkened pathway.

Percy, her dashing soldier hero, had disappeared.

"Charity Stanwood! You will come with me this instant. This instant, I say!" The enormous feather atop her coiffure jiggling royally, Lady Blackthorne stormed forward and grasped Charity, nails digging into her skin like a trap closing in over a frightened rabbit.

Caught with Percy by Lady Blackthorne, London's most notorious gossipmonger.

Though Lady Blackthorne's claws would surely leave bruises, Charity scarcely heeded the pain as the woman hauled her along the path.

Physical pain could be borne.

It was nothing compared to what society would do to her when word of her ruination leaked out and reached their ears. Society liked nothing more than to make a meal of others' misfortunes.

Tonight, she'd given them plenty to feast upon.

◦◦◦

"Enter."

Luke Warren opened the door to his father's study and stepped inside. Rand Warren sat behind a mahogany desk strewn with papers, books, and writing utensils. He looked up from his hunched-over position and flattened both palms on the glossy surface.

Luke crossed the carpeted floor. Whatever his father wanted, Luke hoped it wouldn't take long to conclude. Tomorrow morning, he would be leaving to join his ship, and his mates were waiting for him down at the Red Lion for a send-off, a finale the likes of which he doubted he'd enjoy when once again ensconced in strict military discipline—though since he joined the ship as captain, some leeway would surely be allowed him.

A rule-maker instead of a dictate-follower. Finally.

"You wished to see me, sir?"

"I did." His father lit a cheroot, infusing the air with the scent of smoke. "Care for a brandy, Son?" He gestured with the cheroot to a side table near the desk, atop which rested an array of decanters and glasses.

Behind his back, Luke's hands clenched and unclenched.

Just get on with it, old man. And the quicker the better.

"No, thank you. What was it you wished to discuss?"

"In a hurry, eh?" His father's eyes—the same dusky blue shade as Luke's—lit with a knowing gleam.

"Somewhat, sir." Luke lifted his mouth in a sheepish grin. Father would understand Luke's desire for a night with his friends. Father had once been young too, after all, and would soon finish the conversation and let Luke get on with his evening.

He shifted with anticipation.

"I'm sorry to spoil your fun, but you might as well send 'round a note to whomever you were planning on meeting." Father took another drag, smoke wisping through the air above his head, expression neutral as if oblivious to the wet blanket he'd just dropped upon Luke's plans for a jolly good evening.

Luke's jaw hardened. Blast the man. What could be so deuced important to warrant ruining a night's pleasure?

"I'll get straight to the point, so as not to take up more of your valuable time than necessary."

Too late for that. Luke resisted the urge to roll his eyes.

"When you were a schoolboy, we, the Warren family"—Schoolboy? What was this, a rundown of his father's entire life story? Honestly? Chet and Granby would roar with laughter when they heard what had kept him—"possessed a comfortable amount of prosperity." A frown knit Father's forehead. An unexplainable tightness cinched Luke's middle. Something about the man's expression boded ill tidings.

"Since then, however, we've run into some difficulties. Not large ones, at first, but they've become increasingly so."

"What are you saying?" Luke drew in a deep breath. Somehow, he sensed he'd regret asking this question.

"We've got debts, Son. Creditors. Our mine holdings in Cornwall—well, we haven't discovered any more copper in a good while. The old Jenbrugh load has failed us, bled dry it seems. And you know as well as I do that mining has been the lifeblood of this family, kept your sister in gowns and fripperies, paid your navy expenses, and allowed us to keep on a number of staff. At times, I confess, I've been close to despair, wondering how, when the day comes, I'll tell Harriet we can't afford to foot a dinner for five and twenty. But today, something happened. Something that could pull us back from the brink and get us back on the road to a new start."

"And this something concerns me?" Why hadn't Father told him things were so dire? Luke could have done something. Delayed the purchase of a new riding horse, spent less time at the card tables and more time with his family. He hadn't known. Hadn't suspected even a scrap.

Well, Father had told him now. Now, on the eve of his departure to serve again in His Majesty's navy after taking a three-month leave of absence. Now, when he could do nothing about it. The twist of events was as bitter as it was unexpected.

"It does. In fact, it concerns you more than anyone else. I need your help, Son. You can go a long way in saving us." Father's gaze pierced him, and Luke couldn't help but stand a little straighter. Now that he had attained his two-and-twentieth birthday, Father had at last begun treating him like a man, instead of a stripling playing at seafaring adventures. Pride drummed in his chest. He wouldn't trade this for Chet and Granby's sendoff, nor for anything.

"Just tell me what to do."

"A man came to me this afternoon. John Stanwood, the creditor to whom I owe the most. Three years ago, I took out a loan from his bank, one that came with a substantial amount of interest. Since then, I've only managed to pay the interest, while continuing to take out a further loan at an even higher rate. Today, he paid a call and brought along the promissory note." A gleam lit Father's gaze. A gleam of hope. "He offered to pay the debt out of his own pocket, in full. The debt amounts to ten thousand pounds."

Ten thousand pounds! The vastness of the sum was staggering. Father, under such an obligation? It might as well amount to ten million. But John Stanwood had offered to cancel it, just like that. Something deeper was at play here. Luke's scalp prickled.

"And what does he expect in return?"

Father rubbed a hand across his forehead, shadows from the roaring fire in the hearth accentuating the gray at his temples, the haggard hollows under his eyes. "He wishes you to wed his daughter, Miss Charity Stanwood."

"What?" Last week when Chet had imbibed one too many cupfuls of arrack punch, he'd begun waving his hands wildly and talking as if his dead nanny and old schoolmates stood in front of him. It made reasonable sense, hearing things when under the influence of strong drink.

But Luke hadn't touched a drop all day. Which meant he wasn't hearing things. And that Father spoke truth.

"I know it sounds ridiculous. But it seems the young lady got herself into an entanglement that has led to rather a lot of gossip. Her father wishes her reputation to remain above reproach and feels that having her wed will stay the wagging tongues." He made a weak gesture toward the papers littering his desk. "We each have something the other lacks. Stanwood wants respectability for his family, while we are more than a bit short when it comes to ready capital at the moment."

Luke paced back and forth across the carpet as if his life depended upon traversing from one end of the room to the other. Suddenly, a dram of brandy sounded like a very good idea. But he wouldn't risk muddling his senses. Not when he needed them crystal clear.

He halted in front of the fireplace, facing his father. "You're telling me that John Stanwood expects me to wed his daughter because she got herself into a muck befitting a trollop? The man is outrageous! Besides, I'm leaving tomorrow at first light."

"I told him that. He's already arranged a special license, and the marriage will take place at her home in approximately two hours." He levered himself from his chair and moved to get a glass of amber liquid. Apparently, Father wasn't burdened with reservations about pouring a drink. Luke's fingers itched to do the same.

"I'll say one thing for him. He's not one to waste time." Luke swiveled to face the fireplace while Father downed his drink. Marriage was for staid bachelors who'd had plenty of time to enjoy the freedom of a single life. Not for Luke, hours away from embarking upon his career after years of slogging away as a cabin boy, midshipman, and lieutenant. Though he enjoyed a flirtation well enough, liked making ladies blush and twirling them 'round the dance floor, he was by no means interested in taking a wife. Why, a songbird in a cage possessed more freedom than a married man.

Footsteps sounded behind him, a touch rested on his shoulder. Luke turned and found Father at his side, one hand holding his empty glass. "I wouldn't ask it of you if things weren't so desperate. Goodness knows I don't like the thought of you wed to a woman we know so little of. But I can't help but think what release from the debt would bring to our family." The man's shoulders sagged as if weighted down by all the copper the Jenbrugh load had ever produced. "I'm not asking you, Son. I'm begging you."

Physical battle was a thing Luke welcomed, thirsted after even. Yet the emotional battle warring within him made him long to shake it off and rid himself of it the way one would an uncomfortable coat at the tailor's.

He'd met Miss Charity Stanwood. Once, at a ball. It had been the sort of introduction typical of such evenings—how-do-you-dos and all that nonsense. Even though it had been only a few weeks ago, he could scarcely remember her face. Nor any other distinguishing features about her. She was a typical debutante, dressed in white muslin as they all were.

So she'd gotten herself embroiled in scandal? Well, what did one expect when most girls of his acquaintance possessed naught but air where their brains should have been?

Not exactly the sort of woman he wanted to bind himself to.

But he wouldn't have to do more than sign the marriage certificate, at least not for a good while. His duties in the navy would occupy him for a year, perhaps more. Then after he'd tangled with whatever enemy ordered him by the British military, he could better decide what sort of life he would lead. He wouldn't have to see her. Not much, anyway. They could have a paper marriage, nothing more. It was what the chit deserved, getting herself into a heap of scandal.

And in marrying her, his family would be given financial footing otherwise denied them. He couldn't, in good conscience, turn his back on their needs.

He lifted his gaze, meeting his father's straight on. Man-to-man they faced each other, silence hanging for the space of a few seconds. Luke drew in a long breath of air that smelled of smoke, ink, and raw tension.

"Consider yourself freed from debt, Father." The swords of reason and desire filled his mind with their clash and clang, evidence that the battle had not been won, only subdued. He needed something, anything, to alleviate the deafening noise. For there was no way he'd manage the wedding otherwise.

"Thank you." Father gripped Luke's hand, a look of trust, of gratitude full on his features.

"Don't thank me." Luke returned the handshake. "Just pour me a brandy."

Chapter Two

The taste of consequences proved a bitter tincture to swallow. And like a child being presented with a spoonful of castor oil, Charity desired nothing more than to gag and spit out the nasty taste brought on by the aftermath of her behavior.

"No," she whispered. "I shan't do it." Tears streaked her cheeks, her hair falling in tangled strands over her shoulders. "You cannot make me."

Her papa generally wore a mask of flinty sternness. Yet as he faced her in her bedchamber, eyes cold as ice and hard as granite, his usual expression seemed almost genial.

"It's either this or Scotland with Great-aunt Tabitha. Your choice." His tone held not the slightest shred of compassion, though she did detect a touch of weariness. Not that she cared two straws for her papa's fatigue. Why should she, when he arranged her future as if her own feelings on the subject held the weight of a puff pastry?

"Please, Papa." Rising from her place atop her rumpled bed, she fell to her knees and grasped his hands. Giant sobs engulfed her as she raised her eyes to his. Surely she could get him to see reason. Surely he didn't actually expect her to marry a man she knew less about than she did Alfred, the hall boy. "I'm sorry. . .for what happened. On my honor, I swear to you, it shall never occur again—"

"Your honor?" He tugged his fingers free, her strength no match for his. "In society's eyes, you have none, Charity. I'm sorry to be so blunt, but 'tis time you faced the truth. Now get up off the floor and stop sniveling. It's useless when all has been put into motion. You're seventeen years old, and it's time you behaved like the lady you were raised to be." His voice brooked no argument. His touch, however, as he took her hand and helped her stand, was gentle.

He passed her a clean, folded handkerchief and watched as she wiped her eyes and blew her nose. She crumpled the cotton in her fist and refused to look at him. As if she wasn't already enough ashamed at her actions and tears. She didn't need to look into his censure-filled gaze and compound her misery.

"That's better. You have half an hour to ready yourself and come downstairs. I'll send your maid up." His footsteps sounded across the carpet, then halted as if he'd paused. "Your mother, God rest her, would be saddened by your actions. But she would be proud indeed to see you wed to a member of the Warren family." In the next instant, the door clicked shut.

She needed solitude. But it was not to be granted. Her maid, Wilkes, bustled in scarce minutes later.

"Master says I'm to prepare you for a wedding. In half an hour, no less. Though how I'll manage in that short a time, I don't know." Like a flustered poodle, the woman scampered across the room, her chatter high-pitched and grating as the barking of the dog she shared so many characteristics with.

Charity stood woodenly, watching her maid's frantic attempts to choose a dress. What did any of it matter? What import did a frock hold at a marriage solemnized in dark of night? It wasn't as if her friends would be there to see and admire. Had this been some social event, she'd be at Wilkes's side, debating which gown matched which jewels best. Yet even fashion, a near obsession with Charity, couldn't rouse her from the thick fog of despair.

Her papa had been furious when Lady Blackthorne arrived and announced in a tone syrupy with false compassion what she had witnessed between Charity and Mr. Browne. Not that he'd shown any outward sign of it, listening to Lady Blackthorne without a word. But the moment the woman had departed, he'd pierced Charity with a look that seemed to plumb the depths of her soul and expose the filthy darkness of her actions. He'd turned on his heel and stalked away, while she secreted herself in her bedchamber. She'd expected him to berate her with a lecture, perhaps even an announcement that they were quitting London for a time. She'd been prepared with penitence, assurances of her sorrow over her actions, and promises that such would never take place again.

Instead he'd informed her she could go to the uppermost part of Scotland and become a companion to her great-aunt, a dodgy old lady who never stepped beyond the confines of her little village.

Or she could marry Rand Warren's son.

Catching a glimpse of her reflection in the cheval looking glass, she pressed her lips together. The gown her maid had chosen was one Charity had not yet worn, and with good reason. Pastel blue did not do her justice, and the frock hung wrong, as if the seamstress had neglected to fit it properly.

But she hadn't the least desire to comment upon it and seated herself at her dressing table for Wilkes to arrange the mass of golden curls that now looked dull and mangy. Was it only yesterday she'd sat in the same place, marveling at their loveliness, how they caught the light and glistened when smoothed and coiffed. She'd fancied herself one of the greatest beauties in London, sure to garner marriage proposals from a dozen titled bachelors by her eighteenth birthday.

She let her eyes fall shut as Wilkes pulled a comb through her hair. Well, she'd gotten a marriage proposal. Though how her papa had arranged it at such short notice, she hadn't the faintest idea. To her knowledge, she'd never met Luke Warren. Of course, she could have forgotten, his face drowned out amongst the cadre of others that had courted and danced with her during her debut season. A shiver prickled the exposed skin on the back of her neck. What if he was a corpulent mass of flesh who popped a button on his waistcoat whenever he so much as breathed? The shiver snaked downward. Or worse, what if he were a brute who wasn't above using his fists if she didn't please him. Hadn't she noticed Mrs. Sedgefield using cosmetics to conceal her bruises?

Charity didn't know anything. That was the terror of it. But by the hour's end, it would all be over. She would be his wife, bound to him and his obesity, his temperament, or whatever else made up his character. After the vows were said, all chance of escape would vanish.

Her throat tightened. Had this been one of her novels, Percy would be at the door this very instant, her brave knight to rescue and defend her honor. But a knight would never have left his lady to fend for herself against the machinations of Lady Blackthorne.

So that hope also had been lost.

All too soon, Wilkes put the finishing touches on the ringlets framing Charity's face. At least her hair was neat and properly arranged, though there was naught to be done about the redness under her eyes and around her nose.

"Pretty as a picture, if I do say so myself." Wilkes smiled.

Charity stood, smoothing a hand down the front of her horrid gown. The clock on the mantle announced her tardiness. Already a quarter of an hour late.

She couldn't bring herself to hasten to the door, so she settled upon taking one step at a time. Wilkes stood by the dressing table, hands folded in front of her voluminous apron. Charity couldn't manage a smile for the woman. Her lips just wouldn't curve upward. Still, Wilkes had done her best, no questions asked.

"Thank you, Wilkes. You are very kind." Her words emerged as if they came from the lips of someone other than herself. Then she let herself out of her room and made her way downstairs.

Her feet touched the landing, and she moved in the direction of the drawing room. The closer she approached, the more distinct the voices grew. Her father's and another man's. She hovered on the threshold, stomach roiling.

Every particle within her screamed that she should turn and run as fast as her legs could take her in the opposite direction of what lay beyond that door. Yes. That was what she would do. She'd flee to Percy's rooms. He'd given her the address once. There, she'd beg, convince, demand, do anything to get him to make amends.

Her foot turned.

The door opened. Her father's towering frame filled the doorway. He'd dressed as if going to a ball and held out his hand to her. Like a prisoner realizing only guards stood between themselves and the guillotine, she placed her fingers in his and followed him inside.

Candlelight and shadows. They filled the room with a ghostly flicker, dancing across the patterned carpet, gold velvet drapes, and red damask wallpaper. She'd long since ceased fearing the immensity and grandeur of the chamber, but tonight, those childhood anxieties came rushing back.

A man sat in a chair to the right of the fireplace. Beside him, another man in clerical garb leaned one hand against the mantel. All eyes narrowed in on her at once.

Why, oh why, couldn't a floor sense emotion and open to swallow her up? She'd have responded with a thousand thank-yous for the kindness.

The first man stood and approached her, the clergyman at his heels. Was this her groom then? He seemed closer to her father's age, older even.

"How do you do, Miss Stanwood?" The man's tone was not unkind as he regarded her. If she was indeed to marry him, her legs might cease their trembling for a few seconds. He didn't look the sort to abuse a lady, though the buttons on his waistcoat did seem a bit strained. He turned, glancing over his shoulder. "Luke. Come here and greet your bride."

Slowly, Charity made out a figure emerging from the shadows near the window. Air ceased to enter her lungs as he approached.

Tall. Why if Percy had been standing there, Luke Warren would have dwarfed him by a foot. A coal black tailcoat encased his broad shoulders, and his gaze assessed the room and her in one sweeping glance, as if judging everything in the flash of an instant and finding nothing favorable. And his eyes. The ice in her father's was almost placid compared to his, and no smile edged his firm-set lips. Goodness, he looked exactly like a picture she'd seen in a childhood history book of a medieval soldier preparing to joust. She shivered, despite the room's oppressive warmth.

No. Please, no.

This man—her so-called future husband—was nothing less than a cold monster.

❦

This woman—his so-called future wife—had the look of one who would rather boil in oil than say vows to him tonight.

Standing next to his father, Luke made the briefest of bows. His father looked at him, then back at Miss Stanwood, as if awaiting an exchange of words.

Thankfully, the clergyman spared them. "Ah. Well. Shall we get on with things?"

No one so much as moved. Luke glanced at Miss Stanwood, who appeared to be drilling a hole in the carpet with her gaze, hand on her father's arm.

"Come now. It's late, and my wife will be expecting me." The clergyman clapped his hands together, an impatient edge to his tone. "If you'll both step over here."

Again, Luke looked to Miss Stanwood. The minister's words must have roused her. Either that or her father's quick nudge. Without lifting her gaze, she stepped in his direction. He held out his arm. Finally, her eyes met his. For the barest of instants, he found himself staring into twin irises the color of the Cornwall sea in summer. Then she placed her fingers atop his arm with a touch as tentative as it was unwilling.

They moved to stand in front of the clergyman. The aged man thumbed through a worn black book with knobby fingers.

"Ah. There it is." The man fixed his gaze on both of them, the train of his thoughts written all over his face. *What an odd marriage ceremony this is. Does this couple even know each other? Perhaps it's a mistake to officiate.*

"Please proceed." Luke recognized his father's voice coming from somewhere behind.

"Ah. Yes, of course, sir. Dearly beloved. . ."

Though he tried to steel himself against noticing, it was difficult to ignore the person beside him. A diminutive little thing, barely reaching his shoulder. Her hair, a flaxen shade, shimmered in the firelight. And those eyes—fixed solely on the minister, as if he were her groom-to-be instead of Luke.

Not once did she lift her gaze to his. Not once. Not even when she said her vows. The carpet had her attention then. When Luke said his, the clergyman's collar provided her focus.

Luke had only been to a handful of weddings, but if he guessed correctly, the ceremony was nearing its end. And when they were pronounced man and wife, he'd not give her the satisfaction of noticing he watched her. So he followed her lead and fixated on the painting above the mantel, a lady dressed in the style popular in his father's day. One who bore a remarkable resemblance to the woman beside him now. Her mother? Undoubtedly.

Somehow that knowledge twisted his stomach tighter than the best seaman's knot. Especially as their hands were now clasped together, held out in front of the clergyman. Thankfully, staring at the painting had kept him from noticing how small hers were, a fact which suddenly came to his attention. A fact which he did not like and preferred to forget. He should have consumed more than three glasses of brandy.

"Forasmuch as Luke and Charity have consented together in holy wedlock and have witnessed the same before God and this company, and thereto have given and pledged their troth either to other, and have declared the same by giving and receiving of a ring and by joining of hands; I pronounce that they be man and wife together, In the name of the Father, and of the Son, and of the Holy Ghost. Amen."

Good. It was over. Though he sensed her eyes on him now, he refused to look at her. The quicker this night dimmed in his memory, the better.

Both men—his father and hers—came toward them offering smiles and congratulations that rang as false as an untuned harpsichord, while the clergyman bent over a document spread atop a table that still bore discarded cups and a half-eaten fruitcake.

If there had been anything stronger than cold coffee on that tray, Luke doubted he could have resisted pouring a glass.

The clergyman beckoned them forward to sign the marriage certificate. Luke went first, striding forward and taking up the pen. Drawing in a heavy breath, he scrawled his signature in a manner that would've sent his boyhood tutor into an apoplectic fit: *Luke Geoffrey Warren.*

There. It was over. Done with. He'd discharged his duty. Brushing past his bride, his father, and John Stanwood, he headed for the door. He need not stay, surrounded by people whose very presence stifled him as surely as a rag thrust into the mouth of a choking man. He closed his fingers around the knob and flung open the door.

It slammed shut behind him, a sound that reverberated through the room and his own ringing ears.

As his feet ate up the distance between the hallway and the front entrance, he didn't once look back.

Chapter Three

Three Years Later

Often the greater beauty could be found in what one couldn't control, rather than that which one could. The space of three years had done their best to teach Captain Luke Warren that lesson, but he'd only truly learned it over the past four months.

He took in the sight of London through the carriage window, his first glimpse since he'd rejoined the navy three years ago. It seemed longer than that, somehow. The fault of war, a thing lads such as he ought not view through rose-tinted lenses. There was nothing in the least glamorous about watching men one had supped with at breakfast, bleeding on the deck by noon.

London hadn't changed much. Still the same raw and rank poverty residing in the streets. The faces of the beggars and the crossing sweepers had changed, but only the faces were altered. The essence of the city stayed the same in the poor section, as it did in the rich. In the latter, gentlemen escorted ladies down neat streets, past rows of townhouses with steps freshly scrubbed, no doubt by some scullery maid at a blisteringly early hour.

Having swabbed the deck as discipline for an offense to a superior officer when a mere midshipman, Luke could well pity the servant.

No, it was he, not London, that had done the changing. He cast a glance down at his left hand, lying in his lap. That hand—the catalyst for it all. Sans two fingers and partially crushed after a stack of barrels had knocked him down, one rolling across his hand, it finished the work the Lord had started a year after Luke joined up.

Even now, it seemed hard to believe that he, a man who had never considered God as more than a crutch to provide comfort for the less fortunate, had given over his life in full surrender to the will of Someone greater than himself.

Luke smiled. He hadn't sought God out. The Lord had pursued him relentlessly. Caused pain to come into his life, emptiness, dissolution, all for the cause of bringing him to Himself.

Not that he'd achieved perfection or even become much better than he had been before. Jagged slashes of darkness still marked the canvas of his life. But God had brought light, would remain faithful. Nothing could erase the past though. Nor the pain Luke had brought upon others. It needed to be dealt with, and deal with it he would.

Case in point—his wife. He hadn't seen her since their fateful wedding, and as time passed, her face had faded from his memory, like a piece of patterned cloth left out in the blazing sun until the design had grown indistinguishable. She had written though. Five letters penned in a finishing-school hand, demure and polite, addressing him as Luke and asking about his duties. One had even included a pair of woolen socks, obviously knit by someone who hadn't much skill for the task. Each letter had come, one per month, for the first five months. But he'd been bitter then, calluses still encasing his heart.

He hadn't written back. And then the letters stopped.

After God had shown him the error of his ways, he'd considered writing Charity directly. Yet what weight would a letter have had in her eyes after such an absence? He needed to face her in person.

Now, here he was, discharged from the navy, sitting in a parked carriage outside her father's London house at approximately—he pulled his watch from his waistcoat pocket—nine in the evening.

The driver rapped smartly on the door, as if ordering Luke to remove his posterior from the carriage or hand over more money.

Drawing in a breath, along with a prayer, Luke opened the door and let himself out of the conveyance. He gazed up at the stately townhouse—one of Grosvenor Square's smaller residences, though as elegant as any on the street. Heavy curtains kept all but the faintest glimmer of light from seeping out the many windows. Stars winked in the night sky, jewels amidst a sea of ink. How often during his time aboard ship had he gazed upward, seeing the stars without considering their Maker? Like a man who gorged himself on a banquet without once paying heed to the effort it had taken to prepare it.

He'd been a cad.

And the time had come to face the woman who'd borne the brunt of his actions.

⁂

The crackle of the fire and the rhythmic ticking of the clock on the mantel provided the only sounds as Charity turned another page. She leaned back against her mound of pillows and considered the passage she had just read.

She was stronger alone, and her own good sense so well supported her, that her firmness was as unshaken.

Though she perused novels with less frequency than in prior days, she did savor the half hour before bed when she could shut out all distractions and enjoy a chapter or two. She'd already read this story more than once, but something about the events and characters continued to draw her interest. The novel, entitled *Sense and Sensibility* and written by an author mysteriously referred to only as "A Lady," possessed a grounding in reality that her girlhood gothic tales woefully lacked.

Closing the book, she rested her chin upon her hands and fixed her gaze on the flames dancing in the grate.

Reality had grounded more than her fictional worlds these past years. Perhaps it was the fact that she was no longer seventeen, but twenty. Or that society no longer beckoned to her with its bejeweled hand, wooing her toward pleasure, though in reality offering only poison. Whatever the case, she'd changed. As had her life. And she, for one, was grateful for it.

A smile flitted across her lips as she reopened her book. Elinor and Marianne's paths to true love proved a delightful diversion. Once upon a time, she'd have likened herself to the impetuous Marianne, but these days, practical Elinor suited her best. In the end, both sisters would find love, partners that suited them better than any other would. A lovely ending to a charming story. But there was the difference between real life and fiction. The latter always ended as it ought. The former rarely ever did.

A commotion below shattered the evening quiet.

She started, the book falling from her hands.

Her heart jolted in her chest.

Was someone attempting to break in? Earlier this week, she'd read in the paper of a robbery occurring just down the street, the thieves getting away with a silver tea service and the contents of the family safe. Last she'd heard, the criminals had not yet been apprehended.

She pulled her dressing gown tighter, gaze darting about the room. Of all nights for something to happen, with her papa away and several of the servants out to attend a birthday party. She oughtn't have given them leave to go.

She tiptoed out of bed and across the room, then grasped the poker, curling her fingers around the instrument. Though what she could do against armed criminals with such a measly weapon, she wasn't sure. Perhaps if she came up behind them, she could swing and knock them unconscious. She'd always been rather good with a cricket bat.

Her pulse pounded as she crept out of her room and down the dark hallway. Her bare feet whispered against the carpet, making scarcely a sound as she gained the stairs. Thankfully, she knew which steps creaked.

She squeezed her eyes shut as the third step down emitted a sound between a moan and a shriek.

Oh, all right. Perhaps she *was* being a bit too overdramatic.

Finally, finally she reached the bottom. Though she hadn't thought to bring a candle, one still glimmered on the hall table, casting wavering shadows across the marble tile and illuminating a particularly fearsome portrait of her bewigged great-grandfather.

A shiver ran spiderlike fingers down her back. Which room would they be in?

Rap.

She jumped. The noise. . . It hadn't come from any of the rooms.

Rap.

Outside. Someone was at the door.

It would so happen that the only footman who had remained at home did so because of a chest cough. No doubt Timothy was in his bed belowstairs, hacking into a handkerchief.

I could use a bit of help down here, Lord.

Chills skittered over her bare feet as her fingers tightened around the poker. She drew in a deep breath, focusing on her great-grandfather carrying a sword and bedecked in court dress. Why, he'd be ashamed to think his great-granddaughter a coward.

Ice pooled in her veins as she approached the door. She wouldn't open it—that would be utter foolishness—just call out and see who was there.

"Who are you, and what do you want?" Her tone came out stronger than she expected. Perhaps she had a bit of ancestral blood in her, after all.

"Please, just open the door," came the voice, low and muffled from the other side of the heavy oaken panel. Masculine. One point against him. Two, since he hadn't immediately announced himself.

"No. Not until I know it's safe to do so." Unclenching one hand from the poker, she tugged her dressing gown tighter around herself. Safety wasn't the foremost quality of London at night, and daft was one of many things she'd given up being.

"I can assure you, madam, I mean you no harm." Why this evasion? Why wouldn't whoever it was come out and state his identity? Well, she wouldn't budge until he either named himself or left.

"Your word is worth nothing to me, since I do not know your name." If only she'd shown such foresight three years ago in her dealings with Percy Browne. She'd been young and naive then. Stupid and blind. She was no longer either. She was an intelligent woman who had enough sense not to admit strange, unknown men.

"But I know yours, Charity Warren."

Her lungs gulped in air.

Charity Warren.

It wasn't the fact that he knew her name, but the cadence of his tone as he spoke the words. She'd heard that tone before, on a night as dark as this one, three years prior. Heard it from a stranger's lips as he said vows he did not mean, nor cared to take. Promises that had joined them together, promises that, most days, she tried to forget.

She glanced at the poker. There was no need of it. That sort of defense would not aid her against the person she'd find on the other side of that door.

Her husband.

The poker fell to the ground with an echoing clatter as her fingers fumbled to unbolt the door. For the briefest of instants she squeezed her eyes shut. Why, oh why, could it not have been a marauder? For any criminal villain would have been more to her liking than the man she had been wed to by force.

Yet open it she must.

She grasped the handle. A blast of chill air knifed through her thin nightdress and the dressing gown worn more for ornament than warmth.

Time froze as their gazes met. His eyes, oh, she'd forgotten them. But now each fragment of memory pieced itself together. Gray-blue eyes looking down at her from a face hewn in stone. Her hand, placed upon his arm, by rote, rather than by desire. His frame that seemed to dwarf hers in size and strength, as if he could break her into kindling with a single snap.

The door still in her grasp, night air swirling her loose curls around her face, they studied each other. Husband and wife, alone for the first time in their three-year marriage. A navy uniform, blue and gold, found purchase on his broad shoulders. Though a matching cockade rested on his head, she noticed he wore his jet hair longer, a match to the stubble on his firm jaw.

"Hello, Charity." The words came low, almost husky, as if a band constricted his throat. The faintest of smiles angled his mouth. No, it couldn't really be called a smile. More like an expression that bespoke a hundred different things, none of which she could place her finger upon.

She said nothing. Her tongue couldn't seem to perform, and her mind emptied of all words.

"Do you remember me?" He reached out, as if to hold the door, but she clutched it in her grasp, a mainstay amidst a storm that threatened to send her overboard.

Did she remember him? How could she forget? She had married him, after all, on a night much like this one. Only then she hadn't been wearing nightclothes and he'd looked at her with disgust. Even after all that, she'd written him by command of her father. Five letters, an agony to compose. None of which he'd so much as acknowledged.

So did she remember him? Of course. It was her misfortune, one that had robbed her of night after night of sleep and left her spent and miserable more times than she could count. Oh, how she wished she could forget.

"You'd better come inside." Keeping her tone colder than the metal poker, she stepped aside to let him pass. He filled the doorway with his height, and she tried to make herself as small as possible to avoid brushing up against him as he passed her. Musk and the fragrance of soap swept over her. She held her breath against inhaling his scent.

She closed the door and turned sharply, intent on locating the candle. Her ankle buckled as she stumbled over the poker.

He grabbed her waist, saving her from falling by a split second. Her heart drummed against her chest as she stared up at him, her gaze melded to his.

Meager light illuminated his face. There was something. . .out of balance in his expression. Something that didn't match with the identity of the man who'd deserted her five minutes after being pronounced her husband. The man who had ignored her letters wouldn't look at her with such a myriad of expressions. None of which bore even the faintest hint of anger.

The warmth of his hands pierced through the two layers of fabric separating his skin from hers. Percy's hands had once lingered in that exact spot. Percy, who had treated her with all the courtesy of a vulture picking apart the best parts of its prey, before leaving the rest behind. When he'd left her behind, she'd been no more than a shell.

She wrested herself from his grip.

"I'm sorry. I only meant to keep you from falling." He took a step back, as if her eyes shot fire and he'd been scorched by the blaze.

"Indeed." She yanked her dressing gown closed, wishing she had a sash to tie it with.

"I know you must have questions. There are things we need to say, both of us. But you were abed. I did not mean to wake you." He actually looked as if he'd done wrong.

By waking her? For one thing, she hadn't been asleep. And for another, disturbing her nightly reading was the last item on his list of offenses.

"I won't trespass on your hospitality by asking to stay the night here. I'll go to my father's." He made a move to turn.

"Your father isn't in London. He's in Cornwall, where he's been the past two years. His London house is all shut up, and there are no servants there." Why did she feel the need to offer him the courtesy of this information? It made no sense. Courtesy—the last thing he'd given her.

"I see." He gave a brief nod. "I'll locate a room at an inn then."

Had he given even the slightest impression that he wished her to offer him a room, she'd not have done so. But nothing in his expression hinted at such a desire, and it *was* rather late to be traipsing about town looking for suitable lodging.

"You may stay here. If you wish." She didn't bother injecting any warmth into the words. She'd offered him shelter, and if he didn't like her way of offering, he could depart posthaste.

"Thank you. You're very kind." Why did he say those words as if he meant them? She wasn't kind. Not to him, at any rate.

She lifted the candle, nearly burnt down to the wick, wax pooling around the sides of the holder. "If you'll come this way, I'll show you to your room." She moved toward the stairs.

Stanwood House boasted a total of six bedchambers.

And she'd be sure to give Luke Warren the one farthest away from hers.

Chapter Four

Awakening in a bedchamber belonging to his father-in-law. Donning a jacket and trousers, instead of a uniform. Standing at the head of the stairs, his wife breakfasting below.

Enemy territory he could handle, but when faced with a plethora of unfamiliar things all cobbled together, Luke found himself at loose ends.

Not for the first time in the past ten hours, his thoughts traveled to *that* moment. The moment when Charity opened the door and he beheld the woman whose face had previously been little more than a hazy image, yet now stood out stark and vivid and. . .

Beautiful.

Yes, his wife was beautiful. Her hair, falling to her waist in a cascade of golden ribbons, her eyes a piercing shade of the sea at sunset—deep blue with flecks of amber. One of the things he had remembered was how tiny she was. Her height still didn't reach much past five feet, yet she'd made quite an arresting sight, glaring him down in the entry hall.

Ah. Yes. This beautiful wife of his couldn't stand him. She'd not even attempted to hide her derision, looking positively pained as she offered him a room for the night. A proud enemy regretfully agreeing to terms of surrender.

Of course, he deserved every ounce of her censure. But that didn't mean he looked forward to walking into her hail of verbal bullets and dagger-like glances.

Lord, show me the path. Help me to redeem myself in her eyes, for I know I already have in Yours.

The prayer, along with the half-hour of scripture reading he'd performed just before stepping out, brought the measure of strength he needed to stride downstairs.

It didn't take long to locate the breakfast room, what with all the tantalizing smells issuing forth. His stomach rumbled. Shipboard fare, while filling, didn't exactly qualify as fine dining.

He stepped inside the spacious, sunlit room. A round table sat in the center, a sideboard against one wall piled high with platters and tureens—tempting scents rising up in wafts of steam.

His wife occupied a chair nearest the window and farthest from the sideboard. A half-eaten scone rested on her plate, a cup and saucer adjoining. She looked up from a piece of correspondence.

"Good morning." He tried for a smile, moving to the sideboard and taking up a plate, glancing over his shoulder at her as he did so.

"Likewise." She wore her curls up today, as most young ladies did, a few stray wisps framing her cheeks and brushing her neck. He'd be dashed if he knew the color of her gown. It looked to be a pale shade of orange. No, not really orange, but a lighter variation. From what he'd learned of fashion, every shade had its own particular name. Not usual colors, like red, blue, and green, but complicated ones like scarlet, cobalt, and sage.

Whatever the color, her gown was a very pretty one. It accentuated the gold of her hair and gave her skin a blushing hue.

He turned his attention to the offerings on the sideboard. Scrambled eggs. Fried tomatoes. Ham. Scones and muffins. Kippers.

Adding some of each to his plate, he claimed a seat, leaving a chair between them. Aware of her eyes upon him, though he could tell she pretended thorough absorption in reading her correspondence, he bowed his head and said a silent grace.

When he looked up, she no longer made any pretension of ignoring him but watched him unabashedly. Her eyes took on a curious look, as if a question lingered there.

"Something wrong?" He poured himself a cup of coffee from the pot in the center of the table. Very likely the same pot that had borne silent witness to their wedding ceremony, its silver handle gleaming as if in recognition.

"You never struck me as the praying type." A practiced society smile hovered on her lips. She lifted her delicate china cup as if to mask it.

"Well, now you see that I am." He raised his fork and took a bite of ham, savoring the smoky taste. A thousand times better than ship's biscuits and salt pork.

Silence fell between them. Charity returned to her correspondence. He concentrated on enjoying his breakfast. But the faint sighs emitting from her lips every so often prevented his full enjoyment of the repast. Was he the cause of them?

Vexatious woman. Last night she'd been a hair's breadth away from assaulting him with a poker—he hadn't neglected to notice the detail of the item she'd tripped over—and now she ruined his breakfast. He wiped toast crumbs from his mouth with a napkin, then pushed aside his plate, grateful no servants stood sentry to eavesdrop.

He placed his hands atop the table and spoke loudly enough to make certain she realized he wasn't to be avoided. "We need to talk."

Ever so slowly, she laid down the letter. "Why now? You didn't seem interested in communicating with me when I wrote you all those years ago. I don't see why we should start now." Her tone suggested she'd just as well slap him as look at him.

He swallowed, focusing on his hands—the one still bandaged, the other callused from work aboard ship. "You have every right to think as you do. I don't blame you. But that was three years ago, and I've changed since then. I don't expect you to believe me straight off, but with that in mind, could you at least hear me out?"

He didn't expect her to be very convinced. And he didn't prove his judgment wrong. She released a sigh of resignation and crossed her arms over her chest in the manner of a peevish five-year-old denied some trifle.

"Very well. I'm listening."

Best take what scraps she offered and do his best to add to them. "Thank you. Perhaps I should let you ask me questions, then I could do the same. That way we deal with everything that needs to be dealt with." He added a dollop of cream to his coffee and waited for her to begin.

"Fair enough. Why didn't you answer my letters?"

All right then. Starting with the heaviest surge of cannon fire first. No doubt she'd already lit the fuse the moment he'd walked in the door and had been awaiting the signal to aim and fire.

"Because I was a self-absorbed blackguard."

Her eyebrows rose, as if it surprised her that he so freely admitted his faults. Before handing over his life to the Lord, he'd been too proud to admit his wrongs. Now it went hand-in-hand with his new beliefs—though the actual admission did prove a bit hard to spit out.

"I was angry after I left that night. Very angry. The bargain my father entered into with yours wasn't the easiest thing for me to accept. If it makes you feel any better, I didn't answer my father's correspondence, either. I wanted to forget about my life here, and for me, that involved distancing myself as much as possible from what had happened. It was wrong, I know. But it was what I chose to do, and I make no attempt to mask my error."

As he spoke, some of the hardness in her face seemed to soften just a little. Like wax being held up to intense heat, melting ever so slightly. Or perhaps he only wished to believe she did.

"I see." She unfolded her arms and sat straighter in her seat. "Your turn now."

"How is my family?" His heart still throbbed at the way he'd treated his father and sister. No contact for close to three years, until he'd finally written them while in the early stages of recovering from his injuries. Of course, he hadn't received a reply, since he'd set off for England as soon as he was rendered able to travel.

"So you've finally decided to care about them?" Tartness laced her tone.

Criticism. Censure. That was what he deserved, after all. It was no less than his duty to let those who wished it have a swing at him.

"Yes. And I aim to do the job all the more carefully, and with all the greater devotion for having neglected it as long as I did." He spoke the words quietly, meeting her gaze without flinching, keeping his expression humble and contrite.

"I'm sorry," she whispered, an unexpected softness in her eyes. "That was uncalled for."

He started at her apology. However unexpected, it was a chink in the armor she'd donned against him. "Perhaps. But nonetheless warranted."

"Your sister, I believe, is well. She's in Bath right now, staying with her friend Beth Lacey. But I'm afraid your father is not how you remember him. Due to our arrangement"—her lips curved at the word—"his financial situation improved, but he began to suffer from bad health. He had a—what did the doctors call it? An attack of apoplexy, I think they said. It left him without the use of his right side." A gentleness he did not bargain for and certainly didn't deserve filled her tone. "I believe he scarcely leaves his room."

He rested his forehead in his one good hand. His father ill, and he had not known. Who managed the estate? Who supervised the mines? Who made certain the staff attended to their duties and didn't pilfer the silver? Harriet, undoubtedly tried when at home, but his sister knew as much about mining as a trout did about dry land.

Lord, forgive me.

"I must go to them." Yes. He'd leave straightaway. Take the mail coach and be in Cornwall by tomorrow evening. Then he could begin to make amends. Try, at the very least. He stood, tossing his napkin on the tablecloth.

Yet he'd scarcely reached his full height, before he remembered.

Not only did he have a family to consider, but he had a wife, as well. One who no doubt wished to be made aware of the path their marriage would now take. One who deserved a say in such a decision.

He sat again. Outside, carriage wheels clattered on the street, the horses' hooves clipping rhythmically along. It sounded strange, the absence of one noise and the presence of another. He hadn't heard the slap of waves against the sides of a ship in over a month, yet though he'd heard the noise of horses and carriages many times since then, they still sounded foreign.

Foreign. Like the responsibility of having a wife. *Guide me, Lord. I can see I'll need Your help more than ever.*

"What I mean to say, is, we must decide our course of action together."

"We?" Another incredulous lift of her brows.

"Yes." He added a smile, hoping it looked friendly and not threatening. "We. It's not only my decision, but yours, Charity. And together, we must make it."

⁙

They'd played their little question game, but Charity still had one. One that clanged in her mind and demanded an answer.

Who was the man sitting at her breakfast table?

For he bore no resemblance other than physical to the insolent youth who had stormed from the room three years prior, leaving her behind after less than five minutes of marriage. Nor the person who had spurned her letters. This Luke Warren seemed actually sincere, even gentlemanly, as he took full responsibility for his wrongs. What man did *that*? None she had ever met. And the half smile that played on his lips. . . . Well, she didn't like the uncanny flutter that sped through her insides when it unfurled.

"I'm not one to beat about the bush, so forgive me if what I'm about to say strikes you as blunt." That smile again. "What do you wish our marriage to be, now that I've returned? I should probably tell you I've already quit the navy, due to an accident that occurred while moving some cargo. Though the injury to my hand provided a catalyst for my departure, what you've just told me of my father only confirms my course of action. I, for one, am through with turning my back on my family. I know the circumstances of our marriage were. . .unorthodox, to say the least, but despite that, we *are* married. And together, we must take that fact and decide what to do about it."

At a loss for words was a state in which she did not often find herself. Generally, she could conjure up a reply to any speech—be it serious, scathing, or witty.

Yet though she opened her mouth, no sound escaped.

Yesterday, she'd been a married woman with a figment of a husband, one who rarely crossed her thoughts. Today, a flesh-and-blood man sat beside her, posing a question that would determine the course of both their lives.

And she couldn't even summon an answer. She bent her head, staring at the scattering of crumbs atop the tablecloth. Marriage. A relationship. Two things she knew very little about and scarcely anything favorable. Her parents' marriage had been quite simply miserable, the two of them never managing to do anything but tolerate each other. Why had they even married? Charity had not the slightest idea. They'd been as opposite as north and south, sharing nothing. Papa, consumed with furthering his financial empire; Mamma combating her husband's hedonism by dressing in severe colors and spending hours a day in "charitable obligations."

A shiver crept up Charity's spine and settled deep within her heart. She closed her eyes and tried to block out the lurid memories of her parents' so-called "disagreements." Glass breaking, tables overturning. As a little girl, she would run to the music room, lock the door behind her, and play the piano to drown out the sound—reels and lively tunes, the loudest pieces in her repertoire. She played until her fingers ached and the angry sounds ceased, imagining herself dancing with a handsome duke in a ballroom alight with candles.

Only when silence fell would she allow her own tears to come, dripping onto the ivory keys like raindrops onto cobblestones. Music had been her only escape, for even after her mamma's death five years ago, the shadows of her parents' altercations still crouched in every corner with all the grace of an angry bull.

And then. . .Percy. From the first moment they had met, he had been her knight in shining armor, the handsome man of her piano-playing dreams.

How swiftly he had shown his true colors.

She sucked in a shuddering breath, letting her eyelids slide shut, trying to picture something happier. A memory to fill her mind with, to erase the previous one.

Something warm brushed her hand. She looked up.

Luke had reached across the space between them, his hand now covering hers. Everything in her wanted to jerk away from his touch, as she should have with Percy's. Yet she couldn't deny the comfort that wrapped around her as his fingers closed around hers, a comfort similar to being wrapped in a warm blanket on an icy evening. Similar, but somehow different.

"I know this is rather a lot to take in." A swath of hair fell over his forehead as he bent toward her. "It is for me, too. But I promise you, Charity. You may choose however you wish. You may continue to live here with your father. If you have need of anything, you have only to come to me, and I will provide it. You may continue to use my name. . .or if you wish, I can see a lawyer and arrange to have our marriage annulled.

We certainly have grounds for it." His gaze captured hers much as his fingers did her hand. A touch loose enough to easily release herself from, but holding an unspoken plea to remain where she was.

"Or you could come with me to Cornwall. Become mistress of Cavington Hall. The house hasn't had a real mistress since my mother's death. I promise you, I would ask for nothing save friendship. We can get to know each other, learn about who the other is. I know I haven't done anything to give you much evidence to rest upon, but I will do my utmost to be a kind and faithful husband." He paused then, releasing her hand as if to use nothing to persuade her other than his words—though he did watch her with the intensity of one awaiting a verdict on a long-tried court case.

He wasn't going to force her to bend to his will. Not like her papa had done, marrying her off to a stranger. Not like some husbands did, lording their authority over subservient wives. Luke Warren offered her a choice. And it seemed that he would accept whatever answer she gave with acceptance and without judgment.

So the options lay before her. Remain her father's daughter in a house where everyone considered him the master, her a flighty child. Or go to Cornwall, a place where she knew no one, where no one knew her. Where the person she became rested with no one but herself. Reinvention always held a kind of charm, especially when one had been tainted by scandal.

Or she could but say the word and he would end their marriage. She could seek another husband. Someone of her own choosing.

Though past events had shown her to be nothing if not a poor judge.

What would You have me do, Lord? This is all so sudden, leaving my known little world, shaken. What choice should I make? Which would You have me choose?

The cause of all these uncertainties watched her quietly, posture tense, almost impatient. Of course. This would affect Luke as much as it did her. Yet he did not presume to make the choice, but gave it into her hands. A gift as unexpected as it was unwarranted. A man's place was to decide, a woman's to comply. So she had always been taught, yet he took the notion and turned it upside down, putting them on equal footing.

A marriage with such a man could only be better than a life with her father.

"I thank you for your generosity in allowing me the choice." She spoke the words softly.

"And?" He sat forward. Any enemy who met him during battle had an imposing presence to contend with. At that moment, his muscular frame filled the chair as if the seat were better suited to a tin solider than a navy captain. Her gaze rested on his bandaged hand. What circumstances had caused him to attain the injury?

It was a question she'd never get an answer to if their marriage ended by annulment.

"I'll go with you to Cornwall. I don't know what sort of mistress I'll make at such a house as Cavington Hall, but I'll try. And hope to St. Francis you don't rue the day you issued me the invitation." She tried for a laugh, hoping to crack the tension.

He smiled, but his eyes owned intensity. As if he understood the magnitude of the pledge she made and what they plotted. It was one thing to talk of a life together sitting amongst familiar things in the room she had known since childhood. Quite another to go out into the world with this man at her side and trust him to captain their ship and bring it safe to harbor. To be sure, he'd captained in the navy, but this was two lives, not a seaborne vessel.

A lifetime was a long while to spend regretting a decision made in a morning. She'd already spent three years ruing her rendezvous with Percy. She didn't want another forty lived wishing she had made a different choice today.

"Could you be ready to leave by this afternoon? I hate to ask it, but I'm anxious about my father and wish to assure myself of his welfare without delay."

This afternoon? But what would her papa say when he found her gone? She'd done much less and garnered his displeasure.

The realization burst upon her. She no longer answered to her father's authority. Not when her husband's wishes overrode it. It was a strange thought, considering she'd already been married for three years and was just now learning these things.

"I believe so. I'll summon my maid and assist her in packing." Thus, she began her role as wife. She stood, moving to the door. On the threshold, she paused.

He sat motionless, watching her, as if struggling as much as she to grasp the concept of their new life.

❧

Punctuality. The first of his wife's virtues. She'd overseen the packing and loading of trunks and now bid goodbye to a couple of servants, reaching out and touching the hand of an elderly woman Luke assumed was the housekeeper.

A general could not have arranged the moving of a battalion with such efficiency—giving them an extra hour for traveling.

With a final smile, she turned and came down the steps toward where he and the waiting carriage stood. A dark red, short-waisted jacket hugged her curves, matching the trimmed bonnet secured over her curls. The outfit put him in mind of a cardinal with its vibrant plumage attracting attention among its fellow flitting creatures.

He'd certainly noticed. In fact, since the moment Charity had first appeared on the steps, he'd been unable to stop staring at her. Once he'd attended a party with some of his fellow naval comrades, and a few of their wives had been present. He'd taken note that the men seemed particularly proud to show off their pretty ladies, strutting about the room with them like puffed-up peacocks.

Now he had a wife. One he would be proud to show off. She certainly exceeded the loveliness of any lady his navy friends had married.

Why had he not noticed it the night of their wedding? Had his eyes not been working properly? Or had he been too daft and inebriated?

"Ready?" She stood at his side, looking up at him with a curious expression.

"Yes. Straightaway." Egad, he sounded like a new recruit answering a commanding officer after having not paid attention to any of the orders just issued. Hastily, he stepped aside to allow the footman to open the door of her father's carriage. She'd offered the use of the conveyance, and he'd agreed, though he hoped John Stanwood would have no cause to object. For all Luke knew, the laws of England had changed since he'd been away and absconding with a man's daughter—even if she was his own wife—along with his carriage had become a capital offense.

The servant let down the steps, then held out his hand, palm up, toward Charity.

"Harold! What is the meaning of this?"

Luke glanced in the direction of the burly coachman who looked to be glowering both at the adolescent footman and the trunks arranged atop the conveyance.

The footman's protruding ears turned bright red, as if the lad knew a tongue-lashing awaited him.

"Best go find out what he wants. I'll see to Mrs. Warren." Luke gave the lad a sympathetic look. Why was it that those holding command over others always wanted to wield that power like a battering ram?

The footman walked—albeit slowly—toward the fuming coachman.

Luke turned toward Charity, mimicking the footman's palm-out gesture with his uninjured hand. She placed her gloved fingers in his. He helped her up.

Simple gestures could result in complicated consequences.

Like placing his hand on the small of her back to steady her as she entered the carriage. A gesture that didn't require much thought. . .but then why did the moment sear itself in his memory? The softness of her dress against his palm. The tilt of her head as she looked back at him, as if to convey her thanks. The smile on her ruby-tinged lips, quick, almost mischievous.

Already, the complexities of this marriage were proving too much for his mental capacity. Give him naval maneuvers and he was the man for the job, quick on his feet, instantaneous in his decisions.

Give him a wife to look after and he found himself tongue-twisted, addle-brained, and as befuddled by the effect she had upon him as a schoolboy with a slateful of unrecognizable Latin verses.

Chapter Five

Traveling with a wife proved a sight different than traveling with the navy. Regiments muttered and complained about food, lodging, by turns the heat or cold. A wife, at least his wife, stated her needs once and sweetly, putting Luke at a loss to do anything but instantaneously comply. At both inns where they'd stayed, Charity requested separate rooms—something he quickly agreed to. He already had enough trouble turning his thoughts away from her during the day. What sharing sleeping quarters would do to him, he didn't want to think about.

She also requested dinner in her room instead of in the dining room, as well as hot water at night and then again in the morning. All this had racked up quite the impressive bill.

Another fact to add to his growing repertoire of information about wives. They were expensive.

At least they would reach Cavington Hall by nightfall, in time for a late dinner and a visit with his father before retiring. There, as lady of the house, Charity would be mistress of over twenty servants. Plenty of people to fetch her dinner and carry her water.

He had to give her credit though. She didn't complain. Not when dinner proved to be congealed mutton and cold potatoes. Nor when the water was brought up by a rotund servant who stuck his cabbage-shaped head in the door as if hoping to find her *en dishabille*. Luke had watched from his own room across the hall. Had the man lingered even a second longer, Luke would have been there in a stride, and the man would have found himself sporting a goose egg on his forehead large enough to match the width of his waist.

A gasp sounded from the other side of the carriage, pulling Luke from his thoughts.

"Something the matter?" But she didn't appear to have heard him. Her nose remained pressed against the window.

Of course. He took in the vista outside his own window. They were in Cornwall now. He'd been so caught up in his ruminations that he'd neglected to look upon the landscape that had been the subject of his longings during endless melancholy nights aboard ship.

As far as the eye could see, sweeping green stretched before them. Lush green hills contrasted with craggy cliffs, the sea below a canvas of deep, rich blue. The vastness of the landscape could steal even the most jaded visitor's breath, making one feel naught but a speck amidst this world of wind and rock and sea.

Nearly home. He could depart from Cornwall as often as he liked, yet it would never release its hold upon him. Like a first love, it forever lingered, calling one back with a siren's song.

"It's. . .so. . .indescribable." As Charity gazed at him, he realized he'd been right about one thing.

Her eyes did match the sea. In more ways than one. Both changeable, calm one moment, stormy the next. Both. . . Oh, both transfixed him.

"It's Cornwall. What did you expect?" He smiled at her, a lightness settling upon his shoulders. If ever there was a place to see the past set right, it was here. The tide forever changed. Surely he could, too.

"Oh, I don't know. It's not London, that's for certain."

"Thank goodness for that." He said the words without thinking and started when they prompted a laugh from her.

"I take it you don't care for the city then?" She pressed her lips together, as if to suppress further evidence of amusement.

"No, it's not that. But I find it difficult to appreciate London without filling my lungs with good Cornish air first."

"Like the Lovelace poem?" The staff would definitely know he'd brought them a great lady mistress upon glimpsing her appearance. A velvety green pelisse matched the elaborate feather arrangement topping her bonnet, and tight-fitting gloves encased her hands.

"Lovelace poem?" Poetry was something that, as a schoolboy, he'd done his best to extricate himself from, like a fish wiggling to escape the hook. Shakespeare had struck him as long-winded, and he only had a vague remembrance of a bloke called Lovelace.

"Yes." She looked at him, as if attempting great patience with his lack of ready knowledge. "Do you not know it? In the poem, he's leaving his lady to serve in the English Civil War. And there's this line that says, 'I could not love thee, dear, so much, loved I not honor more.' Cornwall and London are like that for you. You couldn't care about the one, if you didn't love the other."

He had to admit what she said made sense. He'd have to scrounge through his father's library and see if he could dust off a volume of Lovelace.

Perhaps he and Charity could even read it together. He certainly could use some help determining exactly what the poet meant behind all those fancy words and high-flown phrases.

The closer they came to Cavington, the higher his anticipation rose. If he closed his eyes, he could still picture the rambling, great house. As a lad, he'd liked nothing better than to lose himself in one of the rarely used rooms, to the despair of his nanny, who searched for him for hours while he listened to her vain summons from beneath a dusty Holland cover and stifled exultant laughter.

The carriage turned down the avenue.

There. Only a second more and it would be—

His stomach knotted as he beheld the first sight of his childhood home in three years. Not from emotion or anticipation. No, if only it had been that simple.

When he'd left Cavington Hall, it had been a jewel, perfectly situated in its setting. Now, utter chaos reigned.

Weeds grew like tangled serpents amidst what had once been immaculate shrubbery and gardens. Not a single light burned out from the numerous mullioned windows. By thunder, was that a chicken pecking amongst the gravel?

What had once seemed a veritable Camelot had fallen into a level of disrepair that rivaled most graveyards. Though the actual structure of the gray stone building looked to be intact, the place no longer appeared the residence of one of Cornwall's foremost gentlemen.

He only needed to glimpse Charity's expression to see what his own looked like. Her eyes rounded, perfectly matching her aghast features. She clutched her hands together. Probably, her current debate ran something like, *Ought I to risk exiting when the carriage finally stops?*

It did, less than a minute later.

Luke opened the door without waiting for assistance and jumped down. Gravel crunched as he strode. He stopped, hands fisted at his sides, raw anger pulsating through him, taking in the weeds and grass that wavered tall in the wind, to that ridiculous chicken, still pecking away on the same ground that dukes and duchesses once walked.

He took the steps two at a time, throwing open the front door. The ancient entry point grumbled on its hinges.

Viewing the great hall was like looking into something out of one of the ghost stories villagers whispered to each other at dark of night. Dust coated the floor. He could see that much, even in the dark. He made short work of lighting a candle and held it aloft.

The heirloom family paintings now served as resting places for cobwebs. Someone had obviously thrown Holland covers over a few pieces of furniture, but the job had been badly done. A gouge marred a section of the mahogany-paneled wall, a mar that had not been there before Luke's departure.

"Let whoever dwells within these walls show themselves or risk a thrashing!" Years spent raising his voice to be heard above gales and storms had given him quite an impressive shout. His words echoed off the walls and dissipated on the dusty floor under his feet.

A step sounded behind him. He spun around, fingers itching for a weapon.

Charity took an instantaneous step back.

"Oh. It's you." With an effort, he modulated his words.

"Who did you think?" She took in the room, her skirt trailing in the dust. If the front room were any indication of the accommodations they'd find in the rest of the house, she'd soon be asking to be returned to her father.

Footsteps thumped. Finally. Luke tensed, straightening.

The navy had taught him many things, and how to give a good dressing down was one of them.

A woman lumbered into view, her bulky frame swathed in a quilted dressing gown. A nightcap covered her mop of springy gray hair, and she yawned loudly, rubbing her eyes.

"Who shouted? I 'eard someone makin' enough ruckus to wake the dead! What's all this about?" She stumped closer, shuffling the dust with her bare feet.

"You better have a dashed good explanation for what I see before me." Who in the blazes was this woman? Not a housekeeper, that was for sure.

"What do you see afore ye?" She peered up at them through a heavy-lidded stare. Luke wrinkled his nose at the sour aroma of gin emanating from her.

"This." Luke swept his arm wide, encompassing the great hall. "This blasted, bloody mess, that's what."

Behind him, he heard a soft gasp. Reminding him that a real lady was witness to his actions, aiding him in checking the temper that could have blown up in scalding flames and kept on burning for a good while yet.

"Insulting the 'ouse, are ya? Who do ye think ye are?" The woman puffed out her cheeks.

A dry grin edged his lips. He stepped closer, standing nose to nose with the woman, fighting to ignore her stale breath. "I *think* I am Captain Luke Warren, your new master. Yours and every other servants' within these miserable walls. Do I make myself clear?"

The woman bobbed a curtsy, nearly dropping her candle. "Yer Master Rand's son?"

"The very same. Now listen carefully, for I've half a mind to turn the lot of you out this very night. Return to your quarters and inform every member of staff that I expect them—all of them—in the library tomorrow, at 9:00 a.m. sharp. I also expect breakfast served in the dining room at eight. Not a moment later, mind."

The woman fisted her free hand on her hip. "You 'ave a lot of nerve, 'specting such things. What do ye think I am? I'm Master Rand's personal nurse, not some skivvy." She stamped her foot, stirring up the dust.

"That may be so. But on the risk of being turned out this very instant, you take your orders and do as I bid you." He measured out each word for full impact.

The first glimmer of fear kindled in the woman's eyes. "Yes, sir…er…I mean, Captain." She made another bob, before scuttling away.

Luke turned to Charity. Her gaze held questions. Ones that he suddenly had no desire or energy to answer.

"Come." He held out his arm, grateful, at least, that she didn't start in on any feminine tirades about the horror of it all. "Let's see if we can find a clean room for you to spend the night in. Though from what I've seen so far, I can't make any promises."

❦

No two men possessed alike tempers. And when they flared, each did so differently. Her papa bellowed like an ailing bull, throwing the house and servants into a flurry to appease him. Her grandfather—what little Charity remembered of him—sat in stony silence, a fast-emptying snuff box at his side. Some men became cruel when out of sorts.

Others tamped down their emotions with expert skill.

When she'd wed Luke Warren, she'd had an idea of the sort of man he was—one who made no secret of his displeasure. Last night's exhibition only proved it so.

Charity stepped down the second-floor hall, stifling a cough at the envelopment of dust.

Though Luke had been furious, he maintained a certain control lacking in other men. And he hadn't vented his wrath at her, but actually smiled and jested as he showed her to her room—some nonsense about creating a sculpture out of dust and could she cook an egg, because he didn't trust anyone here to make it for him. She'd laughed along, both trying to alleviate the shock of arriving to a state of chaos.

But she hadn't been the cause of his displeasure last night.

Heaven help her if she ever became so.

She descended the stairs, holding her dress well above her ankles. No sense ruining her new lilac-colored muslin just to observe the propriety of letting her skirt trail the floor.

A murmur of voices drifted from the direction of a closed door off the great hall. Stomach rumbling for lack of having breakfasted, she headed in the direction of the conversation. Best find out what had transpired before sating her hunger.

Upon trying the tarnished knob, the door opened with the ease of coffin hinges left to molder for half a century. Charity grimaced at the dissonant sound.

All eyes swung in her direction.

Luke stood in front of a fireplace like a Parliamentarian addressing the House. Seated on white-draped chairs and settees were seven personages—four women and three men. All wore the garb of servants, though admittedly, not very well-kept ones.

Charity tried for a faint smile, though it came out a little shaky, what with it being nine in the morning and her having not yet partaken of her usual cup of steaming tea.

"Good morning, my dear." A smile stretched across Luke's face as he beckoned her closer. She stepped to his side. What manner of meeting was this? No doubt her captain husband considered it a reviewing of his troops. Though if the sorts she looked upon were any indication of the army in his possession, he'd be in a sad state if he ever hoped to outwit the enemy.

"Good morning." What did he mean by terming her "my dear"? They scarcely knew each other. Her smile deepened. After all, every good captain expected the underlings to believe he was on good terms with his second-in-command.

"I'm glad you joined us." Though he couldn't have gotten much sleep, he looked as rested as if he'd spent eight hours in untroubled slumber. His sage-colored coat matched his buff breeches, and he'd subdued his dark hair, though a renegade thatch still fell over his forehead.

"Everyone, allow me to present your mistress, my wife, Charity Warren." He slid his arm through hers, drawing her against his side. Heat brushed her cheeks as her arm bumped up against his, coming against a wall of strength and solidity.

The assembled group chorused greetings. For an instant, Charity remembered her debutante presentation at court and how the assembled royalty had behaved, all subdued nods and polished smiles. Today, it was her turn to play the queen, meeting her kingdom for the first time.

The notion made her dip her chin and unfurl a smile she hoped was gracious.

"I'm very happy to make your acquaintance, and I do hope we shall all get on well together." She glanced up at Luke and found him looking down at her, smiling. "My husband and I look forward to making Cavington Hall a family home again, as it has been in generations past." After someone got rid of the dust first.

"I was just informing everyone that, yes, we intend to take up residence here. And that if they wish to remain, changes must be made. I don't know what you all have been doing in the absence of an able master, but it obviously hasn't been performing your duties." Though any good servant would have taken this as an insult, Luke said it with a polished smile, prompting a few nervous chuckles from the assemblage. His gaze sharpened. "That changes. Right now. If you wish to remain in my family's employ, each of you will conduct yourselves with utmost regard for your place here. You will work hard and perform your duties in a satisfactory manner or risk losing your situation."

A few tenuous glances passed between the younger members of the group—a lanky youth probably employed as a footman and two adolescent girls who were either kitchen maids or housemaids.

"In return, you will receive a fair wage and find me and Mrs. Warren to be a fair master and mistress. There will also be a new butler and housekeeper, both of whom we intend to engage before the week is out. In our decision, we will look for those who will serve as your superiors with intelligence and kindness. There will also be another addition, that of morning prayers. I hope to use this time to provide you with spiritual support, supplemented by weekly church attendance on Sundays. Illness or other extenuating circumstances are the only excuses I will tolerate if you are absent at any of these events." He closed his hand around Charity's, and she found her senses awash in the peculiarly mesmerizing scents of musk and sea air.

Had he been on a walk already this morning? For how else could he smell of the sea? What time did this man rise? No one, at least, could accuse him of laziness.

"I also wish to inform you that I will be hiring a new nurse to attend my father. Mrs. Phipps has regretfully declined to join us in our new venture." Was she mistaken, or did amusement spark in his eyes at the word *regretfully*? She could only imagine the sort of row that had ensued during that conversation.

A grin that was anything but matronly tugged on her lips. She hastily tamped it down and smoothed her expression into one more suited to Cavington's new mistress.

"That concludes what I have to say to you. It is up to you now, each of you, to decide whether or not you intend to remain employed here. I will not judge those who make a decision to leave, and if they choose to do so, I will grant them a week's pay and a reference based upon how worthy I deem their character. Does anyone have any questions?"

"I do." The lanky youth thrust up his hand.

"Yes?" Luke gave him a nod as if granting permission to proceed.

"Well. . ." His neck turned a shade of bright red. "I don't have nothing against morning prayers and all, but sometimes, in the evenings, we like to get up a game of cards downstairs. Not for money or anything like that. Just the sport of it. Would you be objecting to that, Cap'n?"

Though familiarity with her husband's expressions wasn't something Charity could lay great claim to, the studied way Luke glanced up at the ceiling suggested he struggled to contain his amusement as much as she did.

The young man rocked in his seat, eyes darting between Luke and the floor, as if awaiting Luke's verdict from the Almighty.

Her husband finally must have trusted himself to keep a straight face, as he addressed the youth with the slightest of smiles. "No, as a general rule, I don't object to that, Harold. Of course, those we employ as butler and housekeeper will have the final say. But during the interview, I might happen to inquire whether or not they've an objection to cards. Played in good fun, that is."

Harold's shoulders visibly relaxed. "Then you can count me in, Cap'n Warren. I'll be proud to serve you as footman."

"Excellent. Other questions?"

And so it went. When all was said and done, six out of the seven decided to stay. At the end, Luke dismissed them to their duties—foremost being the preparation of decent accommodations for the two of them, followed by a thorough cleaning of the drawing room.

When the room emptied, Luke turned to her.

"Well, that's over with. Thank heaven." He scrubbed a hand across the bridge of his nose. "I'll go into the village this afternoon to see about a housekeeper and butler, as well as more footmen, maids, and some outdoor staff. To look at things now, you wouldn't believe it, but at one time, we boasted a total of five and thirty serving at the hall.

"I suppose with my father ailing, wages weren't distributed regularly. We had a steward at one point, but no one seems to recall what happened to him, other than that he disappeared one day, along with the under cook and a quantity of beef and silver candlesticks." He dropped into a chair, a cloud of dust poofing up from the white sheet covering the upholstery. Resting his forehead in his uninjured hand, he sat in silence. Outside, steady rain pinged and pattered, the sky dull as pewter.

Charity pressed her lips together, hands limp at her sides. Luke looked wretched sitting in a room that had once been a place of beauty but now showed sorry signs of squalor and neglect.

She didn't want to pity him. He'd brought this upon himself, leaving as he had, without giving a single thought to what and whom he left behind. He could have stayed, been at his father's side, taken over the responsibilities as master of Cavington forthwith after his father's apoplexy.

She didn't want to forgive him for his treatment of her, either. If he'd bothered to answer her letters, perhaps she'd have decided to visit his family, could have ascertained the state of things, and then summoned him home.

Yes, the fault lay with him. And he was paying for it.

But though she didn't want to pity or forgive, as she crossed the room and knelt at his side, a bit of both took root deep within her heart.

She touched his hand, kneeling on a rug in need of a thorough beating, heedless of the state of her skirt.

He looked up, in his eyes the angst and frustration he'd masked so well when the servants had been present. A strong man of military bearing, cracking under the weight of walking a path marked by milestones he himself had set in place.

"I saw my father last night, after you were abed."

"How is he?"

"Bearing up as well as can be expected, from what I can gather. He refused to speak to me. I suppose he has a right to his anger. But. . ."

"But what?" She asked the question in a tone meant to coax an answer, the way one might speak to a frightened child.

"Facing the tangible evidence of one's own actions is a fate I'd not wish upon my worst enemy," he muttered.

"Do not distress yourself." She could have settled for drawing his attention by touching his hand and taking hers away. But she kept her fingers upon his, hoping he might gather a bit of strength, something his own presence emanated for others. "I'll help you. With the servants, the house, your father. Even the mine, though I can't claim two pennyworth of knowledge about it." She gave a tremulous laugh, rewarded by a shadow of a smile crossing his lips. "I'll do whatever I can to serve. I promise you."

The look of raw gratitude that softened his features only firmed her resolve. She'd work hard and tirelessly to aid Cavington in its rebirth. It mattered to him.

And thus, inexplicably, to her as well.

Chapter Six

He had one thing to say about Charity Stanwood Warren.

She amazed him.

Luke could scarcely believe his eyes as he took in the great hall. The parquet floor gleamed brighter than new copper farthings. A fire burned in the enormous stone hearth, its glint reflected in the shining suit of armor standing sentry nearby. Not a speck of dust remained in sight. Not. One. Speck.

And it had only been two weeks.

He let the door close behind him, hair and clothes windblown from a ride over to the mine. Things were...well, a bit trickier there. But he wouldn't dwell on such frustrations now. Not when he had this great hall to admire.

A trio of uniformed maids bustled past—new employees. And hard workers, if Luke didn't miss his guess. They eyed him, one of the girls blushing and giggling. Generally, such a display would have annoyed him. But not today. No, today nothing could spoil his good mood.

He crossed the great hall, spying Lyleton, the new butler. One who had no objection to cards played for pleasure, who doubled as a mining expert, having worked in one for half of his two score years, and who knew how to oversee rowdy footmen.

Again, Luke couldn't take a scrap of credit for having found the man. Charity had tracked him down, hired him, and outfitted the burly man with a new suit of livery.

If he hadn't partaken in the conversation, he'd never have guessed that this was the girl his father had told him to wed to obliterate any scandal attached to her name. Though they'd spoken of many things—his navy days, her relationship with her father, the current affairs of Cavington Hall—Percy Browne, the man she'd been entangled with, had not been one of them.

Somehow, Luke sensed that Charity's crime had been mere youth and ignorance. Though he'd never been a womanizing flirt, he'd been acquainted with plenty in the navy and knew how skillfully they worked their charms.

If he ever crossed paths with Charity's seducer, he'd be hard pressed to refrain from inflicting serious injury upon his personhood.

"Do you know where Mistress Warren might be found?" He couldn't keep the smile in check that came from finding Lyleton balancing a silver tray in one hand and a half-eaten cheese sandwich in the other. His staff might be a bit unconventional, but who cared? They were hard workers, and with time, they could be trained in the finer points of their positions.

"Right behind you, Captain." Lyleton swiped crumbs from his mouth with the back of his sandwich-holding hand.

Luke turned. His heart sped up undeniably.

Charity stood a few paces away, her pale pink dress accentuating the roses in her cheeks. She carried a ledger and was making a notation in it with a pencil, her lower lip tucked between her teeth.

"Go belowstairs and finish your sandwich." Luke grinned at the butler, waiting until the man had retreated. In two strides, he reached Charity. A wrinkle marred her porcelain brow, and she didn't look up.

"Mistress Warren?"

"Yes?" She raised her eyes, dropping the pencil. "Oh, it's you." A little laugh escaped. She closed the ledger and bent to pick up the pencil, but he was faster and closed his hand around it. He spun the pencil between his fingers, grinning.

She watched him, an incredulous tilt to her lips. "Why are you smiling?"

"When a man has as fine a wife as mine, the better question is, why would he *not* smile." The words had come before he'd fully pondered them. Though spoken in the midst of the moment, they didn't exactly line up with their plans for a businesslike relationship.

Though not for a moment did he regret them.

She blinked rapidly, as if disbelieving. "Are you quite well?"

"Are compliments a sign of illness?"

She said nothing, her gaze everywhere. Flitting from the floor to the ceiling to the suit of armor. It lingered on the suit of armor the longest, as if seeking a satisfactory answer within the empty shell. If they'd had a real marriage, she wouldn't be looking for chaperone material inside the depths of medieval weaponry.

But then, it would do him good to remember they didn't have a real marriage.

"No. Of course not. But I don't see what I've done to deserve them." Finally, she tore her gaze away from Sir Whoever's battle garments. Her eyes, as vast and untamed as the sea he'd gazed upon not half an hour ago, regarded him in true confusion.

She honestly didn't know? Had his sister, Harriet, taken the trouble to arrange a vase of flowers, she'd not have been content until she informed everyone on the entire estate of her service.

He would have shaken his head, had he not feared Charity would interpret the gesture amiss.

"Allow me to enlighten you then." He swept his arm across the expanse of restored beauty that made up the great hall. "Two weeks ago, this place looked like something out of one of Mrs. Radcliffe's novels. Today, not only could the room be walked in without encountering a speck of dust, but we could actually entertain in here. Oh, and I neglected to mention, we also now have a fully staffed household of servants, each of whom you interviewed and employed. You ask what you have done to deserve a simple compliment. Well, there you have it."

As he spoke, he watched her face transform. From dubious, to incredulous, until finally, finally, something entered her eyes. Wonderment, perhaps. Joy, maybe. Belief. As if accepting his words and their impact. Possibly even their truth.

A warmth spread through his chest. He took a step closer, the light in her eyes drawing him toward her like a moth toward a dancing flame.

"I was only doing what I promised. Trying to help. There is a responsibility that comes with the ownership of such a fine estate. I did not wish you to bear the weight alone." Sincerity shone in her eyes. A sweet sincerity he did not deserve. In fact, all that she'd given him he did not deserve. He'd abandoned his home and family. It was only right he should struggle in reclaiming the pieces. But no. She'd aided him, two weeks of her efforts accomplishing far more than a month of his ever could.

And this was the woman he'd forsaken after their wedding.

Could there be any greater idiocy?

An idea sprang forth, its shoots wrapping around his mind and gaining a foothold. In a sudden gesture, he tugged the ledger from her hands and dropped it onto a table that stood against the wall, holding a vase of fresh-cut flowers.

"I've come to a conclusion." He kept his expression serious.

"What?" Her hands fingered the folds of her dress, as if at a loss for how to occupy themselves now empty of the ledger. Her own expression mirrored his: serious. But it put him in mind of a newly trained kitten awaiting a scolding from its owner. A trifle crushed, as if she expected him to renege the compliment with criticism.

He needed to erase that look from her eyes. And fast.

"That my wife is in need of the afternoon off. And as general of our little army, I command her to take some time for pleasure. With me." A smile crept across his mouth. It sounded even better voicing it aloud.

"But I can't. The menus need to be gone over with Cook. I must discuss the shrubbery with our new gardener, and though the housekeeper plans to oversee the removal of the ruined furniture from the small sitting room, I want to make sure they are only taking the proper items." She'd ticked each task off her fingers and seemed poised to add more.

He captured her hand.

And truly, completely, savored taking it prisoner. Her fingers relaxed within his, their softness brushing against the callous on his palm. *She* relaxed, mouth agape in a small O.

"Nothing unburdens one like a bracing ride across the land. We're going riding. That's an order." A thought struck him like a spark against flint, dousing some of his enthusiasm. Who did he think he was to make such masterful statements? And what if she couldn't ride?

"Unless. . .unless you don't—"

"Wish to?" Her hand remained within his uninjured one. What he wouldn't give for her thoughts to transfer themselves into his mind with the joining of their hands. He'd give the silver in Cavington's safe—well, what little remained of it—to discern what thoughts raced through her mind at this exact moment.

"No." His grin turned sheepish. "Ride."

A laugh rippled from her lips. She pressed her hand against her mouth to cover it. The hand that had been holding his.

How bereft his seemed with the absence of hers.

"You doubt I can ride?" Charity quirked a brow. As if rendering him an idiot with that single gesture, the way a queen rendered subjects banished with one wave of her hand.

No. She hadn't rendered him an idiot. He'd pegged himself as one the moment he walked out the door of her father's drawing room on their wedding night.

"I didn't say that." How could he come up with a reasonable answer with her staring at him in that quizzical way, suggesting she deemed him a wee bit empty in the attic?

"But you thought it." It took him a second to interpret the mischievous glimmer in her gaze. She was teasing him.

The little minx. Perhaps she deserved to be taught a lesson in riding.

Though, in all honesty, there were a few other things he'd rather teach her.

Starting with. . .

Oh, no. Steady on, Captain. He couldn't even be thinking about. . .

Kissing her.

He definitely needed a ride to clear his muddled brain.

"All right." He held up his hands in mock surrender. "I was just asking. Thought it the gentlemanly thing to do before putting you on a horse. Being thrown is a nasty business."

"I know. A knock to the head is always quite unpleasant. As is a tear in a brand-new riding habit." She spun on her heel, heading in the direction of the stairs. "Thankfully, I've since commissioned another. Give me ten minutes to change."

She darted up the stairs, leaving him looking up after her. He waited until she'd disappeared down the hallway before ascending himself.

He'd change into his own riding clothes.

Then dunk his head in a basin of water.

After all, he had to do something to cool off after the heat emanating from her gaze.

❧

Breathless from the exertion of changing far faster than was her wont, Charity nonetheless reached the stables with a minute to spare. She smoothed a leather-gloved hand down the front of her claret-colored riding habit, clutching her crop in the other.

Luke was nowhere in sight.

Good. She needed time to think. Time that had not been afforded her during her mad dash to change outfits.

He wanted to go riding. Not alone, as he had every day since their arrival in Cornwall.

He wanted to go with her.

Something deliciously sweet swept through her, curling her toes and bringing a flush to her cheeks that the bracing wind ought to have alleviated. Not that such a sensation was wrong. The man was lawfully her husband.

Yet it somehow seemed inappropriate. And why shouldn't it? They'd gone from strangers, to acquaintances, to friends in the amount of time most couples spent sharing dances observed by mamas and exchanging calling cards. It was much too soon to be thinking of him as she did. Had. Yes, had. She intended to stop.

She'd labored like a galley slave in reinventing Cavington Hall. Reinventing was probably too lofty a word. She'd simply attempted to unearth it from beneath all that wretched dust. And she'd enlisted a shipload of servants to assist.

The reins of power still chafed in her untried hands. Yet they no longer caused blisters, and she found it easier to keep a grip on them. Or maybe that was simply due to her efficient housekeeper and butler. With such a staff, it would be far too easy for her to become superfluous.

She didn't want that. Not when Luke noticed her efforts and praised her for them.

Sweet nectar, his praises.

The subject of her musings appeared, dressed in riding attire. Gracious, he presented a sight worth beholding. She wasn't deaf to the whispers and titters that emerged from the feminine quarter of her staff every time Luke came within viewing range.

"Oh, he's a fine figure of a man, isn't he?"

She wasn't immune, either. Regrettably. It would have been easier had her pulse not done a twirl at the sight of his broad shoulders fitted snugly within a coal-colored riding coat, a near perfect match to his hair, which tangled in the wind as he walked. Simpler, had she not taken note of the dimple emerging on one edge of his smile. Easier. Simpler. Unfortunately, both evaded her.

"Ready?" he called. Two grooms led horses from the stable. There could be no doubt as to the owner of the first. A jet-black stallion with a perfect white star on its forelock snorted and pranced at the sight of Luke. No doubt anticipating the ride like any hot-blooded horse would.

The other, a slightly smaller, though no less impressive mount, awaited her. Dun-colored, the mare whickered as Charity approached and stroked just above its nose.

"Aren't you a pretty thing?" she whispered, inhaling the scents of warm horse and cool autumn wind. "Let's show those two the stuff we're made of, all right?"

"I see you've met Dearover." Luke's voice sounded behind her, quiet enough to not startle the horse, high enough to be heard over the wind.

She turned, one hand still resting on the horse's body. "Dearover?"

"In the old Cornish tongue, it means 'dear of her.' This girl found Harriet when she got lost as a child. The village spent all night searching for her, but it wasn't until my mother took Dearover out to search that Harriet was found." He patted the horse, affection warm in his gaze. "I thought you'd enjoy riding her this afternoon."

"I would, yes." She smiled. "I'm sure Dearover and I will get along in grand style."

"Then shall we?" Though two grooms stood nearby, one holding the reins of Luke's horse, the over hovering near Dearover, Luke bent, locking his hands together.

She hesitated. Though he no longer wore a bandage around his injured fingers, they couldn't possibly be equal to bearing her weight.

"Ah." He lifted a brow, following her gaze to his hand. "Let's try this another way then, shall we?"

Before she could so much as reply, he swooped her into his arms and placed her in the saddle, the movement effortless, as if she weighed no more than a tot of three. Her breath whooshed out at the magnitude of his strength. No sense pitying the man for the loss of a couple of fingers. He certainly didn't pity himself. And the strength of the rest of him compensated by far.

Atop Dearover, she watched as Luke mounted his own horse, wondering if the sudden crest of her heartbeat was due to the speed in which she'd been transferred to Dearover's back.

It couldn't have a thing to do with the way Luke looked in the saddle—dangerously tempting and as magnificent as the animal he rode. Could it?

Away they went, leaving behind the confines of the stable yard for Cornwall at its finest. Expansive moors edged by plunging cliffs. The blue of the sea, the rush of the wind, and the sheer abandon of being at the center of it all.

When God made Cornwall, He must have been in the mood to create something rare and grand and breath-stealing.

Charity drew her horse alongside Luke's, as the animals' hooves pounded the earth, racing alongside the sea. They fairly skimmed along, her hair streaming in the wind, her lungs full of crisp sea air.

She stole a glance at Luke, and their gazes collided. A spark lit his eyes.

Challenge.

Born and bred city girl though she was, she'd spent several summers of her early teens at a friend's estate in Derbyshire. They'd done little except ride, much to the exasperation of the governess attempting to marshal them into ladylike decorum.

But Luke didn't know that.

She'd always liked surprises.

She pressed her heels against Dearover's flanks, leaning forward in the saddle. Then they flew. Above them, a shaft of sunlight pierced the greyness of the sky, but they rode too fast for it to warm her. Not a soul except Luke, herself, and the horses viewed their afternoon race. For the moment, the moor was theirs.

Cornwall. . .was theirs.

Dearover passed Luke's horse, leaving them behind.

Ah, victory.

Breathless and satisfied, she tugged on the reins, bringing Dearover to a stop beside a lone, gnarled tree. Charity tilted her head and watched as Luke galloped toward them, halting a few paces away.

"I won." She stated the words with a toss of her head and a saucy smile.

"So you did." He dismounted and led his mount to a tree, tying him to it, then walked toward her with the strides of one whose confidence hadn't been dented in the least.

Clasping her waist, he lifted her down. Upon solid ground, she looked up at him.

Temptation owned his grin, as if he knew the havoc his smiles could wreak on the female persuasion. As if he knew. . .and prided himself on besting her with it, since he hadn't in the race.

Infuriating man. One who smelled like musk and let the wind disarrange his hair. One who put his hands around her waist, evoking longings she scrambled to cipher out.

He lifted one hand and slowly, gently captured one of the curls that had come loose and hung against her cheek, tucking it behind her ear. His touch seared her.

Infuriating man.

Chapter Seven

Only one thing could shatter the fog of pleasure that hung over Luke after his ride with Charity. And that was a visit with his father. Yet the time constraints of overseeing the mine and the goings-on at Cavington had kept such visits at the barest minimum. This afternoon, however, Luke intended to temper the guilt eating his conscience, and thus, he stood outside his father's bedchamber.

Luke knocked, but only out of custom rather than necessity. It wasn't as if the man had a great deal of demands upon his time, as in former days. From what Luke could discern, his father hadn't left this room since his apoplexy two years ago.

Receiving no reply, Luke entered. Light filtered between the partially drawn curtains, its sunlit fingers resting on the blue coverlet and his father's face.

His partially paralyzed face. That, along with the loss of use of one side of his body, had been the result of the attack, rendering a once hale and hearty Cornishman a virtual prisoner within these four walls.

Luke couldn't help but pity him.

He approached the bed. "Good afternoon, Father."

"Luke." The man lifted his good hand before letting it fall back onto the bedclothes, his speech audible, though somewhat indistinct.

"It's a fine afternoon outside. Down at the mine, they're working on another load of copper. It's to be a goodly one, the best we've seen all year." Not everything at the mine was quite that simple, but it would do no good to tell his father that. Managing a mine proved a far different endeavor than captaining a ship full of men.

His father nodded, eyes vacant. It wasn't as if he didn't possess the ability to acknowledge or answer Luke, but rather, he chose not to do so.

Such had been the way during each one of their three prior visits. Since his father was unable to command and control, he seemed to have decided to say nothing at all.

It would have been easier had Luke simply been able to chalk it up to the man's indisposition. Yet he couldn't. For the truth of the matter was, his father clutched a grudge the way a beggar child grasped a sovereign. Hard and greedily.

Today, Luke was determined that his father would speak to him.

Give me wisdom, Lord. And humility to acknowledge the wrong I have done and make it right.

"Did you not hear me? What I said about the mine?" Pulling up a hard-backed wing chair, Luke sat beside the bed and clasped his hands loosely between his knees.

"I heard you." Though his impairment prevented the words from emerging sharp and clipped, there was no mistaking the rancor that still existed.

"I wish you would tell me what the matter is. Please. I came to Cavington hoping to mend the past. But I can't mend it, unless you let me." He gazed upon his father's haggard features. They'd once been firm and strong, handsome enough to charm the ladies, with a tongue equipped to issue wit at every card table or dinner party.

The starkness of the change shook Luke.

"You should never have come back. It would have been better if you'd stayed at sea. Or died."

Luke scrubbed a hand across his jaw, fingers raking over stubble. The words pierced him. His father, a man he'd admired in boyhood, now said he wished him dead.

Sometimes, the gall of one's mistakes turned too sour for even the most penitent to swallow.

"I know what I did was wrong. I abandoned you, all of you. But I'm here now, intending to stay and make amends. Why won't you let me? Why can't you forgive me?" A tinge of desperation mingled with the humility of his words. He desired forgiveness. Deeply. Like the prodigal son, he longed for his father to welcome him home. Though Luke wouldn't go so far as to request the fatted calf, it would have been a balm if a dinner of herbs had been offered.

"Forgive you?" His father's sneer was but a shadow of the aristocratic fury he'd have unleashed in former years. "You don't deserve forgiveness. You'll never. . .deserve it." He fell back against the pillows as if the effort of speech had sapped him of all energy. The vacant expression that eclipsed his face assured Luke there would be no more conversation today.

"Rest now, Father," Luke said quietly, standing and quitting the room. He crossed the hallway, the sounds of servants intent upon their duties blending in the background.

He couldn't dwell on his father's words. The wound they'd inflicted wanted only a bandage, not a cleaning. He'd prove himself by his actions, since his words seemed to have no effect. He'd be the best master Cavington ever possessed and the best mine owner, too. He'd already written to his sister, Harriet, requesting she join them at the hall. His family, together under one roof after living scattered to the winds for too long. Perhaps then, with the mine flourishing and his sister home, his father would forgive him.

Jaw firm, he descended the stairs. In the great hall, he spied Charity bent over a hall table, reading a letter.

She looked up, a sparkle in her gaze. The effects of a bracing ride across windswept moors still lingered in the bloom gracing her cheeks. It had done her good, their afternoon outing. Perhaps riding could become a frequent event.

"You'll never guess what just arrived." She passed him an elegant piece of stationery, a bit wrinkled around the edges where she'd clutched it.

He scanned the missive. An invitation to a ball held at the home of Lord and Lady Ashburn, a week from Saturday. Though they'd seen most of the villagers during Sunday services, they had yet to make an appearance among the gentry as husband and wife.

A situation soon to be remedied, from the looks of the letter and Charity's eyes.

"The Ashburns always host an annual party." He handed the invitation back to her. "It's the finest event for miles."

"Then there's no question about it. Captain and Mrs. Warren ought to be in attendance." She laughed, a giddy sound that unwound some of the tightness noosing his nerves.

Captain and Mrs. Warren. Yes, no doubt there was plenty of gossip about that elusive couple. Guests would attend, simply out of curiosity. And in anticipation of the earl of Ashburn's specially concocted punch, of course.

How easily she'd fallen into her role as wife. Charity was born to manage the house and servants, no matter too little for her consideration. And the fire in her eyes after their ride as she'd stood, looking up at him, her bodice heaving with quick breaths, made him wonder if the time might come for a reevaluation of their original plan to have a name-only marriage.

He'd welcome such a conversation.

"Captain and Mrs. Warren, you say?" He smiled down at her, gaze riveted to the curl hanging tantalizingly near her ear. What a temptation to repeat the gesture of this afternoon and brush it away, linger at the soft place under her chin. He flexed the fingers of his good hand into a fist, keeping them determinedly behind his back. "I daresay then, they shall be."

He couldn't stop gazing at her. Maybe it was because she looked heartstoppingly beautiful in her cream-colored ball gown, a single strand of diamonds resting in the hollow of her throat. Or because when Luke stood especially close, the scent of jasmine enfolded him, a fragrance he could get drunk on. Or perhaps it was Charity's rose-tinged lips turned up in a smile, fixated upon him with a frequency he couldn't wrap his mind around.

He didn't like balls. Never had. Never expected to. What red-blooded man wanted to spend five hours in a too-hot, too-perfumed room with preening ladies and their whist-playing escorts, drinking tepid lemonade and eating sugary cake? Not him, that's for certain.

Though, if Charity remained at his side during every ball, he just might change his mind.

After greeting their hosts, they stood in a circle of acquaintances. Luke answered the offered pleasantries and responded in kind. But mostly, he just watched Charity when he thought she wasn't paying attention.

"Oh, yes, Mrs. Burton. You must come to tea and see Cavington Hall. It's truly a beautiful house, and I think you'd particularly appreciate the gardens." Charity's hand rested on his arm, but he might as well have been a stair railing for the little attention she paid him. Instead she was busy smiling at Mr. and Mrs. Burton, behaving as if she'd known them all her life.

And in the doing of it, quelling any gossip about Luke Warren, his new wife, and the circumstance surrounding their marriage. No one would dare speculate in the face of Charity's poise and sweetness.

"What makes you think that?" Mrs. Burton, who had the face of a bewildered goat—or so Luke had always thought—regarded Charity. Even the middle-aged lady's tone sounded like she was bleating.

"Why, the flower in your hair. It shows you have a great appreciation for nature." Charity gestured to the already wilting bloom twined in the lady's greying coiffure.

"You like it?" Mrs. Burton lifted a gloved hand as if to pat her hair. Maybe she thought she'd disarrange her maid's work, because she hastily lowered her hand.

"It's lovely." Charity smiled.

Luke shifted, glancing at Mr. Burton. The man stood next to his wife like a faithful sheepdog, as if he liked nothing better than to listen to the prattle of ladies.

Well, Burton could do as he pleased. Luke, on the other hand, intended to take advantage of the musicians tuning their instruments for the next set and claim his wife for a dance.

"Yes. Lovely." Luke nodded. He turned toward Charity. "You know, I suddenly have a great desire for a dance."

She peeped up at him. Her curls had been arranged in an upswept style, though a profusion of them brushed against her exposed neck. Luke had the sudden, mad urge to swipe the pins securing the rest and watch her hair fall down to her waist in a waterfall of gold, as it had the night when he'd knocked on her door and reentered her life.

He banished the thought from his mind. It didn't quite meet the requirements for appropriate subject matter to ponder during a ball.

"Do you? Is there a particular lady you'd care to partner?" Her tone had a touch of the coquette in it.

"Hmm. Let me think. There *is* someone I've been considering approaching, but I'm sure I'll be refused." Hang the fact that the Burtons still watched them. If his wife had a notion to flirt with him, by thunder, Luke intended to flirt right back.

"What makes you think that?" She tilted her head, the glitter of the gems around her neck catching the light of the chandelier.

"Just a suspicion. But I think I'll ask her anyway." He stepped aside and made move to head in the opposite direction. He'd give a guinea for a glance at her expression right about now. No doubt her pretty little mouth gaped with astonishment at the thought of him asking another woman to dance.

Good thing he wasn't looking in her direction. Whenever her mouth did that, he envisioned his own pressed against it.

He took a couple of steps, then turned. She stared at him, something like barely held back fury smoldering in her blue-green eyes. Approaching, he executed an elaborate bow.

"I would consider it the greatest of honors if you'd dance the next with me, Mrs. Warren."

The way she pressed her lips together made him suspect she was trying not to smile. "Very well. I'd hate to deny you 'the greatest of honors.'"

He led her onto the dance floor, and they took their places near the end of the set. The music struck up its first chords.

Thankfully, he possessed a proclivity to remember the steps of most country dances, which put him at liberty to simply enjoy the pleasure of dancing with her. Each time they linked arms for a half turn or clasped hands to sashay down the center, the rest of the room ceased to exist. Like a trained falconer who held out a gloved arm for the bird to find purchase, she drew him with her spell.

In former years, drink had appealed to him for its ability to lull one into a state of forgetfulness. Yet no amount of brandies had, or could, bring him the sense of utter bliss that the simplicity of partnering his wife on the dance floor had done in the space of ten minutes.

She moved through the steps with fluid grace, drawing his attention to the way her gown accentuated her soft curves. The music continued to play, but he could scarce hear it above the thudding of his own heart.

The dance ended, and everyone broke into spontaneous applause. Charity tilted her head back, clapping along with the rest, laughter on her lips.

His mouth went dry. He offered her his arm, and they exited the floor.

"Thank you for the dance." Wholly unaware. Yes, Charity, his wife, was wholly unaware of the havoc she wreaked in his mind.

"Did you know the Ashburns have a Vandyke in their library?"

"Really?" Her eyes widened.

"Yes." He piloted her in the direction of the ballroom's double doors.

"Where are we going?" She hurried to match his steps, and he forced himself to slow down.

"To see the Vandyke." The hall was blessedly empty, and he headed in the direction of the library with the determination of a captain piloting his ship through enemy waters. They gained the room. He shut the door behind them.

A Vandyke hung above the mantelpiece. But Luke hadn't come here for art. Unfortunately, he didn't have much appreciation for it, which in society's eyes, rendered him unfashionably ignorant.

Oh, he was daft all right. But his current stupidity had nothing to do with art and everything to do with the woman standing at his side, studying the Vandyke. A fire burned in the marble grate, lending the room a low-lit glow.

Shadows.

There had been shadows the night of their marriage ceremony. Nothing but firelight and a few candles to illuminate their faces as they pledged their troth.

That night, he had not kissed her.

But that was then. From the direction of the ballroom came the far-off sounds of music. Gently, Luke turned her to face him. She looked up at him, as forgetful of the painting as he. He reached up and cradled her cheek with his good hand. Time stood still as they regarded each other.

This was now.

So he kissed her. Crushed her against him, his fingers in her hair. She tasted like lemonade and exhilaration. The fragrance of jasmine crashed over him like a wave. He deepened the kiss, savoring the perfection of her against his chest, her lips exploring his as if she too had longed for this. As if she'd tossed away all notion of a business only marriage with sheer and total abandon.

The sound of the door opening punctured his oblivion.

Tamping down a word neither his mother nor the Almighty would approve of, Luke disentangled his fingers from their exploration of the softness of his wife's hair.

A liveried and powdered footman—the cause of their interruption.

"I beg your pardon, Captain Warren. But one of your servants just rode over and brought this." He held out a silver salver, his voice a monotone, as if he encountered couples in the throes of. . .well, never mind, every day.

Luke strode forward and snatched up the note. He broke the seal. A groan rose from deep within his chest as he read.

He crumpled the paper in his fist and turned back to Charity.

"There's to be an emergency meeting of the shareholders in a mine my father invested in long ago. It appears they are in some financial difficulty. I'm to report to Falmouth first thing tomorrow morning." It wasn't that the fate of the mine held much weight with him. The Warren family had their own mines, all beginning to prosper. His father had only invested in this one as a favor to a friend.

He'd need to leave right away to reach Falmouth in time for the early morning meeting. Which meant he wouldn't be able to discover what might have happened had their kiss continued.

Wretched turn of events.

Still, he'd go, even though he could've probably found someone to take his place. But that wasn't what Father would have done, so neither would Luke.

"I'm afraid I must return to Cavington and retrieve some papers. Will you accompany me, or would you prefer to remain here?" After the warmth of their embrace, the words sounded cold, even to his own ears.

But Charity didn't look upset, only confused. Her hair hung in a shambles down her back, a few pins still securing sections. Pink flushed her cheeks, and a darker shade than usual adorned her lips.

She looked like a woman who had been well and thoroughly kissed.

An expression that completely suited her.

"I'll go with you." She made for the door without hesitation. He followed, hoping they could escape out the front entrance without notice.

He'd leave as soon as he could for Falmouth.

For he couldn't return to his wife's side soon enough.

Chapter Eight

Kissing her husband was an entirely different experience than kissing Percy Browne. Like contrasting cheap muslin with fine velvet, there was no comparing the two. When Charity had kissed Percy, she'd been a girl in the throes of physical infatuation. With Luke, everything became a thousand times clearer, like looking into a newly polished mirror and seeing one's reflection in a different light. Yes, every thread of her being came alive when Luke held her in his arms. His kiss muddled her senses and made her giddy all at the same time. But there was more. More than there had ever been in those cheap moments when she'd fancied herself adored by Percy.

And it was the substance of that *more* that left her unable to focus on any task for five minutes flat.

It was eight in the morning, less than ten hours since Luke had galloped off into the darkness. She'd attempted to sleep but hadn't made much progress, so she had risen and dressed without the help of her maid and gone for a ride. Upon her return, she'd attired herself as befitted the mistress of Cavington and now sat in the dining room, pretending not to be achingly, painfully aware of Luke's absence at the other end of the table.

She'd always been a dreadful actress. So over a steaming cup of tea, she gave up all pretenses and let herself imagine what it would be like when he again sat across from her.

Did more kisses like the one they'd shared last night lay in her future? Like a child anticipating a treat, she couldn't help but wish fiercely that it would be so. And if this morning he had occupied his usual chair, she'd have been hard pressed to refrain from locking the servants out of the dining room and discovering if Luke's cravat would untie as easily as she suspected.

A blush flamed her cheeks. As a married woman, none of these thoughts ought to make her feel guilty. They did, though. It would be best to dwell on something else.

She took a ladylike sip of tea, setting the cup down with nary a rattle against its saucer.

How *did* one begin to untie a cravat?

"If you please, ma'am. You have a visitor."

She started, splashing tea down the sides of the cup as she pivoted. Servants were taught to walk noiselessly throughout the house, but sneaking up on her really should be outlawed.

"Very well, Harold. Send them in." The footman exited, and Charity patted the back

58

of her hair, ascertaining its neatness. She picked up a napkin and dabbed at the splotch on the tablecloth.

"Miss Harriet Warren, ma'am."

As gracefully as she could manage, Charity rose from her seat. A twinge of anxiety pricked her middle. Luke's sister. And they were to meet now, when Luke was away, unable to aid in the introductions.

One glimpse of the young lady's face put to rest any social anxieties. A petite girl a few years Charity's junior, Harriet possessed the same dark hair as her brother, as well as the same defined cheekbones. Cheekbones and eyes red and blotchy from tears.

"Miss Warren, what a surprise to see you here." Charity smiled. "You may leave us, Harold." She dared not say more until the room had emptied of listening ears. Harold, unfortunately, had a tendency to gossip, and Harriet looked distressed indeed.

"Mrs. Warren. I'm terribly sorry to arrive without advance warning." Harriet's tone was cultured, though a bit hoarse.

"You needn't apologize. This is your family's home, and you are always welcome in it. Pray, sit down." She motioned to a dining room chair. "May I offer some refreshment? Tea, perhaps?"

The young lady shook her head. "Is my brother at home?" Urgency flashed through her midnight eyes like a lightning strike against a stormy sky.

"Not at present. He's in Falmouth—"

"Good." Harriet grasped one of Charity's hands with surprising strength for one so fragile in appearance. "My brother has written me that you're a kind person. I hope I might dare to trust that such kindness might be extended to even one so undeserving as myself." Tears trailed down the girl's cheeks.

"Of course you may." Charity nodded. She'd do all in her power to help. But what tragedy could have happened to bring the young woman all the way from Bath without first sending word of her impending arrival?

"Thank you. You are too kind." Harriet gulped. "Forgive me, if what I am about to say will shock you. We do not know each other, and I'm ashamed to bring such troubles to you."

A memory niggled the back of her mind. Harriet's expression was familiar. Charity had worn it herself that night so long ago when her folly had been unearthed.

But Harriet couldn't possibly. . .

"I think you should sit down." She kept her tone soft as she assisted Harriet into a chair. Through her tears, the girl gave a grateful smile.

Charity took the chair nearest. "Now, compose yourself, if you can, and tell me what the trouble is."

"I'm ruined." Though Harriet whispered the words, their impact echoed through the dining room. Harsh words. Like *smallpox* or *blight*, *ruined* was the verbal equivalent of a deathblow. Only ladies were ruined, of course. Men simply performed the act and let the woman take all the blame. A hateful state of affairs, but a true one.

Charity forced her features to remain composed. "How?" It was a cruel question, but one that must be asked if she was to help the girl.

"How does it happen for any woman? I met a man." A trace of bitterness simmered in Harriet's tone. "I fancied myself willing to pay any price for his attentions, and I've paid. Dearly."

"How. . .dearly?" Charity considered the consequences of her own situation to have exacted a great price. Yet she sensed Harriet spoke of a cost far greater than her own.

Harriet placed a hand across her middle. She met Charity's gaze with a flinch, like a puppy cowering under a blow.

The air froze in Charity's lungs.

With child. And unmarried.

Harriet Warren had every reason to cry.

But a small smile softened the girl's lips. Why? Was she out of her senses? This wasn't a situation to be smiling over.

"I know what you must be thinking. If my condition is discovered, my reputation will be in shreds. But there is hope." Another smile. "Though I need your help. The gentleman who is responsible for. . .this"—she waved her hand delicately in the direction of her still-flat midsection—"has agreed to pay the consequences."

"Become your husband, you mean." If so, this was promising. As long as the marriage was accomplished quickly, respectability could still be maintained.

Harriet nodded. "He feels great shame in his actions and wishes to make amends. We will travel to Gretna Green and become husband and wife posthaste. But though this man is a gentleman, he's a bit short on funds at present. Some provision for our journey would be useful."

"Perhaps we should wait for your brother to return. He's tending to a business venture at present but will arrive within the day."

Terror filled her eyes as Harriet shook her head. "How could I ever face him? In his eyes, I'm his little sister. Adored playmate. Childhood confidante. Now, I'm scarcely better than a strumpet." Her gaze pierced Charity's, vulnerability mingling with determination.

"But if we were to wed first, before Luke returns, then. . .he need never know. Please, ma'am. I know perhaps 'tis wrong, but I shrink from telling him the truth. The look in his eyes when he hears. . ." Her voice wavered on the verge of a sob. "How can I bear it? I haven't the strength." She lowered her face to her hands, shoulders shaking.

How well I understand her suffering. Perhaps others might not, but have I not tasted the same grief? The same desperation, anxiety, shame all mingled into one? Though I cannot remove the consequences of her actions, I may and can alleviate the severity of her future punishment.

Charity mentally counted the contents of her purse.

Twenty-five pounds.

"Harriet." She rested her hand against the girl's bowed shoulder. "You needn't be afraid any longer. I will help you."

Harriet lifted her face, eyes swollen but face transformed. "You'll help us?" She breathed the words with the look of one pardoned from life imprisonment. "Oh, Percy will be so relieved! He told me we'd get no help from my family, but I assured him we should at least try. He's outside, waiting in the carriage." She stood with remarkable haste for one grief-stricken only seconds ago. "I'll bring him in. If your kindness could extend to seeing your way to providing us something to eat?"

"Why...yes." Charity nodded, though Harriet had already quitted the room. She stood and moved to the bell pull. Again, that odd sense of remembrance. What was it that Harriet had just said to bring it on?

Oh, Percy will be so relieved!

That name. His name. The man who had ruined her and the man who had fathered Harriet's child could not be one and the same. It was too incredible. Impossible.

Her fingers latched around the bell pull. She yanked. On legs that felt as wobbly as congealed gravy, she crossed the room. Fingers finding the back of her chair, she began to pull it out. Her mind twisted and spun like a piece of linen tangled in a sharp wind.

The creak of the door hinges howled in her ears. Two sets of footsteps entered the room.

Charity forced herself to look up.

One never forgot the sight of devastation.

Harriet clung to Percy's arm, looking up at him as if for guidance. Percy released Harriet and took two strides to where Charity stood, clinging to the back of her chair as if her life depended upon it.

"Mrs. Warren." Perhaps it was the ringing in her ears, but something about his tone struck her as different. Less liquid and more substance. More humility and less devil-may-care.

"Mr. Browne." Thankfully, he did not attempt to take her hand or bow or do anything that suggested normalcy. Nothing about this situation or seeing him held even a shred of what was normal.

"Harriet says you've agreed to help us?" It was a question, not a statement. The old Percy was forever making demands. Now, his gaze pleaded with her.

Time suspended.

In the background, Charity focused on Harriet's pale, tear-blotched face. In the world in which they dwelt, reputation equaled the weight of gold. This young girl's was on the way to being annihilated.

How well she herself knew the devastation the Lady Blackthornes of the world could bring.

Percy waited, watching her.

Charity nodded.

One ought to feel a twinge of guilt after galloping one's horse as Luke had just done. Yet Seamus could well handle the speed, enjoyed it even.

And Luke, admittedly, had been anxious to return home. There was much to be discovered about his new relationship with Charity, and the process could not be begun soon enough.

He bounded up the remainder of the avenue and threw open the front door. He'd dash up to his room and change. No lady would appreciate being romanced by a suitor covered in travel grime. After that though. . .

Intent on his purpose, he crossed the great hall. The trip to Falmouth had been a waste. There hadn't even been a meeting. Somehow, the note had reached him with false information. He'd pushed himself and Seamus all for naught. Formerly, the situation would've put him in a foul temper.

But now, no expression seemed more natural than a smile.

Voices from the direction of the dining room caught his attention. He stopped, ears attuned.

Did Charity have guests?

He gave a cursory glance at his attire. Yes, he was dusty. Yes, a bit mud-splattered. But whatever guests within ought to be made aware of his return and, hopefully, sent on their merry way as soon as possible.

Glad he'd never considered himself a dandy, Luke gained the dining-room door and opened it.

Three sets of eyes swung in his direction. Charity. Harriet.

And a man he did not recognize but unaccountably disliked.

Luke gave the man a second glance. Wait. Recognition dawned on him. Years ago he'd encountered this person at social events before his departure for the navy. Years ago, three, to be exact, his father had told him of this man in a conversation that Luke, foxed as he was, by all rights should have forgotten.

Percy Browne. The man Charity, *his* Charity, had compromised herself with.

Every muscle in his body tensed, each coiling into a knot of disbelief and questions.

No mistake about it. Percy Browne sat at Cavington Hall's dining room table beside the two women Luke loved most. His wife and his sister.

The reason for his inconvenient marriage dared to sit at his table, eat his food, and come within mere inches of the woman he had once dishonored?

Luke's jaw hardened to granite.

This was not a moment for civility. Which was good.

Because Luke had no intention of granting this slime in human form a single drop.

Chapter Nine

Harriet's sobs rang through the house, each wail sharp and hollow. Desperate. Achingly desperate.

Charity couldn't stop shaking. Alone in her room, she squeezed her eyes shut, the memories of the past half hour echoing through her mind like a personal town crier.

Tearfully, Harriet had explained the reason for Percy's presence. Luke had allowed less than two minutes for explanation before taking action. He'd dragged Percy through the great hall and out onto the avenue. Before proceeding with the help of a riding crop to let Percy know exactly what he thought of his part in Harriet's ruination. Percy had blubbered and begged for mercy.

Luke had not relented. Finally, he'd thrown Percy into the carriage and bid the driver depart. Charity couldn't tell whether Percy had any hope of making it to the nearest surgeon before losing consciousness from loss of blood.

A shudder trembled through her.

The look in Luke's gaze as he'd stridden inside, riding crop still in hand, would have paralyzed even the staunchest soldier.

He'd locked himself in the library. Harriet had fled to her old bedchamber.

No one had emerged since.

She must go to Luke. Though Percy and Harriet held the largest share of blame in concocting the plot, she wasn't entirely guiltless in agreeing to fund their journey without her husband's permission. She needed to apologize for her actions, and Luke needed a comforter, an adviser. A wife to offer wisdom and encouragement. He'd controlled his temper in her presence once before. Surely he'd do so again.

Letting her eyes fall closed, Charity whispered a prayer for guidance, then rose from her bed on legs that, though not altogether steady, had the strength to carry her downstairs.

After Luke, she'd see to Harriet. Experience had taught her that the tears of the remorseful were best shed in solitude. A witness only added to one's humiliation.

The walk downstairs seemed to take an eternity, and yet ended all too soon. Outside the library door, the heavy wood a barrier between her and Luke—the stubborn, reckless man who filled such a large space in her heart—she raised her fist and knocked.

"Who is it?" His tone emerged low and harsh.

Lifting her chin, she swallowed hard. "It's. . .Charity." She'd have said *your wife*, but it somehow seemed inappropriate against the face of his wrath.

Silence stretched, taut like ropes and just as binding. Had he heard her? Did he intend to leave her out here?

After what seemed like hours, yet probably did not exceed five minutes, the door opened. Without a word, Luke held it as she entered, then crossed the carpet and resumed his seat behind his desk. Shadows dimmed the room, the fire low and candles sputtering.

Charity scarcely resisted pressing a hand to her mouth. In her presence, Luke had never been anything but punctiliously neat and well attired. Now, an empty decanter of brandy shared desk space with a full one, a glass resting next to his hand.

His attire put any wonderment about the removal of his cravat to rest. It lay on the floor like a coiled snake, along with his jacket.

Battles with female emotions she was no stranger to. Surely those that men experienced couldn't be all that dissimilar.

She waited to speak until she stood beside his chair. He slouched in his seat, hand clamped to his forehead, strands of ebony curling over his knuckles. A lion, caged for the moment, but with features no less fearsome.

"Talk to me." Her words whispered above the crackle of the fire and the ticking of the mantel clock. "It will help."

He turned and finally, finally looked at her. As soon as he had, she almost wished he'd remained as he was. Anger smoldered in his eyes, searing her with its sparks.

"You speak of helping?" His tone was hoarse, gravelly. "I beg you, do not. You've helped quite enough for one day. If you've any sense, you'll refrain from doing further damage."

Like a branding iron, his words scorched the raw places in her heart, causing her to catch her breath against the pain. He was right. She had done damage. She'd agreed to alleviate Harriet's shame without a thought for what Luke would think or whether a marriage would be the best course to take. She'd simply acted, with a blindness shocking for one of whom better should be expected.

"What I did was wrong. I should never have allowed Mr. Browne into the house nor agreed to give them money without your permission. I'm sorry." A catch tangled with her words. Still she forced herself to look at Luke during her apology.

He stood. The chair rocked, almost toppling. She took a quick step back, her head bumping the wall.

His face toward the window, away from her, she stared at his strong shoulders. Though she could not see his expression, tension emanated from his frame like an odor, pungent and bitter.

Silence simmered. She dared not break it.

Without warning, he pivoted. "You're sorry? Oh, Charity." A groan rose from his lips. "Do not speak to me of apologies. In the face of all that has happened, they hold little merit. Or weight."

"But why? Nothing—"

"Nothing." His voice rose. "How carelessly you toss the word. Had I returned home an hour later. . .think of it, one *hour*, I'd have found my sister and that worthless swine, aided by your hand, on their way to joining in marriage, an institution durable as flint."

"That did not happen though. You returned. Can things not be mended?" Was his attitude not a bit extreme? She deserved his censure, yes, but to this degree?

"Can trust be mended? It's a difficult fabric to weave from the first. Once rent, I see little hope of repair." The coldness in his tone strangled her, vanquishing the remainder of her calm.

"But I trusted you!" She rushed to his side, grasping his arm, gaze seeking his. When he met her eyes, none of the warmth that had emerged the night of their kiss remained. It had been doused by her actions, and it would be sheer futility to attempt to revive it. "I forgave you, Luke. Remember? When you came back, seeking my forgiveness?"

Something in his expression shifted, stilled. As if she'd chipped away at the barest morsel of ice, revealing his flesh beneath. For a long second, he regarded her.

Before the ice froze over once more.

"Perhaps it would have been better if you had not. Leave me in peace, Charity. For I'm in no mood for conversation today." He brushed past her and returned to his desk, reaching for the decanter as if, with his words, she'd ceased to exist.

She fled. Her heart thundered in her chest, tears falling unheeded down her cheeks. Her feet pounded like drumbeats against the floor. Breathless, she collapsed in the great hall, leaning her cheek against one leg of the suit of armor. Flesh and blood had once existed within these metal confines but had long since died, leaving only this hollow shell as a reminder of their existence.

Luke too, had left her, leaving behind a few beautiful memories and the scattered pieces of what might have been.

She'd trusted him. Forgiven him for abandoning her and letting three years elapse without a single word. Blindly and unreservedly, she'd thrown herself into pleasing him, striving to make Cavington Hall a home he could be proud of. And now this.

The heart could only survive so much trampling. It was not steel, but porcelain. Fragile. Breakable.

She hadn't let him break it after their made-in-haste marriage. She'd held onto it still and been all the better for shielding herself.

This time, he'd shattered her. Because she'd let herself care about him, kiss him. Fall in love with him.

What a mistake.

Through her tears, she poured out her heart to the One who still remained. Unlike Luke, God had never forsaken her nor crushed her heart. In these past weeks, her grip on Him had loosened, while that on her husband had increased. Another mistake to add to her list. Luke was flesh and blood, fallible. God was sovereign, unchangeable.

The realization stung her heart. Putting her trust in the Lord didn't mean Luke's actions ceased to wound her. Yet surrender had consequences.

She needed to forgive Luke.

Swiping a hand against her cheek, she battled the knowledge. It was the last thing she wanted to think of. Everything in her raged against it. She'd done so once before, and he hadn't deserved forgiveness then. He certainly didn't now.

She raised her gaze to the great hall ceiling. Memories spun through her mind, her first glimpse of the house when both she and Luke had been astonished at its state of disrepair. Laughing like a giddy schoolgirl as Luke shared some anecdote from the mine. Exchanging heated glances the night of the ball, when he looked so handsome in evening attire.

It was too much. She couldn't face Luke when he finally emerged from his brandy and dissolution. How could she? When he'd as good as said he regretted everything.

Perhaps, in time, with the help of the Lord, she'd be able to.

But for now, escape was the easiest option.

How long he drowned himself in drink and darkness, Luke couldn't say. Finally, reality took hold of madness and won the battle. A fact which he was simultaneously miserable and thankful for. As the effects of the brandy wore off, guilt, that masterful creature, took over.

"Do not speak to me of apologies. In the face of all that has happened, they hold little merit. Or weight. . ."

"Can trust be mended? It's a difficult fabric to weave from the first. Once rent, I see little hope of repair."

Truth, yes. Charity had done wrong. Come frighteningly close to marrying his sister off to the very leech who had compromised both of them. It scared him how much their actions shook him. He, who prided himself on becoming the ideal master, the perfect son. Meanwhile his sister rushed headlong down a road of dissipation, and his wife had taken steps to aid her in wedding the most worthless sot ever to set foot on English soil.

Thank God, Luke had arrived when he had. Or Browne and Harriet would have been well on their way toward Gretna Green, a legality difficult to undo.

Fear poured down his back like ice water, chilling him to the core.

A rap sounded against the door. His pulse kicked. Charity? He dreaded and needed to face her all at the same time.

Yet the person who answered his summons to enter was not his wife, but the poised and dark-haired young woman he called sister. At the moment, she looked anything but poised, eyes swollen and dress rumpled, her dark hair in tangles down her shoulders.

"Harriet." He stood when she entered and motioned her to take a chair, keeping his movements slow. When last she'd seen him, he'd stood over her intended with a riding crop. Not exactly a memory he wanted to revisit, at least not today.

She didn't take the chair. Instead, she rushed toward him and flung her arms around his waist. He encircled her, the sister he'd not seen since before his departure. Softly, she sobbed against his shirtfront.

"There now," he whispered. "It's all right."

"No, it's not." She drew away, despair raw on her features. "I'm ruined. I'll be notorious. Society's fodder for gossip for the next twenty years. And the man who might've saved me has been sent away, barely escaping with his life. I don't know what you mean by all right, Luke. But this certainly isn't it." She sniffled, looking so like the little girl he'd always sworn to cherish and protect, that his heart wrenched.

"It's better this way. This is not the first time I've been privy to the consequences of Percy Browne's. . .actions. He's a scoundrel of the worst order, and had you joined yourself to him, your life would have been hell on earth. You don't know this, but last night, I was summoned to Falmouth for a meeting regarding a mine Father invested in some years ago. The letter made out that it was urgent, but when I arrived, I discovered there was no meeting. It was only when that man bawled for mercy that he confessed to writing the letter, ensuring I would not be at home when he brought you here. He was out for money, Hattie. Not your welfare, nor that of your child." With an arm around her waist, he led her to a settee and sat beside her.

"I knew that." She released a shuddering sigh. "Not at first, but by the time I'd discovered the. . .the consequences, I'd also learned the truth. I suppose I thought that marrying the father of my child would salvage my reputation. I didn't want to disappoint you. And I know I have."

He pulled her against him. "We've all been disappointments. Myself, most of all. I was gone for so long, Hattie. But that's in the past now. I promise you, now that I'm home, you have a brother who will stand by you and your child, no matter what society says." Leaning his cheek on the crown of her head, a measure of peace filled him. This was who he was meant to be. Harriet's protector.

Charity's—

Another noise against the door. Harriet averted her face, as if ashamed to be seen in such an overwrought state. Luke released her and hastened to the door.

Harold stood outside. Grim anxiety replaced the lad's jovial expression.

"Yes, Harold. What's the matter?" A foolish question to ask, since the footman had witnessed his master inflict vengeance upon Percy Browne mere hours ago. No doubt Harold's opinion of the man who led morning prayers had turned drastically in the wrong direction.

"We just got word of an accident near the cliffs, by Tralin Road. A carriage en route to London. There was a gust of wind—you know how it is—and it overturned."

Luke rubbed a hand across his forehead. All in all, this day had been a wretched one. The last thing he needed was more bad news. Especially when he failed to see how this information concerned him.

"Get the servants to gather blankets and something hot to drink and have it sent over. Anyone who needs medical attention may be brought here." Undoubtedly, some did. One didn't grow up near the cliffs and not hear stories of disaster brought on by harsh winds and unskilled coachmen.

"Aye, Cap'n." Harold made no move to leave.

"Is there something else?" Luke glanced behind him. Harriet waited on the settee.

"I think there might be. Mistress Warren left not two hours ago. She didn't tell anyone where she was going, but I found this note." He pulled a folded paper from his pocket and read aloud: "There's a woman dead, down by the cliffs. I just thought you should know."

Blame it on his consumption of brandy. Or on the footman's lowered tone. For freezing seconds, the words failed to register.

A shrieking howl filled his mind, though Luke's lips remained closed. One word, over and over and over.

Charity.

Charity!

Luke stared down at the paper in his hand. Her flowing script. His name. The letters melded together in a blur.

He tossed the letter to the ground like a piece of refuse. As if by their own volition, his feet moved to the door, each step hard and fast and purposeful.

Outside, bitter wind blasted his face, its whistle like that of the riding crop as it swished through the air and landed again and again.

A horse waited, held by a servant. Who the animal belonged to, Luke had no idea. But like a man possessed, he yanked the reins out of the man's grasp and mounted in the space of time it took to draw a decent gulp of air.

He urged the horse down the avenue, dust and gravel clouding around him.

It would take at least twenty minutes to reach Tralin Road. Twenty minutes for the full impact of Harold's words to seep into his brain like slow-acting poison.

There's a woman dead, down by the cliffs.

Once before he'd seen it. A mangled carriage, two lame horses. Luggage sprawled across the ground like the playthings of a child. He'd been a lad of ten, larking about with one of his mates when they'd come upon it.

A girl in a pale blue dress. Auburn hair. Porcelain skin. Thrown from the carriage in a moment vast in its tragedy, an older man, her companion, badly injured beside her.

The horse's hooves tore up the earth.

The girl's face and Charity's, wide-eyed and pleading like the last moment he'd glimpsed her, swirled together. Became one.

Mistress Warren left two hours ago.

"Because of me." Though none could overhear him, he whispered the words anyway. "She left because of me."

Like a sickening blow to the gut, every word he'd uttered during their conversation reverberated through his mind. With tears streaming down her face, she'd begged him to forgive her. And what had he done? Refused.

Could there be any greater hypocrite? He, who sought forgiveness from others, who'd sought *her* forgiveness, had withheld that very thing. Rebuked her, full to overflowing with his anger, his misplaced self-righteousness thinking it had been her in the wrong.

But I forgave you.

Yes, my darling, you did. You forgave me, a man who deserved only your censure. And when you asked me to do the same, what did I do but coldheartedly refuse?

He was no better than his father, a man who never relinquished a grudge. A man who refused forgiveness to his own son.

A weighted breath heaved its way from Luke's chest and onto the wind. What awaited him when he reached the cliffs? The worst?

Would God hear the pleas of a sinner such as himself? A rash, angry, hypocritical, desperate sinner?

"There was a certain creditor which had two debtors: the one owed five hundred pence, and the other fifty. And when they had nothing to pay, he frankly forgave them both. Tell me therefore, which of them will love him most? Simon answered and said, I suppose that he, to whom he forgave most."

This wasn't the verse he should have recollected. The one about the servant refusing to cancel another's debt, after having been released from his own, greater payment, would have been far more fitting. He was like that servant, deserving of the same consequences.

Would the Lord take Charity from him as punishment for his wrongs?

The second the thought flashed through his mind, he was undone. By the scope of his own sin, by the weight and fear of receiving exactly what he deserved.

"God"—wind buffeted his face, would soon dry his tears, but he shed them anyway—"be merciful to me, a sinner. I've done great wrong. I deserve Your wrath, not grace. And I will accept whatever punishment You choose to give me. But I beg You, don't take Charity from me. Please. Keep my wife safe. Protect her. Don't let it be too late for me to make it right."

He was unworthy for the King of kings to so much as look upon him, much less listen. But the Lord did. Deep inside his spirit, Luke sensed it.

He didn't stop praying for the rest of the ride. No fancy eloquence or high-flung language. Just his heart and soul. Poured out to God. Laid open and bare.

Up ahead, he made out the carriage on its side, a few paces away from the foremost edge of the cliff. A handful of men stood about, heads bent low against the wind.

But no vibrant woman in a dark red spencer.

"Where is she, Lord?" He drew the horse to a stop and dismounted. There wasn't a tree in sight to tie him to, but the animal seemed inclined to stand still after their breakneck gallop.

Luke jogged toward the cluster of men. His heart squeezed like a vice in his chest.

The group looked in his direction, some with recognition. A couple of miners, a few townsfolk.

One of the men met him halfway, his weathered face somber.

"Captain Warren." The elderly man gave an abrupt nod. "As you can see, there's been an accident." He spoke the words slowly, as if each cost him an effort.

Nothing about the gentleman suggested he had good news to impart.

Luke opened his mouth, but no sound emerged. Like a nightmare where danger is approaching but one cannot move arms and legs to get away, Luke stood, frozen.

Everything in him revolted against what this man would say. He didn't want to hear it. Couldn't accept it. The moment the words left the man's mouth, the world would crumble.

Brutally.

"There were three passengers. Myself and two women. It's a sad day, Captain Warren. Very sad."

Luke fixed his gaze on the sky. Nature's audacity was unparalleled.

For how could the sun ever see fit to shine again, much less now?

"But you must be anxious about your wife, sir. The doctor is attending her, though she insists there's no need. She's a feisty lass, pardon me for the liberty of saying so. But I commend her. During the accident, she kept calm as can be. 'Tis due to her levelheaded ways that she and I managed to remain unharmed."

"What did you say?" A surge shot through him, and he snapped his gaze to the man's face, charging toward him.

"Don't be getting all riled up with me, lad. I've known you since you were of an age to be dandled on my knee." The man chuckled, taking a step back. He sobered again. "The young lady that did not survive was a girl from the village. Only eighteen and on her first visit to London. It's one of life's greatest tragedies, when it is cut short too soon."

Luke nodded.

And then he saw her. Leaning on the arm of the doctor, coming closer and closer. Not fast enough, though.

He dodged past the man and reached his wife in the space of instants.

Her eyes widened, registering a hundred different emotions before finally settling on wonderment.

She disengaged herself from the doctor, who nodded and moved toward the scene of the accident.

"You're all right?" Tentatively, he ran his hands across her shoulders, down her arms, assuring himself of her welfare, though the doctor had no doubt just done so.

She nodded. "Fine. A bit shaken."

"But you're alive?" Callous and said without thinking, for although Charity was whole and unharmed, another girl was not. Yet he had to voice the words, if only to confirm them for his own ears.

Another nod. She reached up and swiped a hand across her cheek, where a scratch marred her fair skin.

In a swift movement, he placed his hand against the spot, cradling her hand and her face all at once.

Their gazes melded, vulnerability stark in her matchless blue-green eyes.

His throat tightened. Wind swirled through her curls, catching and spinning the golden strands.

"I don't expect you to want to hear this. I don't even know how to say it. You forgave me once before. It would be too much. . .for you to do so again." He was prepared to turn and walk away, honor her wishes if she wanted nothing more to do with him.

Prepared. But not willing.

She'd taken hold of his heart, this wife of his. In breathtaking, awe-inspiring, all-encompassing ways.

And to deny this would rend his heart in twain.

A solitary tear slipped from her eye, glistening against the mark on her cheek.

Silence hung over them.

She stepped closer, looking up at him, balancing almost on tiptoe. Slowly, sweetly she lifted her fingers, brushing them against the side of his face. Her other hand cupped the other cheek, the feel of her skin against his a manifestation of grace he did not deserve.

Forgiveness could be a word.

It could also be an action.

Though Charity had not spoken so much as a syllable, the gesture said all that was needed. Perhaps she hadn't fully forgiven, fully healed, but it was a start.

Throat tight, he drew her against him, holding her close. Everything inside him ached to join his lips with hers, but he wouldn't. He hadn't earned that husband's privilege, and he wouldn't take what wasn't his to claim.

It humbled him more than he'd thought possible, when, after a long minute, she touched her lips to his. Not a passionate kiss, but a gentle one. Speaking volumes and swelling his heart with tenderness and love.

She stepped back, a tiny smile dancing across her lips.

"I'm not very good at that." She laughed. Then her expression turned hesitating again. "You'll. . .you'll have to teach me."

Again, words he did not merit. But perhaps that was where the beauty lay.

Tell me therefore, which of them will love him most?

"So it will be with me, my darling." He pressed a kiss to her hair, breathing in that beloved jasmine scent. Waves crashed against rock, and wind swept the air like angels' wings.

"What?" She lifted her face to his, eyes shining.

He smiled. "It will keep." He'd share everything with her, of course, but not here, not right now. "But something else will not."

"Yes?"

"Three words that ought to be said on every wedding day, but were never spoken on ours." Imperfect man that he was, he lacked worthiness to say them. Mayhap all good marriages held grace above worthiness. Actions above words.

But not these words.

"I love you." With a heart full of humility and joy, he spoke a truth that far surpassed any other, to a wife who far exceeded any blessing he had merited.

"And I"—she lifted her face to his, eyes ablaze with longing—"love you."

Oh, how he loved her. Not only for the moment, caught up in passion's fire as their lips met again.

But for always.

ECPA bestselling author **Amanda Barratt** fell in love with writing in grade school when she wrote her first story—a spinoff of Jane Eyre. Now, Amanda writes inspirational historical romance, penning stories that transport readers to a variety of locales. These days, Amanda can be found reading way too many books, watching an eclectic mix of BBC dramas and romantic chick flicks, and trying to figure out a way to get on the first possible flight to England. She loves hearing from readers on Facebook and through her website amandabarratt.net.

Masquerade Melody

by Angela Bell

Dedication

In loving memory of my friend Gabriela Pires,
who now dances on streets of gold.
Your radiant smile and worshipper's heart will never be forgotten.

Acknowledgments

Warmest gratitude to my loving family for their continued support!
And special thanks to my critique partner and dear friend, Chawna Schroeder,
whose knowledge and insight as a musician were instrumental
to the writing of this story.

Chapter One

Whoever coined the phrase to "bite one's tongue" was sorely mistaken in believing that silence inflicted mere physical harm. After two years of forfeiting opinions for the safety of agreeable nods, Adelaide knew better. Such silence attacked not body, but soul.

"Are you deaf?" A parasol handle swatted Adelaide's left boot, and Lydia's pampered whine resonated in the all-too-confined carriage. "My greatest hour of need, and there you sit, ignoring my plight. Honestly, for all the good you do, Father might dismiss you as my lady's companion and procure some addle-brained lapdog."

Dismiss? The word roused Adelaide's exhausted mind with a violent shake, and her gaze leapt across the carriage to where Lydia reclined on the opposite green velvet seat. "F-forgive me, Lydia. I weary from our journey." And the incessant need to maintain her cousin's favor. "Please, remind me. . .what is the nature of your dilemma?"

"The exclusiveness of an invitation to summer with the Prince Regent at the Royal Pavilion. All His Majesty's favorite noblemen will be there. Many being unattached officers. The heroes of Waterloo. . . ." Clutching a gloved hand to her butter-yellow spencer jacket, Lydia sighed and fluttered her brunette lashes. "How I adore a man in uniform."

Adelaide mustered her fatigued willpower to keep from rolling her eyes. *Good heavens.* It was going to be a long summer.

A giggle broke Lydia's theatrical interlude. "This being my first time at the Pavilion, it's imperative I make a flawless first impression. Yet how can I do so when I don't know whether the prince favors the colors which best suit my complexion?"

Adelaide blinked, twice. *Lord, provide grace.* Of course, Lydia's *greatest hour of need* would be a fashion quandary. What other plight had she ever known? Her father was still alive. Her provision secure and future certain.

"Well? How do I select a frock for tonight's dinner?"

"Dress to suit yourself, not others' tastes, and you shall be admired by all."

Lydia arched an eyebrow. "Perhaps you are of more use than a lapdog."

How very reassuring. Facing the open window to her right, Adelaide indulged in deep breaths of the refreshing summer air now spiced with a touch of salt from the nearby sea. She allowed her heavy lids to close while the breeze stirred memories of a blissful trip to the ocean's shore, many years ago. When she was one of three and the future had glistened with promise.

"I can see it!" Lydia squealed and thrust nearly half her body out the window to

Adelaide's left, shouting louder still. "I can see the Pavilion. Such a wondrous spectacle!"

One nobody would notice whilst Lydia flaunted her bountiful chest out the window like a peacock on full display. Adelaide wrung her hands. *Tread with care.* "Lydia. . . please, do sit. My uncle wouldn't approve of you carrying on in such a manner."

Lydia plopped back on her seat with an unladylike huff. "I shall 'carry on' as I please. Father may have dubbed you my chaperone, but you're not to ruin my fun. Understand? You shall be as my shadow, disregarded and mute." Her voice assumed an air of acidic superiority. "You may still possess a title, but I am your mistress."

Contrary words surged to Adelaide's mind, but once more, she kept her mouth shut and swallowed them whole. Once more, she could do nothing else. Quitting her situation would dishonor Papa's wishes. Besides, where might she hope to go—a penniless lady without prospects, connections, or serviceable skills?

The carriage slowed and soon rolled no further, jarring Adelaide with the sudden stillness. A pair of footmen approached the window nearest Lydia, one opening the carriage door and the other offering a gloved hand to aid their descent to solid ground. Lydia bubbled with semi-intelligible exclamations while Adelaide just stared. Had their driver taken a sharp eastward turn? Holding onto her bonnet, she tilted her head back to survey the vast structure before them.

Indeed, it appeared they'd arrived in the Orient.

A chilled breeze laced with brine grounded Adelaide. She lifted her loosely hung shawl about her shoulders. Nay, they were yet in England, so by what magic had the Taj Mahal been transported to Brighton? For surely the Royal Pavilion's exotic minarets and onion-shaped domes, shinning brilliant white against the azure sky, echoed sketches she'd seen of India's famed landmark. And what a resounding echo! As if desiring to best its inspiration, each architectural feature was tripled in quantity and lavished with latticework and spires. Marvelous. Whimsical. The Pavilion possessed a beauty all its own, albeit rather extravagant. Like a dream. Adelaide lowered her gaze, restraining wonderment. This dream wasn't meant for her. She must keep a level head and do her utmost to ensure Lydia was the belle of Brighton.

"Welcome, ladies." The Prince Regent appeared in the Pavilion entry.

Adelaide stifled a gasp and reflected Lydia's curtsy. Age and infirmity had wreaked havoc on the prince since she'd last seen him, five years ago at her coming out ball in London. Just a year prior to her world falling apart. In those days the prince still managed to strut—a hazardous combination of coxcomb and rake—ever on the prowl for naive debutants. Now he sported gray hair, sallow bags under his eyes, and a paunch barely kept in check by the stressed gold buttons of his tailcoat.

The prince hobbled forward and extended a hand to Lydia. "How you've blossomed, Lady Lydia." As he kissed Lydia's gloved knuckles, a gleam of the old lecher flashed in his eyes. "Your journey was pleasant?"

"Quite, Your Majesty." Lydia's lashes flitted in mock coyness.

The prince's gaze wandered to Adelaide. "And who is your friend? It's not often I forget a pretty face."

Lydia's buoyant tone slipped only a moment. "This is my cousin and lady's companion, Lady Adelaide Langley. You wouldn't be expected to recall her, Your Highness. Though a relation of mine, she hasn't been amongst society's finer circles."

Not since Papa had taken ill with consumption. Adelaide gnawed the inside of her cheek. One word from a physician had altered her life's course from society parties to invalid care and a two-year battle Papa couldn't win any more than he could break the entail which had given everything to her uncle, Lydia's father.

"Langley, eh?" The prince eyed Adelaide from toe to head. "Who's your father?"

Adelaide glanced at Lydia whose glare smoldered with cobalt embers. Her mouth went dry. Surely Lydia understood she couldn't ignore the prince? "Lord Geoffrey Langley, Earl of Doveton." *Now, for heaven's sake, address Lydia.*

Clearing his throat, the prince tugged at his neckcloth. "Ah yes. . .I remember him."

He ought to, since Papa had been one of the conservative lords who didn't fawn over his every word.

The prince clapped his hands together. "While your things are conveyed to your quarters, what say you to a royal tour of the Pavilion?"

Lydia blushed carnations. "Absolutely. I'm sure you're the most knowledgeable guide."

Allowing the prince to hobble off in the lead and Lydia to flutter at his side, Adelaide took her place as mute chaperone in the rear of the procession.

The Pavilion greeted them with a cream, octagonal hall where chiming brass bells, dangling from the tent-shaped ceiling, bid a fairylike welcome. From there wafts of spiced perfume beckoned them into the Long Gallery—a lengthy corridor the prince said linked all the main rooms. Here, amid pink wallpaper painted with blue creeping vines, enchantment unfurled in a splendid bloom of chinoiserie style: ivory-veneered Chippendale chairs, red tassels dripping from Chinese lanterns, and golden figurines that nodded to Adelaide as she passed by.

The tour continued downstairs to the Great Kitchen where the prince boasted of its modern innovations such as a steam table. Fitted with a cast-iron top and bound in brass, the table was heated by means of an extensive copper piping system which grew from table to ceiling in the guise of palm trees. The technology allowed numerous dishes to be kept warm and ready until served in the adjacent Banqueting Room. An invention which lost its wonder after an hour-long lecture.

Vanity thus elevated by his informative bragging, the prince led them back upstairs. Adelaide almost felt pity for the man, noting how his obese form struggled against obvious pain. Yet it was difficult to maintain sympathy alongside the knowledge that the Regent's ill-health resulted from years of his own self-indulgence, too many enormous banquets, and glasses of cherry brandy.

The prince concluded their tour in the Long Gallery, gesturing to rooms he was apparently too winded to explore. "Beyond this door is the informal Music Gallery, for daytime entertainment, and that door yonder conceals the grand Music Room where evening concerts are held. Tonight Rossini is giving a special, one-night performance with the Pavilion orchestra."

Adelaide's heart leapt. Rossini—the famous Italian composer—was performing here? Tonight? With such music to enjoy, perhaps the summer wouldn't feel so long after all.

"Afterward, I expect every lady to delight us with her singing talents."

Imagine. . .singing before Gioachino Rossini. "How marvelous." The whispered words slipped, escaping capture from Adelaide's better judgment. She bit her tongue, literally. *Please, God, let no one have heard—*

"What was that, Lady Adelaide?" The prince stared at her, waiting.

Lydia's eyes blazed with the ever menacing threat of dismissal.

Of being sacked without notice and sent away without reference. Of being forced to leave her parents' beloved estate and the family-like servants she'd known all her life. Of losing the only home she'd ever known. Adelaide's stomach roiled. To do so would be to watch Papa take his final breath a second time. A pain she'd not risk unearthing.

'Twas better to stay trapped than suffer further loss.

Adelaide pursed her lips. *Think carefully.* "I was only imagining how marvelous Lady Lydia shall be during the concert, Your Majesty. She has a breathtaking voice."

A smile extinguished Lydia's glare and locked Adelaide back in her cage of quiet servitude.

◦◦◦

With an ink-stained hand, Walter crushed yet another sheet of paper and tossed it across the Music Gallery at the pianoforte that mocked with silence. How could he conjure meaningful words whilst staying in this gaudy temple of pointless pageantry? His gaze fell to the empty sleeve hanging at his right side. If only the Pavilion were his real problem.

Unfortunately, one couldn't escape internal deficiency.

"Halloo. . . Glenmire?" Quinby's energetic voice bounced off every wall like a pack of hounds primed for the hunt.

Blast. One afternoon of solitude, that's all he'd wished. One afternoon before the remaining guests arrived and commenced their disgusting parade of shallow festivities. Walter willed himself invisible, leaning against the window in a partially concealed niche. *Go away, Quinby.*

"Come now, comrade. Can't hide forever."

Can too. He managed it in London.

Quinby's boots clomped ever nearer. "As your dearest—handsomest—friend, I'm determined to track you down and make you have fun. Hear that? This summer you're engaging in pleasant activities which may lead to merriment. That's an order, Colonel Glenmire."

Go. Away. Quinby.

"Surrender now or face the bane of my fearsome battle cry."

Walter's eyebrow arched. He wouldn't?

"Very well." Quinby cleared his throat and then shouted as if to scare death. "For God and King and Englaaaaan—"

"Quiet, man!" Walter jumped from his chair and reached Quinby's smirk in three strides. With his lone hand, Walter seized the bellowing bloodhound's cravat and dragged him into the window alcove. "Must you expose my refuge to all of Brighton?"

A dimple tacked a grin to Quinby's rather annoying face. "If that's what it takes for you to rejoin humanity."

Rejoin? A frost-bitten laugh numbed Walter's throat. "My life has been nothing but a swirling pool of humanity since the war. A never-ending deluge of frivolous parties and summers at the Pavilion as the special guest of that pompous. . ." He inhaled a steadying breath. "This year I should have declined the prince's gold-leafed invitation and stayed in London."

A tinge of seriousness tempered Quinby's smirk. "You know us uniformed blokes can't do that. The war might be over, but we're still in service, and a soldier doesn't defy an order. Gold-leafed or otherwise."

Could the societal repercussions truly be worse than enduring the prince's arrogant tales of service at Waterloo? A glorious fantasy in which His Highness emerged the conquering hero—despite having not been there. Bitter cold seeped into Walter's marrow. The pampered simpleton had no notion of the gory day of which he boasted. The death. Carnage. Thousands of men, gone. Abandoned on the field by their comrades and their God. Men like Benjamin.

Like himself.

"Dismiss that scowl, Glenmire. I won't allow melancholy musings and glowering this summer." Quinby flashed his dimpled grin for all it was worth, eyes gleaming with impish glee. "This summer, fun is our objective."

Impossible. He could no sooner have fun in this place than he could pen lyrics to his voiceless aria. The one he carried everywhere, just in case inspiration returned. The one that rested on a table behind him, still unfinished.

"Fine. I'll settle for a half-hearted grin. Consider it a favor for a comrade in arms, eh?"

Walter did not relax his furrowed brow.

"No, chap. The idea is to use those limp muscles on the side of your mouth. . .here." Reaching out with both pointer fingers, Quinby propped up Walter's lips. "Beautiful."

"You're an idiot."

"With the magnanimous face of Apollo."

Walter grinned despite himself, the scars on his cheeks nagging in the stretch. He swatted Quinby's fingers away. "Your father would switch your legs for spouting falsehoods."

"But I made you smile, so 'twas worth it."

"I believe those were your exact words every time you got us in trouble as boys."

"And at university." Quinby's laughter thundered through the gallery.

Blast. Walter put his hand over Quinby's mouth. "Shhh. . .what if the prin—"

Boots clopped on the floor in an uneven, hobbling rhythm. "Captain Quinby?"

The prince's voice hung in the air while Walter held his breath.

"Is Colonel Glenmire with you?"

Walter heaved a sigh through gritted teeth. There'd be no hiding now. "We're here, Your Highness."

Stepping 'round the corner, the prince greeted them with a face born of noble blood and held aloft by a double chin. "Glad I found you, Colonel Glenmire. I've been meaning to speak with you regarding an opera."

Walter's heart fumbled. "An opera?"

"Indeed, or rather an aria. Tonight Rossini is launching the summer festivities by performing an original composition. Come summer's end, our time together will conclude with a masquerade ball, and I wish you to compose an aria for that night to commemorate our great victory at Waterloo. A piece to remind all of the glory of England's crown."

Compose an aria to honor the prince? Preserving the fantasy and lies? Walter forced his clenched jaw to yield a response. "Three months is hardly enough time—"

"Haven't you got some music scribbled?" Quinby's gaze lighted on the voiceless aria, and he snatched it off the table. "Here, the ditty you wrote before the war. Just needs a few words here and there, right?"

Walter reclaimed the sheet music from Quinby and shot his former friend with a glare he hoped hit its mark. "This piece isn't suitable for—"

"I'm sure it will gratify." The Prince Regent settled the matter with a nod that left no room for negation. "Now that nothing hinders the endeavor, Colonel Glenmire, you'll make me proud." His imperial tone beheaded any perception of a question mark into a stark period.

Glaciers of long frozen anger cracked and shifted in Walter's soul. *Make him proud?* His inflated Majesty had pride enough for ten politicians and a legion of dandies. Yet what else could he do but comply? The obligation of duty and convention dictated that he perform the role of obedient officer. Even when repugnant. He must will emotion numb and muster on, alone.

Walter nodded his acquiescence.

With that secured, the prince made his labored departure.

Quinby clapped Walter's back as if a victory had been won. "Now you're sure to have fun, Glenmire. You love that music stuff."

Before Waterloo, yes. When the music still seemed to matter, when he'd believed God could move and heal through the melodies. When he once felt the Almighty's presence in the pulse of every note. Back then, music was a refuge, his way to digest truth. Now it felt like futile noise. A racket he lacked the power to master. Walter sank onto a nearby chair, mute aria choked in hand. "How can I honor the man in song when I detest the fat, pompous, delusional pig?"

Chapter Two

"I come seeking sanctuary."

Standing in the lobby of their chambers, Adelaide peered 'round the half-opened door into Millie's adjacent maid's room finished plainly with white wallpaper and modest wooden furnishings. A common English rose veiled within the Pavilion's exotic lotus garden.

"The ogre banished ye from her den, eh?" Perched on a chair before a Spartan desk, Millie's feet dangled above the floor planks as she polished Lydia's traveling boots. She looked up from the task, brown eyes flashing amber. "And she gave quite the tongue lashin' before kickin' ye out, looks like. Come here now an' tell us what happened. Did ye have to calm her delicate nerves with smelling salts?"

"Nothing so bad as that." *This time.* After shutting the door, Adelaide sat on the nearby tent bed, draped with hangings of white dimity.

"Well, what did happen, then?" Millie set the boots on the desk and crossed willow-thin arms over her apron. "Don't leave me to suspense."

Adelaide worried her hands, tarnished with faded scars. "'Tis nothing unusual. Though we have two bedrooms between us, Lydia retired to the lobby settee for an hour of beauty rejuvenating slumber and didn't wish disturbance from my deafening needle-work or stubborn insistence on breathing."

"Right. Now. . .what really stirred the ogre's ire?" Wisps of strawberry blonde peeked from Millie's cap to tease rosy cheeks, making her the very model of a woodland nymph—until her dainty mouth revealed the colorful personality of a London chimney sweep. "I'll get it out of ye, don't fool yourself otherwise."

An exhausted chuckle escaped Adelaide's lips. She should've known Millie would find her out. After over a decade of service in her family, Millie was more an elder sister than lady's maid. . .or rather, *former* lady's maid. Lydia was now mistress of them both. "I spoke before the prince without being addressed—regarding tonight's concert."

"Ahh, and that girl has enough jealousy in her to bleed green."

"I suppose." Although she couldn't fathom why Lydia might envy her when she was essentially a well-dressed servant with limited privileges. Titled but utterly powerless.

Millie shook her head. "You've had a long journey, m'lady. With a late night yet to come. Why don't ye rest there, now? I'll tend the ogre."

"I couldn't." Not with the concert looming with hurdles unknown.

Rising from the bed, Adelaide paced the diminutive room. Three steps forward, three more back. "How am I to maintain Lydia's favor in this place? 'Twas hard enough at home, with predictable routines, but here. . . . What if the prince should insist I sing tonight? Then who am I to obey—His Majesty or my mistress?" Disregarding the latter's wishes would surely provide grounds for dismissal.

Three steps forward, three more back. "I must avoid the prince's eye somehow. Blend with the crowd so I can't be called upon. I could wear a plain gown, forgo a headpiece, and use Lydia as a screen. Perhaps I might guide her to sit in a back row or—"

"The next fret ta leave your mouth gets throttled by my hand." Millie blocked Adelaide's pacing with her petite frame, two heads shorter but no less imposing. She took Adelaide's hands in her tiny palms and held fast. Steady and strong. "Listen here now. Ye can't control every minute of life, m'lady. Sometimes you've just got to hold tight to the promise that our future's secure in the Lord's hands."

Secure. The word sounded foreign, although familiar. Like a dialect from a native land where she no longer dwelt and had since forgotten. Yet if she thought hard, she could recall.

When apoplexy had taken Mamma in the night, swift and unexpected, God had secured her twelve-year-old heart, alongside Papa. When loss called again, ten years later, at Papa's long anticipated grave, she'd still felt secure. Still believed that all would be well, despite the entail. Then Lydia had usurped her home and reduced that belief to ashes in the course of one night.

Adelaide swallowed the lump rising in her throat. "Oh, Millie. . .if only I could share your certainty."

❧

Be a shadow. Be silent.

Amongst the throng of ornamented guests streaming into the Pavilion's Music Room, Adelaide walked directly behind Lydia. Candlelight sparkled with Lydia's every movement, glittering off her peach gown's delicate, gold net overlay and band of metallic thread embroidery which accentuated its empire-waist silhouette. Hopefully that, along with Adelaide's choice of simple attire, would aid in distracting perilous gazes from veering her way. As they moved forward, she focused on Lydia's peach silk turban festooned with white ostrich plumes. She'd not hazard eye contact or conversation, unless needs must.

The groan of an organ tempted Adelaide's gaze to wander. At the far end of the Music Room, a canopy of imitation bamboo hung above an impressive organ with gleaming pipes that reached to touch the forested ceiling. Her heart skipped. *How thrilling it must be to play.* Gathered in front of the grand instrument, members of the Pavilion orchestra arranged music on stands whilst their conductor conversed with a second gentleman. Rossini, perhaps? She reined in the beginnings of a smile. However marvelous her surroundings she mustn't get swept away. Carried off by the music, she might draw unwanted attention or worse—open her mouth.

To the left of the musicians, the prince sat enthroned with a marbled hearth blazing on his left and a new mistress fawning on his right. Adelaide turned her face away. Following the crowd's procession, Lydia led them to the room's far right wall where chairs had been arranged in neat rows. As the orchestra warmed up their instruments in a delightful cacophony of noise, the guests selected seats with boisterous enthusiasm. She braced her nerves. Now to secure an inconspicuous sitting arrangement.

Placing a hand on Lydia's gloved elbow, Adelaide oh-so-gently offered a guiding nudge toward the back row.

With a flick of her wrist, Lydia disentangled herself and in all boldness claimed a seat on the very front row. Amid a score of decorated officers.

Good heavens. Adelaide ducked into the row just behind Lydia and risked a whisper. "Why don't we sit further back?" Out of the prince's direct line of sight. "'Tis rather warm, and we may need to discreetly exit before the concert—"

"Nonsense. My constitution is quite robust despite my delicate appearance." Lydia giggled loudly for the officers' benefit, then rotated to face Adelaide and whispered, tone noxious with venom. "Utter another sound tonight and you'll again reek of cinders."

A shudder rattled Adelaide. Shrinking into her second-row seat, the smoke wafting from the room's hundreds of candles overwhelmed her senses. Dragging her memory to the pitiless heat of a cackling hearth, to her soot-coated hands streaked with tears and trembling fingers singed black. Burnt and empty. Unable to save her treasured sheet music—and a piece of her faith—from withering in the flames. She wrung her hands, envisioning the blistered scars concealed within the gloves. Remembering how Millie had wrapped poultices around each finger, how the servants rallied to her side like family, and how neither had managed to console.

A quartet of violins freed her from the vision with gentle harmony. Adelaide exhaled as if to blow the smoke far away. *Be a shadow. Be silent. Whatever it takes to avoid the stench of cinders.*

An hour passed.

The orchestra played. Rossini performed. Adelaide sat without reaction, permitting her ears to hear but forbidding her heart to listen.

After two encores from Rossini, the Prince Regent began selecting ladies to sing for the Crown's pleasure. Through each performance the music swept over Adelaide, unfelt. Each soft, clear tone of the pianoforte beckoned her to relax and absorb its healing balm, but she did not lower her guard of reserve. Not while the prince's lecherous gaze combed the crowd for additional performers. A search that drew ever nearer to her location.

Too near. Abandoning posture, Adelaide slumped so as to be better concealed by Lydia's form.

A snap of the prince's chubby fingers summoned a footman, from the foreground to his side, with another glass of champagne. *Good.* The bubbles would blur his powers of observation. Although, perhaps not soon enough. The Regent's drifting gaze alighted on her seat as another recital concluded with applause. Her breath stalled.

Lifting a glass, the prince signaled for silence, beady eyes pinning Adelaide in place like a captured butterfly on display. "Our next performer shall be Lady Lydia Langley."

Adelaide heaved a pent-up breath. *Thank the Lord.*

Springing from her seat, Lydia bowed to the prince and crossed the Music Room to join the orchestra—leaving Adelaide completely exposed.

Adelaide's gaze plummeted, eliminating the chance for eye contact with His Royal Highness. Lydia's fan sat on the chair in front of her, discarded. As the music commenced, Adelaide snatched it up and used the painted silk as a facial shield. A pathetic shield which wouldn't protect her long. She gnawed her bottom lip. If only Lydia had chosen a brief song rather than a Rossini aria. Why her cousin insisted on singing an octave higher than her natural range, she'd never understand.

When Lydia's performance at last ended, a ripple of mild applause rose and fell much too quickly. Peeking over the fan, Adelaide caught the flash of irritation in Lydia's eyes and clenched jaw. *Oh, dear.* Much ego stroking would be required this night.

When Lydia resumed her seat, Adelaide returned her fan. "Well done, cousin." She addressed the officer to Lydia's right. "A captivating performance, was it not, sir?"

The officer swiped a flute of champagne from a footman's tray and offered Lydia a dismissive glance. "Oh yes, um. . .lovely."

Adelaide grimaced. Where was a silver-tongued dandy when you needed one? "I'm sure the prince was most impressed, Lydia."

Without a word of reply, Lydia seized the last flute of champagne and downed it in one draught. Returning the glass to the tray, she shooed the servant away like a fly.

Adelaide reclined in her seat. She didn't know what was more troubling—Lydia's silence or her sudden taste for champagne. A drink she normally couldn't abide and shouldn't now indulge when she'd been too busy flirting to bother with dinner.

After another hour, during which time several ladies received bountiful ovations and two were begged for an encore, Adelaide found herself wishing—nay praying—for the return of Lydia's seething silence.

"I declare, Captain Young, you're the strongest man ever to breathe on this good earth. How do you maintain such fine form?" Lashes aflutter, Lydia ran a hand down the captain's sleeve and gave the muscle beneath a squeeze.

Adelaide's cheeks burned. *Good gracious.* If her position weren't at risk, she'd drag Lydia off this instant. How could she be a proper chaperone with her hands fettered?

Captain Young, now far from disinterested, whispered something all too near Lydia's ear.

"Captain, you're a scoundrel!" Lydia's boisterous giggling echoed in the room, competing with the harpsichord and drawing the attention of many an onlooker. As a footman strode by with refreshments, Lydia reached for another champagne flute.

Adelaide's desperate whisper neared a hiss. "You can't still require refreshment, Lydia. Not after three glasses."

Lydia sneered, words slurring against each other. "Dear bore. You were always better at mathematics." She downed the glass and laughed, cheeks flushed from either too much drink, the crowded room's stifling heat, or both. "Well—" A hiccup induced more loud laughter. "I'm better at fun."

Captain Young chuckled, wiping a droplet of champagne from Lydia's chin. "I'd wager you are, that."

Adelaide's stomach roiled. *Vile rogue.* Shooting to her feet, she hastened to navigate the many pairs of knees blocking her way in the second row. No matter what Lydia threatened, she couldn't in good conscience allow the girl to do something she'd regret come morning. She must get her tucked in bed, safely, quietly, and quickly.

Angling her face away from the prince, she grabbed Lydia's hand. "You need fresh air, cousin." And she'd drag her to it if needs must.

Lydia looked up with glassy eyes, head swaying. "I do nut. I'm f–fine."

"You're ill." Adelaide declared the diagnosis loud enough for nearby judging ears. "Come along." Before the fading music expired.

Slipping an arm around Lydia's waist, Adelaide hauled her charge onto her feet and toward the doors just as the harpsichord's final note died. Adelaide hurried along, towing half of Lydia's weight. *Please God don't let us be—*

"Lady Adelaide?" The prince's voice reverberated through the now quiet room.

No, no, no. Adelaide kept moving, dragging Lydia along as if she did not hear.

"I say, Lady Adelaide Langley. Don't run off without gracing us with a song."

A pair of footmen blocked Adelaide's escape as hundreds of eyes fixed themselves to her retreating back and Lydia's hostile glare seared the side of her face. *What now?*

Chapter Three

I don't know what's more torturous—the number of sharp notes to which I've been subjected or the prospect of collaborating with one of these tone-deaf prima donnas."

Walter massaged his temple, grateful for a momentary lull of silence. Tucked in the Music Room's farthest back corner, seated just to the left of the Pavilion orchestra, he'd hoped to locate a suitable soprano during the course of the evening concert without the drama or competition of a public audition. A hope that had wilted after two agonizingly boring hours.

"You're too particular, that's what." Beside Walter, Quinby nodded in agreement with his own pronouncement. "That last girl was a regular songbird."

"If said songbird were being mauled by a tomcat, then yes, she was quite the canary." Walter tugged at his neckcloth to achieve some relief from the heat—a slight discomfort that had worsened into a stifling oppression after hours in close proximity with hundreds of guests and thousands of flickering candles. If the prince wished to coddle his irrational terror of catching cold, he might at least have the decency to wrap in furs instead of forbidding aeration.

"These girls aren't professionals, old chum. Have a heart."

"I do, Quinby. Along with functional ears, which I employ, whilst you judge every performance on whether the lady graces you with a smile."

"I never!" A satire of indignation elevated Quinby's tone. "For shame, to judge your dearest—handsomest—friend so ill. Everyone knows I'm an avid connoisseur of the arts."

Walter scoffed. "As a boy, you couldn't discern Pachelbel from Handel."

Furrows of thought attempted to take residence on Quinby's smooth brow still crowned with his childhood curls, blithe and fair. "Didn't one of those chaps paint the Sistine Chapel?"

Walter shook his head. "I don't know whether to weep for Michelangelo or your mother."

"Neither. You're supposed to be choosing a maiden to serenade you all summer. That ought to put a smile on your face."

Why couldn't Quinby understand things were not so simple? The war had severed his hand and composing skills—leaving his masterwork aria derelict—and now he couldn't even find a decent soprano.

"There can be no aria without a suitable soprano. On the morrow, I shall appeal to His Majesty with this logic and free myself from obligation." Then retreat to London posthaste. Social repercussions be hanged.

As Walter stood to make his leave, Quinby rose alongside poised for argument.

"Lady Adelaide?" The prince's voice reverberated through the quiet Music Room. "I say, Lady Adelaide Langley. Don't run off without gracing us with a song."

Quinby swatted the front of Walter's red army coatee and flashed a dimpled grin. "There now, you can't slight this girl when you've auditioned the rest."

"I can. And I shall."

Stowing away the defective dimple, Quinby exchanged his previous tactics for a strategy of unabashed pleading. "Please, Glenmire. Give her a chance. She might be your songbird."

She might also unleash the sour note that finally deafened him. However, if he hoped to persuade the prince to release him, he must be certain that said songbird couldn't recognize, let alone carry, a tune.

With a heavy sigh, Walter sat and looked in the direction the audience favored to locate this Lady Adelaide. Across the room, two footmen addressed a young lady with a companion half-draped over her shoulder. The faint companion must have grown ill due to the sweltering heat, and given that they were facing the doors, it seemed the prince's attentions had snared them middeparture. An unfortunate plight, to be sure.

The prince rose with great difficulty. "Our next performer requires encouragement. Honored guests, make welcome Lady Adelaide Langley."

The crowd applauded as bidden by their sovereign. One of the footmen secured the indisposed woman and conveyed her out of the Music Room while his double escorted the timid songbird toward the orchestra. After speaking with the conductor—no doubt regarding song and key choice—Lady Adelaide faced her audience with an expression that could only be described as panic-stricken. Walter studied her downcast frame. Was she suffering performance anxiety or distress for her ill friend?

The opening notes of Thomas Moore's Irish ballad *The Last Rose of Summer* flowed through the air, simple and unassuming. A unique selection compared to the previous performers who'd striven to impress with complex, operatic pieces.

Lady Adelaide's voice tiptoed into the music's current. Almost a whisper. "*'Tis the last rose of summer, left blooming alone; All her lovely companions are faded and gone; No flower of her kindred, no rosebud is nigh, To reflect back her blushes, or give sigh for sigh.*"

Walter leaned forward, straining to unearth something at the heart of that voice. A tone like crystalline water. Yet one muddied by insufficient breath support and lapses in enunciation. Untrained talent? He listened, beyond lyrics and melody.

"*I'll not leave thee, thou lone one! To pine on the stem; since the lovely are sleeping, go, sleep thou with them. Thus kindly I scatter thy leaves o'er the bed, Where thy mates of the garden lie scentless and dead.*"

Nay, this lady was by no means a novice. She was proficient. The vocal fumbles were too precise, too regular in their timing. As if she deliberately sidestepped rather than stumbled over. Why was she endeavoring to conceal the best voice in the whole Pavilion?

Like a child whisked to sleep by a lullaby, Walter reclined in his chair. He allowed his eyes to close, mind to cease scrutinizing. Cease thinking. His breathing adjusted to the music, and for the first time since Waterloo, the notes penetrated beyond his cold skin. Somehow, something in Lady Adelaide's voice breathed life into the music again. Like days long ago. If she sang thus while shrinking back, what might she sound like unreserved?

Lady Adelaide repeated the final stanza, guiding the ballad to its conclusion with a stirring poignancy that couldn't be veiled. "*So soon may I follow when friendships decay, And from Love's shining circle the gems drop away. When true hearts lie withered and fond ones are flown, Oh! who would inhabit this bleak world alone?*"

Her last note flew into the rafters and dispersed, a breathless silence enveloping the room completely for the first time during the evening. Walter opened his eyes, and the crowd was on their feet, applause shattering the magical moment and once more shrouding him in frigid indifference.

Quinby met his gaze with a pleased smirk. "I may not know Pachelbel from Handel, old chum, but even I know there's no chance in Christendom his Majesty will believe you lack a 'suitable soprano.'"

Indeed. With one song, Lady Adelaide had dashed his means of escaping royal obligation and returning to London. Yet for some reason, he was no longer troubled by the notion.

Quinby laughed. "Your songbird's a flighty thing. Winging away without so much as a curtsy."

"What?" Walter's gaze swept the Music Room and caught the hem of Lady Adelaide's swift departure. *Odd.* She seemed to be fleeing the applause, but why? A sense of foreboding unsettled his gut. Convincing Lady Adelaide to perform now presented a task rife with difficulty. And no doubt the prince would be void of sympathy for his plight.

Perfect, just perfect. Now he almost wished she'd deafened him.

Walter bounded to his feet and gave chase, striding across the Music Room. Bursting through the double doors, he spotted Lady Adelaide halfway down the horrifyingly pink Long Gallery, speaking to a footman over the figure of her ill companion, now slumped in a chair against the wall. Why had the ailing woman been subjected to wait thus? He'd best rescue Lady Adelaide from the scrawny lad's lack of experience. Perhaps in so doing, he might secure favor and persuade her to sing. He approached the pair, each step clarifying their whispered conversation.

"I thought you intended to convey Lady Lydia safely to her chamber?" Tremors threatened to unhinge Lady Adelaide's hushed words while she examined her friend's condition. "I never would have left her otherwise."

The footman hung his head as if anticipating a firm ear boxing. "I did try, m'lady. But as I was guiding the lady to her room, she fainted dead away. I thought it best to set her down till your return. A lady ought not be dragged about."

"Dragged?" Horror pierced Lady Adelaide's tone as she whirled 'round. "I should think not. Gracious, how does one even imagine such a notion? The appropriate course of action is to carry her, gently, like —"

"Beg pardon." Walter halted betwixt the pair and addressed Lady Adelaide. "Might I be of assistance?"

Lady Adelaide stared at him, still as a tombstone.

Was she alarmed by his disfigurement or lack of decorum? *Set her at ease, Glenmire.* He offered a bow. "Forgive the intrusion. I know it's irregular for me to approach without proper introduction, but I surmised that your situation was near enough a crisis to warrant dispensing with formal pleasantries. Was I not right?"

Lady Adelaide's gaze darted around the Long Gallery then studied him warily. "Can I depend on your discretion, sir? I don't wish Lady Lydia's fainting spell to be recounted."

Such caution suggested more was afoot than a mere fainting spell. He eyed the indisposed figure slumped against the wall. Face flushed, drool trailing from the mouth—he inhaled—and the lingering aroma of champagne. *Fainted dead away, my foot.* The woman was stone cold drunk. No wonder Lady Adelaide was jittery. Feminine fainting spells were expected and forgiven, but a woman intoxicated beyond consciousness soon found herself without friends or repute—even in the prince's seaside palace of decadence.

Walter stepped toward Lady Adelaide, whispering to avoid the footman's hearing. "My discretion is assured, but the lad's is not. To prevent your dilemma becoming servant tattle, I suggest dismissing his services forthwith, as he's quite obviously unable to carry your friend and too embarrassed to say as much."

Lady Adelaide pursed her lips and then addressed the footman. "Thank you for watching over Lady Lydia in my absence. You may return to your duties. This gentleman will stay with us till she has recovered from the heat fatigue."

The footman bowed and left them in the vacant corridor.

Facing Walter once more, Lady Adelaide wrung her gloved hands. "Urgent though the situation presents, good sir, I feel I must insist on some form of introduction before you accompany us to our chambers."

Walter restrained an impatient huff. Her request for discretion left little time for her want of decorum. *Better have done with it quickly, then.* "I'm Colonel Lord Walter Marlowe, Marquess of Glenmire, as presented at court. You are Lady Adelaide Langley, as announced by His Majesty. And you've referred to this woman as Lady Lydia. Friend or relation?"

Lady Adelaide blinked. "C–cousin. Mistress, rather. I'm her lady's companion."

"Capital. Now that we're acquainted, let's transport Lady Lydia to the privacy of her chamber before the gossipmonger hoard emerges from the Music Room." Kneeling before Lady Lydia, Walter slipped his lone arm under her knees and, rising with a firm grip, hefted her over his left shoulder like an army ration sack of potatoes.

"Good heavens!" Lady Adelaide's hand flew to her mouth. "You cannot mean to carry her that way? Dangling—upside-down—like the spoils of a Viking conquest? It's not proper."

"In drinking herself comatose, Lady Lydia forfeited propriety. That leaves us with two means of aid: speed and secrecy. Let's not squander either with idle conversation." With that, Walter led the way to the Pavilion's main staircase.

As he and Lady Adelaide hastened by the balustrade of faux bamboo, not a word was exchanged. Nor a glance traded as they climbed past a trio of Chinese warriors imprisoned in lighted glass panes. The very silence he'd wished for now spelled his failing. Instead of winning Lady Adelaide over, his impatient quips, tipped with sarcasm, had created a wall of offence. One he knew not how to surmount.

When they reached the blue gallery upstairs, lined with guest chambers, Lady Adelaide opened a door and requested he remain outside. Walter obeyed, and she soon returned with a lady's maid. The women received Lady Lydia from his grasp and working together, laid their charge on a settee.

While the maid tended to her mistress, Lady Adelaide came back to the door. "I don't know how to thank you for your aid and discretion, Colonel Glenmire."

Perhaps this was his way over the wall? "I might have a notion."

The remark awoke a wary glint in Lady Adelaide's hazel depths, and she clutched the door tighter. Walter retreated a step. "Nothing of a Viking nature, I assure you. The prince has commissioned me to compose an aria for the masquerade ball at summer's end, and yours is the only voice in the Pavilion capable of singing it for His Majesty."

All color drained from Lady Adelaide's features, creating a stark contrast between her fair complexion and auburn ringlets. Her voice croaked. "No."

He fought against a grimace. "I noted you suffer from performance anxiety, but—"

"It's not possible." Regret hollowed Lady Adelaide's voice.

"But I know methods—"

"I cannot sing again, not here. Not ever."

Not ever? "Why—"

"My answer is no, Colonel Glenmire. I shall pray you find another singer."

Pray. The empty word pricked Walter's chest, scraping over an opened wound that had never healed. And never would. "Save your voice for *useful* endeavors, Lady Adelaide. It's too precious a thing to be wasted. . .or locked away."

That comment saw the door shut in his face.

Chapter Four

The Prince Regent was mad as King George to construct a seaside palace without a view of the sea. Nestled on a window seat in her bedchamber, pressed against the sun-warmed panes, Adelaide hugged both knees to her chest and stared across the Pavilion's ornamental gardens. A visit to the ocean would do wonders for her nerves. She could be content without feeling the spray's refreshing tingle or watching the expanse of blue undulate to and fro in its unceasing dance, but she longed to hear the music by which the sea's waltz kept time.

The varying sounds of the waves—one minute surging forward with the percussive rumble of timpani, only to crash against the rocks like cymbals and then swiftly retreat to the depths, plucking across the pebbled shore in a fluid pizzicato of strings. A flawless symphony.

But there would be no escaping to it anytime soon.

No avoiding her duties. . .or the phantom which now haunted her every step.

Adelaide's stomach twisted into a plait. She wished to heaven she'd never accepted Colonel Glenmire's assistance two weeks prior. For since the concert, his cold shadow had followed her in an inexorable pursuit. *"Sing my aria at the masquerade."*

"Sing for the Prince."

"Sing for your country."

If it weren't aimed her way, Adelaide might admire the colonel's unswerving determination. But it was aimed her way, pointedly. Therefore, it was only a matter of time before the colonel's focused attentions drew the notice of—

"Adelaide, come here." Lydia's strident command shattered the notion of quiet reflection.

Was a peaceful afternoon too grand a wish? Adelaide shut her eyes and exhumed a memory of Papa's feeble voice. *"I've arranged for you to serve as lady's companion for cousin Lydia when the time comes. With the entail's restraints, this is the best I can provide—security in the house with family. You'll do me proud, I know, and face matters bravely."*

"Adelaide!"

Face matters bravely. For Papa. Rising from the window seat, Adelaide hastened to the chrome-yellow lobby where Lydia tapped a slippered foot. "Is something amiss, Lydia?"

"The lilac gloves, that you and the maid were supposed to pack, aren't in my trunks."

"Why not simply wear another pair?"

An appalled gasp left Lydia's mouth agape. "And risk a disastrous clash of hues? Never. Only the lilac gloves complement my lilac frock with silver netting. If we cannot find them, I cannot wear the dress tonight. Which means the wardrobe rotation I so carefully planned will be upturned. Which means I might be forced to. . .repeat an ensemble." A shudder vexed her countenance.

Heaven forbid they face such a disaster. "Are you certain the gloves weren't misplaced whilst unpacking?"

"The maid assures me they aren't here. Unless you suppose she's lying to cover incompetence or theft?"

Adelaide swallowed a tremor that churned in her stomach. "Of course not. Millie would never spout falsehoods, for any reason." *Nor have need for lilac gloves.* "I supervised the packing, so I'll assume responsibility. Will my white silk gloves remedy the situation? They won't clash, and I've yet to wear them, so no one would be the wiser."

"That might do." Dainty jaw hardening to stone, Lydia lifted her pert nose. "Once again, you've rescued me from societal ruin and necessitate my thanks."

"There's no need for recollection or gratitude." Lydia's sobered decision to forgive her concert performance was return enough. "Only please, adhere to your promise."

"Certainly. Flirting affords little pleasure if one can't remember doing so the following day. Now, I shall fetch your gloves myself—lest they too are *misplaced*—and view them alongside my dress to amend the arrangement of my hair accordingly. A different headpiece will be in order." Lydia sauntered out of view.

Sinking onto a nearby settee, Adelaide heaved a ragged breath she'd been unaware of holding at bay. An internal tremor followed, climbing its way to her hands. She couldn't carry on like this. Not for long. The stresses of serving Lydia were burden enough. She couldn't add the anxiety of avoiding Colonel Glenmire. If matters persisted thus and Colonel Glenmire would not be assuaged, she'd surely break. She'd fail to *face matters bravely.*

Fail to honor Papa's final wish.

"M'lady, did ye grant the ogre rights to your gloves? 'Cause she's snitched 'em bold faced, chittering nonsense 'bout feathers and colors and—" Millie took Adelaide's hand and knelt at her feet like a fairy perched on a toadstool. "What did that tyrant say to ye? You're hands are shakin' like the fire's gone out in winter."

'Twas more like the fire had gone out in her own soul. "What am I to do, Millie? Colonel Glenmire will speak to me again at dinner, I'm sure, and his determination deafens him to any word of refusal. But how else can I answer? Despite Lydia's benevolence regarding the concert, she'd never permit me a moment of limelight during the prince's masquerade." The tremor in Adelaide's hands shivered up her spine with a disturbing chill that numbed her voice. "There's no way out."

Brown eyes glassing over with tears, Millie stared up at her. "What's happened to the strong lady I knew?"

She is gone. Just. . .gone.

Millie squeezed her hand. "There's always a way out, m'lady. But sometimes it's down a harder road than we'd care to travel."

"You cannot mean I should—"

"Sing like you was born ta do? Aye, just that."

Adelaide broke from Millie's gaze, shaking her head frantically. "I'll not risk being separated from you and my home. Papa wanted me to—"

"Be happy. Cared for and loved. And though he did his best, that's not what happened. Though you've been worn into forgetting, your security doesn't come from Lydia or your position. Thanks be! Your future rests with a power higher an' mightier than that girl could ever imagine herself, so stop lettin' her hold a snuffer o'er your voice."

Millie tapped a delicate finger under Adelaide's chin, prompting her gaze upward. "Remember when ye used ta hum traipsin' up stairs? How you'd whistle o'er your needlework? How, after nary every meal, you'd sing for your Papa, warbling carefree as a bird? This is your chance ta get your song back, luve. Tonight, you explain matters to Colonel Glenmire and tell him you'll sing that fancy song o'his. Take the risk an' trust that things will work out."

Hadn't that sort of thinking gotten her into this mess? Adelaide sighed. When the entail gave everything to her uncle, she *had* trusted. She had *faced matters bravely.* Surrendered, believing God would secure her future with an anchor of hope. Unfortunately, the Almighty seemed satisfied to let her sail aimlessly, battered by winds beyond her control.

Menacing winds, swirling with whispers that His anchor might fail.

Adelaide stood, withdrawing from Millie's touch. "I'll take your advice into consideration." As it pertained to explaining her situation to Colonel Glenmire. Hopefully, doing so would diminish his persistence. *Lord, let that be enough.*

❧

"Per the prince's wishes, seating arrangements have been altered this evening to diversify and enliven conversation at table." The footman smiled at Adelaide as if he'd presented her with a Christmas pudding rather than an unsettling announcement.

Beside the dining table that stretched the length of the grand Banqueting Room, Adelaide suppressed the odd desire to grab Lydia's hand. "You mean I'm to be separated from Lady Lydia? We're to be seated with strangers?"

The footman remained oblivious to her discomfort. "You're seated across the table, m'lady. Within each other's sights. I can escort you there, if you like?"

No, she did not like. Not even a fraction. This whole business sent unease creeping up her neck. "Surely we—"

"By jove, there's no need to fret, lady fair." A uniformed gentleman appeared beside the footman, his ruddy face one giant smile punctuated by a well-placed dimple. He bowed, disheveled curls bobbing. "Captain Quinby, at your service. I've been gifted the heavenly task of sitting by Lady Lydia, and I promise, she'll be looked after good and proper. No unwelcome advances or dull conversation."

Lydia's candied giggle turned heads. "If your conversation is as lively as your introductions, any advances on your part would receive a warm welcome, to be sure."

Good heavens. Adelaide bit her lip, then her cheek for good measure. Why didn't Lydia just relinquish ladylike pretense and pen *wanton woman* across her bosom in scarlet ink? "I don't think—"

"Run along, Adelaide." Lydia's cobalt glare communicated with the force of a shout—there'd be no negotiating on behalf of wisdom or decorum.

Praying silently for Captain Quinby to honor his promise of propriety, Adelaide accepted the footman's escort. Dressed in traditional English livery, the footman appeared an ill-prepared adventurer as he led her through the Banqueting Room's mythical jungle. The foliage of a plantain tree decorated the enormous domed ceiling whilst below gilded dragons alighted on elaborate furnishings, from sideboards to lamp bases.

Once seated according to the prince's wishes, Adelaide ascertained that Lydia was indeed within view. Directly across the table beside the jovial figure of Captain Quinby. Who, now that she gave it thought, looked rather familiar. She'd noticed him about the Pavilion, on more than one occasion, but couldn't recall the particulars. The uneasy feeling returned, pricking its way across her skin. Was not the captain often in the company of—

"Good evening, Lady Adelaide." Colonel Glenmire's voice iced down her back.

Adelaide rotated to find the colonel settled on her right. Hundreds of guests resided at the Royal Pavilion, and by chance alone, she'd been paired with the one man who'd assumed the role of her shadow? The very same man considered to be a favorite of the Prince Regent, who'd only this night taken a sudden interest in "diversifying conversation" at table.

Chance, it seemed, donned military regalia and excelled at chess.

Indignation warped the iron bars of Adelaide's restraint and caged words bolted for freedom. "Colonel Glenmire, I don't appreciate being moved here and there like a mindless pawn. I care not if you're a favorite of His Majesty's. Such behavior is manipulative at worst, ungentlemanly at best, and shameful in either case." She flinched at the inadvert rebuke in her tone and braced for its repercussions.

Colonel Glenmire replied with a firm nod. "Agreed."

Adelaide's jaw slacked. "Wh-what?"

"I agree. Wholeheartedly."

While the jagged scars marring the right side of Colonel Glenmire's face remained ominous, his overall countenance thawed. "Believe what you will, Lady Adelaide, but I don't wish to subject you to discomfort. Nor do I wish to compose an aria for the prince. But regrettably, a favorite of His Majesty, I am. And with that association comes certain unpleasant obligations. When my attempts to speak with you incited repeated concerns about neglecting your service to Lady Lydia, my comrade, Captain Quinby, suggested this game of musical chairs. He thought his substitution would eliminate your concern and allow us to talk. I thought the idea a step past ludicrous, but Quinby's gifted at pushing me to that end."

Adelaide glanced at Captain Quinby, now demonstrating for Lydia with childlike glee how to balance a fork on the tip of one's finger.

"You needn't worry about Lady Lydia." The colonel's tone was matter of fact rather than comforting. "Quinby's honorable, if not ridiculous. He'll indulge the lady's propensity for flirtation, but no more."

"Indeed? Then he'd never give chase undeterred by a lady's marked refusal?" Adelaide faced the colonel and raised an eyebrow.

"It's not the natural inclination of his character, no." A glint restored vigor in the colonel's dark eyes. "Although, if pressed by outward circumstances, he might inquire as to the reason behind said refusal." His unuttered question hung in the air.

This was her chance to explain matters, but would it do any good? "What if the lady were bound by certain…unpleasant obligations? Would he respond with understanding?"

"He would." Colonel Glenmire's cold manner returned with the menace of frostbite. "Assuming the lady ceased veiling every word in subtextual nuance and came straight out with it."

Right. Adelaide fortified herself with a deep breath. "As you know, I serve as a companion to my cousin Lydia. What you don't know is that I have no other family or resource. I need my position, Colonel Glenmire. A position which depends upon my maintaining Lydia's favor. If I sing publicly, she's made it clear I shall be sent away without so much as a reference. While Lydia forgave my concert performance, for reasons you may well imagine, I cannot hazard an encore. I apologize if this subjects you to His Majesty's ire. Nevertheless, I cannot sing and beg you relent in pursuing the matter further."

A grave air entombed Colonel Glenmire, and he turned away without reply.

Adelaide exhaled. Freed of one less concern, she might eat in peace.

Over a dozen footmen emerged from the nearby Great Kitchen, carrying silver trays, and commenced the fashionable *à la russe* dinner by serving the guests at table. Cooled white wine accompanied the dish, but Adelaide refrained, in order to keep an alert eye on Lydia. As the courses progressed into the tens, Colonel Glenmire maintained his silence. Thankfully. Meanwhile, Adelaide joined the lady on her left in admiring the room's magical centerpiece—a crystal chandelier held in the claws of a giant, silvered dragon. Amid the dazzling nest of crystals, six reptilian offspring sprang forth and exhaled light through glass, lotus-shaped shades.

As the twentieth course was served, Adelaide felt herself watched.

"What if I contrived for you to sing without discovery?"

Adelaide lowered a spoonful of pink champagne jelly to her plate. "Do you never give up, Colonel?"

"Not when it's within my power to mend."

"But it's not in your power, sir."

"Nonsense. It can be managed. We arrange rehearsals around your duties. Practice in secret. Keep your identity hidden from the Pavilion populace, easily done as the performance is during a masquerade. Lady Lydia never need know you sang a note."

This wasn't how he was supposed to respond. He was supposed to leave her be, not increase his determination. "Even if I managed to sneak away and wore a mask, Lydia would still recognize my voice."

"Not if an attractive solider whisked her to the moonlit gardens during your performance." Colonel Glenmire's head motioned toward Captain Quinby.

Forge a romantic liaison? "You cannot be serious?"

"Why not? Lady Lydia enjoys his company. Quinby enjoys an elaborate ruse. As I said, he's honorable, so no need to fear anything untoward. At least consider a trial rehearsal where I may judge your voice properly. Without your futile attempts to water it down."

He'd noticed that? Adelaide's nerves tangled in a fraying knot. She could heed Millie's advice, take the risk, and trust that things would work out, but. . .what if they didn't? What if things went awry and God failed to intervene?

"Allow me to present a new question." Colonel Glenmire propped his arm on the table and leaned closer, intense gaze searching her own. "Do you *want* to sing?"

No one had cared what she wanted in ages. Did she even know anymore?

"If you honestly don't want to sing, I'll desist. But if you want to sing, permit us a trial rehearsal." The colonel resumed his distance and stared ahead. "As I said, your voice is too precious a thing to be wasted or locked away. Especially if music is your passion."

It had been. . .long ago. A quiver unsettled Adelaide's bottom lip. Did she dare risk everything to sing just once more? It seemed such a great risk, for such a little thing. Yet, for her, it was no little thing. *"This is your chance ta get your song back, luve."*

Adelaide unfurled her clenched fingers. If she released but one hand from the task of navigating her life, might she rekindle the passion which had once sparked life in her soul?

Chapter Five

Walter still couldn't believe Lady Adelaide had agreed to a trial rehearsal. Yet there she stood, on the opposite end of the Music Gallery, performing a series of vocal exercises as the first timid rays of dawn crept in through floor-to-ceiling windows. He ought to feel relieved, one step closer in securing her talents for the masquerade ball. However, the solving of one problem only served to heighten the bleakness of his original quandary. He sat on a piano bench and fanned out the sheet music for his aria. Barren strings of notes unadorned by a single lyrical gem. If Lady Adelaide gave consent, could he mine lyrics for her to sing in time?

Walter set the papers to rights. *Tackle one problem at a time.* Hopefully, this experimental practice would convince Lady Adelaide to perform and, in turn, provide inspiration to revive his creativity.

Rising from the piano bench, Walter strode to the nearby sofa where Quinby snored, chin drooped onto his chest. *Lazy louse.* He gave Quinby a sound kick to the shins.

Quinby startled and whacked his head against the ivory wall. "Owww! Treason and tyranny, Glenmire. What the devil did you go and do that for?"

"Because you're supposed to be chaperoning this clandestine rehearsal." Walter lowered his voice to a whisper. "I assured Lady Adelaide we'd preserve her reputation, as well as her position, which means you must endeavor to stay awake."

"Who can stay awake at this ghastly hour? The sun hasn't even crested the horizon." Rubbing sleep from his eyes, Quinby reclined on the gold-gilt sofa and stretched his legs out on the red carpet, propping one boot atop the other. "It's unnatural, that's what."

"Servants rise at this 'unnatural' hour daily—scullery maids earlier still—and put in a full day's labor, besides. I think you can manage to sit and keep your eyes open, Captain."

"We're not at war, anymore, old chum. You can't just pull rank whenever you like."

Oh, he couldn't, eh? Gripping Quinby's ear and yanking upward, Walter helped the yelping captain onto his feet. "What are your orders, Captain Quinby?"

"Stay awake, Colonel Glenmire, sir. Eyes wide open and vigilant against impropriety, sir. Like a wrinkled hag of a spinster, hovering in bitter black, out to ruin a chap's good time, sir."

A female-toned *harrumph* drew Walter and Quinby's attention to Lady Adelaide, who now stood rather close with an eyebrow raised in censure. "If you gentlemen are through behaving like schoolboys and disparaging the plight of unmarried women—who are unfairly left with little means or resources besides guarding naive debs against the 'good time' intentions of rakes and coxcombs—then perhaps we might proceed with this rehearsal? I should very much like to conclude before I am missed at breakfast."

Heat scalded Walter's neck and face. *Schoolboy, indeed.* Whenever the shy woman dared voice an opinion, it reduced him to an addle-brained youth in a manner that was as disquieting as it was pleasant. Walter released Quinby, and with a wave of his hand toward the pianoforte, invited Lady Adelaide to walk ahead.

As Lady Adelaide passed him by, a hint of amusement seemed to flash in the gold flecks of her hazel eyes and then disappeared behind her shroud of unreadable silence.

For the life of him, Walter couldn't understand why she kept that shroud so tight in hand. Was the fear of losing her employment that great? Or did her cousin hold a worse threat over her head? Not that he had any personal interest, of course. The details of Lady Adelaide's life were neither his business nor concern, unless they affected the task at hand.

As Lady Adelaide assumed the pianoforte's bench, Walter gathered his sheet music and set the papers on a nearby table topped with red marble. "Proceed when ready, Lady Adelaide."

With a demure nod, Lady Adelaide played the familiar opening of Handel's *Messiah*—part three, air for soprano. Music flitted about the room as if buoyed by the sun's warm emergence, now painting upward strokes of light across the gallery. Walter tapped the side of his breeches, fingering the notes played. *Fine selection.* The lady had excellent taste.

Lady Adelaide closed her eyes, hands never faltering as if they knew the piece by memory. Nay, by heart. Opening her eyes once more, she sang the dormant words off the page. "*I know that my Redeemer liveth.*"

The ever-present tension in Walter's shoulders dissipated. His heartbeat slowed, calmed by the melody's gentle sway. He tried to study Lady Adelaide's vocal range, take note of qualities in her voice to showcase in the aria he must write, but his mind was latched fast onto the song's lyrics. To the words he'd once believed. The words now searing through the ice encasing his numb heart.

"*I know that my Redeemer liveth.*"

Focus, man. Walter turned away from Lady Adelaide and faced the window. *Focus on the performance.* The words didn't matter anymore. Perhaps they never had.

"*I know that my Redeemer liveth.*"

A blanket of warmth fell upon Walter, wrapping him with overwhelming peace. One he used to feel whenever music played. Whenever he'd been inspired to compose. The very same peace that held him close now, in a father's embrace, soft and comforting in its strength. Lady Adelaide's voice faded to the background of his conscience and then vanished from hearing altogether. All his awareness centered on the divine peace. The holy Presence. Right now, in this moment, he was no longer that solider wounded and forgotten on a bloodstained battlefield.

In this moment, he wasn't alone.

A tear slipped down Walter's cheek. *God?*

Next thing Walter knew he was seated and hunched over the marble table, graphite pencil dredged from his pocket, scribbling furiously on sheet music to capture the lyrics breezing through his mind to the tune of his masterwork aria. He examined the words jotted down. *I cling to Christ, my refuge. I surrender to His Shepherd fold. The past I cannot change; the future I cannot control.* Such lyrics wouldn't please the prince, but they fitted to the music like gems cut for a custom setting. These were the words he'd waited for so long.

Lady Adelaide's faint voice seeped back into his consciousness, and her song again met his hearing. *"He shall stand at the latter day upon the earth."*

He shall stand. . .even after Waterloo? Peace held Walter secure while the thought wandered in his mind, searching for a place to take root. Was it possible that God hadn't abandoned him? That He'd stood there, peace amid the chaos? That He stood here now, waiting for Walter's frozen anger to thaw and once again make His presence welcome?

Reaching off the page, the new lyrics seemed to knock on his heart and ask for admittance. *I surrender to His Shepherd fold. The past I cannot change. . .the brother I could not save?* A second tear escaped Walter's guard.

No. Never.

The heat had thawed too quickly, awaking old pain once dulled. Walter turned his back on the table, and the peace fell from his shoulders, exposing them to the unlit room's chill. What right had God to make His presence known now? If the Almighty loved as the scriptures professed, He'd have met Benjamin in his hour of need. He'd have ended Benjamin's pain.

Saved his life.

Walter spun back and glowered at the sheet music, which now contained more lyrics than he'd written in the entire four years since Waterloo. Since he stopped praying, stopped believing, stopped caring. He scoffed at the harsh reality. While he hadn't lost the physical skill or mental acuteness for composition, he couldn't create on his own, and he'd severed himself from the very Source that provided his creativity.

A Source he refused to rely on ever again.

Chapter Six

"Enough!"

The word pierced Adelaide like a shard of ice, freezing her fingers above the ivories and silencing her song. She gawked at Colonel Glenmire across the pianoforte, his tear-wetted face darkened by anguish. What had she done? "Should I try another song?"

"No." A deathly chill coursed through the response. His lone hand formed a fist atop the pianoforte and snapped a pencil with which he must have been writing. Staggering away from the point of destruction, his russet eyes widened by the horror of something she couldn't perceive. The vision reduced his voice to a haunted whisper. "We're through."

Without explanation, Colonel Glenmire marched out of the Music Gallery.

Unable to articulate a single muddled thought, Adelaide stared at the spot where the colonel had stood, now occupied exclusively by golden serpents coiling around ivory columns. What happened? All had been music and sunrise and seeming perfection. What could have caused such a stark alteration in Colonel Glenmire's countenance?

Certainly the colonel appeared naught but a chilling shadow at first glance. However, as she drew closer, she'd thought herself witnessing a different side of him. A lighter side that broke through the gloom every now and then. Such as during their conversation at dinner last night or moments earlier, in an exchange of lighthearted jest with Captain Quinby. Seconds ago, when a song of praise moved him to tears. What kept dragging Colonel Glenmire's soul back into the tortured darkness?

"Lady Adelaide, you have my thanks." Captain Quinby now stood on her left, expression as somber as his mischievous dimple would allow.

Adelaide shook her head. "Whatever for, sir?"

"For giving Glenmire a moment's peace." The captain leaned against the pianoforte. "He's spot on, you know. That voice of yours is top notch. More than mere talent, I'd say."

"For that I cannot take credit."

For while singing Handel's poignant lyrics, Adelaide had felt the Redeemer Himself step into the room and lift her spirits with the grandest sense of liberty. As though she had finally emerged into the fresh, welcoming air of a spring day after a winter's seclusion in stale darkness. A feeling she hadn't experienced since days long past when she'd found gratifying joy in comforting through song. Ministering peace to Papa after Mamma's death. Spreading joy to the servants amid the monotony of daily chores.

Consoling her own heart when Papa's chair sat empty by the hearth.

When had she become so content with silence? Resigned to a future of endless winter? Adelaide turned, stroking the pianoforte keys, and then indulged in a chord. As the notes faded, she could almost hear Papa's voice. *"Sing me a ditty, darling."*

In a moment, the chord of harmonizing notes vanished into still, quiet vapor. Adelaide's heart ached at their departure. Even if Papa hadn't intended for her to become trapped in silence, what hope was there of things changing now?

"Lady Adelaide." Captain Quinby's voice dragged her from the chasm of thought.

Oh dear, he was still here? Uncertain what to do, no doubt. And she was being terribly rude. Adelaide stood. "Forgive me, Captain Quinby. Consider yourself relieved of chaperone duty. I best return upstairs for breakfast." *And face matters bravely.*

"Don't run off just yet, lady fair." Captain Quinby rushed to the other side of the pianoforte and soon returned with the stack of papers belonging to Colonel Glenmire, presenting the lot to her keeping. "Look here. A song more beautiful couldn't be found, I'd wager. Surely a fine singer, such as yourself, would have a great lark performing it. Am I right?"

Adelaide studied the sheet music. The arrangement was beautiful, indeed, although the lyrics were not yet finished. *I cling to Christ, my refuge. I surrender to His Shepherd fold. The past I cannot change; the future I cannot control.*

The future she couldn't control. . .no matter how hard she tried. A lump caught in her throat. She couldn't fathom such complete surrender. "Colonel Glenmire penned this?"

"He did, and composed the music. You'll sing it at the masquerade, won't you? I swear on my love of figgy pudding to distract your cousin and keep it a secret." Fair brows furrowing, Captain Quinby's signature grin disappeared. "Please, Glenmire needs this."

He wasn't the only one. Gnawing on her lower lip, Adelaide examined the aria's every note. Something deep within her needed to hear it completed, even if her circumstances couldn't be altered. Perhaps this song was God's way of allowing her to enjoy the spring air one last time?

"Where might I find Colonel Glenmire, do you think?"

Captain Quinby's eyes gleamed, awakening his impish dimple. "Try the gardens. Glenmire always hunts down fresh air when he's upset. But don't let that shady scowl of his frighten you off. If you cast enough sunshine on it, the bugger loses its bite."

A fleeting chuckle relaxed Adelaide's frame. "You're a good friend, Captain Quinby."

"The best and handsomest. Although, truth be told, I think Glenmire's the better man."

Chapter Seven

The July sun awakened bright as a copper penny to find Walter pacing beside a pianoforte in the Music Gallery, once again listening to Lady Adelaide sing. For the past two weeks, they had met thus, rehearsing whilst the prince's guests slept off the effects of their late-night revelry. Quinby, suddenly keen about secrecy, had taken to standing guard outside the gallery doors like an excitable watchdog.

Walter's pacing carried him closer to the windows where golden-yellow curtains framed the Pavilion's unique landscape of shrubbery and flower beds. Even now, he couldn't shake the memory of Lady Adelaide approaching him on one of the garden's winding paths. No longer hiding behind persons or pillars. No longer cowering, avoiding eye contact, or clinging to her silence. She'd strode to meet him, donning a new mantle of boldness—shoulders back, head erect, and hazel eyes unwavering in their gaze.

"I will perform your aria, Colonel Glenmire. But I have two petitions. First, that Lydia never find out, as promised. I know you'll strive to make good on your word. The zealous loyalty exhibited by your friend isn't something of which a man without character can boast. Second, you must finish this aria."

Then Lady Adelaide had handed him the sheet music for his voiceless aria, now scribbled with three lines that he couldn't bear to complete. *"I'm confident that you're capable, both in talent and resolve, to finish this. For it is a masterpiece in the making. But more importantly. . .these lyrics have the potential to balm wounded hearts. People must know how it ends. I must know how it ends."*

Moved by the fervor of her encouragement, awed by the bravery she'd mustered to overcome her initial wariness, Walter had gained a new determination. He couldn't let Lady Adelaide down. He *had* to write her a song. . .and so he had, that very night. Locked away in his private quarters, he had chased down lyrics and notes with a club of willpower. Written an entirely new aria arranged perfectly for Lady Adelaide's voice— and the prince's haughty expectations. A gleaming tribute to His Majesty's victory at Waterloo.

One that turned his stomach during every rehearsal.

Rotating toward the pianoforte, Walter inspected Lady Adelaide's countenance. While she'd yet to comment, he knew she wasn't pleased about the song change. Her voice still hit the right notes, mouth forming the right words, but all joy and passion had vanished from the recital. The last two days she'd not even met his gaze. She was retreating into her shroud of silence. Somehow he must prevent that from happening and revive Lady Adelaide's enthusiasm. A need he chose not to examine for its motivation.

As the ending notes of the aria faded, Walter approached the pianoforte. "That was tolerable enough, but I think we can do better."

Lady Adelaide's fixed stare leapt from the ivories to his face, a fiery spark in their hazel depths. "Agreed. This aria is a travesty. Notes forced together like mismatched puzzle pieces jammed in place on a child's nursery table. Lyrics hollow as a bird's dry bones—void of life and truth and hope. It doesn't bear repeating. You are better than this, Colonel."

Walter didn't know whether to be offended or impressed by her keen observation and musical insight.

"What happened to the other aria?" Disappointment pinched Lady Adelaide's mouth and creased around her eyes. "Why did you not finish it?"

Because the very prospect hurt too deeply. "What does it matter?"

"In case you've forgotten, Colonel Glenmire, I am taking a great personal risk in agreeing to perform again. One I chose to hazard for the sake of singing a song with a noble theme. Now I'm risking everything for what, exactly? To indulge the prince's ego? To better your reputation?"

"No. This has nothing to do with me."

"Which may be why this aria lacks poignancy. You composed it without feeling, so the music is without feeling. Consequently it's irrelevant to you or anyone else."

The truth punched Walter in the ribs. Why must she expose his insufficiency? "You're not here to critique my work, Lady Adelaide."

"And you, Colonel, no longer frighten me with your glacial scowl."

Walter's jaw went slack. His presence had frightened her? A shudder unsettled his gut, casting his gaze to the floor. *Dear God. . .perhaps he had died that day with Benjamin.*

The somber hush of a graveyard stilled the Music Gallery, ominous and overwhelming.

After a few moments, Lady Adelaide's gentle tone breathed life into the room once more. "We need a reprieve, I think. Too much work is bound to breed quarrels."

Walter nodded, accepting her gracious offer to leave well enough alone.

"Why do we not play a duet on the pianoforte?"

She couldn't be serious? Walter dug his fingers into his palm. "You know that's impossible."

"Nonsense." With a graceful air, Lady Adelaide slid to the bench's far right side. "You play left, while I play right. My Mamma and I did so many times with great success. When I was a child, I loved nothing more than creating music with my parents. Mamma and I sharing the pianoforte while Papa stood with his violin tucked under his chin. After dinner we'd play airs and reels, well into the night, Papa urging us faster and faster with his bow until our aching fingers could no longer match him."

A wistful smile softened Lady Adelaide's features and seemed to make her forget his presence. "I've never felt so loved as on those nights. Sheltered and liberated all at once."

She ought to feel that way every night.

And such thoughts of Lady Adelaide ought *not* cross his mind.

Regaining her composure, Lady Adelaide stood and leafed through a drawer containing a portion of the Prince Regent's collection of costly, machine-printed sheet music. "Now, Colonel, what shall we play? Robert Burns? I adore his 'My Luve is Like a Red, Red Rose' but perhaps you'd prefer a piano concerto?"

He actually preferred Burns, but that didn't matter a whit, because he couldn't play. *Could. Not.* "Why are you determined to humiliate me?"

"Why are you opposed to a moment's fun?"

He huffed and raised an eyebrow. "You've been exchanging nonsense with Quinby."

A coy smile brightened Lady Adelaide's face as she set a selection of music atop the pianoforte. She sat, leaving room on the bench, and gave him an anticipating sideways glance.

Blast. "You'll not be diverted, I suppose?"

"Surprised by how obnoxious persistence can be, Colonel? Since you're adept at doggedness, I expected you'd be familiar with the paradigm."

How did she manage to look so alluring while driving him mad? "One. Song."

As Walter assumed his place on the bench, he tensed, keenly aware of Lady Adelaide's proximity. A sliver of space separated her from the tailcoat sleeve that concealed his stub of an arm. No doubt if she were to see the mangled deformity, she'd recoil from him appalled. Frightened by him worse still. Neck and cheeks heating, he focused on Lady Adelaide's musical selection, Haydn's Piano Concerto No. 11 in D Major. He couldn't play such a difficult piece. Not now.

"Ready?" Lady Adelaide's right hand floated above the keys.

Not in the least. However, the confidence radiating in her eyes made him want to believe he was capable. The impossible, possible. Walter raised his left hand and nodded.

The concerto fumbled off the page and limped across the gallery, hindered by Walter's lack of practice. His awkward fingers cramped. Staggered like a drunkard, intent on murdering Hayden's stunning arrangement. With the fall of every butchered note, Walter winced and ground his teeth, but Lady Adelaide never grimaced. She simply played, allowing him to grow accustomed to the change of playing with one hand.

After a while, Walter's fingers relaxed and recalled their training. Soon he was able to mimic Lady Adelaide's rhythm and thus remove the concerto's burden. The notes sprinted, leaping and bounding, with an energizing strength as if the war had never happened. As if life hadn't altered and he wasn't useless. Time, which for Walter had been frozen, started to tick again to the melody's cadence, and for a rare moment, the cold weight that oppressed him receded, freeing his mind from the snare of Waterloo. For a moment, he was fully present. Every color restored to vividness. Every note felt to his bones.

When the concerto ended, Walter tolerated only three seconds of silence. *One song wasn't enough.* With lightened fingers, he struck up *Sir Roger de Coverley*, once his favorite dance to play at his family's estate.

Lady Adelaide flashed a smile, curtained by auburn ringlets, and picked up the tune.

Together their fingers nimbly skipped back and forth across the keys like partners at a country dance. No better dance had Walter ever enjoyed. For in this jig Lady Adelaide wasn't obligated to frolic away from him down the line or take a turn with another partner. Instead she remained at his side, delicate shoulder glancing his as they played.

Inspired by a mischievous notion, Walter increased the jig's tempo a beat.

Gifting him a sideways smirk, Lady Adelaide matched his swiftness.

He upped the speed a little more.

Lady Adelaide bit her lower lip as her fingers scurried to keep pace.

Holding back a chuckle, Walter sped the jig as fast as his fingers would permit.

Lady Adelaide nudged him with an elbow, her fingers scrambling. "Have mercy, Colonel, lest my fingers break."

"I never surrender, dear lady." Walter fought to contain a grin.

"Fiend!" The word broke forth on her laughter. "Then you must be taken prisoner." Lady Adelaide grasped his hand with tiny fingers, halting their dance with a startling abruptness. She beamed a broad smile, raising one eyebrow like a victory banner. "I win."

Completely captured by her gaze, a mere breath away, Walter lost all will and desire to restrain a smile. "Indeed, you have, my lady."

Realization of their nearness dawned in Lady Adelaide's expression. A blush seized her cheeks as she snatched away both hands and leapt to her feet, retreating with small steps toward the doors. "Breakfast. They will be serving breakfast. Upstairs. Now. I. . . until, tomorrow, Colonel." She curtsied and then fled as if chased by fire, speeding right past a smirking Quinby.

Once she'd exited the room, Walter turned to gather the sheet music. "Out with it, meddlesome watchdog. How much did you see?"

"Enough to be jealous." Behind him, Quinby's boots traipsed across the gallery, and his voice assumed a serious tone. "And to know it's high time you set aside what happened at Waterloo."

Chest constricting, Walter spun 'round and stood. "You've no right."

"As your handsomest and dearest friend, I've every right. We're not on the battlefield anymore, Glenmire. Back there, surrender was a treacherous word. A weakness that spelled defeat. But it's not like that now. Not when yielding to the Divine Commander." Quinby gripped Walter's shoulder. "Surrendering to God doesn't make us prisoners of war—it liberates us from having to carry that awful day around forever. Let Him carry it for you, chum."

The ache clutching Walter's chest sliced deeper still and garroted his words of all feeling. "If God cared a wink, He would've carried us *then*."

Tears welled in Quinby's eyes, turning them fragile as glass. "How do you know He didn't? How do you know He wasn't right there, holding you, carrying you both into what was to come? Just because we can't understand His ways. . .can't see Him move. . . doesn't mean we're alone."

That's exactly what it meant.

"Don't stay trapped in that horrible day forever, chum. Benjamin wouldn't want that. He wouldn't want you to look back so long that you miss what's right in front of your face."

Struggling for breath, Walter glanced at the doors. "What are you talk—"

"Mark my word, Glenmire. If you let that songbird fly away, you'll never get her back."

Chapter Eight

Another morn arrived in stillness, noted only by the delicate chimes of the lobby clock and Adelaide's dancing heart. Rising before the sun, she dressed in the shadows, each creeping step leaden with the risk of discovery and quickened by the delightful chance to be heard. To be fully herself, without reproach, in a temporal haven of music. Perhaps today Colonel Glenmire might even smile once more as he had three days prior.

Warmth flooded her cheeks. With silly thoughts such as that, perhaps she'd best ask Captain Quinby to resume his chaperone duties *inside* the Music Gallery.

After donning her slippers, Adelaide opened her chamber door a fraction and examined the lobby, dimly lit by a few wall sconces. *Empty. Thank heaven.* Emerging from her room and shutting the door behind quietly, she tiptoed through the gloom toward the main door.

"Where are you off to at this wretched hour?"

Lydia! Adelaide whipped 'round to face her cousin, heart stunned still.

"Well?" Standing beside a flickering sconce, Lydia wrapped a shawl about the shoulders of her flowing white nightgown and stared with a gaze all too alert and determined.

The hairs on Adelaide's neck bristled as her heart resumed its beating with urgency. *Lord, don't let her destroy everything. Please, not again.*

Lydia's double-edged tone sharpened against a grindstone of impatience. "I will have an explanation."

An explanation, right. Captain Quinby had devised a plan, instructed her to give a certain excuse were she ever caught, but what was it? What was she to say? Adelaide inhaled, gathering her thoughts. "Forgive me, Lydia. I didn't intend to disturb your rest."

"Obviously." Lydia folded her arms over her chest. "Were you off to meet someone?"

Adelaide feigned a thwarted sigh, which required little acting on her part. "He shall be so disappointed that I ruined things. He wished it to be a romantic surprise. You were to awake and find the note on your bedside table along with a rose." The deception tasted bitter on her tongue.

"A rose? From whom?" Interest, melded with desperation, dulled the edge in Lydia's voice. "Come now, I demand you stop talking in riddles and speak plainly."

Mustering her resolve, Adelaide repeated the captain's instructions verbatim. "You have an admirer. Captain Quinby has nurtured a fervent affection for you since you dined together at the prince's table. However, when it comes to matters of the heart, it so happens that the jovial captain is rather shy. Which is why he sent word to me, privately, requesting that I meet him before all had risen in order to convey a letter on his behalf."

"A love letter, for me? And from an officer too?" With a triumphant squeal, Lydia twirled around and around, shawl fluttering behind her shoulders.

The demonstration curdled the guilt in Adelaide's stomach. *Lord, forgive me.* "Why do we not preserve the captain's pride? Allow me to fetch the note as agreed upon." And inform Colonel Glenmire that today's rehearsal must be cancelled.

Lydia ceased twirling, her face flushed. "Indeed not. You shall take me to my Romeo."

"T–take you? Now?" *That wasn't part of the plan.*

"As soon as I can be dressed. If the captain wishes to woo me, then he must be informed that hiding behind paper and ink isn't the way. I wish to hear the avowal of feeling from his very lips, declared with the passion of brave Romeo. Besides, I'm sure Captain Quinby would rather see his Juliet than speak through a bumbling Cyrano." As Lydia hastened to her chamber, her frothy giggles lathered from delicate bubbles to foamy suds. "He shall be so surprised!"

Adelaide gulped. "Indeed." She prayed Captain Quinby was prepared for such a shock.

After helping Lydia to dress and primp and compliment herself, Adelaide descended the magnificent Pavilion staircase, clutching the faux bamboo railing with paled knuckles. To her left, Lydia floated on a cloud of mirth, unaware that it was naught but a vapor. Hopefully, neither of them would be dashed to the ground of reality when it dissolved.

Setting foot in the effervescent pink Long Gallery, Adelaide spotted Captain Quinby standing a ways off, just outside the closed Music Gallery doors—the very same doors which concealed Colonel Glenmire's presence. According to Captain Quinby's contingency plan, the colonel was not to emerge from the gallery unless given the all clear from their dimpled watchdog. A sound plan in theory, but now she worried they'd overlooked a perilous defect. Might their designated meeting place, in front of the Music Gallery, ignite Lydia's suspicions?

If it did, Lydia said not a word. Instead, her cousin rushed across the corridor and nigh flung herself into the arms of Captain Quinby.

A gasp fled Adelaide's lips.

The captain, however, didn't so much as blink at the impropriety, but rather transformed into a gallant lovestruck hero of yore, swinging Lydia 'round thrice in the air. When he returned her feet to the ground, he took a step back and grinned at his pretend Juliet. "Fair maiden, your boldness has liberated me from my insecurity. 'Tis a miracle. Nay, a sign that you and I are but two stars in one sky. A new constellation, gracing the heavens."

Adelaide contained an unladylike snort, just barely, and forced herself not to smirk. Colonel Glenmire had understated his friend's puckish nature—the captain not only enjoyed an elaborate ruse, he was a roguish imp incarnate.

Clutching the sleeve of Captain Quinby's red coatee, Lydia batted her lashes.

"Then we shall spend the remainder of the summer at each other's side, my dear captain. From now on, the Music Gallery threshold shall be our secret meeting place." She turned toward Adelaide, gaze flickering hot as coals. "Cyrano's services are no longer required."

Adelaide bit her lip, stilling a slight tremor. In other words, the Music Gallery was now forbidden and she under heightened scrutiny. *God above, what were they to do now?*

Chapter Nine

As Colonel Glenmire led the way into the Prince Regent's anteroom, Adelaide found herself marveling at the colonel's perseverance anew, the quality that once exasperated now rather endearing.

A monochromatic menagerie of dragons, dolphins, and birds inhabited the anteroom's mint-green walls and seemed to watch the invasion of their royal domain. Pile of sheet music in arm, she kept her voice at a cautious whisper as if the fanciful creatures might overhear. "I still can't believe you arranged for us to practice in His Majesty's private apartments."

Nor could she believe the lengths to which Colonel Glenmire had gone to ease her concern since Lydia's suspicions were ignited two days prior. Along with the precaution of changing locations, he'd also thought to move their rehearsals to late afternoon and ordered Captain Quinby to keep Lydia occupied with his *"horrid attempts at poetry."*

The enchanting mint walls preceded them into the adjoining library where gilded bookshelves housed, what must be, thousands of volumes of literature. Adelaide glanced over her shoulder, half expecting to find a disapproving guard. "Are you certain His Majesty doesn't mind us being here?"

Colonel Glenmire shut the library door. "He cannot mind what he does not know."

Panic strangled Adelaide's whisper. "You didn't ask his consent?"

"Discretion is paramount. Every individual privy to our location increases the odds of discovery through the Pavilion's gossip network. Not even Quinby knows where we're rehearsing now." A tilted half-smile lightened Colonel Glenmire's rich brown eyes. "So you can stop whispering. The prince is off for a day of Dr. Russell's sea cure, bathing machine in tow, and won't return for hours. All will be well."

Adelaide's cheeks warmed. She looked down at her sheet music to conceal the traitorous blush and dispel the memory of holding Colonel Glenmire's hand whilst he'd beamed that same smile. Easily the most foolish thing she'd ever done. She took a breath. Entertaining notions of perceived feelings on the colonel's part was ridiculous. He was a marquess who could, and must, make a fine match. While she was a lady's companion without a dowry or prospects. Their time together was an "unpleasant obligation" to the prince. Nothing more.

She must keep that in mind and focus on her personal objective—to somehow help Colonel Glenmire finish the surrender aria.

Adelaide looked up and caught Colonel Glenmire's smile still fixed on her face as if comfortable there. The blush rekindled in her cheeks with a vengeance. *A chaperone.* Tomorrow she must bring Millie along as chaperone—for appearance's sake. She was *not* falling in love with Colonel Glenmire. Breaking eye contact, her gaze roamed the vast library. "I don't spy a pianoforte hereabouts."

"Couldn't risk having one moved. However, I thought we might manage with this." Striding to an object draped in white cloth, Colonel Glenmire pulled the covering away to reveal a magnificent harp fashioned like a golden palm tree. "Do you play, or must we soldier on without musical accompaniment?"

Adelaide traced a thumb across one of her scarred fingers, forever ruined by flames. "I'm afraid my meager talent for the harp has waned from lack of practice. Besides, I thought we might try something different today." Leafing through the papers she carried, Adelaide retrieved the music for his unfinished aria, concealed behind his operatic ode to the prince's ego, and held it aloft.

A shadow of anguish smothered his smile. "You shouldn't have—"

"Retrieved it from the Music Gallery? Then you should find a more creative hiding spot than a cabinet filled with music." Adelaide infused her tone with jest, hoping to keep him at ease. When she'd stumbled upon the aria the day after their duet, she couldn't bring herself to leave it buried away. It must be finished. *Lord, provide the right words.* "Colonel, part of you must wish to see this piece completed or you wouldn't hold on to it still. Perhaps together we might—"

A clatter resounded in the anteroom followed by a female's mutterings.

Adelaide held her breath and strained to listen.

Footsteps echoed, growing louder as they approached the library.

Someone was coming. Adelaide clasped the sheet music to her chest, wishing to quiet her pounding heart. They were going to be found in the Prince Regent's apartments, unchaperoned.

"Quickly." Colonel Glenmire covered the harp as before and then, placing his hand betwixt her shoulders, guided her to the rear of the library. Halting before a wall lamp crowned with winged serpents, he grasped one of the four candles and pulled it down like a lever. The wall where the lamp was mounted cracked open to expose a dimly lit passage. She gasped, but the colonel remained unfazed as he nudged her into the tunnel and followed. Seconds later the secret door closed without a sound.

Adelaide exhaled a long breath, fluttering the pages of music in her grasp. "Gone for hours, you said. All will be well, you said."

"All *is* well." Removing his warm palm from her back, Colonel Glenmire raked his fingers through his dark, wavy locks. A sheepish expression contrasted with his austere scars. "I just neglected to consider the possibility of a maid being sent to clean the apartments during the prince's absence."

Adelaide smirked. "Suppose I omit the part where I say 'no one is perfect' and you tell me where we are."

"This is the Prince Regent's famously rumored secret tunnel that runs under the Royal Pavilion gardens."

Good heavens. It was real? "The one which leads to the home of his mistress, Maria Fitzherbert?"

"Facts are less romantic than gossip. The tunnel was constructed to allow our stout prince to reach the stables during inclement weather. . .and to spare his pride the injury of gawking onlookers." Colonel Glenmire pressed an ear to the secret door. "We best head for the stables ourselves. The poor maid has many a shelf to dust."

Assuming a natural silence, the pair walked side-by-side down the passageway. Utilitarian lanterns tucked into wall niches stood sentry at regular intervals, casting a dim glow upon the brick floor and arched cement ceiling. The earthen aroma of clay permeated the air, making the narrow tunnel feel somehow comforting. Sheltered. Enough so that Adelaide dared once more to surmount the colonel's barricade and free the song imprisoned therein. "This place is perfectly suited for airing out secrets. Will you not tell me yours—the reason you refuse to finish the aria?"

Steady pace unaltered, Colonel Glenmire responded with neither word nor glance.

As they continued their subterranean stroll, Adelaide ran her thumb along the music she carried, flicking the papers' edges. Was he angered? Had she pushed too far?

Raw emotion pulled Colonel Glenmire's words taut. "It's that important to you?"

More than she dared admit. "Your aria is too significant to remain unfinished."

The colonel observed another period of silence. "I'll consent to an exchange: my secret for one of yours."

An interesting proposal. One that meant she was making a bit of headway. "Very well, Colonel. Here's a secret for you. The night we first met and climbed the Pavilion stairs, I was desperately trying not to laugh at the sight of Lydia flung over your shoulder." She chuckled.

"That's not a secret, Lady Adelaide. It's neither shocking nor tragic."

"You wish a shock, sir?" Inhaling a draught of clay-steeped air and then letting it go, Adelaide uttered the first thought that sprang to mind. "I hate deceiving Lydia with a false Romeo and feel that I ought to make amends." Although, if the truth came out, Lydia would make her pay dearly enough.

"That won't serve either. Our exchange must be equal in gravity to be judged fair. Besides, I have a specific matter in mind."

Specific? What could he wish to know?

The colonel's tone softened, aching with concern. "Tell me, truthfully, what intimidation does Lady Lydia hold about your neck like a noose?"

The question halted Adelaide midstride and constricted her breath. "That, sir, is a complicated tale."

"We've time." Colonel Glenmire's countenance shone with a compassion and warmth his scars could not disfigure, and his gaze tenderly implored her to go on.

Adelaide gnawed on her bottom lip. *It would be so nice to finally tell someone.* Hugging the music close to her heart, she swallowed a knot of uncertainty and let the story unfold. "Shortly after my uncle assumed possession of Papa's estate, Lydia hosted a party at our— *their* home. The guests took turns at the pianoforte, playing and singing, but my recital received the longest ovation. For the rest of the evening, conversation repeatedly diverted to compliments of my performance." If only she'd known to hush them.

Shaking away the regret, Adelaide sighed. "Later that night, Lydia confronted me with accusations of ruining her party. I foolishly attempted to reason with her, but she was too livid for coherent thought. An argument ensued, and before I could prevent her, she seized my collection of printed sheet music. . .a lifetime of gifts from my parents and. . . tossed it into the fire." That last word unsettled her jaw with a tremor. "Lydia swore to ensure that my uncle would dismiss me if I dared sing again. That was now a year ago."

Colonel Glenmire's dark brows knit together, forming creases around his eyes. "Can't you explain matters to your uncle?"

"Though kindhearted, my aunt and uncle are blind to their daughter's faults. And Lydia is careful not to exhibit questionable behavior in their presence, so I bite my tongue. To stay in my home, remain with our servants, and prevent Lydia from destroying the one precious heirloom that remains—Papa's violin."

"You mean the she-devil has it?"

The marked outrage in Colonel Glenmire's tone was somehow comforting. . .a validation of feelings she struggled to repress. "While I vainly tried to save my music from the fire, Lydia took the violin hostage. That's why she must never discover us." Fresh grief crashed over Adelaide in a wave, eroding through another layer of strength and hope, rendering her voice hollow. "She'll make me watch it burn. . .make me lose my parents all over again."

A gentle hush wrapped the pair in its arms, enfolding them in a cocoon of stillness where words could be absorbed and felt and understood. And though he said nothing, she knew Colonel Glenmire understood her all too well. Not in a rational manner of mental process, but at a depth that penetrated to the heart. He understood because, standing before a looking glass, they saw the same reflection—weary eyes emptied of tears, furrowed brows haunted by tragic days, a fragile image held together by gritted jaws.

All at once, the aria no longer mattered. All that mattered was Colonel Glenmire's story. Listening, as he had listened, and consoling as best could be done. "We had an agreement." Adelaide mustered a timid smile. "I kept my end."

"And this time I can't fault your barter." Turning his face away from scrutiny, Colonel Glenmire moved forward, walking through the tunnel while she followed alongside.

After an interlude, he cleared his throat. "I've a younger brother. *Had* a younger brother. Benjamin. Gangly, sprig of a lad. He followed me and Quinby everywhere as children. Irritated me to no end with his questions and determination to mimic my every action. As we grew older, he continued to follow in my footsteps, and I grew not to wish otherwise. When I joined the military, he enlisted beside me. A decision I should never have encouraged. I should've insisted he stay home."

Adelaide's heart descended to her stomach with each slow step, now leaden, for she could already guess at this story's conclusion.

"I kept assuring Benjamin that someone would save us." The statement snagged

Colonel Glenmire's low voice on a shard of pain, shredding each word that followed. "We lay injured at Waterloo till nightfall. Men stacked like kindling all around, some groaning, others forever silenced. Still I promised Benjamin a rescue, praying under my breath. . .but no one answered. No one came. Eventually, I rallied strength and tried to drag Benjamin to aid with my remaining hand. . .but it was for naught."

No wonder Colonel Glenmire thought her prayers wasted effort.

Inhaling a ragged breath, the colonel stood still. "My brother died. . .alone."

Alone? The tragic word gored Adelaide. "You were with—"

"I blacked out!" The confession tore from his being and echoed through the tunnel, rattling Adelaide to the core. Colonel Glenmire whipped around to face her, his countenance now blackened by tangible loathing. A mere shadow of himself. "I was weak, and Benjamin died. Alone."

Adelaide's heart wrenched at his belief in the morose statement. "That's not true."

Jaw gritted and gaze vacant, the colonel moved to walk away.

Adelaide dashed forward and blocked his path, forcing him to meet her gaze headlong. He glowered, but she stood firm. He must hear the truth. "Listen well, Colonel. No one who is in Christ ever dies alone. We who remain earthbound simply can't see the One who welcomes our beloved on the other side of eternity."

Tears glistened in Colonel Glenmire's eyes, unshed. "I wish I could believe that."

His words broke her heart. "They *are* welcomed, Colonel. By love greater than we can fathom. Christ suffered the loneliest death imaginable to spare us that very fate."

Colonel Glenmire shook his head and his bleak gaze fell, dragging Adelaide's attention down to the space between them, now much too narrow.

She stepped back over the invisible but heavy cord of decorum she'd so recklessly crossed and restored an appropriate distance between them. What was she thinking? Intention to comfort didn't condone such forwardness. Such intimate conversation. Besides, after this summer, she'd never see Colonel Glenmire again.

Adelaide hurried down the tunnel, paying no heed as to whether Colonel Glenmire followed. The pages of music bit into her arms, so tight were they now clutched. She needed to reach the surface. Bask in the sunlight where boundaries were visible and romantic feelings obviously impractical. She must focus solely on the song she'd agreed to sing and above all—find a chaperone.

Passing through a door at the end of tunnel, Adelaide entered the stables. The scent of hay refreshed her senses. A colossal domed ceiling reached toward the sun, bidding rays welcome through glass panes. Equine whinnies and snorts echoed in the palatial building.

"Remarkable structure, isn't it?" Colonel Glenmire's presence at her side, and the restoration of his calm cadence, put Adelaide on alert.

She nodded, not hazarding a glance his direction.

"I've always preferred ships and limitless ocean to carriages and narrow streets. Would've joined the navy, but centuries of family tradition dictated otherwise. Marlowe men always join the army." The colonel's gaze warmed her neck. "Ever been to the sea?"

"Not in many years." Not since Papa had taken ill her debut season.

Colonel Glenmire appeared to study a passing white steed, led on a rope by a groom. "No rehearsal tomorrow, I think. We need a reprieve."

Indeed, she'd benefit from time away from him to collect her thoughts. "Fine."

"Will you come here instead, Lady Adelaide? For a surprise."

Adelaide sought the colonel's face before she thought to refrain. "A surprise?"

"Just that." A smile danced in Colonel Glenmire's russet eyes. "And it might be prudent if you brought a chaperone."

Chapter Ten

Y**ou're smitten and preening like a turtledove."**

If Walter were the blushing sort, Quinby's pleased chortle would've lit his cheeks a blazing scarlet. Shooting a hard glare in the looking glass, aimed at Quinby's reflection, Walter persisted in the vain struggle to straighten his neckcloth one-handed. "I never preen."

"But you are smitten?"

"No." *Possibly. . .*

Dainty chimes pealed in the lobby of Walter's private apartments, the song of a butterfly-shaped clock, which was alighted on a wall painted to resemble a bamboo forest.

Quinby prodded Walter's ribs with an elbow, blasted dimple a teasing court jester. "Want me to help write the songbird a poem? 'My love is as soft as a horse's nose. By Adelaide I'm smitten, everyone knows!'"

"And to think, your father wonders why you couldn't keep a tutor employed for more than three months together."

"Don't change the subject. Look at yourself, Glenmire. Spiffing up with more spit and polish than you used in our army days, all for an afternoon with Lady Adelaide. Admit it, chap. You're smitten by the songbird, and she's done you good. Jolly good. You're playing pianoforte and smiling and having adventures in secret tunnels." With an air of smug triumph, Quinby crossed his arms and waggled his eyebrows. "What's more, you've scribbled new words on that song of yours."

Walter lowered his hand to the dressing table where his aria now rested. Yesterday in the stables, Lady Adelaide had returned the music with an apology for meddling in his private affairs and then walked away before he could articulate a response. After watching her swift departure, he'd tucked the papers inside his buttoned tailcoat where they'd burned against his chest. Just as Lady Adelaide's confident declaration had seared his heart and mind.

No one who is in Christ ever dies alone.

That night, unable to shake those words, he'd thrown them at God as a question. Praying, for the first time in years. While he'd not received an answer, lyrics for his aria had rained down almost faster than he could write, clear and refreshing—until he'd stopped them.

Once more consumed by anger.

Once more freezing himself in the past.

Throat constricting tighter and tighter against the flow of air, Walter's lungs ached. He ripped the neckcloth off with desperate fingers. Pressing his fist atop the dressing table, he slumped forward and let his head hang. "I can't keep doing this."

A hand gripped Walter's shoulder, and he met Quinby's gaze in the glass.

Quinby pointed a thumb over his shoulder at the gold-leafed butterfly, ticking away the minutes. "It's past time, Glenmire. Are you ready?"

Was he? Was he ready to accept God's healing? Walter dragged in a labored breath. He wasn't sure, but God help him, for the first time since that awful day, he wanted to be.

He wanted to let go.

"I can't let go."

Hiding from the first glorious rays of August, Adelaide clutched Millie's hand in a vice-like grip and peered through the carriage window. Colonel Glenmire waited for her on Brighton's pebbled beach. Within just four and twenty hours, he'd arranged every-thing to the smallest detail—fresh distraction for Lydia in the form of a military picnic with Captain Quinby and the Pavilion's entire reserve of officers as well as a lavish royal carriage to convey Adelaide hence—all to give her a day at the sea. His surprise.

The gesture both thrilled and terrified Adelaide to the core.

She let the curtain fall and mask the view. She shouldn't have agreed to come. Shouldn't have indulged in the thought of an attachment between a dowerless lady's companion and a decorated marquess. An idiotic fantasy. To exit the carriage, here and now, was to invite heartbreak. "I can't, Millie. I can't let go of your hand and meet Colo-nel Glenmire outside of a music rehearsal." Adelaide's free hand fiddled with the ruffles that trimmed her cerulean spencer sleeve. "Ask the driver to turn 'round, will you?"

"Not for three shillings an' six pence." Extracting her wisp of a hand from Adelaide's grip, Millie flung open the curtain, inviting an ocean breeze to tease the feathery curls peeking from her white lacy cap. A flint of spunk sharpened her tone and amber gaze. "You're meetin' that colonel o'yours if I must put a sack o'er your head and drag ye down the beach."

"He's not my colonel—"

"And I'm batty King George." A nymph-like grin brightened Millie's rosy cheeks as she opened the carriage door. "Stop fearin' and frettin' and see if ye can find that strong lady I once knew. Tell her I miss her, eh?"

The ache of loss dug a hollow grave in Adelaide's chest. She missed that lady, too. Might she yet be found? A few measured breaths unearthed a new sense of resolve. *Time to find out.* Securing the ribbons of her straw bonnet in a tight bow, Adelaide stepped down to the pebbled shore and ventured toward where Colonel Glenmire surveyed the frolicking waves. She glanced over her shoulder. The sight of Millie standing near the carriage, keeping watch, provided further reassurance. With her faerie chaperone pres-ent, all was proper.

Colonel Glenmire turned and met her gaze, hitching Adelaide's breath. Goodness, was he blushing? Surely not. The brisk air and sunshine must have ruddied his cheeks. The colonel bowed in greeting. "You had me on edge, Lady Adelaide. I feared you'd never exit that blasted carriage."

Heavens, he noticed? Her stomach performed a somersault. "Forgive me, I—"

"No need for explanation." Colonel Glenmire stationed himself at her side, his expression donning a new mantle of hope. "Let's be off. There is much beauty to behold this day."

Warmth bloomed in Adelaide's cheeks, but caution prevented it from taking root in her heart. *Lord, let this not end with another painful good-bye.*

Side by side, the pair ambled along the shore and conversed with an ease as refreshing as the sea air. First they compared favorite composers. Then preferred instruments and beloved operas. Adelaide cast many a backward glance throughout, anchoring herself with the sight of Millie following several paces behind. However, the ocean's tranquil ballad of waves, ebbing and flowing to the rhythm of cawing gulls, soon stilled the anxious practice.

Thus soothed beneath the azure sky, Adelaide related stories of her youth. Not once hushed or censured in the telling. Colonel Glenmire spoke fondly of his relations in turn, regaling her with memories of his childhood at Whitecliff Park, the Marlowe family's estate by the sea, where his mother and two younger sisters yet resided.

Colonel Glenmire chuckled without restraint. "That gull chased Benjamin across the beach, swooping and pecking with ravenous beak. Until, fearing for his life, Benjamin took drastic measures. He shoved the prized cherry tart into his mouth and dove into the ocean, wearing his Sunday best—shocking my mother and the gull both."

Adelaide laughed till her sides ached, imagining four-year-old Benjamin's antics and wishing she could have met him but once. "His frock was ruined, I suppose. Your poor mother."

"Indeed. . .poor mother." The colonel's buoyant laughter sank hard and fast, drowning in a deep undertow of silence. He halted their procession and stared off into the vast expanse of undulating water. "How do you do it. . .trust in a God who abandons?"

A sigh escaped Adelaide's lips and joined the breeze. "By clinging to the truth of His Word for dear life." A difficult task on good days, made seemingly impossible when blinded by pain's deceptive haze. "One such truth being that God never abandons."

Colonel Glenmire's expression remained an unmoved stone.

Adelaide gnawed on her lip, searching for something else to say. Something of use. *Lord, provide the words and help him see beyond the fog.* A memory floated to the surface of her mind. "Once. . .when I was young, my family summered by the sea. We enjoyed weeks of sunshine and peaceful tides, but on our last day, a horrid gale forced us to stay indoors. Watching the storm from an alcove window, I spotted a fishing vessel caught unawares and struggling to remain afloat. One moment, it was there. The next, violent waves swallowed it whole. I turned away in fright, but Papa gathered me to his lap and spoke words I've never forgotten."

Pausing, Adelaide looked to her left and verified by his alert countenance that

Colonel Glenmire was indeed listening. "Papa said, 'Sometimes God stands between us and the waves, so their force isn't felt. But sometimes He stands at our side and holds us in a strong embrace as the wave hits full force, knocks us off our feet, and drags us under. In that moment, submerged in frigid waters, we don't yet realize that if we but remain in His grasp, eventually, at the appointed time, God will see us to shore and sun again.' Then Papa pointed out the window, where the ship had resurfaced, battered but afloat. 'Though we may sink, dear one, there's no need to fear drowning when serving the Lord who walks on the sea.'"

Adelaide's lips lifted in a quaking smile. "That's how I trust, Colonel. Because though I've been battered by waves, I have also been held and led back to shore." A truth she'd forgotten to cling to this last year.

God *had* faithfully conveyed her to solid ground after the deaths of Mamma and Papa both. But instead of remaining held, Adelaide had broken from God's embrace in the wake of Lydia's cruel actions and gotten lost in the fog without realizing it.

"But why does God let us go through it at all?" Colonel Glenmire's words staggered out, tired and worn. "Surely knowing why would make it easier."

"I thought the same, once." Salted wind tossed Adelaide's ringlets and ribbons as new waves broke into foam against Brighton's pebbled shore. "But *why* isn't always granted an answer this side of heaven. Eventually, we must choose which we will relinquish—the desire to know why, or God Himself." And yet, now it dawned clear, that she'd been holding God at a distance. Remaining in His presence, but not in His keeping. A divide she'd not the courage to bridge.

"You're a remarkable woman, Lady Adelaide." Colonel Glenmire gifted her a smile, tender and fleeting, which revived lightheartedness in his demeanor. "And here I've cast a gloom on your day. Before we turn 'round, it must be dispelled. Why don't you sing something?"

Adelaide gulped. "Now?"

"Why not?"

"You'll again reek of cinders." A jolt of panic stunned Adelaide, and her gaze darted about the shore as if Lydia might appear. "We've n—no music." *And someone might hear.*

"You don't need music. Go on, sing anything you like. Sing for the joy of music itself." Hand stationed on his hip, Colonel Glenmire waited expectantly.

Adelaide could only gawk at him, mouth stripped dry and lips terrified even to tremble.

Concern knit his dark brows. "Dear Lady Adelaide. . .will you never sing freely?"

"I daren't even hope." The strength she'd once had could never be restored. Tears gathering in pools, Adelaide blinked them away as she took a step back and then another. "Brighton. Singing. Today. . .it's all a mirage. Naught but shifting mist. I can no sooner take it home with me than I can capture a dream."

Colonel Glenmire drew closer, tracing the steps of her retreat. "You trusted God with yesterday's trial. Why not trust Him with tomorrow's dream?" His throat bobbed and, lifting his arm, he offered it to her like an anchor. "Let us make a pact: I will finish my aria if you will sing with the hope of one day capturing a dream. Perhaps we can move in trust, together?"

Together. The word settled in Adelaide's heart, and for just a moment, dispersed ashen fears of loss with its gentle light. She accepted Colonel Glenmire's arm. "Perhaps we can."

Chapter Eleven

Masquerade morn was upon them at last.

As the orchestral company assumed their seats for one final rehearsal, the Music Room sparkled amid a full bloom of August sunshine. And Walter couldn't stop beaming like an idiot. Not while distributing sheet music. Nor during the raucous cacophony of tuning instruments.

Since that afternoon by the sea, everything had changed. Time itself seemed to have hastened its ticking, zipping through minutes and hours with the blithe passion of a frenzied violinist's bow, severing string after fraying string. One evening felt the whole of his anger and *whys* poured before God. Three nights of unhindered worship saw his aria complete. Five days more heard Lady Adelaide commit it to heart. Another two weeks stirred the sweet fragrance of nearing triumph with one rehearsal after the next promising a recital to remember. And through it all, Walter beamed because he wasn't forsaken.

Despite being battered by waves, he'd been held and led back to shore.

"Colonel Glenmire, shall we begin?" The Pavilion Orchestra's conductor met him with a glower. "I'm not accustomed to delaying rehearsals for tardy performers."

Tardy? Striding away from the conductor, Walter sought out the nearest clock, which confirmed that Lady Adelaide was now fifteen minutes late. His nerves bristled. Why would her habit of punctuality alter, today of all days? Had she awoken with performance day jitters. . .or had he failed to perceive a resurgence of her paralyzing fear?

"If you let that songbird fly away, you'll never get her back."

Quinby's words ricocheted through Walter with cold foreboding.

◌◌◌

"Lydia, have mercy. I might perish if I go on thus."

Legs aching and breath cut short, Adelaide halted midway on what was no doubt the tallest flight of stairs in all Christendom. No exaggeration. If one could die by staircase, this winding dragon's tail would be the one to do a body in. She looked up at Lydia, now two steps above. "Will you not reconsider this venture? You really ought to be getting ready for the masquerade." Primping for hours as planned whilst she escaped for final rehearsal.

Lydia rolled her eyes. "Do quit grousing. There's plenty of time yet, and I refuse to leave the Pavilion without having explored every glorious nook and cranny. The Saloon

Bottle is the last thing I've yet to see—as all my friends have done—and I shan't be the one to miss out."

"Surely viewing the Bottle's exterior is sufficient? The interior is only servants' quarters." *Male* servants' quarters that ought to be avoided by unwed, young ladies.

"And those quarters have windows that frame the most spectacular view of Brighton, or so I've been told. If I'm to see it for myself, this is my best chance. All the servants are busy preparing for the masquerade, either in the kitchen or assisting their lords and ladies, so the Bottle will be deserted. Turn 'round if you wish, but I will not." With a huff, Lydia stomped up the stairs alone.

How could she allow Lydia to sashay into a beehive, possibly buzzing with handsome valets? Adelaide sighed, leaning against the wall. She couldn't in good conscience. Which is why she'd come along in the first place. *Face matters bravely.* Gripping the plain wooden banister in one hand and lifting her skirt with the other, she trudged after Lydia's shadow. If they didn't dally, she might have enough time to pamper Lydia's whim and still attend rehearsal.

Assuming the dragon didn't kill her first.

After traversing more steps than she'd cared to count, Adelaide finally reached the snaking monstrosity's head. The Saloon Bottle met her sight with an unimpressive landing and four doors, one of which stood ajar as if bidding her to enter. She stepped through, expecting to find Lydia giggling over her escapade, but instead found only a simple bedchamber. Quiet and empty. Was Lydia sulking in an unseen corner or swooning in a valet's arms?

Adelaide covered the whole room in a few strides, looking here and there as if Lydia were a child one might find hiding in a trunk or under a bed. Her search turned up nothing. Had Lydia gone into one of the other rooms? Turning to investigate this possibility, she spotted Lydia in the doorway and paused. "There you are."

Lydia's cobalt eyes hardened in a glare, and she slammed the door shut.

Adelaide startled, heart dropping to her feet. Lydia knew.

Somehow Lydia knew everything.

Rushing across the room, Adelaide gripped the latch but it would not turn. Indeed, the door pushed back as if someone leaned against the other side. She inhaled to keep her voice steady, to rein in panic. "Lydia? Are you still there? Please. . .let me out."

"I'm not stupid, you know." Lydia's voice seeped through a crack in the door. "I have eyes and ears. I noticed your strange behavior—unusual fatigue, the lack of nagging about my outings with Captain Quinby, sneaking off at odd hours, looking so. . .happy." She spat the last word.

Adelaide flinched, birthing a tremor that spread from stomach to lips. She had to get out of here and find Colonel Glenmire. "Please open the door and let's talk—"

"About what, Adelaide?" Lydia's sharpened tone hacked through the door like an ax. "Shall we talk about how every week of my childhood delivered a new letter from your parents to mine, bursting with detailed praise of your latest accomplishment? About how my parents read said letters aloud, promising if I practiced more and studied harder

I might be *as bright as Cousin Adelaide*? Shall we discuss how that never happened? How I was still never good enough?"

The confession stunned Adelaide's breath. How long had Lydia felt this way? She shut her eyes, still grasping the latch. "Your parents love you, Lydia. I know they never meant their words to be taken in such a way." Her own statement hit the door and bounced back. And Papa never meant for a loving entreaty to "face matters bravely" to render her mute, had he?

A thick silence filled the Saloon Bottle, noxious and murky as smoke.

"Lydia? Please don't—"

"I'm leaving to attend the masquerade now, and you're not to follow." A chilling calm tempered Lydia's words. "You are to sit behind this door for the rest of the night. I bribed a couple valets for the use of the room, so you won't be bothered."

"You're going to lock me in?" Adelaide's heart thrashed within her chest, each beat wanting out, out, out. *Lord, please don't let this happen.*

"Of course not. Then you might imagine yourself some persecuted princess locked in yonder tower." The chill in Lydia's tone slowly froze over, developing ice crystals with jagged edges that cut and burned. "No, you'll stay of your own choosing. Because if you do, I'll secure your employment. For at least a year. But if you dare appear at the masquerade, I'll have you and Millie both sacked immediately."

The threat wrapped its bony fingers around Adelaide's throat and wrung out her breath.

"It's your choice, Adelaide. Sing or save your friend's situation. Either way, the moment we return home your precious violin's as good as cinders."

Chapter Twelve

Like a bird in a covered cage, denied flight and song, Adelaide was trapped.

Alone in the Royal Pavilion's Bottle she stood with eyes fixed upon the door, imprisoned not by iron lock and key, but by the paralyzing fear of what might happen should she dare touch the latch. The time for final rehearsal was long past. The dinner hour was now nearing its end. Soon the Prince Regent's guests, adorned in finery from plumed turbans to silken slippers, would follow their liege into the Music Room and commence the Masquerade Ball.

And she could not move.

"Your precious violin's as good as cinders."

Tremors coursed through Adelaide's veins, dispersing an unnatural cold as the polluted life source circulated. Her stomach caved in on itself. Her heart thrashed in its den, faster and faster. Each panicked beat a scream to run. *Run.* The door taunted, enticing her to burst forth and flee its unlocked confines, only to shove her back with the unknown future that lay beyond, tormenting with circumstances she could neither predict nor control.

"I'll have you and Millie both sacked immediately."

Where would she and Millie go? What would they do? However might they survive?

The questions rushed up Adelaide's throat, obstructing airways and stifling breath.

She gasped and wrenched away from the door, retreating with feeble steps to the rear of the chamber, seeking the relief of fresh air seeping through the windows. A search proved vain. Unlike the door at her back, the windows could not be opened by choice.

Adelaide leaned against the chilled panes and shut her eyes, willing Lydia's words unsaid. *"It's your choice, Adelaide. Sing or save your friend's situation."*

The internal quivers seeped through Adelaide's skin, shaking her through and through with a familiar panic that had defeated her two years ago. Swathing herself with both arms, she clung to One unseen. Pressing through the fear, she spoke in fractured shards. "Lord? D–don't let go. . .hold me fast. P–please. Remind me of Your truth. I. . . I c–can't remember."

"Though we may sink, dear one, there's no need to fear drowning when serving the Lord who walks on the sea." Memory of Papa's embrace warmed Adelaide through, parting the fog.

"*Your security doesn't come from Lydia or your position. Your future rests with a power higher an' mightier than that girl could ever imagine herself.*" Millie's bold faith steadied her nerves, calming her every tremor.

"*You trusted God with yesterday's trial. Why not trust Him with tomorrow's dream? Perhaps we can move in trust, together?*" Colonel Glenmire's words encouraged Adelaide to open her eyes.

The most spectacular view of Brighton greeted her gaze, framed by the Pavilion's elliptical windows. Heaven had donned an evening gown. With effortless grace, it draped across the night sky and flowed earthbound, star-dusted indigo train finished with a periwinkle hem that swept along the sea's ebony floor. Brighton admired the beauty with tranquil awe while candles burned, twinkling in numerous windows as if to reflect the stars.

A world of wonderment outlined in a window pane.

One she might embrace by simply walking through an unbarred door.

Adelaide stood tall and stared down the flimsy wooden barrier, stretching out the wings of strength she'd not used in so long. She bridged the room in four strides. Seized the latch. Took a breath. *Face matters bravely.* Swinging the door open, she soared over the threshold and into God's keeping without a backward glance.

After racing down the dragon's tail and making a mad dash to change attire, Adelaide's rapid pulse still thought itself on the run. Yet now, descending the main bamboo-railed staircase, she was running toward something rather than hiding away. Heart beating with exhilaration, rather than fear.

With knees and feet aching, Adelaide at last conquered the final step. She found the Long Gallery deserted but for one masked gentleman, pacing the width of the pink corridor in a frenzied panic. *Might it be. . .* "Colonel Glenmire?"

The gentleman halted. "You came." Relief saturated the familiar baritone voice.

Adelaide smiled. "Indeed, I did, Colonel. Though I almost failed to recognize you in costume. I thought you might forgo the social convention."

Colonel Glenmire bridged the distance between them in a few strides. "I look—"

"No clues, good sir. Masquerade etiquette requires that I guess the nature of your disguise, unaided." Placing one finger under her chin, Adelaide made a study of his apparel.

Shinning brass clockworks decorated Colonel Glenmire's boots and ivory breeches. Diamonds and rubies sparkled across his military coatee, sewn with metallic thread, while a tiny crank peeked from the coatee's squared shoulder on his right side. Topping off the fancy dress ensemble, the colonel sported a half mask over the scarred portion of his face, which featured an array of gears, diamonds, and musical notes fashioned from gold.

Adelaide chuckled. "You're a music box."

"Correct. Quinby's idea, but I've grown to like it." The colonel's unmasked cheek quirked in a lopsided grin. "And you're a nightingale. Most fitting."

A blush unfurled beneath Adelaide's delicate mask trimmed with downy feathers. "Millie made it without my knowing." She'd expected to don an out-of-season gown of Lydia's choosing, but instead Millie had revealed her creation—skirt fluttering with white plumes, empire waistband glittering with crystals, and periwinkle silk bodice gleaming with silver filigree notes. After helping Adelaide dress, Millie had stood back and beamed. *"There's my lady, strong as ever she was. Ready ta get her song back."*

More than ready, she was eager. Adelaide glanced at the Music Room doors, then back to the colonel. "Am I too late?"

"Not at all. When I couldn't find you, I—"

"You searched for me?" Adelaide's rapid heartbeat quieted.

"Everywhere I could think to look." Colonel Glenmire's baritone infused with tenderness. "That's what I tried to tell you earlier. . .I wanted to be sure you knew."

A smile warmed Adelaide through. How did being missed and sought for make one feel so delightfully happy?

"As I was saying. . .when I couldn't find you, I convinced the orchestra to delay things by starting with a few dances."

"Then let us not dally another minute." Adelaide turned toward the Music Room. "Wait."

At his abrupt plea, Adelaide paused. "Something amiss?"

Colonel Glenmire raked his fingers through his dark waves, disheveling their neat arrangement, while lines of concern disturbed the unmasked portion of his brow. "Lady Lydia has taken to shunning Quinby. Wouldn't even acknowledge him at dinner. I fear she won't accompany him to the garden as planned, so you mustn't perform unless I can devise a new means of protecting you."

His consideration tugged at Adelaide's heart. "We're past the point of anonymity, Colonel Glenmire. Lydia knows everything, so Captain Quinby might as well enjoy the recital."

The lines did not release Colonel Glenmire's brow, but rather deepened as he examined her with penetrating gaze. "I won't hold you to your promise, Lady Adelaide. I'll pacify the prince and do my best to restore your standing with Lady Lydia, if that is your wish. You're under no obligation."

"No, but we did make a pact, Colonel. And I wish to honor my part." Adelaide raised a gloved arm, inviting him to be her escort.

Colonel Glenmire beamed a broad smile that chased away every furrow and line. Reaching out, he supported her arm with his own. "Then let us not dally another minute."

Escorted by Colonel Glenmire, Adelaide did not cower on this entrance into the Music Room. Slippers nestled by Axminster carpets, she walked in boldness and permitted herself to feel the orchestra's melody while her liberated gaze wandered. A crush of masked nobility swirled on the dance floor's cloud of perfume, beneath the glow of nine lotus-shaped chandeliers. Higher still, golden cockleshells overlapped by the thousands across the domed ceiling, creating the illusion of scales.

Guided by the colonel's steady arm, Adelaide strode past crimson walls garnished with oriental landscapes and floor-to-ceiling windows draped in sapphire satin, each alive with serpents and winged dragons. Each paling before the grand Royal Pavilion Orchestra.

When the dance concluded, Colonel Glenmire issued instructions to the conductor and led her in front of the musicians as a hush settled. He addressed the masqueraders. "At the beginning of the summer, I was commissioned by the prince to compose an aria for this night. I now thank His Majesty for the privilege. May this song honor Him who is worthy above all." Releasing Adelaide's arm, the colonel bowed to her and then faded into the crowd.

Hundreds of eyes now fixated on Adelaide alone, and somewhere among the sea of masks, she knew Lydia watched, glaring cobalt embers. Plotting her ruin.

A quiver coursed through Adelaide's hands. As the opening notes of the aria filled the room, she closed her eyes, letting her heart listen to the music once again. Then, though her hands yet trembled, she spread her wings of strength in the whole of their smallness.

Though she stood before many, Adelaide wet her lips and lifted her voice to sing for an audience of One. "*Trust the Lord, my weary heart. Lean not on finite understanding. Whatever chaos I might see, His thoughts toward me are peace. Whatever darkness might surround, He lights my future with hope.*"

As the music built, the presence of God met Adelaide with an overwhelming peace that stilled all trembling and lifted her beyond the Pavilion's dome to the night sky. "*Be still, my fearful heart. God will not fail, nor abandon. Be still, my broken heart. He is faithful to make all whole.*"

Tears pooling and breaking free of her mask, Adelaide unveiled her heart in worship. Fears bared alongside faith. Brokenness alongside hope. "*Hold on, my doubting heart, to the promises assured. Though I walk through lonely valley, sink in the cold depths of the sea; Though I face death's tragic timing and lament what could not be, He is ever, with, me.*"

The music reached its peak, and Adelaide's heart soared. No threat could cage her now. "*God's ways, no man can fathom. His love, no shadow dim. His goodness, no storm destroy. Therefore, I cling to Christ, my refuge. I surrender to His Shepherd fold. The past I cannot change, the future I cannot control. I surrender all I have, all I am, all I know.*"

Adelaide's high note seemingly resounded off the moon. Breathing deep, she and the music descended from the clouds. "*Take every question without answer, preserve them with my bottled tears. My consoled heart now rests secure. Surrendering to Thee is my liberty. You're all I have, all I am, all I know.*"

The aria's final note echoed, then plunged headlong into silence.

Applause, thunderous in its fervor, grounded Adelaide once more to the Pavilion floor. Without hesitation, she opened her eyes to a future as unknown as the faces hidden in the ocean of dazzling masks. Her employ was forfeit in one song. She knew not what to expect come the morrow, and yet she was no longer shaken by such a prospect. Her consoled heart did indeed rest. Whatever circumstances might arise with the dawning of Brighton's sun, she could now *face matters bravely* as Papa had intended all along—with her future held secure by the Lord who walked the seas.

A refreshing, salted breeze fluttered the plumes of Adelaide's costume while gentle waves lapped at Brighton's shoreline in a serene lullaby. One she wished never to forget.

The *clack-clack* of shifting pebbles announced that someone drew near. Colonel Glenmire appeared on her right, pale moonlight shimmering off the gems of his clockwork mask. "Was the masquerade so dreadfully tedious?"

"Tedious, no. A stifling crush, absolutely. I much prefer the fresh air. Besides, I couldn't let such an exquisite night go to waste." Adelaide wiggled her toes, restoring feeling in her aching feet. Dainty slippers provided little protection from the beach's smooth rocks, but she hadn't wanted to fetch boots from her room. There would be a time to face Lydia and sort out the consequences of her performance, but not tonight.

Tonight she was free to roam, wherever she pleased.

Tonight she would savor her last few hours in Brighton, bidding a fond farewell to the sea and Colonel Glenmire.

She mustered a smile. "Tell me, Sir Music Box, what did the prince think of your aria? Was he pleased?"

"Not likely. However, overwhelming praise of the evening from his respected guests soothed any kindled ire before it fanned to flame. Unfortunately, I am still a 'royal favorite.' Blasted shame, really. I'd rather looked forward to losing his esteem."

Adelaide laughed. "What an unfortunate turn of events, indeed, sir. You have my deepest sympathy." Inhaling another draught of precious sea air, she released it in a wistful sigh. She would miss this lovely shore, almost as much as the man at her side.

With their visit to the Royal Pavilion near its end and their pact fulfilled, there was nothing left to keep them in the same sphere. In all their time together, Colonel Glenmire had made no declaration of feeling. No offer of marriage. Either the colonel's considerations toward her were mere kindness offered in friendship, or any deeper feelings on his part weren't strong enough to overcome their circumstances. After all, she was nearer destitute now than when they'd first met.

Adelaide swallowed a lump in her throat. *Lord, help me trust You still. . .help me say goodbye.* She glanced at the driver and carriage that had conveyed her to the beach, now accompanied by a matching pair. "I don't relish the thought of tomorrow's journey home."

"Why, Lady Adelaide? Do you suppose—pent up in a carriage for hours on end—that my company will soon bore you?"

His company?

The colonel's tone remained level in its matter-of-factness. "Quinby insists on joining us as our chaperone, so perhaps he can make up for any dullness on my part. I may be quite lackluster with my mind focused on the business ahead."

Slowly turning to face him, Adelaide's masked eyes narrowed. "Business?"

"Indeed, I'll have much to do." Uncurling gloved fingers one by one, he outlined a swift list. "First there's meeting with your uncle to ask for your hand, then discussing the safe transfer of your violin dowry and securing the services of your Millie, then I'll have a plethora of travel arrangements to make, all before whisking you away to plan a spring wedding at Whitecliff Park—that is, if you will have me?"

Adelaide's heart did not quicken its beating, for it did not believe him. This could not truly be happening. It was too wonderful, much too wonderful to be real.

Lowering one knee onto the clacking pebbles, Colonel Glenmire took her gloved hand, and his steady tone seemed to falter. Break. "*Will* you have me?"

Adelaide ran her thumb along the colonel's fingers and smiled. "Is this how it feels, Colonel Glenmire? To catch a dream?"

Moonlight revealed Colonel Glenmire's mouth tilting in a half grin obscured by his mask. "Not quite." He stood and reached across his chest, winding the tiny crank fixed in the fringed shoulder pad of his coatee. With a tinkling metallic tone, music emanated from the jeweled fabric. A delicate rendition of *Red, Red Rose* by Robert Burns seemingly played by silver pixies.

Placing his hand on the small of Adelaide's back, Colonel Glenmire led her in a gentle waltz and sang in his rich baritone. "*O my Luve's like a red, red rose that's newly sprung in June: O my Luve's like the melodie, that's sweetly play'd in tune. As fair art thou, my bonie lass, so deep in luve am I; and I will luve thee still, my dear, till a' the seas gang dry.*"

As the music slowed and ended with a final metallic chime, Colonel Glenmire pressed a kiss to Adelaide's brow. "Have I ever told you that you're a remarkable woman, dear Lady Adelaide?"

"Indeed you have, Colonel Glenmire, but I've always been one to enjoy an encore."

Author's Note

The Royal Pavilion is a former royal residence located in Brighton, England, which can still be enjoyed by visitors today! Beginning in 1787, it was built in stages as a seaside retreat for George, Prince of Wales, who became the Prince Regent in 1811. The current appearance of the Pavilion with its exotic domes and minarets is the work of architect John Nash, who extended the building, starting in 1815 and ending in 1823. While my story takes place in 1819, I chose to describe the Pavilion in its completed form to showcase its full whimsical splendor. I also took creative liberties when describing the real secret tunnel's entrance and had Italian composer Rossini appear at the Pavilion prior to his actual visit in 1823.

ECPA bestselling author **Angela Bell** is a twenty-first-century lady with nineteenth-century sensibilities. Her activities consist of reading voraciously, drinking copious amounts of tea, and writing letters with a fountain pen. She currently resides in Texas with pup Mr. Darcy and kitties Lizzie Bennett and Lord Sterling. One might describe Angela's fictional scribblings as historical romance or as Victorian history and steampunk whimsy in a romantic blend. Whenever you need a respite from the twenty-first-century hustle, please visit her cyberspace parlor www.AuthorAngelaBell.com where she can be found waiting with a pot of English tea and some Victorian cordiality.

Three Little Matchmakers

by Susanne Dietze

Dedication

For Laura Hopkins. It's been a long time since we were in school and wrote silly Regencies of our own, but some things never change. You're still my sister in my heart.

Acknowledgments

Thanks to my children and our three young friends who bring joy into my life and inspired bits and pieces of the Little Matchmakers.

See what great love the Father has lavished on us,
that we should be called children of God! And that is what we are!
1 JOHN 3:1 (NIV)

Chapter One

Spring 1817
Staffordshire, England

So, the rumors about Henry Graves, the Earl of Marsden, were true.

Caroline Dempsey had always enjoyed Henry's wide, welcoming grins, smiles so warm they could thaw a frozen pond—or incite her to blush. But as she stepped down from the carriage onto the gravel drive of Marsden Hall, there was no trace of Henry's exuberant smile as he stood on the Doric portico of the sandstone manse to greet them. The polite upturn of his lips couldn't melt an ice chip, much less invite the children to take a liking to him.

He was stoic as stone, just as the gossips claimed. She'd thought it a lie, of course, even though his letter inviting her and the children to Marsden Hall had been just as stiff as the set of his shoulders was now. She never would have believed Henry had changed this much, were she not seeing it with her own eyes.

She could muse about this later, however. She beckoned the children from the carriage. They lined up beside her as they'd been taught, three little brown-haired stair steps dressed in mourning black.

Her entire world.

"Lord Marsden." Caroline turned to Henry and curtsied. She also smiled, hoping it might prove contagious to him as well as the children, whose eyes were large and wary. "May I present your nieces and nephew? Julia, Lucy, and Rupert Stapleton—Julia, set down the dog, please."

Eight-year-old Julia lowered the wiggling liver-and-white spaniel to the drive and then bobbed her knees. "Uncle."

Lucy, six, imitated her sister, although her voice was nowhere as loud as Julia's. Rupert, four, executed the serious bow Caroline had been practicing with him for a week, but it was cut short when the spaniel weaved about his little legs.

"Miss Dempsey, children, welcome to Marsden Hall," Henry said at last, nodding his head at each in turn. "You must be eager to settle in. Would you care to see the nursery?"

These children were his flesh and blood, orphan offspring of his only sister, relatives he'd never seen, and he dismissed them to the nursery first thing? Not to mention that he and Caroline used to be—

Never mind. They were nothing now but a lord and his wards' governess.

Caroline's next smile was forced. "You are too kind, my lord. We should like to see the nursery and pay our respects to your grandmother, and then perhaps stretch our legs in the garden after such a tedious journey—"

"We came from Spain." Julia broke rank and stood so close she could lean her head against her uncle's mourning-black coat, if she tipped her head that way.

"A long journey." He looked down at her.

Lucy patted his sleeve. "Mama and Papa died."

Henry's impassive expression didn't alter. "Yes, I know. I'm very sorry."

"This is George." Rupert held up his favorite toy, a wooden horse that accompanied him everywhere, even to bed.

"I see," Henry said with a fixed smile.

Oh dear. Where had her Henry gone? He looked the same—broad shoulders, square jaw, eyes still the shade of storm clouds—although his wild brown locks had been tamed into submission, and now that he was thirty, faint lines crinkled around the edges of his eyes. But the resemblance to the Henry she used to know seemed to be only a physical one. His unfortunate incident in London eight years ago had changed him into someone else.

"What's that?" Julia pointed to the copse of trees at the edge of the yard.

"The deer park," Caroline and Henry said together. She bit her lip. She shouldn't have spoken over a lofty earl, no matter that they used to be friends.

"I want to see a deer." Lucy cast her begging gaze up at Caroline.

"Not now, darling."

Perhaps not at all, the way Henry was frowning. How odd, considering how much they'd enjoyed playing in the wooded park as children. They'd created a sort of playhouse out of the old hunting lodge at its center. What a dingy old heap that had been. Was it still there?

"You mustn't venture into the park without an adult. It is overgrown and one could easily get lost." Henry's gaze flitted to where the spaniel snuffled about the grass. "This is your dog?"

"Cinders is their pet, yes." Caroline answered when the children didn't.

"There hasn't been an animal in the house in decades." Henry's brows lowered.

"There was indeed an animal in the house at one time, if you recall."

If she'd hoped the memory would coax a smile from him, she was to be disappointed. Julia hopped past Caroline. "We'll meet Mama's grandmama?"

Henry shook his head. "Grandmama isn't up to visitors today."

"She's ill?" Lady Marsden had resided at Marsden Hall as long as Caroline could remember. She'd always been kind to Caroline, but tended toward infirmities that kept her to her chambers.

"Her humors are off."

Gout, probably. "How sorry I am to hear it. May I be of assistance?"

"She is resting, but expressed the desire to see you all tomorrow." Henry looked like he'd like to say something more, but instead he tipped his head at the house.

She took the hint and squeezed Rupert's hand. "Let's see the nursery then, shall we? Come Cinders—no, Cinders, stay out of there!"

The girls stepped into line, but Cinders didn't twitch an ear. Instead, she frolicked on the wide expanse of lawn where Caroline used to play with Henry and Esther, the children's mother.

The tall blond footman who'd assisted her from the carriage came forward. "I'll see to the spaniel, ma'am."

"Thank you. Your name, please?" She'd need to learn the servants' names, the sooner the better.

"Edgar." He dipped his head.

She smiled her thanks and returned her gaze to Henry. She'd spent so much of her childhood playing here at Marsden Hall, but she'd never expected to live here. Then again, she'd never expected she and Henry would behave like strangers.

But that was clearly what they were now. They were no longer children. She was a governess and he an earl, and a wide gulf separated them. She curtsied. "Thank you, my lord."

"Miss Dempsey." His curt tone forestalled her from going into the house. "I should like to speak to you in the library in an hour, if you please."

She nodded. He probably intended to discuss particulars with her. "One hour, my lord."

When she reached the large, bright nursery with its familiar green wallpaper and wide windows that overlooked the south lawn, she had no time to fall into nostalgia. Servants rushed about to unpack their belongings, and a reed-thin young woman with light-brown hair introduced herself as Polly, the nursemaid. "Mrs. Byrd, the house-keeper, thought I might be of use."

"Indeed you shall." Caroline would have to thank Mrs. Byrd for her thoughtfulness.

In the midst of the bustle, the children spread out to explore the space, peppering her with questions about the toys and beds and what they would eat for supper.

"What's a deer park?" Lucy fingered the leaf-green damask drapes.

"It's a parcel of land to keep fallow deer."

"Like a menagerie?" Julia clasped her hands under her chin.

"No, they're for hunting." She scooped George, Rupert's toy horse, from the middle of the floor and set it atop a small table so no one would trip on it. "There is also a small lodge, hardly even a cottage, really, at the park's center, which I always thought was amusing, because Marsden Hall is but a mile away. The earl who had it built could have hunted deer and then gone home to sleep in his own comfortable bed."

"Perhaps the earl liked to pretend he was traveling. Or he wanted his own bed-chamber." Julia glanced side-eyed at her siblings.

Caroline's lips twitched. "Perhaps he did."

"Can we see the deer?" Lucy spun from the window.

"I do not know if any are left. Your grandfather did not care to hunt, and your uncle has not lived here in many years. He said you may not go alone, but I will find out if we can go together soon." It could be an enjoyable outing. Caroline had always thought the fallow deer were lovely, with their large brown eyes and white-spotted chestnut coats. "There are also sheep here."

"Cinders will like that." Rupert patted the resting spaniel.

"Indeed she will." Hopefully, Cinders wouldn't be the only one of them to find something to like about Marsden Hall. The children should be happy, too. This was their new home, and Caroline's, too.

She'd grown up in the parson's cottage beside the old stone church in the village. If her papa could see her now, living in Marsden Hall, he'd be astonished.

Truth be told, Caroline was astonished herself. She'd always secretly longed to live in the hall with her darling Henry.

But she'd never imagined it quite like this.

❧

This was much, much harder than Henry had thought it would be.

Although he should be working on the ledgers, he stared out the library window overlooking the lawn, not seeing much of anything except the images in his mind.

For a moment when Caroline Dempsey stepped out of the carriage, he was young again and full of hope and lightness, glad to see his friend. So happy he'd almost reached for her. How had she been all this time? He knew she'd taken employment with his sister Esther and her husband, Richard, after her father, the vicar, had died, and that she was well and happy.

But how was she really? He was not the boy Caroline Dempsey had known, and it stood to reason that she was greatly changed, too.

That one moment, however, was all he could allow himself of such foolishness. There was nothing familiar or comfortable about this situation. His sister was dead. He was now the guardian of her three children. Caroline was their governess and he was the Earl of Marsden, striving his hardest to execute his duty as would please his father.

Today was all about duty. He'd thought himself prepared for the arrival of the children and their governess here at Marsden Hall, but then he'd seen them. It was indeed much harder than he'd thought it would be.

"My lord?"

Henry turned at the soft voice. Caroline was still slight of build, still bright-eyed, but her blond hair was a shade darker than he remembered—or maybe it only appeared that way because her high-necked gown was a deep, mourning black for Esther and Richard.

Maybe that also explained the tentative look in her eyes.

"Miss Dempsey. Please, sit. Would you care for tea?"

"No, thank you." She lowered into the striped chair he'd indicated by the fire, glancing at the ecru-and-gilt walls, the ornate ceiling, and the shelves of leather volumes. They'd never been allowed in here as children, because this had been his father's domain. Maybe she felt as ill at ease in this room as he did.

He'd written a list of things to discuss with her, but he couldn't dislodge his thoughts from his sister as he took the seat opposite Caroline. "The children look like Esther.

Especially the younger ones."

If Caroline was surprised that he'd blurted out something so obvious, she didn't show it. "Lucy and Rupert favor her, don't they?"

They didn't just favor Esther. They were her duplicates. All three children had his sister's brown hair, but Lucy and Rupert had her dark eyes, her rosebud mouth, and the curve of her cheek. "Julia seems more like her in manner, though. Esther was never shy."

Caroline chuckled. "Julia is as stalwart and bold as Esther, but she looks more like Richard."

"What are the other two like?"

Her smile softened. "Lucy is sweet and gentle—even her touch is soft, which is a good thing, I suppose, since she is in a phase where she touches everything. Rupert is exuberant and imaginative. They remind me each day of the best parts of Esther."

Why did she seem happy about it? Thinking about Esther caused pain, and it took a good deal of strength not to succumb to his grief. But he wouldn't yield to sorrow or any other strong emotions again. He'd learned the hard way.

"Are the children settled in the nursery?"

"Unpacked, yes, but they aren't there now." She smiled as barking sounded from outside the window. "Your grandmother was kind enough to arrange for a nursemaid, Polly, for them, so I sent them on a tour of the house with her. I expect they'll find themselves at Cook's table in the kitchen soon enough, plied with cake, just as we did once upon a time." Her smile fell. "My lord."

He must have been scowling. He hadn't meant to, but the dog and its incessant barking was something Father would never have allowed.

She glanced at the window. "Cinders will quiet down. She's a good dog, truly, and important to the children. She's the pup of Richard's spaniel. He was so attached to her."

Henry had forgotten Richard even had a dog. He'd hardly known the fellow, since he and Esther had left the area promptly after marrying against Father's wishes. "Why is she named Cinders?"

"A good question, since she isn't the least bit gray. But she has flecks on her paws that Julia thought looked like she'd been playing in the ashes. She's creative with stories, that one, but Lucy is creative like you. She shows promise with her artwork already, and she's only six." She nodded at something behind him. "That's lovely. Did you paint that?"

He followed her gaze to the landscape painting set on a decorative easel, a bucolic scene of the River Sow in spring. "That's stood in that spot for ages. No, I don't paint anymore."

Her head tipped to the side. "I'm sorry to hear that. Not only were you talented, but it seemed to be such a big part of you. Always sketching. Perhaps now that you're back at Marsden Hall, you'll paint again."

It wasn't appropriate for a man who would be earl to paint. Artwork was a display of wealth to boast in one's home, but creating it? Improper, according to Father.

A curious thump sounded in the hall. Henry cocked his head, but didn't hear it again, so he returned his gaze to Caroline. They had business to discuss, but seeing her again seemed to let loose a torrent of questions.

"Is it odd, being back?"

"My lord?" Her pale brows rose.

"I find it odd. I haven't been here since Father died. The steward was more than capable of running the place, so I let him while I was occupied in London."

She bit her lip. She must have already known from Esther he avoided Marsden Hall. Those two had always been close, but as friends, not as lady and governess. "It's been years since I've been back. I confess I'd like to see the village again."

"I am certain everyone will be delighted to see you. I think you picked flowers for half the village when you thought them downhearted. You even did it for me."

He almost smiled, but stopped himself. He was a man now, not a boy. Nostalgia was not a becoming trait.

But she laughed, sounding as light and clear as he remembered. "You were mortified."

A little. Even more so when Father found out. "It was a heartfelt gesture."

"I promise not to deplete your gardens by sharing your flowers any longer."

"The garden won't be in full bloom until you go, at any rate."

She blinked at him. "Go?"

He was sure she'd be happy about it. Or at least relieved. "Being a governess wasn't the life you expected, I'm sure."

"Perhaps not, but Esther was kind to take me into her household when Papa died. I had no other recourse."

"Well, you do now." He'd ensure it. "I was thinking autumn would be a good time to release you from your duties."

"You're dismissing me?" She jumped to her feet.

He rose too. "I'm enabling you to live however you like. I'm prepared to offer you a generous pension, and you can start afresh. Independent, with no need to find employment."

"And the children?" She stared at him as if he'd suggested selling them.

"The girls are old enough to attend a reputable school in Bath, and in a few years Rupert will follow. In the meantime a nursemaid can—"

"School?"

"That is what I said, yes."

Her gray eyes narrowed. "While they are in mourning, in a new country, among strangers, you would send them away."

"School is not unexpected for children of their class."

"It is unexpected when they are so young. You hated school. So much so that your father relented and brought you home again until you left for Eton."

Henry's stomach clenched. "That is true, but—"

"This is the worst time imaginable to separate the children. Their parents have been gone three months. They need each other."

Thump. Someone shuffled in the hall outside the library. The servants were generally quieter than that.

The servants didn't whisper, either, but high, hushed voices carried from beyond the gaping door, followed by the retreating patter of small feet.

He lowered his voice. "The children?"

"The children." She sighed, not looking at him.

Why didn't Caroline see that he offered her a life of her own? She clearly wasn't made to be a governess. She wasn't doing a good job of it at all.

"They've dodged the nursemaid and taken to eavesdropping. School might be just the thing, considering their manners aren't what they could be," he murmured.

"And you are not the same boy I once picked flowers for. My lord." She tacked the last on like a barb. "You may take umbrage with the children running loose in the house, which I might remind you we did once upon a time. You may dismiss me from your employ, but I beseech you to consider their needs before you send them away. They require something constant in their lives. They need a home."

She started to leave the room, but spun on her heel, as if remembering her place as his servant.

He nodded in dismissal. She curtsied and bolted from the room in a flurry of black bombazine.

Marsden Hall used to be his home and Caroline one of his closest companions. But Father had been right about that too. Henry couldn't be friends with her, but not because she was beneath him in station, as Father believed.

Too much had changed. She was not the same sunny Caro who never challenged him, and he was someone else altogether, someone who could shoulder the earldom in the way Father would have wanted.

Caro wouldn't like him anymore. He couldn't blame her. He didn't always much like himself.

◆◆◆

The little eavesdroppers lounged on the nursery floor as if they'd been there for hours, but their pink cheeks betrayed them. They'd run into the nursery right ahead of her.

Caroline shook her head. "Really, you three. Snooping is most impolite."

Discarding all pretense, Julia rose to her knees. "You heard us?"

"Indeed." Caroline sat on a low stool close to them. "Where was Polly?" The nursemaid was young, but eager, and seemed more than capable of keeping an eye on the children.

"Rupert left George in the rose garden. We said we'd get him while she talked with Cook."

Rupert held up the toy horse for Caroline's inspection. She nodded. "Very well, but that gives you no leave to lurk outside open doors when you hear adults talking."

"But he said he was sending me and Julia to school." Lucy looked about to cry. "Why doesn't he like us?"

"He does like you. Very much."

"Why doesn't he like you, then? Maybe you should give him flowers again."

Oh dear. They'd heard quite a bit. "It isn't a question of him liking me. He just doesn't quite know what to do with a houseful yet. He's a bachelor, you know."

"What's a batch-ler?" Rupert's nose wrinkled.

"A gentleman who is not married."

"Like me." Rupert shrugged.

"Precisely." Caroline's thumb wiped a crumb from his chin. "Your uncle must grow accustomed to this new situation, as must you three. Try not to worry, dear ones. We should pray together for God's guidane and help." Caroline was praying even as she spoke to the children.

"If we pray, he might change his mind?" Julia's blue eyes widened.

"Indeed." *Lord, let it be so.*

"But you'll still tell him not to send us?" Lucy patted Caroline's sleeve.

"I cannot tell him to do anything. Your Uncle Henry—Lord Marsden—is in charge of you."

"But you're our governess," Julia protested.

"I am a servant. I am not your mother, with authority to make decisions."

Three little mouths frowned and foreheads furrowed. Then Julia's lips leveled, her brow smoothed, and a bright gleam sparked in her blue eyes.

Caroline had seen that look before. Now it was her turn to frown.

Chapter Two

A good night's sleep could do wonders for a person's outlook.

Caroline had expected the children's first night at Marsden Hall to be fretful, especially after they overheard Henry's plans about separating them and sending the girls to school, but all three of them—and Caroline, in her pleasant yellow chamber next door to the nursery—rested until sunrise.

But no later than that. Maybe someday Rupert would sleep past dawn.

"It's not me, it's George. He wants to play," Rupert said around a spoonful of mush when they breakfasted in the cheery nursery.

"A gentleman doesn't speak with his mouth full." Caroline turned her gaze from Rupert to George, propped on the window sill. "And you really must let Rupert sleep, George. He requires his rest."

Rupert giggled. So did the girls.

"I am going to visit your great-grandmother." Caroline rose from the table. "Polly will see you are occupied until I return, and when I do, we shall study geography."

Julia groaned. Lucy clapped. Rupert shoved another spoonful into his mouth.

Lady Marsden's chamber was on the same floor as the nursery, but on the opposite wing of the house. Caroline found it easily enough and knocked on the door to the dowager's sitting room, attempting to ignore the flutter of nerves in her stomach.

It was bold to visit Lady Marsden. As a governess, Caroline was not quite considered one of the servants. Yet she should not expect to be treated as a member of the family either. Esther and Richard had welcomed her at their table and hearth, but that was different, and they were gone now. Last night, had Caroline not dined with the children, she would have supped alone.

But Caroline was once the vicar's daughter, and Esther and Henry's friend. She'd known the dowager when she was young and would have called upon her regularly had she remained in the village.

Lady Marsden's flint-eyed maid bid Caroline enter an overwarm sitting room, where a black-gowned, plump woman with lead-gray curls reclined in a chair before a roaring fire, her swollen feet elevated on a plush ottoman.

"Miss Dempsey? Is that truly you?" Lady Marsden beckoned.

Caroline curtsied. "It is, my lady."

Lady Marsden grinned and lifted her hands. "Come close and let me look on you. You've changed, haven't you?"

Of course she'd changed in six years. They all had. She squeezed the dowager's cool fingers. "It is good to see you, although I wish you did not suffer."

The dowager glanced down at her swollen leg. "Gout is the bane of my existence. That, and Henry."

"What has Lord Marsden done?"

"Nothing. For years, other than to write uninspiring letters of his dull London life." She released Caroline's hands and gestured for her to sit opposite her. "Henry hasn't done much of interest since the incident with Augusta Davies-Thorpe."

"By all accounts he's done plenty of interest, ma'am. Esther would read his letters to me. He's served well in Parliament."

"Boring stuff. I liked him better when he was love-mad. I say, your being here is just the thing. You'll coax Henry to act like that again."

Caroline, make Henry act love-mad? Her cheeks warmed, and not because she sat in a room so hot it could roast a joint of beef. "I'm sure I don't know what you mean."

"He's turned into his father, I fear, but you are just the one to revive him. Influence him so he's animated once again, like he was when you were both here last."

"We were children then."

"You're a child now."

"I am five-and-twenty." Decidedly on the shelf. "And a governess. We do not know one another anymore. In fact, he suggested I leave my post so the children might attend school."

The dowager's lips parted in a loud pop. "Incredulous. You've just arrived. You've scarce had time to displease him."

"I—" This was not going well. And she really shouldn't be casting Henry in a negative light to his grandmother. Caroline was nothing more than the governess. "He is their guardian."

The dowager pushed herself into a straighter position on the chair. "He is an idiot."

"He's—he is new to the idea of children in the house, is all."

"But he's not new to the idea of you. You are his Caro."

A soft knock drew their gaze to the door, where Edgar the footman stood with a stoic expression, but his eyes were sympathetic. "Miss Dempsey, his lordship's asking for you."

It was clear his lordship didn't summon her for pleasantries. Henry was upset about something or poor Edgar wouldn't look so pitying.

She rose and curtsied to Lady Marsden. "I do not think I have been his Caro for some time, ma'am."

And she was quite sure she never would be again.

Henry stood the moment Caroline entered the library. "Miss Dempsey."

She nodded, making the blond curls at her temples bob against her rosy cheeks. Caroline had always had a becoming flush to her pale skin that bespoke vitality and exuberance. If she weren't in mourning for Esther and Richard, she might wear a hue more complimentary of her coloring, like apricot, instead of her serviceable black gown. Caroline had been a pretty child, but she was even prettier now—

"You wished to see me, my lord?" Her brows rose in expectation.

What a fool he was, staring at her like that. Imagining her in colorful clothes? How ridiculous. "Er, yes. I've something to show you." He gestured to the desk.

As she stepped forward, her eyes narrowed. "I do not see—oh, my, what is that?"

"A vase of flowers."

"Well, yes, of course, not flowers precisely, but it makes no sense."

No, it did not. The porcelain vase, recognizable by the pastoral scene of a shepherd- ess and sheep painted on the front, was one that usually sat on the table by the window here in the library. It had been moved to the desk, however, and so much water had been added to it that liquid spilled over the side and puddled on the mahogany. Henry handed her the note that he'd found propped against the vase.

"It must make some sense to you, since you are the one who sent these to me."

She took the soggy vellum and read. Her eyes widened. "This is Julia's handwriting. The children did this."

"Yes, the misspelling of *Dempsey* was a particular hint that you were not responsible, despite the claim these came from you," he said, not holding back the sarcasm. "That, and the, er, cuttings aren't quite up to standard."

She peered closer at the small yellow blooms on scraggly-leafed stems. "What are they?"

"Calendula. I summoned the housekeeper, who informed me the stillroom maid is up in arms this morning because she'd been waiting for these very blooms to open so she could make a salve to ease the groom's joint pain."

Caroline's eyes shut. "Those little imps."

"Why would they do this?"

"They overheard our discussion yesterday. I imagine they thought if I picked flowers for you, as I did a million years ago, it might make you happy." She gestured at the mess. "I will call them at once to tidy up."

After she'd pulled the bell, Henry folded his arms. "I'm happy."

Happy enough, at least.

"They were trying to be kind." She turned to give instructions to Edgar before walk- ing back toward Henry. "They only want you to like them."

"What nonsense. Of course I like them."

"You do not know them. Yet. And children sometimes do things like this." She nudged a stack of papers on his desk away from the ever-increasing pool of water. "You certainly did your share of silly things when you were young."

And he'd lived to regret them. "None were quite like this."

"What of Barnaby?"

"Barnaby was different."

"He was a sheep."

Henry had been young. Older than Julia, but young, and Father hadn't been here, so he'd taken advantage of his absence. "Barnaby had the kindest black face, and he followed me like a puppy. You saw it."

"I also saw you cajole him into the ballroom."

"I didn't cajole. I wooed." When Caroline snickered, Henry waved his arm. "Where else was I to put him? He required space to romp."

"And graze?"

"Well, the ballroom wasn't ideal for that, true." And he hadn't known quite how loud a sheep's bleat could echo in a vast, empty chamber until that moment either. "I didn't have a plan, other than to save him from the butcher."

"Which you accomplished. I wonder if Barnaby remembered his ballroom adventure whilst he lived out his long, sheepy life? In between munching grass and wandering the hills, did he think of you with fond recollection?"

Henry laughed. He couldn't help it. It burst out of him before he could stop himself.

And once he'd started, he didn't want to stop. It felt good, laughing over something, anything, even a memory as ridiculous as this one. It had been a long time since he'd allowed himself to laugh, but Caroline still had a way about her. She made him feel like a carefree lad again—

A chambermaid with a bucket and rags lingered in the doorway, curtsying. Behind her, his two nieces and nephew watched him with wide eyes.

Henry's laughter died and his breakfast curdled in his stomach. Pity the children had seen him in such a weak moment. Now he had to communicate disapproval of their action but at the same time, not frighten them. How was he supposed to do that? *Don't stand like Father, if you don't wish to instill fear.* Henry forced a stern look, but tried to keep his hands loose at his sides.

They looked so much like Esther and Richard, it was easy to not feel angry with them. Actually, he wasn't angry at all, come to think of it.

Children did indeed do silly things, didn't they?

Caroline beckoned the children into the room with one dainty hand. "Julia, Lucy, and Rupert, you will apologize to your uncle for making such a mess on his desk. Oh yes, we know it was you. Your handwriting is not much like mine yet, Julia. You will help clean the desk, and then you will apologize to the stillroom maid for plucking herbs she needed today."

"We thought they were pretty," Julia protested.

"And they were right in the garden by the kitchen." Lucy shrugged.

Rupert craned his neck to look at the books on the high shelves.

"Ahem." Caroline's head tipped forward.

"Sorry, Uncle," the girls said in tandem. Rupert echoed them.

Caroline took their small shoulders and guided them to the desk. "Come along, before the wood warps."

The maid removed the vase and gave the children rags. Henry scooped up the stack of papers from the desk which required his attention. Fortunately, the edges were not yet moist. "I'll see to my business in the morning room, then. Thank you, Caro."

Her pretty eyes went wide before her head dipped in a nod.

He was settled at the rosewood escritoire in the morning room before he realized he'd called her Caro. Not Miss Dempsey.

The name had slipped out. At once, shame lapped over his skin, but it receded as quickly as it had come. They were friends long ago. Little wonder he reverted to the name he'd called her in their youth, after seeing each other again after all this time.

After laughing about Barnaby.

From his spot in the morning room, he could hear traces of the children's high-pitched chatter. Esther's offspring in the house brought some life into it, reminding him Marsden Hall hadn't always been a place of pain and shame. It had been a place of joy as well.

He'd romped and laughed and sprawled on the floor to draw and sketch—everything, from maps of the grounds and the park to houses and sheep and portraits of the girls to things he only saw in his head. Esther and Caroline had been at his side through it all. Esther was three years younger than he, Caroline a couple of years younger than that, but they'd managed to get into mischief and fun quite well during those happy times.

Remembering them felt strange, but good, too.

He never thought he'd admit it, but it also felt satisfying to return to estate business. This was his birthright. His home, his land, his longhorn cattle and Southdown sheep. The figures and sums on the pages before him reminded him of his blessings and the home he'd ignored for so long so he could ignore the pain associated with it.

Maybe Marsden Hall could be a place of happiness again, like parts of his childhood. Not the parts when Father was home, of course, but in Father's long absences, life here had been smooth. Sweet. Quiet.

A place of fun and peace.

Henry was still thinking about the blessed peace of Marsden Hall two hours later when a resounding crash echoed through the house and sent him bolting from his chair.

Chapter Three

W hat was that?" Caroline stood from the basin, sloshing warm salt water over her arms.

"What was what? I heard nothing." The dowager shifted in her chair, flexing her swollen foot in the bath Caroline had prepared.

"Something fell." Something loud. Like a piece of furniture. Nothing echoed now, though. Perhaps Caroline was mistaken.

Ka-thunk!

No mistake there. Or that the shrill cry that followed came from one of her young charges. And Cinders had found something to bark about.

"Pardon me, my lady, but something is amiss."

"I shall stay here and soak," the dowager called after her.

Caroline descended the stairs two at a time, a most unladylike pace, but urgent voices rose from below, punctuated by barks and thumps and bangs. She rounded the landing, looked down, and would have lost her footing had she not been clutching the newel post.

Something large and grayish-white blurred past, followed by Cinders. "What was that?"

"Nothing," Lucy called, dashing past the foot of the stairs in the opposite direction of the grayish blur.

Loud footsteps sounded behind her. Henry hurried downstairs, his dark brows pulled low in a worried expression. "What's this commotion?"

She could only point before he passed her and called for the butler, Anson. She hurried after him.

Not a single footman stood at attention in the front hall. The front door yawned open onto the portico, and the gilt Italian side table flanking the door lay on its side on the polished stone floor. Opposite the front door, a lacquered stand sat at an odd angle in the center of the room, as if it had caught on something and been dragged.

Henry shoved past it to the Portrait Hall, the long hallway that led to the drawing, dining, and morning rooms as well as the library. Caroline pursued him, about to call for the children, when a maidservant screeched and the jowl-cheeked Anson burst panting from the drawing room, his face purple as a turnip-top.

"My lord!" Anson exclaimed.

Caroline dashed around him. The elegant drawing room was in utter disarray, its delicate Chippendale chairs askew, the plush salmon-pink sofa that matched the wallpaper nudged from its standard placement, music from the pianoforte scattered on the rug—

A horrifying moan sounded from another room. No, not a moan.

A bleat.

Caroline hurried through the connecting door to the morning room, where a maid gripped Cinders by the collar and begged the barking dog to hush. Good. The spaniel might be causing as much damage as their woolly intruder.

Following the sounds of wreckage, Caroline returned to the Portrait Hall. In an instant, her foot caught a table leg and she spilled forward. A pair of hands gripped her arms and pulled her upright against a broad chest.

Henry's gray gaze traversed her face. "Are you hurt?"

She couldn't speak with her heart filling her throat, but she managed to shake her head. She hadn't been in Henry's arms since she was fifteen and he helped her learn the waltz. She'd been mad with infatuation for him then, afraid he'd be able to guess her affection by her sweat-slick hands.

That experience, memorable and pulse-ratcheting as it was, was nothing like this, with him so close she could see the traces of stubble on his jaw and her senses filled with the rich scent of his shaving soap.

His brows met. "Are you certain?"

"Fine," she managed, her voice breathy.

"Why are you soaking wet?"

What? Oh. Yes. "Mineral soak. Your grandmother." The last word was eclipsed by a howl and crash. Henry's arms fell from hers, but he took her elbow and guided her around the overturned table.

Caroline rolled her eyes at herself. While she was lost to a most inappropriate appreciation of being in Henry's arms, an animal was on the loose in the house.

They trailed the noise back to the front hall, where they'd been moments before. Two footmen were there, now, as was the tsking housekeeper Mrs. Byrd, and Polly, tears streaking her face as she moaned about how she was sure to lose her employment.

Also present was the fluffy, ovoid silhouette of a creature in the doorway to the portico.

"Baaaaaah." The sheep blinked.

Anson stomped past Caroline, his jowls quivering. "A thousand pardons, milord. I don't know how the beast got into the house."

"I've a good idea." Henry frowned down at Caroline. "Barnaby, I expect?"

Heat suffused her chest and face. "We don't know that the children are responsible. Or that they eavesdropped on our earlier discussion, and this is their version of Barnaby. It isn't as if the sheep wears a ribbon and tag declaring its name."

Henry's brow quirked.

"All right, it was the children."

The footmen's attempts to shoo the sheep accomplished naught. With an exasperated exhalation, Henry plunged between them, grasped the sheep around the shoulders, and hoisted it into his arms. "*Oof.* Stained-glass windows depicting King David the Shepherd make this look easy."

"David is holding lambs in those windows, Lord Marsden, not fully-grown ewes in need of a good shearing."

He shook his head at her.

Despite the circumstances, she rather liked the look of him carrying the sheep, his dark hair mussed over his broad brow the way it used to be when he was young, his black coat and neckcloth disheveled. He had the look of the old Henry about him.

He hauled the sheep outside, issuing instructions as he went. Edgar shut the door behind him. Caroline met the manservant's gaze. "Bring the children here. And will you please stay a moment, Mr. Anson?"

"Yes, Miss Dempsey." But his worried gaze took in the upturned furniture. He waved for the second footman to right it.

"Oh, no." Caroline stood tall, hand extended in warning. "Leave the mess as it is. Leave it all."

❧

Henry's coat was ruined. So was his peaceful mood. The sheep was bad enough, upsetting the furniture. Now the house would be in an emotional upset, too, with crying children and an exasperated staff. The mess on the ground floor could be fixed and freshened, but emotional spectacles like the ones certain to be displayed by the children and staff were not so easily tidied. He did not know how to handle such a thing without becoming like his father.

God, if You hear me, help me remain as calm as possible.

He'd hurry upstairs to change and bury himself in paperwork, away from the literal and emotional upheaval on the ground floor, so he wouldn't be faced with such unpleasantness.

But first things first. He lowered the sheep to the ground when he reached Goodman, the man who'd overseen the flock since Henry was small. "The sheep were close by the house this morning, I take it?"

Goodman crumpled his hat in his gnarled fingers. "Aye, milord, and the children wanted to pet one. I didn't see no harm in it, recalling how you were with yer sheep when you was a lad, if you don't mind me saying so."

"No." The legend of Barnaby would never die now. "How did the children acquire the sheep?"

"I was tending another of the ewes. Bad leg, milord, but I think it'll heal right up." Goodman bowed his thick shoulders. "I didn't notice the missing ewe until ten minutes passed, but it was too late, they'd gone with her. Never did my eyes expect to see that happen twice in my lifetime, with someone from the house takin' a sheep. Never thought I'd see your lordship carryin' her back out, neither."

Henry brushed a clump of grayish wool and broken bits of dried leaf from his sleeve. "Yes, well. I shan't make a habit of it."

"No, milord."

Henry stomped back to the house, pushing down every feeling in his chest. Not that he was angry at the children. Vexed—annoyed, perhaps, but not angry. They were trying to make him happy, in their own strange way.

But some other emotion rattled in his chest, something that stirred when Caroline tripped and he caught her. His heart had started thrumming in a way that hadn't happened since Augusta Davies-Thorpe. In a way that would cause him nothing but trouble.

He paused on the portico. He'd go inside, spare one moment in the front hall to express his appreciation to the staff for their uncommon efforts after an uncommon situation, endure a moment of the moaning and weeping of the children and maybe Polly, too, who might well lose her position now that the children had escaped her supervision, and then he'd hurry upstairs.

He braced himself and opened the door.

To a party.

"O waly, waly up the bank,
And waly, waly doun the brae,
And waly, waly, yon burn-side,
Where I and my love wont to gae."

Henry hadn't heard that old Scottish air in ages, much less sung it, and while it was about wailing over love, the way Caroline's high, sweet voice led them in an upbeat tempo, it sounded almost jolly. She hoisted half of the gilt table to its upright position while Lucy pushed up the other side, singing along. Julia worked a broom over the floor, belting the lyrics as loudly as an opera singer. Polly warbled along as she held the dustpan for Julia. A humming Mrs. Byrd gestured to the footmen in the opening to the portrait hall to carry on, and Anson was smiling while he hoisted Rupert in his arms to straighten a portrait on the wall.

Polly looked up at Henry and stopped singing. They all did.

Julia dropped the broom and plowed into his legs with such force he almost fell backward. "Uncle, we are sorry."

"Sorry." Lucy gripped his knees.

"Very sorry." Rupert wiggled in Anson's arms and was set down at once so he could join the mass embrace.

Never had Henry had anyone attached to his limbs like this. It felt unsettling, like he might fall. Emotionally unsettling too, because it was sweet and uncomfortable all at once. He wasn't sure what to do, so he patted their heads in turn.

Caroline stood before them, a look of approval softening her eyes. She truly did care for the children, didn't she?

Her expression grew more businesslike as her gaze settled on Henry. "We are attending to the mess we created."

"So I see."

Julia tugged his coattail. "And we're sorry!"

Caroline's head tipped. "About eavesdropping and the sheep."

"Yes, both." Lucy sighed and let go of Henry. Julia released him, too.

Rupert followed suit and moved to lean against Caroline's legs. Her fingers absently played in his fine dark hair. "I'm glad we all understand one another now."

Should Henry say something, too? Probably. "You mustn't steal sheep."

"We didn't steal Barnaby." Julia picked a broken leaf off her skirt. "He belongs to you, and we were bringing him to you."

"He wouldn't go into the ballroom," Rupert said with a shrug.

"Alas, the ballroom is not as appropriate for a sheep as the outdoors. And another thing. Barnaby is a girl."

"No, Barnaby's a boy." Rupert's mouth pinched.

"She's most assuredly a ewe."

Rupert's jaw set. "I like boy sheep."

Caroline sent Henry a warning look. "Yes, Rupert, you prefer males in all things. At any rate, this room is put to rights now. You three go to work in the drawing room. Do not touch anything except what Mrs. Byrd or Polly tells you to. No touching the porcelain. Or the candles."

Julia started up the "O Waly, Waly" song while they dashed through to the Portrait Hall, followed by Polly and Anson, leaving Henry and Caroline alone.

He'd thought to be the one to leave the hall first, hadn't he? Nothing had gone quite as he planned since Caroline and the children returned to Marsden Hall.

Father would be furious to see it.

Caroline did not look the least bit furious. Her eyes turned down in apology, but she was smiling. "Barnaby was, like the flowers, supposed to be from me. They confessed at once, the little scamps. I hope that in cleaning the messes, they'll learn a lesson."

Childish laughter carried from the drawing room. "They don't sound as if they're being disciplined."

Caroline's brow quirked. "In addition to cleaning up, they're not to have any sweets today and must go to bed early. But while they know they are being disciplined, they also know they're being loved."

Henry had never understood those two things could go together. Mama didn't discipline at all, and Father, well, he didn't love.

He'd always preferred Mama's way, but for eight years now, Henry had accepted that Father's way was right. Emotional displays led to hurt, to both heart and body.

Still, his nieces and nephew were just children. "It's good that they've found something happy today, considering."

"Considering Esther and Richard? It's been three months to the day. Can you fathom it?" She sighed. "The loss has been terrible for them, but day by day, they are starting to experience joy again."

"Yes, but I meant, it's good the children will have a pleasant memory of something, considering they will soon be off to school."

Caroline's eyes narrowed. "You still insist on sending them away?"

"They need school."

"What they need is a constant in their lives."

"That's what school is, Caro."

"No, Henry, that's what family is. People and a place that never changes, that welcomes them and supports them and loves them." She shook her head, clearly not aware she'd used his Christian name. "You are their family."

He willed his hands not to shake. "By blood, in name, yes, but I'm not their real family. Esther and Richard only chose me as their guardian because Richard had no relatives. I'm all that's left, but I can't raise children. I don't even live here anymore—I stay in London for Parliament. I'm a bachelor with no intention of having my own family. Not anymore."

Her head lifted a fraction. "Not since Augusta Davies-Thorpe."

"Not since—" He bit it back. "Not since the aftermath of it."

"Pardon my saying so, but you have allowed that incident to guide your life for too long. She was not worth it."

"No, she wasn't. And it wasn't her, it was Father." But he didn't want to talk about it now. "I've matters to attend to, and a coat to send to the rubbish bin."

"But what about the children and school, my lord?"

"Henry." He walked backward to the staircase, meeting her cross gaze. "You called me Henry, you know. And I think you should keep doing so. We've known one another far too long to be Lord Marsden and Miss Dempsey, and we aren't precisely speaking to one another as employer and governess, are we?"

Her rosy cheeks flushed a deeper shade, and even though he shouldn't, he found the effect of her blush quite charming.

His valet was, of course, horrified by the dirty state of Henry's coat, pantaloons, and Hessian boots, but within minutes Henry was changed into fresh clothing and situated in his bedchamber's sitting room with the post, including a letter from his particular friend, Sir Montague Hurst.

It was difficult to concentrate, however. The children's laughter carried upstairs.

Maybe Caroline was right. He'd let the incident with Augusta Davies-Thorpe put him off marriage, but perhaps he should reassess his choice. Funny enough, Monty mentioned in his letter about his cousin Cassandra's court presentation. She was pretty, well bred, and available for marriage. Monty's hint at matchmaking couldn't have been stronger.

What was he thinking? Marriage? Family?

Ridiculous. He had no business being involved in a child's life. He didn't know how to be a family man, and if he tried, he'd no doubt wound his children as his father had done. Not on the outside, maybe. But in other ways.

It was best for all of them—Esther's little ones, but Caroline, too—to get away from Marsden Hall as fast as possible.

For their own good.

Yet he caught himself humming "O Waly, Waly" along with the children as their voices carried from below.

Chapter Four

The next day, Caroline took the children with her to visit the dowager.

"You must be quiet," she warned as they strode to Lady Marsden's chambers. "Hands to yourselves."

It would not be easy for Lucy. Even now, Lucy brushed Caroline's overskirt with her fingers, seeking out the embroidered lavender-on-lavender pattern of her gown. Since it was past three months since the carriage accident that took Esther and Richard, it was now appropriate for the children to move into a period of half-mourning. Caroline instructed Polly to set aside their black garments and dress the girls in lilac frocks. A black armband encircled the tiny bicep of Rupert's dark-brown coat, and while Caroline wished the children were not in mourning at all, it was good to see them in some color again.

In three more months when the children were out of mourning altogether, Caroline would dress them in vibrant hues. Red shoes and sashes for the girls, and vibrant green and blue coats for Rupert. They'd play on the lawn, as she used to years ago, running through the summer grass—

Would Henry have sent them all away by then?

"You're frowning." Lucy patted Caroline's forearm. "The dowager's not one of those ladies who eats children, is she?"

Caroline stumbled. "Wherever did you get such an idea?"

"Polly told us a story about a boy and girl in the woods." Rupert hopped. "I like the boy better than the girl."

Of course he did. "I do not approve of this story at all. And no, the dowager is most kind. I believe she has biscuits awaiting us."

"Biscuits!" Rupert dashed forward.

"Manners," Caroline warned.

Lady Marsden sat in her chair by the blazing fire, her foot propped on the overstuffed ottoman, but she wore stockings today. The children curtsied and bowed and let their great-grandmother fuss over them.

Lady Marsden eyed the younger two. "You look like your mother."

"Not me," Julia said. "I look like Papa."

"Indeed. He was a handsome fellow, too." Lady Marsden grinned at Caroline before returning her gaze to the children. "Are you hungry?"

"Biscuits!" Rupert hopped.

When they settled to their snack, Caroline leaned toward the dowager. "How is your leg? Did the mineral soak help?"

"It did, and I had another this morning. I'm doing so much better, I've told Henry I should like to join him in the dining room tomorrow evening."

"That's wonderful."

"I'll rest all day for it."

"A true cause for celebration, Lady Marsden."

"And you, of course, will join us."

Caroline stiffened. "Me?"

"Are you concerned you have nothing suitable to wear to dinner? Governesses always worry about such things." Lady Marsden looked up and down Caroline's ensemble.

"Not at all. I dined with Esther and Richard, and have appropriate garb."

"She has a gray dress," Julia announced.

"And jet jewelry?"

"No," Caroline admitted.

"Never mind. It's half-mourning now, you can bring out your pearls. None of those either?" Lady Marsden shook her head at Caroline. "Without jewelry, one always looks like the poor relation at the table."

Which was, in a way, what she was. Esther's poor friend. But Caroline didn't mind, and she was not without jewelry. "I have a fine gold cross necklace to wear."

Lady Marsden leaned toward Julia in a conspiratorial pose. "If it's not her attire, then why does your governess look so cross about the prospect of dinner?"

"It's Uncle Henry." Julia spun on her seat to face the dowager. "He wants to ship us to school and give her a pension."

Caroline's stomach swooped. "Julia!"

Lady Marsden blinked at Caroline before dipping her head back to Julia. "You're a little young for school, if I may be so bold as to voice my opinion, and I do not like the idea of Miss Dempsey being dismissed. She seems a fine governess."

"She is, and she's Mama's friend."

"Mama wouldn't like Miss Dempsey in a prison." Lucy shook her head.

Rupert's legs swung. "Prisons are bad."

Caroline held up a hand. "Not a prison. A pension is an altogether—"

Lady Marsden ignored her. "Your uncle and your Miss Dempsey used to be such thick friends. He and Miss Dempsey and your mother ran wild, dancing and sneaking biscuits."

"What sort of biscuits?" Julia scooted closer on the settee to the dowager.

"Oh, any kind," Lady Marsden said. "Miss Dempsey was never particular. Why, the stories I could tell you about your governess!"

As if she wasn't sitting in the room. Caroline had never been so thankful to spy Polly's face in the threshold. "Oh, here is Polly, come for you, children. Cook has a project for you in the kitchen. Cracking nuts, I think. Say 'thank you' to Lady Marsden."

They thanked their great-grandmother and kissed her plump cheeks.

Caroline prepared to follow after them, but paused. "Would you like another foot soak? I can assist you—"

"I'll have one later. I thought Henry would forget the idea of sending the children to school once you set him to rights. He hasn't?"

Caroline shouldn't discuss it. She was a servant. Henry was the dowager's grandson. But the words came out anyway.

"He doesn't want a family, not after Augusta Davies-Thorpe."

"Oh, that." Lady Marsden's eyes rolled. "Yes, she hurt him, but the reason he remains unwed isn't her. 'Tis his father."

"He said something to that extent." Curiosity rooted Caroline to her chair. She had never cared for Henry and Esther's stern father. He was in London much of the year, not often at Marsden Hall, but when he came home, he disapproved of everything and didn't seem to like anyone, not even his family. All the fun stopped when Henry's father was around. "I don't understand, though. Wouldn't Henry's father want him to have a family? Because it's his duty as earl?"

"Henry didn't propose to that horrid Davies-Thorpe person out of duty. It was a rebellion against his father."

"No, my lady. Henry proposed because he cared for her. Esther said so, as did the gossips."

"He was smitten, yes. Never before had he experienced a matter of the heart, and he was what, all of twenty?"

"Two and twenty." And Caroline had been seventeen and heartbroken by the reports of Henry's slavish adoration of the beautiful, wealthy, highborn Miss Davies-Thorpe.

"Henry was young, impulsive, and thought to prove to his father that love triumphed over all, because love was not the least bit important to his father. It was the same with Esther, you know. My son had much loftier potential husbands in mind for her than Richard, but she, too, chose love over a dynastic match."

Caroline had known Esther's father didn't care for Richard, who came from a good family but lacked connections and immense wealth. Esther had somehow managed to gain permission to marry him, but there was a cost: after the wedding, Esther's father cut her off from the family, ignoring her letters and pretending she didn't exist. Esther didn't seem to mind, though, even though she and Richard had little money. Things were so strained that when a diplomatic position arose six years ago, they saw it as a gift of God.

It was a gift of God for Caroline, too, since her father had just died. Esther was eager to bring Caroline along on their grand adventure in Spain. They'd had a happy life together.

Henry could have one, too, but the shadow of his father seemed to loom long and dark over him. "Forgive me, my lady, but your son has been gone some five years now. I don't quite understand his continued influence on Henry when it comes to a family—"

"Never mind. I'm prattling on." The dowager patted Caroline's hand. "Go enjoy a moment to yourself. You get so few of them."

Caroline didn't want a moment to herself. She wanted to understand what had happened with Henry to change him from the boy she used to know.

But Lady Marsden's lips pinched shut, and it was not Caroline's place to pry, no matter how curious she was. "You are too kind. Very well, I shall settle with a book." A look of relief smoothed Lady Marsden's features.

Caroline returned to her bedchamber adjacent to the now-quiet nursery. The children were still busy with Cook and Polly, but it became clear the moment Caroline crossed to the comfortable chair by the window that the children had been here quite recently.

Alongside her book, a delicate plate crafted of local porcelain sat on the side table. Atop it lay two sugared biscuits, and beside it lay a note, bearing her name. She took up the paper and frowned.

The biscuits remained untouched when the children and Polly returned to the nursery. Caroline took a deep breath through her nose before joining them. "Children, a word in my chamber, please?"

The children followed her, accompanied by a tail-wagging Cinders.

"What is it, Miss Dempsey?" Julia's round-eyed look of surprise was rather well done. The child might have a future as an actress.

"Your biscuits are still here." Lucy was genuinely surprised about that.

So was Rupert. "I'll eat them if you don't want them."

Julia frowned at her brother. "They're Miss Dempsey's."

"I'm not hungry." It was true; Caroline's appetite was nonexistent. "I'll send them back."

"Uncle wouldn't like it if you don't eat the biscuits he sent," Lucy blurted, giving up the jig.

"He didn't send them." Caroline held up the note. "This writing does not match the letter he sent inviting us to Marsden Hall."

"Maybe his secretary wrote it for him." Julia shrugged.

"No more lies. Lord Marsden did not request Cook send me these biscuits any more than I picked those flowers for him—or brought Barnaby inside."

Julia's eyes widened. "We never said you brought in Barnaby. We thought he'd like it."

"I understand you want your uncle to be happy, and to like—us." She almost said *me.*

"We don't just want him to like you, Miss Dempsey." Lucy fingered the biscuit plate. "We want him to marry you."

Caroline blinked. They wanted *what?*

"You should get married," Julia said, hopping on her toes. "Then you will be our new mother and you will have the authority to make decisions about us—that's what you said, only our mother could do that. Then we won't have to go away to school."

Poor dears. They wanted a family. Could she blame them for that? Hardly, even if their attempts to secure one were meddlesome, at best.

Embarrassing, to be sure.

And possibly heartbreaking, because she'd always had a soft spot for Henry Graves, long before he was Earl of Marsden, and it wouldn't take much to send her tumbling into something far more dangerous and real than the cream-pot love she'd had for him as a girl.

Lord, help.

But there was no help for it. She lowered to the plush rug by the hearth and extended her arms. The children snuggled into her embrace, Rupert's small body curling perfectly under her left arm.

"My darlings, I do not know if your uncle will marry someday, but his wife will not be me."

"Whyever not?" Lucy plucked at Caroline's overskirt.

"I am not noble born. I am a vicar's daughter. A respectable female, to be sure, but I did not inherit jewels or fortune or land." That was the main reason she'd had to become their governess, because she had no other means to survive once Papa died.

"Uncle has a big house. He doesn't need your fortune or land."

Caroline laughed. "True. But that changes nothing. I am who I am; he is who he is. Someday if I wed, it will be to an honorable gentleman, and should your uncle wed, it will be to a fine lady who wears baubles around her neck."

"Oh, I see." Lucy gently touched Caroline's bare throat.

"So do I," Julia said.

And if there was a gleam in her eye, Caroline couldn't see it before Julia's gaze turned to the window.

❧

The note lay square atop Henry's desk in precisely the same place the vase of "flowers" had, demanding his full attention. LORD MARSDEN was scrawled across a sheet of the expensive vellum he kept in the top drawer.

It did not require much thought to deduce the true author of the note. Caro's admonitions to the children that they stop such nonsense weren't proving effective. Maybe there was another way to put a stop to their antics.

Henry jotted down a message on a cheap scrap of foolscap and rang for Anson.

"Yes, milord?"

"Send Miss Dempsey to me, at her convenience, and then bring tea for us. But first, instruct my valet to send these down." He handed Anson the paper.

Anson's brow quirked. No wonder. Henry's request was odd.

But it was also fun, something Henry hadn't had in a long while. "Thank you, Anson."

"Indeed, milord." The butler bowed and withdrew to execute his task.

Within ten minutes, Henry's valet delivered the soft velvet pouch. He'd not been gone a minute when Caroline appeared in the doorway, her eyes wide with curiosity.

"Ah, come in. I have something to loan you." He handed her the wine-hued pouch.

"What is this?"

"Open it."

Her dainty fingers unfastened the clasp and reached inside. Tentatively, she withdrew a silver necklace set with five amethysts. The largest of the gemstone pendants, hanging at the center of the necklace, was the size of a black currant—a modest piece but an exquisite one, with delicate filigree work and a rich, deep quality to the stones.

She looked up at him. "You're loaning me a necklace?"

"Of course." He held up the note. "You asked for them."

"I did no such—oh." Her eyes shut. "The children."

"Yes. The note was signed with an impressively large *D* for *Dempsey.*"

"What did I supposedly say in this note?"

"That you did not wish to be embarrassed tomorrow, dining without gems. No, pardon me." He consulted the note. "'Fancy, fancy gems.'"

"Those rascals. I was not at all embarrassed, but I am now."

"I certainly don't wish for you to be embarrassed. I'd rather you feel we had the upper hand for a moment where those three are concerned." He broke off at the arrival of the tea things. At his request, Caroline took a seat and set about pouring their cups, adding a snip of sugar to his without him having to ask.

She handed him his cup. "I take it that you wish me to wear the necklace as if you believed I truly asked to borrow them?"

He carried the cup with him to stand near the hearth. "It would be amusing to view their reaction, but actually, I was thinking about their concern for you being comfortable at dinner."

Whatever she'd been about to say melted away, and a faint smile toyed around her lips. "Henry, are you worried about the appropriateness of my clothing? I assure you, I have suitable attire for the dining room. The ballroom, too."

"Everything you own is suitable and becoming. You could wear a riding habit to dinner and I wouldn't care."

She chuckled. "A riding habit isn't genteel dining apparel."

"You know what I mean. What you have on is fine." He waved at her lavender frock.

"Not for a formal dinner, it's not."

Of course not. Even a bachelor like him knew women wore altogether different gowns for evening, but that wasn't what this was about. "I'm not talking about fashion. Neither were the children, not really. They demonstrated a true concern for your well-being. Esther cared for you, too. Do you have something of hers to remember her by?"

Her chin quivered. "No. But I don't need anything. She's in my heart."

That settled it. "Keep the amethysts."

"No, Henry." She rose, scooped the necklace, and shoved it at him.

He didn't take them. "She'd want you to have them."

"I don't want anything that should go to her children."

"I said you should have something of Esther's, but this actually isn't hers. She liked it and called it the black currant necklace. I shouldn't tell you this, but when she was tiny she tasted the stones—I'm certain they've been cleaned since then. Regardless, it's mine to give. The children will receive other pieces. They'll never see want, Caro. Take it."

Her hand still stretched out toward him, holding out the necklace. "I couldn't."

"I insist."

He took her fingers and curved them tighter around the necklace. So soft, those fingers, and warm, too, against the cool silver of the necklace. The last time he'd touched Caro's hand was a quick clasp when he'd gone to London eight years ago. Then he'd kissed her knuckles as a jest.

Her touch didn't scorch him then the way it did now.

He should let her go. He was being inappropriate. And the last time he was inappropriate scorched his memory for an altogether different reason. He'd proposed in public to Augusta Davies-Thorpe, and the Lord knew what a disaster that had been.

His hand fell. She ducked her head, avoiding his gaze, and tucked the necklace back into its pouch. "I really shouldn't—"

"Caro, please." He looked out the window, not seeing much. "You knew Esther better than I these past six years."

He heard and felt Caroline move away and resume her seat. "She loved you."

Talking about Esther hurt, but it was easier than thinking about Augusta. Or why Caro's touch felt altogether different to him now. "I should have visited her."

"Spain is a long way, Henry."

"But her children don't know me at all. They think I'm such an ogre they need to pull tricks to get me to notice them."

"No, it's not that at all." Her tone held a curious quality.

"They think I need sweetening with flowers. They clearly think I'd judge you if you didn't wear 'fancy, fancy gems' to dinner."

"You're not the sole object of their efforts. They sent me biscuits accompanied by a note from you. And they. . . well, I hesitate to tell you." She busied herself with the teapot.

"What?"

"It's a trifle."

Clearly it wasn't. "What is it, Caro? They don't care for us arguing, is that it? They're bang up to the mark there. If they're sending you biscuits from me, they want us to be friends, and I shall endeavor to be an even better one."

"They want us to be more than that." She met his gaze for a half second while he took a sip of his tea. "They'd like us to marry."

The tea seemed to stop halfway down his gullet. "Pardon me?"

Her cheeks pinked. "They entertain the ridiculous notion that if I become their aunt, I can convince you not to send them to school."

Married. Him and Caroline. He stared into his teacup, grasping all the while for something to say. "Astonishing."

"Mad."

"Creative, I'll give them that." He drained his cup.

So did she. "A little too creative."

Father would suffer an apoplexy, had he been alive.

"So will you at least wear the amethysts tomorrow?" His voice sounded a little strangled.

"I don't know." She hopped to her feet. "If that is all, I should check on the children."

"This is my last chance to convince you, then. I'm dining with the neighbors tonight, and at dawn I'll ride out with the estate manager to view his suggested improvements. So please trust me when I say Esther would have liked you wearing the black currant necklace."

Her gaze met his and held it, but her chin quivered. "I shall think on it."

He nodded. He could ask for no more from her.

But it was time he asked more of himself, perhaps. It was time he got to know the children better.

And if doing so required him to be around Caroline more, so be it. He shoved down the sense of joy such a prospect engendered in his chest. He must take care to keep his burgeoning feelings for her in check or he'd make a fool of himself all over again.

No, he'd send Caroline away before he humiliated them both by allowing himself to start feeling things like that again. It wouldn't do either of them any good.

Chapter Five

Caroline hastened to her bedchamber and stuffed the velvet pouch in the top drawer of her bureau, an effort far clumsier than it should have been, but her fingers still trembled from Henry's touch.

How ridiculous. He was only ensuring she didn't drop the amethysts.

Caroline spun from the bureau, hand pressed against her chest as she fought to steady her breath. She was no longer a girl with a *tendre* for her childhood friend. She was a governess, and he was her employer. Those old feelings for him must not resurface. They had no place here, anyway. She was not the same person now, and neither was he. Not at all.

Lord, please help me. I mustn't allow anything to muddle my determination to care for the children.

Their high voices carried from the hall, accompanied by Polly's soft alto. Caroline took one last deep, steadying breath and joined them in the nursery.

The little rascals didn't ask about the "fancy, fancy gems" they'd requested from their uncle on her behalf. Caroline wouldn't say a word, either, but tomorrow, she'd keep them so busy they wouldn't have a moment to write another note in someone else's name, much less contemplate another matchmaking plot.

And if she kept herself too busy to think of Henry and his gift of the "black currant" amethysts, well, that would be of benefit to her, too.

In the morning, Caroline and the children assisted the stillroom maid in the kitchen garden and then helped her organize the herbs and flowers they'd collected. Afterward, with Cinders in tow, they tromped up and down the damp green hills behind the house to count sheep, sketch wildflowers, and play fetch with Cinders and a small rag ball.

The girls skipped, and Rupert pretended to fall so he could roll down a small knoll, staining his nankeen pantaloons. Caroline sighed, but he was about to grow out of them anyway.

In fact, Rupert was about to grow out of everything. She'd have to speak with Henry about new clothing for the children.

Heat prickled her face that had nothing to do with exertion from tromping the hills. Thinking of Henry reminded her of how the simple touch of his fingers had jolted her to her leg bones.

It might not be so bad had she not told him about the children's matchmaking plan. Such a thing was mortifying, but it was best to have it out in the open. They were adults. Mature. Able to discuss matters rationally.

Henry was all about being rational these days. Too bad Caroline's insides seemed incapable of holding fast to logic, because allowing herself to feel anything more familiar than a gentle appreciation of her employer was not only illogical. It was dangerous.

She must smother those feelings, once and for all, before she saw him at dinner tonight.

That got her thinking of the amethysts again. And Henry's touch.

Lord, help me cease being such a cabbagehead about Henry. But whilst we're on the subject of Henry, will you heal whatever has plagued him for so long? Augusta Davies-Thorpe or whatever changed him from who he was. Please mend his heart, Lord.

At noon, Polly and one of the footmen brought them a picnic of pigeon pies and thick buttered bread, as well as a blanket to lounge upon. She and the children feasted and laughed and watched the clouds saunter across the sky.

"Why are we having a holiday?" Julia's face scrunched.

"It is not a holiday. We've had lessons. You did your sums, adding the groups of sheep. You learned some housewifery with the stillroom maid, and practiced your sketching."

Lucy frowned at her brother's sketchbook. "Rupert didn't draw the flowers like he was supposed to."

"I don't like flowers." Rupert had drawn roundish lumps instead. Sheep, with dotted eyes, smiling mouths, and legs sprouting directly out of their faces. He was getting better at holding the pencil, and soon he'd be able to write his numbers and letters as well as the girls.

A hot rush of affection swelled in Caroline's chest. How she loved these children. It would devastate her to part from them. It would devastate Esther, too. These little ones must grow up knowing they were loved by their parents, and they deserved to be loved by whoever was in charge of their care. She must convince Henry that Esther wouldn't have wanted them to be sent to school so young.

Perhaps if he spent more time with them, he'd come to love them, too.

"Are you crying, Miss Dempsey?" Julia peered in her face.

"I suppose I am, a little." Caroline dabbed a hot tear from her cheek.

"Because Rupert's drawing is so bad?"

Rupert kicked at Julia's dress, missing her leg, but Julia squawked.

Caroline scooped Rupert onto her lap. "No kicking, Rupert. Julia, his drawings are perfect for a young gentleman. Apologize, both of you."

They mumbled *sorry* while Lucy patted Caroline's damp cheek. "Why are you crying? Do you miss Mama and Papa?"

"Yes."

"Me, too." Lucy snuggled against Caroline's side. Julia laid her head on Caroline's knee, and even Cinders curled alongside. They sat that way, in a comforting knot, for a full minute before Rupert stirred.

"Can I play with Cinders again?"

"Yes." Caroline patted his back. The girls wanted extra hugs, but soon they were playing too.

Caroline was rising to return home when Edgar ascended the hill. "Miss Dempsey?"

"Yes, Edgar?"

"Lady Marsden requests your presence in the ballroom at three. Yours and the children's."

"The ballroom?"

"Oh, yes." Julia ran in a circle around Caroline and Edgar. "For our dancing lesson."

Caroline had planned no such lesson, but all three children hopped in excitement. Weren't they exhausted after running about outdoors all day? Caroline was. Even Cinders had had enough, flopping onto the wet grass with her tongue lolling out of her doggy-smiling mouth.

Then again, if the children were dancing, they wouldn't be plotting a new way to put their uncle and their governess together.

"Very well. I confess I'm surprised Lady Marsden organized such a thing for you." Caroline marched down the hill with them.

"We're not." Lucy trooped alongside. "We discussed it yesterday."

"Where was I?"

"With Uncle Henry in the library."

How did they know that? Did they know about the necklace, too? "You were supposed to be in the kitchen."

"We finished cracking nuts. Cook didn't need us anymore."

"That didn't give you leave to bother Lady Marsden again."

"She was happy to see us, and to arrange a dancing lesson, too."

Caroline nevertheless felt out of sorts after she and the children washed up, changed clothes, and made their way to the ballroom.

Lady Marsden sat at the elegant pianoforte in the corner. At the sight of the children, she didn't rise, but a wide smile parted her lips and she trilled the keys.

The girls spun in circles while Rupert ran about the room's perimeter. Caroline crossed to Lady Marsden and curtsied. "What a surprise, my lady."

"Isn't it? I told the children I would summon them when I felt strong enough, and I do." She played a slow but accurate scale. "My leg may not work, but my fingers are still nimble, so I shall play while you show the children how to execute the waltz."

"Why do we not start with a reel?" Something they all could do at the same time.

"Reels bore me." Lady Marsden began a piece in three-quarter time. "You do know how, do you not?"

Of course Caroline knew how to waltz. All genteel females knew how. Her father was a vicar, but he hadn't scrimped on her education. "I attended a few balls in Spain with Esther."

Lady Marsden's fingers froze. "Did you dance with any charming Spaniards? I am agog with curiosity."

"A few." Let Lady Marsden make of that what she would. Caroline spun. "Stand here, children. We are going to learn the waltz. We will start by tracing a box with our feet."

She lifted her hem an inch so they could see her feet, and demonstrated. At once, Julia and Lucy executed the basic steps, but Rupert, of course, hopped instead.

Laughing, she hoisted him in the air and landed his small feet atop hers. "Rupert, as a gentleman, you must go backwards. Like this."

Clinging to her hands, he squealed and laughed. "More!"

"Now we turn." She craned her neck to look back at the girls. "Follow the steps, but turn in time to the music. One-two-three, one-two-three, perfect."

"I'm dizzy!" Lucy twirled so fast she stumbled.

"I'm a princess!" Julia swung her arms.

None of them were really dancing the waltz at all. But it was fun.

The music stopped abruptly. "Henry, come here at once," Lady Marsden ordered.

Rupert still propped atop her toes, Caroline spun toward the door. Henry stood in the threshold, dressed for riding in tall boots and a functional brown coat. "What's this ruckus? Is there another sheep in the house?"

Julia giggled. "We're waltzing."

"And Caroline needs a man." Lady Marsden nodded at Caroline.

Henry's brows rose halfway up his forehead. "Is that so, Caro?"

Caroline shook her head. "I do not—"

"Dance the waltz with her, Henry, so the children see how it is properly executed." Lady Marsden began playing again.

Caroline's head hadn't stopped shaking no. "Lord Marsden is busy—"

"Not that busy," Henry said, walking toward her. "Rupert, may I borrow your partner?"

Rupert tugged back his hands and hopped away while Henry removed his gloves and offered them to Julia. Then he extended his hand to Caroline.

Caroline gulped. She had no choice but to oblige.

Henry bowed. "Forgive me if I smell like a horse."

She curtsied. "Earlier this week you smelled like a sheep."

His lips quirked as he lifted their joined hands into the proper posture. "I probably dance like one, too. It's been a while."

"Caroline has danced with charming Spaniards," Lady Marsden shouted over the music.

"I am sure to disappoint, then, but at least the children will see how the dance is done." Henry smiled as his warm right hand rested on her back, just above her waist. Perfectly proper. Nevertheless, the touch burned through to her spine.

They were perfectly proper in their distance apart, too, but she was so close she could see the ring of green around his gray irises and make out the faint fragrance of his soap. Oh dear. Oh dear, oh dear. She lowered her gaze to the neat knot of his neckcloth.

He cleared his throat and gestured with a flick of his eyes to his shoulder. Caroline hurriedly put her left hand there, and then he led her in the motions of the dance.

One two three, one two three. Don't quake like a leaf in the wind, Caroline. You're made of sterner stuff than this.

He led her in a turn. "Remember when you and Esther forced me to dance with you in this very room some years ago? Esther threatened me with bodily harm, I think."

"That was not it. She threatened to tell your mother about your astronomy marks at university."

"You recall such detail."

She recalled everything. Dancing with him that day was the moment she'd thought herself in love with Henry Graves, the future Earl of Marsden.

Dancing with him now, with him smiling and teasing like the old Henry, she found herself in grave danger of repeating that particular folly.

If it wasn't already too late.

It had been a long time since Henry thought of that waltz with Caroline. He'd been twenty or thereabouts and not particularly enthused when Esther saw him pass the ballroom and urged him to dance. She was close to making her come-out in society, fretting about making a good impression, so he'd given in and waltzed with each of the girls in turn.

That day, he'd realized Caroline was not the bony, long-limbed child she'd been when he'd left for university. He'd thought she'd become rather pretty, in fact.

She was even prettier now.

But she didn't smile, and Henry craved it, so he did what he'd done when they'd danced those years ago. He tightened his hold on her and spun her far too fast to be a model couple if they were, indeed, instructing the children. The only reason to spin her like that was to make her laugh.

She gasped instead, gaping at him while her lavender hem twisted about her ankles, but the children cackled.

"Again!" one of the girls shouted.

He wiggled his brows at Caroline. Ah, there it was—her smile. "Ready?"

"You wouldn't—"

He did, spinning her hard and fast. Her head tipped back, exposing the line of her neck. He pushed her out so she twirled on his arm and then he pulled her back. They were both laughing, hardly able to one-two-three in a box pattern, much less turn about the room.

"Me next." Julia hopped up and down. Lucy spun in her own circle, holding the black-trimmed hem of her skirt out like a ball gown. Rupert twirled and fell onto the floor in a dizzy-looking heap.

Loath as he was to break his hold on Caroline, Henry had decided to spend more time with the children, so he released her hands and bowed before Julia. "May I?"

"Oh, yes." She gripped his hands while Caroline turned to take Lucy's.

Henry turned Julia in a sort of waltz, but it was obvious she only wanted to be spun about the room like a top, so he did. Her blue eyes curved into happy crescents and she laughed, revealing a hole where a bottom tooth should be. She was losing teeth already? When did that start? Henry had all but forgotten such a thing happened. He didn't know a thing about children.

Except that they apparently liked being spun into frenzies.

"Switch partners," Grandmama called, starting the song over again.

Giggling, Lucy pranced to him and took his hands with her tiny ones. She looked so much like Esther it ached his chest, but only for a moment. It was difficult to mourn when one's arms were being tugged on by a giggling sprite. "Faster!"

He obliged, glancing up to where Caroline made a lopsided circle dance with Julia and Rupert. They skipped, he twirled, and then it was time to switch again. Rupert plowed into Henry's legs.

Rather than spin him, Henry hauled the lad into his arms—he weighed almost nothing—and tossed him in the air, catching him around the ribs. A high-pitched squeal erupted from his tiny frame—had Henry broken him?

"Again!" Rupert's voice was almost as high as the squeal. "Again."

"Again, *please*." Caroline spun Lucy under her arm.

"Pweese!"

So Henry did it again. And again before capturing the boy to his chest in an impulsive hug.

He was so small, this nephew of his. He smelled of milk and soap, and his brown eyes crinkled when he laughed, just like Esther's eyes.

"My turn!" Julia grabbed his sleeve.

Henry spun her, then Lucy, then Rupert, until Grandmama abruptly stopped the music. "This lesson has deteriorated into something altogether ridiculous."

"And altogether delightful." Caroline's cheeks were pink and round as young apples.

"Indeed," Henry surprised himself by saying. He hadn't done anything this silly since. . .well, since Augusta, if one didn't count him hauling a sheep out of the house. These past eight years, he'd been dignified, proper, and unobjectionable. But just now he'd forgotten himself and joined the frenzy of laughter and fun, and he'd liked it, although it felt strange, too.

Would Grandmama view him differently after seeing him toss and whirl children? Would Caro?

Her wide smile for him was unchanged, so he guessed not. Then again, she was a governess, accustomed to playing. And when she was younger, she'd had no qualms about appearing undignified. Father had called her a hoyden.

Henry had defended Caroline, at least in his mind. He could never have told Father aloud how much he liked Caroline's spirit.

She clapped her hands for Grandmama, nodding at the children to do the same.

"We are grateful for your skilled playing, as well as your arrangement of such a fun activity."

"Yes, thank you." Julia was still spinning.

Lucy and Rupert followed suit.

"You're welcome," Grandmama said coyly, glancing at the children.

Who started giggling.

Ah. It all made sense now—

"What is it?" Caro's brows knit.

"I shall tell you later," Henry answered. "I must see to some correspondence now. But you'll still be joining me for dinner tonight? I mean, me and Grandmama, of course."

"Yes." She looked away, as if suddenly shy.

He shouldn't be so happy about her coming down to dinner. Or about the dancing lesson, especially since it had been manufactured by the three little matchmakers—there was no doubt about it, spontaneous though it had been made to appear.

Mayhap that explained why, a few minutes later, instead of finishing a letter to Sir Montague, he found himself sketching for the first time in several years. Caroline twirling about the dance floor, the little black currant amethysts about her neck.

He should stop sketching. He should stop thinking about Caroline, too, but the joy in his chest was a difficult thing to ignore. He'd indulge it a little longer, even though it was probably a dreadful mistake.

Chapter Six

Caroline dressed for dinner, leaving the amethyst necklace for last. Should she really wear it? The stones were cool in her hands, their polished edges reflecting the candlelight, but they were not so brilliant that they would be inappropriate for half-mourning.

They felt utterly inappropriate for a vicar's daughter, however. Heavy. Rich in hue. Old enough to have belonged to Henry's mother, who was the daughter of a viscount.

Henry had been right, though—she did enjoy having something of Esther's like this. It was like her best friend was here again with her. And this might be her only opportunity to wear such a fine piece of jewelry. She fixed the clasp behind her neck and straightened the silver chain so the middle pendant was at the hollow of her throat.

Henry may have offered them as a gift, but she'd give them back.

Gazing at her reflection in the narrow looking glass in her chamber, Caroline had to admit the necklace went rather well with her dinner gown, a simple design in slate gray with tiny puffed sleeves. The evening might be a little cool for the cut, but Caroline wasn't the least bit cold. At the last moment, she scooped up her white shawl, but she doubted she'd need it.

The nursery door yawned open, and she paused in the threshold. Julia, Lucy, and Rupert were dressed for bed, nightcaps and all, playing with Cinders on the rug. "Goodnight, dear ones. I trust you'll behave for Polly?"

"Oh, yes." Not one of them met her gaze. Their widening eyes focused on her throat.

Henry was right. They hadn't expected him to go through with it.

"I like your fancy gems." Lucy rose to her feet, reaching to touch the necklace.

"Your uncle loaned them to me. They were your Mama's."

Julia grinned. "How thoughtful of Uncle."

"Yes, indeed." One final embrace for each child and a pat on Cinders's head, and Caroline bid them goodnight.

She was still smiling when she arrived in the coral-pink drawing room. Lady Marsden was not yet down, and Henry was alone, leaning against the mantelpiece, looking so handsome in his black evening coat that her ankles wobbled.

What nonsense.

His expression eager, Henry strode toward her and bowed. "You look lovely, Caro."

She did? Of course not. He meant the necklace. She curtsied. "The amethysts are stunning, are they not? Thank you."

"The amethysts? Oh. . .yes." He glanced at her throat before his gaze met hers again. "So the children noticed?"

"Rupert didn't care a whit, Lucy touched each gem, but Julia, well, she seemed rather pleased with herself."

"Did she think she'd fooled us?"

"I think so. I tried hard not to laugh at her expression." She sighed. "I hope they sleep well after such an active day. It was kind of you to help demonstrate the waltz for them."

"I do not know if I would call it a demonstration. No one learned to waltz. But I do not think that was their idea, anyway."

"What do you mean?"

"It seems they have a new conspirator among their ranks. Grandmama." He glanced around Caroline as if ensuring Lady Marsden didn't linger in the threshold. "We were duped into participating in yet another matchmaking scheme."

"That isn't possible. Lady Marsden summoned us, but you were out. You dropped by because of the noise."

He shook his head. "Edgar informed me that Grandmama requested my presence in the ballroom at once, so I didn't even change from my riding attire."

Shame coursed, hot and fast, through Caroline's veins. It was one thing for the children to scheme at making her their aunt and guardian. Surely Lady Marsden was not in agreement with them?

"I doubt she was matchmaking, Henry. She probably only listened to the children's wish to see you happy and she thought to involve you in a fun activity."

His brow quirked. "Dancing?"

"Well, it is not as if your grandmother is in robust enough health for lawn bowling."

"Ah, Grandmama." Henry's gaze fixed behind Caroline's ear. "How good to see you downstairs, ma'am."

Dressed in a black evening gown, Lady Marsden leaned on a silver-tipped cane that matched her curls. "No one is more pleased than I to be out of my chamber. Caroline's ministrations have proved beneficial indeed, but I do not wish to overdo on this leg. Shall we go straight into dinner, or do you insist on standing on ceremony and forcing us all to chat in the drawing room first?"

Caroline bit back a smile as Henry offered his arm to his grandmother. "I am delighted to forgo formalities. Shall we?"

Caroline followed them into the dining room, a chamber she'd always loved but had seldom had opportunity to visit. It was painted in the palest of blues, trimmed in white and gilt, and crowned with an elaborately decorated ceiling. Square windows overlooked the front lawn, and the other walls boasted large paintings, mostly landscapes, but above the fireplace hung the portrait of one of Henry's ancestors, wearing a pleasant smile and his ermine-trimmed earl's robes.

If only that ancestor knew what his youngest descendants had planned—marriage between Henry and a lowly governess—he'd scowl down upon them.

Once they were seated around the polished table, Henry offered grace and they started on bowls of delicate pea soup. The flavor was exquisite, but Caroline couldn't appreciate it, not with wondering what Henry thought of the children's scheme.

He probably wanted to send her away now more than ever.

Now, more than ever, Henry wanted to make Caroline smile again. When she grinned, she seemed to glow from within, and that glow spilled its invisible light onto Henry. There was something addictive about her smiles, and he wanted to be the one to coax one out of her now.

At the moment, however, he couldn't think of a thing to say to her.

Well, that wasn't true. He thought of plenty of things. He just couldn't say any of them aloud.

I like your hair like that.

Did you have a suitor in Spain?

Your eyes are liquid in this light.

He cleared his throat. "The fish is delicious."

"Yes, the watercress is an excellent complement. I believe Cook prepared a similar dish the last time I dined here."

He'd forgotten that night, until now. "Esther was about to leave for her season in London, wasn't she? She was eighteen."

"Nineteen. It was her second season. Your mother invited Papa and me to dine and bid her farewell before she left."

Caroline was nearly two years younger than Esther, but as a vicar's daughter, never had a season of her own. Had it bothered her? Henry couldn't tell, but she smiled now, so he did the same. "It was a lovely night."

"Your memory is addled. I kicked you under the table for telling Papa I took off my shoes and waded in the stream."

There was her smile. Warmth suffused Henry's chest. "If I tattled on you, you must have deserved it."

"I probably did."

Grandmama squinted across the table at Caroline. "Why, those were your mother's, Henry."

It took him a moment to realize what Grandmama was talking about, but her gaze was fixed on Caro's throat. "Yes, and Esther's favorite when we were small. She called the amethysts black currants. I always thought she'd want it after Mama passed, but she chose other pieces. She told me these were mine to do with as I wished, and I thought Caroline should have them as something to remember Esther by."

Upon reflection, what Esther had actually said was, "*These are for the next Lady Marsden.*"

"A far too generous token." Caroline looked imploringly at Grandmama.

"Nonsense. You should have something of Esther's. What a thoughtful gesture,

Henry." Grandmama made it sound like a question. Now that he thought of it, Grandmama might well have been present when Esther told him the amethysts should be for his wife. Henry quickly finished his fish.

Grandmama dominated the rest of the conversation on the prices of muslin, sprigged and Indian, at various linen drapers she'd visited before her most recent gout flare—not a subject on which Henry was well versed, but he appreciated the fact that they weren't talking about the amethysts anymore. Caroline seemed relieved, too, helping keep the conversation on muslin alive until the last bite of sponge cake.

Henry rose and helped his grandmother to stand. "If you don't mind, I'll come through with you ladies." The convention might be for gentlemen to remain in the dining room a while, but he far preferred the ladies' company tonight.

"Of course." Grandmama took his arm and they ambled to the drawing room, where she settled in a plush armchair by the fire. "What was I saying a moment ago?"

"The muslins in Newcastle-under-Lyme were vastly overpriced." Caroline assisted Grandmama with the ottoman and then found a seat on the settee perpendicular to the older woman.

"I suppose I said all there was to say, then. So Caro, what adventures do you and the children have tomorrow?"

"Sums and poems. A little French. They have been asking to see the fallow deer in the park, so if it is well with you, Henry, I may take them for a constitutional."

Ah, yes. Henry had told them not to go alone on their first day here. "Perhaps I should go with you. I've been told some of the trees have fallen, and I'd hate for anyone to get hurt or lost."

"We can't get lost if we stay on the path to the lodge." She smiled.

"I imagine that old place is in shambles now." Henry dropped into the chair opposite the settee. "I wanted to live there."

"You adored that rustic place." Grandmama stifled a yawn behind her hand.

"It was quiet. Peaceful." Father never darkened its door. He could take a sketchbook and stick of charcoal and draw for hours without fear of being caught.

"I do not recall peace there so much as carryings-on," Caroline contradicted. "Blind Man's Bluff and Bridge of Sighs and Cat in the Corner."

Such silly, fun games. "You're right."

An inelegant snort sounded from Grandmama's chair. She'd fallen asleep, her head tipped at an uncomfortable-looking angle against the back of the chair. She'd have a terrible crick when she woke.

Caroline sighed. "I should wake her."

"Let her rest. If you don't mind sitting up and talking to me when our chaperone is asleep."

"We do not require a chaperone. I am but a governess." She laughed a little. "What a silly notion the children have, trying to make a match of us."

"We are not an expected pair, are we?"

"I am not highborn. You're meant to marry an heiress."

"That is what my father instructed me to do, yes."

"If I married, my husband would be scholar. Or a vicar like Papa."

"I suppose so." But Henry didn't like the thought of her marrying a vicar. In fact, his mood soured considerably.

"The whole idea of matchmaking an earl and a governess is absurd." She shivered.

"Are you cold?" Henry rose. "Come move closer to the fire."

Caro's head shook. "I don't wish to wake your grandmother in the commotion. I'll just put on my shawl." She opened the white rectangle and attempted to wrap it around her.

Somehow it hadn't quite unfolded enough to cover her bare arms. "'Tis twisted." Henry bent down and reached around her, taking the silky edge of the shawl in his fingers. He spread it so it draped over her shoulders. "Better?"

"Yes."

He was closer to her than when they waltzed, his face inches over hers. His hand still rested on her arm, holding the shawl, and his gaze fixed to her shell-pink lips.

"Henry?"

"Yes?"

She didn't continue. Neither did he. His brain had ceased working, other than to think Father might have been wrong after all. About everything. Maybe with God's help he could be that old Henry again, not just as he was before Father punished him, but before he even met Augusta. He could be the person he'd been when Caroline was his dear friend. They could have that closeness again.

Maybe more.

Creak.

Caroline bent back, away from him. "What was that?"

"Nothing." A servant. A shift of logs on the fire. Henry had to tell her now. "I've been thinking about our discussion about the children's schooling. I—"

Crick-crick. "Shh."

Henry went cold and flinched, as if cool water splashed him. "Is that the children?"

"I fear so." Caro's eyes shut.

Henry was off the settee before he took another breath. Sure enough, three little figures in white nightcaps huddled in the threshold, eyes wide. "Go to bed, the lot of you."

"But we're thirsty." Julia pirouetted.

"There is a pitcher in the nursery. You know what Miss Dempsey has said about eavesdropping. Go to bed."

"We couldn't hear everything," Lucy insisted. "Like what you said about our schooling."

"Do you like Miss Dempsey's fancy gems, Uncle?" Julia spun again.

Rupert ran past them into the drawing room and flopped on the settee beside Caroline. "I want to go to the lodge and play Blind Man's Bluff."

"How long have you stood there?" Caroline gaped. "No, young sir, there will be no Blind Man's Bluff."

Rupert kicked in protest. "Pweese."

"Please!" The girls jumped up and down.

"Enough." Henry's bellow startled Grandmama into wakefulness and drew every wide eye. "You are out of bed, listening to conversations that are none of your affair, breaking all sorts of Miss Dempsey's rules."

"He's cross," Rupert observed to Caroline, which somehow only made Henry angrier.

Lucy reached for her governess's hand. "Miss Dempsey, come—"

"No." Henry willed his voice to calm. "She bade you goodnight at your bedtime. You do not get another chance, because you broke her rules and snuck out from bed. Go now."

They stared at him for a moment before dashing from the drawing room.

It was only when he turned back from the door and faced Caroline that he realized he'd shouted. Just like his father.

The old Henry was far too gone to come back. There was no hope for him after all.

Chapter Seven

Caroline hopped to her feet, her hands extended. "I'm sorry. They're not usually so. . .disobedient."

"They're a persistent lot," Lady Marsden corrected, pushing herself to stand. "I'm to bed now as well. And no, I do not require assistance from either one of you. Stay and enjoy the evening."

There would be no enjoying the evening now, though. There was much to say, and Henry paced the plush gold rug like a caged bear. She'd never seen him angry like this before.

"I am sorry," she repeated. "It's no excuse, but they're worried."

"I'm not angry at them. Well, I am, but I'm far angrier at myself. How could I have done that?"

"Done what?"

"Raise my voice. Shout at them. But it's good it happened now, with you here, so now I know for certain."

This made no sense. "Know what?"

He stopped on his heel and turned to her. "Did you ever make the acquaintance of my school friend, Sir Montague Hurst?"

"You brought him home with you one holiday." He'd worn the tallest hat she'd ever seen to church, and from her seat behind him, she couldn't see the pulpit. What had he to do with the children eavesdropping?

"The children aren't the only ones interested in making me a match. He's written to me about his cousin Cassandra as a potential bride."

Oh. That was what Sir Montague Hurst had to do with the subject. Matchmaking.

She shouldn't be surprised that Henry would wed. Hadn't they discussed him marrying an heiress, not an hour ago? But it had been hypothetical. And then, on the heels of that discussion, he'd seemed like he might kiss her on the settee when he helped her with her shawl.

She was such a bacon-brained ninny.

He was an earl. She was a governess. If they cared for one another, it wouldn't be the most shocking marriage in the *beau monde*, but he did not care for her the way she did for him. How many times must she remind herself of their differences?

She should say something to cover up the pain sluicing through her chest. She forced a smile. "You're thinking of taking a bride, then?"

"Yes. No. I mean, for a moment, I considered it. It's what normal people do, isn't it?" She swallowed hard. "In your position, yes."

He ran a hand through his hair, mussing it. "I hadn't even put the letter from Monty down before I came to my senses. After Augusta, I knew I couldn't ever marry. Or have a family."

That was one of the things the gossips said about Henry. He was forever scarred by Augusta's rejection, and it rendered him incapable of feeling anything for anyone else. Her heart ached in a new way now. "You must have loved Augusta Davies-Thorpe a great deal."

"I thought I did."

But he'd been refused as publicly as he'd proposed. "She broke your heart."

"I was hurt, yes, but it was worse when I returned here to Marsden Hall afterward." He stared into the fire. "Father was home, too. . ."

He couldn't finish, so Caroline took a tentative step toward him. "Pardon my saying so, but your father was not a kind man. We were all afraid of him. I imagine he scolded and shamed you."

Henry shrugged—no, not a shrug. He rolled his coat from his shoulders and pulled it off entirely, leaving him standing in his shirtsleeves and embroidered gray waistcoat. Then he loosened one of his cuffs and rolled up his sleeve, revealing a raised cluster of long, thin scars on his forearm.

The injuries were no accident. Nauseated with horror, Caroline laid her fingers atop the scars, which had been left by a narrow cane or lash. "He beat you. My poor Henry."

"Whenever he was home from London, if I showed any behavior he found undignified of my position, he attempted to correct it. Rambunctious play with you and Esther. Having sticky hands. Or when my tutor told him I showed promise in my artwork. Art is something to possess and display, not to create—it's improper for someone like an earl to engage in such wastes of time, you see. After that, if he caught me sketching, he caned my arm so I'd remember it the next time I was tempted to draw anything. When I cried or defied him or got angry, the beatings were doubled. Emotions are weakness, you see."

Caro's dinner crawled up her throat. "He was wrong."

"I thought so, too; you know I did. That is why I determined to be an artist, when he forbade it. A person who saw joy in life, when he valued dignity. A romantic fool for the lofty cause of love. That's why I proposed to Augusta at Almack's in front of the so-called polite world, so Father would hear of it and know I was not going to be like him. He could cut me off as he had Esther, but he couldn't prevent me from inheriting the title, or Marsden Hall. I felt I had the upper hand. But Augusta said no to my proposal, as you and everyone knows, and when I came home, well, I cannot show you what he did without removing my shirt altogether."

"But you were a grown man then." Why did Henry not fight back?

"I feared what he'd do to Mama if his wrath against me went unsatisfied. The way she cowered around him, I long suspected he struck her sometimes, too, but she never admitted it. In any event, it was far preferable to let him dole out his punishment."

She wanted to embrace him, to comfort him, but they were alone in the drawing room and he was in his shirtsleeves and it was most improper, so all she could do was keep holding his scarred arm. "How horrible. I know not what to do but pray."

"I could scarcely pray for myself, because I was certain God was in agreement with Father. Since being back here at Marsden Hall though, I've wondered if I've been wrong about God. I think I've always known God wouldn't have wanted Father to strike me like he did."

"Hurting you like that? Attempting to beat your talent and joy out of you? Never."

"But Father was right. After Augusta's rejection, I was the subject of gossip. If I'd behaved with more decorum as Father insisted, gone about things properly, I would have spared myself, and Augusta, a great deal of embarrassment. After that, I closed myself off from everyone, and lo and behold, I didn't get hurt. If I didn't laugh, I wasn't ashamed later by my lack of dignity for laughing too loud. If I didn't dance, no one could judge me for being too enthusiastic. If I did things Father's way, I was spared pain." He gestured to the scars. "Physical as well as internal."

"You closed yourself off from Esther. Your grandmother. From your home. From sketching and painting, which is part of who you are. From happiness." He'd gained a reputation as an unsmiling, serious, stoic man. Some said even a bitter one. Now she understood why, but it was tragic.

"It is easier to be the earl Father envisioned me being when I am not around people who knew me when I was younger. And it's far easier to avoid painful memories of Marsden Hall if I am not here."

"Happiness is not an old, bad habit. As for Marsden Hall, there are good memories, too. And new ones to make with the children."

"What I did today, making a fool of myself in the ballroom? Even though I'm scared to be around the children because I fear I'll hurt them, because all I know is intimidation and beatings, I chose to get to know them. To be joyful with them and with you. I liked it, laughing and dancing and spinning. But there was a price. Shame."

"You feel ashamed? Why?"

"Because I behaved without dignity."

Poor, dear Henry. "You were not in the least undignified. You were charming and caring and gentle. God gave us joy and laughter. Enjoyment. You showed care to Esther's children, and that is a good thing. Happiness is a good thing, too."

"Happiness is hard for me to experience without feeling guilty. I fear I'll make another poor decision. Tonight I almost thought I could be the old me again, I almost gave into it, before the children made noise and you and I—"

His mouth clamped shut. He turned away from her, and she had to release his arm. He took a long breath, and then turned back. "But look what happened. In my weakness, I grew angry at the children. I yelled at them. I was like my father."

"You were stern but not abusive, Henry. There is a great deal of difference. I am vexed with them often, but the world does not end. Neither does my care for them."

He fixed his cuff. "You would have handled things differently."

True. "I try to coax them first, but I've been known to raise my voice."

"What about next time? What if I turn into my father and do more than raise my voice?"

"Esther didn't act like your father."

"Esther was his daughter. He didn't beat her; he allowed her and Mother their so-called feminine weaknesses, although I suspect he struck Mother."

Maybe that explained why Henry's mother never defended him, then. She, too, was frightened. But with all her heart, Caroline wished someone had intervened and protected Henry and his mother.

Papa would have, had he known. A wave of grief for her father swept her, swirling with her grief for Henry and all he'd suffered at his father's hands. Tears pricked her eyes, but she blinked them away.

"You are not your father. I know you. I do not think you would ever hurt the children, Henry."

"I'll ensure I won't. I'll stay far away from them for their protection."

Caroline's heart skipped a beat before pounding fast in her ears. "You were going to tell me before we were interrupted—you're sending them away to school after all? Them and me?"

"No. I was going to tell you I won't send the children away. Or you either. You were right. They deserve consistency and love, and that's what you are. I could never tear you from them. But I was also going to say that I wanted to learn how to be their uncle." He donned his coat. "I don't anymore."

"What?"

"I'm leaving. Tomorrow is best. Back to the townhouse in London. I was supposed to go back for a meeting for one of the charities I assist, but I shall leave early. Fear not, Caro. You will be cared for. So will the children. Their every need will be met."

"They need you. Their family. Your care. Your acceptance."

"They'll have you and Grandmama. Goodnight, Caro. Pray excuse me, but I've arrangements to make if I'm to leave in the morning."

"Henry." She reached for him, but he was already gone.

Oh, Lord, guide me now. How could she fix this? What could she say to Henry to help? *There may be nothing I can say or do, Lord. Only you can heal this wound.*

But she hurt, too, for every lash and harsh word Henry had received. For his broken heart. For the years of self-preservation and shame that kept him closed off from love. It was such an irony, too, because the house was full of people who wanted his love desperately.

Caroline swiped the tears from her cheeks and prayed. She spent most of the night praying, too, hardly sleeping.

She rose before dawn, dressed, and donned a cloak and bonnet. A walk might do her good, and the children wouldn't be up for a while yet. Besides, Polly was with them.

The morning air was cool against her face and in her lungs, but she warmed quickly as she tromped over the knolls. Her prayers were scattered things, unfocused but desperate. While she was grateful Henry no longer intended to separate her and the children, the future nevertheless looked unbearable. Perhaps she could convince him to reconsider before he left this morning.

She was stomping excess mud from her boots at the kitchen stoop when Edgar saw her from the window.

He flung the door wide. "Thank God, Miss Dempsey. You must come inside right away. The children are gone."

❧

"Gone?" Henry rose from his seat at the library desk, where he'd been jotting down final instructions for the estate manager. "What do you mean, gone? Out to find another sheep? Hiding from you and Polly to avoid their lessons?"

Caroline, splattered in mud from what looked to have been a long walk through tall grass, thrust a paper at him. "Gone, as in looking for the hunting lodge."

The note was scribbled in a familiar, childish scrawl on another piece of his expensive vellum. "They took the dog and went to the lodge to play Blind Man's Bluff."

"They eavesdropped on that particular part of the conversation last night, remember? But I suspect it's a scheme to get us to follow them."

To get him somewhere he'd been happy. He must scowl a great deal for the children to think him so miserable.

Well, he was scowling again. "They know I'm leaving, then?"

"No. They were asleep when I looked in on them in the nursery last night, and it was quite early when I left for my walk. Rupert rises at dawn, but he knows to play quietly until Polly brings breakfast. I planned to speak to you again before I told them."

And try to talk him out of leaving, no doubt. Her persistence was one of the things he admired most about her. That, and the way she made him feel safe and far less broken than he was. Like he could be a loving man.

If he hadn't been too damaged to take a wife, he would have gladly fallen prey to the children's matchmaking scheme. It had opened his eyes to what a lovely, dear, wonderful woman Caroline truly was, and that was why he'd almost kissed her last night.

"I'm sorry my nieces and nephew are such imps. They'll stop such antics once I've left Marsden Hall, I trust."

"I wish they'd stopped with the flowers." She backtracked to the door. "They have truly put me to the test with this, especially since they are forbidden from wandering the park alone. I'll take Edgar with me, but I wanted you to know what was afoot. Especially since you are leaving this morning."

The urge to go along rose in Henry's chest, but what if he lost his temper again? "I shall bid the children farewell when you return."

"I wish you wouldn't."

"Tell them good-bye?"

"Leave." Her fingers fidgeted at her waist. "You should stay here at Marsden Hall. With all of us."

He rubbed the back of his neck. "Caro."

"Postpone your departure by a day or two, then, so we can speak more on the matter. You might speak to the vicar about it, too."

He rubbed his sleeve, just over the scars. "I know in my head God can help me with my feelings, to not become like my father, but I am not sure my heart believes it."

Cinders's loud barks sounded from the hall. Father would have shuddered at the impropriety of it all, loud children and a barking dog indoors, but Henry exhaled in relief. The noise meant the children were back safely. He didn't like the idea of them wandering the park or playing in the dilapidated lodge. It had been years since anyone used it, and it probably hadn't even been safe when he, Esther, and Caroline played there. The floorboards were half rotted—

"Miss Dempsey!" Julia cried.

Caro's face contorted, and she dashed to the door. Cinders leapt on her legs a second before Julia plowed into Caro's hip, her face red and wet. "I'm sorry! I'm so sorry!"

Henry's stomach dropped to his boots. "Where are your brother and sister?"

Julia's words were difficult to make out between sobs, but Rupert's name was clear enough. Myriad scenarios flashed through his mind, from scratches to head bumps to far, far worse.

The stricken look on Caro's face revealed that she, too, tried not to think the worst. "How is he hurt, darling?"

"There was a crack and he fell through the floor."

Rupert's little leg, caught in the rotten floorboards. Poor fellow must be scared out of his wits.

Henry didn't think, just dashed out the door.

"I'll have him home safe in a trice." Henry spared Caroline a backward glance. "I'll take a horse to bring him home. Don't fret."

Chapter Eight

How could Caroline not fret? Rupert could be scraped, stuck, perhaps even bleeding. He was probably crying for Esther.

All he would get was Caroline, a sorry substitute.

What sort of governess was she—what sort of friend to Esther was she—that she'd left the house without checking on the children this morning? True, Polly dressed and fed them. Also true, the children were at their home, not imprisoned, and could play outside.

But not in the park. And not a mile distant at the lodge.

Henry was probably reconsidering his decision to let her stay on with the children now. She was a terrible governess. A terrible friend.

But she couldn't love Rupert or Lucy or Julia more if they were her own. Panic welled in her chest at the thought of not being with Rupert when he was hurt and frightened. Henry wouldn't lose his temper—she was sure of it, even if he was not—but she nevertheless wanted to be at the lodge.

She cupped Julia's head in a brief pat. "Stay here. I'm going to help Rupert."

"On a horse?"

"Alas, I do not ride, as you well know. I must do the unladylike thing and run like a hoyden."

Henry's father would gape.

"I'm coming, too. I'm fast."

Caroline could put down her proverbial foot, but there wasn't time. Besides, Julia was worried about Rupert, too. Caroline took her hand and they made haste out the front door to the portico, Cinders running ahead. She released Julia's hand once they reached the grass. "We must lift our hems, darling, so we don't trip and fall."

If they were going to cause a spectacle by running, they might as well go a step further and show their ankles to the world, too.

Pale morning light streamed through the canopy of trees as they entered the wooded park, and it took a moment for Caroline to adjust to the dimness. Cinders dashed ahead, followed by Julia, who scrambled into the carpet of decaying leaves and soft earth.

"Stay on the path," Caroline called. There was no risk of getting lost that way. While she'd tromped through this park countless times growing up, that was long ago, and nothing looked familiar anymore.

"This way is faster than the path," Julia yelled back at her.

Caroline almost lost her footing. "What do you mean, *this* way? How would you know that?" The children weren't allowed in the deer park. They couldn't have snuck out here before today without Caroline knowing.

Julia pointed as she ran on. "Turn right at that bent tree."

"I'm glad you thought to look for landmarks so you could find your way home." The words came out in pants as Caroline ran after her, pressing the sudden ache in her side.

"We didn't. It was on our map."

"You have a map?" Who would dared have drawn one for them? Lady Marsden?

This matchmaking scheme had gone too far, for too long. It must stop once and for all. Once they'd seen to Rupert, of course.

They broke through to a rise above the simple wooden lodge. It looked smaller than she remembered, and the years had not been kind to it. The windows were dark with dinge, and even from this distance of twenty or so yards, cracks were visible in them.

Untethered, Henry's horse grazed outside the lodge. Caroline exhaled in relief as she scampered down the slope. She could hear Rupert's cries, but Henry probably had the child in his arms already.

The interior of the little lodge was dim, but not so dark she couldn't see Lucy huddled against the far wall, crying, knees curled into her chest. Or Henry lying on his stomach before a hole in the floor, his head inside and arms reaching down to the cellar below. Rupert's frightened wails emanated from beneath Caroline's feet.

Rupert's leg hadn't fallen through the rotten wood. All of him had.

She dropped to her knees at the edge of the hole. At once, Henry's arm shot out to hold her back. "I don't want you falling in, too."

She scuttled back. "I'll go outside to the cellar door and get him that way."

"I've already tried. It's locked and chained." Henry's voice was muffled. "Rupert, try once more, lad. Stretch your arms."

"I'm here, Rupert, my love. I'm here." Caroline willed her voice to sound hopeful and calm for him while she skirted Henry to wrap a comforting arm around Lucy. *Lord, help us.*

Henry pushed backward and swung his legs into the hole. "Be ready to take him when I lift him out."

"Henry!" Caroline reached for him, but he'd shoved himself into the dark pit below. She flopped to her belly and peered down into the cellar, but it was too dark to see much of anything. Rupert's cries echoed in the small space, but Henry's gentle words and the squelch of boots on thick mud were audible, too. The smells of rot, must, and damp made Caroline's nose twitch, and her chest and stomach ached as jagged pieces of floorboard pushed into her.

How much worse it must be for Rupert and Henry. Clearly the cellar had been flooded at some point and was still wet, slick, and uncomfortable.

"Here he comes." The top of Henry's head came into view about two feet down, and then Rupert's as Henry lifted the boy above his head. She grabbed Rupert under his arms and heaved, rolling her body sideways to pull him the rest of the way. He lay on her chest, sniffling, his breath hitching, his clothes wet and muddy, but whole and hale.

She squeezed him tightly and kissed his hair. "My little one, where are you hurt?"

"He's bleeding." Julia sounded panicked.

A quick inspection revealed a scrape on his spindly calf, probably from the rotten floorboards when he fell through, but it would heal. "He'll be fine. Rupert, darling, where did you land?"

He patted his bottom.

She clasped him tighter and then shifted him out of her arms. "Stay here, my darling."

"George!" he shouted.

"We'll find him."

Lucy and Julia embraced him while Caroline rolled back to her stomach, leaning down into the hole, her arms extended. Henry was gone.

Panic filled her throat. "Henry?"

"Here." He reappeared, holding up a muddy George. Stretching, he handed the horse up to her.

Caroline grabbed the damp toy and scuttled to Rupert before returning to the hole in the floor. Henry looked up at her.

"I don't think we'll be playing any Blind Man's Bluff today," he said, his lips twitching.

"Your face is bleeding."

He absently fingered the cut on his forehead. "It's rather dark down here. I walked into something."

"Give me your hands."

"Caro." His smile was sad. "You're the strongest woman I know, but I don't think you can pull me out."

"Give me your hands, Henry."

"Go back and get help. I'm quite comfortable down here."

She didn't budge, other than to smile back. "Your hands, Henry."

"You aren't going to listen to reason, are you?"

"When have I ever?"

"Very well, but you're not going to get me out that way. Move back, my dear Caro, but not too far. Be ready for me."

She'd been ready for him since he waltzed with her ten years ago. When he jumped and gripped the jagged edge of the hole, she grabbed his coat and tugged with all her might.

Henry pulled himself up and swung his legs up and over the edge, praying all the while the broken floorboards would hold. Caroline's grasp on him helped, but the way she gripped his coat and shirt choked him, cutting off his air.

But he loved her for it.

How had it happened, him falling in love with her? When? He'd fought against caring for anyone, built a wall so high and thick no one could get over or around it. But God had found the cracks. So had Caroline.

And his nieces and nephew.

God had given him these children. They were a gift as much as a responsibility. They were not here for him to simply clothe and educate and feed. He was meant to love them, too. And he did love them. At the thought of Rupert being hurt, Henry had been terrified. All he could think about was getting the lad out of the pit, and he hadn't thought a moment about how he'd get out of the hole himself. His own well-being was not a priority.

He'd jump into a thousand pits of mud for these children.

Once on the debatably solid ground of the floor, he pulled Rupert to him, cradling his nephew against his chest. "I heard you have a cut."

Rupert pulled up his trouser leg, and Henry exhaled in relief. A bandage would be all the treatment necessary. "Any bumps? Goose eggs?" He rubbed Rupert's head, then the girls' heads for good measure.

"Silly Uncle, we did not fall down." Lucy patted his knee. "Why is your voice shaking?"

Was it? "Because I was scared, and one doesn't always recover from being frightened in an instant."

"You told us not to come here. Are you going to punish us?" Lucy's eyes went wide with uncertainty.

"I don't know." His gaze met Caroline's. What was he supposed to do?

She simply stared at him, waiting.

"I shall speak to Miss Dempsey, but at the moment I'm of the mind this experience is punishment enough. You won't come here again, and maybe now you'll obey the rules."

"That's it? Aren't you angry we disobeyed you?" Julia looked confused.

"Of course I am." In fact, a fresh wave of frustration flooded his chest and made his pulse pound in his temples. "I told you expressly not to come here, yet you did. *This* was why, because I wanted to keep you safe. I don't like your disobedience at all."

Caroline grinned, as if something wonderful had happened.

"What?" He adjusted Rupert's gentle weight on his lap, feeling suddenly frustrated with Caroline, too. "What's funny? Are you laughing at me?"

"You're *angry.*"

"Yes. I am. I—"

Something sparked alive in him, like a wick caught flame and cast light in a dark room. He was *angry with the children.* He was upset they'd disobeyed him and put their precious lives in danger.

But he hadn't clenched a fist or shouted or threatened to beat obedience into them, as had been done to him. He wasn't remotely tempted to spout lectures about propriety and decorum. He didn't care a whit that muddy George had left streaks on his waistcoat, or that Lucy played with his coat buttons and might well pull one off, or that Cinders barked outside the lodge, or that the lot of them were a filthy mess.

They were safe. They were together, and all he wanted to do was hold them close, even though frustration still pumped through his veins.

"I'm angry." He grinned at Caroline.

"Yes, you are." She grinned back. "And you are not your father."

Thank You, Lord. You've been with me all this time, haven't You? Thank You for these children, this opportunity to be happy again. To be who You want me to be, not who my father wanted me to be.

He laughed. He couldn't help it. He laughed and squeezed Rupert so hard the boy wiggled in protest. "Sorry." He let Rupert go, but Rupert didn't crawl off his lap.

"I don't know why you're laughing about being angry," Julia said.

"Well, we're happy, too," Caroline said, hugging her.

Lucy grimaced. "About what?"

"That you are safe."

Julia sighed. "You might not punish us when we get back to the house, but we're surely going to school now."

"I don't want to go away to school." Rupert pulled George over his eyes.

Caroline took his small hand. "Oh, darling, you're not going to school. Your uncle has already decided that you three will stay here at Marsden Hall."

"He has?" Lucy straightened, sure enough forgetting to loosen her hold on Henry's coat button. Off it went in her grasp.

"No school?" Rupert waved George in the air, almost knocking Henry on the chin.

"Our plan worked!" Lucy marveled.

Julia clapped. "You're getting married?"

"Of course not." Caroline flushed. "Your uncle is leaving for London—"

"I must attend a function," Henry interrupted. "But I will come back."

"But—" Caroline blurted then cut herself off.

There would be time to explain to her soon. First, he must reassure the children. "I loved your mother very much. I've been sad for a long time, but you've reminded me what it's like to be happy. You will stay with me, if that is well with you."

"Yes!" they said together.

"Good." He grinned. "But no more sheep in the house."

"May I still run over the grass with my hem up to my knees?" Julia demonstrated. "Miss Dempsey and I didn't wish to trip when we ran here, even though it was unladylike to hoist our skirts—"

"That was an exceptional case," Caroline said, her cheeks pinking.

"Indeed." Henry forced himself to keep a straight face.

"So, no school?" Lucy repeated. "What about Miss Dempsey?"

He glanced at Caroline. "Your mother picked the finest person to raise you, if she was not able to herself."

"You?" Lucy touched his face.

"No, sweetheart. I meant Miss Dempsey."

"You," Caroline amended. "You're their guardian. Esther and Richard chose you."

"And they chose you to be a loving, guiding presence in their children's lives."

"They chose both of you." Julia stuck out her lip. "You should get married."

"About that," Henry began.

Cinders's barks increased, alerting them to the appearance of three groundskeepers from Marsden Hall. They burst into the lodge, and one bore a coiled rope over his shoulder.

At the sight of the group on the floor, they gaped and offered hasty bows. "Milord."

Henry rose to his full height, setting Rupert on the ground. "How good of you to come. Who sent you?"

"Once word went to Lady Marsden there might be a problem here, milord, she urged us to make haste in case help was needed."

"It is much appreciated. As you can see, we are well, but the lodge is in desperate need of repair. I've neglected the matter for too long."

One of the men tugged his forelock. "We'll see to it right away, milord."

"When convenient." Henry tipped his head at the door and met Caroline's gaze. "Shall we get Rupert's leg cleaned up?"

They made their way back to the house on the path, Rupert astride the gelding and the girls taking turns in the saddle with him. Cinders ran ahead, out of sight. They were almost to the edge of the park when a flash of white-mottled chestnut dashed through the trees ahead of them.

"A deer!" Julia's voice was soft and high.

"I want to pet it," Lucy announced.

"Is it a boy deer?" Rupert clutched George.

"I did not see antlers, but I suppose it could be a young buck," Caroline said.

"And bucks are not much for petting." Henry smiled.

"I want to see another one." Lucy sighed.

"Soon, perhaps." Henry led them across the grassy yard to the portico. "We'll take a walk together in the park another day, shall we?"

"We have a map." Lucy slid off the saddle into Henry's arms. Then he hoisted Rupert to the ground.

"Ah, yes, the map." Caroline had almost forgotten. "Did Lady Marsden draw it for you?"

Julia shook her head. "We found it in a nursery drawer."

Henry's breath caught. "May I see it?"

She pulled it from her pocket. The paper had been folded multiple, imprecise times into a strange lump, but Henry recognized it immediately.

"I drew this. A long time ago."

Caroline's gaze met his. "So you did."

"I shall have to draw a better one now."

"You'll draw again?"

"I confess I already started something." The sketch of her dancing.

Her eyes were damp with tears.

Within minutes, they were ensconced in the nursery, seeing to Rupert's leg. Grandmama joined them, and the children regaled her and Polly with the tale of their adventure. Once Rupert was bandaged, Caroline stepped away.

Henry followed her. "Is everything all right?"

"I was going to order biscuits and milk for the children. And bathwater."

"Afterward, may I have a moment?"

A look of fear flashed her countenance, but she nodded.

Chapter Nine

For some ridiculous reason, being alone with Henry sent a flutter of nerves from Caroline's stomach to her throat. No doubt he wished to discuss his new plan to be a family with the children and keep her on as governess. Nothing to worry about.

But she couldn't help wishing she'd had the chance to wash up and change out of her dirty clothes first.

How trivial of her. Henry didn't care what she looked like. She was his wards' governess. She really mustn't fixate on her feelings for him anymore. Indeed, she should be jubilant that the children weren't seriously hurt and that Henry's heart had begun healing today.

God, for this happy outcome, I thank You.

Nevertheless, she was patting her hair as she accompanied Henry to the library.

His hair was a darling, messy disaster. She loved it. One curly lock was stuck to the scrape on his forehead, however.

"You should see to that now."

"This?" His hand absently found the wound. "It's nothing."

"It requires bandaging."

"In a moment. I wanted to tell you something." He indicated that she take a seat by the small fire burning in the grate, and he sat opposite her. "Whilst I'm in London I'm obliged to attend a dinner with Sir Montague Hurst where he'll no doubt introduce me to his cousin Cassandra. The one he thinks to make a match with me."

She'd all but forgotten that, but now that he mentioned it, her stomach felt sour all over again. "You've reconsidered your decision not to marry then?"

"I have. Now that I know I can be angry and not be my father, I realize I would like a family more than anything."

It took a minute to make her mouth work. "I see."

"But I do not wish to marry the fair Cassandra."

"You haven't met her to know whether or not she is fair. Or whether you'd suit."

"You're quite right. I've no idea if she likes spaniels or sings while she sets furniture to rights or runs across the grass with her skirts lifted above her ankles in a most unladylike display."

Why was he teasing her about that? "I was in a hurry. Rupert could have been—"

"I am not chiding you, Caro." He rubbed the bridge of his nose. "I cannot say this right."

"Say what?" That he was going to get married? He'd already done that.

"First, that I owe you everything for showing me I could choose a way to live other than what my father taught me. That just because emotions and children and dogs and sheep and life are messy, that doesn't mean it's not a mess worth relishing. I'd forgotten the joy, perhaps on purpose, because it was easier to believe Father was right than to get hurt again."

"You were protecting yourself, and then you thought you were protecting the children."

"I almost made a dreadful mistake, sending them away."

"But you didn't."

"Thanks to you."

"I only told you the truth. You do not need to be afraid of what you feel. You are not a violent, cruel man. There is life and joy and hope inside of you."

"And love. For the children. And more."

Yes, that. She avoided his gaze. "You'll look for a wife in London then?" A horrible thought occurred. "She'll want to find her own governess."

"Indeed, she probably shall."

Caroline stood. "So what you said at the lodge, about Esther choosing me to be part of the children's lives? All this talk about—"

"I don't want you as their governess." He stood, too.

He was dismissing her. Sending her away from the children she loved as her own. A sudden protective rage coursed through her veins. She might be a mere governess, but she couldn't go without a fight. "But at the lodge you said—"

"I don't want you to marry a vicar, either. In fact, the idea of it sets my teeth on edge."

"Of all the bold, arrogant—"

"Arrogant?"

"—unkind things to say to me, after knowing me my entire life. Henry, I am astonished. Outraged. Angry, and it may be most improper for a lowly governess to speak in such terms to her employer, and an earl at that, but this is madness. You may dismiss me without reference, and even send me from the children. You've the right. But you may not tell me whom to marry."

"I don't want to tell you, but I'd like to ask." He dropped to one knee and reached for her clenched hand. "Could you marry someone as broken and wretched as I?"

"What?" Her anger dissipated like vapor.

"Not someone *like* me, though. Me. I want you to be my countess, Caro. Not because the children love you, although it helps. Because I love you. I don't know when it started. Maybe when you told me I was not my father. Maybe when you got that Scottish air in my head and all day I sang "Waly, Waly," and you reminded me what it was like when we were young, or told me to sketch and paint again or I held you in my arms for the waltz and didn't want to let you go. Maybe it was even when you stepped out of the carriage that first day and you looked like home to me. In my eagerness to forget my happiness, I forgot how beautiful you were, too."

Her smile grew with every phrase, and her cheeks ached from the width of her smile. "I never forgot you, Henry."

"You are a far better person than I, and I like how you encourage me and challenge me and remind me God can take a mess like me and bring joy and hope into my life again. I trust you and I rely upon you, and I want you to rely upon me. But I want you to be happy, and if that means rejecting my proposal, I understand. I know I'm more trouble than I'm worth, and I'll require a heap of patience. I don't want things to be awkward, so if you don't wish to marry me, but wish to stay on with the children, I won't speak a word of this again. Only know how much I love you."

His lips pressed gently against her knuckles, shooting a jolt of liquid fire up her arm.

"Oh," was all she could manage to say.

"I want you to raise Esther and Richard's children with me, and to mother whatever children God sends to us. I want you to never leave Marsden Hall but to help me make it a home again. Caro, could you love me?"

If he only knew. "I loved you when I was fifteen and you waltzed with me. I knew I loved you again when we waltzed with the children. Perhaps I never stopped. I tried, for years and years."

He was on his feet again, pulling her against his chest while his free hand cupped her cheek. "Please don't try to stop again."

"I won't. I can't—"

Then he was kissing her. Quite thoroughly.

When his lips left hers, she smiled against his cheek. "I don't think you ever asked the question, though."

"Didn't I? Hmm." His lips traced her ear. "Will you marry me, my darling friend, my beautiful love?"

"Yes, Henry. Yes, if you think the children will be well with it."

"They're the ones who started us down this path. At least they think they are. Will you marry me soon? I can speak to the vicar and post the banns Sunday."

She couldn't answer, because his lips had found hers again.

A soft squeal sounded from the threshold. Henry pulled back. "Our three little eavesdroppers?"

"Three little matchmakers," she agreed. But they weren't alone. Lady Marsden stood with them, grinning, her hands clasped to her heart.

"Come along, children," Lady Marsden said. "The most important part of matchmaking is stepping back and leaving the pair alone so they can settle the betrothal."

"It looks settled to me," Julia protested. "They were kissing."

"Blech." Rupert pulled George in front of his eyes.

Henry kissed her hand and then beckoned for the children to join them. "Come, family."

Lucy patted Caroline's hand. "You must admit we were good matchmakers, Miss Dempsey."

"She is to be Lady Marsden," Julia corrected.

"I like 'Aunt Caro' better." Henry smiled.

"I do, too." Caroline smiled back. "And yes, you were good matchmakers indeed."

Henry ruffled Rupert's hair. "You and Grandmama set a fine trap for us, and I am happy for it."

"Do not congratulate me on the idea." Lady Marsden chortled. "I merely agreed with them and insisted on a waltz instead of a reel, that's all."

"Nothing was more romantic than waltzing with you lot," Henry teased.

They embraced the children and laughed and accepted Lady Marsden's kisses and were undoubtedly a noisy lot. The previous Earl of Marsden would not have approved.

But Caroline could live with that, and it seemed Henry could, too. God had given them love. Joy. A family.

Caroline kissed Henry's cheek. It hadn't just been the children's matchmaking scheme, though. It seemed the Lord had one in mind, too. Not just for her to marry Henry, but to match them all together—Henry, his grandmother, the children, and Caroline, too, into one family.

Thank You for making such a match of us, Lord.

Susanne Dietze began writing love stories in high school, casting her friends in the starring roles. Today, she's the award-winning author of a dozen new and upcoming historical romances who's seen her work on the ECPA and *Publisher's Weekly* best-seller lists for inspirational fiction. Married to a pastor and the mom of two, Susanne lives in California and enjoys fancy-schmancy tea parties, the beach, and curling up on the couch with a costume drama and a plate of nachos. You can visit her online at www.susannedietze.com and subscribe to her newsletters at http://eepurl.com/bieza5.

The Gentleman Smuggler's Lady

by Michelle Griep

Dedication

To the One I lean on when there is no one else and all the
Poldark fans out there who love a great gallop along the Cornish cliffs

Acknowledgments

Julie Klassen: Brainstormer Extraordinaire
Kelly Klepfer: Male POV Guru
Shannon McNear: Horse Aficionado
Ane Mulligan: Fierce First Reader
MaryLu Tyndall: Editor Supreme
Chawna Schroeder: Plausibility Princess

Chapter One

Pretend I am courageous.
Pretend my heart still beats.
Pretend all manner of blissful things. . .
and that I shall find him alive.

Recreasing a worn scrap of foolscap, Helen Fletcher tucked the paper into her valise, then snapped shut the clasp, wishing most of all she'd never received such horrid news. No one had ever warned her about the dangers of parchment.

Pretend the world is right and well. . . For it would be—or she would die trying to make it so.

She rose from her sleeping berth and paced the few steps to the small mirror on the wall. Grey-blue light, the last from the end of a melancholic day, leaked through the porthole into her tiny accommodations. The vessel *Nancarrow* had never been meant to haul passengers, but the captain had made an exception because of her plight, thank God. Removing her hat from a hook, she did her best to pin up her dark hair beneath the brim, then tied the ribbon securely. Now that they were docked, she'd not be sorry to leave this tucked-away compartment.

"Of course Father will be fine," she whispered to her reflection, taking courage in the voicing of such a hope. She lifted her chin, staring into her own eyes. "And you will be, too."

Whirling about, she retrieved her valise and left her sanctuary of the past fortnight. The corridor was a maze and a dim one at that. Very few vigil lanterns lit the way. She edged past stacks of crates secured against one wall, then turned sideways to squeeze through a narrow throat of a space next to a post. Though she ought be used to it by now, the tight quarters smelled of brine and dampness and overworked ship hands—an odor she wouldn't miss.

At last she made it to the stairs leading to fresh air and England. She'd never been to Cornwall, Bath having been her home before leaving for Ireland as a governess. But as long as she was with Father, it would no doubt feel like home.

She gripped the railing with one gloved hand and ascended the wooden rungs. Her other hand held tightly to all she owned in this life, which was precious little. No matter. God would provide. He always did. Was not the very fact she'd been sent passage to attend her ailing father proof enough of God's surprising provision?

The closer she climbed toward the top deck, the louder shouts echoed and boots thudded. Strange. When they'd set sail from Ireland's green coast, the crew had sung ditties of brisk winds and prows cutting through the ocean blue. Ought not the ballads of mooring at a friendly port be jolly as well? She frowned. No, those rumbles and curses were decidedly not merry at all.

She cleared the last step. Three paces later, she froze. The crew stood against one rail, hands behind their heads. Two masked brigands aimed guns their way. In the center of the deck, the trapdoor of the hold flung wide with more masked scofflaws descending into it like an unholy swarm. Not far from her, the largest man of them all trained a pistol on the captain's chest. A nightmare on the wrong side of slumber.

Captain Ogden's gaze darted her way, the slight tip of his head urging her to retreat back below.

Too late.

Before she could consider the possibility, the scoundrel threatening the captain slipped her a sideways glance. Though brief, she'd never forget the intensity in those brown eyes, commanding her without words to stay put.

"Blast!" the man roared at the crew. "I thought you said you cleared the cabins."

One of the men, the first in a chain of thieves leading from the hold to the gang-plank, grunted as he passed a crate on to the next man. "Aye, sir. I did."

"Apparently, you missed one." The cloth tied over the bottom half of the big man's face riffled with a growl. "You, my lady, over here, if you please."

Though her heart beat hard against her ribcage, she got the distinct impression he meant her no harm—but that didn't mean she'd comply. Biting her lower lip, she studied the distance between her and the side of the ship. Could she jump from railing to wharf? How big the gap? How great the fall?

And why was no one stopping these thieves? Though it was dusk, surely not all from the village could be abed. Perhaps if she merely screamed for help, there'd be no need to risk a twisted ankle. . .or worse.

She opened her mouth—and a glove pressed against her lips. A strong arm pulled her against the side of the man dressed in black. How had he moved so quickly?

"Hush, lady. I'll have none of that. Do you understand?" His free hand yet aimed the gun at the captain, but his terrible gaze stared into her soul.

Pretend that I am brave. Pretend that fear is strength.

For her father's sake, she had to get off this ship. Now. She blinked up at him and nodded.

His hold on her slackened.

She twisted and jerked up her knee, driving home a solid blow he'd remember for a very long time.

⌘

"Oof!"

Wind rushed out of Isaac Seaton's lungs. Sharp, sickening pain rose up his throat.

Thunder and turf! The little spitfire. Scarcely able to breathe, he released the woman. It was either that or drop the gun, which could be deadly.

But so could the snippet of skirt who even now lurched toward the side of the boat. Blast! Sucking in salty air, he barely snagged her arm before she was out reach. She was fast. He'd give her that.

"Join the captain," he strained out then he shoved her toward the man. Stunning, this fiend he'd become—all thanks to Brannigan. Thank God this was his last raid.

She stumbled forward, still clutching her valise. When she joined the captain's side, she turned and glowered, the fury in her gaze calling down the wrath of God upon Isaac's head.

He stifled a smile. A worthy opponent. But no time now to dally with such thoughts. Glancing past the woman and the captain, he checked on progress. Wooden crates passed from man to man, slowly filling the wagon on the wharf. Too slow. The free flow of ale at the Pickled Parrot was paid for until the last of light, at which point some very drunk dockhands could pour out the door and discover this little escapade.

"Make haste, men!" he barked.

"God sees your evil deed." The captain's eyes burned like embers, his glower condemning him to the pits of Sheol.

"Yes, God sees. But evil deed?" Beneath his kerchief, Isaac's mouth curled into a half smile, one that tasted bitter. "That's debatable."

The lady gasped. "Thievery is wrong."

Indeed. A principle he knew as intimately as a lover—one no honest man should ever have to bed. He narrowed his eyes, considering the slip of a woman who accused him. What kind of lady would speak her mind so freely while at the wrong end of a loaded pistol? She stood barely the height of his shoulder, and that with a bonnet atop her head. Brown eyes, not as dark as his own, stared back at him. She was fine of bone, almost birdlike. So slight, should a good wind come along, she might fly off.

But there was nothing fragile about the way she denounced him. Her indictment crawled beneath his skin. "One man's theft is another man's restitution." His voice came out harsher than intended, and he cleared his throat. "Tell me, is it wrong to reclaim what was yours in the first place?"

The captain snorted. "This shipment belongs to Brannigan, unless you wear the Brannigan crest on your finger."

"You are mistaken. Part of this shipment belongs to me." The sight of a barrel—not a crate—slipped by, just past the captain's shoulder. Isaac's free hand curled into a fist. "Blast it! Put those spirits back."

"Aww, but one barrel ain't gonna—"

"Do it." He growled.

Young Graham Ambler, easily distinguishable by the gimp in his step, wheeled about and disappeared into the hold.

Isaac turned back to the captain. "Leastwise the blasting powder is mine. I assure you nothing more will be taken." He fumbled with a pouch tied to his belt and tossed the leather sack to the captain. "For your trouble."

The man caught it, a mighty frown tugging the corners of his mouth. "This does not atone for your behavior."

The captain's words struck him as brutally as the pain leftover from the woman's knee. "I don't expect it to, sir."

A sharp thwack rent the evening as the cover on the hold slammed shut. The last of the crates hefted from man to man, until finally the men themselves emptied down the gangplank.

He whistled for Rook and Hawker to withdraw from guarding the *Nancarrow's* crew, then lowered his pistol. "For future reference, Captain, I suggest you comply more agreeably should smugglers or pirates ever board one of your vessels. Others will not be as forgiving as I."

A curse flew from the captain's mouth, tingeing the lady's cheeks with a fine shade of scarlet.

The wagon rolled down the wharf—just as bawdy drinking songs belched out of the Pickled Parrot, farther up the shore. Clearly if Captain Ogden could not control Isaac's band of well-intentioned smugglers, he'd not be able to contend with besotted dockhands should any decide to ramble this far.

Isaac glanced at the lady, her outline smudging into the darkness nearly upon them. It was neither safe for her to remain here nor to venture into town past those men. He huffed out a sigh at both alternatives, feeling the weight of responsibility. Bending slightly, he hooked her into his arm and up over his shoulder, like a sack of grain.

"Put me down!" She whapped his back with her satchel, a far cry easier to bear than her former attack.

The captain bellowed for his men to pursue—and the chase was on.

Isaac sprinted down the gangplank then swung the lady and himself onto Duchess, his dappled grey waiting where he'd left her. By the time Captain Ogden's crew cleared the deck, Duchess was already crushing gravel beneath her hooves and tearing up toward the village proper.

The lady wriggled in his grasp. "Put me down!"

"In due time." He flexed his arms into bands of steel as she flailed. Clearly, she hadn't the horse sense to know she'd probably be killed if she fell from a galloping mount.

Ahh, yet he could not help but admire such pluck. A slow smile stretched across his face. He might almost enjoy this were he not posing as a felon.

He reined Duchess to a stop in front of the Candlelight Inn. Swinging his leg over, he dismounted and pulled the woman down along with him. She squirmed, and in the scuffle, his kerchief fell to his neck.

His hand shot up, about to tug the cloth into place, but as she glowered at him, he froze. Locks of raven-coloured hair had loosened, lending her a wild appearance—yet altogether lovely. The flush of fear and wind pinked her skin to a most becoming shade. Beneath the fabric of her sleeve, frailty and strength contradicted one another.

Without thinking, he pulled her close and breathed in her sweet rosewater scent—and lost any reason whatsoever. "It is customary, lady, to reward a good deed with a kiss."

"Good deed! You've taken me from the sanctity of a ship to God knows where—"

"The Candlelight Inn," he interrupted.

Her eyes narrowed. "For what purpose I can only imagine."

"For the purpose of saving you from a drunken band of longshoremen and delivering you to a coaching inn that will provide you with the means of getting to wherever it is you're going." He retreated a step and flourished a bow. "Now, about that kiss?"

"After delaying me from my father's sickbed? You, sir, are a miscreant." She sidestepped him and darted toward the safety of the inn.

He watched until the hem of her skirt disappeared through the inn's front door. Then he hoisted himself back into the saddle. Of course, he'd never see her again.

But that didn't mean he wouldn't like to.

Chapter Two

Helen nudged open the door to her father's chamber, her hands full with a morning tea tray and her heart filled with a fresh hope—for Father's smile, albeit weak, greeted her from across the room. She'd been hard-pressed to decide which had frightened her more these past two days: her disturbing encounter with smugglers or the deadly state of her father's health. But perhaps today would be the day he turned the corner toward healing.

Pretend it will be so.

"Good day." Her father's words wavered on a wheezing breath, ravaged by age and dropsy.

"It is a good day, for you are awake." She set the tray on a bedside stand and pulled over the only chair in the small room. "I am glad of it."

"And I am glad for another day, Daughter."

"So should we all be, hmm? Now, let's prop you up." Sliding her hand behind his shoulders, she lifted him and his pillow, choosing to ignore the swelling in his neck and fluttering breath.

Once settled, she retrieved the mug of tea and bottle of chamomile syrup, stirring a spoonful of the tincture into his drink. "Here you are."

Some of the mixture leaked from the sides of his mouth, and she snatched a coarse cloth from the tray, the cheap fabric a bit rough for his frail skin. She frowned. "Would that I had been a son, and a prosperous one at that."

"Pish!" His bare head, long removed of the dark hair she remembered, shook against the cushion. "I couldn't have hoped for a better daughter. Nor a better patron."

"Forgive me, Father. I did not mean to sound ungrateful. I *am* thankful for the Seatons' generosity, and I shall let them know how much as soon as you are on the mend."

He reached for her hand, his fingers swollen to the size of sausages. "There will be no mending. Not this time. My breaths are numbered, and the sum is small."

"Do not speak so. You must live, for me, for your congregation."

"We are all mortal, Daughter."

She patted his hand, unwilling to acknowledge the grotesque changes destroying his body. "It benefits no one to accept defeat, even death, and so I shall endeavor to fight against it—for both of us, if need be."

"This is not your fight."

She squeezed his hand, then let go of his hold and his words. "I will not concede.

You are all I have left."

"No, child. There is *always* God."

"Yes, of course, but. . ." She sighed. Why could doubts not be as easily exhaled?

"But what?"

"Well, I know in my head God is always present, but in my heart? I cannot credit it."

A sliver of morning light angled through the single window, washing her father's face in a pool of yellow light. "You keep your heart too well guarded, I fear."

Of course she did—and always would. There was no better protection against hurt. "In the homes where I've served, I've seen what men do to women's hearts."

"You can't judge all men by the actions of a few. Did you ever stop to think that by shutting off your heart from man, you've closed the door to God's love as well? Those who leave everything in God's hand will eventually see God's hand in everything. . .even in man."

A rap at the front door jarred her as much as her father's words, and she patted his shoulder. "I shall return."

Exiting his chamber, she crossed the small main room and opened the door. An angel of light appeared—or so it seemed.

Sunshine haloed a woman slightly taller than herself, but judging by the smoothness of her skin and brilliance of eye, she was roughly the same age as Helen. The visitor was dressed in an emerald pelisse devoid of any decoration or embellishments. Blue skirts peeked out beneath, their former brilliance subdued by several years of wear. But whatever elegance the lady's clothing lacked, her lovely smile more than made up for it. Portrait artists would pay dearly to capture a beauty such as this.

"Good day," she said. "Are you Helen Fletcher?"

"Yes." Helen nodded at the wicker basket clutched in the woman's grasp. "And you must be the good fairy who's left food at our door the past two days."

"I am Esther Seaton, but I adore the alias *Good Fairy.*" She angled her face, and a true pixie could not have looked more mischievous. "Mind if I borrow it sometime?"

"Not at all. Come in." Helen stepped aside, allowing the lady to pass and setting her offering upon the table at the center of the room.

"Welcome to Treporth, Miss Fletcher. I trust you are settling in well." The lady swept out her hand, encompassing the interior of the small cottage. Then slowly her fingers dropped, as did her smile. "I heard of the scuffle at your arrival, and for that, I apologize. Truly, the folk around here are not a bad sort, and I am sorry for the impression you must have."

"It was harrowing, but I will not allow one bad experience to taint my opinion of all."

Miss Seaton's grin returned in full, and she crossed the room to gather Helen's hands in her own. "I have the feeling we shall be the best of friends."

A cough rattled out from Father's chamber, and Esther's gaze drifted toward it. "How is your father today?"

Shame tightened Helen's throat. Had she not moments earlier begrudged the roughness of a cloth, given along with a roof overhead and food for their bellies? She squeezed the lady's fingers then pulled back. "He is rallied this morn. I am hoping he shall be on his feet in no time."

"Really? I'd been led to believe otherwise." The lady's brow knit together, but unraveled as quickly. "Still, I am glad of your report."

"And I am glad for your provisions. You have been more than generous."

A delicate shrug lifted Miss Seaton's shoulders. "Do not thank me. I merely deliver. It is my brother who provides."

"Then I hope to meet him someday and thank him in person."

Miss Seaton arched a brow. "Would you?"

"Of course."

"Then come to dinner this evening at Seaton Hall. There's a government official recently arrived, and the conversation will no doubt turn tedious. Politics is not my topic of choice." She leaned closer. "I am sure you and I can find much to divert ourselves. Do say you'll come."

Helen bit her lip. Should she spend an entire evening away from Father? Somehow, it did not seem right, for he was the sole purpose she'd come here. "I am grateful for your invitation, Miss Seaton, but—"

"Esther, please."

She couldn't help but smile at the warmth in the woman's voice. "Very well, Esther, I should like to go, but—"

"Your father wishes you to go, child." The words traveled out the open door of her father's chamber.

"There you have it." Esther grinned. "Will you?"

Helen studied the worn floorboards, as if an answer might be found on the swept wood. She hadn't left Ireland for socializing, but this would be a prime opportunity to thank their benefactor. What was the right thing to do?

Slowly, she lifted her head. "My answer is yes."

Yes! Yes, yes, yes!

Isaac set the pen in the holder and leaned back in his chair. Two years of hard work had finally elevated the negative numbers to zero. A blessing, that. As was the improved state of his tenants. Perhaps his Robin Hood days were truly behind him.

But...

Sighing, he scrubbed a hand along his jaw. The relief was strange—like a rotted tooth pulled from his mouth, one that had festered far too long. It was good to have the thing removed, but hard not to continue probing the gap left behind. If he gathered his crew for just one more shipment, positive numbers could seed the new venture he'd been planning, and then some. Yet would that not be dangerous with a revenue man sniffing about?

Or as greedy as Brannigan?

He laced his fingers behind his head and stared up at the ceiling. *Well God. . .what would You have me do?*

The clock ticked overloud on the mantel. Windowpanes rattled from a gust of wind. In the hearth, flames licked lumps of coal, the low crackling the only other sound in the room.

Isaac grimaced. *Just as I thought. No answer. Again.*

"Here you are." His sister flounced through the door, a sweet pout painted on her lips. "I sent Roberts half an hour ago to retrieve you. Can you not be finished with your paperwork? Our guests are arrived."

"Guests?" Sitting upright, he closed the ledger and frowned at her. "I thought only Mr. Farris would be joining us."

"Oh! I forgot to tell you." Lamplight sparkled in his sister's amber gaze. "I invited the parson's daughter, Miss Helen Fletcher."

"She's arrived, then?" He shoved back his chair and stood, doubt rising along for the ride. How many other matters had he let slide these past months? "I didn't realize she'd be here so soon."

"I daresay you'd not notice should the world stop spinning."

"Such saltiness from you, Esther?" He rounded his desk, trying in vain to keep a sheepish grin from twitching his lips. "I suppose I deserve it."

She returned his smile. "That and more."

Isaac's heart warmed. This sister of his would make a fine wife for some deserving man—yet another thing he'd put off pursuing. But no more. Now that his financial pre-occupation was at an end, he'd have more time to escort her to dinners and dances where she could meet some eligible bachelors.

Crooking his arm, he offered her a wink along with it. "Shall we?"

She rested her fingers atop his sleeve, and they left behind the confines of his study.

"I think you shall like Miss Fletcher." The way his sister tipped her chin, a cat with a saucer of milk couldn't have looked more pleased.

"And why is that?"

"Besides her beauty, she seems quite amiable, especially given the circumstances of her arrival."

"Indeed." He blew out a low breath. Taking in Parson Fletcher despite his poor health had been a gamble—a wager all would be sorry to lose. "How is the parson faring? I own I've neglected him of late, but I intend to rectify that."

"Despite what Miss Fletcher says, I fear he's not long for this earth."

He patted her hand, a worthless consolation, but what else could he do?

The hallway emptied into the foyer, and he steered his sister to the farthest door on the right. Allowing her to pass before him, he trailed her skirts.

"Brother, may I introduce Mr. Farris and Miss Fletcher?" She beamed at their guests then swept her hand toward him. "And here, at last, is my wayward sibling, Mr. Isaac Seaton."

Before he could get a good look at the parson's daughter, a curly-haired man, red of lips and cheeks, dashed up to him and reached for his hand, pumping his arm as he might a well handle. His clothes were surprisingly tailored in the latest fashion, odd for a government official whose job could sometimes turn violent. Whose nephew or cousin was this? For surely the fellow had not landed the position by merit alone.

"Delighted to meet you, Mr. Seaton." The man's voice was as overeager as his grip. Even more irritating, the fellow's gaze never left Esther. "I am thrilled to have met your fine sister. I know we shall get on quite merrily."

Isaac cleared his throat, shoving down a remark every bit as salty as his sister's. "I trust your business here will not take very long, Mr. Farris."

Hopefully. For beside the fact that Farris was a revenue man on the prowl for smugglers, Isaac could not stomach the man's obvious interest in his sister, in spite of his wishing to see her married. Something was wrong about Farris.

"I shall do my best to remain in the area as long as possible." Farris finally let go and swooped over to Esther.

Which gave Isaac full view of Miss Fletcher.

Her gown flowed along delicate curves, so slight her bearing, so small her frame. The woman floated toward him, almost like. . .a bird.

His gaze shot to her face, where brown eyes flashed recognition. Her lips parted.

His breath caught.

One wrong word, and a noose would bite into his neck.

Chapter Three

What did one say to an abductor? A smuggler? A thief? So many accusations clogged Helen's throat that none got out. What manner of man was this Isaac Seaton, to so brashly pillage a ship at dock, dare to take her by force on a wild ride, yet now stand here calmly in the guise of a gentleman?

A very polished one, apparently. He captured her hand in his and bowed over her glove, pressing his lips to her fingers. Straightening, he arched a brow, his gaze tethering her to him in a way that quickened her pulse. "I am enchanted to meet you, Miss Fletcher."

She snatched back her hand, denying the urge to rub where his breath had heated her skin. Perhaps such charm would silence other women, but not her. She opened her mouth—

But before she could speak, he continued. "I am happy you are arrived safely from Ireland. No doubt your previous charges shall miss their governess, yet your father must be exceedingly grateful for your presence here."

She clamped her lips, trapping angry indictments behind her teeth. So, that was his game. Remind her of Father's debt before she snapped at the hand that fed. An audacious move, yet not surprising, for had he not shown such boldness aboard the *Nancarrow*?

Esther swooped over and linked arms with her. "Let us take this conversation into the dining room, shall we? I, for one, am famished."

Grateful for Esther's rescue, Helen kept step with her hostess, leaving Mr. Farris and the smuggler to follow.

Esther dipped her head toward her as they traversed a hall, their steps echoing on a floor absent of carpeting. "I am glad you are here." Her voice lowered for Helen's ears alone. "I'm not certain I trust that Mr. Farris. He seems an awfully forward fellow."

La! She could say the same of the lady's brother. Helen's step hitched, and she begged off Esther's arm. Did this lady know of her brother's smuggling escapades?

They entered a dining room surprisingly devoid of finery. Plain paneled walls surrounded them. Drapery, striped with too many years spent in the sun, hung on the windows. The table was set with plain white ironstone on linen a step above sailcloth. Ought not a thief have more riches than this?

Confused, Helen sank into a chair.

And the smuggling gentleman sat next to her.

Directly across the table, Mr. Farris leaned forward, nearly colliding with a bowl of soup being placed in front of him by a servant. "Tell me, Miss Fletcher, as Mr. Seaton intimated you are recently arrived from Ireland, did you by chance happen to hear of the fate of the ship *Nancarrow*?"

She sipped a spoonful of beef bouillon, savoring the saltiness along with the thought that she might be the one to bring criminals to justice. "As a matter of fact, sir, I was aboard that very ship. Furthermore—"

Isaac Seaton's spoon clanked against the edge of his bowl. "Excuse me, but how does your father fare, Miss Fletcher?"

Drat the man! Well did he know her father would've expired long ago had he not intervened with medical care. She lifted her face to the bully. "He is weak, yet lives."

He flashed a smile, the gleam in his eye far too knowing. "I am glad of it."

Mr. Farris shoved his bowl aside, ignoring the broth. "Were you on board for long after it harbored, Miss Fletcher?"

"Indeed." She glanced sideways at the big man next to her. "I was there when the brigands attacked."

"Were you? Splendid!"

Mr. Seaton's gaze shot to hers. Was that slight dip of his head a request or a threat?

Esther motioned to a servant for the first remove. "I fail to see how such a frightening experience could be splendid, Mr. Farris."

"Nor I." Isaac Seaton's deep voice filled the room. "This is hardly a conversation fit for dinner. Tell us of your own travels—"

"I shall." Mr. Farris waved off a refill of his wine glass. "But first I must know, Miss Fletcher, what you saw, or more importantly *who* you saw. Would you be able to recognize any of the men should I apprehend them?"

The smuggler at her side ran his palms along his trousers, a movement only she could witness. Clearly, he waited to see if she'd hand him over as easily as the footman passed a platter to Esther.

Should she? There was no debating Isaac Seaton had broken the law and therefore ought to be held accountable. But by implicating him, was she sentencing her ailing father to destitution? Was it right to repay her benefactor with such a harsh retribution? She'd not even thanked him yet for his provision. How had something so straightforward tangled into such a snarl?

She set down her fork and nodded for her plate to be removed. "It all happened very quickly, Mr. Farris, and it was near to dark."

"Justice might hinge upon your word, so please, consider. This is a serious matter, for the shipment taken belonged to the Brannigans. They do not take loss lightly."

She studied Mr. Farris's fleshy face for a hint of what that might mean, but he merely blinked. "What exactly would justice imply?" she asked.

The man's thick lips parted in a smile. "Why, the noose, of course."

Isaac Seaton tossed back the contents of his entire drink.

Esther placed her hand on Mr. Farris's arm. "My brother is correct. This conversation is not fit for dinner."

Mr. Farris looked from Esther's hand to her face. "Forgive my manners, Miss Seaton. I would do anything to please you." Then his gaze shot back to Helen. "But I must ask, Miss Fletcher, is there any hope of you identifying the lawbreakers?"

"If you please, sir!" Isaac Seaton's fist rattled the tableware. "I believe my sister and I have made it quite clear this conversation is ended."

Mr. Farris's lower lip quivered, like a tot who'd been scolded.

And the sight kindled the first ember of compassion Helen had felt for the man all evening. She offered him a weak smile. "I am sorry to disappoint, Mr. Farris, but every one of the brigands wore a mask. I am afraid I wouldn't be much help to you, and so there truly is nothing more to say."

"I am sorry to hear it." His quivering ceased, and his voice hardened to a sharp edge. "Such thievery has got to stop, and so it shall, for I will not leave Treporth until the criminals are caught."

<hr />

Every bite of dinner stuck in Isaac's throat like a fish bone—and fish was not on the menu. Mr. Farris alternated between fawning over Esther and Miss Fletcher, though Esther tallied the lion's share of the man's compliments. At least the fellow had dropped the topic of smuggling, for now.

Esther dabbed her mouth with her napkin then pushed back her seat. "Shall we retire into the drawing room? Unless you men would prefer to take port beforehand?"

He stifled a smirk. No doubt Farris would jump at the chance to drink with the leader of those he sought.

"I think not, Sister, for I trust Mr. Farris would agree that your company, ladies, is more desirable."

"Well said, sir. Shall we?" Farris shot up from his chair and immediately offered his arm to Esther.

She slipped Isaac a withering glance, then ever the gracious hostess, allowed the man to lead her toward the door.

Miss Fletcher followed—until Isaac stopped her with a touch to her sleeve before she could escape. "A word, Miss Fletcher."

The fabric between her shoulder blades drew taut as a sail in the wind, but she turned with a quirk to her brow. "Yes. I should like a word with you, sir."

As master of Seaton Hall, he'd met women from all stations of society—but none so curious as this petite governess. "You are quite the contradiction."

She tipped her pert little chin. "What do you mean?"

"You wish to speak with a. . . . What was it you called me when we last met?" In his mind he traveled back to that darkened night in front of the Candlelight Inn, with those big brown eyes assessing him and a severe retort on her lips. "Ahh, yes. You called me a miscreant. By your own word, you disdain who I am, so why not reveal me to Mr. Farris?"

"I came here to thank you, sir, not indict you. You paid my passage, you provide for my father, and for that I acknowledge your generosity." Her gaze hardened. "But for keeping my silence, I consider that debt now paid in full."

"I required no repayment. It was a gift, free and clear."

She retreated a step, angling her face to study him. "You are wrong, Mr. Seaton. It is you who are the contradiction."

He sucked in a breath. The same rosewater scent she'd worn the night he'd abducted her hung in the air, a fragrance as delightful as her intriguing mind. "I?"

"You play the part, no"—she swept out her hand—"you embody the essence of a gentleman. Upright. Noble, even." Her eyes narrowed. "Yet it is an undeniable fact that you led a mob to rob a ship and threaten the lives of the crew."

A chuckle rumbled in his chest. "I'd hardly call eight men a mob, nor were any of the crew's lives in danger. I merely removed what was mine in the first place."

"Mr. Farris said that shipment belonged to Brannigan."

The name curled his hands into fists, a base reaction, yet entirely unstoppable. "You have no idea who that is. Or what the Brannigans are capable of."

"What I know, sir, is that smuggling is wrong. Stealing for any reason shows a lack of trust in God's provision. And deception is as equally abhorrent. You are guilty of both."

Deception? Yes. But smuggling? Not if he ended his ventures now that he'd broken even from his losses—his *stolen* losses. He stared at the small woman, so unwavering in her beliefs that she didn't flinch beneath his assessment. Was this petite beauty God's answer to his earlier prayer for guidance? A smile lifted the corner of his mouth. If so, a very pretty reply.

"I do not deny your charge of deception, madam, and for that I freely repent. But I am no smuggler."

Her nostrils flared. "I saw you!"

Ahh, but his fingers itched to smooth that angry furrow on her brow. How soft the skin? How warm and—

He clasped his hands behind his back, lest they touch her without permission. "Sometimes what we see, Miss Fletcher, and what is truth are two different things. The world is not as black and white as you seem to believe. More often it is grey."

"Then you are no God-fearing man, Mr. Seaton."

"On the contrary, I acknowledge God as the creator of all colours."

A small snort blew from her lips. "You play with words as easily as you disregard the law."

"Come with me and my sister tomorrow, and I will show you grey." He pressed his mouth shut. What was it about this woman that made him issue such an invitation? He ought keep his distance from this parson's daughter, for her convictions did strange things to his conscience.

She shook her head. "I cannot leave my father for long periods. In truth, I should stay here no longer tonight."

"Then I will provide a maid to sit with him."

Her brow creased, not much, but enough to hint she considered his offer. "Have you an answer for everything?" she asked.

"Usually."

But not for her. She neither feared nor revered him. What kind of woman was Miss Helen Fletcher?

Chapter Four

Sunshine dappled light through a canopy of elms. Helen grasped the side of the pony cart and angled her face upward, closing her eyes. Esther was a competent driver, and the steady plod of Mr. Seaton's horse ahead of theirs set an easy pace. Yet the pattern of dark and light against her lids was as splotchy as her thoughts.

Each of the families they'd called on this morning had widened the crack in her heart, until she feared visiting any more would bleed out the last dregs of emotion. And then what? Was it possible to sympathize so thoroughly that no feelings would remain? These people were in dire need—and there was nothing she could do about it.

Could she?

"Nearly there." Esther's voice ended the debate.

Helen opened her eyes to a small cottage built into a rise of grassy earth. Mr. Seaton dismounted and offered her his hand as Esther set the cart's brake.

He leaned toward Helen as he helped her to the ground. "Are you starting to understand the plight of these people, Miss Fletcher?"

"I believe that I am, yet I fail to understand what any of this has to do with your..." She glanced to where Esther retrieved a basket from the cart, then lowered her voice. "Other diversion, shall I call it?"

"No, not a diversion. A necessity." He flashed a roguish grin. "One I will no longer pursue, thanks to you."

Her brows shot skyward. "Me? Why?"

"Master Isaac!" The screech of his name upset a swoop of martins from the neighboring elms.

The three of them turned toward the cottage door.

Out flew a grey-haired lady, mob cap askew and apron strings flapping like an extra pair of legs. If she could move this spritely now, what kind of whirlwind had this woman been in former years? She plowed into Mr. Seaton. "How I've missed ye, lad."

He wrapped his arms around her and chuckled. "Good to see you also, Mrs. Garren."

Esther set the basket down by the lady's door, beaming at the sight.

Helen pursed her lips. The man was a paradox: one day brandishing a pistol at a captain and another embracing an elder half his size.

Isaac set the lady from him then bent on one knee. Taking her hand into his, he kissed her fingers. "My deepest apologies for my absence, madam. Forgive me?"

"Posh!" She swatted him on the head. "Who can stay angry with you, lad? Now then, who is it ye've brought?"

The lady's gaze landed on Helen. Her eyes were like two tiny coals, deep and dark, and entirely warm and cozy. Hopefully this woman had many grandbabes to dandle on her knee, for such was the love in her scrutiny.

"Annah, I present to you the parson's daughter, Miss Helen Fletcher." Esther joined Helen's side. "Helen, this is Mrs. Annah Garren."

Helen dipped a bow. "Pleased to meet you, Mrs. Garren."

"Oh posh! Only Master Isaac gets away with such formalities. Call me Annah." Her right eye winked—or was it a tic? "Come in, come in! Take a cup o' nettle tea."

Esther placed a hand on the lady's shawl. "I am sorry, Annah, but we must be off."

"So soon?"

"I've yet to see to the village children. And Miss Fletcher's father is very ill. We shouldn't keep her from him for too long."

Without so much as a goodbye, the old lady pivoted and darted into her house. Mr. Seaton swung back into his saddle, and Esther crossed to the pony cart. Was that it? Helen frowned. Not a very fond farewell after such an intimate welcome.

Annah reappeared before Helen could climb back up on the cart. She dashed toward them, her speed once again belying her age. Drawing close, the old lady pressed a stained piece of fabric into her hands. "For your father, child."

"Thank you for. . ." She turned the small piece over in her fingers. It was too small to be a kerchief, though clearly the scrap was a gift of some kind. She smiled at the old lady. "Thank you."

"Posh!" Annah waved her off then lifted her face to Mr. Seaton. "Hie yerself back here more often, Master Isaac. Take care of our lad, Esther."

Then Annah vanished back into her cottage.

Helen climbed up on the cart and sat next to Esther, puzzling over the odd encounter. "That was. . .interesting. What is this?" She held out the scrap for inspection.

Esther glanced at it and urged the pony to walk on. "Except for the shawl from her shoulders, I suspect it's all Annah had to give you. Since her husband died, my brother has provided as best he can for her and all the tenants you've seen today. Isaac is a generous soul—overmuch at times. Often he goes without sleep or meals to come up with a way to continue providing."

Continue providing? The cart juddered over a rock in the road, and Helen grabbed hold of the side while also trying to grasp Esther's information. Thinking back on the sparse decor at Seaton Hall, it all started to make sense. "So, I take it finances are an issue, then?"

"Well. . .Mr. Farris did mention the Brannigans last evening, so I don't suppose Isaac would mind me telling you." Though her brother rode ahead of them, well out of earshot, she dipped her head closer to Helen. "My father owned a successful enterprise, shipping over the finest Irish blasting powder for the copper and tin mines hereabouts. When he died, the business went to Isaac."

Helen's gaze shot to Mr. Seaton. The fabric of his suit coat stretched across his shoulders like a mantle of power. "He seems well suited for such a venture."

"Indeed—were it not for Richard Brannigan. There's bad blood between the two. When Richard heard of my father's death, it's rumoured he put into play a smuggling scheme to relieve all incoming ships of Isaac's cargo."

"But wouldn't whoever had insured those loads pay your brother for his losses?"

Esther sighed. "Not if the insurance company is so heavily burdened by payouts that they are driven out of business. Such was the case."

"Why not simply employ a different company?"

"Brannigan's *is* the only remaining insurance provider in these parts." She jutted her chin toward her brother. "And he can't bear the name, so please, hold in confidence what I've told you."

"Of course."

Esther fell into a silence, and while she drove on, Helen tried to reconcile the ill-treated gentleman trotting in front of them against the bold thief who'd accosted her only days before. She tapped a faint pattern against the square of cloth on her knee as they rattled along, yet could not solve the mystery of the fellow even by the time they slowed near the outskirts of Treporth.

A salty breeze welcomed them. They stopped in front of a collection of row houses, leaning against one another like sailors after a night of ale. Mr. Seaton had barely assisted her and Esther down before a mob of children burst out the doors, one after the other, like a tumbling chain of dominoes falling all over themselves. Eventually they huddled around Esther.

Helen peeked up at Mr. Seaton. "What's this about?"

He grinned. "Not a day goes by Esther doesn't come to tell Bible stories to the children. As you can see, they love her for it."

She looked from one Seaton to the other. In all the fine homes she'd served, all the gentlefolk she'd encountered, none compared to the heart she'd witnessed in these two.

Behind them, horse hooves thundered. Esther ushered the children forward, while Helen and Mr. Seaton turned toward the sound.

The rider reined his mount to a stop in front of them. "Mr. Seaton, sir." The man tugged the brim of his hat in respect. "I'm looking for a Miss Fletcher. I was told you'd know her whereabouts."

Mr. Seaton looked from the rider to her. "You have found her."

"This be for you, miss." Bending, the man handed over a folded slip of paper.

Her heart thumped hard as she opened the note.

Pretend it is not parchment. Pretend it is good news.

But as she scanned the words, her world tipped sideways.

❧

Isaac studied Miss Fletcher's face as her gaze dropped to the note. The more she read, the more her lips flattened, until eventually her whole countenance deflated. He stood at the ready should she hit the ground.

"What is it?" he asked.

"My father." Big brown eyes peered into his. "He's taken a turn for the worse."

"Then we must leave. Now."

After a word with Esther to explain their haste, he left his sister in care of the children and retrieved Duchess. Miss Fletcher allowed him to lift her, and he waited a moment for her to straighten her skirts as she sat sidesaddle. He swung up behind her, feeling like a beast stationed behind such a small woman.

"What of your sister?" she asked.

"She'll return shortly." He jabbed his heels, and Duchess took off, though he held her to a canter. The set of the woman's shoulders in front of him, the quietness of her small frame caused an ache in his belly. Would that he could protect her from the inevitable end of her father.

"Thank you for your kindness, Mr. Seaton."

He'd been thanked before, and often, but coming from this lady, the gratitude sank low, filling him like the pleasantness of a fine meal. He leaned closer, breathing in her sweet scent, then immediately drew back. What the deuce was he thinking? The woman rode toward a father who might be dying and here he was, playing the lovesick schoolboy.

He cleared his throat. "Tell me, what did you think of the people you met today?"

She turned toward him, a small smile curving her lips. "I understand your affection for them—and theirs for you."

"Really? A miscreant such as myself?"

"Well. . ." Her smile spread. "I suppose I was a bit harsh in my first assessment."

"So, you've grown to appreciate my charms, hmm?"

Her grin twisted into a smirk. "I wouldn't go that far."

The road forked, and he urged Duchess eastward, onto Seaton lands, though he needn't have. The mare could travel this route with a hood on her head.

Miss Fletcher faced him once again, yet she said nothing. What went on behind those brown eyes?

"Go on," he encouraged. "I see by the quirk of your brow you have more to say."

"I am wondering. . .what did you mean when you said you had me to thank for your decision to stop smuggling?"

"Just that. You voiced aloud concerns I've often thought. If one cannot trust in God's provision, then perhaps one has no business professing a faith at all."

"Then why did you not stop sooner?"

Her question struck harder than a well-aimed right hook. How did one explain the loss a man feels when income, inheritance, even justice were ripped from his grasp? "It's. . .complicated."

"I suppose you have a point, somewhat. Stealing *is* wrong—but so are the miserable lives of your tenants. Why is it that good things do not always happen to good people?"

"You have no idea how often I've wrestled with that very question."

She angled her head, like a sparrow considering a worm to be devoured. "And the outcome?"

"My only conclusion is that we are not in control, and we never were." He reined Duchess to a halt in front of the parsonage and leapt down, then reached up to aid Miss Fletcher.

"I don't know whether to thank or condemn you for such frank conversation." Her breath warmed his cheek as he lowered her to the ground.

"Neither. The gratitude is all mine."

For a moment their gazes locked, and the space between them rippled, like the charge in the air just before lightning struck earth. Was he addled—or did she feel it, too?

Without a word, she pulled from his hands and dashed into the cottage.

He hesitated long after she disappeared. For the first time in a long time, he dared hope that God not only would answer his prayers—but in fact, already had.

Chapter Five

The loamy scent of earth washed fresh by rain would make a fine cologne. Helen breathed deeply as she tread the road into town, pondering such a fragrance. She'd label it *hope* and purchase a bottle to keep in her pocket. The past several days at her father's bedside had drained her reserves.

Rounding a bend, she stepped to the side of the thoroughfare, happy to see Esther's pony cart drawing near—and happier still to see her new friend smiling back at her.

"Good afternoon, Helen." Esther halted her horse. "What an exotic sight you are, my dear. Your blue skirts are so vibrant against a backdrop of dampened wildwood. You are a picture."

Helen laughed. "Someone's been reading novels, hmm?"

"I wish it, but no time." Her smile faded. "Is your father faring any better since his attack?"

For three days now, her father had mumbled nothing but gibberish—but at least he still breathed. She straightened her shoulders. *Pretend that you are strong.* "As of yet, he's unable to move the left side of his body, but with effort, he manages to smile, albeit crookedly. I thank you for the care you and your brother have provided—oh, and especially for Gwen. I hope by lending her to us, you are not short staffed at the hall."

"It's the least we can do. Isaac and I are both truly sorry. Your father is a fine man." Leftover drops from the earlier rain dripped like tears from the canopy of trees, adding a gloomy encore to Esther's lament.

Helen forced lightness into her tone. "I trust he will recover with sufficient rest. Even now, I am on my way to the apothecary for a sleeping draught."

"I could use the opposite." Esther glanced at the bundles heaped atop the seat next to her and at her feet.

Helen peered at the piles of fabric. "What is all this?"

"A boon *and* a load of work. Old Mrs. Turner headed up a charity drive for the poor of the parish."

"What has that to do with you?"

Esther sighed, the force of which distracted her pony—who stamped a hoof, eager to be off. "I offered to mend and reissue any garments she collected. I had no idea she'd meet with such success. With this much sewing, I'm afraid I'll have to cut short my story time with the children." For a moment, a shadow darkened her lovely face, like the flash of a spring storm, then surprisingly cleared away. "But on the bright side, it's a ready excuse should Mr. Farris come to call. Which he does. Far too much for my liking."

If nothing else, the man was persistent, for Helen had seen his mount passing by her own cottage several times on his way to Seaton Hall. Thankfully, he'd been too focused on Esther to pay her any mind.

"I have plenty of time to sew while sitting with my father. If you wouldn't mind stopping by the cottage, you may drop off some of your load." Helen stepped closer and smiled. "Not so much as to take away your excuse, though."

"You are a dear—and so I've told my brother on many occasions."

Her cheeks heated. But such warmth ought be blamed on the ray of sun breaking through the branches, not on the mention of Esther's brother.

Esther's brow rose, her brown eyes twinkling almost golden. "Good day, Helen. Godspeed."

"Good day." Grasping her skirts to keep clear of mud, she whirled about and hastened her step. Though Gwen sat with her father, it wouldn't do to dawdle.

The road to Treporth truly was a lovely walk, from flatlands higher inland down to the more wooded stretch just before town. Despite the chore of keeping her hem from the dirty road, she relished the break from sitting indoors.

Closer to town, pounding hooves rumbled, and a horse appeared, the rider dressed in the official coat of a revenue officer. Once again, Helen stepped to the side of the thoroughfare.

Mr. Farris reined in his horse and tipped his hat. "Miss Fletcher. Delighted."

"Mr. Farris." She dipped a bow. "On the hunt for more smugglers?"

"Actually, I'm on my way to see Miss Seaton."

Helen stifled a frown. If he caught up to Esther on the road, her friend would have a hard time avoiding the man. "I am afraid you will not find her at home."

"Oh?" His lips folded into a pout. "Do you know when she will return?"

"I do not. She is a very busy young lady. Good day, sir." She strode away before he could needle her with further questions. It would be wrong to lie—but just as devious to reveal Esther's whereabouts.

The rhythmic stomping of the horse caught up to her side. "Where are you off to this fine afternoon, Miss Fletcher?"

She peered up at him yet did not alter her stride. "Not that it signifies, but I go to the apothecary for my father."

"Then you must allow me to give you a ride."

"Do not trouble yourself. It's not that much farther."

"No trouble at all, since my errand seems remiss at this point." Bending toward her, Mr. Farris held out his hand. "Come along."

This time a frown would not be stopped. Should she? Despite the man's odious company, riding would be faster, shaving at least a quarter hour—maybe more—from her task, and she'd be back to her father's side that much sooner.

Grabbing hold of his hand, she raised her foot to use his boot as a step, then allowed him to hoist her up in front of him. She sat sideways, as she had on Mr. Seaton's horse, but Mr. Farris sidled against her far closer than Mr. Seaton ever had.

She faced forward, straining away from him. *Pretend this wasn't a mistake.*

"It is dangerous for a lady to roam alone in this wild countryside."

Indeed, for she'd run into him. The retort died an anguished death on her tongue, so dearly did she wish to speak it.

"It's a good thing I came along to rescue you." He scooted nearer.

The pride of the man! She scowled. "I was hardly in danger, sir."

"Still, one never knows with smugglers about. You would do well to think on finding a husband." His arm reached out, pulling her against him.

She plucked his sleeve aside, refusing so much as a glance over her shoulder. "You are very forward, sir."

"I find I must be in my line of work." His words warmed her ear, for he bent near, almost cheek to cheek.

She stiffened. "Put me down. I shall walk the rest of the way."

"No, no. I won't hear of it. We are nearly there."

No wonder Esther clung to an excuse to stay away from this determined rake. Helen leaned so far forward, the horse's mane tickled her nose. Thank God the road opened onto the outskirts of Treporth. With witnesses, surely he'd stop his advances.

Wrong.

He grasped the reins with both hands, closing his arms against her—a hold only an intimate couple might dare in public. "With Miss Seaton so occupied, perhaps I should call on you instead."

She squirmed. The crazed ride she'd endured with a masked smuggler had been far more desirable than this. "Mr. Farris, if you've finished with your job here in Cornwall, I suggest you go back to wherever it is you came from. Now put me down."

"London, Miss Fletcher. I hail from London. And there are many ladies in that fine town who are hoping for my return as a bachelor." His lips brushed against her ear. "But I wonder if you will be the crusher of their dreams?"

"No!" She wriggled and wrenched—but his grasp was relentless. "Put. Me. Down!"

"You heard the lady." A deadly still voice rumbled like a coming storm. "Let her go."

Vile words sat on Isaac's tongue, spiky and bitter. He bit down until the salty taste of blood kept them from spilling. Seeing Miss Fletcher struggling in this man's embrace left a putrid aftertaste.

"Mr. Seaton." Farris smiled down at him, entirely fake. More like the mask of a boy who'd been caught dipping snuff and scrambled for a reason to deny it. He loosened his hold of Miss Fletcher—but did not release her. "Good afternoon."

Isaac glowered. "It will be good once you let the lady go as she asked."

Dropping his arms, Farris gazed at Miss Fletcher. "Allow me to revise that. It's a *beautiful* afternoon, actually."

Isaac shot out his hand for Helen to grab hold of, better that than yanking the scoundrel off his horse and pounding him a good one. Wait a minute. . .

Helen?

A charge raced through him. The last time he'd thought of a woman by her Christian name, things did not end well.

She reached for his hand, allowing him to lower her to the ground. Her face was dangerously close to his as she whispered, "Thank you, Mr. Seaton."

Her gratitude—or dare he hope, admiration—stoked the fury in his gut for Farris's bold moves. He glared up at the man. "Is your business in Treporth not yet finished?"

"No." His eyes followed Helen's step. "There is much here to keep my attention."

"Then I suggest you see to your work and leave off the ladies."

A leer slashed across Farris's face. "All work and no play makes one very dull."

Isaac's hands curled into fists. If he listened to any more of this, he'd be charged with assault. He wheeled about and caught up to Helen. "Are you all right?"

"Yes, but good thing you came along when you did." She slid her gaze to him, a pert lift to her brow. "Or I would have been forced to hurt him."

He snorted, remembering their first encounter—or rather his meeting with her very strong knee. "No doubt. Shall I accompany you to. . . Where are you going?"

"The apothecary's, and yes, you may."

He matched his step to hers, fighting the urge to speed her along. If he were late to his meeting for such a reason as this, well, then may his punctual reputation be hanged.

"If you don't mind me asking," he glanced over his shoulder to make sure the revenue man was gone, "why did you agree to ride with Mr. Farris in the first place?"

"I was on my way to town when he came along. I thought it would be faster."

"Hmm. I suppose I shall have to remedy that."

Her brown eyes studied his for a moment, curiosity adding a lovely sparkle to their depths, yet she said nothing more—nor did he, all the way to Krick's Powders and Pills.

Stepping from her side, he bowed, flourishing his hat in one hand. "I bid you good afternoon, my lady."

"Thank you, Mr. Seaton." She dipped her head. "I am in your debt once again."

He watched as her skirts slipped through the door then turned on his heel and yanked out his pocket watch. Blast!

He darted past pedestrians and a few street hawkers selling their wares, running all the way to Mr. Henry Green's, esquire and banker extraordinaire. He slipped through the man's office door, out of breath and cravat askew.

Green looked up from a stack of paperwork. "What's this? Isaac Seaton late?"

"Sorry. Had to save a damsel in distress."

Green chuckled. "Ever the hero, eh lad?"

He advanced, pulling out a packet of banknotes from a leather wallet and slapping them on the desk.

"What's this?"

"The rest of what I owe." He sank into one of the leather high-backs.

"So. . ." A smile spread across Green's face, erasing years from his weathered skin. "Ready to get back in business then?"

"No." He sniffed, the scent of spent cheroots and sweaty men striking trade deals thick on the air. "I'm ready to own the business."

"Really?" Green reared back, staring down his nose. "And what would that venture be?"

Isaac planted his hands on his thighs and leaned forward. "An old friend of my father's recently stopped in for a visit, mourning the decline of the Anglesey mines. Opencast mining was never the way to go, in my opinion, and so I wasn't surprised. But our discussion sparked an idea that's since burned out of control."

He paused, the concept so stunning yet so organic in its conception, he was almost afraid to voice it aloud, lest it disappear.

"Yes?" Green prompted.

"As you know, the Tregonning mines are putting out ore like never before. Why it never occurred to Father or to me is. . . Well, I suppose we were too focused on supplying mines rather than running one. But Seaton lands touch Tregonning Hill!"

"Are you saying you want to open a mine?"

He jumped up, spreading his hands. "Is that not a brilliantly simple idea?"

Green folded his arms, and they rode the crest of several large breaths before he answered. "Perhaps. But the scope of opening a new mine is immensely expensive."

"I know."

Green narrowed his eyes. "So why are you grinning at me like a lovesick bridegroom on his wedding night?"

"You, my friend," he grinned in full, "are just the man to find some investors. Sir Francis Bassett, George Hunt—"

Green's hand shot up. "Stop right there. Your reputation will precede you, Isaac. Bassett, Hunt, and everyone else knows you'll throw caution to the wind in order to thwart Richard Brannigan. I'd have to be able to assure them you will not continue your vendetta against the man. Your focus would have to be solely your new mining venture. Can you agree to that?"

He paced the length of Green's office. A fair question, but one he wasn't sure he could answer. He and Esther had suffered two years of barely getting by with meager fare and threadbare clothing. Even worse, he'd been unable to buy seed for his tenants—and farming was hard enough on this rugged patch of land even with prime seed. The deprivation, the worry of debtor's prison, near starvation and disease, all this was Brannigan's fault.

Isaac stopped at the hearth and stared into the coals. Was it right to let a thieving bully like Richard Brannigan escape justice?

Chapter Six

Outside the cottage, the lonely cry of a collared dove hovered on the air, so bittersweet, Helen couldn't decide if she should weep or sing along with the beauty of the sound. But neither would do. Not when there was sewing aplenty and her father to tend. She drained her tea and pushed away from the table.

The bird suddenly silenced, and Helen cocked her head. Horses' hooves pounded closer. She crossed to the window and peered through the curtain, then stood there, mesmerized. Coming up the drive were two horses. One occupied, the other tethered to Mr. Seaton's mount. But it was the man that captivated.

He swung his long leg over the saddle and dismounted, landing on the ground like a reigning king. Morning light warmed his face to a burnished, almost golden hue. La! Everything about the man was royal. From the confidence in his stride to the broad shoulders that could carry the weight of the world he lived in—or she did. What might it feel like to have such a man care for her?

She jerked back from the glass. What was she thinking? The only safe love was God's, not man's.

Pretend that you are happy. Pretend you are fulfilled.

A sharp rap rattled the quiet inside the parsonage. She opened the door to Isaac Seaton's smile flashing brighter than the April morn.

"Good morning, Miss Fletcher."

"Good morning." Her voice was breathy. A miracle, really, that it worked at all. How was one to speak—let alone think—with such a direct gaze consuming hers?

"I. . ." She cleared her throat, willing the traitorous thing to allow words to pass. *Pah!* What was wrong with her? Surely he wasn't here to see her. She greeted him with a smile as melancholy as the bird's cry. "I am happy you called, yet sorry to refuse you. My father still isn't well enough to receive visitors."

"Though I wish your father well, in truth, I did not come to check on him." He bent, face to face, a rogue tilt to his chin. "I came to call on you."

"Me?" Her hand flew to her chest.

He straightened, his grin growing. "I've brought you something." But instead of handing over whatever it was, he pivoted about and strode away.

Pursing her lips, she hesitated. Was this real? Or was she pretending again?

She followed to where he untethered a beautiful Irish hunter. Rich brown in colour, surprising flashes of a red undertone gleamed where the sun painted with a broader brush.

Helen stroked the mare's nose. "My, but she's lovely."

Isaac's gaze slid to her, a curious sparkle in his eyes—one that did strange things to her stomach.

"Yes. I quite agree." The words were husky, as if, perhaps, he may be speaking of more than the horse.

Of course he spoke of the horse! Regardless, heat crawled up her neck and flushed her cheeks. She turned to the mare. "What's her name?"

"Red Jenny. Jenny for short." He patted the mount's strong neck. "And she's yours."

"Mine?" She snapped her face toward his. "But I cannot accept such a gift."

"You can. . .unless you prefer riding into town with Mr. Farris?"

The question constricted as tightly as Mr. Farris's embrace of the previous day. No, that was not an experience she wished to repeat. She ran an absent finger along the mare's muzzle, thinking aloud. "Even so, this is too much. How would I keep her?"

"There's a shed around back. I'll send Sam over to clean it out, lay fresh straw, and deliver some hay and oats."

Did the man have an answer for everything? She shook her head. "No, this is well beyond my means, not to mention highly improper, and—"

"Miss Fletcher." He planted himself firmly in front of her. "Think of this as a gift for your father, if you please. A means to get him pills and powders when needed. Now, are you going to spout more excuses as to why you should not have ready transportation into town, or shall we take a jaunt around so you get the feel of her?"

"No—yes—I mean. . ." She retreated a step from the horse—and the man. "I hardly know what to say."

"How about that you'll go grab your hat and gloves and join me?"

Should she? Riding the countryside with a handsome gentleman was not at all what she ought to be doing. Her brow pinched. Then again, nothing about this trip had happened as she'd planned. And he was right. Getting to and from town would be a lot easier. Well. . .for Father, then.

Whirling, she strode back inside and peeked into her father's room. By all appearances, he slept peacefully.

Gwen, the serving girl sitting at his bedside, lifted green eyes toward her. "Everything a'right, mistress?"

She nodded. "Think you can manage if I'm gone for half an hour?"

"Aye, he's resting well."

With one last glance at her father, Helen withdrew to the main room of the cottage. Gathering her spencer, bonnet, and gloves, she donned each, mind wandering. Was this the right thing to do? It seemed decadent to ride away a spring morning while her father lay abed.

But she revised that opinion when she paced back outside and caught sight of Mr. Seaton's fine profile, all muscle and strength.

Pretend this isn't wanton.

He turned at her approach, holding out a riding crop. "Ready?"

Was she?

She grasped the thin rod in her hand. "Ready."

Crouching, Mr. Seaton laced his fingers together, allowing a hold for her foot. As she climbed, she caught a whiff of his clary sage aftershave—a fine addition to a glorious morning. She grabbed hold of the pommel and, once seated on the sidesaddle, settled her skirts while he mounted Duchess.

Jenny took an impatient step sideways, and though horsemanship wasn't Helen's mainstay, she knew enough to rein the animal under control before they took off.

Mr. Seaton led them on a merry ride, past Seaton Hall and through the woods sheltering the manor. Eventually the land opened up onto a grassy flat with a sliver of grey sea beyond. He continued to skirt the edge of the trees, but slowed, allowing her to catch up.

"How is she?" he asked.

What a question. The mare was perfect in every way—just like the man. "Wonderful."

He said nothing, yet didn't pull his gaze from hers.

"I, uh. . ." Where were her words this morning? She wetted her lips and tried again. "I feel as if I shall never stop thanking you or your sister."

"No need. It's entirely my pleasure. Besides. . ." He faced forward then, and the loss was as tangible as the clouds suddenly hiding the sun. "It is I who should be thanking you."

"For what?"

"Helping Esther. Not many governesses would so willingly take on the menial task of repairing worn garments for the sake of poor fisherfolk."

"Nor many gentlewomen, so perhaps you ought to be thanking your sister. But such a trait runs strong in your family, does it not?"

He reined Duchess around to face her. "What trait?"

"Doing the unexpected."

"Me?" His brows rose.

She quirked her lips into a saucy grin. "You are a gentleman smuggler, are you not?"

With a tap of the crop to Jenny's side, she urged the horse ahead before he could reply—but then the flash of a brown wing flapped up from the tall grass at the wood's edge, startling Jenny. The horse broke into a gallop.

Helen grabbed the pommel. Tight.

Stay on. Just stay on.

Wind caught her hat, flinging it behind her. The ribbon cut into her neck. Tears stung her eyes, and the world blurred.

She bent nearly double.

Stay on!

In her mind, she screamed for the horse to stop—but screaming was impossible. So was breathing.

Her legs ached. Her hands. Her back. How much pain would a body feel before all went black? If she fell now, there was only one of two outcomes.

Either her skirt would catch, and she'd be dragged.

Or she'd break her neck.

◦◦◦◦◦◦

"Helen!"

Was that primal shout really his? Had to be, for Isaac's throat burned.

He spurred Duchess headlong after the nightmare. Helen's horse stretched full-out, racing toward the cliffs. Racing toward death.

God, no!

Leaning into his mount, Isaac became one with the horse. An animal. Ferocious in speed and bent on his quarry.

He drove Duchess on, urging her to pass the runaway mare. Helen's hat and hair streamed behind her, but she held. Thank God, she held.

Sound receded. No more thundering hooves. No sea or wind. Just a rush of breath. In. Out. Focus. *Focus!*

The instant Duchess gained enough lead on Jenny, he jerked his mount close to Helen's. Reaching. Stretching. His fingers spread to grab hold of Jenny's rein, which slapped like a crazed lash, scaring the horse further.

He strained a little more and. . .

Contact.

He veered right, commanding both animals into a circle. Wild spree thus interrupted, Red Jenny eventually submitted, though not without a few, fierce jerks of her head. After several circles, both horses trotted, until he could halt them and jump down.

He dashed around to Helen's side, where she yet clung to the mare's neck, breathing hard.

"Helen!" He reached for her, pulling her down into his arms. "Are you all right?" He leaned back for a better view. "Are you hurt?"

A wide-eyed stare met his. Face mostly pale, except for the unnatural redness of her cheeks. Dark hair, loosened and long, curled past her shoulders. She was a savage picture, untamed and fierce. Yet a pampered London lady could not have looked more ravishing.

"I am shaken." Her voice caught on a little hiccup. "I might have. . .I could have—"

She broke then, trembling so violently, tears cut loose.

He drew her close, wrapping his arms around her. "Shh. All's well now." He spoke as much to himself as to her. Indeed. He very well could have lost this precious woman. They shuddered in unison. With effort, he forced his thoughts from what could have been and instead focused on meeting her need for the here and now.

How long they stood there, he couldn't say. An eternity wouldn't have been long enough, so right, almost holy, did the moment feel.

But eventually she pulled away, her big, brown eyes gazing up into his. Her lips parted.

And he immediately put his finger against them. "Do not thank me again."

Beneath his touch, her mouth curved into a smile. If only he weren't wearing gloves and could feel the softness of those lips. If only it wasn't his finger pressed against such temptation, but his mouth. Desire stoked a long-banked fire in his gut.

He retreated, unwilling to look at those lips a minute more. Any longer and he'd act on the impulse. Duchess stood nearest, so he strode to collect Jenny first. Once both horses were gathered, he handed the reins of the Irish hunter to Helen.

She accepted them, but a fine flare of her nostrils revealed remnants of terror.

"How about we lead them a bit before riding?" he asked.

The admiration shining in her gaze was a pleasure so intense, he nearly moaned with the pain of it. He strode ahead.

She caught up to his side. "You are very thoughtful."

"So now I am a thoughtful gentleman smuggler, eh?" He smiled at her.

She swatted his arm.

What kind of a woman went from terror to brokenness to playful, all in a manner of minutes? He blew out a long breath. One that he wanted, that's what.

"Why did you never marry?" The question flew out before he thought. Would she even answer? Not that he'd blame her if she didn't. He'd taken a slap for questions less delicate.

She merely shrugged, never missing a step. "A governess doesn't have much opportunity. And you?"

Her response hit him broadside. The woman parried with more speed than an expert swordsman. He hadn't spoken of Catherine in over a year. Should he now? Was that hurt not long buried?

But unbidden, words tumbled out of his mouth. "I almost did, once."

"What happened?"

Memories crashed against him like the dull roar of the sea just past the cliffs. A bitter taste filled his mouth. He'd sworn off women, yet here he stood, walking side by side with one. "Perhaps you can tell me." He gazed down at her as they plowed through the grass. "How is it a woman can pledge undying love for a man—until his business fails and wealth is no longer part of the equation?"

With one hand, she pulled hair from her eyes, and gathered the thickness of the loosened bulk at the back of her neck. "Shortsightedness, I suppose."

His brows shot up. "In what respect?"

"Clearly the woman in question did not take into consideration the determination and probability of said man to eventually conquer the world."

Unbelievable. Helen Fletcher was a jewel with so many facets, he longed to see which side of her would shine next. A slow smile stretched his mouth. "I own that reason never once came to mind. . .but I like it."

And her.

A blush deepened on her cheeks, a healthy colour, not the fearful scarlet of before. They walked in silence for a ways, the breeze cooling their mounts so that riding again would not be a concern.

"Might we get a view of the sea before we head back?" Helen pointed to a worn path leading downward.

He frowned. Tremawgan's trail. One he knew well. Too well. And had vowed to never know again.

"No." The refusal sounded abrupt even to his own ears.

She peered at him. The sting of his harshness weighted her brow, like a young girl showing her father a treasure and having it slapped from her hand.

He softened his tone and his frown. "It's a risk not worth taking. That trail is treacherous even for the best of riders. Stay away. Your horse is too skittish."

She tipped her chin to a saucy angle. "*And* I might run into smugglers?"

"Would you not say, lady," he stepped closer, "that you already have?"

Chapter Seven

The following day, Helen stood inside Seaton Hall's receiving room, waiting upon Esther. Drawn toward the only ornament gracing the chamber, she crossed to the mantel and traced her finger over a carved box. Somewhat rough-hewn, this was as common a cheroot case as she'd ever seen. Nothing hinted at pomp or pretense, so like the master of the house. Her pulse quickened. Had Isaac's hands also touched the wood this very morning?

For a moment she gave in and closed her eyes, reliving the way he'd held her. The feel of his strong arms sheltering her against his chest. The heat of him. His scent. If she breathed deeply now, would she catch a leftover remnant of clary sage?

"Helen! What a surprise, yet lovely to see you."

Helen jumped at Esther's voice. Good thing the woman could not see into her mind. She sucked in a breath, shoving down the shameless thoughts of the woman's brother. "Good day, Esther. I was hoping to catch you at home."

"Oh, dear." The curls framing Esther's face trembled as she crossed the room and reached for Helen's hands. "I hope you're not here because of your father."

"No, thankfully, though I am sad to say there has been no improvement." She squeezed Esther's fingers then let go. "I came because I've finished that load of mending you dropped off and wondered if you might send someone by to pick it up?"

"So soon? You are more proficient with a needle than I, for I've barely made it half-way through my pile."

"Would you like me to take on more?"

"Don't even think of it, but it is sweet of you to offer." Esther swept over to the settee and patted the cushion beside her. "I daresay Isaac thinks you sweet as well."

Pretend her words are true. Pretend he cares for you.

Shirking off the notion, she settled her skirts next to Esther. Of course he wouldn't think of her in that way. He was kind to everyone. Romance was for storybooks and naive girls, not a governess tending to a sick father.

She lifted her face to Esther. "His opinion of me may have lowered since yesterday after the way I lost control of my horse."

Esther shook her head, light catching copper strands in her hair, so like Isaac's. "Any time my brother gets to play the champion is a boost for his confidence, which believe it or not, is sorely needed. The past few years have been hard on him." She went silent. Though Esther still sat on the settee, clearly memories crowded behind her eyes, so faraway her gaze.

Helen patted her arm. "I am sorry to hear it."

"Hmm?" Esther jolted at the touch, but a smile soon curved her lips. "All that's changed since you arrived. My brother is happier now. Lighter of spirit. You are good for him."

"Don't be silly. It can't be because of me."

"No, you're wrong. I really think he—"

"Pardon me, miss." A black skirt entered the room, ushering in a red-faced house-keeper and the waft of linseed oil. She dipped a bow to Esther. "There's a Mr. Farris here to see Master Seaton. I told him the master weren't home, so he insists on speaking with you instead."

Esther shot a gaze to Helen. A trapped fox couldn't have looked more desperate.

Helen leaned near and whispered, "I will stay until he leaves."

A flicker of gratitude lit Esther's eyes, then she flattened her lips and faced the housekeeper. "Very well, send him in."

They stood as the revenue man entered.

He wilted into a sloppy bow, hat in hand. "What's this? Two beautiful women when I anticipated only one? It is my lucky day, is it not?"

To her credit, Esther dipped a polite nod. "Perhaps not, Mr. Farris, for my brother is gone to town, and it's my understanding you were calling on him."

"Pish!" He fluttered his fingers. "Only a slight inconvenience, and besides. . ." In three strides, he closed in on them. Taking each of their hands, he pressed a kiss to their skin simultaneously. "I'd much rather call on pretty ladies."

Helen yanked her hand away. Did the man think of nothing else? No wonder he failed at the task for which he'd been sent. Taking Esther's arm, she guided her friend back to the settee and made sure to spread out her gown so that the fellow couldn't barge in between them.

Planting his feet wide, he frowned at her maneuver.

She smiled up at him. "Mr. Farris, have you any news of the smugglers you were after?"

"None about the scoundrels who raided the *Nancarrow*." A squall raged on his creased brow, the jaunty curls of his hair unwinding a bit. Then he snapped his fingers and perked up. "But not to worry. I have a plan afoot to entrap those thieves. Actually, that's what I was hoping Mr. Seaton might help me with."

"Oh?" Alarm lifted gooseflesh on her arms. "I hope it's not dangerous."

The man's chest filled out, straining the buttons on his waistcoat. "I thrive on danger, Miss Fletcher, but don't fret. I shall keep Mr. Seaton perfectly safe. I merely need an extra pair of eyes."

Next to her, Esther stiffened. "Are you expecting trouble, sir?"

"What I am expecting, ladies, is a ship to arrive in three days. The perfect bait for those who cannot keep themselves from pilfering others' goods."

Helen leaned forward. "And if none do?"

"Hadn't thought of that." He rubbed his jaw, the rasp of poorly shaven whiskers overly loud in the room.

A slow smile slashed across his face, entirely too suggestive. "You have a quick mind, Miss Fletcher, one I should like to know better."

She stood. Enough was far more than enough. "Allow me to be plain, Mr. Farris. Your attentions toward me are not only a waste of your time but are unwelcome. I am not now, nor ever will be, inclined to foster your acquaintance."

Deep red spread up his neck like a wound.

Good. She stepped closer. "Furthermore, sir, since Mr. Seaton is clearly not at home, I suggest you go and find him, for there can be no more for you to say to us."

Behind her, Esther gasped.

Mr. Farris jammed his hat back atop his head. "Well," he blustered. "Good day, then, ladies."

He stalked from the room, steps stilted and neck stiff. The picture of a reprimanded schoolboy.

Laughter begged to run free past her lips, but she slapped her hand to her mouth. Oh, what must Esther think of her to so rudely upbraid a guest in her home? She spun, horrified, and held her breath.

Esther stood, wide-eyed. "Did you see his face?"

"I did."

Slowly, Esther's lips curved, higher and higher, until she burst into laughter so merry that Helen couldn't help but join in. They giggled like girls, and finally Esther had to dab at the moisture in her eyes.

"Oh, Esther, please forgive my breach of manners, but the man was simply not to be borne."

"No apology required." Esther flew to the window and parted the curtain, then winked back at Helen. "There he goes. I wouldn't have known how to shoo him off so efficiently, but I am a quick study. I shall endeavor to be as forthright as you in the future."

She gained her friend's side and stared out at the retreating backside of Mr. Farris's horse. "In the case of Mr. Farris, pride is his Achilles' heel. Strike that, and he'll leave you be."

Her smile faded as the man galloped off. She'd steered him away from herself and Esther for now, but hopefully she'd not shoved him more forcefully into seeking out and arresting the area smugglers.

Namely Isaac.

⸎

Patting the signed document in his pocket, Isaac stepped out of Mr. Green's office. The man was a miracle worker. Only one more investor—*one*—and the mine wouldn't be merely an idea, but a money-making reality for him and his tenants.

He strolled down High Street with a lift to his step. Out of debt. A lovely woman living in the parsonage. A new business venture to pursue. He tugged his hat with a smile and a hearty, "Good day," as he passed old Marnie Winkler, selling last year's apples. Then on second thought, he doubled back and flipped her a coin, just for the joy of it.

She dipped her head. "God bless ye, Master Seaton."

"Indeed, He has, Mistress Winkler."

He continued on, but as he crossed over to Fore Street, his step hitched. He paused, listening hard.

Cack. Cack.

There it was again. The raspy cry of a corn crake—a bird more inclined to a hayfield than a village.

And one that sang only at night.

Slowly, he slid his gaze across the street, to a thin gap between two buildings. The black outline of a bony man emerged, but even as daylight engulfed the fellow, he was little more than a dirt-coloured smudge. Stained breeches. Soiled dress coat. Even the man's shirt had yellowed into the dull drab of hopelessness. His dark gaze met Isaac's, then he slipped back into the shadows.

Billy Hawker. A growl rumbled in Isaac's throat. Glancing up and down the street, he waited for a dray to lumber past, then took off at a run. The gap between buildings was barely wide enough for Billy, let alone Isaac's shoulders. Sideways, he scraped on as best he could, until the passage opened into a narrow alley, hidden from the street on one side by a stack of crates. The other end curved slightly, blocking pedestrian views.

Isaac grabbed the man by the collar and shoved him up against a brick wall. "Blast it! I told you we were finished."

Hawker's eyes bulged. "But there's something you should know."

"Not in public! Never in public." Isaac ground his teeth. If anyone saw him with a known free trader, the gossip could not only tarnish his reputation, but raise Farris's suspicions. Isaac's fingers clenched tighter, cutting off Hawker's air supply. The man wriggled beneath his grasp.

"Bah!" He let go.

Any damage was already done.

Hawker slumped over, gasping. "I din't...din't know how else...to reach ye."

Isaac sighed, flexing out the leftover rage still tingling in his hands. "What is it?"

After a few more gulps of air, the man straightened. "I were slinging back a pint at the Pickled Parrot last eve when in walks Grimlox."

Folding his arms, Isaac leaned against the opposite building. "Jack Grimlox?"

"Aye."

The leader of a rival gang of smugglers? He frowned. "What's he doing showing his face around here?"

"That's what me and the boys thought." Hawker's thin shoulders raised like tent posts holding up a worn canvas. "Din't much care, though, after he bought a few rounds o' drinks."

"That doesn't make any sense." Isaac shook his head. "What's he after?"

"Silence."

"What?" He stepped away from the wall, studying Hawker's face. Was this some kind of ruse?

Hawker retreated, until his backbone smacked against the bricks. "I can explain. Seems there's a shipment on the move, three days hence. Grimlox and his gang aim to relieve her and want us to lay low."

"So, he bribed you."

"Aye."

"Well, well." Isaac chewed on that morsel of information, the fat of which satisfied. "I'd say that round of drinks was Grimlox's loss, for we aren't in the smuggling business anymore. But"—he narrowed his eyes—"why was it so important to tell me this?"

Hawker dragged his sleeve beneath his nose, leaving a darkened smear on the cuff. "I never saw Grimlox looking better. He were all cleaned up, he were. Dandy clothes. A jingle in his pocket, e'en after he paid for our night o' ale."

The man advanced a step, glanced both ways, then leaned in close to Isaac.

"And he were wearin' a seal ring."

Isaac's muscles clenched. If Hawker took the risk to single him out on a public street, then the ring must be of deadly importance. "Whose?" he asked.

"Brannigan's."

"Blast!" He reeled about and smashed his fist into the wall, wishing to heavens it was Richard's face. "I knew the two were connected. I knew it!"

"I say if you really want to take a jab at ol' Brannigan, then we lift the goods before Grimlox and his gang can get to it. Brandy, tea, rum, tobacco. . .it's a mite fair load. Bring a fancy price."

Breathing hard, he lowered his hand, ignoring the pain and the warmth of blood dripping down his fingers. Hawker's words were a temptation, a strong, flaming temptation. The chance to lash out at Richard Brannigan pounded louder with each beat of his heart.

Until the quiet voice of a small woman murmured in his mind.

Thievery is wrong.

His shoulders slumped. This wasn't a shipment to recoup blasting powder that'd been taken from him. This time it truly would be thievery.

He turned back to Hawker, the weight of the document swinging his coat hem against his thigh. Had he not just minutes ago promised Mr. Green to leave his vengeance against Richard to God?

"Well?" asked Hawker. "What say you?"

"I say no. You and the boys will not plunder this shipment. It's too dangerous with that revenue man sniffing about."

"Danger don't mean nothin' when I've a wife and five littles at home. We be fine now, but winter comes the same time every year. I won't be list'nin' to their cryin', not when I've a chance to set something by."

Reaching out, Isaac rested a hand on the man's shoulder, the bone of which cut into his heart. "I understand, Billy. Truly. Just be patient. I'm near to striking a deal that will benefit us all—for years to come."

"I'm glad for it. I am. But the thought o' Grimlox and his lot gettin' the whole load..." He shook his head. "Don't seem right."

"I'm coming to believe neither was it right for us to engage in the same dubious activities as Grimlox in the first place." He let go of the fellow. "We must put our trust in God alone, not in our own feeble attempts to enact justice. Let them have it, Hawker. All of it."

For a moment, the man stood there, his grey eyes agleam with a strange light. Then slowly it faded to a hollowness seen usually in the gazes of fisherfolk after a bad pilchard season. Hawker sniffed, and after a last swipe of his nose, stalked away.

Yanking out a handkerchief, Isaac pressed the cloth against his knuckles. Would Billy Hawker do as he said? Lord knew. And Isaac wouldn't blame him if he didn't. Only a month ago, he'd have done the same.

Balling up the cloth, he shoved it back into his pocket. Funny how a small governess could change his whole world.

Chapter Eight

Three sleepless nights. Three never-ending days. Helen lived and died in jerky starts and stops, and it seemed Father did, too. He rarely opened his eyes anymore, let alone consumed any food or drink. On the chair next to his bedside, she planted her elbows on her thighs and her chin in her hands. Fatigue barged in like an unwelcome guest, and this time, she opened the door. Closing her eyes, she matched her prayers to Father's breaths, which wheezed in then slowly bled away.

Oh God, please. Heal this man. The world needs him. I need him. You can do this, for nothing is too hard for You.

"Helen."

She tensed. Her name was little more than a sigh in the afternoon quiet. Or was it a vain imagining? Not that she didn't believe God could answer in an audible voice, but here? Now?

Yes, Lord. I am listening.

"Helen."

Her eyelids flew open, and she lurched upright. "Father?"

Cloudy brown eyes stared at her—or did they? Father gazed as if he looked right through her. She shivered, recalling St. Stephen peering into heaven itself, moments before he died.

She shifted from her chair to his bed, reaching out to press her palm against his cheek. Cool skin met her touch, parchment thin and far too fragile. "You're awake. I am glad of it."

His lips worked, the left side lagging behind the right, but nevertheless working. "Let," he said.

Let? What on earth did he need her permission for? She bent, leaning close. "Let what?"

His face moved almost imperceptibly beneath her hand, but this time his voice was a sail catching wind, stronger and with more force. "Letter."

She couldn't help but smile. "Oh, a letter. You want to write a letter?"

"Nay, already written. For you."

Her throat tightened. "You've written a letter to me?"

"No. God did." His gaze strayed to his Bible on the bedstand. "His Word is a letter to you."

Reaching for it, she retrieved the book, running her hand over the cracked leather cover. How many messages had he prepared from this text? How many words of wisdom gleaned? She shook her head. "Oh Father, I cannot take this. You are getting better. You shall need it."

"It is yours now." His withered hand crept atop the counterpane, inching toward her own. "This isn't. . ." His fingers met hers, resting like the last leaf of autumn fallen to the ground. His Adam's apple bobbed, and he sucked in a breath. "This isn't the day I would have chosen to die, but it is not of my choosing."

She shook her head, over and over, as if the movement could prevent his words from reaching her ears. Hugging the Bible to her chest, she drew what strength she could from the feel of it then laid it back where it belonged. "This is the most you've spoken in a fortnight. You are on the mend."

"I love you, child."

"Oh, Father. . . I love you, too." She pressed her lips shut, lest sorrow suddenly break loose.

"Now," she stood. "How about some broth? Gwen made a pot of stock before she left at noontide. She even made biscuits to hold us over until her return on the morrow. Would you like some?"

The clouds billowed back over his gaze, thick and milky. Nevertheless, he nodded, and while only once, the movement was sure and strong.

She darted out to the main room. A bit of broth and watered ale, both would surely feed this sudden strength he'd shown. She dipped some soup into a bowl, letting it cool as she gathered a mug—but then a rap on the door pulled her from filling it.

Isaac's broad shoulders crowded the doorframe, his presence a brilliant light in the grey afternoon. He doffed his hat, and his dark hair glistened at the edges where mist had snuck beneath. "Good day, Miss Fletcher."

"Good day, Mr. Seaton." She swept out her hand. "Will you come in?"

"No, I was merely on my way home and thought I'd check on your father." His gaze held her in place. "And on you."

Despite the chill moisture seeping in the open door, warmth spread from her tummy to her chest. "My father seems to be rallying. I think he is finally and truly on the mend."

"I hope it, for his sake and yours." He cocked his head, his eyes narrowing as he searched her face. He reached, slowly, as if she might skitter away, and his thumb traced the curve beneath her eyes. "You look weary. How are you faring?"

She bit her lip. Besides her father, was there ever a more thoughtful soul?

"Bearing up," she murmured.

"You're a brave one." His hand dropped, and he grinned. "You know, I think you'd make a fine smuggler."

"An offer I heartily refuse, sir. . . Oh, but that does remind me, has Mr. Farris caught up with you yet?"

"No." His smile faded. "Why?"

She tensed. Would it be spreading gossip, since clearly the man hadn't tried very hard to find Isaac? "Well, perhaps Mr. Farris has changed his mind, but he did mention to me and Esther that there's some shipment coming in he intends to use as a lure for smugglers."

Isaac grunted. "What has that to do with me?"

"Nothing—I hope?" Holding her breath, she studied his eyes, first one then the other, fearing yet needing to read the truth.

His gaze bored into hers, steady and sure. "I give you my word, I am well and truly finished with such a trade."

She blew out her relief. "I am glad of it."

"Yet. . ." His voice lowered to a gentle command. "There is something I should like your word on as well."

It took everything within her not to gape. What could he possibly want from her? "Such as?"

"While your independent spirit does you credit, when the time comes for your father to. . ." Sorrow creased his brow. That he cared so deeply was a testament to the compassion of this man.

He stepped closer. "I would not see you grieving alone. Know that I am always available for you, no matter the time of day. Promise that you will lean on me for support." Her pulse quickened. Surely he meant that not in a literal sense, yet she couldn't help but remember when he'd held her the week before, so strong, so compassionate. She swallowed the lump in her throat. "You are very kind."

"I am glad your opinion of me has altered since we first met."

"And I am glad your occupation has changed."

"Touché, Miss Fletcher." He donned his hat, his rogue grin returning. "Good day to you."

"Good day." She watched him stride away then slowly pressed the door shut behind him. How wicked was it to wish her father well, yet not so well that she would have to leave Seaton lands? With a sigh, she filled her father's mug, collected the broth bowl, and returned to his chamber.

As soon as she crossed the threshold, she stopped. The bowl hit the floorboards, soup splattering against her hem. The cup cracked like a broken bone. Father stared at her wide-eyed.

And dead.

༄

Isaac hunched his shoulders against the unrelenting mist, clicking his tongue to urge Duchess onward. The coming evening would not be kind to man or beast caught unawares. Thankfully he'd be pulling off his boots in front of a warm hearth and drinking a glass of Madeira by the time a thick fog rolled in with the tide. Leaning forward, he patted his mount's neck. "And you'll be glad of a warm stall, eh girl?"

Despite the threat of poor weather, he whistled an old folk tune as he rode from the parsonage to Seaton Hall. Life hadn't been this good since Father's death. His shoulder bag bounced against his back, containing the signed contract for a new mine. The sweet smile of Helen lingered in his thoughts. Life was very good.

He turned onto the gravel road leading to home. Ahead, just in front of the manor, a blur of red poked a hole in the grey afternoon. His blood ran cold.

Redcoats. Four of them. Mounted and at the ready.

Oh, God. Was this it? Had his past sins come to haunt in a way that would choke the breath from him at the end of a noose? What would happen to Esther? What of Helen?

The four men said nothing as he rode by, their stoic faces impossible to read—even when he tipped his hat to them. But they let him pass without hindrance, so surely that meant something. It *had* to mean something.

God, please.

He dismounted in front of the stairs, fully aware of the men at his back, just as a scarlet-faced Mr. Farris erupted out the manor's door, hat in hand.

Farris took the steps two at a time. "About time you show your face, Seaton!"

Isaac grabbed onto Duchess's headstall, calming the animal from the revenue man's advance. "Were you looking for me, Mr. Farris?"

Farris spit out a curse. "I've been looking for you these past three days, sir!"

"And so you've found me. But surely I am not the cause for your friends here"—he hitched his thumb over his shoulder—"or for your hasty departure from Seaton Hall."

"No. I have your sister to thank for that."

He frowned. What was he to make of that? Men generally ran toward Esther, not away from her.

"My sister?" he asked.

Ruddy splotches bloomed on Farris's face. "I suggest you spend more time at home, Mr. Seaton, schooling her in the proper arts of decorum and etiquette. I've never been so insulted."

"What's she done?"

"She cast me out, sir!" Tiny flecks of spittle flew from the man's mouth. "A finer catch she couldn't have found, nor will she. Her loss, though, not to mention yours."

An enraged child couldn't have looked more petulant. Tempted to laugh at the man, Isaac settled for clearing his throat instead. "I'm sorry, but did you say you were looking for me, not my sister?"

"Indeed." Farris yanked on his hat, his heaving chest slowly coming to rest. "I need your assistance in navigating the coastline hereabouts. You'd know it better than any since it's your land."

"What are you looking. . ."

Beyond Farris, a dark shape peeked out from around the corner of the manor, then immediately jerked back. Had Isaac not recognized that thin collection of bones, he'd have tallied it up to imagination. Blast it! Why would Billy Hawker show up here? Now? The redcoats at Isaac's back would need no encouragement to string Hawker up if they caught sight of him.

Farris narrowed his eyes at Isaac's sudden silence.

Immediately Isaac forced a cough, pulling out his handkerchief for extra measure.

"Sorry. Been fighting a raw throat the better part of the day. Now then, what is it exactly that you're looking for?"

"You'd know if you weren't so deuced hard to track down." Farris stomped over to where his horse was tethered to a post, mercifully opposite where Hawker hid. "There was a ship to arrive this morn, yet it's now nearing dark. I suspect it was waylaid by smugglers last night, or worse, wreckers. I need you to mount up and help us find them." Farris swung into his saddle.

Isaac planted his feet. "Smugglers there may be, but you'll find no wreckers in Treporth. The people here are not that kind of folk."

"So. . ." Farris's eyelids tightened to slits. "You admit to smugglers, eh?"

Isaac shook his head. "I admit to nothing."

"Then mount your horse and let's be off."

"In this weather?" He threw out his hands. "It's a fool's errand. That ship is likely hunkered down in Galwyn Bay, not sailing through in a fog sure to come."

"Are you refusing to do your duty, Mr. Seaton?" The man's voice was a growl. One of the redcoat's horses stamped the gravel. Both indicted in a way that augured violence.

"Consider the possibilities." Isaac spread his words out slow, like a soothing balm. "If you make any headway, you won't get very far before you'll have to turn back. The tide rises in a few hours, and along with it a fog so thick, you'll be hard-pressed to find your way home."

"Then we'll move from shore to higher ground—as the smugglers must." Farris flipped aside the hem of his coat, revealing the handle of a pistol tucked into his belt. "Now, mount up."

A sigh emptied the last of his fight. There'd be no reasoning with this mad man. "Very well, but my horse is done for. I've ridden her hard to Truro and back. Be on your way while I see to her and gear up a fresh mount."

Mist gathered like a shroud on Farris's shoulders, nature proclaiming this fool was on a death ride. Nevertheless, the man lifted his arrogant nose. "Do I have your word, sir?"

He'd have to give it or Farris would never leave. "You do," he said simply.

The pack of men heeled their horses about and rode down the road. Isaac waited until the last hint of red blended into grey.

Leaving Duchess where she stood, he took off at a sprint and rounded the corner of the manor. "Hawker! What the devil are you doing here?"

A sack of dark clothing rose from the shrubbery like a ghoul. Dark eyes drilled into his. "There's been a rockslide. Tegwyn and Rook are trapped."

"Blast!" Though the redcoats were long gone, he lowered his tone. "Where?"

"Blackpool Cove."

"The cove?" Growling, he yanked off his hat and slapped it against his thigh. It was either that or pummel the man in front of him. "You boarded that ship and pulled off goods, did you not?"

Hawker's thin shoulders shrugged. "She were fair picked over by the time we reached her."

"No doubt by Grimlox and his gang." He blew out a breath, long and low, and crammed his hat back atop his head. "You'll be the ones to hang if Farris finds you with the goods—and you know that's where he's headed."

Fear darkened the man's face like a thundercloud. "Then we must hurry."

Isaac's gut clenched. This was wrong. A trap. Certain death.

But did he even have a choice?

Chapter Nine

Death was no stranger to Helen Fletcher. As a young girl, she'd held hands with the black specter while weeping at her mother's bedside. But here in a Cornwall parsonage as she knelt beside her father, tears spent, grief already unpacked and settled into the cavern of her heart, she knew instinctively this was different. She was alone in the world now. An unmoored ghost. Deserted. The fear she'd tried to ignore all her life suddenly rushed at her, stealing the breath from her lungs. Pretending wouldn't work this time.

And never would again.

She closed her eyes. *Oh God, how am I to bear this?*

Prickles tingled in her feet from her cramped position, heaping pain upon pain. It was all too much. She rose and fled from her father's chamber. Wild to be among the living, she grabbed her spencer and buttoned it haphazardly, then tied on her bonnet. Shoving her hands into her gloves, she escaped out the door into a world seeping with tears.

The mist followed her to the shed where Jenny stood, and though it took her several tries, she managed to saddle the horse. She dragged over an upturned bucket and mounted. Hopefully Isaac had meant his offer of support.

She straightened her skirts then urged the horse out into the monochrome afternoon. Fitting, really, that colour should die the same day as her father. She gave Jenny free rein, prepared for speed and heedless of the danger should she fall. So be it.

Fine rain needled her cheeks. The world smeared by. In no time, she rounded the bend to Seaton Hall—only to see a black horse taking off across a nearby field, heading toward the woods. Slowing, she squinted in the fuzzy light. The horse was definitely not Duchess, but the man astride? Wide shoulders. As animal as his mount. A silhouette of strength. It had to be Isaac.

She frowned. As the gap widened between her and the master of Seaton Hall, panic welled until something inside her broke. Something only he could fix. She needed his arms around her more than anything.

"Isaac!" she shouted, as stunned by the passion in her voice as by the use of his Christian name.

But he was too far ahead to hear. And once he entered the copse, she'd lose sight of him as well. Should she let him go? Turn back and seek some measure of comfort from Esther's company? She glanced over her shoulder at the manor as she rode. Small comfort was not the same as leaning on someone, and she'd promised to lean on Isaac.

With a crack of the crop, she plunged after him. The field was easy enough to cross, but once she entered the trees, she was forced to slow. She had to settle for simply keeping him in sight, and even that was a stretch, for he rode with far more experience. By the time she navigated to the end of the woods, her skirt hem was ripped, her bonnet dangled by the ribbons at her neck, and Isaac had already crossed the grassy ridge leading to the coastal cliffs.

Cupping her hand to her mouth, she yelled his name again.

But the misty air blunted the sound as effectively as a damp blanket dulls the roar of a fire. Defeat tasted bitter in her mouth.

She swallowed it back and pressed on, desperate. An insane chase were she of a right mind, yet nothing was right about this day—nor ever would be again, now that her father was gone. She drove Jenny across the ridge and reined her to a halt at the rocky trail disappearing over the cliff, the one Isaac had warned her about. She leaned as far as she dared without tumbling from the saddle, trying to catch a glimpse of the man. He was right. The path was narrow, jagged, and altogether foreboding. But down a ways, it flattened out before it hooked into a switchback. She'd go that far, and no farther, whether she glimpsed him or not.

Clicking her tongue, she gripped the reins until her fingers ached. Jenny's nose jerked up and her ears twitched, but she moved on. Leaning back for balance, Helen held her breath as the horse picked her way along the thin route and didn't release it until Jenny made it to the rocky landing.

This time Helen didn't dare to peek, so treacherously did the ground give way beside her. *Don't look. Don't look!* She forced her focus along the snaking trail. As Isaac had said, it plummeted at an alarming slope, nearly down to the rocky beach, then turned and disappeared into the mist. If Isaac had come this way, he was out of sight.

She frowned. He'd never admitted this was a smuggler's trail, yet she couldn't help but wonder. What was left of her heart sank to her stomach. Surely Isaac was a man of his word. He said he'd given up such thievery. But why disappear down to the coast on a foul day such as this? La! What was *she* doing out here? She'd heard of the grieving committing strange acts, but she never expected to yield to such behaviour.

Nor would she. She'd wait for him at Seaton Hall. Pulling on the left rein, she attempted to turn the horse. "Let's go, Jenny."

But Jenny's rear hoof slipped. The horse panicked.

And Helen plunged.

She hit the ground at the same time Jenny's hoof smashed into her ankle. The horse galloped down the trail. Helen groaned, reaching for her foot.

But the rocks of the path gave way.

Helen bounced down the side of the cliff like a rag doll tossed from a coach window. Sky and ground blended together. Rocks cut. Scraping, scratching, ripping fabric and skin.

Then the world stopped.

How long she lay there, God only knew. Long enough to hate the pain, the drizzle, the hopelessness throbbing with as much agony as her bruised body. Most of all, she hated herself. What a reckless thing to have done.

Weary to the bone, she rolled over and pushed up. But when she tried to put weight on her ankle, a cry tore out her throat, and she dropped to her knees. Walking was out of the question.

Lifting her head, she scanned the immediate area. Nearby, a gaping hollow opened onto the beach—not a cave, really, but shelter enough to get her out of the spitting rain.

Crawling in a wet skirt sapped the small store of strength she had left. Once inside, she stretched out her legs and leaned back against the rocks, weary beyond measure. Oh, to quit breathing, just like Father, but her body wouldn't oblige.

"God," she whispered, "what am I to do?"

Only the crash of wave against rock answered.

She lifted her voice, hurtling her words as viciously as the sea. "I cannot bear this. I cannot!"

Rage, sorrow, torment, all tore out her throat in a ragged cry. Was this how Jesus felt before he died, broken by a grief so great that He committed his spirit to God?

Committed His spirit to God.

The words played over and over in her head, cresting with each swell of the sea until suddenly it made sense.

Her head dropped, and she closed her eyes. For the first time in her life, she surrendered instead of pretending.

"Your will, God," she murmured. "Your will."

⬤⬤

Isaac vaulted off his horse, his heels barely digging into the sand before he took off at a lope. To his right, a wall of fog crept closer with the tide. On his left, a cliff, pitted and gouged from the rockslide. And ahead. . .

Oh, God.

It wasn't much of a prayer, but it was the best he could muster while speeding past one wagon and sliding to a stop at the back of another. Hawker squatted next to Rook, who propped himself up on his elbows, one of his legs trapped. A pace past Rook, Tegwyn lay insensible, the left side of his body hidden by the same boulder crushing Rook's leg.

Isaac crouched next to Hawker. "Hang on, Rook. Hawker and I will have you and Tegwyn out of here in no time."

"Aye, Master Seaton. No doubt ye will." Rook's brave words traveled on a groan, the pain distinguishable even above the crashing waves.

Rising, Isaac yanked Hawker up along with him and pulled him aside. "Where's the rest of the crew?"

"Davey musta run off when I come get you, the blackguard. He were gone by the time I got back." Hawker swiped his nose then averted his gaze. "No one else come."

"Do you mean to tell me you attempted this with only four men? Of all the incompetent, foolhardy—" He clamped his jaw shut. Hard. No sense berating Hawker. The man could hardly count to ten. Tegwyn must've been the brains behind this scheme—and now suffered the consequences of it.

Isaac sighed. "Come on."

Leaping over several scattered crates yet to be loaded, he dashed to where the rowboat was grounded. The bow was secure, hauled up on slippery green rocks, but the stern floated higher than when it had landed. Much longer and the sea would take it.

Leaning over the gunwale, Isaac grabbed the two oars and tossed one to Hawker. Not much daylight remained, and even that a poor gruel. Still, he strained to examine the top of the ridge for any flash of redcoats. Farris was out here, somewhere.

He sped back to the injured men.

"We'll have to wedge this boulder upward. We won't be able to move it much, but a little may be all we need." He crouched, searching for the best angle to drive in the oars, then shouted up at Hawker. "Cram an oar, paddle end down, in here."

Leaving Hawker behind, Isaac searched for the right size rock to use as a hammer. Big enough for powerful strokes, but not so big that he couldn't hold it, and—there. He scooped up a great, craggy chunk and ran back.

He nodded at Hawker. "You hold the oar, I'll pound it in."

Hefting the rock, Isaac whaled on the wood. Each strike juddered up his arms. Slowly, the oar sank, wedging the boulder up by hairline increments until—crack! The oar tip broke.

Hawker swore.

Isaac merely dropped his rock and grabbed the broken wood. A small space had opened where the paddle had sunk deep, and he crammed the shortened piece of oar into it.

Hawker frowned as he grabbed onto it, and Isaac didn't blame him. Now that the oar was shortened, if Isaac were to miss his aim, he'd snap the man's arm in two.

Praying for a good eye, Isaac threw all he had left into driving the rock against the oar. Sweat stung his eyes. His muscles screamed. But the wood inched earthward. When there was nothing left to pound, he met Hawker's gaze and nodded. They yanked Tegwyn free first. He didn't wake, but at least his crushed arm was still attached.

Rook screamed when they pulled him out. His boot stuck but his leg pulled free, a bloody pulp at the end of his smashed foot, leastwise what was left of it. He'd need that foot attended to immediately or risk losing it. Even then, there were no guarantees.

With Hawker's help, they hefted Rook up and heaved him into the back of the wagon. With his elbows, Rook scuttled over and propped himself against a crate.

They raced back to Tegwyn. Isaac grabbed the man's feet, Hawker his shoulders, and together they hoisted the fellow up next to Rook, then closed the wagon's back gate.

Isaac turned to Hawker. "Get these men out of here."

The mist ran rivulets down Hawker's face. "But the rest o' the load!"

"These men need help. Now!"

Ignoring him, Hawker stared at the goods, eyes transfixed as if nothing else in the world existed.

A growl rumbled in Isaac's chest. The dull-witted fellow was so focused on the goods that he couldn't see the need of his friends. If Isaac drove the injured men himself and left Hawker on his own, the scrawny man would no doubt struggle long to load the big crates and likely end up being drowned by the rising tide or caught by the redcoats.

"Blast!" he shouted at Hawker, the tide, the sky—and the frustration of the whole situation. "I'll see to the last crates and meet up with you. Go!"

It was all he could think of to get Hawker to move. But was it enough? Did the man even hear him?

Thankfully, it worked. Hawker rounded the side of the wagon and hiked his bones up into the driver's seat. With a snap of the reins, he got the two horses going—though truly it wouldn't have taken even that, so eager were the animals to escape the water lapping closer and closer.

Soaked by sweat, sea spray, and anger, Isaac loaded the last four crates into the second wagon. All the while, he scanned from an ever-narrowing beach up to the top of the cliff, keen to spy any hint of scarlet. By the time he finished, white foam licked his heels. He retrieved his own mount, for the horse had shied off to higher ground, then he tethered the beast to the back of the wagon. Crawling up to the driver's seat, he barely grabbed the reins before the workhorses set off.

He drove the length of the beach to where the sand cut away between an archway of rock. Passing beneath, he tensed. This road would likely be where he'd run into Farris—if indeed the man haunted this stretch of coast. It ascended to Isaac's left, fresh ruts ground in the earth by Hawker's wagon. To the right, the treacherous trail leading to Isaac's own lands, wide enough for only one horse—the horse bolting toward him. A flash of reddish-brown mane flew past him.

Isaac yanked the reins of the workhorses, heart dropping to his boots. Jenny. That was Red Jenny. Sidesaddle attached.

And riderless.

He jumped to his feet and stared as far as he could see along the narrow path.

"Helen!" he shouted.

No movement. Just mist and mud, rock and fear. Why would her horse be out here, unless she'd—?

Blast!

A rising tide. A missing woman. And a revenue man only God knew where with Hawker and two injured men hauling a load of contraband. Isaac roared along with the crashing waves and jumped down from the wagon.

There was only one thing to be done.

Chapter Ten

J erking upright, Helen startled awake. Or was she? Darkness surrounded her. Her bones ached, her ankle throbbed, and dampness soaked her backside. But none of that mattered as much as the swell of cold water lapping at her feet. The rising tide. Soon it would reach in and drag her out to sea.

And she couldn't swim.

Fear unhinged her jaw, and she screamed, then held her breath, listening. Were this a dream, there'd be no echo—but the remnants of her cry hung in the darkness like a living thing. Indeed, this nightmare was very real.

"Helen!"

Her name was a lifeline, but did she only imagine Isaac's voice? Was the call of a loved one the last thing one heard before death?

"Helen!"

Did it matter?

"Isaac!" She crawled to the edge of the rocky recess, hands and legs submerged. "I'm here!"

Booming surf drowned her voice. She waited, listening for the break between waves, then invested everything into her next bellow. "Isaac!"

The silhouette of a man on a horse, black against the night, splashed close and stopped in front of her. Isaac sprang from his mount and swept her into his arms.

"Thank God." His breath warmed her brow.

"Oh Isaac! I was so—"

"There's no time."

He hefted her up into the saddle, and she sat sideways, allowing him to swing up behind her.

"Hold on, tightly," he directed.

Wheeling the horse about, he spurred the animal on. The rain had stopped and the sky had cleared, but sea spray broke over them with shocking force as they tore along the beach, drenching her already damp clothes. Knee-deep water hampered the horse's pace.

Isaac took a hard right, steering them onto a steep incline. Instinctively, Helen leaned forward against the horse's neck. Isaac's chest pressed against her back as he did the same. Hooves scrambled for purchase of earth, the horse frantic for a foothold. Were it not for Isaac's strong arms cocooning her, she'd surely fall.

Another turn, and the slope lessened. The narrow track widened and eventually changed into a road. The slap of waves shushed the higher they climbed. Finally, the track evened out, and Isaac stopped the crazed pace, slowing the horse to a walk. Hard to tell where they were, for shadows painted the landscape with an inky brush. But once they passed beneath the bower of a great brambly hedge, the ground flattened onto an open sward. Her eyes adjusted, and she could now see a road bathed in starlight. She had no idea where it went, but apparently Isaac did, for he clicked his tongue and swung the horse to the left.

He crooked his head close to hers. "Are you well?"

The question was too big to consider. Of course she wasn't well, not when Father lay cold in a bed. But the words were too awful to say, so she settled for a lesser pain. "I'm afraid I hurt my ankle. Jenny threw me."

"Then we shall get that attended to as soon as we reach Seaton Hall. What were you doing on Jenny in the first place? Why are you out here?"

"I. . ." Her tongue lay fallow in her mouth. Too many emotions wrestled for first place, and to her shame, the strongest one was to turn her face and rest her cheek against his. Fighting against it, she blurted out, "My father is gone."

He reined the horse to a stop, and before she drew another breath, he cradled her in his arms and pressed his lips against the top of her head. "Oh, my sweet Helen, I am so sorry for your loss. Would that I could take your pain."

Her throat closed, the compassion in his words breaking and mending at the same time. She leaned against him, allowing his strength to shore her up. "This is why I sought you," she murmured.

He pulled back, the horse shifting beneath his sudden move. "But how did you know I was out here?"

"I saw you riding off, and I didn't think. I simply followed." She peered up at his dark shadow of a face, his eyes unreadable beneath the brim of his hat. "What *are* you doing out here?"

〜◦◦〜

Wide brown eyes stared into Isaac's soul, searching for truth. Though he wore layers of soggy garments, he felt as exposed as the day he'd graced the world with his first cry. "I'll answer you as we ride. You've got to get out of that wet gown, and I have yet one more engagement to attend to."

With pressure from his heels, he prodded the horse on toward Seaton Hall, where he'd deposit Helen with his sister for the night. Sleeping alone in a cottage with her deceased father was beyond a grievous act.

She faced forward, her loosened hair brushing against his chin as she turned. "Thank you, but all the same, I should like that answer now."

A grin stretched his lips. Even while suffering loss, she remained as determined as ever. "Mr. Farris asked me to help ferret out some smugglers. Seems there was a shipment running late, and he had his suspicions."

She quirked her head, like an owl listening for the slightest rustle of undergrowth.

"After working with young charges the past five years, I've developed a knack for discerning deception. You are not telling me the full truth, I think."

His brow fairly raised the brim of his hat. "Are you really a governess or an interrogator for the Crown sent here to bedevil me?"

"If you are bedeviled," she glanced over her shoulder, "then I suggest it is your own conscience wreaking such turmoil."

His gaze landed on her lips. A slow burn ignited in his gut. How well she molded against his chest. How right the feel of her in his arms. What would her response be if he acted on such rising desire?

Instant remorse punched him hard, for he ought not feel such things toward a grieving woman. Even so, he couldn't purge the huskiness from his voice. "On that account you are entirely wrong."

She turned forward again, and for a while, they rode in silence, the horse's steady plodding sucking up mud.

"I think that before you intended to meet with Mr. Farris," she said at length, "you were warning those smugglers, were you not?"

"Not warning, helping."

She jerked back to face him. "You promised you were done with thievery!"

The look of admiration in her eyes vanished, replaced by cold shadows, and the loss cut deep and bloody. He shook his head. "I have not broken that promise. A few of the men were in trouble, caught beneath a rockslide at Blackpool Cove. I went to free them—and a good thing I did, or I'd not have seen your horse running loose."

Her shoulders sagged, the rhythm of the mount's gait dipping her head—or was it due to her disappointment in him?

She blinked up at him. "It seems once again I am in your debt."

Her words taught him to hope. The scent of the sea clung to her, every bit as pungent as the loamy smell of the wet earth his horse trod upon. A lock of dark hair drooped on her cheek, as wild as on that first ride they'd shared. He reached for it and tucked the strand behind her ear, wishing for all the world there weren't a barrier of leather glove between his skin and hers. She shivered, from a chill or from his touch?

Oh, hang it all. He yanked off his glove and swept his fingers over her cheek, cupping her face in his hand. She did not pull back. "You are wrong, you know. It is I who owe you. I am a changed man since your arrival. Your candor has caused me to think about my actions, that the end does not justify the means. For so long I've been bent on revenge, thinking I was right by taking back what Brannigan had taken from me, but I've come to see that none of it was mine in the first place. It's always—only—been God's. You helped me see that."

Her head shook beneath his hand. "Not me."

"You." He bent toward her, resting his brow against hers. "Tell me, Helen, what will you do now that your father is gone?"

She edged back from him, the small space between them gaping like a wound.

"Return to Ireland, I suppose. Though I hope you'll help me with arrangements for a proper burial before I leave."

Blast! He could hardly bear the inches between them, let alone the entire North Sea. Loosening the reins, he let the horse walk at will and focused his entire attention—and heart—on the woman in front of him. "Of course I'll help."

Her mouth curved into a half-smile. "And a good deed requires a kiss, does it not?"

She remembered? He cocked his head, studying her by the shadow of night. "Who told you that?"

"You did," she poked him in the shoulder. "That first night we met."

A charge shot through him, and he captured her hand, pressing it to his chest. Dare he hope the evening they'd met was as indelibly etched onto her heart as it was on his? "You are not as adept at discerning the truth as you claim, for that night I did not speak the full truth."

"Oh?"

He swallowed. Was he ready for this? Was she? The timing was off, couldn't be worse, in fact. But there was no stopping now.

"A deed of such magnitude requires your hand in marriage." His voice lowered to a rasp, not for want of asking, but for fear of the answer. "Will you give it?"

Chapter Eleven

Everything was overloud. The creak of saddle and jingle of tack as the horse shifted weight. Leftover drips of mist working their way down blades of the sward's scrubby grass. Helen's racing heart. How could she accept a proposal on the night of her father's death?

Isaac stared, waiting, rock still. Everything hinged on her answer—for them both. She'd never known such a kind man, such generosity and compassion, and to think he would offer to spend the rest of his days with her. . . . How could she not accept such a gift? Had not Father himself admonished her to open her heart to love? And she did. She loved this man more than life itself.

Twisting her hand in Isaac's grip, she laced her fingers through his, palm to palm—a perfect fit.

"Yes," she whispered.

A simple answer. Or was it? She tipped her face to his, straining to read Isaac's response. And what she saw stole her breath.

Despite the shadow of his hat brim, his eyes lit with an intense fire, with her the sole focus of a love so pure, it shimmied across her shoulders. Her lips parted, dumbstruck. How did one respond to such unbridled passion? She swallowed, fearing she might never be worthy of such adoration.

And then his mouth was on hers.

One taste, and she knew it would never be enough. She'd endured a stolen kiss before, but nothing like this. She leaned into him, clinging to his shirt, pulling him closer. He smelled of the sea, of wind and waves and distant horizons. Warmth spread through her body, driving off the pain of loss and hurt. By the time he pulled back, she nearly slipped from the horse.

"Whoa, now." He chuckled, bracing her up with his strong arms. "I know it is wrong of me to be so happy on the day of your bereavement, but you have made me so." Cupping her face in his hands, he pressed a kiss to her brow. "I love you, more than life and air."

"Oh, Isaac—" Her voice broke, and she licked her lips, the leftover taste of him still there. "I love you infinitely more."

She could live here, in this moment, his breath warming her skin. But despite the heat of the man and the fervor of the moment, the chill of her wet gown crept beneath her skin, and she shivered.

He leaned back, gathering the reins. "Time we get you home."

She turned and nestled against his chest as he drove the horse into a canter. Her thoughts sped as quickly as the passing black landscape, too dizzying to sort through. Eventually, her head sank, and she stared at the woolen sleeve of the man—her future husband—holding the reins in a loose grip. It was fine fabric, that of a gentleman, but matted with sand and smelling of hard work. He was a contradiction, indeed, but he was her contradiction. How could a single day hold such exquisite pain and joy?

"Nearly there," Isaac's voice rumbled close to her ear.

The road rounded the swell of a hillock. They followed the curve, and once they cleared the mound, Isaac jerked the horse to a stop. Not far ahead, torches lit the night, four of which were gripped in the hands of mounted redcoats and bobbed alongside a wagon.

Helen squinted at the bright offense. "Why would—?"

"Shh," Isaac warned.

Too late.

The two soldiers at the rear charged toward them. "Hands up! Behind yer heads!"

Isaac stiffened. "Do as they say."

Slowly, she lifted her fingers to the back of her neck. The loss of Isaac's arms around her felt like death.

The larger of the two reached for the reins and led their horse. Were Isaac's strong thighs and his back not a steadying rock, she'd surely have slipped from the saddle. What kind of trouble was this?

A horse tethered to the back of the wagon pawed the ground when they passed. As they moved on, a low groan rumbled in Isaac's chest. In the wagon bed, two men sat upright, torchlight doing crazy things to the whites of their eyes. Another man lay next to them, bloodied and still.

Gooseflesh lifted along Helen's arms. Were these the smugglers Isaac had come to help?

Mr. Farris turned on the driver's seat, a pistol lying beside him. A torch mounted on the wagon's side tinted his face with devilish light. "What's this?"

"You're the one who wanted me out here, and so you find me." Isaac's voice thundered at her back. "Now call down your men. You're frightening Miss Fletcher."

"No, that one fears nothing." Farris's dark eyes landed on her. "Tell me, Miss Fletcher, what are you doing out here on such a wicked night?"

"I—I—" The words stuck in her throat, trapped beneath the stare of the soldiers. Sucking in a breath, she tried again. "I was looking for Mr. Seaton when my horse threw me. My ankle turned, and he found me."

Mr. Farris narrowed his eyes. "A very pretty story, lady—yet I believe not a word of it. Dismount."

Behind her, Isaac shifted, and Mr. Farris snatched up the gun at his side, aiming it at them. "Ah-ah-ah, not you, Seaton."

"For the love of all that's right, man, she's hurt!" Isaac's shout hung on the air, savage in intensity. "She'll not be able to stand."

Farris cocked the hammer, the click of it as sharp as a bullet's report. "That's exactly what I intend to find out."

She lowered her hands, careful, like a piece of glass. One wrong move and the crack of gunfire might shatter bones and lives. Holding tightly to the saddle horn, she eased earthward. If she landed on her good foot, she could surely stand, for she'd played many a game of hopscotch with her charges.

But at the last moment, the horse shied. She teetered. Hundreds of knives stabbed her foot and ankle. A fiery scream burned out her throat, and she crumpled.

Before muddy gravel bit into her cheek, sturdy arms scooped her up.

And the barrels of four more guns swung their way.

❧

Isaac clenched his jaw so hard, it crackled in his ears. How dare this upstart treat them like criminals? He hadn't even done anything wrong this time! Helen gasped in his arms, from pain or fear, hard to say. Either way, Farris was to blame. Despite the brilliance of the flaming torches, rage painted the whole scene purple.

"Tell your men to stand down!" Isaac's voice shook like a peal of thunder. Good. May they all cower at his fury. "You can see the woman's not playacting. Allow to me put her back on my horse."

"No." Farris lifted his chin and stared down the length of his nose. "Put her up here with me."

Was the man mad? He'd as soon sit her next to the jaws of hell. "I will do nothing of the sort!"

Farris's head lowered like a bull about to charge. The soldiers closed in, eyes bright with the promise of a fight. Farris cocked the hammer of his gun to full open. If that thing went off, Helen would bear the brunt.

Isaac pivoted back a step, shielding her by exposing his own side. "I swear to God, if you so much as—"

"Stop it!" Helen squirmed in his arms, shifting to face Farris.

Isaac widened his stance.

Farris widened his eyes.

"Mr. Farris, there can be no hope for you and I." Helen spoke as to a schoolboy, her tone confident yet instructive. And in that moment, Isaac couldn't have been more proud. Any other woman would have swooned by now.

"This very night I have committed my hand to Mr. Seaton," she continued. "I am certain, however, that with your capture of these ruffians, you will be lauded a hero. Better women than I will vie for your attention."

What? Was she seriously complimenting the buffoon? Isaac cocked his head. So did Farris.

"Why would you say..." The words died on Isaac's lips as an interesting transformation took place up on the wagon seat.

Farris's chest expanded a full two inches, and his shoulders stood at attention. A toad couldn't have puffed up to a greater swell. "No doubt you are correct," he sneered. Even so, he tripped the hammer closed on his gun. "Stand down, men. These two are not involved with the smugglers. Go ahead, Seaton. Hoist her up."

Isaac heaved a sigh and breathed out, "Well done," into Helen's ear, then he lifted her so that she could reach the saddle and released her when she sat secure.

Turning from the horse, he caught a glimpse of Hawker and Rook, fettered in the wagon's back. A sickening taste soured his mouth. He knew that wild-eyed look. He'd seen it the instant before he'd had to put down one of his best geldings. The comparison punched him in the gut, but what was he to do? Outmanned and outgunned, words and timing were his only allies.

God, please. A little help, here.

He faced Farris. "I would have a word with you. Alone."

Farris snorted. "I don't trust you that far, Seaton. Whatever you have to say may be said here, in front of witnesses."

"Fine." He shrugged. "Though sensitive information is usually heard by the commanding—"

"*Sensitive*," Farris drawled out the word. "Information?"

Isaac strode the few steps to the wagon seat, acutely aware of the redcoats' gazes stabbing him from all angles. "Besides my rescuing of Miss Fletcher, why do you think it took me so long to get out here? I gave my word to help you, and I have information to do just that."

Farris eyed him. Would he bite the bait? Isaac drew in a breath and held it.

"Very well. Men, keep guard." Farris jumped down from the wagon, his boots slogging hard into the mud as he landed. He kept his gun, but at least he tucked the barrel into his trousers.

Isaac led him to the side of the road, making a show of taking the fool into his confidence—while stalling to come up with something to say.

Farris folded his arms. "Well?"

Exactly. Well what? He scrubbed his jaw, hoping to work loose a magical concoction of words—when a perfectly wonderful idea took root. And grew.

Thank You, Lord.

"These men you have"—he hitched his thumb over his shoulder—"while a fine catch, they are not the real villains."

Farris's brow crumpled. "What do you mean?"

"Look at that wagon. Do you really think those few crates are the sum of what was taken from that cargo? No." He shook his head. "That ship of yours was first waylaid and picked over farther up the coast, four miles from here. The true smugglers are led by a man named Grimlox. Jack Grimlox. If you hurry, you can catch them in the act, with a far better haul than this sorry lot."

Farris stared at him, his gaze unreadable so far from the torches. Would this work?

"So help me, Seaton," Farris rumbled as he unfolded his arms. "If you are lying. . ."

The threat twisted on the air like a rope from a gibbet.

Isaac advanced, towering at least a hand span above the man and using that intimidation to the fullest. "This is the thanks I get for giving you intelligence? You offend me?"

Farris retreated a step, uncertainty rippling across his large lips. "I—I—no, I never meant to offend. My apologies."

Isaac held the stance a breath longer, then backed off, allowing a slow smile to spread. "Well, don't just stand here, man." He swept out a hand. "Go get those law breakers!"

"But I'll need my men if I'm to capture an entire gang." His head shook from side to side. "I cannot free the scoundrels I've already caught."

"Not to worry." Isaac cuffed him on the back, the restraint of keeping the swat playful burning his muscles. "As local magistrate, I will see to these men."

"Singlehandedly?"

"You've already subdued them." Playing to the man's pride nearly choked him. He scrubbed the back of his neck to keep from tugging at his collar. "I'll lock them up until the circuit judge arrives in Truro, then transport them with the help of a few tenants of mine. Naturally, I shall give you all the credit, for it was you who bagged them."

Farris's eyes narrowed. "Why so accommodating?"

He placed his hand on his heart. "I take my duty to God and country very seriously."

Farris gaped. "I fear I have misjudged you, Mr. Seaton. You are a true loyalist, sir, and I salute you." He clacked his heels together and snapped his fingers to his brow.

Isaac bowed, hiding a smile. "Godspeed, Mr. Farris. May your return to London be victorious."

"Oh, that it shall be. I vow it." Shoving his hand into his greatcoat, he pulled out a key and handed it over, then he pivoted and sprinted away, shouting out orders and untethering his horse from the back of the wagon.

Isaac watched the man go, certain that he was the real victor in this. . .or rather God was.

Chapter Twelve

Mr. Farris and the soldiers thundered off, but despite the danger disappearing into the dark, Helen's heart still beat an irregular tattoo, for Isaac strode toward her. Determined of gait and singularly focused on her, she nearly shrank from the force of his gaze.

He grasped the horse's headstall and shushed away the skittishness of her mount, all while searching her from head to toe with a fearsome eye. "Are you all right?"

"I am." The words were weak. Her smile weaker. But after the events of the day, it was a wonder she functioned at all.

She lifted a hand toward the retreating men. "How on earth did you manage that?"

His teeth shone white in the dark, the only torch remaining on the wagon seat. "Some things aren't black and white, but one thing is for certain—the arrogance in Mr. Farris. I simply used his pride to my advantage."

She couldn't help but return Isaac's grin. "You, sir, are a rogue."

"Is that a step up or down from a smuggler?" He winked, then wheeled about and swung himself up into the back of the wagon.

He worked with sure yet gentle movements while caring for the wounded men. What a husband he would be. What a father.

Father.

Her shoulders sagged. No, her whole body did. Her own father yet lay cold in the cottage, alone but not forgotten. A fresh wave of tears blurred the world, and she forced herself to the present, anchoring her gaze on Isaac's broad back as he moved from man to man.

He squeezed the arm of one. "Bear up, Rook. We'll soon get you to a doctor." Then he crouched in front of another and pulled out a key.

"So, yer a miracle worker now, eh?" The man, all sharp angles and shadows, lifted his face toward Isaac. "Don't know how ye did it, but I thank ye."

"Save your thanks, for your other wagon is lost to the tide, and it was your information I gave to Farris. Now hold out your hands."

The fellow complied but not without complaint. "Flit! What ye goin' on about?"

The sound of shackles clacked onto the wagon bed. Isaac and only one of the other men stood.

Isaac clapped the fellow on the shoulder. "I let it slip that Grimlox and his gang were the true culprits. If Farris is able to haul them in, Brannigan will be implicated.

Maybe not a killing blow, but a blow nonetheless."

"Fitting end to 'em both, I say."

Isaac released the man. "Drive this rig onward, Hawker. See that Tegwyn and Rook get care and fast. I've a lady to attend to."

"And a right fine one at that." The dark eyes of the thin man met her across the gap between wagon and horse. "Ma'am." He tugged the brim of his hat.

Helen dipped her head in greeting. "Mister. . .?"

Isaac hoisted himself up behind her, snugging her back against him. "That's Billy Hawker. Hawker, meet the soon-to-be Mrs. Isaac Seaton."

The pile of bones crawled onto the wagon seat and faced them. "Ho-ho! Welcome to the ranks, m'lady." With a nod of his head, he reached for the reins and nudged the horses into action.

Helen turned to Isaac. She shouldn't be surprised if she awoke from this scene to find it was all a dream. Lifting her hand, she ran her fingers along the cheek of the man who would be her husband, the rasp of unshaved whiskers very real beneath her touch.

"You know, as impoverished as I was, I never thought I'd marry such a fine gentleman as you, so I used to pretend I was a grand lady," she murmured, afraid that if she spoke too loudly, this moment would dissolve. "But you have made it so."

He shook his head. "Once again, you have it wrong, my love. You. . ." He bent, and his lips brushed against her cheek. "Always have. . ." His mouth moved to the hollow near her temple. "And always will be. . ." Heat traced a line down her jaw. "A lady."

He kissed her soundly then turned her from him, enfolding his strong arms around her. She smiled shamelessly as they rode off into the night. Weeks ago he'd been a smuggler—and now she was his lady. Despite the heartache of the day, the irony of it all released a small laugh.

Isaac leaned over her shoulder, nuzzling her cheek. "What delights you so?"

She reached and caressed the side of his face, getting lost in the feel of his skin against her fingertips. "Life. It's a glorious thing."

Michelle Griep has been writing since she first discovered blank wall space and Crayolas. She is the author of historical romances: *The Innkeeper's Daughter, 12 Days at Bleakly Manor, The Captive Heart, Brentwood's Ward, A Heart Deceived, Undercurrent,* and *Gallimore,* but also leaped the historical fence into the realm of contemporary with the zany romantic mystery *Out of the Frying Pan.* If you'd like to keep up with her escapades, find her at www.michellegriep.com or stalk her on Facebook, Twitter, and Pinterest.

When I Saw His Face

by Nancy Moser

Chapter One

August 30, 1807
Chancebury, England

The carriage pulled away from the church. The wedding guests waved and cheered as the bride and groom began their new lives together.

Esther Horton raised her hand to wave, but returned it to her side before the action could be completed. "Petunia didn't even say goodbye."

The words were said for her own benefit, but overheard by her brother-in-law. "You expected otherwise?"

"Hoped otherwise."

Clarence put an arm around her shoulders. "You've done well with her since Stephen died."

"Well enough?"

He shrugged. "Petunia has always owned her own mind."

"Which she does not hesitate to share with others."

"Often and vociferously."

They shared a resigned smile and looked in the direction the carriage had gone.

"Will they be happy?" Clarence asked.

"I pray it will be so," Esther said.

"But?"

Esther fingered the fringe on her shawl. "I expect Petunia will make her husband quite..." She didn't wish to say the word.

"Miserable?"

There was a disconcerting satisfaction in having someone else understand the situation. "We both know if making people miserable is a talent, Petunia can easily be considered a girl with unparalleled expertise."

Clarence chuckled. "'For better or worse,' she is John's problem now."

"If it goes badly, it's your fault. You introduced them when she visited you last spring."

He sighed. "May she become his blessing."

They watched as the wedding guests dispersed and Pastor Wilkins closed the doors of the church. The wedding was over. The task fully accomplished.

Esther sighed. "Now what?"

"What, you say?" Clarence asked.

She hadn't realized she'd spoken the words aloud. "Nothing." She took his arm. "Walk me home."

After a dozen steps, he said, "You should move back to Manchester with Sarah and me. Your parents have died, and with Petunia moving to London, there's nothing to keep you here in tiny Chancebury. It was Stephen's choice to move here. I never understood why the countryside was always a lure to him."

"It's a fine village. We were happy here. I *am* happy here."

"So you say, but it's not like you were born here."

"I believe living in a village for twelve years provides even the most grudging resident the opinion that I am a full citizen of Chancebury in body, loyalty, and emotional connection."

"But with your stepdaughter gone, this is your chance to start over. Elsewhere. Fresh and new."

The simple notion of it made her shake her head vehemently. The action made her think of another "fresh and new" beginning, instituted after Stephen died. "If I left, what of my pies?" she asked. "People have grown to depend on them."

"People depend on meat and milk and even a pint of ale. They do not depend on pies."

"You offend me."

"I mean no offense. I simply speak facts, Esther. If you shutter your pie shop, the world would not shudder."

She stopped their progress to face him. "You offend me again."

He studied her face a moment, then offered her a bow. "Forgive me. I merely want you to be happy. Losing Stephen, bringing up Petunia on your own, then having her leave. . ."

She took his arm and they resumed their walk. "I appreciate your kind hopes. But what you are not considering is how important the pies are to *me*. The shop saved me these past six years. Beyond earning a living, the pies gave me a purpose. The shop is more than something to do, it is something to be."

"I misspoke." He patted her hand. "I have tasted your pies. There are none to rival them."

She had a new thought that might make her point. "Did the eating of my pies make you happy?"

He nodded. "And quite content."

"The baking of those pies has the same effect on me, Clarence. They make me happy and content. Therefore, I will not give them up and risk some possible betterment of life elsewhere for what is already good right here."

"Your point is duly taken."

Finally.

They reached the garden gate of her cottage. "Would you like to come in for some tea?"

"Do you desire the company?"

She considered this a moment. "Actually, I am quite done in."

"Then I will be on my way. Sarah will not sleep well until I am snoring beside her."

Esther kissed his cheek. "Tell her I hope she feels better soon."

"I will." He turned to leave, then stopped. "Remember, Esther. We are always here for you."

"I know, and I thank you for it. Good evening, Clarence, and safe travel home."

He tipped his hat and walked back to the church where his carriage waited.

Esther closed the garden gate and took a moment to look upon her home. For the first time in her life she would live here alone. No Stephen. And now, no Petunia.

Just me.

The day had brought a crucial change that could not be undone. From this moment forward, everything would be different.

She paused to let the thought settle, for surely such a monumental change demanded a monumental response. She took a breath in and let it out, willing for despair or regret to fall upon her and demand release.

Suddenly, another emotion stepped forward, one that was so foreign yet so insistent it would not be denied.

Rather than let its release be public, she quickly stepped inside and latched the door behind her. Assured in her privacy that she would not be the next subject of village gossip, Esther bent her knees low and then jumped into the air, her arms skimming the low ceiling, her shawl flying toward the rungs of the rocking chair.

She landed awkwardly but without a turn of her ankle, and celebrated by laughing aloud at her folly. She covered her mouth, but her joy caused her hand to fall away. Surrendering to the fullness of the moment, she raised her arms above her head and called out, "I am free!"

A giggle followed, and then a waltz among the furniture. She held the skirt of her dress, allowing a porcelain figurine of a shepherd full view of her ankles.

She offered him a curtsy then giggled as if she were a girl of seventeen and not a widow of forty-one.

She retrieved her shawl and hung it on the back of the chair. But another shawl lay where it shouldn't. She plucked Petunia's weekday shawl from a heap at the bottom of the stairs and gathered a pair of her shoes from the edge of the rug. In truth these castoffs were hers now, as Petunia had told Esther she could have them "as a gift."

Upon closer inspection, Esther found a tear in the shawl and holes in the soles of the shoes.

She shook her head at their condition but knew she shouldn't have expected more. "I've been living with Petunia's cast-offs for a long while now."

Since Stephen's passing to be exact.

His untimely death from falling off a horse represented not just the loss of a husband. His death had meant there would be no more babies for Esther. The two she had carried had not lived, so with Stephen's death, so died the chance of a miracle. Coming to terms with that awful fact she'd thanked God she had Petunia to help her through her grief. But as the fourteen-year-old girl grew older, her attitude worsened. Without the firm hand of her father, she became demanding, selfish, and disobedient. It was as though Petunia felt the world owed her a wage of happiness that she wasn't willing to work for. Esther had done her best to contain and restrain the girl's temperaments, but had cried herself to sleep on many a night, praying for wisdom, patience, and peace.

In order to win her daughter's favor, and in the hope of helping the two of them overcome their grief, Esther had given in too much, accepting the role of second fiddle in her own home.

But no more!

Esther raised the lid of the woodbox and tossed Petunia's discards inside, letting the lid fall with a satisfying *clump.*

She found herself grinning for the second time in a very few minutes. Which made her grin all the more.

Energized by her glee, she got another idea. She moved to her late husband's chair—the only comfortable chair in the front room, the chair Petunia had claimed as her own after her father's death. And then she did something she'd never done before.

She sat in it.

Esther nestled into the cushions and stroked the well-worn arms, a habit of Stephen's when he was deep in thought. She closed her eyes and sighed. "Oh, Stephen. I miss you so much. I had six years with you, and now six years without you. We didn't have enough time, my love." She smiled at the memory of him, the way he'd wink when he teased her, his smile that made everything right, and his loving touch that made the world go away.

"What now, darling?" she whispered.

She didn't expect an answer—certainly not from Stephen. Yet she hoped God heard her plea and would answer her, if not in regard to the moment, in regard to the long run.

Esther took a deep breath of the here and now and looked at her basket of knitting, at the shawl she'd been making for a friend's birthday. Then her eyes strayed to another pastime that remained unfinished. She retrieved a book she had been trying to read for weeks. Perhaps now she would finish it. Perhaps now, in the silence of her cottage, she would read all the books waiting for her on the bookshelf.

She had just found her place when there was a knock at the door.

Perhaps God is answering my "what now" question?

Or else John was returning Petunia, having already had his fill of her.

Esther opened the door and found Chester Mayfield, hat in hand.

"Evening, Esther."

"Chester."

"It was a fine wedding."

"Thank you." At the lag in the conversation, she knew he expected to be asked inside, but she held her ground.

"I. . .I was just checking on you, to see how you be."

"I am fine. Thank you." *Now go on with you.*

He made his hat go full circle in his hands. "Well then."

"Thank you for stopping by," she said.

His double chin turned to triple, but he nodded. "I will see you tomorrow then?"

"I will be at the shop. You may pick up your daily pie, as usual."

She closed the door on him, suffering a twinge of guilt.

But only a twinge. She would not let anything taint this first night of freedom.

Back to her book. But first, she decided to make herself a cup of tea.

With two sugars.

Chapter Two

Esther knocked on the bedroom door. "Petunia, it's time to get up." She waited to hear the familiar groan that indicated Petunia had heard.

There was no groan.

It took Esther a good five seconds to remember the reason for the silence.

Petunia wasn't there. Petunia was married. Esther was alone.

Neither revelation upset her.

She chuckled at her mistake and went downstairs for breakfast. It was then she discovered something else that was different: she didn't need to start the fire. Since the house would remain empty all day—until she came home that evening—there was no need for the added work or the added expense.

She had tea in the pot leftover from last evening and found it quite agreeable to drink cold. She deliberately took out one cup and saucer. One spoon. And one scone from the batch she made last Friday.

The scones would certainly go further now that Petunia wasn't there to gobble up two each morning. Or three. Her appetites were John's problem now.

In further recognition of her freedom, Esther grabbed her shawl and left the house. She'd eat the scone on the way to the shop.

Despite being earlier than usual, she was not the first to arrive. That chore went to her faithful helper, Sadie Morrow. It was Sadie's job to start the fire in the beehive oven each morning, a task that was begun a good hour before Esther usually arrived, its proper heat not attained until at least an hour after.

When Esther entered the Horton Pie Shop, she found Sadie in the back, sitting near the stove, a pile of wood at the ready to add to the already blazing fire. She held a book in her hands.

She looked up. "Is it that late?" Sadie set the book down and moved to add more wood.

"Calm yourself. It's not late at all," Esther said. "I am simply an hour early." She pointed to the book. "Sit and do as you do every day before I come in. Do not let me disrupt your routine."

With a glance and poke into the oven, Sadie returned to her chair.

"I am happy to see you reading," Esther said. She'd taught Sadie how to read.

Sadie retrieved the book. "I am *trying* to read more than actually reading. I still can't untangle some of the words."

"Show me one that makes you stumble."

Sadie perused a page and pointed to *acrimony*. "Ache-*rim*-on-ee?"

"*A*-cri-mo-nee."

Sadie studied the word a moment, then said, "Pronounced or not, I don't know what it is."

"It means being spiteful or bitter about something."

"Ah." She set the book spread-open on her lap. "Is the house peaceful with Petunia gone?"

That the definition of *acrimony* led to the question was telling. "It is."

"Quiet, too, I imagine."

"Quiet, too."

Sadie nodded. "I'm happy for you."

"It's traditional to be happy for the bride."

She shrugged. "We both know Petunia will keep happiness at arm's length, just to have something to complain about."

If the statement had been made by another, Esther might have taken offense and come to Petunia's defense. But whether right or wrong, wise or foolish, Sadie knew much about Esther's life, being a willing ear whenever Esther needed to purge her emotions rather than die of them.

"Are you lonely yet?" Sadie asked.

"Not yet." Then she thought of something. "You live alone. Are you lonely?"

"At times it scrapes me from the inside out."

Esther was taken aback. "I am ashamed I didn't know that."

"'Tis nothing unexpected. A woman of thirty-six who's not been wed is used to loneliness sitting by her side. You were lucky. You had a man. And a daughter—such as she was."

Esther said a silent prayer of contrition. "I apologize for not knowing about your struggles. It is apparent that over the years I have done most of the talking and you have done most of the listening."

With a glance to the oven, Sadie added more wood, pushing it in deeper with a hoe. "My life is of little interest. I always enjoy listening to details of yours, for it adds spice to mine. You're going to dinner at the Woodsons' tonight, yes?"

"I am."

"See? Far more excitement than mine." They heard commotion out front. "That will be Fergus with the meat delivery," Sadie said.

"I'll tend to him." Esther vowed to do a better job of tending to Sadie, too. It was time to give as much as she'd taken.

The hours flew by, as they did every morning. The first pies were in the oven, and Esther crimped the edges of the next batch, made of mutton.

With a single rap on the door, Chester slipped into the shop.

"We're not open yet, Chester," Esther said. "You know that."

"I do. But I want to order a pie."

Esther had to smile. "Your pie is already in the oven."

"Not the usual meat pie. A different kind. And not for today. For Thursday."

Esther looked up from her work. "What's happening Thursday?"

"You're coming to dinner."

"I am?"

"Will you?"

They had never dined together at his home. The thought of it made her stomach dance a leery dance. She had felt comfortable occasionally sharing a meal at her own house, mainly because Petunia was always present. But to be completely alone with him. . .

She was being silly. They'd known each other for years. He was a good man. "I suppose I could."

"Good," he said with relief. "So make me a special pie on Thursday."

"What kind?"

"Apple."

"You don't like apple pie," Esther said. "Too sweet."

He focused on Esther. "But you like it. It's *your* favorite. Come now, Esther. Dine with me."

She deemed her nerves silly. "Do you cook?"

"I make a mighty stew. I'll buy some bread from the baker's, and with your pie we shall have a fine meal."

She could think of no reason to say no. "I'd be happy to come."

His chubby face lit up as if a light shined from within. "See you at half past seven on Thursday." He glanced toward the back. "I'll come later for me pork pie." With a smile and a nod he left her.

Sadie came into the front of the shop. "You're going to his house for dinner?"

"You shouldn't eavesdrop."

"A woman can't help hearing what a woman can't help hearing."

Esther looked at the door and sighed.

"What's the sigh for?"

She hadn't realized her sigh spoke so loudly. "He's on the press now. Full out."

"The press?"

"Now that Petunia's gone he'll want us to marry."

"Oh."

Esther went back to crimping the pie. "For the past six years, when my 'no thank-yous' fell on deaf ears, I kept his attention at bay with the promise that once Petunia was gone I would be ready."

"Are you?"

"I thought I'd be. But. . ."

Sadie waved an arm toward the door. "If you don't love him, tell him so. Don't be cruel and leave him hanging, more than. . ."

"More than I already have?"

"Six years is a long time for any man to wait."

❧

The door to the Woodson home was opened by their twins. "Mama made potatoes with butter," April said.

"Lots of them," May added.

"Do you like buttery potatoes?" Esther asked.

Both eight-year-olds nodded. "We'll eat yours if you don't want 'em."

"You will do no such thing." Their mother, Anne, shooed them away. "Come in, Esther." She jostled little Joe on her hip.

"Chee!" he said, pointing at Esther.

She took his plump little hand and kissed it. "What does 'chee' mean?"

"We have no idea." Anne handed him off. "Will you? I need to check the chicken on the fire."

Esther loved the feel of a young one in her arms, but it was short-lived, as Joe wiggled his way to freedom. He ran to his father's lap as Alexander sat by the fire with his pipe.

"Evening, Esther," the man said. "Have a seat."

"A good evening to you," she said, sitting in the chair opposite. "Thank you for having me."

"Anne was afeared you'd be lonesome in your empty house."

She didn't answer.

"So, are you lonesome?"

"Not yet."

The twins began playing bilbocatch, their voices loudly counting the number of times they caught the ball on the handheld pedestal. Esther expected them to be chastised for their volume, but instead, Alexander set Joe on the floor and took a turn himself to much cheering and applause.

"Twelve!" Alexander said.

"That's not the best, Papa," April said. "I've had fourteen."

"May I try?" Esther asked.

She was handed the toy and twice hit herself with the ball that was attached to the base with a string. "I'm not very good."

"Keep trying," May said.

"Didn't Petunia have one of these?" Alexander asked.

"She did, but she never let me play with it."

Finally, Esther got the ball to land where it should. The room erupted with acclamation, but when she tried for number two, she missed.

"You just need practice," April said.

May darted into a bedroom and came back with a second one. "You can borrow mine to practice at home, if you wish."

"How kind of you, dear." Esther wasn't used to children who willingly shared.

"Dinner is served!" Anne transferred a chicken from a spit on the fire to a serving plate.

They gathered around a table at the other end of the room, with Joe in Anne's lap. Alexander said the blessing, and delicious chicken and very buttery potatoes were served with asparagus and fresh bread.

Esther experienced the dinner as a full participant, but found herself distracted by poignant moments of reflection. The love between the Woodsons was palpable and made Esther remember the good times with her own family. She'd become Petunia's mother when the girl was the same age as the twins. The transition from an unmarried twenty-nine-year-old to a wife and mother had not been easy, but Stephen's love had carried her through.

Did she want to be alone the rest of her life? Or did she wish to be a wife again? A mother?

"You're quiet," Anne said as she wiped Joe's mouth with a corner of her apron.

Esther offered them a grateful smile. "Your joyful home is an inspiration."

Anne exchanged a mischievous smile with her husband. "You don't have to be alone. We all know there is someone who is very willing to make your one two again."

"Has Chester proposed yet?" Alexander asked.

"Darling!" Anne said. "That is too blunt a question."

"One that mirrors your own curiosity, wife."

Anne's cheeks reddened. "With Petunia gone, the entire village is wondering."

"I know."

"So?"

"I am thinking on it."

"You've had six years to think on it, Esther," Anne said. "You are too young and too delightful to be alone."

"I don't plan to be," she said.

Alexander's eyebrows rose. "You have someone else in mind?"

"I don't," she added quickly. "Not specifically."

Anne shook her head. "I cannot think of a single man in Chancebury who might pique your interest."

"Wife, you make the men of the village sound quite abysmal."

"Not abysmal, but they *are* too old, too young, too married, or too. . .tedious."

"Tedious?" Esther asked.

Anne took a moment to think. "Too bashful, boring, brash, boorish, or barbarous."

"Who in Chancebury is barbarous?" Alexander asked.

"Reginald Collins. Have you heard the oaths that come out of his mouth?"

He nodded once. "Agreed."

Esther laughed. "I will admit the male pickings in the village are slim. But does that mean I should settle?"

"Do you think marrying Chester would be settling?" Anne asked.

"No, not at all." *At least I don't think so.*

Anne rose to clear the dishes, and Esther stood to help her. "If you expect some dashing man to ride into town and sweep you off your feet, I'd suggest you toss away the novels you've been reading."

"It could happen," she said.

"When pigs fly," Alexander added.

Esther wouldn't mind seeing a pig fly.

Chapter Three

Thursdays were Esther's favorite day. Any who heard of this preference would find it puzzling, for no one preferred a work day over the freedom from work that Sundays afforded. And why Thursday of all days?

Esther looked forward to Thursday because it wasn't Friday or Saturday when the shop was especially busy with people wanting a pie for Sunday dinner. Or Monday and Wednesday that were also busy with customers wanting a new pie to last them a few days. Tuesday and Thursday were the pie shop's slowest days.

So why Thursday and not Tuesday?

Because Thursday was the day she visited her friend Lady Tomkins. Thursday was the day she could fully be herself.

Each and every Thursday since the pie shop opened, Esther took Verdelia—Verd—two pies—one meat and one sweet. In her economy Verd made the pies last a week, having taught her maidservant to cut them into an exact seven pieces. Esther often wondered what Nelly ate, but since the woman had some heft to her, it was clear she ate well enough when she went home to her husband. Nelly and Sam lived in the caretaker's cottage just a stone's throw from the main house. They were the only servants left at Coventry Hall.

Esther admired Verd for making do. It was difficult to fall from the status of one of the county's elite families to obsolete. From wealth to ruin—or near ruin. For only by Verd's thrift and determination had she been able to stay in the house after her husband's death when the consequences of his gambling debts came to light.

Since then, shame kept Verd in seclusion. Esther was her only friend, her only contact, and though they'd known of each other twelve years, it was only since Stephen's death that their acquaintance had blossomed into friendship.

Esther turned up the driveway leading to the hall. She and Lady Tomkins first met because Stephen had been the hall's estate manager. His brother, Clarence, and Esther's father had been the solicitors for the baronet and had found Stephen the position when they'd heard Sir Thomas was in need of a manager. That duo had also been instrumental in introducing Esther to Stephen. His wife had died when Petunia was born, and by the time he met Esther, the girl was eight and he had a great desire to finally be a full family. Their marriage and Chancebury had given him his wish.

After the baronet's death—he was shot during a poker game in London—Stephen had helped keep the estate running. But upon Stephen's sudden death a few years later, the hall had slipped into further decay and now was a melancholy survivor of the once-grand estate. Only then had the widow Lady Tomkins and the widow Esther Horton found the common bond that had lured them into true friendship.

Esther neared the door—that needed a goodly coat of paint. Sam was slacking.

Or perhaps there wasn't money for paint.

She pinched some dead stems from a clump of daisies, then knocked on the door.

Nelly answered. "Good day to you, Mrs. Horton," she said.

"And good day to you, Nelly." She leaned close. "How is she today?"

"*She* is fine," called Verd from the parlor. "How did you think she'd be?"

Esther and Nelly shared a smile, and the pies were handed over for Nelly to take to the kitchen building out back.

Esther entered the parlor and leaned down to kiss her friend's cheek and give her cat, Christopher, a scratch behind the ears. "If I remember correctly, last week you had a headache."

"You didn't think it bad enough to visit me between then and now," Verd said, nodding toward Esther's usual chair that had been drawn close.

"I had a wedding to attend."

Verd blinked twice. "Ah. Yes. So Petunia is finally someone else's problem."

Esther removed her bonnet and set it on a side table. "You are too harsh."

"I only know what you tell me, girl. If I am harsh it is because you have presented her so."

Esther smoothed her skirt over her knees. Only Verd would call Esther a girl. Yet compared to Verd's seventy-some years, age was relative. "Perhaps I *have* been too harsh."

"Perhaps you haven't."

Esther chuckled softly. "Perhaps I haven't."

"There now," Verd said. "At least we have that truth settled. So tell me what else is new in the world of Chancebury."

Esther knew it was best to get to the base of it, especially since Nelly was otherwise occupied making tea. The fewer ears that heard, the better.

"Chester is taking me at my word—about *after* Petunia leaves home."

"So he hasn't forgotten about you?"

"Not in the least."

Verd stroked the length of Christopher's black coat. He began to purr. "You *are* rather unforgettable."

"You flatter me, Lady Tomkins."

"I only speak the truth."

"It is your greatest gift." Her words were more than flattery. "*That* is the truth."

"My, my, we are replete with compliments today. Yet I long for otherwise."

"You do like the gossip."

Verd spread her arms wide. "These walls have told me all the stories they are going to tell. I depend on you to keep me entertained."

"You could venture out. Come to dinner. Just us two."

"What would I gain by that? I have your company here. I do not need to go elsewhere for it."

"No one in the village blames you for your husband's. . ."

"Nastiness?"

Esther nodded. "It has been a long time. I promise your reentry into the village would be painless."

"But I rarely went to the village before Thomas died. I knew of their suffering under his so-called patronage, for it was my own." The wrinkles on her face multiplied.

The discussion was interrupted by Nelly bringing the tea. The smell of earth and smoke toured the room. Verd poured milk and sugar in both cups, just the way Esther liked, then handed her a cup.

"There now. Chester. Are you enjoying his attention?"

"Partly."

"You have been partly enjoying it for six years. I assume he wants the all of you?"

"He does."

Verd's grey eyebrows rose. "He has proposed?"

"Not yet. Though he has invited me to dinner tonight."

"What are your thoughts on the matter?"

Esther held the cup beneath her chin, letting its aromatic vapors calm her. "I am not certain I wish to marry anyone."

"Ever?"

"That, I don't know. But certainly I hesitate regarding now. I am only forty-one."

"That old?"

"You should talk."

"I agree. There is time for you. But your hesitance involves issues more than age, does it not?"

"Although it is new to me, I think I enjoy having the house to myself."

"That statement is as weak as this tea." Verd set her cup down. "I swear Nelly uses the leaves leftover from her morning pot with Sam."

Esther ignored the complaint. "There is a quote from Cicero that I hold dear."

"Since when do you read Cicero?"

"I have read him off and on. But I've been keeping this quotation in my pocket to pull out when it suited my life."

"And the quotation is. . . ?"

" 'I am never less alone than when alone.' "

Verd clapped her hands together. "Aye! That is a good one. Well said."

"I've always thought so." She took a sip of tea. "When Petunia was home I felt glimmers of satisfaction, but never felt it fully until this week when I have the house totally to myself."

Verd nodded. "I understand. I do not mind being alone these seven years. For I have my own good company, yours on occasion, and the Lord's on all occasions. What more do I need?"

"Perhaps your example has inspired me."

She moved her arm so Christopher could jump to the floor. He meandered out of the room and up the grand stairway.

"I enjoyed the love of one good man," Esther said. "I do not need another."

"I did not enjoy the love of one good man, and never found another."

Esther had heard many stories of Verd's husband—from Verd, from Stephen, and from the citizens of Chancebury. A more contrary man had never lived. Sir Thomas held all things in contempt, whether they deserved his judgment or not. He never graced Chancebury with a stroll through the square, but arrived and departed in an enclosed carriage, with not even a wave to mark his passing. The only time anyone saw him was when they fell into his ill graces by not providing perfection of some item or service. His tenants would sell their youngest child to pay the rent on time, for Sir Thomas had never been averse to calling in the law. Which of course had led to eviction or debtor's prison on more than one occasion—in spite of Stephen's best efforts and calls for mercy and understanding. And financial intervention. For also, on more than one occasion, Stephen had paid the debt—without Sir Thomas' knowledge.

It was ironic the baronet had died in debt. It was a bad end to a bad man, who had left a good wife and a spoiled and willful son.

Speaking of. . . "How is your son?"

"According to his rather insufficient letters, Thaddeus thrives on the Continent, having no interest in the hall or the duties of baronet. Or his duties as my son."

"Does he plan a visit soon?"

She flipped the question away with a hand. "He, his wife, and their daughters are busy being busy. They have no time for me."

Their lack of interest saddened Esther. Unfortunately they shared the grief of ungrateful children.

Verd shook her head in a short burst, as though dispelling the subject. "I do have a visit to look forward to."

"Who is coming?"

"My nephew."

"Henry?"

"The same. He comes next week."

"All the way from London?"

She raised a finger. "He is not in London anymore. He recently became the headmaster at a school in Manchester."

"How delightful. He has never been the head before, has he?"

"He has not. He has been a teacher for sixteen years. It is time he rises up. And *he* writes a delightful letter."

"I would like to meet him sometime."

"I am sure that can be arranged."

Esther noticed Verd's smile was slightly wicked.

"Do not match us up, friend," Esther said. "Did I not just say I enjoy my newfound freedom?"

Verd offered an exaggerated sigh. "Alas, you did." She winked. "But you can still meet him." Verd set her teacup down. "Actually, I have something even more important to speak with you about."

"What's that?"

"I have a confession to make."

Esther grinned. "Do tell."

"Nothing scandalous, I assure you. It's rather pitiful, really."

Esther leaned forward and touched her knee. "What's wrong?"

"In spite of our courageous talk, I have been feeling rather lonely of late."

"I am sorry for that. I could come visit more often."

Verd held up a hand. "I appreciate your offer, but at Henry's suggestion I have decided on another remedy."

"You have my attention."

"I have locked myself away for years. You have been my only contact with the village, but now. . . It is time for a change."

"Are you going to town?"

"Pooh. Not that much of a change. But I would like to meet the people of Chancebury. I was thinking it was time to let some people in—people other than you. Are you jealous?"

"Not at all. I think it's wonderful. But how—"

"I wish to invite them here."

It took Esther a moment to comprehend her meaning. "All of them?"

She seemed taken aback. "The village has not grown by that much, has it?"

"I have no knowledge of the actual population, but I would imagine it is close to two hundred, all told."

"Oh dear. That many."

"You could invite a few."

She shook her head. "It will be all or nothing. For I turn eighty on the sixteenth of next month."

A few weeks from now. "I congratulate you, but to arrange a party so quickly. . ."

"A person only turns eighty once, and such a milestone deserves a mighty celebration. And so I say, let them come—at least let all be invited." She pointed to her desk. "Fetch the paper there, noting the details."

Esther found the piece of paper in question, which listed foods to be served.

"Add your pies to the list."

"Of course."

"Do you think people will come?"

Esther chuckled. "They will. For you and this house have been the subject of their curiosity for years."

"Ha," Verd said with a grin. "I do like keeping them in suspense."

Esther looked at the information. "How do you propose to spread the word?"

"I thought you could post a sign at your shop and on the windows of a few other shops in the village. And perhaps Pastor Wilkins could mention it next Sunday?"

"Would you like help making the notices?"

Verd nodded toward the desk. "I have pen and paper right there. How many do you think we shall need?"

⚬

Back in the shop, it was time to close up and go to dinner at Chester's. Esther draped her shawl over her shoulders and tied it with a knot, needing her hands for the apple pie.

"Shouldn't you go home and put on a nicer dress?" Sadie asked. "Eating at Chester's is a special occasion."

Esther glanced down at the blue-sprigged dress she'd worn the entire day. Although she'd worn an apron, she could see flour on the skirt. She brushed it off and made a decision. "I should, but I'm not going to. I don't want to encourage him by dressing up."

"Don't you think going to dinner will encourage him?"

Esther gave the shawl's knot an extra tug. "Maybe I shouldn't go."

"Maybe you shouldn't."

Sadie's words made Esther look at her. "You think so?"

Sadie wrapped her own shawl close and headed to the door. "Just go. You need to eat."

Esther nodded and took up the pie.

"Be nice to him," Sadie said as she closed the door behind them. "Chester deserves that."

⚬

Esther had walked past Chester's cottage a thousand times before this evening. It was near his smithy, though sufficient steps away to escape the smoke and cinders.

She could see firelight through the window. Her thought of *he's in there* was absurd. Of course he was in there. She approached the door.

"Good evening, Esther," came a familiar woman's voice.

Esther turned around and saw Myrtle Cray strolling by. "Evening, Myrtle."

"Say hello to Chester for me," she said with a smile as she passed.

Esther faced the door again, hating that of all people to see her at Chester's, it was the town gossip. Myrtle was a fly in the peaceful ointment of Chancebury. She buzzed from this to that, listening in, seeing what she shouldn't, and annoying people until they wanted to swat her away. She was as small in mind as she was in stature.

The door opened. "I thought I heard someone out here."

"It's just me." *More absurdity. Esther, gather your wits!*

He stepped aside. "Come in."

She entered a cottage that was ablaze with a cozy fire and a lit candle on the small table—which was set with two pewter bowls, plates, and spoons. In the center of the table was a tankard filled with wildflowers.

"How prettily done, Chester."

"I wanted to make it nice. Since we're having stew, I wasn't sure we needed the plates, but then I thought of the bread and pie and—" He noticed her holding it and took it from her.

"You did a fine job of the setting," she said.

He let out a breath. It was then she noticed he had also done a fine job in regards to his own appearance. He wore his Sunday vest, and his hair was slicked back from its usual tousle.

"Is that pomade in your hair?" she asked.

He moved to touch it, but stopped short. "Anne at the mercantile sold it to me. I thought I would give a go of it. I know it's silly but—"

"You look very nice," she said. And she wasn't lying. Not really. Although Chester could never be considered handsome and was a bit more portly than most, his countenance was agreeable enough. His smile made up for any lack in his looks.

At this point she felt badly for not going home to change clothes. "I feel underdressed."

"You look beautiful," he said, "as always."

She felt herself blush but didn't need to worry about him seeing it, as he moved to stir the stew on the fire.

"It smells delicious."

"There's not much to go wrong with meat and vegetables." He moved the wrought-iron cooking crane aside so it was away from direct heat. "It appears ready. Shall we?" He motioned to the table then held her chair.

He took the bowls to the pot and ladled a goodly portion. Then he sliced the bread and offered her a piece.

"Here's some of Mrs. Cooley's blackberry jam, and the stew may need some salt." He pushed a wooden saltcellar toward her. "But you might taste it first."

He began to pick up his spoon, but stopped when he saw her bow her head.

"Oh. Sorry. I's out of the habit."

At his request, she said a blessing, and the meal commenced. Blessedly the conversation centered around town news. Mr. Parker bought a new horse. Mrs. Donnelly had a fifth child—another boy. And the Wilsons were expecting his cousins from London for a visit. Esther told him about Lady Tomkins' birthday celebration. When they spoke of Petunia's wedding, Esther feared Chester would bring up her vow to marry him.

He didn't mention it.

As they ate the last bites of the apple pie—which of course, was delicious—Esther could finally breathe freely. She'd made it through the dinner without talking about their relationship.

Chester pushed his empty plate away and sat back, groaning with contentment. "I am full to overflowing."

Although his words could be construed in an indelicate way, Esther agreed. "It was a delicious meal. Thank you for inviting me." She heard the clock strike nine and began to stand. "I must get home. The mornings come early for both of us."

He helped with her chair, but as she stepped aside, he took her hand in both of his, their large size engulfing hers. "Esther."

With that one word, she knew what was coming.

She wanted to flee, but smiled as much as she could manage and gently pulled her hand free. "Again, thank you for your kind hospitality."

His face contorted with panic, and he took her hand again. "Esther. It's time."

No, it isn't!

Before she could stop him, he got down on one knee—with a groan—and gazed up at her. "Esther Horton, I love you. Will you be my wife?"

A thousand words sped through her mind, and she feared she wouldn't find the right ones. But then she said, "I will think about it."

He looked confused, then smiled and rose to standing. "It is a more positive answer than, 'no thank you.'"

She smiled back. "I believe it is."

"Let me walk you home."

She glanced outside and saw that the summer sun had not fully set. "I will be all right," she said. "I will see you tomorrow for your Friday pie?"

"You will."

On impulse, she kissed him on the cheek and left. She did more than leave, she fled like a released prisoner fearing the jailer would change his mind.

Esther felt dreadful for her attitude. She'd just received a proposal from a very nice man, and as the Woodsons had pointed out, one of the only eligible men in Chancebury. He was also a very patient man. She should be flying down the road on the wings of love.

Wings of like. For I do like him.

But it was not enough. Not nearly enough.

Chapter Four

And they all said, "Amen."

Esther sat next to Sadie in their usual pew. Everyone in Chancebury had their spots, which made it easy for the pastor to see who had found something else to do with their Sunday mornings. In the days following Sunday, Pastor Wilkins made it a habit to check on each absentee. Those who had good reason—their deathbed—would be comforted. Those who slept late or decided the morning too perfect for fishing would receive Pastor Wilkins's rebuke. And if repeatedly tested, there were opportunities to weed the cemetery or scrape candle wax from the sanctuary floor and altar.

The possibility of the pastor's reprimand had no bearing on Esther's loyal attendance. In actuality, his sermons were not the draw, either. What did draw her to her self-appointed place was her need for peace. Apart from the busyness of everyday life and the drama that spun around Petunia and Chester, church allowed Esther the chance to close her eyes, fully invite God in, and banish the world. At least for a little while.

Her head bowed, she half-listened to the pastor's prayer—which leaned toward verbosity and lofty language meant to impress. She could not be certain, but since Jesus came to earth in such a humble manner, and since all accounts of His life featured His love and concern for His flock devoid of self-aggrandizement, Esther had long ago chosen to drown out Pastor Wilkins's drone of a prayer in preference for her own simple entreaties to the Lord. Gratitude, hallelujahs, and cries for help wove together into a durable, threefold cord.

She was just bringing the subject of Chester before the Almighty, when she heard him—Chester, not the Lord—clear his throat in the pew behind her.

There he is, Lord. What do I do with Chester? Are we to be together? Should I remain alone? Or is there someone. . . ?

The congregation stood to sing a hymn, forcing Esther to leave go of her prayer. She shared a hymnal with Sadie and sang:

> *"Give me a new, a perfect heart,*
> *From doubt, and fear, and sorrow free;*
> *The mind which was in Christ impart,*
> *And let my spirit cleave to Thee."*

She smiled as she sang, for as often happened, the words suited her state of mind, as if God Himself had chosen the hymn just for her.

Chester's mellow baritone rang out behind her, causing her to share a smile with Sadie.

"'*Cause me to walk in Christ my Way,'*" he sang, "'*and I Thy statutes shall fulfill. In every point Thy law obey, and perfectly perform Thy wi-ll-ll.'*"

By holding out the last note—beyond every other voice in the sanctuary—Esther knew Chester wanted her to turn around and smile at him. Although she knew she shouldn't, she couldn't help herself.

He gave her a smile in return. And a wink. Somehow the wink seemed a bit cheeky for the house of God, so she quickly faced forward.

Cheeky or not, Chester made her think happy thoughts.

Had God answered her prayer already?

The congregation exited the church, taking turns shaking Pastor Wilkins's hand. Esther welcomed the chance to thank him for mentioning Verd's eightieth birthday party on September sixteenth.

At the bottom of the steps, Esther spotted a mighty contingent of Chancebury's finest gossips.

"Good morning, Esther," Myrtle Cray said. "Chester."

"Do you two have plans for the rest of the day?" another asked.

Another looked to the sky. "'Tis a fine day."

Chester touched Esther's arm. "Indeed it is. Mrs. Horton, would you care for a walk?"

In an instant Esther knew that rejecting him would cause more unwanted gossip than agreeing. "If you'd like."

Chester offered his arm, and together they walked away from the church.

"They were lying in wait for us," she said. "Ready to pounce."

"I don't object to their suggestion. Do you?"

"I object to their assumption."

"Ah." He nodded once. "'Tis not a horrible assumption, is it?"

She sighed. She was making a mess of things. "Not at all. Forgive me. I simply object to having any part of my life be a foregone conclusion."

He laughed. "Like Myrtle being a gossip and the boredom of Pastor's sermons?"

She had to laugh with him. "I find both of interest—on occasion."

"Not often enough." He pointed toward the sky. "God is up there and we are down here. When I die I want to be up there, too. Beyond that, I don't need a pastor spouting off shalt-nots at me."

"That's a rather simplistic notion of faith."

He shrugged. "I am a simple man."

"But what about trying to deepen your faith? What about the power of prayer?

What about somehow discovering why we are here, now?"

He shook his head and pointed at a path that led from the main road into the meadow and woods beyond. "Shall we?"

Esther mourned his lack of interest in discussing anything profound. Their conversations were always amiable but occasionally she would have liked to discuss subjects beyond the moment.

"Come on," he said, pulling her toward the path.

She glanced behind and saw the other churchgoers walking home, including Myrtle and her cronies. "I think it best we stay on the road."

Chester glanced back, too. "Perhaps I should shock the lot of them by gathering you in my arms and leaning you into a low dip."

She swatted his arm and let go. "You will do no such thing."

"I will not. But it is pleasurable to think about."

Actually, it was.

<hr/>

Although Esther knew the Sabbath was supposed to be a day of rest, once home from church her thoughts whirled in such a frenzied fashion that she failed all seemly Sunday pursuits such as reading a book, praying over the Bible, or knitting. She was spurred into bodily action lest she burst—which would be the essence of unseemly.

She retrieved a basket and went to her garden—her pride and joy. Stephen's pride and joy. She hadn't shown much interest in it until he passed, but then she discovered it held much satisfaction. It was also highly integral to her livelihood. For without the vegetables and fruits from said garden, her pies would bring less profit. She already had to purchase the meats for the filling. And the flour and sugar. And butter and eggs. To self-provide the other filling ingredients was a godsend.

She strolled through the rows and gathered ripe berries. That an occasional berry never made it to the basket was payment for her work. But bending down so long made her back ache, and she stood and arched it with a groan.

"No rest for the weary?"

She looked over her shoulder and saw Chester standing on the road, a bouquet of flowers in his hands. "It appears you've been doing your own picking."

He walked to the low fence that formed an edge between them and held them out to her. "I meant to get you some flowers this morning on our walk. You can blame Myrtle Cray for the delay."

She left her basket on the ground and stepped over a row of berry plants to take the white flowers. "Thank you."

"They are forget-me-nots."

"I think not. They are fool's parsley."

"No! They are forget-me-nots."

"I appreciate the sentiment, but as it is nearly September, forget-me-nots are past. You hold fool's parsley."

His countenance fell and she felt badly for being too specific. "Whatever they are called I thank you for your effort."

"I considered bringing you some bachelor's button, but I didn't want to be associated with such a flower anymore, and so..."

She held the flowers to her nose, but disliked the scent. "Thank you, Chester."

He nodded. Sighed. Then looked to the fruit trees. "You have apples that need picking."

"I was going to get the Tanner boy to help me."

"No need. I am here. Where is your ladder?"

"Remember it's the Sabbath, Chester. I don't want to lure you into sin by making you work."

"I heard Pastor say something about the harvest being plenteous, but the laborers few."

"So you were listening."

"Occasionally."

"I believe he was referring to harvesting souls, not apples."

He paused but a moment. "Your pies are a harvest to my soul, Esther."

She wasn't sure if it was an apt analogy, but again appreciated his effort. She pointed to the ladder on the side of the house.

As she got into bed that night, Esther found herself smiling and knew there was only one reason.

His name was Chester Mayfield.

They'd had a very enjoyable afternoon picking apples and a very enjoyable evening eating a simple dinner of bread, cheese, and chopped apples mixed with cinnamon and sugar.

"I am far satisfied," she told the bedroom as she blew out the candle.

The smell of burnt tallow wafted over her, encircling her words.

She sat up in bed. "*Am* I far satisfied? If so, it is Chester's doing." She thought of her prayer that morning when she'd asked God if He wanted her to be with Chester.

And then Chester had shown up with flowers and an eager spirit.

Esther looked heavenward. "It's him, isn't it, Lord? You want me to be with Chester."

She snuggled into the cozy comfort of her bed and let God's answer tuck her in.

Chapter Five

Chester beamed as he came into the pie shop. "Good afternoon, ladies. Are you ready for the September Festival?"

Esther looked to Sadie, and the two women nodded. "Fifteen pies ready to sell by the slice," Esther said. "Help us get a few of them to the table outside. People are already gathering in the square."

With Chester's help, half the pies were transferred, as were a mishmash of plates and forks that Esther had gathered over the years for just such an occasion. She placed small notes next to each pie to mark the selection: lamb, beef, apple, raspberry, cherry, and even trout—caught by Chester in the river.

He adjusted the bench behind the table. "Will this suit you, Sadie?"

"It does. Thank you, Chester."

Was Sadie blushing?

Esther didn't have time to ponder the question, as their first customer arrived. "Mr. Bowens, how can I tempt you today?"

The music was infectious.

Chester approached and held out his hand. "Shall we?"

Esther glanced at the table.

"There are only five slices left," he said. "I'll buy them all myself if it will get you to dance with me."

"Go on," Sadie said from her place nearby. "Dance."

Esther was drawn into the crowd of revelers and let the music of the fiddle, pipe, and drum transport her to a place of pure pleasure and merriment. Those who weren't dancing offered their encouragement by clapping in time—and hooting when the music gave special delight.

One dance led to the next, and Esther felt a catch in her side. She begged off the next song then saw Sadie, standing forlorn. "Chester, go ask Sadie to dance."

He looked in her direction, nodded, then added, "But only because you look done in."

She waved him off and moved to the bench. Chester stood before Sadie and bowed like a gallant. "Miss Morrow? May I have the pleasure?"

Sadie looked to Esther for permission. "Please," Esther said with a wave. "Wear him out."

Sadie looked absolutely gleeful as Chester whirled her around.

Myrtle approached and handed Esther a folded fan. "It appears you need this more than I."

She accepted the offer. The breeze of the fan refreshed in spite of the foul wind of its owner. "Chester is quite indefatigable."

"He is indeed tireless." Myrtle smiled. "And persistent, I would guess?"

Luckily, Esther's face was already reddened.

"Come now, Esther," Myrtle said. "Everyone in Chancebury is waiting for Chester and Esther to tie the knot. For with those two names, how can you not? Has he not asked?"

"Mostly," she said.

"What an odd way to put it."

I've said too much already.

"So if he has mostly asked, what did you mostly say?"

"I said I would think about it."

"And have you?"

"Very much."

Myrtle tossed her pudgy hands in the air. "Then what say you, woman? Give the poor man an answer or set him free."

Esther was shocked by her choice of words. "He is free already."

"He most certainly is not. He has set his cap on you and you alone. You're not being fair, Esther Horton. Nor even polite."

Esther hated being lectured about courtesy by the likes of Myrtle Cray. To put an end to the conversation, she handed the fan back. Luckily, the song also ended, and she saw Chester turning in her direction with a glowing Sadie by his side.

Myrtle leaned close. "Give him your answer this very day—before you lose him."

Lose him?

She watched Chester and Sadie chat happily as they came closer.

Sadie?

And Chester?

She had not seen any attraction between them.

Or had she?

They reached the table.

"Thank you for the dance, Chester," Sadie said. "You are a fine dancer."

"As are you, Miss Morrow." He turned to Myrtle. "I may have to borrow your fan."

She handed it to him, and he let himself look silly with its use.

"Why don't you and Esther take a walk?" Myrtle said. "Find a nice breeze along the lane."

He looked confused—as was Esther, until she received the busybody's pointed look. Oh. Yes. That.

Chester returned the fan then offered Esther his arm. "I will never reject a stroll with my Esther."

My Esther.

Although she hated being propelled to action by Myrtle, with a glance to Sadie—who looked troubled—Esther took his arm and together they walked away from the square.

She was suddenly tongue-tied. Had the time actually come for her to answer Chester's proposal?

He noticed her silence. "You are quiet. And your face melancholy. Is something troubling you? I only asked Sadie to dance because you asked me to."

She shook her head. "That's not it. I *did* ask you to."

"Then what is it?"

She waited until some children ran by then stopped to face him. "Ask me the question you asked in your cottage."

He blinked, then smiled. "Really?"

She suffered a wave of panic and could only nod.

He took her hands in his. "Esther, will you marry me?"

Although she knew she should say yes with enthusiasm, she found she couldn't respond without full honesty. "I don't want to say yes, but can think of no reason to say no."

"Good enough!" He drew her into his arms and kissed her on the lips.

"Kissy-missy!" a boy called out.

"Oooh," said another.

The couple separated, but Chester kept his arm around her. "Be nice, boys, and perhaps you too can win the hand of a good woman someday."

"Yer gettin' married?"

"We are."

The boys ran toward the square, shouting the news. "Mr. Mayfield and Mrs. Horton are getting hitched!"

To have the entire village know in such quick fashion overwhelmed. Yet what did Esther expect?

Chester kissed her forehead. "Shall we go accept their congratulations?"

Esther didn't want to say yes, but could think of no reason to say no.

Chapter Six

I *am betrothed.*
  Esther lay in bed the morning after saying yes to Chester and let the thought settle.

She did not smile. She did not frown.

A white butterfly entered her room with the morning breeze, fluttered about, then escaped outside again. Carefree. Without responsibilities or consequences to weigh it down.

Being betrothed was all about responsibilities and consequences, but it was also about joy and anticipation. Oddly she felt little of anything. She was lukewarm. Neither hot nor cold. It was not a pleasant sensation.

God does not like lukewarm. She remembered a verse and repeated it aloud. "'Because thou art lukewarm, and neither cold nor hot, I will spue thee out of my mouth.'"

That this nothingness of feeling left her joyless *and* disgusted the Almighty, meant something had to be done about it.

But what?

To clear her head, she felt the need to talk it through with someone. She dressed quickly and walked toward the church—toward the cemetery where Stephen was buried. Stephen would know what to do. She knew the thought ridiculous but still hoped talking to him—hearing her words said aloud in the coolness of the cloudy day would nudge her one way or the other.

It looked like rain. But if she hurried. . .

As she passed the path that she and Chester were going to take into the meadow the previous Sunday, she turned upon it to gather some wildflowers for Stephen's grave. She chose asters and bachelor's buttons—the latter making her smile.

As she retraced her steps toward the road, she heard a carriage coming. Just as she paused to let it pass, an awful racket sounded as the wheel of the carriage cracked. The cabriolet tilted precariously to its side on half a wheel. The horse dragged it a few feet, nearly losing its footing, forcing spokes to pop and splinter.

Esther ran to help.

When the carriage fully halted, she saw that a man had fallen toward the lower side of the chaise, an awkward leg extended outward for balance.

Esther tossed the flowers aside. "Sir! Are you all right?"

He glanced at her while pushing himself away from the tilt, with effort gaining his feet upon the ground. He staggered a few steps and took a deep breath, straightened his clothing, then assessed the damage. "I appear to be in one piece. Thank God."

"I thank Him, too," Esther said. "It could have been far worse."

He put his hat to his chest and looked heavenward. "Again, I thank You, Lord."

Esther had her first free moment to give him her full attention. She was impressed. He was very tall and had tousled hair the color of wheat. He was dressed beautifully in buff trousers, a blue weskit, and a dark cutaway coat covered with a black cloak.

"Now that the dust has cleared. . . Madam," he said with a bow.

"Sir." Esther bobbed a curtsy and found her heart flutter. How unusual.

He returned his hat to his head and smiled at her. It was not an ordinary smile, but it seemed to signal the completion of a pleasurable transaction, as if one plus one equaled. . .

"Are you here to save me?" he asked.

She smiled. "Perhaps."

He helped her negotiate the tall grass at the edge of the road so they could speak in closer proximity.

She pointed at the wheel. "There is a wainwright in town. You should ask for Mr. Mayfield."

Just as the information was exchanged, she felt a raindrop. And then another.

The heavens opened.

"Come!" He removed his cloak and held it as a shield over Esther as he helped her into the tilted chaise. He quickly pulled the leather roof over them. Together they held the cloak over the front opening, creating further protection.

The rain pelted. Thunder rumbled.

She could smell coffee upon his breath.

"Well then," he said. "That was unexpected."

She saw him press his feet against the floorboard as he tried to keep a respectable distance.

"I apologize," he said. "Tight quarters."

"It cannot be helped." And actually, she didn't mind his closeness. For he had fascinating eyes, as pale as a foggy sky. She wished it were possible to see them in full light. To stare at them.

Stop it, Esther. You're acting like a lovesick girl.

"You say the name of the wainwright is Mayfield?"

"Chester Mayfield," she said. Then she noticed his hand was bleeding. "You cut yourself."

He couldn't inspect his hand without compromising their shelter. "It appears I did. It's nothing that won't heal."

"As I said, it could have been far worse. If the horse hadn't stopped, you could have been flung out."

"A broken wheel can be mended."

"Far easier than broken bones."

Suddenly there was silence. The rain stopped as abruptly as it began. "Well then," he said.

Esther endured a wave of disappointment, as though she'd been told there would be no Christmas.

"Here. Let me take the cloak for both of us." He took over her handhold of it, and their fingers touched. His lingered mere seconds, yet with that brief contact, Esther felt like she'd enjoyed a full caress. How utterly odd. And magnificent.

He tilted the cloak outward, then quickly swept it to the far side amid a flurry of droplets that spattered the back of the horse.

They sat in the carriage a moment, confirming the obvious. Since the rain had stopped, regrettably, their need to sit close was over.

"Let me get out, and then I will help you." He stepped to the ground then extended his hand toward Esther. She welcomed the chance to touch him again.

But there was more.

Due to the precariousness of the tilt, he took hold beneath her arms and lifted her to the ground.

Don't let go! met with *Why am I responding this way?*

His hands moved to her upper arms for a fleeting moment. "Are you all right?"

"Not even damp, thanks to you."

He swept his top hat into a bow. "I thank you for your company, milady. I. . .I guess I will be on my way."

"You are welcome, sir." With a curtsy she reluctantly turned in the opposite direction of the village and walked toward the church. She enjoyed an uncommon spring to her step. She should not be smiling, for there had been a carriage accident. A broken wheel. A close call to dire injury.

The source of her smile belonged to the man.

Then—

"I don't know his name!"

She stopped in the road, looked back, and saw him rounding a curve. At that moment he also looked back. And waved.

Esther waved, too. At the man. Without a name.

"Why didn't we exchange names? We spoke of the rain and the wheel, but not our names? What is wrong with me?" She remembered her lukewarm emotions that morning. Her current feelings were far from lukewarm. But for the wrong reasons.

Her need to talk to Stephen increased.

She continued her walk to the cemetery and to his headstone. She regretted tossing her flowers away but knew Stephen would forgive her. She would have knelt but for the wet grass. Instead she stood, faced the stone, and sighed deeply. "Oh, Stephen." She wasn't sure what to say next, so settled for the obvious. "I miss you. And I'm so confused." She continued with her confession. "I am engaged to Chester, but I feel little for the fact, as though I am numb or uncaring. I shouldn't be uncaring about such a happy event, should I?"

She peered back toward the road, her memories returning to the man in the carriage.

"I met another man today, Stephen. I know nothing of him but for a feeling of immediate connection. I remember feeling such a way when I met you, how the hint of your touch would course through me as though I were on fire." She shook her head and plucked a weed from the grass. "'Tis silly. Completely and entirely. I don't even know his name."

She heard movement behind her. Her heart leapt. *He's come back!*

But it wasn't the man. It was Pastor Wilkins. She forced a smile to cover her disappointment. "Pastor."

"Mrs. Horton. How are you today?"

She nodded toward the headstone. "I am chatting with Stephen."

He smiled. "How is he?"

"Probably very fine, tending to God's garden, but I. . ."

Should she say something?

"Yes?"

"I am not so fine."

He looked surprised. "You are newly engaged to a fine man. I would think your heart would be soaring."

You would think.

"Is your betrothal at issue?"

"No. Not. . .exactly."

"You have been married before, Mrs. Horton. Surely you approve of the institution."

She glanced toward Stephen's grave. "I had a very happy marriage."

"You have known Chester for many years."

"As long as I have been in Chancebury."

"He has been attentive during the years since Stephen died."

She let a nod be her answer.

His brow furrowed. "Do you know of any defect of his character?"

"None. He is a fine man. Of impeccable character."

Pastor Wilkins spread his arms. "There it is then."

She let out a breath. "There it is."

"You have been through much lately, what with Petunia's wedding. Be happy in the change, and look forward not back."

"I am looking forward, I just. . ." There was nothing more to say that he would understand. "It's nothing. I should go. I'm late. Sadie has been all alone at the shop far too long."

He put a hand to his chin. "Perhaps she could man the post a while longer?"

"You have a task for me?"

"An opinion, if you will. About candles." He gestured toward the church. "Shall we?"

❦

After long deliberation, a decision regarding the church candles was accomplished. While Esther wished to be anywhere but there, Pastor Wilkins painstakingly detailed

the dilemma: should they continue to use the low-light—and ill-smelling—tallow candles which were offered for free by Mrs. Collins who made them out of pig fat from her
farm? The alternatives were whale-oil candles for brighter light or the even more expensive beeswax candles. Apparently the alternatives offered a longer life, no bad smell, less
mess, and brighter light. But they were not free.

To finish with the matter—and in an attempt to prevent herself from screaming in
frustration because Esther didn't care which candles were used and saw no need for her
opinion in the first place—she offered to pay for the first lot of whale-oil candles from
her proceeds earned during the festival. Only upon leaving did she wonder if that was
the pastor's intent all along.

Free at last, she hurried toward the village with new purpose. For halfway into Pastor Wilkins' candle dissertation, she realized the man from the carriage was in Chancebury right that minute. He was at Chester's. If she wanted to see him—and find out his
name—she had to hurry and catch him before the wheel was repaired and he was gone
from her forever.

She ignored the intimacy and idiocy of the latter phrase, her need to know overrid-
ing common sense. A mantra of *please be there, please be there* spurred her to walk so fast
her heart raced and a trickle of perspiration tickled down her back.

But then she saw him in the road beside the carriage, assisting Chester as the wheel
was replaced. She forced herself to slow down and put a hand to the strands of hair that
had escaped her bonnet.

He turned in her direction. And smiled. Esther waved and hurried the last few
steps. "I see it is nearly fixed."

"It is," the man said. "Due to your recommendation of Mr. Mayfield."

Chester continued to work. "So you're the woman who helped him?"

"I am."

The man stepped forward. "I believe we parted without being introduced. I am—"

Chester stood and wiped his hands on his thighs. "Mr. Waters, meet Mrs. Horton, my—"

Esther stopped him before the word *fiancée* could be placed in the air between them.
"Nice to meet you, Mr. Waters," she said with a curtsy.

"It is a pleasure to properly meet you."

Chester turned toward him. "That will be half a crown."

Mr. Waters produced the payment. "Thank you for your service, sir."

Chester nodded.

"Well then," Mr. Waters said. He paused as though wishing to expand the moment.
But it could only be expanded so far. "I will be off. Good day to you both." He climbed
into the carriage and, with a tip of his hat, was on his way.

A wave of regret swept over Esther, making her heart heavy and her feet leaden.
Don't go!

Chester gathered his tools and placed them in his wagon. "You are just going to the
shop?"

"Pastor Wilkins needed my advice."

"Better you giving him advice than the flip of it. Come. I'll drive you."

Getting into the wagon, Esther realized Chester might be able to help her. "What an interesting man."

"Who?"

"Mr. Waters."

He shrugged. "Just a man. I'm glad for the business. I usually charge two shillings, but thought he could afford the extra."

"That wasn't very nice."

"I was nice enough to go out and get his wheel in the first place, bring it back, fix it, then go back again to replace it."

He was right. "Where is he from? Where is he going?"

"What's that to me? Or you?"

She looked to the side of the road so he would not see the flush she felt in her cheeks. "We don't get many strangers through Chancebury. I was just curious. You spent much time with him."

"I spent little time *with* him. I was with his wheel. His personal business is not my concern."

She thought of something else. "Did he seem curious about the village?" *Or me?*

"As I said, we did not idly chat. I had work to do, woman."

Sadly, whether she liked it or not, that was the end of it.

The end of Mr. Waters.

Chapter Seven

"Y ou're daydreaming again," Sadie said.

Esther tore her gaze from the shop window. "Hmm?"

"You've spent more time looking outside the past two days than you've spent the entire time I've known you. Are you waiting for something?"

Someone. Esther pulled her eyes away from the square and her mind away from the daydream. Reluctantly.

"I'm sorry to be distracted." Then she lied. "I don't know why."

Sadie wiped crumbs off the counter. "I thought you'd be brimming over with plans for your wedding."

Me, too.

"By the by, what is the date of it?"

"We haven't decided."

"I imagine Chester wants to be married sooner rather than later."

He did. Chester repeatedly brought up the subject. Esther hedged, giving lame excuses about wishing to enjoy the time of their betrothal, wanting to create the perfect day for such a momentous event.

The truth was, she needed time to wait. For something.

Someone.

"Let me know if I can help," Sadie said. She tied a cloth around a pie and did the same for another, tying each with a knot. "Here you are. Tell Lady Tomkins hello."

"I will." Today, more than any other Thursday, Esther was eager to talk to Verd. Isolated as she was, had Verd heard about Esther and Chester's betrothal? Esther hoped against it, because it wasn't Chester she wished to discuss. Maybe Verd knew of a Mr. Waters.

A half hour later, Esther was welcomed into Verd's parlor with the usual hospitality. Christopher was scratched behind the ears, and Esther was invited to sit in a nearby chair. She set her bonnet on her lap.

But then she noticed there was a second chair pulled close. "You have another guest coming?" She was disappointed at the thought. Her topic of the day was too personal for sharing beyond her friend's ears.

"I do indeed," Verd said with a grin. "Henry?"

Esther recognized the name as the nephew's, but when she turned toward the doorway, she was stunned to see that the man who entered was none other than—

"Mr. Waters?"

His eyebrows rose. "Mrs. Horton?"

"You two know each other?" Verd asked.

"We met by accident," she explained.

"Quite literally," he said. "Remember I told you about the wheel of my carriage?"

Verd looked between the two of them. "Why didn't you say you'd met my Esther?"

He sat in the appointed chair. "Because I didn't know she was your Esther. She was introduced by Mr. Mayfield as Mrs. Horton. And if you remember, Auntie, you kept me busy all of yesterday with bookwork and business."

"Indeed I did," she conceded. "But now you can meet properly. And a good time for it too, for I have been singing your praises, one to the other."

"She thinks very highly of you," Esther said, enjoying his proximity.

"And you," he said.

A silent moment passed between them. She felt heady looking upon his face, the face of the man in her daydreams, the man who refused to leave her thoughts.

Her bonnet slipped from her lap to the floor, and the two of them bent to retrieve it, their fingers once again touching, making Esther want more.

"Well, well," Verd said.

Esther returned the bonnet to her lap and felt herself blush. It was disconcerting to know their connection was so easily noticed.

Suddenly Verd stood—she never stood during their meetings—and Henry stood in deference. "Sit, sit," she told him. "I will check on the tea."

As she left the room, the couple shared another moment of silence—this one awkward.

"Subtlety is not your aunt's strongest suit," Esther said.

"It is not. But. . .do you mind?"

"Not at all. It is good to have a chance to speak with you beyond the wheel problem, beyond its resolution."

"I agree." He moved to the mantel, fingered a porcelain bird in passing, then faced her.

Esther appreciated seeing the whole of him. As she'd noticed before, he was tall and lean, two attributes that showed his waistcoat and breeches to their full favor. He stood with the confidence of one who was used to addressing others, and his countenance offered her his full attention, as if her presence and her words were the most important details of his day. She willingly gave in kind, quite willing to be lured into his realm—a realm that felt regal yet relaxed.

He cleared his throat. "When we first parted, when I proceeded to town and you in the other direction, I chided myself in the strongest fashion that I had not asked your name."

"I suffered the same chiding," she said.

He let the bird be. "So what if we begin again? I have met you and you have met me, and so. . ."

And so we are free to explore. . . "Verd says you recently obtained a headmaster position in Manchester."

"I did." He returned to his chair and angled it toward hers.

The scent of manly spice made her feel warm inside.

"The Hillston Preparatory School for Boys."

"No girls?"

"Alas, no."

"But you are not against the education of females?"

"I am not. I encourage it. If only society would catch up to modern thinking on the matter."

"I commend your modern thinking—for it matches mine. There should be more purpose in a woman's life than reading approved books, having children, running a household, and supporting a husband's endeavors at the expense of her own."

He smiled. "Such as running a pie shop?"

"Exactly like running a pie shop."

"My aunt said you are a widow. I am sorry for your loss."

"Thank you. Stephen was a very good man."

"But she didn't say. . . Do you have children?"

"I have a stepdaughter, Petunia. Her mother died soon after her birth, and she was eight when I married Stephen. She herself was recently married and has moved to London."

"The next step will be grandchildren, then."

She waved her hands. "I pray not too soon. Although I enjoy the idea of being a grandmother, I am only one and forty." She put a hand over her mouth. "Oh dear. A woman is not supposed to reveal her age—especially at first meeting."

"Third meeting actually."

"Indeed it is. So perhaps it is acceptable." She grinned. "As I have revealed, so must you."

"I am not quite forty."

She laughed. "A younger man."

"Only barely."

Then she realized her *faux pas*. "Forgive me, for my comment about your age compared to mine assumes. . ."

His voice softens. "I must admit I like the assumption."

A wave of pleasure embraced her.

Verd came in the room with Nelly carrying the tea tray. She took her seat, and Christopher immediately appeared and took his. "So then. Have you become fast friends as yet?"

He answered for them. "I believe we have."

She handed Esther a cup, and then served Henry.

Although Esther wanted to know more about him, she was hesitant to ask personal questions with the eager Verd as a witness, so she chose a broader subject. "Although I have been friends with Verd for years, I would love to hear more about your family as a whole. Where did you grow up? Do you have siblings? Are your parents still living?"

"Right to the point," Verd said.

Esther felt her face redden. Although the questions were innocent, they were notably personal. "Forgive me. I have never met any of Verd's relatives beyond her son—and that was years ago."

"She wants to know our family secrets," Verd said.

"I want to know no such thing." But Esther smiled. "Unless they are titillating and riveting."

Henry chuckled then leaned close in confidence. "I have an aversion to rabbits."

"Rabbits?"

"He does," Verd said. "Completely and utterly."

"To eating them, or in general?"

"I believe the one caused the other."

"He got sick once after eating rabbit."

"I have avoided them ever since."

Esther studied their faces. When she saw hints of their smiles, she knew she'd been had. "You are teasing me."

"Absolutely," he said.

"It's quite enjoyable," Verd said.

"Is this a delaying tactic for answering my too-many questions about your family?" she asked.

"Just a diversion." Henry sipped his tea then set the cup on the small table between them. "Perhaps we diverted the conversation because our family is rather ordinary. No recent scandals. And on the reverse, no accomplishments to impress the world."

"Ordinary can possess elements of extraordinary," Esther said.

He shrugged. "To get to the root of it, my parents are living."

"His mother is my sister."

"I have three older siblings—two sisters and a brother. They all live in London."

"So you are the lone sheep, lost to Manchester?" It did seem odd he would leave the rest of them.

"If I may be blunt?"

"Please." She braced herself.

"All of my siblings are happily married, and I have six nieces and nephews."

"How nice. I am an only child and my parents have died, so I will never have such a blessing."

His face turned serious. "The happy marriages and children are enormous blessings, blessings that have eluded me to the point of envy." His face reddened, and he avoided her gaze. "I could never confess such a thing to them."

"Only to me," Verd said. "I hear his confessions and he, mine."

"I thought you confessed to me," Esther teased.

"I have so many sins, I need two sets of willing ears." She stroked Christopher's back, then said, "It must be stated that Henry's unmarried status is not due to lack of female interest."

"I would never think such a thing," Esther said with complete sincerity.

"It is simply due to his discerning nature," Verd said.

"I am choosy."

"Pickity-snickity," Verd said.

"I do not believe in marriage for its own sake. I believe God does the choosing."

What a refreshing opinion. "So. . ." Esther said. "If two people get married, it is God's doing?"

"Not at all," Verd said. "People can make mistakes."

Henry nodded once. "God will let two people find each other, and He ignites a spark between them. It is their choice whether they fan the flame or extinguish it."

She liked his reasoning. "So you have not yet felt a spark?"

He retrieved his tea cup and sipped around his answer. "Perhaps."

"Perhaps indeed," Verd said.

Esther was pleased with their answer. If he had said "Not until now," she would have been overwhelmed—even if she had an inkling it *was* his full reply.

A question surfaced. "Do you believe God has chosen *one* spouse for each person?" *What about me? God brought Stephen and me together. If I marry Chester. . .if I marry. . .*

"I believe," Henry said quietly, "there are seasons to life. A marriage made in youth may only be for that season. But I believe it is possible that God can and will choose another spouse for the one left behind, so the two can travel through the next season together."

Out of nowhere, Esther felt tears threaten and hurriedly set her tea aside and ran from the parlor into the dining room.

She overheard Henry say, "I'm so sorry. Did I say something wrong?"

"Not at all," Verd said. "I'll go after her."

Before Verd appeared, Esther swiped her tears away. "I'm so embarassed," she told her friend.

"As a widow, you *can* find happiness again."

"I know. And I appreciate his words."

"As do I. For they sound like truth." Verd handed her a handkerchief.

"I've made a fool of myself."

"I assure you, you have not. If anything, you have piqued Henry's interest—more than it is already piqued."

"But I shouldn't do that!"

Verd looked at her askance. "And why not?"

Because I am betrothed to Chester!

Esther kept that truth to herself and said instead, "I have only met Henry, and here we are talking of husbands and wives and God doing the choosing. . ."

"When last here, you mentioned Chester's persistent interest. Do you think God chose him for you?"

It was the question of the century. "I don't know."

Verd took the handkerchief and dabbed Esther's cheek. "Then it behooves you to wait until you *do* know. Until then, let us finish our tea."

Esther took a deep breath, calming her unease. "I *would* like to make amends for my outburst."

"T'will not be difficult. Let us go discuss the details of my upcoming party."

Esther left Verd's home with an invitation to come pick the berries from Verd's garden tomorrow evening—with Henry to help her.

Although she knew she should have declined the offer, she could not. And did not.

Her walk back to the shop was made without conscious thought. One foot found its way in front of the other, her breath moved in and out, and her destination was reached without the realization that time had passed.

"Did Verd like her pies?" Sadie asked upon Esther's entrance.

"As usual."

"Any interesting news?"

"It was an ordinary visit." Esther felt guilty for the immensity of the lie. But she did not correct it.

Chapter Eight

Chester came in at closing time, on his way to the Boar's Head for his Friday night ritual of ale and friends. Esther had never minded before and certainly did not mind on this particular Friday.

He kissed her on the cheek. "I will see you tomorrow."

She was glad he did not ask her how she was going to spend her evening. She didn't wish to lie to him—even though she *was* lying by her omission.

After closing the shop, Esther rushed home to put on another dress, the one patterned with pink rosebuds. She combed through her hair and refastened it into a bun at the nape of her neck. She pinched her cheeks but found them already blushed with anticipation. Then she carefully set her bonnet and tied the pink ribbon in a pretty bow to the side. She peered at herself in the mirror above her bureau. "What are you doing, Esther Horton?"

She looked away, unable to look herself in the eye.

&c.

"Do you often pick berries here?" Mr. Waters asked as they took their baskets into Verd's garden.

"Never before this evening. Your aunt usually has Sam bring me the bounty."

"But today she is making you do the work."

"I don't mind at all." She heard the deeper meaning in her words, and added. "I have grown to love gardening."

"You did not always love it?"

"Not at all. My late husband was the one who had a passion for it. He was never happier than in his garden, planting, weeding, watering, or picking the harvest."

"A man of the earth."

"Completely. Though he grew up in Manchester, his heart belonged to the countryside."

"And to you."

"And to me."

They began at a row of blackberry bushes, each taking a side. "So you grew to enjoy it?"

"I have. Actually, I think the Almighty had a plan."

"He is known to use gardens." He winked.

She ate a berry. "Our payment for the work."

"A fine pay it is." He ate his own berry. "So what plan did God implement in your garden?"

"I hesitate to say, because it may seem presumptuous to suppose upon God's deeds."

"There is no way for us to fully know the extent of His ways in this world. But I do not believe He objects to us seeing His hand."

She stooped to get the berries at the bottom of the bush, which gave her slight cover for her story. "I would never have gardened if not for Stephen. And after he died, it turned out I needed the garden for my very survival."

"The pie shop."

She nodded. "We had some money saved from his time as the estate manager for your aunt, but I realized that money would run out. I did not wish to rely on the charity of others, so I needed to do *something*. One evening while Petunia and I were eating a pie I'd made, she remarked on its tastiness and told me I should make them to sell." Esther stood and faced him straight across the bush. "And so I did. The shop has saved me from poverty and provided me diversion and satisfaction."

"I believe it has also provided the whole of Chancebury with the latter."

"At the risk of boasting, I believe you are right."

In concert, they moved to the next bush. Then Mr. Waters said, "I believe God sent me to Manchester."

"What were your clues?"

"A door closed."

"In what way?"

"The school where I was teaching in London hired a new headmaster. It is fair to say we did not agree on our methods."

"I ask again, in what way?"

"He believed boys could be forced to learn by using a ruler in ways other than its original purpose."

"He hit them?"

"With gusto. And pleasure, I believe."

"How despicable."

"I attempted to get him to change his ways but was dismissed for my efforts." He spread a hand. "A door closed."

"And one opened in Manchester?"

"It did."

"Why Manchester? There are many miles between it and London."

"Nearly two hundred, I believe." He popped another berry in his mouth and seemed to ponder his next words. "Two hundred miles was not too far for God. The opportunity presented itself over mutton chops and Banbury cakes. I was dining at my sister's one evening while they were entertaining a friend, a Mr. Connelly."

"Who happened to live in Manchester?"

He smiled. "You jump ahead."

"Forgive me. Continue."

"His son attended Hillston in Manchester, and he noted that the headmaster was retiring due to ill health. The subject of my situation was mentioned, and by the last bite of cake, it was arranged for me to travel back to Manchester with him, to interview for the position."

Esther hung her basket on her arm and applauded. "Bravo, Mr. Connelly."

"Bravo, God."

She retrieved a fallen berry and dropped it in her basket. "I like how you see God's hand."

"How we both see God's hand."

"I fear I have been lax in that regard these past years."

"You have been busy raising a child. Surviving."

She shook her head. "That is a poor excuse." Esther swiped a hair away from her eyes with the back of her hand. "Stephen was the godly one. He taught me by example more than words."

"I wish I could have met him."

She studied him a moment. "He would have liked you."

"And I, him?"

Esther nodded with complete certainty. "You have much in common."

"How so?"

She suddenly feared she'd said too much, for in actuality her knowledge of Mr. Waters was limited. "You are both honorable men who stand up for what you believe in. You both seek God and love Him."

He put a finger to the brim of his hat. "Thank you, Mrs. Horton. I appreciate the generous words."

"You're welcome."

"But I believe there is more we have in common."

"And what's that?"

"We both enjoy the company of. . ."

Oh dear. He's going to say it!

He winked, and tossed a berry in his mouth. "We enjoy the company of delicious fruit."

"Oh, you." She couldn't help but feel a tad bit disappointed.

⟨❧⟩

Mr. Waters stood on the bench of the wagon, took Esther's hand, and helped her up to the seat beside him. The bed of the wagon was loaded with baskets and crates full of berries, apples, carrots, cabbages, and green beans.

"I can't believe we picked such a bounty," Esther said.

"I can't believe it is near dark," Mr. Waters said. "The time flew by."

"Good conversation and hard work will do that."

He took up the reins, but then Verd came outside. "Wait!"

Esther was shocked twofold: at the sight of her friend outside her home *and* hearing her shout.

"What's wrong, Auntie?"

She took a moment to catch her breath, her hand to her chest. Then she said, "I wish to order a blackberry pie from Esther."

That was the reason for her sudden appearance and shout? "Very well," Esther said. "Next Thursday, I will make a blackberry—"

"Not next Thursday," Verd said. "Tomorrow. For it is Henry's favorite pie."

"That it is," Henry said.

"Then I will make you one," she told him with a nod.

But Verd wasn't through. "Bring it over when you come for dinner."

Previously, sharing tea had been the extent of Verd's hospitality. "Dinner?"

"You do eat dinner, don't you?" Verd asked.

"Of course I do, but—"

"Then join us for dinner tomorrow evening." Verd turned toward the front door, but kept talking. "And bring the pie." The door closed behind her.

"It appears I am coming to dinner," she said.

Mr. Waters chucked at the horses. "I, for one, look forward to it."

Dark had tucked the world in shadows as Esther and Mr. Waters unloaded the garden's abundance.

She lit a candle in the pie shop—which was obviously closed for the day.

"Sadie will be so surprised when she comes in tomorrow morning," she said, placing the last basket of blackberries on a table.

He turned in a circle. "So this is where the deliciousness happens."

"It is," Esther said.

"Where is the oven?"

"Come, I'll show you." She took up the candle and led him into the back room that had been built to allow access to the front of the oven, while the bulk of said oven remained outdoors. "Sadie comes in very early to get the fire hot enough for the baking."

"How does she know what hot is hot enough?"

Esther shrugged. "Experience. I am lucky to—"

"Esther?"

She turned to see Myrtle Cray in the doorway. Her stomach flipped. "Good evening, Myrtle."

"I saw the wagon outside, and then a flickering within." She gazed at Mr. Waters, top to bottom. "Are you the man with the broken wheel?"

"I am he. Mr. Waters." He offered her a small bow. "And you are?"

She bobbed an awkward curtsy. "Miss Cray."

"A pleasure."

But it wasn't a pleasure. Who knew how Myrtle would skew this moment?

"If you'll excuse me?" he said with a tip of his hat. He bowed to Esther, too, and she was ever so glad he didn't say, "See you tomorrow."

As they heard the wagon pull away, Myrtle asked, "Where is he staying?"

Although Esther was tempted to lie, she told the truth—or a portion of it. "At Coventry Hall, I believe."

"Where is he from?"

Enough truth. "If you see him again, you will have to ask. Now, if you will excuse me, I need to get home." She blew out the light and held the door for Myrtle. "Good night, then."

"But—"

Esther hurried away before more questions could be asked.

Chapter Nine

Esther went to the pie shop early, knowing the work of handling the cornucopia of produce from Verd's garden. She was hulling her second bowl of strawberries, remembering the pleasure of the picking, when Sadie came in.

Sadie's eyes grew wide. "Where did all this come from?"

"Lady Tomkins's garden."

She ate a berry. "She must have had every available lad in the county picking."

"Just me," Esther said, "And her visiting nephew."

"It must have taken hours and hours."

"Until nearly dark." She needed the conversation to move on. "Since much bounty demands much work, I came in early."

Sadie put on her apron. "Let's get to it, then."

"Also, to let you know, Lady Tomkins ordered a blackberry pie for today."

"It isn't Thursday."

"Apparently her nephew likes pie."

Sadie tucked her hair beneath a cap. "Good for him. Good for us."

"I. . ." Should she say it? "I have been invited to dine with them this evening."

"At the hall?"

"Yes."

"You've never dined there before, have you?"

"No."

"How odd."

If only Esther hadn't said anything.

❦

Esther looked up from her work when Chester came in. "Your pie is ready."

He took offense. "No 'good day'? No kiss on the cheek?"

She chastised herself for treating him like any other customer. She had to pull her head out of the clouds and act normally. She took his pie off the shelf and handed it to him—adding a kiss to his cheek.

He held the pie to his nose. "What kind today?"

"Mutton with cabbage, carrots, and onions."

"Sounds tasty."

Sadie stepped in from the oven room. "Afternoon, Chester."

"Sadie."

She looked to Esther. "Lady Tomkins's blackberry pie is just out."

"A pie for the hall? It's not Thursday," Chester said.

It seemed everyone knew the schedule. "Her nephew is visiting."

"Esther is going there for dinner," Sadie said.

Esther felt herself blush. Why had she told Sadie about the invitation?

"Dinner?" Chester asked.

She busied herself rolling out a crust. "I was as surprised as you. I have never been invited for a meal." She hoped her words minimized the event. "I believe I am invited for my contribution to the dinner conversation."

"So her nephew is dull?"

Not at all. "I believe he is a teacher."

"Dull."

"That is unduly harsh."

"I dislike people who know books but don't know real life."

"One does not have to negate the other."

He shrugged.

She knew she should let it go, but had one more question. "I am curious. Who in Chancebury knows books but not real life?"

He was saved from an answer when Myrtle swept into the shop like a foul wind. "Afternoon, Esther. Chester. Sadie."

The woman avoided Esther's gaze, which usually meant she had gossip on her mind—about Esther.

"What can I do for you today, Myrtle?"

Her eyes scanned the pies cooling on a shelf. "You work far too hard, Esther. Being here even after dark last night. . ."

Esther's stomach flipped. "I do what must be done."

Chester took the bait. "You were here after dark?"

Myrtle beat Esther to the answer. "It was well past dark when I spotted a lone candle flickering in the shop. I thought it odd, so investigated and found Esther and Mr. Waters here. Together." Her jowls twitched.

"Waters?" Chester asked. "The man with the wheel?"

"The same," Esther said. "He helped me unload produce from Lady Tomkins's garden."

"How does he know Lady Tomkins?"

"Yes, Esther," Myrtle said. "You never did specify."

There was no circumventing the truth. "Mr. Waters is Lady Tomkins's nephew. Just visiting."

Myrtle twirled the ribbon of her bonnet around a finger and grinned. The action of an ingenue looked ridiculous considering her fifty-some years. "He is quite handsome. Is he married?"

"I don't believe so."

Luckily, Chester had little patience for small talk. "I best be getting back to the forge." He tipped his hat and left with his pie.

Esther let a breath of relief escape before asking, "Which pie would you like, Myrtle?"

The woman spun around toward the door. "None today. Ta-ta."

Esther let the air settle. "That, I didn't need."

"That?" Sadie asked.

"Nothing." Only it wasn't nothing. At all.

Why do I blush every time I see him?

"It looks delicious." Mr. Waters eyed the blackberry pie Esther carried into Coventry Hall. "Can we eat dessert first tonight?"

"You most certainly cannot," Nelly said, taking possession of it. "I spent all day cooking a nice meal for you, and you will do nothing to curb your appetite before it is served."

He saluted her. "Yes, ma'am."

She turned on her heel and left them.

"I think she likes you," Esther said.

"How can you tell?"

"If she scolds you, she thinks of you as family."

"I *am* family."

"There you are."

"My aunt is waiting in the parlor," he said.

"Impatiently waiting," came Verd's voice from the next room.

Esther entered and kissed her friend on the cheek. "Patience is a virtue," she said.

"I have never claimed to be virtuous," Verd said. "Sit now, you two. Let us have a nice chat before Nelly calls us to dine."

Esther noticed an open book on the small table beside Verd's settee. "What are you reading?"

She put a hand upon it. "*A Vindication of the Rights of Woman.* Henry lent it to me."

Esther had not heard of it. "Rights of women? Are you a radical thinker, Mr. Waters?"

He pointed to his head. "I am a rational thinker who believes women are, too."

"Now that *is* radical," Esther said.

Verd adjusted Christopher's paws upon her lap. "Henry says women have the same ability to reason as men do."

"Mrs. Wollstonecraft says that, in her book," he explained.

"Of course we do. It's only logical," Esther said.

"You prove the point," he said. "But she goes further in saying that because of that fact, women deserve the same rights as men."

"Namely?"

"The right to an education for one."

Esther tossed her hands in the air. "I have been touting that for years. Females are not born to be mindless, emotional creatures, yet we are encouraged to be just that. We have good minds, and God wants us to use them."

Verd applauded. "Well said, Esther. I wish I had been allowed to voice my opinions. I would have liked to be a true partner to my husband."

"He would not allow it?" Mr. Waters asked.

"He believed I existed for his pleasure."

"And not your own," Esther said, remembering Verd's stories of oppression.

"Not my own. At all." Verd's face had turned haggard.

"It makes me so sad for you," Esther said.

"I survived it."

"But you shouldn't have merely survived, but thrived. Women are more than pretty faces and polite manners."

"Indeed you are, and I am glad for it," Mr. Waters said.

She was taken aback. "Why?"

"Because women who reveal an innate intelligence—like you and my aunt—inspire me to be a better man. We should be *more* together than apart."

Verd snuggled Christopher under her chin, making him purr. "My husband encouraged me to be weak, frivolous, and silent on all subjects outside the doors of this house. If I questioned him on any issue beyond the domestic, he suggested I calm myself and retire to my room lest I become agitated."

Esther shook her head. "He wished for you to remain mute and ignorant."

"Completely. One time I chose a volume from our library on the history of English kings, and he snatched it away from me, forbidding me to read it. To this day I remember his words: 'There is no reason for you to know what came before this moment. Nor should you worry for the future. Focus on today, on my dinner, our son, and the betterment of our household.'"

"Those are also admirable tasks," Mr. Waters said.

"But I could do more, think more, be more." Verd's voice rose, causing Christopher to escape her lap.

Mr. Waters pointed toward the book. "That is why you will appreciate Mrs. Wollstonecraft's book."

"I already do."

"I would like to read it, too," Esther said. "Stephen often brought home books from the hall, and we'd read them together."

"Did you read them to your daughter?" he asked.

"We tried to teach Petunia—in all subjects, in all ways. But she was not interested. Perhaps if there had been a real school in Chancebury, she might have been willing to learn." Or not.

"I will see you get the book when Auntie is through with it." He smoothed his trouser against his leg. "Tell me more about your husband, Mrs. Horton."

She thought a moment, trying to think of how to best describe Stephen. "He was kind, capable—"

Verd interrupted her list. "He was a first-rate estate manager. And he was invaluable after Thomas was killed and we had the difficulties with the debt he had incurred."

"Stephen enjoyed working at the hall, though more for its sake than your husband's, I'm afraid."

"No one liked Thomas. It is a fact I cannot and will not dispute. But back to Stephen's attributes."

The mental list was long, but Esther chose a highlight. "Beyond his abilities and character, he adored me. And I him."

Verd put her hands to her chest. "Oh, my. To be adored. . .there can be nothing more fulfilling."

Esther looked to her lap, thinking of Stephen's smile, his soft touch, his encouraging words. "He never made me feel like 'just a woman,' but instead as if we were joined together, two for one, moving through life." She glanced up and saw Mr. Waters nodding.

"Everything you have told me about him confirms him to be an exceptional man."

"That he was."

Nelly entered, wiping her hands on her apron. "Dinner is served."

Mr. Waters helped his aunt to her feet, and she wrapped a hand around one of his arms. He offered his other arm to Esther and led them toward the dining room.

"I am the luckiest of all men this night," he said, "to be in the company of two beautiful, intelligent women."

Esther felt rather lucky herself.

⁓

After dinner, Mr. Waters drove Esther home.

"Is something wrong?" he asked. "You have grown quiet."

Everything is wrong. Even while everything is right.

"I must be tired," she said. "I had a marvelous time this evening."

"As did I. I enjoy a lively discussion."

"As do I." She decided to share one factor of her silence. "Such discussion is a phenomenon I now experience too seldom. My friends do not read much, except the Bible. Perhaps."

"There are many thought-provoking stories in the Bible."

"Which would do well to be discussed."

"Perhaps you could bring them up in conversation?"

She unsuccessfully stifled a laugh and clapped a hand over her mouth. "I apologize. I must seem prideful, raising myself above others. I do have many dear friends." *And one is my fiancé.*

"It is understandable they are focused on the issues of the here and now rather than past history or biblical stories that often take a bit of effort to discover their moral lesson."

He had pegged the main issue. "How do we inspire people to expand their knowledge?"

"By sharing it with them."

"What if they won't listen? What if they change the subject?"

He pulled the reins, stopping the carriage so he could face her. "'Who hath ears to hear, let him hear.'"

Esther remembered numerous times when Chester had cut her off and shut down a conversation that delved into deeper subjects. "What good does it do if they don't hear? Don't listen?"

"We have to keep telling the stories—as Jesus did. Hopefully by repetition, their hearts and eyes will be opened, and they will see the full meaning."

"It's not just Bible stories they avoid, but subjects that are important to our lives right now—and to Chancebury's future. I think of all the children here who know next to nothing, not even how to read. We need a school for them. A simple school. Nothing fancy. But somewhere where they can learn something beyond how to feed a chicken or dip a candle."

"Those are also important tasks."

She looked to the stars overhead then pointed at them. "I have only to look up to see the expanse of what is available to learn. There is always more."

"Then teach them. Expand the borders of their world."

She chuckled and let her hand fall to her lap. "How can I teach what I myself do not know?"

"Learn it. Then share it."

She loved the idea, but the implementation would be difficult.

"You told me you are teaching Sadie to read, yes?"

"I am."

"Then you can teach others who wish to learn."

"But there is more to life than reading and basic arithmetic."

He raised a finger. "But reading opens the world. Start there. The rest will come."

Esther felt a stirring inside, as though a breeze had blown through an opened door. There were too many logistics to determine, but the idea of learning—and teaching—left her giddy with possibilities.

Once they reached her home, Mr. Waters got down from the carriage and helped her alight. He bowed, and she curtsied, but then she did something more. She extended her hand to him. "Thank you, Mr. Waters. For the fine conversation and for proposing an even finer challenge."

He shook her hand then put his free hand on top, keeping hers captive. "Don't you think it's time to call each other by our given names?"

"I would like that. Thank you, Henry."

"A good night to you, Esther."

She stood by the front door of her cottage until the sound of his carriage faded into nothingness. In the silence, she realized that more than anything in the world—even more than wanting a school or knowledge—she wanted Henry Waters to remain a part of her life.

Chapter Ten

Esther and Chester took a walk after church. She held his arm, but looked ahead, seeing nothing. If someone had covered her eyes and suddenly asked, "Where are you right this moment?" she would not have been able to tell them.

Chester stopped their progress. "Where *are* you today?"

"I'm sorry. My mind is wandering."

"Tell it to come back. I feel as though you don't even need me to be here."

Esther blinked, forcing herself into the present. She touched his cheek. "Again, I apologize."

"Pastor Wilkins's sermon wasn't that thought provoking."

"Actually, I wouldn't know."

"At least I'm not the only one you're ignoring."

She tried to corral her thoughts, but they fled from her like sheep out of a pen.

"How was dinner last night at the hall?"

She ignored the entire subject of Henry and turned to the subject she *could* share with him. "I would like to start a school in Chancebury, for boys *and* girls."

His head drew back. "A school? Whyever for?"

"To educate the children. Too many don't even know how to read. Look at Sadie. She didn't know until I took it upon myself to teach her."

"Does she need to know how to read? Does she have some secret stash of books she's been wanting to read all her life? Does she even own a book?"

"Don't be rude."

"'Tis a logical question. I don't know how to read either, and I've never missed it."

She felt her mouth gape open. "You don't know how to read?"

"I shoe horses and fix wagons. Why would I need to read?"

"To find out more about worlds beyond Chancebury."

"I've been to Manchester. That's enough of the world for me. Too much."

How could he be so utterly closed-minded? Chester disparaged new worlds; Henry embraced them.

Esther embraced them.

Chester kicked a pebble away from the space where he stood, just like he kicked away Esther's idea. "People don't want their children to take time away from chores to learn something they'll never use."

It was her turn to be incredulous. "Even if it means they can better themselves? Or at least tap into the knowledge the world has to share?"

He started walking again. "I'd say 'no thank you' to that."

None too gently, she pulled him to a stop. "Then you are an ignorant fool."

His brow furrowed. "What's got into you, Esther?"

She tried to put a word to it. "Opportunity."

"To stir a pot that doesn't need stirring?"

"I believe it needs a good whipping."

"What about your pies? Are you giving that up—and the income it earns—to create this school no one needs or wants? A school where you'd get paid nothing?"

She'd thought about this. "I don't think it would come to that. I could set up the school in my spare time."

"Where? Where would it be?"

She hesitated. "I don't know."

"Who's going to teach there?"

That was the largest issue. "I could—if I let Sadie take over the shop. Or. . ." She thought of Henry. "Perhaps someone else."

He scoffed. "We know every soul in Chancebury. There isn't a scholar among us."

She knew he was right—which was part of her conundrum. "Perhaps there is a hidden scholar here."

This elicited a full laugh. "I suppose old Mr. Grundsby recites poems while he shears his sheep? And I'm certain the butcher's wife knows all the kings of England in proper order."

"They could."

"No one needs that kind of nonsense in their head. Be practical, Esther. People in Chancebury need their brains to survive. Nothing more."

He'd quieted the wind in her sail to the point of feeling adrift. "Walk me home, please."

"Nay now, I didn't mean to upset you. I just spoke the truth; you know I did."

He'd spoken *a* truth. That didn't mean there wasn't more truth to be had.

Esther closed the book she'd attempted to read all afternoon. Checking the pages, she realized she'd only read two. In an hour. And remembered none of it.

"This is absurd," she told the room.

She bowed her head, needing the peace that only God could provide. "Lord, help me wind my way through my thoughts about the school. It seems like such a good idea. It would be a blessing to many and might give some of the young people hope for a more productive life."

"They would be able to read My book."

Esther grabbed at the new thought. "They would! They would be able to read the Bible for themselves! Is that not a glorious goal?"

Her thoughts suddenly turned to Chester. He was against the entire notion—which had made her think less of him.

Which in turn made her think more of Henry.

Chester and Henry. Neither man knew of the other beyond passing. Two men who had gained her attention for far different reasons. Chester, because he was someone she'd known forever and was a comfortable, familiar friend who helped her enjoy what was. And Henry, because he was a fascinating man who challenged her mind and made her think of what could be. One was her fiancé, and one was. . .not.

There was the core of it. The full fact of it. To think of Henry and all the things he made her envision—many of which were beyond common reason—was that wise? Or was she being foolish to a fault?

She put her elbows on her knees, grasped her hands in prayer, and bowed her head. "Help me see what You want me to see. Help me do what You want me to do. Keep me from mistaking what is exciting and new for Your will. If these thoughts of a school and—and Henry—are not pleasing to You, take them from—"

A knock on the door interrupted her prayer.

When she answered it her heart fluttered. "Mr. Waters. Henry. How nice to see you."

"I hope I do not disturb."

"Not at all."

He held a book. "My aunt has finished Mrs. Wollstonecraft. You mentioned wanting to read it?"

"Why thank you. How thoughtful."

While he stood there, she made a decision. Although she wanted to invite him in, to do so was improper. But that didn't mean she wanted him to leave. "Would you like to sit in the garden with me? It's a beautiful evening."

"I would enjoy that very much. For I leave tomorrow."

"No!" She realized she had overreacted. "Forgive me, but this comes as a surprise." She led him to a bench near a trellis of clematis and sat beside him. Their bodies touched side to side, and she was glad for the contact that could not be avoided by the usual protocol or propriety.

"Leaving was a surprise to me, also," he said.

"What about your aunt's party Wednesday?"

He sighed deeply. "I received word that I was needed at the school for some issue. As I am new at the position, I feel the need to obey their request."

"Of course." The thought of him leaving—even though she'd known his time in Chancebury was temporary—pained her as surely as a slap.

He raised his eyes to gaze at the sky, and then the garden. He closed them and took a deep breath. "There is peace here."

"This is the place I run to when I am unsettled."

"Hmm. Close your eyes and listen."

Although she knew there was the chance of feeling silly, Henry's request seemed anything but. So she closed her eyes. And listened.

"What do you hear?" he asked.

"I hear bees, the wind in the trees, the soft bleating of my neighbor's sheep down the road."

"I hear music."

She opened her eyes. "Music?"

"Are you a fan of Beethoven?"

"Who?"

"He is a composer whose fame is continuing to grow. I happened to hear his *Eroica* Symphony in Vienna two years ago."

"Vienna," she said wistfully. "I cannot imagine such a place."

"You have not traveled?"

She touched her temple. "Only in here. Stephen and I often talked about going to the Continent once Petunia was grown." She sighed. "But then he died, and the dream was set aside."

"It need not be. Perhaps postponed?"

She knew the next would sound presumptuous. "I have no one to travel with, no one to help with the logistics of it, nor anyone who has the desire for it."

"Perhaps your daughter—?"

She laughed. "Petunia is busy with her new life as a married woman—as she should be. The last thing she would want is to travel with her mother."

He gave her a simple nod then raised his face and closed his eyes again. "When I hear glorious music I like to close my eyes and let the music surround me. I give it free rein to create images in my head that are far beyond the here and now."

"I have never heard a symphony or any music besides hymns and local folk songs."

He studied her. "I would love to share music with you. And more, for there is so much in the world to experience. And it is better experienced with. . .with someone."

Esther longed to spring to her feet and say, "*Yes! Let me go with you! Let me be that someone!*"

Instead, the knowledge that there was no chance for any of it to become reality, caused her imagined spring to turn into the simple act of standing.

"Shall we walk?" she asked, knowing of nothing else she could say.

"Of course."

She led him through her rows of flowers. Her heart pounded in her chest, revealing what her body understood and her mind would never acknowledge.

She loved Henry Waters. She wanted Henry Waters to love her. She wanted to marry Henry Waters.

She leaned over to pinch a dead blossom, letting the words that needed to be said find their voice. "I need to tell you something, Henry. Something I should have told you a long time ago."

"What is that?"

When she straightened to face him, her balance bobbled, and she would have fallen if Henry had not reached out to steady her.

"Thank you. I'm so clumsy." But as she righted herself, she spotted Myrtle standing at the corner of her fence. "Evening, Myrtle."

The smile that crossed the woman's face spoke volumes as to the mischievous workings of her thoughts. "Evening, Esther. And Mr. Waters, is it?"

Henry tipped his hat. "Good evening, ma'am."

"Miss," she said.

"I stand corrected. Good evening, miss."

"Mr. Waters stopped by to lend me a book," Esther said, realizing too late her explanation would only add to Myrtle's smoldering fire.

"I see."

"I should be leaving," Henry said.

"No need to hurry off on my account," Myrtle said.

"I'm not. It is getting late, and I must get back to the hall." He nodded toward Myrtle. "Good evening, miss." Then turned to Esther. "Mrs. Horton."

And he was away.

All that was within Esther wished to run after him. *Don't go, Henry! You're leaving tomorrow! I need you to stay! I need you to know the truth about me and Chester, and. . .*

I need you to love me anyway.

Myrtle stood at the fence and watched him go. "A bit unusual, me seeing you two together at odd hours, not once, but twice."

Esther felt the full weight of her predicament. If she explained it would seem she protested out of guilt. Yet to say nothing would hint at that same.

The latter seemed the lesser of two evils. "Good evening, Myrtle."

She escaped inside her cottage. Upon the click of the door, her legs gave out beneath her, and she slipped to the floor like a puddle.

"Lord, what shall I do?"

Chapter Eleven

S leep eluded her.

Esther turned over in bed and opened her eyes to the morning, which had come too soon.

Although she longed to know God's will in her life, and usually had a good sense about it due to the peace that was its companion, last night's sleep—or lack thereof—seemed a good indication that her current situation was not God's will.

She surrendered to that truth. Yet she still wasn't certain what came next.

Did God disapprove of her tenuous situation with Chester? Her own doubts hinted that the Almighty might be against their match.

Or did God disapprove of her burgeoning feelings for Henry?

She found herself smiling. The sudden appearance of Henry in her life did not seem a coincidence. Coming upon him on the road with a broken wheel, perhaps. But being caught in the rain with him inside the carriage, seeing him at Verd's. . .

If she had decided to visit Stephen's grave an hour earlier or later, she would have missed meeting him altogether. If his wheel had not broken just then, if the rain had not forced them to take cover—a rain that ended soon after. . .

She might have met him at Verd's when he came to visit, but would meeting in that formal situation have sparked the same intensity of feelings?

Was there a reason she hadn't married Chester yet, or even set a date?

If she weren't betrothed to Chester, would she rush into Henry's arms?

Would he want her there?

She threw aside the covers and sat on the side of the bed. "You are a fickle woman, Esther Horton. Fickle and vain. Two men cannot—cannot—be in love with you. It is impossible." She looked heavenward. "Forgive me if I've offended You in any way, Father. I mean no harm to either man, so help me. Thy will be done."

❧

Esther crimped the edge of a beef pie and slit the crust with steam holes. "Another one, ready," she called out to Sadie.

"Coming."

Esther moved to slit the next two pies, a strawberry and a raspberry. She looked up as Sam came in.

"Sam. Is everything all right at the hall?"

"Right as rain." He handed her a folded note with a seal on it. "Mr. Waters asked me to bring this by for you."

She held it to her breast. "Has he left for Manchester yet?"

"First thing this morning."

He is really gone then. "Thank you, Sam. Let Lady Tomkins know the pies will be ready for her party Wednesday."

He tipped his cap and was gone.

Sadie came out of the oven room, swiping her forehead against its heat. She spotted the note. "Who's that from?"

Esther hedged. "Coventry Hall. If you don't mind?" She nodded toward the door, stepped outside, and sat on the bench beneath the window. Before breaking the seal, she ran a finger over her name. *Esther* was written in a beautiful cursive with extra embellishments on the E. "Henry," she whispered.

"Morning, Esther," said the butcher's wife.

"Morning."

Luckily, the woman moved on, but the square had come alive with people going about their business. Esther best get on with it before someone stopped and asked about the note.

She unfolded it and read:

Dearest Esther,
I hope you forgive me the endearment, but I found I could not write this note without including it. For despite our short acquaintance, you have become very dear to me.

I can honestly say that I have never met another woman—yea, another person—who has given me so much pleasure by their mere presence. That presence would be enough in itself, yet it is enhanced by the blessed contribution of good conversation about subjects near and far, and dialogue that ignites new ideas and deepens old ones.

I regret missing my aunt's party and having to return to Manchester so soon. Too soon.

May God grant us the joy of another meeting in the very near future.

Yours truly,
Henry

A wave of grief engulfed her, and she felt tears threaten. She bowed her head. *Lord, what shall I do? His words mean the world to me.*

"A distressing note, Esther?"

She looked up. Why was she doomed to see Myrtle around every corner?

She quickly slipped the note into her apron pocket. "I am not distressed."

"You looked so. You looked very much so. You had your head bowed and—"

"Perhaps I was taking a nap."

Myrtle shook her head violently. "I watched you reading the note, and then you bowed your head. There was no time for a nap."

Esther stood and glared at her. "Have you nothing better to do than trace my every move?"

Myrtle held her gaze. "Not every move—though who knows what mischief has occurred beyond my gaze."

"What mischief could ever occur beyond your gaze, Myrtle Cray?"

With that, Esther went inside the shop.

Sadie was there to meet her, an incredulous look upon her face. "I cannot believe you said that to her. She deserved that, and more, but. . ."

In the moment between outside and in, Esther had regained her senses. "Oh dear. What have I done?"

"No good, that is for certain," Sadie said. "You know Myrtle lets no slight go unpunished."

Esther put a protective hand upon her pocket. "I have done nothing wrong." *In public or private, yet I have sinned aplenty in my heart.*

"The truth doesn't matter," Sadie said. "You know that. Myrtle can take a speck of dust and create a blinding dust cloud."

Esther looked out to the square. "Did you see in which direction she went?"

Sadie pointed to the left. Toward Chester's smithy. Then she said, "Go make amends. And be quick about it."

Esther ran out of the shop, and tried—as unobtrusively as possible—to hurry toward Chester's. She received curious looks, but dared not lessen her pace. Her future depended on reaching Chester before Myrtle did.

She turned the final corner and spotted the two of them together. Unfortunately, Myrtle was doing all the talking, gesticulating toward the pie shop.

Chester looked up and spotted Esther. She forced herself to smile and wave as though nothing were amiss.

Unfortunately, when Myrtle saw her, she stormed to her side. "Come now, Esther, it's time you tell Chester—your betrothed—about your secret liaisons with Mr. Waters."

Esther let her brow dip—hoping her expression feigned surprise. "Secret liaisons? I hardly think dining with Lady Tomkins or feeding Mr. Waters' curiosity about the pie oven deserves such a phrase."

"I saw you together at your cottage."

Esther forced herself to remain calm. "Outside my cottage. In my garden, to be exact."

Chester spoke up. "He was at your cottage?"

"In my garden. He was kind enough to bring over a book he and Lady Tomkins wished for me to read."

"What book?"

Oh dear. *A Vindication of the Rights of Woman* was not the title of an easily enjoyed novel. "A book by a Mrs. Wollstonecraft."

"What a name," Chester said.

Esther shrugged. "She is the one who must endure it."

"Sounds made up," Myrtle said.

"You would know about made-up things," Esther said.

She huffed and fuddled. "Well, I. . ."

Chester remained true to his dislike of gossip and took Myrtle by the shoulders, spun her around, and gave her a little push. "On with you, woman. Mind your own house before sullying someone else's."

"But—"

"Go!"

She scurried away, murmuring to herself.

Esther tried to calm herself. "I'm sorry you had to endure her nonsense. You met Mr. Waters. He's a gentleman beyond reproach."

"I met him long enough to fix a wheel."

"Well, let me assure you, he is a man of honor."

"How do you know that?"

She thought quickly. "Lady Tomkins has always spoken highly of him. He just took a headmaster position in Manchester. The term begins soon."

"Good. So he will not be coming back to Chancebury often." He hesitated, then added, "We wouldn't want to fuel Myrtle's imagination."

"Indeed not," Esther said. She kissed his cheek. "I best get back to the baking."

He called after her. "She mentioned a note?"

Esther nearly put a hand on her pocket but stopped the action in time. "I received a note from Mr. Waters, telling me goodbye. He has already left for Manchester."

"May I read it?" He glanced at her apron. "I see the outline of something in your pocket."

"I hardly think that's necessary."

He cleared his throat. "I do. For the note is not Myrtle's doing. It is paper I can feel and words I can read." He held out his hand.

She handed the note to him, her mind racing, trying to remember the words that were said. *Dearest Esther. . .dear to me. . .pleasure. . .good conversation. . .joy. . .see you again. . .*

But then a reprieve.

Chester looked at the letter and handed it back to her. "I forgot. I can't read."

A nervous laugh escaped. "Well, let me assure you that—"

"Read it to me."

Esther felt her breath leave her. There was no choice but to edit the words between eye and mouth. Not of their content but of their intimacy.

"Dear Mrs. Horton." She sped past the entire first paragraph, summing it up thusly, "It was a pleasure to meet you. I enjoyed talking with you about books and travel. Feel free to borrow other books from my aunt. I will try to keep her supplied. I wish I did not have to return to Manchester so soon and miss my aunt's party. I am nervous about my new position. Hopefully, we can meet again. Signed, Mr. Henry Waters."

She looked up, unable to speak another word due to the rapid beating of her heart and a sudden dearth of breath.

Chester considered this a moment. "He's a polite one, he is."

She quickly folded the note and returned it to her pocket. "I really must be getting back. Myrtle has caused me to get behind making the pies for Lady Tomkins's party."

"Myrtle *is* a behind—if you ask me."

She gave him a smile. "Have a good day, Chester."

On the way back to the shop, Esther roiled against her deception. Yet how could she have read Henry's exact words aloud? They were private. And they would do nothing but hurt Chester.

And Chester didn't deserve to be hurt.

She repeated that fact as she walked. *Chester doesn't deserve to be hurt.*

Chapter Twelve

E sther stared at her reflection, yet saw nothing. Henry was the focus of her mind's eye, meaning her eyes saw no other. She hated that he would miss Verd's party. With the school term starting soon, who knew when she would see him again?

Her thoughts circled back to when she stumbled in the garden and Henry had righted her. How could such a simple act of assistance seem romantic? Yet it was. For in those few moments of contact she'd felt his strength and his caring nature. But more than that, she'd felt a connection, as though by that simple touch they were weaving a bond, like two strands of a rope, winding around each other, being made stronger by the union. A verse came to mind: "'A threefold cord is not quickly broken."

Yet she and Henry were only two.

"I am three. I am the first cord. Wind yourselves around Me."

Esther shivered and pressed a hand against her heart. "So Henry is Your choice, Father?"

She waited for an answer, but received none. Yet with one fresh breath and then another, the doubt that had plagued her dissipated. "So Chester is my past and Henry is my future?"

She was shocked by the look of surprise and then calm that passed over her reflection, as if the words had not been mentally formed before they were uttered. She smiled at the knowledge that they—that she—had spoken the truth.

Esther made a vow. "I will speak with Chester after the party. And then write to Henry."

Speaking of, she needed to hurry or she'd be late.

◦◦◦

Esther arrived at Coventry Hall in Chester's wagon—for they had pies to deliver. She had let Sadie sit in the seat beside Chester, and in spite of their objections, she had sat in back, ostensibly making sure the pies did not slide. But there was another reason for the seating arrangement. To sit so close to Chester when she had all intentions of breaking their engagement was beyond her ability.

Sam opened the door for them—a door that had a fresh coat of paint. He was dressed in fine livery that was a tad too small around the middle. Verd rushed to greet her first guests.

Rush? Verd did not rush.

But the woman took Esther's hands and squeezed them, drawing her into the parlor, leaving Sadie and Chester to deal with the pies. "I am so nervous. This is the first time I have seen the people of Chancebury in eight years since Thomas's funeral procession. And I had little contact before that. Other than having you come visit, I fear I have lost the art of being a hostess. I have hired three village girls to help with the food, and Sam had a lad help with the setting up, so all the logisticals are in place. But as for me. . ."

"Just smile and be yourself." Esther added, "The guests will be nervous, too, for they have never been invited to such a fine house. They will be on their best behavior."

"As will I," came a man's voice.

Henry walked into the room.

Esther nearly swayed at the sight of him.

"I didn't mean to frighten you."

"I am not frightened," she said, regaining her composure. "Only very surprised. You said you could not attend."

Verd pinched his cheek. "I persuaded him to hurry through his work issues as a birthday gift to me." Her pinch turned into a gentle hand against his cheek. "The finest gift I could ever receive."

"You flatter me, Auntie."

"I do no such thing. Now come along you two. Peruse the buffet with me to see if the layout is appealing as well as functional."

They moved through the dining room, out some double doors, and into the garden where tables were already brimming with food. Sadie and Chester were placing the pies with the other delectables: sandwiches, fruit, breads, smoked meat, cheese, and sweets. "The offerings are plenteous," Esther said.

"I hope there is enough."

Esther noticed a mismatch of chairs littering the grounds.

Verd followed her gaze. "I had Sam bring out every chair in the house, yet I know it is not half enough."

Esther laughed at the sight of an ornate French-styled chair with a silk seat set near a simple wooden chair, probably taken from the kitchen. "It is delightful."

"Do you think so? I was hoping the children wouldn't mind sitting on the lawn."

"I am sure they won't mind at all." Henry pointed to the buffet table. "But aren't those stacked dishes your very best China?"

"And my other two sets as well. What is it for, if not to use?"

Esther scanned another table which held crystal goblets, an enormous punch bowl, and forks of fine sterling. "I hope no one snatches a piece."

"Nelly and Sam mentioned that, too," Verd said. "But what are my guests to use if not forks?"

"It will be a temptation to some," Henry said.

"A temptation they will overcome," she said.

"You trust mankind too much."

"God will witness their actions." She shook her head, dismissing the subject. "They are but things. I have lived among things long enough. It is time I live among people—among my neighbors."

Sam appeared in the doorway. "They are arriving, Lady Tomkins."

Verd touched the simple ruby necklace hanging around her neck. "I'm coming."

Esther and Henry followed her in. There was only time enough for Esther to say, "I'm so glad to see you again, Henry."

"You received my note?"

"I did. And I thank you for it."

"I meant every sentiment. Every—"

The first guests flowed into the foyer, their eyes wide as they took in the lush surroundings: the sweeping staircase, the gilt-framed paintings, the intricate pattern in the rugs. Verd turned to Esther, her eyes panicked. "Help them along to the garden, Mrs. Horton. Henry?"

Esther and Henry hurried to her rescue.

⸎

Esther looked over the garden and grounds that were littered with people eating, talking, and laughing. Children ran along the garden paths, playing tag and hide-and-seek among the lilac bushes and rhododendron. The buffet table had been gleaned of all edibles, and Esther saw Nelly, Sam, and the hired help collecting china, forks, and glasses from every imaginable place. She'd been doing the same, helping as she could. Not because her help was needed as much as it kept her busy and solved the problem of whether she shared a conversation with Henry or Chester. To have them both present caused her nerves to fray like an unhemmed dress.

And it wasn't just their presence that caused her stress. It was the fact that others made no secret of their interest in the trio. Whispers abounded, along with wicked smiles. Myrtle seemed in her element, flitting from this group to that, spreading her mischief.

Esther spotted Chester watching Myrtle. His brow was dipped, his head cocked to the side as if trying to make heads or tails of it. What had he heard? What was there to hear?

His eyes met Esther's, and he came toward her, a question evident on his face.

"Are you enjoying the party?" she asked.

"Yes, yes. It's a fine party. But something's going on. People are looking at me oddly."

"You *are* especially handsome today."

He gave her the look she deserved. "I heard people whispering."

Esther's stomach tightened. "Chancebury always has someone whispering about something."

"But I heard your name mentioned. And Mr. Waters'."

Her thoughts traveled from words of self-defense, to words that could break their engagement, once and for all.

Unfortunately, neither set of words found release before she heard Henry call out, "Attention, everyone! Attention."

Conversation quieted.

"I want to thank my dear aunt for inviting us into her home. She is the most gracious, kind, and loving aunt a man could want. I hope you all get to know her as I do. Happy eightieth birthday, Auntie, and may you have many more!"

There were toasts to Lady Tomkins, huzzahs, and applause.

Verd acknowledged their well wishes. "Thank you for coming. I guarantee this will not be my last soiree."

More cheers.

But she wasn't through. "I would also like to make an announcement." She glanced at Henry, then Esther. "I have hopes of opening a school in Chancebury soon. A school for boys *and* girls."

Really?

Esther looked to Henry. He smiled at her and nodded. Why hadn't they said anything?

The mason's daughter raised a hand. "I could go, too?"

"You could go, too."

Murmurs rustled all around—not all positive—but Verd quieted them. "It is just in a planning phase, but since you are all here, I wanted to share it with you. Again, thank you for coming."

As people began to disperse, Chester quickly stepped forward. "Since we are toasting, I want everyone to raise a glass to my lovely fiancée, Esther. I cannot wait for her to become my wife."

There was applause and shouts of affirmation, but Esther only heard it vaguely, as sounds heard through a wall. What loomed large was the look of shock and betrayal on Verd's face.

Chester linked Esther's arm in his.

The dip in Henry's brow and the pale wash of his skin was a knife to Esther's heart. He came close and shook Chester's hand. "Congratulations." Then he bowed formally to Esther. "Best wishes for the future."

But. . .but. . . Let me explain!

"Now if you will excuse me, I must return to Manchester." He rushed past his aunt.

"Henry?" Verd said.

"I must go, Auntie. I'm sorry."

"Oh dear. I will see you out." With a glare to Esther, she added, "I need to talk to you."

Esther turned to Chester. "Lady Tomkins needs me. I will be right back." She hurried into the house, hoping to catch Henry before he left. But she was moments too late as his horse galloped down the drive.

"But I need to tell him. . .explain. . ."

Verd took her arm none too gently and drew her past the parlor, past the dining room, into a room that served as a pantry. She closed the door.

"You wish to explain. Explain. Immediately," she demanded.

"I didn't know Chester was going to say anything."

"So it's true? You are betrothed?"

Esther focused on a bag of opened flour that had sprinkled on the floor. "It is true. But I. . .I don't want it to be true."

"You hurt Henry. And myself. You betrayed our trust. You know the feelings he has for you."

"To hurt him pains me greatly. Just this morning I made the decision to break my engagement with Chester."

Verd crossed her arms. "You waited too long."

Esther pressed her hands to her face. "It is such a muddle."

"Then do something about it."

"What can I do? Henry has left. The pained look upon his face. . . I will never forget it."

"Nor should you. Tell me this: when did you accept Chester's proposal?"

"At the September festival."

"Why didn't you tell me?"

"I was going to, but then Henry was here, and I discovered he was the man with the wheel—the man who had made me think true love was possible. I was so happy to see him again."

"Some way to show it."

"You know I was happy in his company. I enjoyed talking with him and walking in the garden. . ."

"So you have feelings for Henry?"

"I do. I. . .I love him."

"A disturbing way to show it."

"I was going to tell Chester after the party, and write to Henry. But then he was here and—"

"Good intentions mean little. I thought you were a woman of honor."

"I am. I was trying to be. Chester is a good man, and I hate hurting him."

"So now you've hurt Henry."

"I didn't mean to. I was going to sort it all out today."

"Too little, too late." Verd flipped a hand at her. "I must say goodbye to my guests."

"May I come by tomorrow and talk? Help me repair this. Please."

"I see no repair to this, Mrs. Horton. Do not come again."

She left Esther alone in the pantry. With her pain. And her guilt.

◦◦◦

Chester stopped the wagon in front of Esther's. "I'm sorry for your headache. I was hoping to come in."

"Not tonight." *I've caused enough pain for one day.* She watched as Sadie moved from the back of the wagon to the seat beside him. "See you in the morning, Sadie."

Esther went into her cottage but kept the candles unlit. She made her way to her room and fell upon the bed, fully clothed. She pulled a pillow close, hugged it, and prayed the pain of losing her best friend *and* the love of her life would subside.

Knowing very well it wouldn't.

Chapter Thirteen

First Chester. Then Verd.

That was the order of the day. Break her engagement with Chester, then mend her relationship with Verd.

As for Henry? He was gone. His reaction to her engagement proved his feelings for her. Deceived, he had left with a broken heart. Could his heart be mended? There was no way to know. But either way, Esther knew she could not marry Chester.

She reached the smithy, but he was not there.

"Where is Mr. Mayfield?" she asked his helper.

"In the barn, ma'am. A horse is foaling."

She detoured to the barn and heard commotion inside. She didn't want to intrude, nor was she comfortable seeing the process. Instead, she peeked through an opened window.

She was surprised to see Sadie with Chester, helping with the birth.

Her second reaction was anger. He'd called Sadie in to help and not her?

He knows of your squeamishness. He knows you care little for horses.

Logic calmed her reaction. She sat on a trough to wait.

As Chester and Sadie—and the mare—worked, she could hear them discussing horses. Esther had never known of Sadie's fondness for them. *What else don't I know?*

Suddenly, there was a lot of commotion, and then exclamations of joy. "There she is!"

Esther peeked through the window a second time and saw the newborn foal in the straw. Chester and Sadie laughed and congratulated each other.

Then Chester asked Sadie, "What's your middle name?"

"Matilda."

"Then I will name the new foal Mattie, after you."

Sadie awkwardly hugged him. "Thank you."

Esther's throat tightened at the touching moment. There was a definite connection between them. But what made it even more telling was the knowledge that there was no such connection between herself and Chester. Their affection was amiable enough, but matched to what she'd just witnessed, it was a shallow stream compared to a mighty river.

And then, in a rush, all of Sadie's half-hearted support for Esther and Chester's engagement came to mind. Plus her utter joy when she'd danced with him at the festival. And her quick smile and her penchant for coming out of the oven room every time he came in the shop.

Could it be. . . ? Did Sadie feel romantic affection for him?

"Open your eyes and see what I have done."

Had God brought them together? Beyond a flash of jealousy, Esther's thoughts moved to a different avenue: Could Sadie's feelings for Chester be a way to soften the blow of Esther breaking their engagement?

She heard Sadie say, "I need to get to the shop. I started the ovens before I came, but Esther will be wondering where I am."

Esther knew she couldn't speak to Chester just yet. She had to speak to someone else first.

She hurried to the shop.

"I'm sorry I'm late," Sadie said as she came in just moments behind Esther. She pointed to the ovens. "I was here, but then I got called away."

Esther measured some flour for a crust. "It must have been something important for you to leave."

Sadie tied on her apron. "It was. Chester stopped by in a tizzy. Annabelle was foaling."

The simple fact that Sadie knew the name of Chester's horse—and Esther didn't—loomed large. "You went to help?"

Her face glowed with the memory of it. "To see a birth like that. . ." She beamed. "He named her after me—after my middle name, Matilda."

"That's very kind of him."

"Yes, well. . ." She looked away. "Chester is a very kind man."

Father, let the truth come out. "You two have a special bond."

Sadie hedged. "Perhaps we do."

"I saw it."

"You did?"

"When Mattie was born. I was outside."

Sadie looked embarrassed. "We do have a connection, but don't worry. . ."

Esther had to ask the difficult question. "Do you care for him? Beyond friendship?"

Sadie stepped toward the oven room.

Esther caught her arm. "Do you? Don't worry about what I might think about it, tell the truth."

Sadie's face battled a storm of emotions. Finally she said, "I do. I know I shouldn't because he's yours, but. . .but I do. I love him." She took a new breath and said more softly, "I do."

Esther was silent a moment, gauging how she felt about this new knowledge. She expected to feel regret or anger. She did not expect to feel relief. "How long have you loved him?"

"Since always. And we might have been married, too, but when your husband died,

Chester turned his sights on you and made winning your hand a quest. I didn't have a chance."

"Does he know how you feel?"

Sadie shook her head. "He only has eyes for you. I do everything I possibly can to make him know I care, but he doesn't see it."

It was time for Esther to share her truth. "I don't want to marry him."

"Since when?"

Since Henry. But it was more than Henry. "Chester is a decent man—a very persistent man. He wore down my defenses until I agreed."

Sadie bit her lip. "What are we doing to do?"

"There is only one thing we can do, and I must start the process."

"By. . . ?"

"By breaking our engagement."

Sadie's face brightened then grew serious. "It will hurt him. He's wanted you for so long."

"But you love him."

"That doesn't mean he loves me or would marry me, even if he was free. Love often comes unbidden. I didn't mean to love him."

As I didn't mean to love Henry. And just because Esther was free didn't mean Henry would come back to her.

"We must take the risk, Sadie. True love is a gift from God, but love that is lacking in truth offends Him." By making this choice, Esther knew she might end up without a man. Yet being alone was preferable to living a lie.

She remembered her gleeful "I'm free!" moment after Petunia married. She could be alone and happy. Perhaps God wanted her alone.

Hopefully not.

Esther extended a hand toward Sadie. "Let us pray all works out exactly as the Almighty wishes it to."

"And may God give you the words to kindly tell Chester it's over."

Amen.

Esther waited for Chester to come in for his daily pie. When he didn't and she saw the stable boy running by outside, she hurried out of the shop to stop him.

"Hey, boy. Where are you going so fast?"

"Mr. Mayfield slipped off a ladder and sprained his ankle bad. I'm going for me ma. She knows about such things."

Esther knew nothing about such things, but she said, "I'll go."

Sadie stepped out to the square. "No. I know what to do. I'll go." She looked at Esther. "Yes?"

Absolutely. As Esther watched Sadie hurry off with the boy, she knew she had witnessed God in action. He had opened a door for Sadie. It was a chance for the bond between her and Chester to deepen. And as such, God had shown Esther her own door. And closed it. *Please do Your work, Lord. Let everything fall into place as only You can.*

Sadie returned at midday. Esther was glad to see her because she herself had burned the first pie. But she was also glad to see Sadie because she was desperate to know what had happened.

And how Chester was doing, of course. Yet that seemed secondary. For if God was behind all this, Chester's sprained ankle was a part of His handiwork. God would take care of Chester's injury. As He would take care of Chester. And Sadie. And Esther.

As soon as the ovens were stoked to Sadie's satisfaction, she came into the main part of the shop.

"Well?" Esther asked.

"Firstly, Chester will be fine."

"I'm glad. But give me more."

Sadie grinned. "He said I was a very special lady."

"You are. He is wise to see it."

"We talked about Mattie."

"He was happy to see you then?"

"He was."

"Did he ask where I was?"

"Well. . .no."

Esther beat down her disappointment. Her pride was injured while her hope was curried. "It's time, then?"

"For you to speak to him?"

Esther nodded. "I'll bring him his pie." She removed her apron. "Wish me luck."

"You have it. And my prayers."

"So you see, I don't want either of us to settle for what could be. I want us to find the kind of love that should be. That has to be."

Chester sat in a chair, his right foot on a stool. He stared at his fireplace, though in the warmth of September there was no fire. "I was wondering about that."

"About love?"

"About our sort of love. It just didn't seem. . ." He searched for the word. "Full enough." He stroked his chin. "Kind of like a pie that's got half the pieces missing."

Esther laughed. "I can think of no better analogy."

The deed was done, and Esther offered God a silent thank-you.

But there was more to be accomplished.

"Sadie told me about Mattie."

"She was a big help to me."

"Then, and also with your ankle."

He looked at his ankle as if studying it. "She's a very good woman."

"The best." She wondered if she should say more. And then she said it. "She loves you."

"What?"

"She always has, but I got in the way."

"She always has?"

He was like a lad being told a girl fancied him. Esther could have stayed but felt it was time to leave. Let Chester work through the rest on his own.

She leaned down and kissed his forehead. "I do love you, Chester, as a dear and trusted friend. I wish you the best always."

He grabbed her hand and kissed it. "As I do for you, Esther."

As she left Esther remembered her "What now?" question after Petunia had married. She'd thought the answer was to marry Chester. Now that door was closed. So once again she asked God, "What now?"

The answer was unknown. Yet Esther Horton did not simply walk away from Chester's. She flew on the wings of hope, and the assurance that God was in control.

∞

Esther was greeted at the door by Nelly. "Lady Tomkins does not wish to see you, Mrs. Horton."

"Tell her it's imperative I speak with her. Essential." She saw Christopher walking out of the parlor and suspected Verd was sitting nearby. Esther raised her voice. "Tell her I am despicable and deserve her wrath. I come to her, asking forgiveness. If she values our friendship at all, I beg her to—"

"Gracious!" Verd called out from the parlor. "If you are taking the route of confession and absolution at least give me the satisfaction of being a full witness."

Nelly rolled her eyes as she let Esther enter. As expected, Verd was sitting in her usual place. Esther stood directly in front of her. "Good afternoon, Lady Tomkins."

"It's Verd to you."

Esther smiled.

Verd pointed at her. "Do not smile. One does not smile while groveling."

"Does one sit?"

"I'd prefer a full kneel, but yes, I suppose you can sit and grovel."

Esther pulled a chair close and sat with her hands clasped in her lap. "I am truly and utterly sorry I hurt you."

"And my nephew."

"Especially him."

Her eyebrow rose. "So he takes precedence over me?"

"In this sin, yes, he does. For I hurt you by a sin of omission in not telling you that Chester and I were engaged."

"Indeed you did."

"I meant to tell you on the day Henry stepped into the room. But once I met him..."

Verd's eyebrow rose again. "Yes?"

A thousand words stood by, waiting their turn. "I have never met anyone like Henry. When I saw his face during that first meeting on the road, my heart shifted." She clutched her hands to her chest. "I can honestly say I have not stopped thinking of him since."

"He is a memorable man."

"He is. You arranged for us to spend time together—and I knew your intent and did not set it right by being honest with you. In truth, I enjoyed our time so immensely that I chose to ignore what was real for this lofty other-world that existed when I was with Henry." She gazed into her friend's eyes with full intensity. "He ignites something in me that makes me see more, be more, and want more."

"Little good it will do since you're marrying Chester."

Finally, the good news. "I broke my engagement right before I came here."

Verd sat taller. "How did he react?"

"He was more gracious than I deserved."

"I believe that."

Esther accepted the barb. "I still see the horrified look on Henry's face when Chester toasted our engagement. To love him yet see him hurt like that. . . Will he ever forgive me for hurting him?"

"You will have to ask him."

"When is he—?"

Henry stepped into the room.

Esther stood, her heart racing. "You're here."

"I am. I rode away in anger, but I returned."

Verd beckoned him closer. "Tell her why you returned."

He extended his hands to Esther. She felt tears threaten as she anticipated, hoped, and prayed for what would come next. She took his hands, forming a circle between them.

"I returned because I was not willing to let you go so easily. Without a fight."

"Really?"

"And?" Verd said. "Get to the point, boy."

"The point is, I love you. I adore you." He lowered to one knee. "Esther, would you do me the great honor of becoming my wife?"

"Yes! Oh yes!"

Their embrace was accompanied by Verd's applause.

And God's. For Esther felt God's blessings encircle them. "Thank You, Lord," she whispered against Henry's shoulder.

He let go enough to see her face. "I agree, my darling. For you are an answer to prayer."

Esther touched his lovely face, the face that had made her love him at first sight.

He gazed into her eyes. "Remember when we first met, I asked if you'd come to save me?"

"I do."

"I believe you've done just that. For I have been saved from a life made lonely by your absence."

"As you have saved me, dear love. As you have saved me."

Epilogue

Henry stood in Coventry Hall in his uncle's old study, a room commandeered to a new use as the Chancebury Academy of Learning. It was a scholarly room with three walls lined with walnut shelving that held a treasure of books about subjects from horticulture, to the strategy of war, to the classics of Plato, Descartes, Shakespeare, and of course, Daniel Defoe. For what child could grow up without reading *Robinson Crusoe*? If that story didn't ignite the imaginations of the students, nothing would.

Henry had repositioned his uncle's desk so it was at the opposite end, facing the books. In between were long tables and benches that would seat five children in four rows. Positioned at each place was a slate, chalk, a rag for erasing, and a copy of *The Protestant Tutor*, which would teach the children their alphabet with a few morals thrown in for good measure.

Esther set the last book. "There. We are ready."

"Their places and supplies are ready, but am I?"

She went to him and gave a kiss. "This is a good thing we're doing, Henry. For many children, this may be the only schooling they ever receive."

"Do not add to the burden of my responsibility, wife."

"I will be here to help."

He drew her hand around his arm. "Will you miss the pie shop?"

"Not a bit, for it is in good hands. Sadie knows more about making pies than I do."

"And Chester is made glad for the free lifetime supply."

Esther was ecstatic for her own marriage, but also for the marriage of Sadie and Chester. It was unfortunate they'd had the wedding while she and Henry were on their honeymoon, but there had been no reason for them to wait. Life was short. Best grab onto happiness as soon as possible.

"I am eager for the maps we purchased in Italy to arrive," Henry said.

"And the etchings of the masterworks. We did well in Florence. And Rome. And Paris. And Vienna."

He looked down at her and winked. "Very well."

She felt herself blush.

Suddenly, he patted his vest pocket. "Oh dear. I forgot my watch."

"I'll fetch it. I will be but a minute." Another change in their lives had been moving into Coventry Hall. There were obviously rooms enough, and Verd appreciated the company and was very good about giving the newlyweds their privacy.

Esther was leaving to get the watch when she heard young voices in the foyer. "They're here," she whispered.

"May God have mercy on our souls!"

Esther stepped back as Verd entered the study with a little girl on each hand. "Here we are, children." Four boys streamed in behind, their eyes scanning the room in awe.

"Crikey," said the oldest, who looked about ten. "I didn't know so many books were in the whole, entire world."

"Take a seat, everyone," Esther said.

Verd flicked one of them on the nose. "I will see to the scones and milk."

"We get to eat, too?" a girl asked.

"It is a known fact that learning is enhanced by a full belly," Verd said as she left.

Just then five more were ushered in by Sam. Eleven students. A goodly number.

A godly number.

Henry clapped to get their attention. "Welcome to the wonderful and amazing world of learning, children."

A wonderful and amazing world indeed.

Nancy Moser is an award-winning author of over thirty novels that share a common message: we each have a unique purpose—the trick is to find out what it is. Her genres include contemporary and historical novels including *The Pattern Artist*, *Love of the Summerfields*, *Mozart's Sister*, *The Invitation*, and the Christy Award-winning *Time Lottery*. She is a fan of anything antique—humans included. Visit her website at www.nancymoser.com.

The Highwayman's Bargain

by MaryLu Tyndall

Chapter One

April 1811
Hertfordshire, England

Sophia Crew closed the door of the humble cottage that had been her home for the past twenty-one years and gazed at the elegant coach-and-four waiting in her driveway. Drawing a deep breath, she moved forward, knowing that with each step, she left behind her old life and moved toward her new—from the daughter of a poor yeoman farmer to the wife of a nobleman, from a life of hard work to one of ease, from worry to security, and most of all from poverty to wealth.

She examined the Henley coat of arms emblazoned on the door of the fancy carriage that had pulled up before her home in a glittering blaze of glory just an hour past—the one in which already sat her mother and father, their luggage hefted on top by the footman. Excitement sparkled from her mother's eyes as she smiled at Sophia from the window and urged her to hurry.

Truly, it was an exciting day!

Then why did Sophia feel as though she'd eaten rocks that morning instead of oatmeal?

Nerves. That was all. She was to be married within a week. What lady wouldn't be nervous?

Gathering her pelisse around her shoulders, she halted and turned one last time to look at her home—the chipped stone walls, the slate roof in need of repair, the front door framed by two mullioned casement windows, the chimney rising on the right side of the house, where many a fire below had provided warmth for her family.

Gertrude's low brought her gaze to the left, where the milk cow chomped on grass in the field. Chickens squawked across the yard, while a family of pigs grunted in the mud. Beyond the barn, the rest of their meager twenty acres rolled in waves of golden-brown barley, soon ready for harvest. The first harvest in which Sophia wouldn't be here to help.

A chilled breeze brought the scent of roses and lilies from her mother's flower garden, lifting her dour mood. She smiled. So much joy had filled this home, so many fond memories. She had been happy here. Despite the hard work and want, her childhood had been filled with love and laughter.

"Come, dear. We don't want to keep Mr. Pratt waiting," her mother said.

Forcing back tears, Sophia turned and took the footman's hand, allowing him to assist her. He closed the door and hopped to his position at the back as Sophia sank into the seats. "Such luxury." She eased her gloved fingers down the soft leather, drawing her father's gaze.

"Get used to it, pumpkin." His aged eyes crinkled. "This is your life now."

Why did her father suddenly look so old? Even dressed in his finest—his only—suit of black wool trimmed in velvet, the one he only wore at weddings and funerals. She'd always remembered him as being strong, virile, and handsome, working out in the fields from dusk until dawn. As a little girl, she'd believed nothing and no one could ever defeat him. Strong as the mighty oak trees that lined their farm and just as sturdy and ageless. But time had crumbled her childish vision. He was human like everyone else, and like everyone else, he aged and grew weak with each passing year.

The whip snapped, and the coach jerked forward. Sophia glanced out the window, soaking in every detail of her home. Mercy, what was wrong with her? She'd return of course. But deep in her heart, she knew things would never be the same.

"You must be all a jitter, my dear." Her mother reached to take Sophia's hand in hers. "I can see it on your face. Such an exciting week ahead of you."

Before Sophia could answer, her mother's coughing began. Short bursts at first but then quickly morphing into uncontrollable hacks so deep and rumbling that Sophia cringed at each one. Handing his wife a handkerchief, her father swung an arm around her and drew her close, his features drawn tight.

"Mama, I fear you shouldn't have come," Sophia said, her voice shaky. "The apothecary insisted you stay abed."

"And miss"—she coughed again, holding her chest and trying to regain her voice—"my only daughter's wedding? If I was dead and buried, I'd still find a way to attend," she squeaked out before another fit struck her.

Sophia's gut tightened. "Don't say such things. I could not bear it." Moisture filled her eyes, and she gazed out the window again. Pleurisy, the apothecary had told them, an infection in the chest that if not treated could turn into consumption, a deadly disease. Yet none of the elixirs he had given her were helping. She needed a physician, one they'd soon be able to afford.

"I agree, my love. There will be no talk of death here." Her father kissed his wife on the forehead, and once again, her parents exchanged that loving glance Sophia had witnessed thousands of times during her childhood—the one that always warmed her heart and made her long to be gazed at with that same affection.

The coach turned onto a more well-traveled road, settling into a gentle sway instead of the jerks and jars of moments before. The green hills of Hertfordshire rolled out before her, bursting with wildflowers and crops of oats, barley, corn, and potatoes. Cows roamed across grassy fields while sheep dotted a slope in the distance. If she strained her eyes, she could even spot the tall, spired roof of Longworth, the estate of Lord Cramsford, who owned most of this land.

What little remained of the morning sun was soon swallowed by dark clouds as a breeze laden with the sting of rain whipped through the coach, luring Sophia's gaze back inside.

Her mother leaned against her father, hand still pressed on her chest, though her breathing had settled. Thank God. She had been ill and confined to her bed for nearly six years now, leaving Sophia to do all the cooking, sewing, gardening, and cleaning, along with assisting Papa with the farm. Not that she minded. She'd do anything to ease her mother's burden, to help her get well again. Yet with her father's advanced age slowing him down more and more each year, well, suffice it to say that if things didn't improve, her family would lose their farm and end up in the poorhouse.

But Sophia would not allow that to happen. No, she—or should she say the comely face God had given her—had caught the eye of Mr. Edward Pratt, second son to Lord Henley, a well-to-do baron. Once she was married, she'd have enough money to save her parents' farm and grant them a life of ease. Edward had promised as much.

The reins snapped, the coach jerked forward, and horse hooves pounded the road as thunder growled from the darkening skies.

"Oh, dear," her mother said. "I hope it doesn't rain too hard or we shall be delayed attending our first dinner party."

"Not to worry, my love." Sophia's father patted his wife's hand. "There are plenty of parties planned for the entire week. I dare say we shall be sick of such frivolity by the time Sophia walks down the aisle." He winked at Sophia.

Her mother playfully swatted him. "Never! The only parties I've attended have been simple country balls, and I am beyond excited for all the festivities the Pratts have planned. Can you imagine? Mingling with society, with lords and ladies as if we were one of them? And to see London itself! St. Paul's Cathedral, Westminster Abbey, St James Square, Piccadilly, and Hyde Park. I cannot wait to see it all!"

Joy filled Sophia that she could bring her mother such happiness. "You will love London, Mama. There is no city like it." Yet her tone lacked enthusiasm.

As if sensing her apprehension, her father leaned toward her. "Pumpkin, I have said this before and I shall say it again. I pray you are marrying Mr. Pratt for love and not to help your mother and I." He looked at his wife again and smiled. "We are very happy and thankful to God for all He provides and for what He will continue to provide. 'I have been young, and now am old; yet have I not seen the righteous forsaken, nor his seed begging bread,'" he quoted from his favorite psalm.

Sophia wasn't sure about that. It seemed many righteous people suffered hunger and want. Regardless, she smiled. "Father, I adore Edward. Can I help it if he happens to be wealthy? Why, he is a true gentleman, educated, mannerly, cultured...the son of a baron. And quite handsome." She thought of his dark brown hair, always expertly styled and curled at the tips, his tall figure, sharp noble features, and deep-set eyes.

"I'll not argue that the man has many good qualities, but you sound as though you are reciting a list of qualifications for a post, not expressing the passion of your heart. Do you love him?" he asked pointedly, as was his way, always direct and unapologetic.

"Of course," she answered before she took time to consider it. She *couldn't* consider it. She had no choice to consider it. She loved Edward. And if she didn't, she would grow to love him.

"Praise be to God!" Mama squealed. "Our daughter marrying the son of a baron.

Who would have thought such a thing possible?"

"Second son, Mama. He won't inherit."

"But he is a nobleman, dear, and his family is worth a fortune."

Her father huffed and gazed out the window. "Titles and money mean nothing to God."

Because He has no need of them. Sophia bit her lip and immediately chastised herself.

Several minutes passed as they each retreated into their thoughts. Finally, her father faced her.

"But what of Nash, Sophia?"

Nash. The name never failed to stir something deep within Sophia, something alarming, exciting, and yet deeply sorrowful.

"I haven't seen Nash in six years, Papa."

The coach jostled over a bump in the road, and her mother shifted in her seat. "But he's been writing you recently, has he not?"

"I suppose I've received a few posts."

Her father laughed. "More than a few, I'd say. I counted at least seven in the past two weeks. I heard he's back from his adventures with the East India Company."

Sophia fingered the ruby bracelet Edward had given her, pulling it around her wrist.

"Why don't you answer him?" Papa asked.

"I *have* answered him. To inform him not to write again, that I am about to be married and it wouldn't be proper to entertain his company. But the man is as stubborn as always."

"I doubt the impropriety of a short visit. After all, you two were inseparable as children."

They were. Every memory of her childhood included Nash. The son of a gentleman farmer whose land bordered theirs, he had found Sophia huddling beneath a bush, soaked to the bone and shivering in fright from a thunderstorm. She was eight and he was ten, and they were rarely seen apart for the next seven years.

"That is the point," Sophia returned. "We are no longer children."

Her mother's lips tightened, and she pressed a handkerchief to her chest as the pains began. Father withdrew a small vile from within his coat. "Drink this, my dear. Quickly." She gulped it down and closed her eyes.

Thunder so loud it seemed to come out of nowhere shook the carriage, jarring Sophia. A torrent of rain began to pound the roof, and Sophia's father swept aside the velvet curtains to find the scenery blurred in a gray sheen.

"Merely a small storm. It should soon pass," Papa said, and she smiled at his optimism. In truth, she envied his strong faith in God, his belief that all things worked for good for God's people. Perhaps, if she could believe that, she wouldn't be so nervous all the time, so anxious to ensure the safety and security of her family by means other than simple prayers.

As her father predicted, the hard rain soon transformed into a light drizzle as the carriage rambled down the road, past more grand estates and small farms, through a village whose streets were deserted due to the downpour, and finally into a copse of trees that formed a barrier against the rain.

Leaning against her husband, Mama closed her eyes to rest, and conversation dwindled. Sophia tried to do the same, but her nerves were as tight as wool on a spinning wheel. In less than three hours she'd be in London, where she'd be introduced to the remainder of Edward's family and no doubt be whisked away to don one of the gowns Edward's mother, Lady Henley, had insisted on having made for her. Sophia glanced down at the travel gown she had sent ahead—a lovely lavender sprigged muslin, trimmed in lace at the neckline and cuffs. A purple spencer and silk embroidered slippers completed the ensemble. Sophia was sure there was more than altruism at work in the gift, for the lady of the house would not want to be embarrassed by Sophia's drab wool gown.

A loud crack broke the silence, followed by a shout and the screech of horses. The coach jerked to a stop. Sophia gripped the edge of the seat to keep from being tossed to the floor. Her father held tight to her mother, annoyance and then fear crossing his eyes as more shouts were heard.

"What is the meaning of this, sir?" The voice came from the driver's perch. "This is Lord Henley's private coach."

"Capital! Precisely the one I seek," another stronger voice replied with a bit of sarcasm, followed quickly by, "Ah ha ha, I wouldn't do—" The pop of a pistol sent Sophia leaping from her perch, hand on her heart. Her father drew her close and positioned her beside her mother.

"We carry no coin or jewels, sir."

"Ah, but something far more precious, I believe."

Papa rose from his seat.

"No, Papa, please." Sophia grabbed his arm, but he gently nudged her back. "Stay with your mother." His voice was firm, but his gaze loving as he cast one last glance at them both. He exited the coach, and Sophia moved to the window, craning for a glimpse of the man who dared waylay their journey—one of the notorious highwaymen who plagued England's roads, no doubt. Her breath escaped her. *God in heaven, help us!*

"For goodness sake, stay away from the window, Sophia." Mama tugged on Sophia's arm just as she heard her father bravely say to the bandit.

"What is the meaning of this, sir? I demand you stand aside and allow us passage at once."

Silence reigned for a moment, save for the pitter-patter of raindrops on the leaves and the whistle of wind. Her mother began to sob, and Sophia held her tight.

"Get the women," a man said, and before Sophia could react, her father shouted, "I beg your pardon!" Then she heard his loud grunt and a thud. A man jerked open the coach door. His ruddy, pock-marked face peered inside, smiled upon seeing them, and then grabbed Sophia's arm and pulled her and her mother from the carriage.

Their feet landed splat in the mud. Jerking from the man's grip, Sophia found the perpetrator of this horrific crime sitting astride a horse, pointing a pistol at the driver and two footmen on the driver's perch. Dressed all in black, he wore a mask over his eyes, half his face shadowed by a wide-brimmed hat.

A groan sounded.

"Papa!" Sophia dashed to her father, who was struggling to rise from where he'd been shoved to the ground.

"No damage done, pumpkin." He slapped mud from his breeches as Sophia's mother flew into his arms.

Too angry to be afraid, Sophia charged the man on horseback. "Such bravery, sir. How proud you must be to accost an old man and two women!"

He smiled, a cocksure half grin that bristled her anger even further.

The pock-marked man mounted his horse and leveled his pistol at the driver, allowing the masked man to holster his weapon.

"Sophia!" Papa shouted. "Get back here at once."

She started her slow retreat, maintaining a glare upon the brute. "We have nothing of value, sir. You've done your damage. Now, you may take your leave."

"May I? How kind." The smile widened, the blue eyes twinkled through the mask holes, and Sophia suddenly knew he was not after jewels at all. Terror squeezed every inch of her, but before she could turn and rush to her parents, the bandit slid from his horse, grabbed her by the waist, and lifted her with ease onto his saddle. Then with minimal effort, he leapt behind her and imprisoned her with his arms.

No amount of struggling, kicking, or screaming freed her even an inch.

"Sophia!" her mother yelled.

"What on earth? Unhand her at once!" Papa rushed for them.

Sophia continued to struggle, terror causing tears to flow, but the cullion surrounded her with thick arms covered in black leather and held her so tight she could hardly breathe.

"Papa, Mama!" she screamed in desperation as her mother collapsed to the dirt, sobbing.

But the man only tipped his hat toward them. "Never fear, I shall take good care of her."

Turning his horse, and with a nod to his companion, he galloped down the muddy road.

Chapter Two

Terrified, all Sophia could do was hang onto her kidnapper as he galloped through the countryside—so fast there was no chance for her to free herself from his tight grip. Though surely if she could, she would probably fall off the horse to her death. In a strange twist of mercy, fear began to numb her senses, transforming the horrifying event into a mere nightmare. A nightmare from which if she could just wake up, no doubt she'd find herself sitting in the Henley coach across from her mother and father and apologizing for falling asleep.

She was vaguely aware of passing hills of green and tree trunks from poplars, pines, and oaks waving at her as she sped past, like an audience cheering for a race. Before too long, fingers of dark clouds doused the sun as it sank toward the horizon—a candle put out for the night. She was more aware of the beast behind her, imprisoning her with an arm of steel; his hot breath spewing on her neck; his scent, oddly familiar, mixing with the spice of rain and loamy smell of moist earth. He made no conversation, no quip of whatever ill-intentions he had toward her, only a persistent and determined gallop toward some destination that would no doubt seal her fate.

The rain started again, a drizzle at first, but soon icy pebbles stung her face and neck, waking her from her daze. Crouching forward, the highwayman attempted to shield her—or was he only protecting his prize?—as he urged his horse to the left down a smaller road. Minutes passed, maybe hours. She lost track of time as her mind retreated into a safer place where the sun was shining and she was home, surrounded by those she loved.

God, why? Why have You allowed this to happen? When she was about to be married to a man who adored her, when she could have saved her family, could have situated them all securely and happily. Nothing made sense. She had done everything right. Been a good girl all her life. Obeyed her parents, followed all the rules—well, most of them. "God, help me, please." Her whisper was stolen by the brisk wind, dissipating just like her faith.

The last glow of light abandoned them, casting a death shroud over the scene. Wind transformed her damp gown into ice. She shivered, and the man drew her close.

"We are almost there," was all he said, and she hadn't the strength to ask him where *there* was. Not that it really mattered.

Light flickered in the distance, growing larger and larger with each plod of the horse's hooves in the mud. They passed through a gate, a row of trees, and finally the man halted before a small cottage. Smoke puffed from a chimney, while golden light poured from the small window in front. Sliding from the horse with ease, the rogue grabbed her waist and pulled her down beside him. She wanted to be strong. She wanted to be brave, punch him, and make a dash for freedom. But her legs turned to pudding, and he swept her in his arms before she fell.

"Put me down!" Her shout faltered on trembling lips as the man barreled through the front door opened by a squab, rough-looking fellow.

"I didn't 'xpect you so soon, sir."

The beast set her down on a chair before a roaring fire.

"There were no complications." He reached in his pocket and pulled out a small velvet bag that jingled as he handed it to the man. "Tend to my horse before you leave."

It was as if all her senses returned at that moment. Sophia lunged from the chair and dashed toward the servant. "Sir, I beg you. This man has kidnapped me! You must help me!"

The foul smell of alcohol bit her nose as a chuckle rumbled from his lips. "Beggin' yer pardon, miss." He tipped his hat at her as if they'd just met at a country dance then nodded toward the foul ruffian and left, closing the door behind him.

Leaving her at the mercy of this highwayman, who now stood before her smiling. *Smiling!*

"Your gown is wet. I have dry clothes for you to wear."

She slowly backed away, eyes on the door, wondering if she should make a dash for it. "What do you want with me?"

He moved between her and the only exit and gestured for her to sit before the fire. "You have naught to fear from me, Sophie."

Sophie. "How dare you use my Christian name." Not only her Christian name, but a pet name—one she hadn't heard in many years.

He moved toward her, the stomp of his wet boots echoing across the room. Water dripped a *tap, tap, tap* from his coat onto the floor, joining the whistle of wind against the windowpane and the crackle of the fire.

"I apologize for frightening you." He took off his hat and tossed it onto a table, then ran a hand through his hair—the color of chestnut streaked with gold—dislodging strands from his tie.

"Frightening me? You have kidnapped me, taken me from my parents, my fiancé, *and* my wedding! For what purpose, I can only guess, for we have no wealth to pay your ransom." She narrowed her eyes. "Oh, I see. You think my fiancé will pay, is that it?"

"I want no money, especially not from him."

Sophia swallowed a burst of fear. "Then I can only imagine what you want from me."

He smiled again, blue eyes twinkling through the mask holes. Yet it was a playful smile, not one full of malice. He drew off his disguise, cocked his head, and stared at her, brows lifted.

His face was strong, angular, his chin square and shadowed with stubble. A scar ran down the right side of his cheek that did not detract from the noble nose and proud eyes that completed what could be called a handsome visage. . . .

If he weren't an insolent cur.

Yet something familiar about him made her squirm.

The fire sparked and spit.

Shock tingled her feet, crept up her legs, and slowly made its way to her heart. Faltering, she sank into a chair behind her, breath squeezing from her chest.

Nash?

No. Couldn't be. Nash was but a dark-haired lad, lithe of limb, smooth of face, gangly, and full of life and humor.

Before her stood a man, thickly muscled, tall, austere, commanding, and without a trace of gaiety.

"Have six years changed me so much?" he said.

⬥⬥⬥

Nash Barrett had not thought it possible for Miss Sophia Crew to have grown any more beautiful than when he'd last seen her. But the years had been kind to her. Damp golden hair, loosened from her pins, dangled in coils over her shoulders into her lap, accentuating a figure that had filled into all the right womanly curves. Jade-green eyes, forested in thick lashes, stared at him in wonder, confusion, anger, but thankfully no longer fear. Her bottom lip quivered slightly, that soft pink pillow his own lips remembered so well.

"What are you. . . I don't understand." Her brows collided in that cute way of hers before they shot up like arches in a cathedral. "Why have you kidnapped me?" She tried to stand, but sank back into the chair and squeezed the bridge of her nose.

"To save you. You really should change into some dry attire, Sophie. Let me put on some tea."

"I don't want tea, and I don't want to be dry! Do you know what you have done?"

"I believe I do, yes." Nash eased into a chair across from her and leaned forward on his knees. "Why would you not see me these past two weeks?"

"Is this what this is about?" Her chest heaved as she snapped her fiery gaze to his. "I wouldn't agree to meet you, so you kidnap me! Have you gone mad?"

"Quite possibly." He rubbed his chin, finding it difficult to take his eyes off her, regardless of her fury. Rising, he moved to the sideboard where he'd instructed Brant to leave biscuits and a pot of tea and thankfully found them there. He poured her a cup and set it before her, along with a biscuit.

She stared at the fire, refusing to look at him. Yet he knew from the tremble of her lip, the crease in her brow, and the way she clasped her hands that she was frightened again. And he felt like a cad. How many times had he rescued her from danger, soothed her fears, comforted her when she was distraught? And now he was the cause of all three. But it couldn't be helped.

Grabbing a quilt from a stool, he swung it around her shoulders. "If you won't change, please stay warm."

She shrugged it off.

So, she had acquired a bit of pluck these last six years. Good. She would need it. He smiled.

"You find this amusing? You scared me to death. And my parents. What they must be going through! Not to mention, I'm supposed to be at an engagement party this very minute. My reputation! You've ruined it. You've ruined everything." Standing, she gathered the quilt and threw it at him then turned her back and began to sob.

Nash had never known exactly what to do when a woman cried. Neither as a young lad, nor especially after living aboard a ship for six years with hardened sailors. Yet he couldn't help but feel his heart crack in two.

Setting aside the quilt, he moved to stand behind her, lifted his hands to grip her shoulders in a gesture of comfort, then dropped them. "Sophie, allow me to explain. I have my reasons. You know I would never hurt you." Absently, he fingered a lock of her hair—just to touch her again as he'd dreamed of doing for so many years.

Whirling, she slapped his hand away. "I know no such thing. I knew a boy once named Nash. I do not know this highwayman before me, this knave devoid of decency and conscience."

The hatred in her eyes stunned him. "I knew of no other way to stop you from making the gravest error of your life."

"What are you talking about?" She squeezed her eyes shut for a moment before moving to the hearth.

"Marrying Edward Pratt."

"You know my fiancé?" Her gaze snapped to his.

"To my great misfortune, yes."

"How could you possibly?" She waved him away. "You are a sailor, the son of a farmer, and he is the son of a baron."

He bristled at the insult. Though he shouldn't be surprised. Position and wealth had always occupied Sophia's dreams.

The tears came again as she sank into her chair and hugged herself. "I can't believe you've done this. What is to become of me now? What is to become of my family?"

"Sophie," Nash began and then realized it was best if he just told her everything, no matter the shock. She may be in love with Edward, but he had no choice. He knelt before her. "Edward is not the man he portrays. He's a gambler, drunkard, and libertine. He is only using you to get revenge on his father who forbade him to marry beneath their family."

She stared at him, wide eyes moist with tears, lips pinched, anger rising up her neck in a torrent of red. "What rubbish is this? Do you find it so outrageous, so unbelievable that a true gentleman would fall in love with me, a poor yeoman's daughter? Or does your jealousy insist you make up such scandalous tales?"

"Jealous? Of Pratt?" Nash huffed and ran a hand through his hair. "He is the last man worthy of any one's envy." He softened his tone. "And it would never be impossible for any man to fall in love with you." *As he had done.*

She searched his eyes, no doubt spotting the affection he tried so hard to hide. "You *are* jealous."

He shook his head. "You broke my heart, Sophie. I'll not deny it. But I was a boy of only seventeen. Six years aboard an East Indiaman does much to mend one's heart." Or at least it should. "Sophie." He inched toward her, peering up into her face. "I'm telling you the truth. If you marry Pratt, you'll be miserable the rest of your life. You'll have to deal with his drunkenness and debauchery as he flaunts a parade of mistresses before you, humiliating you and breaking your heart. I could not stand by without at least warning you."

"I don't believe you. Edward has always been loving, kind, the perfect gentleman, a man of breeding and distinction. I've never once seen him overindulge in spirits, nor gamble, aside from the occasional game of whist. Indeed, he attends church every week and is good friends with the vicar."

"More proof that you do not know him at all, lamb."

"Do not call me that. We are no longer children."

Indeed. Of that he could attest. For if so, he would have wrestled her to the ground until she acquiesced, or better yet, challenged her to a horse race. Now, he could only swallow his frustration. "How much time have you actually spent with the man?"

She pursed her lips and stared at the flames.

Grabbing a log, Nash tossed it onto the fire, pondering how to proceed, how to convince this stubborn girl of the danger she was in. "I owed it to our friendship to warn you."

"A simple letter would have sufficed."

"Surely you must know I could not write such accusations in a letter."

"So you kidnap me instead," she shot back.

Sighing, he slowly rose. "I did not fully consider the repercussions, I admit."

"Repercussions?" She all but growled. "I am ruined, Nash. And my family."

"I see you have not lost your flair for drama, Sophie."

"I am here with you alone. That is enough to ruin me, whether you are an old friend or not."

"No one need know."

"So, you intend to release me?"

Wind shook the window, twirling a spindle of cold air around him that fluttered the candle flame. Nash chastised himself under his breath. Fool! What possessed him to think he could change the lady's mind with only his word? Yes, they had trusted each other implicitly as children, but too much time had passed, and they had both been tainted by life. Now, he had but one recourse left.

Clearing his throat, he faced her. "I propose a bargain, Miss Crew. One in which, if I lose, you can turn me into the constable in London as a highwayman and then proceed with your plans to marry Mr. Pratt."

Suspicion crinkled her brow. "And if *I* should lose?"

Chapter Three

Then you will promise not to marry Mr. Pratt. 'Tis that simple." The man who claimed to be Nash, the young boy Sophia had loved since she was eight, stiffened his jaw, awaiting her response.

But of course it was Nash behind all the muscles and stubble and severity. She caught glimpses of that boy—the playfulness in his eyes, kindness in his gestures, humor upon his lips. The way he looked at her, as he always had, as if she were made of precious crystal and he was assigned to keep her safe. Still, he *was* different—more serious, determined, stronger, and perhaps a little sad.

"I make no bargains with highwaymen," she said with conviction.

"Good to know."

"What if I refuse to play your game?"

"Then I will refuse to release you."

"You would keep me prisoner? You wouldn't dare."

"Since you have already admitted I am not the same man you knew, how would you know what I am capable of?"

Sophia ground her teeth. "You cannot hide me away forever. Lord Henley and his son have the wherewithal to search for me in all of England."

"Are you so confident they would spare the expense?"

Another cut to her pride. Of all the. . . "What are you impl—"

He held up a hand. "Please, I meant no insult. I beg you, hear my terms."

"I see I have no choice." She lifted her chin, feigning a courage she didn't feel.

Nash rose and moved to the fire, placing his boot on the hearth. "I will escort you safely to London where you will grant me two days in which to prove Edward's fallacious character. Afterward, if I have convinced you, you will not marry him. If I have *not* convinced you, you may turn me in to the constable as your kidnapper and proceed with your nuptials."

She searched his eyes for a spark of humor, insincerity, or even madness, but found only the young lad who had been her champion for years. "You would risk the noose merely to prove a point?"

He swallowed as if suddenly overcome. "Sophie, I would risk my life to see you happy." Shifting away his gaze, he cleared his throat. "We are friends forever, remember?"

Ignoring the emotion she saw in his eyes, she quipped in return, "Friends don't kidnap friends."

"It is a good bargain. Either way, you come out the winner."

"The sea air has made you mad."

"Yet pray, lamb, indulge my madness." There was that appeal again in his eyes, his voice, as if she had a choice. But she didn't. That he would keep her against her will, she had no doubt. Some things never changed. And Nash's stubbornness was one of them.

The scent of fried eggs tickled Sophia's nose, spreading relief down to her toes. She must be home. Or better yet, at Pratt House waking up from the worst nightmare she ever remembered having. *Thank You, God.* Surely, all would be well now. But then, as her mind crept out from the bliss of slumber, other smells became distinct—fire smoke, aged wood, damp muslin, and a unique scent from her childhood—*Nash.* She moved her hand and felt the lumpy edges of a straw cot, not the wool-stuffed mattress of her own bed, while from another room the soft whistle of a tune she'd long forgotten met her ears.

She sat up. The warm quilt covering her dropped to the bed, allowing chilled air to prick her arms. She rubbed her eyes and found she lay in a private chamber, modestly furnished with bed, table, lantern, and a gown and underthings draped over a chair. The door was closed. Heart clambering up her throat, she glanced down. Her gown was still on.

And *still* damp.

Her heart continued its climb as memories returned of her sitting before the fire with Nash, refusing to change into dry clothing or retire for the night. Heaven's mercy! She must have fallen asleep.

Pots clanged and the whistling continued. Sophia scrambled to free herself from the quilt and stood, instantly assaulted by a chill that sliced to her bones. Foolish girl! Why had she not changed? It would do no good to be ill at her wedding. Quickly discarding her damp attire, she donned the fresh petticoat, stockings, and gown, amazed at the fine quality provided by a mere sailor. Hesitantly she opened the door and peered into the next room.

"Ah, just in time to break our fast." Nash smiled her way from the hearth, where he stooped over a pan of eggs and two slices of bread on an iron grill. *Smiled* at her as if he hadn't kidnapped her and forced her into his jealous bargain.

She bit back an angry retort and sneezed as she approached the fire, relishing the warmth that instantly blanketed her.

He raised an incriminating brow, his eyes playful. "You should have changed last night."

"And you should not have stolen me away."

His smile remained as he examined her. "You look lovely."

She gazed down at the cream-colored gown with embroidered rose-petal trim and then patted her attempt at a chignon with far fewer pins than required, suddenly nervous beneath his scrutiny. "When can we leave? I'm most anxious to get to London."

"After we eat." He slid eggs onto a plate, added a slice of toast, and handed it to her.

She shouldn't take it—should take nothing from this man—but her stomach ached at the sight, and she couldn't help but lower herself to a chair and take a bite of toast.

He poured hot tea from a pot sitting amongst the coals and set the cup on the table beside her, then helped himself to a plate.

The tea was sweet with a dollop of cream, just how she liked it. How had he remembered after all these years? Cupping her hands around the warm mug, she studied him—this boy who had proposed to her six years ago and who, after she had rejected him, had joined an East Indiaman, never to return.

But the boy had become a man. No doubt 'twas working on a ship that caused the rounded muscles not easily hidden by his white linen shirt and waistcoat. A scar ran down the right side of a tanned face, disappearing into the stubble on his jaw. He had been handsome enough as a youth, but as a man, he had a rugged allure, a strength about him that far surpassed appearance. Shifting her gaze away, she took a bite of eggs, perfectly prepared, not too dry, not too mushy.

"You always were a good cook," she remarked.

He smiled, and that dimple she remembered appeared on the right corner of his mouth—at such odds with his rugged appearance. "Stolen eggs taste far better."

She laughed. "Indeed. Remember that time we were so hungry, we stole Mr. Paulson's eggs and you cooked them over a fire in the woods."

"Best eggs I ever made."

"Best I ever ate."

What was she doing? Bantering with her kidnapper. She sighed and sipped her tea. Yet this particular kidnapper was Nash, and that made it all the more confusing. "When my father discovered our thievery, you took the blame for me. Though it had been my idea."

He shrugged and tossed the last piece of toast into his mouth. "'Twas the gentlemanly thing to do."

"It was not the first time you took my punishment." Or the last. Her childhood memories were filled with Nash coming to her rescue.

He finished his last bite of eggs and gazed at her with that look she knew too well. . .but had desperately tried to forget.

But she *must* forget. This Nash was not *her* Nash. He had more than proven it by his actions. This Nash was a grown man, scarred inside and outside by life. He was no longer her champion, her protector.

He was her enemy.

Her anger returned. "Can you imagine what you have done to my parents?"

He sipped his tea, frowning. "They will soon discover you well and unscathed."

"My mother is ill, and Father is old. The fright may kill them both."

"I am sorry to hear your mother is unwell. You know I always loved them both."

"You have a strange way of showing it."

Standing, he gathered her empty plate and cup and set them on the hearth then poured a bucket of ash over the fire to douse the flames. "We should go."

◦◦◦

It didn't take long for Nash to regret not hiring a coach to take them the entire journey to London. He hadn't thought being so close to Sophia would affect him after all these years, but the warmth of her body pressed so tightly against his chest and her constant squirming was driving him to distraction.

"Be still, lamb." He urged the horse down the road, muddy from last night's storm.

"This saddle is uncomfortable. Why could you not at least have purchased fare on a coach?"

He laughed. "A kidnapper transporting his victim by coach?"

"Well at least you admit your crime."

"I never denied it." He drew in a deep breath of her hair, the scent of rose water and rain, invoking delightful memories.

She turned her head slightly, enough for him to see her lashes outlined in golden sunlight. "I give you my word I will not scream for help. You have your two days, sir."

"Sir now, is it?"

"Would you prefer villain, blackguard, or scoundrel?"

"I have been called worse."

"No doubt." Shifting again in her seat, she sighed her frustration. "Are you planning on galloping into London with me astride your horse like some country hussy?"

"Galloping? Nay, I planned on a mild canter."

"Insufferable cur!"

He leaned toward her ear. "Never fear, I have made plans to protect your reputation, Sophie."

"I wait eagerly to hear them."

"You can trust me. I have not changed so much."

At this, she gave a ladylike snort.

The countryside rolled past them in waves of green speckled with sheep and cows, farmhouses, and inns. A rare bold sun stood above the horizon, forging a path across a blue sky painted in billowing clouds. Nash slowed his pace, trying to prolong his time with Sophie before they reached Northolt. But her constant moans, fidgeting, and occasional shudder made him doubt his ingenious plan to rescue her. Clearly, she was afraid, and he suddenly felt like the worst scoundrel for putting her through such a harrowing adventure.

Indeed, she may have blossomed into a woman on the outside, but inside she remained the same old Sophie—nervous, timid, sensitive, and naive.

Which is precisely why he had to protect her from Pratt.

A brisk wind brought the scent of livestock, earth, and wildflowers, and he drew in a deep breath. So different from the brine, salt, and fish he'd grown accustomed to at sea. In fact, he would still be sailing the world if he hadn't received the post that had changed his life. Nothing else could have drawn him home, nothing could have made him risk seeing the woman he loved married to another man, as he assumed she would be by now.

Imagine his surprise to find her on the cusp of an ill-fated match that would forever seal her doom.

Providence at work, for surely God had sent him to rescue her.

She moved again, and in an effort to shift his thoughts in a purer direction, he began to whistle a tune that never failed to calm his nerves.

After a few moments, she laughed. "You still whistle that silly song, 'Ward the Pirate'?"

He joined her laughter. "Old habits, I suppose."

"Tell me of the East India Company. What was it like out at sea?"

"Ah, daring to converse with your kidnapper? Shocking, Miss Crew."

"Only to pass the time quicker, since you insist on such a slow pace."

"Cold and wet."

"What was?"

"The sea." The horse started down a steep incline, and instinctively, Nash wrapped an arm around her waist.

She pushed him away. "Surely it was beautiful as well. You must have seen many exotic lands."

"Indeed, India, China, Africa. . .even the West Indies."

"How very exciting. You always were the adventurous type."

"Something I'd hoped to bring out in you." He'd seen something in her as a child. A yearning, a desire to live life to its fullest—a zest held back by fear and unbelief.

"You take far too many risks, Nash, which is another reason—"

"You rejected my proposal?"

She shifted in the saddle. "We would never have been happy. I have accepted the nature God gave me—one which seeks safety and security."

"You didn't always act safely, lamb."

"Quit calling me that! Besides, when I didn't, 'twas your fault."

"Like the time we raced horses bareback in the rain?"

"I was absolutely horrified!" She laughed. "But I would not be made a coward by your challenge."

"Which proves my point." Nash eased the horse around a huge puddle. "You have pluck. And a strong urge to win. At least against me." He laughed. "You never stopped trying to beat me at something, anything—cards, milking cows, collecting eggs, baking bread, mucking stalls, and especially racing horses. Not exactly an activity for a timid girl."

A rather large dragonfly buzzed near Sophia's face, and she shrieked and batted it away, making a fool of his last statement. "I was tired of you winning at everything. And with nary a speck of fear. I suppose I wanted to be more like you and not so nervous all the time."

He leaned toward her ear. "It takes courage to do something that frightens you—courage and trust in God."

She turned her face, her silky skin brushing against his stubble, her tone sharp. "God does not expect us to behave like fools, rashly risking our lives as you did many times when we were young."

"Yet I'm still here."

"Indeed, and still behaving the brazen child, it seems."

Her angry tone made him attempt to lighten the mood. "Do you remember the time we put toads in Mrs. Cropley's picnic basket?"

"We? It was you who put them there. I wouldn't touch them."

"Yes, but it was your idea."

She laughed, and the sweet sound stirred his senses to life. "I never expected you to agree."

"Didn't you? I fear that you preyed upon my reckless nature, Miss Crew."

Silence descended as Nash led the horse onward. A hawk flew overhead, issuing a shrill call as a breeze spun dirt across the path.

"Did you encounter any pirates while out at sea?"

He chuckled. "A few."

"Are they as vile and evil as they say?"

"Some. Others are gentlemen hoping to aid their country and make a fortune in the process."

"Such adventures you have had, such a life you have led."

He wanted to tell her he would gladly have stayed home, given up all his adventures, if only she had agreed to marry him.

Wind danced through the golden tendrils at her neck. "Why did you return? Not simply to destroy my life, I hope."

"Nay, destroying your life was a mere afterthought."

Growling, she shoved from him. "You are incorrigible and ridiculous, and I will never forgive you for this!"

He regretted his statement. "I was teasing, Sophie."

"Perhaps I would find it amusing if it weren't true. Please urge this beast faster. I cannot stand your presence another minute."

Her words stung, deflating Nash's rising hope. Still, he must continue, regardless of whether she would hate him in the end.

Conversation lapsed, and they entered a small village. People milled about, attending their chores, sparing glances their way. Pigs and chickens wandered over the streets as a blacksmith's hammer echoed down the lane. Nash's nerves tightened. Would Sophie scream for help? Though he sensed her body tighten, he prayed she was the same honorable girl who always kept her promises.

An hour outside the village, how delighted he was to discover that she was. The sun stood above them, its fiery rays only occasionally shielded by passing clouds. Nash spotted a small pond beside the road where a large willow provided shade. He led the horse there and dismounted.

"What are we doing?"

"Resting. You need to eat."

"I don't want to rest." She spoke like a princess on her throne. "We should be in London by now."

Ignoring her protests, Nash took her by the waist and brought her gently to the ground. "I don't wish to tire you."

"You tire me with your insolence." She stomped away from him. "Heaven's mercy, I have forgotten myself. My parents are no doubt overcome with fear, my fiancé drowning in sorrow and worry, and I sit atop my kidnapper's horse, which moves no faster than a snail, making idle conversation as if we were still children." She spun to face him, eyes fiery jades in sunlight. "This wasted time counts toward my two days."

Nash frowned and was about to protest when two horses appeared in the distance, galloping toward them down the road, spitting up mud in their wake. Sunlight glinted off something in their hands. *Pistols!*

Nash stiffened. No time to mount his gelding and make a run for it should these men have ill intent. Perhaps they would pass them by.

No such luck. The two men reared up their horses on the road and headed toward Nash—slovenly looking characters, one plump, red of face with a hook nose and jagged yellow teeth, the other built like an ox wearing attire fit for a gentleman. Both grinning like children at Christmas.

They stopped before them, enveloping Nash in the stench of brandy and horseflesh.

"Now what have we here? A gentleman an' 'is wife."

"A fine-lookin' woman a' that."

Instead of shrinking in fear, Sophia arched an angry brow toward Nash. "More of your associates, I assume? Another ploy to keep me from Edward and delay us even further?"

Grabbing her hand, Nash attempted to pull her behind him. "Shsss, woman."

She jerked from his grasp and charged the two men. "I've had about enough highwaymen to last a lifetime. Whatever he is paying you will not be worth the trouble I will cause you. Now, turn around and go back the way you came this instant."

She emphasized her point by stomping her foot on the ground.

And they emphasized theirs by pointing their pistols at her.

Chapter Four

Sophia couldn't remember being angrier. Angry at herself, angry at these ruffians, and most of all angry at Nash. She'd been too trusting, too naive all her life, and she refused to be played the fool any more.

"Sophie," she heard Nash grind out behind her. "Get back here."

The men laughed. One rubbed his chin and stared at her as if she belonged in an asylum.

"Paid?" The other man dismounted, leveling his pistol her way. "Not yet, but we's hopin' you can remedy that."

Despite the trembling in her legs, Sophia would not be intimidated. "You will get back on your horse, sir, and leave immediately. We have urgent business in London and cannot be delayed."

The man who resembled a tomato chuckled from atop his horse. "Urgent business? Then by all means, miss, be on your way. After you hand over your jewels an' coin." He eyed the ruby bracelet on her wrist.

She covered it with her hand. "This was a gift from my fiancé. I dare you to come and take it."

Behind her, Nash groaned and moved to stand in front of her. "Gentlemen, you must forgive my wife. She's quite out of her mind, you see. In fact, we are on our way to Bedlam."

She struck him in the arm. "How dare you!"

Nash gripped her wrist as the men chuckled.

"No business of mine if she's got the mind of a gnat. We'll be taking your jewels an' coin now, or they'll be somethin' else we'll be takin', as well." The man as large as a tree eyed Sophia with a salacious twinkle that made her almost believe him.

The other villain dismounted and joined his friend.

She jerked from Nash's grip. "Are you daft, gentlemen? I told you to leave. I'm having none of this charade."

Yet the men continued moving toward her, snarls upon their faces—far better acting than she expected from such ill-bred mongrels.

Nash shoved her behind him. Yes, *shoved*. So hard, she tumbled backward, barely keeping her balance.

"Faith, gentlemen, there is no need for such unsavory behavior." He made a gesture of peace with open arms. "We have nothing of value, and my wife is clearly ill."

"I am not your wife!" Sophia spit out.

Halting just a yard before Nash, the men snorted, both their pistols aimed at his chest.

Sophia huffed, brushing aside her unfounded fear. They weren't loaded, of course.

"If you're goin' to stop us, best do it now, or step aside, dandy, an' let us to our business."

"Very well." Nash gave a casual shrug as Sophia started forward again. In a move too fast to make any sense of, Nash clasped one of the men's wrists between two arms and twisted. Sophia could swear she heard bone snap as his pistol fell to the ground. At the same time, a kick to the other man's pistol sent it spinning into a shrub a yard away. The crack of a shot bellowed across the clearing. Sophia halted and stared at the smoke curling from the fallen weapon.

Shock widened both men's eyes, followed by fear. . .and finally rage. The tall one swung a fist at Nash. He ducked and slammed his own fist into the man's gut, sending him reeling back.

Sophia could only stare dumbfounded as Nash blocked the second man's strike with his arm and then slugged him across the face. His head whipped around, and he stumbled back, blood spurting from his mouth. Nash grabbed the first man by the collar and hauled him to his horse.

"As my wife requested, I suggest you rats return to the hole from whence you crawled." He shoved the man against his animal then charged the second villain who was rubbing his jaw and uttering curses that burned Sophia's ears. Upon seeing Nash, he backed away in horror and dashed to his mount.

Both men leapt upon their horses, cast one last scowl toward Nash, then galloped away in the same direction they had come.

Sophie's heart refused to settle. The pistol had been loaded! These men were *real* villains? Villains who could have hurt her, even ravished her. If not for Nash. With more skill then she'd ever seen, he had easily defeated them both.

"Heaven's mercy." She breathed out what felt like her last breath as her legs gave way beneath her.

Darting to her side, Nash caught her. "Now, now, lamb. All is well." He led her to sit on a boulder overlooking the pond.

"How did you. . .? They were real highwaymen!" The sky spun around her head, and she felt herself tipping over.

Lowering to sit beside her, he wrapped an arm around her shoulders and drew her close.

He smelled of man, smoke, and a hint of the sea. And as much as she hated to admit it, she felt safe in his arms.

He chuckled. "Your courage is exemplary, Miss Crew."

She leaned her head on his shoulder. "I thought they were actors."

"Do you think me so low as to hire highwaymen, real or not, to torment you further?" He rubbed her arm. It felt good. . .far too good.

A sensation she must put a stop to immediately.

"I didn't think you so low as to become one in the first place," she returned angrily.

Her harsh tone bore the intended effect. He rose, straightened his waistcoat, and held out his hand. "We should go. You are right. I have been delaying our trip."

His voice was devoid of its usual playfulness, and despite her traitorous remorse, she knew 'twas for the best.

He hoisted her onto the horse, she climbed on behind, and they proceeded at a canter down the road. Before long, they entered Northolt, where, much to her surprise, they stopped before an inn. Fearing he intended to spend the night, Sophia was relieved when, after Nash spoke with a gentleman at the stables and gave him a pouch of coins, they were transferred to a coach, complete with driver and footman.

Taking the gloved hand of the servant, Sophia stepped inside—thankful to be off a horse—and was greeted by an elderly woman, plainly dressed in wool, with cheeks as round and soft-looking as kneaded dough.

"Mrs. Simons." Nash introduced her as he entered. "Your companion for the remainder of the journey."

Sophia greeted the kind-faced lady, who smiled in return and cast a knowing glance at Nash.

"Dear lady," Sophia said. "I don't suppose it would do any good to ask for your help to escape this beast who has taken me against my will?"

Mrs. Simons's chuckle filled the coach. "Now, miss, why would you want to be doing that? He's a good man, straight as an arrow flies, and more honor in his hat than most men have in their entire body. Besides, he's taking you where you want to go, eh?"

Nash smiled at Mrs. Simons before facing Sophia.

"I told you I would not ruin your reputation. As far as Mrs. Simons is concerned, she has been with you the entire time after I rescued you from the highwayman."

"*You* rescued me? *Pshaw!* And if I choose to turn you into the authorities as the highwayman himself?"

He flattened his lips. "Mrs. Simons is prepared to say she helped you escape my vile clutches before we were ever alone and then traveled with you to London."

Reaching his hand out the window, Nash slapped the side of the coach. Reins snapped, horses neighed, and the coach jerked forward on its way.

"He must be paying you a fortune, Mrs. Simons."

"Paying me? Nah!" She shared a smile with Nash. "I would gladly do anything to help Mr. Barrett."

Sophia frowned. Was it her, or did it seem the entire world was against her and on the side of this rapscallion? She ran her fingers down the leather seats, noting that the same leather covered the walls as well. Red velvet curtains framed windows on either side, while lanterns perched outside provided light within. "Pray tell, Nash, how does a poor sailor afford such a luxurious coach?"

"Prize money, Miss Crew." He winked. "I acquired a fair sum during my six years at sea."

Not much was said as the carriage ambled down the road, past the boundary of Northolt, and down a much busier highway than before. The sun began its descent, and, as if portending doom, clouds moved in to paint everything in dreary gray.

Sophia tried to concentrate on her upcoming nuptials. Surely Edward would be beside himself with joy to see her unscathed. Perhaps this little scare would even enhance his love for her when he realized he might have lost her forever. She tried to envision his expression when he first saw her—his utter glee. Then, of course, the joy of reuniting with her worried parents, followed by the lavish parties hosted in her honor. But no matter how hard she tried, she could not cast from her thoughts the man who sat across from her—the man who smelled of spice and the sea and who filled the coach with his presence. The man whose intense gaze repeatedly found its way to her. And within that gaze she could find no malice or ill-intent, only care, concern, and a lingering sorrow that gave her pause.

After some time, snoring filled the coach, and both Sophia and Nash chuckled at Mrs. Simons curled up in the corner.

"Where did you learn to fight so well?" Sophia asked Nash.

"A necessity aboard a sailing ship." He replied, his somber gaze fixed out the window, wind tossing his hair behind him and flapping the top of his shirt.

She hadn't thought of how hard life must have been aboard a ship. No doubt that was the reason Nash seemed so changed—rough, powerful, yet teetering on edge, like a powder keg about to ignite.

"You have no need to continue protecting me, Nash. I know what I am doing."

"Do you?" He faced her and moved his legs, booted to the knee, inadvertently touching her and sparking something within her she could not deny.

Nash Barrett had saved her more times than she could count. Once from a rabid fox intent on chomping her leg and another time when she fell down an old well. He'd held her during thunderstorms, patched up her wounds, tended her when she'd been sick, fought off bullies. Once he'd even risked his life to climb to the top of a tree during a storm to rescue her cat.

In truth, he had been her protector, her champion as far back as she could remember. Until she turned down his proposal and he walked out of her life. She had never felt so lost as she had that first year after he left. But how could she blame him?

Now as he sat so close to her, those same feelings began to spark to life. And she hated herself for it.

She knew they had entered London when the air became clogged with soot. The sunset disappeared behind a black shroud as they ambled through narrow streets. She'd never seen so many people in one place. Merchants hawking their wares, men in top hats and silk coats walking alongside others in rags. Taverns, shops, and crumbling brick buildings stacked atop one another, looking as if they'd fall should anyone knock on the door. Children barely dressed running barefoot through the street, chimney sweeps with black faces and brooms in hand, hackneys and wagons crowding the cobblestone streets. And the stench. A mixture of smoke, human waste, manure, and rotten fish.

She coughed, and Nash plucked a handkerchief from his pocket and handed it to her. "Takes some getting used to."

"I've been here before." Though she'd forgotten the horrid odor. She held the cloth to her nose.

"Then you know we are on the east side by the docks. Soon you will see a difference."

Indeed, within minutes the coach turned this way and that, and more stately buildings lined the street.

Craning her head out the window, she spotted the seven gates and ominous spires of the Tower of London. Next London Bridge came into view, golden lights flickering from its massive pillars. The coach made another turn onto a wider street, where the rounded dome of St. Paul's Cathedral reached toward heaven. Making their way down the Strand, they passed St. James Church and various theaters and museums. So much to do and see! Sophia couldn't help but feel excited at the prospect of living in such a place—for at least part of the year.

More turns were made as they ambled down streets lined with stately townhomes rising high into the night sky. They halted before one of them, and Nash hopped out and assisted Sophia and a groggy Mrs. Simons from the coach.

"This is not the Pratt home. Where are we?" Sophia's fear rose once more.

"The townhome of a friend who is currently on holiday. There is a full staff who will attend your every need." Nash paid the driver, and the man tipped his hat and drove away.

"I demand you return me to my fiancé!"

"You gave me two days." Nash extended his arm, unruffled by her outburst.

"You have one left, sir. And I assumed you would merely recite a litany of slanderous allegations against Edward and be done with it."

"If that would convince you, lamb, I'd have done so already. Nay, you must see things for yourself." Taking her hand, he placed it in the crook of his elbow and proceeded toward the door.

"I don't see how—" She pulled back her hand as the door opened and a tall, middle-aged man in a butler's livery appeared.

Nash gestured for her to proceed up the stairs. "I will agree to one more day, Sophie. Will that appease you?"

"I will be delivered to Edward safely this time tomorrow evening?"

"You have my word."

He escorted her inside where a butler took his coat and a flurry of maids came to greet them. Overwhelmed by the number—equal to the Pratts' staff—Sophia glanced up at the winding marble staircase and the crystalline chandelier hanging above them from the tall ceiling.

A maid curtseyed and took her cloak while Nash drew his butler aside. Mrs. Simons greeted the other servants as if she'd known them all her life. Sophia could make no sense of it, nor how Nash had procured such lavish accommodations.

Dismissing the butler, Nash approached and addressed Mrs. Simons. "Escort

Miss Crew to her chamber, prepare her a bath, and allow her to choose a gown for the party."

"What party?" Sophia asked, her ire rising once again.

"Not truly a party, lamb, but a masquerade ball." He winked and walked away.

Chapter Five

"That is well enough, Benson. Stop fidgeting." Nash waved away his steward and examined himself in the mirror. He'd never grown accustomed to being dressed by a servant. It seemed downright unmanly to not put on one's own clothing. But it was the way of things in a gentleman's world. And it seemed to please Benson, who fussed over him like an old mother hen.

"Very well. Shall I tie your cravat?" The pudgy man could barely reach Nash's neck, but he nodded his agreement. If only to keep the man happy. As Benson struggled with the silk monstrosity, Nash's thoughts drifted to Sophia—as they usually did. He could hardly believe she was so close—in this very house! After all the years he'd spent far away, thinking of her, wondering where she was, what she was doing, now he would see her again in only minutes. Yet, what did it matter? She had made it more than plain that her heart was not his. In his foolishness, he had hoped that a day or two together would remind her of the bond between them, the love they had once shared. But he had been wrong. Perhaps too much time had passed, or perhaps she truly *did* love Edward Pratt, as unfathomable as that thought was.

Yet, what was clearly now even more unfathomable was the way Nash had gone about rescuing her from Pratt! What had he been thinking? He knew she was the nervous sort, frightened by a mere mouse skittering across the path. So, what had he done? Kidnapped her. Then to make matters worse, they'd been attacked by ruffians, who had no doubt spotted them as easy prey when they'd traveled through Northolt. Nash had put Sophia in danger, something he never intended to do. The look on her face after the event—the way she trembled and then her anger toward him—convinced him that he'd yet again made a muck of things.

Benson stepped back to admire his work and started to gather Nash's dirty attire.

"Thank you, Benson. You've made a gentleman out of me yet again." Indeed, the man staring back at him from the mirror bore no resemblance to the rough, wind-beaten sailor he'd been the past six years.

"Have Jackson prepare the phaeton and bring it around front, if you will, Benson." The steward nodded and left.

Nash picked up the ridiculous mask Benson had provided and held it to his eyes. Black, like his highwayman's mask, but trimmed in red and sequined with jewels. Still, it covered the top half of his face, effectively shielding his identity from all but the closest of friends. Smiling, he headed out the door.

An hour later, as he waited at the bottom of the stairs, sweat beaded on the back of his neck in anticipation of Sophia's appearance. Chastising himself, he began whistling to calm his nerves. What was wrong with him? He was no longer a schoolboy waiting for a glimpse of his first love, nor did the lady wish to spend the evening with him.

Movement alerted him, and he gazed up to see her grip the bannister and begin her descent. Candlelight glittered over a white satin gown with a square neckline and epaulet sleeves. A lace over-gown was draped upon it, extending to her knees and fastened down the front with rosettes of pearls, which were also inlaid on her sleeves and neckline and trimmed the silk band around her waist. Her hair was pulled back into a loose chignon from which golden ringlets dripped like watery jewels. Her pearl necklace rose and fell with each nervous breath as her satin slippers made barely a sound on the treads. She glanced up at him briefly, halted for a moment, and smiled before she started down again—an angel daring to descend from heaven to share her beauty and charm with mere mortals for but a moment in time.

He knew now why he was nervous. He had only one night left with her. Just one night to convince her of Pratt's character. If he failed, she'd not only walk out of his life forever, but she'd be walking into a prison of sorrow with a life sentence. And there was nothing he could do about it.

⋐⋑

Sophia couldn't resist smiling when she first saw the elegant gentleman standing at the bottom of the stairs. Before she had left her chamber, she'd heard him whistling the tune from "Ward the Pirate." If not for that, she wouldn't have believed it was truly him—from farm boy to sailor to highwayman and now dressed in such grandeur and elegance, he could easily compete with the regent himself. His black suit was expertly tailored, from his trousers that fed into knee-high boots, to his cream-colored silk waistcoat, to his black tail coat and a neck-full of bubbling silk. His sun-streaked hair was slicked back from a clean-shaven jaw, strong mouth, Roman nose, and eyes that would melt the prudest matron. Goodness, but the man was handsome. Even as the thought crossed her mind, she chastised herself and fingered her ruby bracelet, reminding her that she was betrothed to another. Besides, Nash had kidnapped her! Why could she not remember that when she was with him?

But as she stopped before him and he took her hand and leaned to kiss it, she could not deny the warmth spiraling through her at his touch.

"You look ravishing, Sophie." His blue eyes assessed her, and once again she saw within them the old Nash she had loved so dearly.

"And you look like a lord. How have you pulled it off?"

He smiled, his eyes flashing. "Miracles do happen."

"Miracles, indeed." She glanced down at her attire and still couldn't believe her eyes. "I've never worn anything so extravagant. Where did you get it? And how did you afford it?" More importantly, why did it fit as if it were tailored just for her?

"No more questions tonight, Sophie. Let us just enjoy the evening. Shall we?" He gestured toward the door where the butler stood with their coats.

"We must be careful not to disclose our identities," Nash said once they were in the carriage and on their way.

She stared down at the ridiculous mask in her lap. With jewels sprinkled across bright green silk and a layer of feathers sprouting across the top, it looked more like a wounded bird caught in a web of glitter. "Not until midnight. Despite my upbringing, I am aware of the rules."

"Not *ever* at this party."

Sophia shook her head and gazed out the window. A thousand questions shouted in her mind—how was Nash suddenly transformed into a gentleman? Where did he get the money for a coach and such fine attire? How did he procure an invitation to a society party? And to what purpose were they even going?

She could only think of one answer for the last question.

"Edward will be at this ball, won't he?"

Nash drew in a sigh, not meeting her gaze. "In all honesty, I have no idea."

She huffed. "How long must I endure this?"

"Not long. Indulge me this one night, Sophie."

The carriage bounced down the street, this way and that, and Sophia realized that should she try to escape her captor, she'd be hopelessly lost. Street lanterns flickered in the chilled breeze, lighting the way down crowded avenues.

The landau halted before a grand, two-story home with white columns and a small garden in front lit by torches. Music and light spilled from open windows, along with laughter and chatter as various couples, decked in their finest, made their way to the front door. Sophie swallowed and strapped on her mask. The only parties she'd ever attended were country dances, and she certainly had never met any of the ton, as London society liked the call themselves.

Indeed, Edward's parents had held a dinner party in her honor when she'd first come to meet them two months ago, but it had been small and not well-attended. She had always wondered whether it was her status that had kept people away, though Edward denied it.

The footman opened the carriage door, and Nash leapt out and held a hand for her. He looked incredibly mysterious—even dangerous in his mask, especially with his scar angling out from beneath it.

"Are you sure you aren't truly a highwayman?" she teased, hoping to alleviate her nervous jitters.

"Tonight, I vow to be anything you desire, miss. . .miss. I shall call you 'Lady Gillingham.'"

"And who shall you be?"

"Lord Gillingham, of course."

"We pretend to be titled, then?" She huffed. "If discovered, we will be escorted out in disgrace. Is that your plan? To disgrace me, besmirch my reputation, and force Edward to break off the engagement?"

"We will not be discovered, and nay, I would never disgrace you in any way."

His tone was so soft, his eyes so sincere, she found she believed him. "How did you come to be invited to such an affair?"

"'Tis Lord Gillingham's home in which we stay. As I said, he is a friend."

Sophia wanted to laugh at the ludicrous story. "You must take me for a fool. Just how do you know a member of the aristocracy? And why would he lower himself, risk the disapproval of his peers, by allowing you to stay in his home?"

"I saved his nephew's life while out at sea. In return, he offered his home to me when he was away." He spoke matter-of-factly as if it was an everyday occurrence, but their arrival at the front door forbade further questioning.

Nash handed a card to the man, who, after examining it, allowed them entrance. An elderly lady dressed in exorbitant finery greeted them next, studying Nash with interest and offering him her hand. He kissed it, thanked her for the invitation, and she waved them on, giving him a flirtatious smile.

The foyer was as large as Sophia's entire childhood home, brimming with people chattering gaily and flitting about in their silks and satins, ladies with pearls in their hair and feathers atop their coiffures. . .and everyone wearing an elaborate mask.

Nash escorted her through the crush as if he'd done so a hundred times, making his way to another large room also filled with people hovering around a long, white-clothed table covered with food and drink—tea, lemonade, iced sherbet, small cakes, and bon-bons—to which many of the guests were helping themselves.

The smell of roasted pheasant and baked apples wafted up from below stairs, waking her stomach to life, and she placed a hand atop it.

"You must be famished," Nash said. "If we stay long enough, they will provide sup-per downstairs. For now, allow me to get you some cakes."

"I couldn't possibly, Na—I mean, milord." She smirked. "My nerves."

He frowned. "But you haven't eaten since this morning."

"Mrs. Simons brought me soup."

"A drink then?" He grabbed a glass of lemonade from a passing tray and handed it to her.

The sweet refreshment helped calm her as she stared in wonder over the scene. Tall, arched ceilings boasted what appeared to be carvings of cherubs in ivory. Tapestries and paintings lined the wall, while soft-cushioned chairs and tables were spread about. Music from the room next door floated on a layer of perfume that nearly choked her—expensive French perfume she imagined.

Yet through it all, she couldn't help but smile. Here she was, a simple yeoman's daughter at a society function in London. Of course, she would attend many more of these affairs once she married Edward, but she still could not believe that finally, after all these years, she would be important. She would *be* somebody. Her status would demand respect, not engender avoidance, or, as was usually the case, dismissal.

Even better, with everyone behind masks, no one knew who was who or what title belonged to whom or whether Sophia was a duchess or a farm girl. She supposed her introduction to society couldn't have worked out better, for at least she could hide from those who would sneer at her position until she could marry Edward.

Nash glanced over the crowd as if he were looking for someone, completely oblivious to a group of ladies eyeing him behind fans from across the room. A flare of jealousy surprised Sophia and deflated her giddy mood. She set down her glass. "Why are we here?"

"Come." He led her into the ballroom, even more elaborately appointed than the refreshment room. Garlands of fresh flowers festooned walls that were decorated with paintings of the English countryside. Cut-glass chandeliers rained glittering light upon the people below. An orchestra was perched on a dais at one end before a floor where couples twirled and spun. Surrounding the dancers, people stood watching and conversing—young ladies waiting to be asked to dance, older women assessing the prospects for their daughters, old men drinking and talking politics, while young bucks eyed the pretty women.

A man stumbled up to them and gripped Nash's shoulder. "I haven't seen you in months, Northum. Ah yes," He leaned toward him and winked. "I can see it's you behind that mask." He faced Sophia and grinned, dousing her in the scent of brandy. "I do insist, Northum, introduce me to this ravishing lady."

"She is my wife, sir!" Nash replied, feigning indignance.

"Ah ha." The man chuckled and pointed a finger at Nash, lowering his voice. "I see. 'Tis part of your disguise." Looking both ways, he leaned toward them. "Mum's the word." His gaze traveled back to her—or rather to her low neckline. "Yet surely you can lend her to me for one dance?"

Sophia took a step back, appalled at the man's forward behavior.

"I fear I must disappoint you." Nash dipped his head and extended his arm toward her. "My wife has promised me the first dance."

"Who was that?" Sophia glanced over her shoulder as Nash led her away. "Why did he call you Northum?"

Nash shrugged. "The man is drunk and mistook me for someone else."

He escorted her onto the floor before she had a chance to protest. The beginning quadrille had ended and a cotillion began. Nash faced her and bowed. She had a decision to make, curtsey and continue with this devilish man in dance, or embarrass them both by running off the floor. Part of her truly wanted to dance, had always wanted to dance at one of these grand affairs, twirling in a beautiful gown before a crowd of people like a princess at court.

Nash took her hesitation as compliance and laced his hand with hers. The dimple appeared at the right corner of his mouth, and she found she could not resist him even if she wanted to. The music began, and the couples grabbed hands and began spinning in a circle. Then separating, they exchanged partners and swung about, moving from dancer to dancer. But Sophia's gaze was on Nash. . .how he all but floated across the floor in moves too polished for a farmer or sailor. Once again, they met hand in hand, he spun her around, and her heart betrayed her with a leap and a warmth that spiraled down to her toes. When she raised her gaze to his, she found his eyes adoring her, and she looked away, confused.

That's when she saw him. On the edge of the crowd.

Edward. Standing far too close to a dark-haired lady. Though he wore a mask, she'd know him anywhere.

She pushed from Nash and threw a hand to her throat. "I must—" She started toward Edward, her one thought to let him know she was here! Alive and well and returned to him. But Nash grabbed her arm, led her off the floor, and dove into the crowd. Leading her to a corner, his grip tight, he whispered into her ear. "You promised me one night."

"You'd knew he'd be here!" She turned her back to him, trying to settle her anger. People began to stare. "Why are you torturing me?" she sobbed out.

He gently turned her to face him. "That is my last wish. I merely want you to observe."

She stared at him, her eyes brimming with tears. "Observe what?"

Chapter Six

How could Sophia stand by and simply observe her fiancé without making her presence known? Surely that was beyond cruel to do to a man who was no doubt overwrought with worry for her safety. She drew a breath and faced the dance floor again.

There he was, just yards from where she stood. She could be by his side within minutes, alleviate his agony, and finally be rid of Nash Barrett and his vile plans. Not to mention be escorted to the Pratt residence and reunited with her parents this very night!

But she couldn't. She had promised Nash, made a bargain with him when they were but children that they would never break a vow to each other. He had promised to deliver her to Edward tomorrow, and she believed him.

Two ladies walked past, fluttering fans and eyeing Nash as if he were a sweet cake. Ignoring them, Nash's gaze remained locked upon Sophia. At least she could feel it locked upon her, for she could not take her eyes off Edward.

Friends hailed him from across the room, and he proffered his arm and escorted the lady he'd been speaking to—a young, attractive woman with raven hair netted with rubies, rouge on her high cheeks, and a full figure—to join them.

"What now, Nash?"

"We wait."

They didn't have to wait long. Edward finished his drink, set it on a tray, and laughed at something one of his friends had said. *Laughed?* A jovial, carefree laugh. A rock sank to the bottom of Sophia's stomach. Was he aware his fiancée had been kidnapped by a highwayman? Attending a party was one thing, particularly if he needed the company of friends to comfort him in his fear and anguish—something she knew Edward was prone to do when distraught. But enjoying himself was quite another matter.

Nodding to his friends, Edward led the lady from the room. Who was this lady who clung to her fiancé's arm? Perhaps just a family friend, someone to attend the party with in Sophia's stead. That must be it. Then why did Sophia suddenly feel like the biggest fool ever? Taking her arm, Nash all but dragged her from her spot and followed the couple at a distance, through a crowded solarium, and then out a back door. Gardens extended into the darkness where a few intermittent lanterns on poles attempted to light a path among cultured shrubs and flowers. Laughter and other sounds—disturbing sounds—emanated from the thick hedgerow that fringed the outskirts of the yard.

"Where could he have gone?" Sophia whispered to no one in particular, even as perspiration broke out on her neck.

"Perhaps, we should leave." Nash's tone bore regret as he started to turn.

"No, I want to see." Though she had a feeling what she would encounter, she forged down the path, following sounds of female giggling and lusty groans.

Everywhere she looked, behind bushes and beneath trees, she found couples' bodies intertwined. Yet there was no sign of Edward. Perhaps he hadn't come outside after all.

Relief began to spread through her as the outline of a gazebo appeared in the moonlight ahead. What could it hurt to check one last spot? Halting, Sophia pushed aside leaves of a bush and peered behind it.

Edward. There was Edward! Sitting on a wrought-iron bench, trailing kisses down the woman's neck as she moaned in ecstasy.

Sophia's lungs collapsed. Her blood became a raging torrent. Everything in her wanted to rush him and slap him across the face, demand an explanation, and tell him he was the worst kind of scoundrel. But that would no doubt end their engagement.

Along with all her dreams.

"Come, Sophie." Nash's tender voice urged her as he tugged her away.

In a daze, she allowed him to lead her back through the ballroom, the refreshment room, the foyer, ignoring hails from those who thought they knew him. Gathering their cloaks, Nash swept hers around her shoulders before escorting her out into the cold air and ordering their carriage brought forth.

The ride home was a blur of lights angling across the carriage seats and onto the floor, and a multitude of sounds in the distance—the *clip-clop* of horse hooves and snap of reins, people's voices from the street. . .and the tearing of Sophia's broken heart.

She wanted to cry, to scream. She *should* be crying, sobbing hysterically. But she couldn't seem to muster a single tear. "You must think me a fool," she finally said to Nash who sat across from her, silently watching her.

"I would never think such a thing."

"You wanted me to see Edward with another woman."

"I'm sorry, Sophie. I never wanted to hurt you, but you needed to know the truth."

"How did you know where he'd be. . .that he would behave so reprehensibly?"

"I have my sources."

"Heaven's mercy." She rubbed her temples where a headache formed. "With my whereabouts and my very safety unknown, he. . .he. . ."

Tears finally spilled down her cheeks, and Nash handed her a handkerchief.

He started to rise, perhaps to sit beside her and offer his comfort, but she raised a hand, and he plopped back down.

The landau ambled on, her mind awhirl, her emotions more shock and anger than pain.

"Do you know what marrying Edward would do for my family?" She bunched the handkerchief in one hand. "Do you understand that he was my last hope to save us from the King's Bench?"

"Whatever do you mean?"

"Mother is ill. She needs a physician we cannot afford. Father is fast approaching sixty and can hardly work anymore. I cannot run the farm by myself, and our landlord threatens to evict us. Edward's money would save us. Mother would receive the care she needs. Father need not work another day. They will be well-cared for."

"I'm sorry. I didn't know." Frowning, Nash leaned forward on his knees. "Yet knowing your parents, I doubt they'd want you to sacrifice your life for them." He studied her. "Perhaps there is another reason." He sat back, his tone suddenly bitter. "You always wanted to join society."

"That isn't fair," she shot back.

"It is quite fair, especially since 'twas for that very reason you turned down my proposal."

Sophia tossed the handkerchief at him. "So this is your way of getting revenge?"

"No." Picking up the cloth, he fingered it as if her tears were precious. "Seek your status and wealth, Sophie, if that is what you desire. I pray you find it someday, but with a man who loves you, who is worthy of you."

She sighed and shook her head. "How often do you think the son of a baron wishes to marry a yeoman's daughter? Do you think it happens every day?" Forcing down her anger, she gripped the seat as the carriage bounced and jangled around a corner. "God answered my prayer. For myself and my family. And I intend to accept His gracious gift."

At first shock claimed his features, then disappointment as he leaned toward her again and arched an incriminating brow. "At what price, Sophie?"

"Are my parents' lives not worth my unhappiness?"

Sitting back, Nash ran a hand through his hair. "Do not play the saint with me. I know you too well."

"Doesn't our Lord say we should put others' needs above our own?"

"It also says we are not to consort with evil nor be unequally yoked. Do you really believe this is God's will for you?"

"What else could it be?"

"A test, perhaps?"

The air inside the carriage seemed to grow heavier with each passing minute.

"Where is your faith, Sophie?"

She huffed and shook her head. "I don't know whether I believe God even answers our prayers."

"He does. I can attest to that. But in His own time and His own way. We must be patient and trust Him, and we must put God first, above our desire for anything else."

He paused, and she could feel his eyes upon her. "Following after the things of this world is like living in a mud hut when God has a castle prepared for you."

"You should have joined the church instead of set out to sea," she replied a bit more harshly than intended.

Nash rubbed his jaw and reached across for her hand. "Sophie, I beg you. Trust God to take care of you and your family. Don't place your life on the sacrificial altar. God does not require that of you. He loves you too much."

She tugged from his grasp. "Believing in Him always came easy for you."

"You think so?" He snorted and ran a finger down the scar on his face. "Then you have no concept of what I've been through the past six years." He stared out the window. "Yet through all of it, there's one thing I've learned. Trust in the One who died for you."

Sophie followed his gaze to rows of passing townhomes, candlelight flickering from their windows.

"Tell me one thing, Sophia. Do you love Edward?"

She ground her teeth together, restraining a growl. Why was everyone asking her that? A question, in all honesty, for which she had no answer. But she knew one thing. She needed Edward. Without him, she and her parents were lost. "I do."

Nash dropped his chin to his chest as if praying, thinking. . .gathering himself before he lifted his gaze to hers. When he did, the boyish gleam was absent from his eyes, replaced by a resolute acceptance and a hard sheen. "Very well, then I shall return you to his home straight away."

❦

"Thank you, Mrs. Simons. You have my sincerest apology for not only waking you at this hour, but for asking you to stretch the truth for me." The plump, elderly housekeeper sat across from Nash in the same carriage they had just used to convey Sophia to Pratt House.

"Stretch the truth?" she laughed. "'Twas lying, it were."

He arched a brow. "In truth, you *are* Lord Gillingham's housekeeper, and you were on holiday to visit your sister in Dunstable. And you did rescue Miss Crew from the highwayman's company and escort her to London."

She smiled. "I suppose if you put it that way, there's more truth than lies. Nevertheless, I know it were for a good cause. I'm sorry your plan didn't work."

"So am I, Mrs. Simons."

They reached the Gillingham Townhome, and two footmen sped out to care for the horses, while Nash escorted Mrs. Simons within, handing his cloak to the butler.

"I'm leaving first thing in the morning," he said to them both.

"So soon?" Mrs. Simons stared up at him. "Lord Gillingham is set to return in a fortnight, and I know he will be sorry to miss you."

"I'm afraid it can't be helped. Good night to you both."

He sped off to avoid further conversation and took the stairs two at a time, making his way to his chamber. Closing the door, he leaned back against the hard wood, staring into the darkness, wanting to shout, wanting to put his fist through the wall, wanting to leap upon a horse and gallop back to the Pratt home and steal Sophia away. Anything to ease the pain ripping his heart in two.

But none of those things would help. Sophia had made her choice. And now Nash would make his. Tomorrow, he would ride as far away from London as he could and vow to never see Miss Sophia Crew again.

Chapter Seven

Sophia sat nervously on the sofa in the Pratt drawing room, alternating between staring at the hot coals a servant was trying to coax to life in the hearth and the doorway that led to the foyer. Across from her sat Lord and Lady Henley, Edward's parents, while on either side of Sophia sat her mother and father who, by their fidgeting, seemed as nervous as she.

To say her parents had been ecstatic to see her would demean their reaction. Having been just roused from their beds, Sophia feared they would faint from the shock as they stood staring at her, mouths agape, rubbing their eyes. Then she feared for the strain on their hearts as they swallowed her up in their arms and shouted with such glee, they were instantly hushed by servants in the hallway fearing they would wake his lordship.

To say that *said* lordship and his wife were less than exuberant to see her that morning at breakfast would be a charitable description of their reaction. Of course the servants had already informed them of Sophia's late arrival the night before, so they were somewhat prepared, but their greetings of relief that she was unharmed lacked conviction in both tone and expression.

Apparently, Edward was "out on business" and had not arrived home as expected last night. Yet now as they awkwardly awaited his arrival, all Sophia could think of was Nash. The last time she'd seen him standing outside the Pratt home, he'd taken her hands in his and kissed them ever so lovingly. Then he'd simply wished her the best, told her his prayers were with her, ordered the driver to meet him down the street, and walked away. She'd stood there beside Mrs. Simmons, watching him until darkness had stolen him from sight.

She had rejected him twice now. But this time she knew in the deepest part of her heart she'd never see him again. And the thought crushed any joy she may have at her upcoming status and wealth.

Noise from the foyer brought everyone's attentions to the door, where Sophia heard the butler informing Edward his parents wished to see him in the sitting room. That declaration was soon followed by mumbling and cursing and the appearance of the man himself in the doorway. He was a mere shell of the elegantly dressed man she'd seen last night. His waistcoat was open, revealing a stained shirt; his cravat was untied and hanging about his neck; and his hair, normally perfectly styled, stuck out in a dozen angles.

He scanned the room with eyes so bloodshot, Sophia could see them from where she sat, until finally they locked upon her and a look of consternation tightened his features. He stared at her for a rather long, awkward moment before he shifted his gaze to his mother, who sighed and rose. "Edward, can you not see Miss Crew has been found? Alive and unscathed."

Edward blinked and approached Sophia. The smell of alcohol bit her nose, along with body odor and perfume. And she knew he'd spent the night with that lady.

"What happened to you?" he asked, staring at her as if she were an unwelcome apparition.

Where was the expected delight—the relief, the joy at finding her unharmed and well? Despite his philandering, she'd hoped for at least that.

She opened her mouth to respond but no words formed. Her father struggled to rise and wrapped an arm around her shoulder.

"She was taken by a highwayman as we told you, but miraculously rescued by Lord Gillingham's housekeeper, who safely escorted her home."

"Gillingham's housekeeper. . ." Seeming to wake up from a dream, Edward made a bumbling attempt to straighten his cravat.

"Pull yourself together, Edward." Lord Henley huffed in disgust as he stood and moved to the fireplace. "You bring shame to our family."

Edward pasted on a smile. "As you have informed me on multiple occasions, Father."

"He does no such thing, Robert." Lady Henley wrung her hands, her earbobs quivering. "Can you not see he's been quite distraught?" She faced her son with a look of adoration. "Mrs. Simons recognized Miss Crew at Dunstable and was able to sneak her away while the blackguard was purchasing a fresh horse."

Edward shifted his gaze to Sophia, the barest hint of affection returning to his eyes. "An incredible story, indeed. How frightened you must have been." He took her hands in his. "And you are not harmed?"

"No. Mrs. Simons found me only a few hours after the vile man stole me from my parents. But since it was late, we spent the night there and purchased fare on a mail coach in the morning."

"Mrs. Simons is such a brave woman," Sophia's mother offered. "We are indebted to her."

"Indeed." Lady Henley turned toward her husband, who was staring at the flames. "We should give her a reward."

"I'll not pay a housekeeper," he mumbled.

Edward kissed Sophia's hand. "More importantly, you are returned to me! What a fright you gave us all. I've been overwrought, as you can see." He gestured to his disheveled attire.

Yes, she could. And her disdain for him rose in light of his lies. How easy it seemed for him to speak such untruths, how simple a thing to hold her hands and kiss them affectionately when those same lips had been on another woman's only hours earlier.

"However, I must beg your forgiveness," he said. "I have been away on urgent family business and must rest. We shall talk later. And mother, we should notify our guests that the engagement party is to commence as planned." Then he staggered out the door and up the stairs, rubbing his head as if seeing her again pained him greatly.

∽⥲∾

"They have certainly not made us feel welcome," Sophia's mother exclaimed as she walked beside Sophia and her father down the wide dirt paths of Hyde Park. The Pratts had generously given them the use of a barouche and footman for a drive through the city, and being the country folk they were, they'd ended up at the biggest park in London.

"Come now, my love," her father said. "They've been most courteous, attending to our every comfort."

"Comfort, yes, but welcome? I have felt merely tolerated, not valued as soon-to-be relations. And other than alerting the constable and sending a few servants out to search, they did nothing to find you, Sophia."

Sophia tried to hide her shock and the pain that followed.

"And Edward," her mother continued, "what a disgrace he was this morning."

"I quite agree," her father answered with a sigh. "How hard that must have been for you, pumpkin." He squeezed Sophia's hand as it rested in the crook of his elbow.

Two gentlemen atop horses passed on their left, tipping their hats at Sophia.

"Perhaps 'twas his anguish over my safety that drove him to his cups." Sophia knew if she told her parents the truth, they would insist she call off the engagement and return home at once.

Her mother's sudden cough only confirmed Sophia's decision.

"Perhaps we should sit," her father offered.

"Not yet—" More coughing prevented further speech until she collected herself. "It is such a lovely park. Why, look at all the dazzling couples strolling arm in arm, the gentlemen atop high-bred horses, and the fine carriages. . . . I never thought to see such opulence. Yet here I am walking among the ton, as if we were one of them."

Indeed. Sophia had never seen such fine walking gowns nor such rich suits on the men—all Mechlin ruffles and silk—red-heeled shoes, white gloves, gold-headed canes, and an assortment of other accessories.

This would be her life after Friday's ceremony—driven about in fancy carriages, wearing fine clothes, greeted as if she were highborn instead of baseborn. Yet more than that, it pleased her immensely to see her mother happy.

Still, the coughing continued, and soon her father led them off the path to sit on a bench before a pond. Reaching into his waistcoat, he handed Sophia's mother her medicine, and thankfully after a few sips and deep breaths, she calmed and sat back.

"Pumpkin," Sophia's father began, lined face full of concern. "I beg your patience, but I must ask you yet again, are you sure you wish to marry Edward?"

Sophia flattened her lips and stared at the pond, glistening like glass on a rare sunny day. Two geese skated across it, squawking and lurching at each other. "Why do you keep asking me that, Papa?"

"After meeting his parents and witnessing Edward's treatment of you, I cannot in good conscience proceed unless I am convinced of your happiness."

Sophia attempted a reassuring smile. "Do not fear for me, Papa. Edward was not himself. He was merely overcome with grief and then shocked at seeing me safe. Can you blame him?"

Her father growled as if he could. "Very well."

Her mother squeezed Sophia's hand. "The engagement party promises to be such a delightful affair. I am very excited to meet some of London society."

"Indeed, Mother, and they will adore you. But you must rest and get well."

Conversation drifted off as her parents held hands and gazed over the beautiful scenery. But Sophia could find no rest. The *clip-clop* of horses and hushed conversations kept luring her to study each carriage, each horse, and each passing group of people, looking for Nash.

But he wasn't there. He was long gone.

Forever.

Sophia didn't see Edward all day. Apparently from the hushed whispers of the staff, the youngest son of Lord Henley often slept long into the afternoon after a night about the town. She accidentally ran into the eldest son, Richard, when she entered the library for a book to read. Tall, thinner, and far more serious than his brother, he merely smiled, inquired as to her health, expressed relief over her safety, and promptly left. Edward had often confessed to her how much he hated his brother, how conceited he was, and how he had fooled his parents into believing he was competent when, in fact, he was naught but a wastrel who would devour the Henley estate after his parents died. Yet the few times she'd conversed with Richard provided Sophia no proof of such a claim.

Sighing, she took a candle and searched the shelves for a book to occupy her time until dinner. Darkness had stolen the rare sunny day and had cast a cloud of gloom over her as well.

Picking up a book, she absently sifted through the pages, trying to keep her mind off Edward, her wedding, and especially Nash. Voices drifted her way, at first muffled but then stern and growing louder. Replacing the book, she set down the candle, slipped into the hall, and followed the sounds to the back of the house and Lord Henley's study. The door was shut, but the voices of his lordship and Edward were quite clear. She dove into the shadows of a dark corner.

"Why do you insist on marrying the little strumpet? Especially now, that she is no doubt sullied. Are you aware of the rumors propagating around town about her so-called abduction?"

"Does it displease you, Father, to have her reputation defiled?"

"Dash it! Of course. Our name is everything. It's reprehensible enough that she is a poor farmer's daughter, now we discover her wanton."

Sophia's breath caught in her throat as anger heated her.

"Which only makes my desire to marry her all the stronger."

"You defy me on purpose! Why are you so intent on ruining this family?"

"Because you have defied me my entire life, Father. You favor Richard. You always have. Perfect, obedient Richard. All your praise goes to him."

"I praise Richard because he isn't an implacable tosspot like you. He is respectable and honorable, and worthy of his inheritance. As for you, you could have joined the church, been appointed a commission in the navy—made a life for yourself, instead of wasting it away on women and cards."

"Didn't you tell me to find something I'm good at?" Edward quipped in return.

"As you have more than proven by your shameless parties and gambling debts. I should cast you from this house, disown and disgrace you."

"But you won't because of Mother. She has always been my advocate."

Silence ensued, broken by the loud crash of broken glass. "Do not try me, you useless sot. One of these days I may not give a care to your mother's weak heart."

Sophia's own heart was beating so fast, she was sure everyone in the house could hear it. Despite his philandering, Sophia had held onto the hope that Edward loved her in his own way. But now. . .now it was clear he was using her as revenge against his father.

Just like Nash had said.

The door opened, and she melted into the shadows as Edward stomped out and headed upstairs, cursing under his breath.

⟪∾⟫

Begging off from supper with the excuse of not feeling well, Sophia paced her chamber. Her parents had checked on her before retiring, and a chambermaid had stoked the fire and turned down her bed, but Sophia couldn't sleep. Tomorrow was her engagement party, and two days later she would be married. These should be the happiest days of her life, but instead, she felt as though she were attending a funeral—her own.

What should she do? She gripped the window ledge and stared into a blackness so thick, barely the twinkle of street lamps could penetrate it. In light of Edward's character—and perhaps with a bit owed to Nash's influence—the allure of title and status had lost its appeal. But the money. . .oh, how she needed the money to save her parents. Even now, through the thick walls, she could hear her mother coughing in the chamber beside hers and her father's gentle reassurance that all would be well.

But that would only be true if Sophia married Edward. Pushing from the window, she took up a pace before the fireplace. Nash had told her to trust God, that God loved her, that He always answered prayers but in His own way and time. Had Sophia's anxiety over money and her parents caused her not to hear from God? Caused her to rush into solving her own problem her way? Perhaps it was her lifelong yearning to become part of the aristocracy, along with the need for money, that had blinded her to the right path. But what was the right path?

Sophia did something she hadn't done in a long while. She got on her knees, bowed her head, and prayed.

"Father in heaven, please help me. I'm sorry if I didn't wait for Your answer. I'm sorry if I didn't believe You cared. I need You now. Please tell me what to do."

Moments passed with nothing but the crackle of flame and whistle of wind against the window. Still she waited, settling her mind and heart, remembering Nash's words about mud huts and sandcastles. *God, if You're there, answer me.*

A warm breeze stirred her hair, easing one strand across her face. Wiping it aside, she opened her eyes, seeking the source. But the window was shut. Warmth flooded her, not a natural warmth, but one that grew from the inside out, as if someone had placed a hot coal in her spirit.

"God?" She bowed her head again, sensing a presence—a holy presence. So holy, so pure, she fell with her face to the ground and was instantly aware of all her failings, her mistakes, her selfishness, and her lies. "I'm so sorry, Lord. I'm so sorry." She was all darkness in the presence of pure light. And pure love. Overwhelming love poured over her, crystalline water washing away the dirt in her soul. And still she sobbed.

A hand touched her shoulder. *Trust me, Daughter.*

Rising to sit, she wiped the tears from her face and glanced around the room. How could she trust someone she couldn't see, couldn't hear? Yet. . .she *could* hear Him, sense Him.

"Father, tell me what to do, and I'll do it. No matter the cost, I want to trust You. Help me to trust You."

There was no answer, at least none she could sense. But there was peace, incredible peace the likes of which she'd never felt before.

Chapter Eight

Sophia took her position beside Edward in the foyer as the first guests arrived.

"Where have you been all day?" she asked him, sounding more like a nagging wife than a blushing bride.

He cast her a quick glance as he greeted Lord and Lady Ashford and smiled, that familiar twinkle returning to his eyes at the sight of her.

Sophia curtseyed and greeted the earl and countess of Ashford and thanked them for their congratulations.

"You look lovely tonight, Sophia." Edward winked at her before turning to greet the next guests.

She ran her hands over her pink gown, embroidered with red roses across the neckline and hem and overlaid with a silk netting. She'd been fitted for the gown two months ago on her prior visit to London, and in all the angst had forgotten how beautiful it was until a servant delivered it, along with her wedding dress, that morning. She hadn't opened the latter. She couldn't. If she took it out of the package, her future would become all too real. In truth, she hadn't yet decided what to do. She wanted out of this marriage more than anything. She wanted to trust God, but every time she gazed at her father's withering body and her mother's weakening condition, fear consumed her.

At the very least, she had hoped to spend time with Edward, searching for a glimmer of the man she once thought he was, some speck of decency, some sign from God that would give her hope. But he'd been absent all day.

She had not sought out his parents either, for she could still feel the sting of Lord Henley's harsh words. In fact, she could hardly look at him now as he stood at the front of the receiving line, greeting his guests warmly as if his son weren't marrying a "strumpet."

Judging by the cold reception she received from most of the guests, she assumed they agreed with his assessment. Some gave polite smiles, some barely looked at her, and others she heard whispering as they walked away.

"Never fear, my dear, they will soon fall madly in love with you as I have." Edward faced her when they were done and kissed her gloved hands. "Do forgive me, but I must speak to Lord Gerham on an important matter. I shall return shortly, for we must be the first couple to dance." And off he sauntered, leaving her alone once again.

Sophia sought out her parents and found them sitting in the corner of the grand reception room. Her mother looked stunning in her French white cotton gown with blue silk sash, and her father appeared the dapper gentleman in his suit of fine broadcloth. Yet they sat alone, being ignored by the same ton with which her mother was so enamored. Regardless, her mother's eyes were aglow as she gazed over the room at the people laughing and chatting in their elegant attire.

"Oh, dear, what a marvelous party." She reached out to Sophia from her chair.

Her father's smile was tight.

"Have you had refreshments yet?" Sophia asked. "I hear the sweetcakes and punch are very good."

"Not yet, dear, my stomach is all aflutter with the excitement."

"Then allow me to introduce you around." Her ire pricked, Sophia had not a care what these people thought about her, but she'd not let them dismiss her parents. She only hoped she remembered some of their names.

As it turned out, she did. And quite well. Her mother was aghast, meeting an earl, a duke, and a marquis. Her father behaved with more dignity than many present, and she admired him all the more for his lack of intimidation regarding title or wealth. Everyone was polite enough, though after a few minutes, conversation lagged, and Sophia ushered her parents on. After several introductions, her father stayed her with a touch to her arm.

"Pumpkin, I believe your mother and I will have those refreshments now. Do not worry for us. This is your night, and you should be with Edward."

"He's busy, Papa," she said, bitterly, just as she saw the man himself strolling toward her from across the room. He *was* handsome, if she admitted it, in a very polished sort of way, and the way he looked at her now reminded her of the first time they'd met—he on horseback, riding through the country, and she on foot, picking flowers and enjoying the scenery.

He stopped before her and took her hand. The sting of alcohol wafted over her like a foul breeze. "May I have this dance?" His grin was boyish and charming, and she smiled her acquiescence as he led her through a crush of people into the ballroom.

Guests parted the way and stared at them as they passed, women whispering behind fans, while some of the men eyed her in a most uncomfortable way. Mercy, but her pigs had more manners than most of London society. Shaking off the thought, she entered the ballroom and drew in a breath at the magnificent decorations. Garlands of ribbons and pearls circled the room while sparkling light from chandeliers reflected off a wall of mirrors to her left and bounced off a marble floor so polished she could see herself.

Edward led her into the center of the room, and she felt like a princess for the first time in her life, escorted by her prince. But when they stopped and she turned to face him, she realized Edward was not her prince. This man was an imposter, and the thought made her sick to her stomach. He bowed, and for a moment, she glanced at the door, longing to make her escape. But then she saw her parents standing on the edge of the crowd, smiling at her.

Other couples joined them in a circle and the orchestra began the first quadrille. The good thing about a quadrille was that Sophia kept switching partners, hence she could avoid intimate touch or conversation with Edward. Even so, her thoughts filled with memories of the last time she danced—with Nash—and she felt a smile form on her lips. But when she glanced up, it was Edward not Nash, who stood beside her.

After two sets, he led her from the floor and escorted her through the crush of joyful guests, stopping to converse with several of his friends. Along the way, he grabbed drink after drink from passing trays and downed the liquor as if it was lemonade.

"Are you not the least bit curious as to my ordeal, Edward?" she asked at an unusual moment alone. "I would think being kidnapped by a highwayman is not the sort of thing that happens every day."

Edward patted her hand. "It only matters you are safe now. I have no wish to bring back memories that would cause you alarm. You really should try a glass of brandy, Sophia. It will loosen your nerves."

"I prefer to keep my wits about me."

He grinned. "I find it rather increases mine."

She wanted to say that evidence was to the contrary, but she kept her mouth shut.

Placing yet another empty glass on a servant's passing tray, he led her down a hall toward the back of the house. Before she could ask him where they were going, he halted, slipped into the shadows, and pulled her toward him. "I am mad for you, Sophia. I always have been. Perhaps, a kiss for your fiancé? Something to ease my pain?"

The stench of brandy swirled over her, and she turned her face away just as he lowered his lips toward hers. "Let us not spoil our wedding night, Edward." She pushed from him, but his wet lips struck her cheek.

"It's just a kiss, Sophia. And we are as good as married," he breathed out in a husky voice as he pinned her against the wall and slobbered down her neck.

"I beg you, control yourself! We should not be here alone." Sophia shoved him back, relieved when he stopped his assault. She attempted to move past him, but he stood in her way.

"Forgive me, Sophia. I didn't mean. . . I'm sorry. I'm merely anxious for you to become my wife."

Was that true contrition in his eyes or merely the haze of alcohol?

She released a sigh and made one last appeal. "Tell me you love me, Edward. Tell me we will be happy." *Tell me you didn't mean what you said to your father.*

"Of course, Sophia. You are my special treasure." He brushed a thumb down her cheek as was his way. The gesture had always delighted her, but this time, it left her cold. "Forgive me for not spending more time with you, but we shall soon have all the time in the world."

He straightened his cravat, held out his elbow, and led her back to the reception room. Lifting another drink from a passing tray, he sipped it and glanced over the crowd, his gaze latching upon a comely lady, smiling at him from behind her fan. "If you'll excuse me, my dear. I see someone I must speak with on a personal matter. I'll rejoin you for the toast before dinner."

Sophia merely curtseyed and watched him as he pushed through the throng, returning greetings from those who hailed him. She wanted to cry, to curl in a ball and sob, to run as far away as she could. Instead she retreated to a chair against the wall and prayed.

In all her confusion, in all her sorrow, and, she supposed, in the final desperation of her mind, she heard someone whistling "Ward the Pirate." Above the music and din of the crowd, the tune flowed like sweet nectar, stirring her soul and bringing a smile to her lips. One scan of the guests told her she was losing what remained of her sanity. Before the last shred of it escaped her, she must admit the truth.

She could not go through with this marriage.

Everything within her shouted warning after warning. She had hoped God would give her a sign tonight, some indication that Edward loved her and that she was doing the right thing. But now she knew without a doubt, it was wrong to marry such a man, no matter the reason. Clasping her hands in her lap, she closed her eyes and whispered a prayer. "Father, I'm trusting You to watch over my family, to provide for us and protect us like Nash said You would, like Your Word says You will."

That same sense of peace she'd felt in her chamber dropped over her like the sudden appearance of the sun from behind a cloud, scattering the cold darkness and filling her soul with hope.

Feeling as if a massive burden had been lifted, Sophia Crew rose and started across the room, her head held high, meeting the gaze of all. She would find her parents and spend the remainder of the party with them, then retire early. In the morning, she would inform Edward of her decision and then somehow hire a coach to return her and her parents to their farm in Hertfordshire. A tremble ran through her, and she took a deep breath. *I trust You, Father. Help me to trust You.*

That's when she saw him.

Nash Barrett standing at the doorway, wearing a black satin suit that made him look like a prince. His sun-bronzed hair was pulled behind him, his jaw stiff but clean-shaven, and the look on his face as he surveyed the crowd was one of desperation.

She must be seeing things, for why would he be here? No one without an invitation was allowed entrance, and surely Lord and Lady Henley wouldn't invite a mere sailor to their son's engagement party.

Yet there he stood. His eyes finally found hers, and at that moment, it was as if no one else existed. The music and chatter faded, the people blurred, and all that mattered was Nash standing there, staring at her as if he had found buried treasure.

He was here!

Smiling, he walked toward her, his eyes never leaving hers. Her heart nearly burst through her chest. Her knees became liquid. Yet before she could falter, he gripped her arm and steadied her.

"May I speak with you alone, Miss Crew?"

That voice, like thunderous waves crashing on shore.

Could he speak to her? Was he kidding? She could spend a lifetime listening to the love in that voice.

"In private?" he pressed.

Nodding, she retreated to the hallway and stopped in an alcove beneath the stairway.

"Why are you here? How are you here?"

"I was halfway to Newbury. . ." His jaw stiffened and he looked down, shaking his head before he faced her again. "But I forgot to ask you something. Something I must ask you or I shall ever live to regret it."

She could only stare up at him, wondering what was so important that he would sneak into her engagement party and risk being tossed out.

Taking both her hands, he knelt on the marble floor and gazed up at her. "Sophie, I know you need money for your family, but I'm asking you one last time to trust God. To trust God and marry me. Will you marry this poor sailor?"

Tears instantly blurred the vision of him and spilled from her eyes. Her thoughts whirled nonsensically, her breath halted, but all she could feel was the joy filling her heart.

Frowning, he rose. "Forgive me. I shouldn't have asked such a question. And at your engagement party no less. I am a fool."

Sophia found her voice and mumbled out, "Yes."

He nodded and turned to leave. "I will bother you no longer."

She tugged on his arm more forcibly than she intended, spinning him around to face her. "I mean yes, I *will* marry you." She smiled.

His brows shot up as a wide grin spread over his handsome face. "You will?"

She nodded, giddy with joy.

Nash hoisted her in his arms and spun her around, his laughter joining hers.

"What is the meaning of this?" Edward's slurred shout echoed off the high ceilings.

Releasing Sophia, Nash turned to face him, taking a position in front of her.

"Lord Nor—"

"Miss Crew and I are old friends, Mr. Pratt." Nash interrupted him.

"Friends is it?" His shout lured a crowd from the reception room, Sophia's father one of them. "Friends don't embrace other men's fiancées!" He approached, eyes narrowed, expression twisted in rage.

Sophia sidestepped Nash. "Edward, I'm sorry. I cannot marry you. I pray you forgive me and we can part amicably." She wanted to tell him she knew about the other women, the gambling and drinking, but she would not disgrace him in front of his friends.

"Whore! Common, baseborn strumpet! I didn't want to believe the rumors." He lifted his chin and took up a regal stance. "I stood up for you, even against good opinion and advice, but you have made me a fool. Run back to your farm and wallow in the muck with your pigs where you belong." Spit flew from his mouth like venom.

Nash fisted his hand and slugged Edward across the jaw. Arms flailing, the man toppled backward and fell to the ground in a heap and a curse.

"It's about time." Sophia heard her father say.

Chapter Nine

"Stop the carriage." Nash yelled out the window to the driver.

"Why are we stopping?" Sophia sat beside him and glanced at her parents, who were perched across from them. The two had not stopped smiling at Nash since early that day when he'd ushered them into the hired coach and then joined them and Sophia on their way home.

"I have something I want to show you." He smiled as the carriage slowed, pulled to the side of the road, and stopped.

She didn't care what he had to show her as long as he never left her side. Of course her parents were thrilled to see Nash again after all these years and even more thrilled that Sophia and he were to be married. Even though they'd remain poor, and even though they'd not be able to pay for proper medical care for her mother, they both seemed relieved to be free of the Pratts and even happier to see Sophia beside herself with joy.

After the incident with Edward—which still made Sophia smile—Lord and Lady Henley dismissed the guests and ordered Sophia and her parents to leave their home immediately. Nash was more than happy to receive them at the Gillingham house, where he settled them comfortably in chambers for the night.

Sophia's father had scolded her vehemently for keeping the truth about Edward from him. In light of Edward's character, even her mother had cast aside her dreams of high society more quickly than Sophia would have expected.

"Do you think we wish to see you miserable on our account? I'd rather die!" her mother had said.

Now all Sophia could think about was spending the rest of her life with Nash. It would be a life without parties or fancy clothes and carriages, a life without servants, a life of hard work and simplicity. But so had her parents' lives been, yet here they were, still looking at each other as if they were recently wed.

Sophia had tried to fulfill the desires of her heart her own way. She had not believed God had her greatest good in mind. So she had settled for living in a mud shack when a castle made of gold stood just behind her. She knew now that God's plans were always the best, if she would just seek Him with all her heart and believe. Yes, God would take care of them. And maybe He would even heal her mother. All things were possible with Him.

Nash opened the door, hopped out, then reached for her hand.

"I'll return her in a moment, I promise." He smiled at her parents.

"What on earth are you up to?" Sophia said as she wove her arm through Nash's.

He only smiled as he pushed aside branches and leaves and led her through a copse of trees and up a small hill. Halting at the top, he drew a deep breath and glanced over the scenery.

Below them, grass rolled over hills in waves of green and gold, while a river snaked a sparkling blue trail between hills, forests, and farmland. Sheep, horses, and cows appeared as mere dots scattered across the scene. A little village sat comfortably on a stretch of flat land to her right. And far in the distance, a stately castle perched on a hill, its spires and pinnacles reaching into the blue sky.

"It's beautiful."

"Lord Northum's estate. Everything you see—the farmland, the village, the forests—all belong to him."

"He is truly blessed, this Lord Northum. I hope he appreciates it."

"He does."

Shielding her eyes from the sun, she faced him. "And how would you know such a thing?"

Taking both her hands in his, he rubbed them gently. An unusual sparkle lit his blue eyes, playful yet excited. His dimple appeared.

"Because Sophia, I *am* Viscount Northum."

She laughed. She didn't mean to mock him, but surely he was joking. She stared at him. Wasn't he? Yet instead of joining in her laughter, he just stood there smiling at her.

Nash had always loved to tease her, but never in a cruel way. She glanced at the land again then back at him, confused. "Why are you doing this?"

"Doing what?"

"Teasing me so."

"I am not teasing you, Sophie. Lord Northum recently died with no heir. Having no other sons and no brothers, the title and estate would then go to his cousin, but the poor man is also dead, as is his first son, who died without an heir. As it turns out, I'm a distant relation to the cousin's second son. Or at least that's what I'm told." He shook his head. "In truth, I didn't believe it either when the barrister came to my door."

His words rampaged through her mind, trampling all reason. The sky spun, and she wobbled.

"Forgive me, I didn't mean to shock you so." He led her to sit on a boulder then knelt beside her and eased a lock of hair from her face.

"How long have you known?" she asked.

"I took over the estate six months ago."

She could only stare at him, her mind recalling every detail of the past week. "That's how you could afford a coach. . .and the clothing, the invitations. And the Gillingham townhome. . .yours?"

"That is, indeed, my friend, Garret Hamrick, Lord Gillingham's house."

"And you are a viscount?" She stared at him, mouth agape.

He closed it with a finger. "Hard to believe."

She giggled and shook her head. "Heaven's mercy, your rank is higher than Edward's!"

"Heaven's mercy, indeed."

"You actually *were* invited to my engagement party."

He smiled sheepishly. "I've had the misfortune of dealing with Edward in the past."

"Why didn't you tell me? All this time we were together and you said not a word."

He took her hand and kissed it. "I wanted you to trust God first. I wanted you—no, after your rejection six years ago—I *needed* you to choose me over wealth and status."

She looked down. "You always were the wise one."

"Finally, you admit it." He teased.

"I will spend my life admitting it. And loving you, viscount or not." She cupped his jaw. "I have always loved you, Nash."

"I know."

She laughed. "Ah, your ego, sir."

He raised a teasing brow. "The one you attempted to deflate by beating me on horseback?"

"Indeed. And, if you recall, *Lord Northum*, I nearly won two of those races."

"*Nearly*, being the important word."

"In case you haven't noticed, I am no longer a little girl."

"Indeed, I have taken note of that." The twinkle in his eye warmed her as he leaned forward and placed his lips on hers.

Sweet madness! Her body trembled at his touch. Warmth flooded her, inciting a need for him, a yearning she did not realize she possessed. He tasted of spice and coffee as he lifted her to her feet and drew her close, caressing her with his lips, driving her mad with his touch.

Finally, he pushed back and leaned his forehead against hers.

"We should leave," she breathed out.

"I reluctantly agree." He kissed her forehead and withdrew.

Patting her hair in place, she waited for her heart to settle. "I can't wait to tell my parents."

"Race you to the carriage?" He winked.

"In my gown? Are you mad?"

"Quite possibly." He grinned and took off running.

Grabbing her skirts, Sophia dashed after him, her heart overflowing with joy at the thought of spending her life loving this man. But most of all she thanked God for pulling her out of the mud and ushering her into a castle.

Award-winning and best-selling author **MaryLu Tyndall** describes herself as an introvert, tall ship enthusiast, friend of pirates and mermaids, control freak, history lover, hopeless romantic, and a sword wielding, princess-warrior for the King of Kings. Her books are filled with adventure and romance guaranteed to touch your heart. Her hope is that readers will not only be entertained but will be brought closer to the Creator who loves them beyond measure. In a culture that accepts the occult, wizards, zombies, and vampires without batting an eye, MaryLu hopes to show the awesome present and powerful acts of God in a dying world. She has published over twenty novels and currently lives in California with her husband, six kids, three grandkids, and various stray cats. Visit MaryLu's website at www.marylutyndall.com.

Jamie Ever After

by Erica Vetsch

Dedication

For my daughter, Heather, I hope we get to explore London together someday.
For my son, James, who always challenges me to see things differently.
And to my husband, Peter, the hero of my story. Every. Single. Day. I love you all!

Chapter One

March 1813
London

W e lived through it, and that's about all I can say to recommend the experience." Lady Jamie Everard leaned on the oars, lifting them from the water. One of the oarlocks was loose, making rowing difficult. She really should have insisted on a better watercraft than the one the boatman had rented to her. "All I could think about was not stepping on my train as I backed away, and that I was glad that stomachers have now gone out of fashion because mine was cutting off all my air."

Polly Crofton lay back on the pillows in the bow of the rickety rowboat, giggling. "All I could think about was not sounding daft if the queen should speak to me. I'm glad she didn't, though I know it's supposed to be a great honor. What did she say to you? I meant to ask yesterday, but your Aunt Minty whisked you away so quickly, I didn't have time."

"Her Majesty was quite nice, although I'm sure she could hear my knees knocking. My mother was one of her ladies-in-waiting once upon a time, and the queen said she remembered her fondly and hoped I would have a successful season."

"Once word gets out that you received a personal comment from the queen, your season is assured to be a success. You'll have a full dance card and visitors and flowers delivered every day and rides in Hyde Park and evenings at Vauxhall Gardens and all the things we couldn't ever do before because we hadn't been brought out yet." Polly pretended to swoon. "You might even be dubbed 'The Incomparable' this year."

Jamie wrinkled her nose. The season was finally upon them. Or it would be this evening when they were formally "brought out" at their debut ball. Anticipation scampered across her skin. The ball was being held at Crofton House, the London home of Polly's brother, William Crofton, the Earl of Beckenham.

Her heart fluttered a bit faster. She would see him tonight. Would he notice her? Well, of course he would notice her. He was the host of the party, and she was a guest of honor, a debutante being brought out the same evening as his sister. But would he really *notice* her?

"I'm glad you could sneak out of the house this morning for one last jaunt." Jamie took a lazy pull on the oars, frowning as the left one slipped in the loose oarlock. "This is our final fling before we're ladies of the *ton*." She put on her most plummy accent. "I imagine by next week, you'll be the one besieged by suitors, my dear." She grinned at Polly. For years while they were away at boarding school, they'd dreamed and anticipated, wondered and speculated about what it would be like once they were old enough to be "brought out." So far it had involved a tedious amount of time at the dressmakers, dancing lessons, deportment classes, and being told over and over all the things one simply must *not* do.

"Sneak is exactly what I had to do. Mother would have the vapors if she knew I was out rowing on the St. James Canal instead of resting up for tonight." Polly's laugh filled the air.

"Aunt Minty won't care a bit. In fact, she might be disappointed that I didn't invite her along. But she couldn't have come anyway. She was up and away even before I was. She's interviewing new nurses for the veteran's hospital. No doubt she's also having another run-in with the hospital administration."

"Sometimes I think if your Aunt Minty had been put in charge of the war effort, she would've routed Old Boney, horse, foot, and artillery, years ago, and the war would've been over in a month."

"Even so—and I'm not saying you're wrong—hospital administrators are the bane of her existence. It seems she's always having to concoct ways to get around their petty little dictatorships to do what is best for the patients."

"I think you're brave to help her so much, going to the hospital and nursing soldiers."

Jamie liked the work, liked meeting the infantrymen, marines, sailors, and soldiers. They were so appreciative of anything she did for them. Though it broke her heart, too. War was so costly. But she'd learned a lot about herself and about medical care for invalids. She didn't know where she would use it in her future life, but Aunt Minty always said no lesson learned was wasted and she'd just have to see what God had in store for her.

Of course, Aunt Minty and Father had gone 'round and 'round over Jamie's helping at the hospital. Father feared it would damage her chances of marrying well. After all, what gentleman wanted his wife to consort with wounded ruffians and brigands who had taken the King's shilling? Aunt Minty stood her ground—as she always did—and said a real man would want his wife to help those less fortunate and that hospital work was both charitable and generous. Jamie could have her pick of titled gentlemen once she made her debut. It was just a matter of finding one that came up to scratch in every area—by which Aunt Minty seemed to mean a man who would let Jamie do whatever she wanted.

If such a creature existed. Would such charitable work as volunteering at a soldier's hospital matter to someone like. . .say. . .The Earl of Beckenham?

Polly sat up with a start, rocking the boat. "Hey, what's this?" She lifted her hem, which was soaked, streaming water into the bottom of the boat. "Are we sinking?"

Jamie let her feet drop off the seat in front of her, and they plopped into several inches of canal water. "Oh no." While she'd been daydreaming, they'd been taking on water. The gunwales were only inches above the surface, and the boat was as far from shore as you could get on the St. James Canal.

The oars splashed into the water, and she pulled hard, bracing her feet, but feeling them slip along the bottom of the boat. The left oarlock snapped, and the oar jerked out of her hand. She tried to grab for it, but the shift in her weight sent a wave cascading over the side and into the craft, sinking it further.

"Oh, hurry!" Polly, scattering soggy pillows, began bailing water with her cupped hands.

Jamie tugged on the right oar, but the boat, already waterlogged and heavy, spun in slow circles, and before she knew it, the rowboat slipped beneath the surface of the canal. Water rose to her waist, and then her shoulders.

Polly screamed as she disappeared, thrashing and flailing, churning the water.

Aunt Minty is going to kill me. Jamie tread water, her skirts wrapping about her legs. "Polly! Stop it." A gout of water hit her in the face, toppling her straw bonnet off her head to drag by its ribbons around her neck.

More splashing and squealing from Polly.

"Reach down with your toes." Jamie's slippers just brushed the bottom of the canal, and if she tipped her head back, her face cleared the water. "It isn't that deep. Reach down."

It might not have been overly deep, but it was cold. Early spring wasn't a time to take a dip in neck-deep water. Jamie's fingers and toes began to tingle as she stretched out to grab Polly. Her friend's agitations sent water splashing over Jamie's head, plastering her hair to her face and neck.

"For mercy's sake, Polly, will you stop it?" Jamie laughed and sputtered as she gripped Polly's hand and dragged her toward the shore. "You're going to drown both of us."

Polly gasped, blinking, and stopped slapping the water. She snorted, beginning to giggle as her feet touched bottom and her head remained above the waterline. A brocade pillow floated in front of her, and she pushed it out of the way. "You look like a drowned duck."

"Ducks don't drown," Jamie shot back. "And you look no better. Hurry. I'm freezing."

They clambered up the bank. Polly staggered onto the grass and sank down. "I lost my shoes."

"Me too. The bottom was pure mud." Jamie collapsed beside Polly on the grass, shivering in the early morning breeze. "What are we going to do?" Out on the canal, the oars floated and the pillows bobbed, half submerged. Of the boat there was no sign. So much for their rental deposit. Though she would be having a few words with the boat rental man. How could he send them out in such a craft?

"Do you have your reticule? I think mine's at the bottom of the canal." Polly shoved a sodden curl off her forehead. "I can't think that a hackney cab will pick us up in this condition."

Jamie laughed through chattering teeth. "I know I wouldn't." She crossed her arms, hugging herself. "How are we going to explain this to our families? On the day of our debut, no less?"

"I'm not going to explain it." Polly shook her head, sending water droplets scattering. "I'm going to sneak back into the house and never tell a soul."

Jamie gathered her clinging, heavy skirts, wringing them out as best she could and preparing to stand. "If we're going to do that, we'd better hurry. The question is, how?"

"I have no idea." Giggles gone, Polly's brow furrowed. "William is going to kill me."

"He just might."

The masculine voice had both girls whirling around. Jamie's heart fell to her toes. William Crofton, the Earl of Beckenham, stood on the bank above them.

❦

His sister was going to be the death of him. Napoleon couldn't do it. The army surgeons didn't quite manage it, though they gave it a good effort. But Polly seemed to be doing her best to hurry him to an early grave.

William swirled off his cloak one-handed, dropped it around Polly's shoulders, and shrugged out of his morning coat. "What are you doing out here so early? And without a chaperone." He handed the garment to Polly's companion, a girl of about the same age as his sister, painfully conscious of his useless left hand without his cloak and coat to hide it. "It's a bit early in the year to be swimming, don't you think?"

Her friend wrapped his coat around her shoulders and laughed. "We were rowing on the canal. Sort of a last lark before our debut tonight."

"Rowing usually requires a boat, does it not?" He put his hand on his hip. How could she be jovial at a time like this?

"So it does," she agreed. "Our craft, however, proved to be less than seaworthy." Humor sparked in her eyes and then erupted, gleeful and unrestrained.

Polly put her hand to her mouth, stifling laughter as she clutched his cloak around her shoulders.

Her friend had dark brown, sodden rat's tails of hair hanging in her face, and her bonnet lay on the grass, a woeful heap of straw and ribbon. Polly looked no better, dripping positive streams of water onto the grass, a good foot of her hems covered in mud and muck. And yet they couldn't stop laughing.

They were both daft. If anyone saw them, they'd be the talk of the *beau monde* drawing rooms and Polly could kiss her debut season good-bye.

"Pull yourself together, Polly. We need to get you out of here before someone sees you. It's a good thing I came along." He shook his head at their heedlessness.

"How *did* you come to be here?" Polly asked, sobering.

"Beckett came to my study this morning and told me you'd snuck out early, so I headed out to fetch you home. You're a young lady now, not a hoyden. It's time you put schoolgirl pranks behind you and acted your age." He clasped Polly's elbow to hustle her up the bank.

Polly blinked. "You followed me?"

"And a good thing too. What do you think would've happened if I hadn't? How were you going to get home unseen? You're drenched, you look like you've been dragged through a knothole backwards, and your clothes are clinging to you in an unseemly way. Mother is going to be furious."

Holding Polly's elbow with his good hand meant he had to either ignore her friend or offer his damaged arm. What would she do? Would she recoil as other ladies had done? He steeled himself, still undecided, but she took the choice from him by slipping her hand through his permanently-bent left arm as if he were a whole man and they were out for a stroll.

William startled. Her touch felt strange on the old scars, sort of there but not there, though for a moment he was more aware of her fingers through the linen of his shirt sleeve than he was of anything else.

His carriage stood at the curb just up the slope. London was wide awake with carts, carriages, and cabs trundling down the streets and pedestrians already filling the sidewalks. "Hurry up. We'll talk more later." William bundled them into the safety of the closed carriage. The girls crowded into the forward-facing seat, dripping water everywhere, while William took the rear-facing one.

"Where to, my lord?" the coachman asked as he held the door.

William raised his eyebrows, glancing at the girls.

"Portman Square, if you please," Polly's friend said, smiling at the coachman as if nothing out of the ordinary had happened to her this morning.

Hmm, a lofty address. The coachman closed and fastened the door, shutting them in. The carriage rocked as he climbed aboard and lurched as the horses took off.

"You aren't going to tell Mother, are you?" Polly asked, her voice tinged with the first hint that she understood the severity of her escapade.

"Serve you right if I did, but I am well beyond the years of tattling." William rested his scarred and useless left hand in his lap and covered it with his right. Polly was well-accustomed to his appearance and never mentioned it, but he didn't know if her companion would feel compelled to comment as some people did.

Thankfully, she said nothing about his disability.

His coat nearly swallowed her. She had her head down, probably realizing the seriousness of her situation. No one must get wind of these shenanigans. Then she looked up at him from under lashes that were gathered into points by canal water.

The velvety brown of her eyes impacted his chest like a shove. His collar grew tight, and the air inside the carriage closed in. When not looking like a drowned dormouse, the girl must be more than passably pretty.

He cleared his throat. "Polly, we're forgetting our manners. Introduce me to your friend."

"Will, this is *Jamie*." Polly rolled her eyes. "Lady Jamesina Everard. Baron Everard's daughter? You've met her before. At Beckenham Hall. She came to stay for the summer when we were both fourteen. I wrote screeds about her in all my letters." Polly nudged her friend with her shoulder. "Jamie, you remember my brother? The Earl of Beckenham."

"My lord." Lady Jamesina bowed slightly and very charmingly caught her lower lip between her teeth.

William studied her for a moment. So this was the infamous Jamie? Polly's partner in crime through her boarding school days. The girl who had written sweet, funny postscripts to Polly's letters to him while he was in Spain. She had a heart-shaped face, long brown hair, a bow-shaped mouth that looked as if it smiled often. . .but it was those eyes, brown as the heart of a pansy—intelligent eyes, intriguing eyes.

He jerked his chin in acknowledgment of her greeting. If he had met her four summers ago, he didn't remember it. She would've still been in the schoolroom and he home on leave from the war. His father had spent William's entire leave urging his only son to resign his commission and return to the Beckenham estates, but William had refused, rejoining his regiment early to avoid continued confrontation.

It had been the last time William had seen his father.

Now here he was, the Earl of Beckenham, invalided home from the front, crippled, jilted, and jaded.

Polly caught Jamie's eye, lifted a hank of hair off her shoulder, and wrung it out, streaming water onto his cloak. The pair dissolved into another fit of giggles.

William felt ancient. When was the last time he had laughed like that?

Chapter Two

Villiam had heard it all so many times before, but never this frequently and with such urgency.

"It is beyond time for you to take up your responsibilities. You have a duty, both to the peerage and to your family. It is beyond time you married and set up your nursery. You need an heir. I refuse to allow the title to go to your cousin Cedric. He's a wastrel, gambler, and womanizer." Mother fanned herself with such vigor the ostrich plumes in her hair wafted. "I can't believe I had to drag you to Town. You'd spend your entire life moldering away in the country if I let you. Tonight you will begin the search for a countess, or I will do it for you."

William tried to loosen the muscles in his shoulders, both grateful for the high cravat and disgruntled by it. It hid the worst of the burn scars on his neck, but it had decidedly noose-like qualities.

"Are you listening to me?" Mother's rings caught the light as she fanned. The more agitated she became, the faster the fan fluttered.

"Guests will be arriving soon. Where's Polly?" He consulted the ormolu clock on the mantel. "The orchestra is tuning up."

Crofton House had been in an uproar for the entire two weeks since they had arrived for Polly's debut season. William could scarcely find a quiet corner in his own home these days.

"Don't try to change the subject." Mother snapped her fan shut then flicked it open and set it in motion again. "William, I know you find all this tedious, but I hope you'll put yourself out to be pleasant tonight. There will be a wonderful selection of young ladies on display who would be more than eager to be your countess. All you have to do is settle on one."

She made it sound so simple. Like walking into a haberdasher's and picking out a new shirt. The entire notion of the Marriage Mart was distasteful, but it seemed there would be no escape for him.

Deep down, he knew if he didn't have a title and money, no woman would consider marrying him. Hadn't Mirabelle said as much when she ended their engagement? Her visit stood out in his mind, one of the few sharp memories he had of the first few weeks after being invalided home. Her tears, which he sensed masked a feeling of relief. Her assurances that it was for the best. Her handing back of the engagement ring.

And now he was supposed to set about finding a new fiancée, a new bride. But what woman wanted to be tied to a cripple who had somehow died on the battlefield but survived? An empty, one-handed shell? He tucked his useless hand into his pocket and tugged at his collar with the other.

"How do I look?"

William turned toward the door, grateful for the interruption of his thoughts.

"Oh, my dear." Mother fluttered over to Polly. "You look lovely."

A burst of pride shot through William at the sight of his little sister, standing on the cusp of womanhood. She seemed quite a stranger to him, dressed all in white with high gloves and perfectly formed curls. Because she was a debutante, she wore no jewels, but she had a pretty, bright-blue ribbon threaded through her golden hair.

"Do I really look all right?"

Her eyes were big as a doe's, and her voice trembled, though with fear or excitement William couldn't tell. Was this the child who had written to him so faithfully, spilling all her girlish secrets, buoying his spirits while on campaign, regaling him with the minutia of her life that both amused and encouraged him?

"You'll do," he said, gruffly. "Though I'm wondering how long you can keep a white dress clean before you decide to climb a tree or slide down a banister." He offered his elbow, and she grinned up at him, giving him a glimpse of the old, familiar Polly.

They walked through the portrait gallery toward the ballroom at the back of the house, passing masses of flowers in tall urns and hundreds of candles in wall sconces and candelabras. William tamped down the question of how much all this was costing him. If Polly was successfully launched, that was all that mattered.

The ballroom itself, though not large, was beautifully appointed. Gilded mirrors threw back the light of the chandeliers, and the french doors stood ready to open onto the terrace should the room heat up too much. And far overhead, a frieze of cherubs and clouds and blue sky soared in diffused detail.

The butler appeared in the doorway with the first guests. "Baron Everard, Lady Araminta Everard, and Lady Jamesina Everard."

A rather short, balding man entered first, attired in breeches and tailcoat. Behind him came an older woman, resplendent in turban and jewels and peacock-blue silk.

But it was the youngest of the trio that drew William's attention. He barely recognized her as the girl he had met this morning. Her white dress seemed to glow in the candlelight, and her eyes were luminous. With a smile, she went right to Polly, holding out her gloved hands. A fan and dance card dangled from her wrist. Like Polly, she wore no jewels, but she sparkled enough without them.

William shook his head. Fanciful thoughts, and very unlike him, pragmatist that he was. He went to greet his guests.

"Everard. Lady Araminta." He nodded.

"Beckenham. Thank you for having us, for hosting Jamesina's debut." The baron held out his hand, giving William's a firm shake. "My sister and I are grateful."

Lady Araminta offered her gloved hand, looking William over from his light-brown hair to his shined boots, her brown eyes—similar in shape and color but sharper than her niece's—not missing a thing. They lingered but a moment on the hand he kept tucked into his pocket, sliding over and revealing nothing of her thoughts about his infirmity.

"My lord. A pleasure to meet you. Jamie and Polly have been such friends through the years, it seemed appropriate for them to share a 'come out.'" Gray-brown curls clustered tightly around her face, and a trio of peacock feathers stood up on the left side of her turban. "We're honored that you agreed to host us this evening."

Which was news to William. He'd agreed to no such thing. Probably because he hadn't been consulted on anything regarding tonight's festivities.

"Jamie?" Everard called his daughter. She left Polly's side and came to them. "Beckenham, may I present my daughter, Lady Jamesina. Jamie, his lordship, the Earl of Beckenham."

"My lord." Lady Jamesina put her fingers in his, sending a jolt up his arm, and executed a perfect curtsy. Her hand felt light in his, small-boned and delicate.

"Lady Jamesina." William inclined his head. "It's nice to see you under such felicitous circumstances." She little resembled the half-drowned kitten he'd rescued this morning. "I hope you're feeling well?"

Her lips twitched. "Most well, my lord, though I will admit to some butterflies." She put her hand to her midsection and bit her lower lip. She was most fetching, and he was sure the swains would cluster around her tonight. Her loveliness would be irresistible to rake, rogue, and roué alike.

Guests began arriving, and William was forced to stand in the receiving line, between his mother and Polly, accepting bows and curtsies, keeping his withered hand in his pocket, enduring for Polly's sake the looks and deliberate 'not-looks.' How many invitations had his mother issued? The line seemed to stretch forever. At this rate, there wouldn't be room enough to dance in the ballroom.

Eventually the newcomers dwindled, and William bowed to his mother and sister, prepared to excuse himself. He'd had enough of the crowds, of the young ladies with horror in their eyes when they looked at him, and of their eagle-eyed mamas with nothing more on their minds than to marry their daughters off to a title and money, regardless of their daughters' feelings on the matter. He was also weary of his own mother nudging his elbow every time an eligible woman came through the line.

The worst had been when Mirabelle—Countess Fordham now—had swept past him with a mere flick of her eyes, her hand firmly on the arm of her husband. Her smile had been bright, her laugh loud, as she greeted Polly. And William had had to stand there, the jilted suitor, and watch. His mother turned her shoulder slightly, no doubt knowing he was simmering that she had invited Mirabelle into his house. She seemed to think all that was in the past and he needed to get beyond it. As if it were that easy.

He didn't want Mirabelle back. She'd shown her true colors. But he did want his life back, his life before his injuries.

What William needed was some solitude and fresh air. What he wanted was to escape to Beckenham Hall, to his dogs, his horses, and his land, where it was easier to forget.

"Where do you think you're going?" Mother stood before him now, tapping his chest with her folded fan. Suddenly, he felt much as he had when his governess had caught him sneaking out to the stables in his Sunday clothes.

But he was a grown man, not a boy in short pants. "To tell the footmen to open the french doors. It's stifling in here."

"You're expected to lead Polly out in the first dance."

William closed his eyes, feeling his jaw tense. "Mother, I won't be dancing, and you know very well why not. I arranged for Cousin Cedric to do the honors. He's the next closest male relative, and he enjoys dancing."

"How do you intend to find a bride if you don't ask anyone to dance?" Exasperation laced her tone, and she tossed a glance at the cherubs overhead.

"I will accomplish the task in my own way and in my own time." He bowed. "If you'll excuse me. I'll have a word with the footmen. I'm sure you'll want to be waiting when Polly's dance is over."

Mother stepped aside, and William threaded his way through the onlookers around the perimeter of the room. He caught a glimpse of Lady Jamie and her father and Polly and Cedric twirling and circling on the polished floor. How many times had Polly written to him bemoaning the dance lessons and her "pinch-faced, cranky dance master"? Still, it appeared the lessons had paid off.

Cedric led Polly with all the confidence of Beau Brummell, but he kept turning his head to watch Jamie as she danced with her father. Speaking of rogues and roués. Cedric would bear watching. He'd always put it about that he intended to marry money, but he never minded dallying with beauty. And Jamie was a rare beauty.

William once had been a better than fair dancer himself. And hadn't he enjoyed the attention his red coat and gold braid had garnered from the young ladies? Now he wished he could fade into the background. When a footman opened the nearest french door, William availed himself of the escape route and stepped out onto the terrace.

If his mother had her way, he'd most likely met his bride somewhere in the receiving line tonight. The thought made him shudder.

⚬≪≫⚬

Jamie curtsied to her father as they finished her first official dance at a society event. He tucked her hand into his elbow and walked to where Aunt Minty waited.

"That was nicely done, my dear." Aunt Minty raised her lorgnette and surveyed the room. "Ah, here they come." Party guests, most of them male, clustered around.

After that, it was a whirl of introductions, new dancing partners, and trying to make intelligent conversation while not tripping up on the steps. And through it all, searching the room for the Earl of Beckenham while trying not to appear to do so.

By the end of the second set, disappointment weighed upon Jamie, and it was difficult to maintain her smile. Her partner, Cedric Crofton, returned her to Aunt Minty's side with a bow and a request to be allowed to call upon her sometime. . .perhaps tomorrow?

"That is most kind," Aunt Minty answered for her. "We'll be making calls ourselves tomorrow afternoon, but perhaps our paths will cross."

"I shall endeavor to make it so." He smiled and bowed and backed away. Feathers of unease traipsed across Jamie's skin. He was altogether too bold, too knowing, too worldly and urbane for her taste.

"We're making calls tomorrow?" Jamie asked.

"Of course. The Countess of Beckenham has asked us to call, and Polly will be eager to talk over tonight's ball. Anyway"—Aunt Minty smiled—"it wouldn't do to appear too eager for gentlemen callers. I imagine you'll have your share of nosegays and bouquets delivered tomorrow as it is."

The fourth set was a waltz, and because Jamesina hadn't been given permission from the patronesses of Almack's yet to perform such an intimate dance, she wasn't allowed to participate. Aunt Minty greeted an old friend and fell into animated conversation, and Jamie took the chance to escape the ballroom for the fresh air of the terrace. It really wasn't the done thing, to stroll unchaperoned, but the party had been deemed a "squeeze," and the packed room was stifling.

Standing on the terrace, she took a deep breath of night air. Along the perimeter, lanterns had been lit, and several couples strolled. Jamie studied the night sky, the stars barely visible here in the city. At Chelmsley, the boarding school she and Polly had attended near Bath, the stars had been so bright, it had always seemed to Jamie she could reach up and pluck one from the velvet backdrop.

She missed Chelmsley, the open sky and the rhythm of the waves, and the freedom. Hard to reconcile freedom with boarding school, but when compared to the restrictions of the ton, boarding school was a lark. Jamie felt as if she walked on soap bubbles, fearing she would do or say something that would violate one of the screeds of unwritten rules. And she hadn't the confidence of Aunt Minty to do as she pleased and not worry about the rules.

So far, her debut had been. . .disappointing. And she had no one but herself to blame. In her girlish fantasies—which she must get over as soon as possible—she'd imagined William, the host of tonight's event, would be waiting to escort her onto the dance floor for the second set. It would have been customary. But he hadn't danced at all, not even with Polly. Instead, their cousin had done the honors.

Jamie wrinkled her nose. Cedric. He had squeezed her hand much too tightly, staring boldly into her face, letting his gaze wander over her in a much too familiar way. Polly said he was brazen, and she hadn't been exaggerating.

"Lady Jamesina, shouldn't you be dancing?"

Her heart jerked, and she turned in surprise. "You startled me." She toyed with her fan. "I have not yet been given permission to waltz, my lord, so I thought I would take advantage of the chance to get some fresh air. It's a bit crowded in there."

William leaned against the side of the house where the stone railing joined the wall. His face was half in shadow. "I found it the same. No doubt my mother will be in raptures at the success of her evening. Are you enjoying yourself?"

"Yes, thank you." She bit her lip, but when she realized it, she forced herself to stop. "Are you?"

He raised one eyebrow. "I could lie and say yes." Pushing himself off the wall, he strolled over to her. "But it would be just that, a lie."

"Where would you rather be?"

"With my regiment." The answer came quickly, as if his regiment had already been on his mind. "But, barring that, at Beckenham Hall."

"Your estate in Kent?" She knew the location. After all, some of her fondest memories were of that summer at Beckenham Hall. . .the first time she had met William.

"Yes, on the coast between Herne Bay and Margate."

"The house is lovely, and if I remember correctly, from the upper floors you can see the sea. I love the seaside, the waves, the blue, the. . .I don't know. . .the vastness? I think to myself, 'How immense the sea is, and how small I am, and yet, God is bigger than the sea, and He still sees me.'" She laughed. "I suppose that sounds silly. I can't explain it."

"I thought you explained it rather well." William cocked his head. "The music is finishing. We should both return before we're missed."

The other guests walking the terrace were heading inside, and William offered his right arm. Jamie placed her hand on his sleeve, feeling the warmth through her glove and all the way up her arm.

They were halfway across the terrace when they met a couple. Did she imagine it, or did William's arm tense under her fingers?

"William, so nice to see you," the blond woman exclaimed. She introduced the spare, pale man as Earl Fordham, and waited, brows raised expectantly.

"Countess, Fordham, may I present Lady Jamesina Everard?"

To Jamie his voice sounded tight, and to her surprise, he squeezed her hand against his side and gave her a warm. . .affectionate?. . .smile. His eyes looked deeply into hers, and her heart hastened its beat. She answered his smile with one of her own.

"I'd best get you back inside, my dear."

My dear? What was going on here? He inclined his head to the beautiful countess and escorted Jamie in the direction of the ballroom.

Aunt Minty met them at the door. "Where have you been, child?" Her cheeks were flushed, and she grasped Jamie's arm. "It isn't done to wander off, especially not at your debut." She stopped. "Oh, she was with you, my lord."

"Not for long, I assure you, Lady Araminta." William—in her heart, Jamie always thought of him as William, not the Earl of Beckenham—stepped back with a slight bow. "I shall tender her into your care."

He was leaving. Jamie's spirits fell. It had been so nice to finally talk to him, and she hadn't even remembered to thank him for his rescue of the morning. And she was still puzzled by what had just happened on the terrace. The tension between him and the Fordhams had been palpable.

"My lord." Aunt Minty stopped him. "Could I prevail upon you to escort Jamie into the dining room? I see an old school friend I would love to catch up with." Without giving him time to refuse, she turned and disappeared into the crowd.

Jamie bit her lip, dismayed at being foisted so obviously on William, and to her surprise, he chuckled, albeit wryly. "Don't worry. I can find you another escort, if you'd rather. I don't want you to feel shackled to me when there are handsome, eager men waiting for the honor of taking you in to supper."

As if he wasn't handsome.

"I don't mind, my lord. I would be happy to be your dinner companion." If he only knew.

He held out his right arm again, and she placed her hand on his sleeve. "You can act as a smokescreen. My mother is determined I marry this season, and if I don't take someone in to dinner, she'll come along with an eligible female for me to escort. This way, I can appear to be doing my duty as host and not have to worry about entertaining a prospective bride."

Jamie blinked. So, he didn't see her as a prospective bride? Of course he didn't. He probably still saw her as a child, a playmate of Polly's. And this morning's little escapade certainly hadn't helped.

She took his arm, determined to at least cherish the time she did have with him.

Chapter Three

William stood at the drawing room window, listening to the prattle of the guests but not hearing it. People had been arriving all afternoon, come to talk over the party and to gloat with his mother over the successful bash.

He should've escaped to White's while he had the chance. He could be reading newspapers and talking politics with his peers instead of listening to post-mortems on his sister's come-out. He had a niggling suspicion as to why he hadn't gone out, but he refused to acknowledge it. Whether Lady Jamesina Everard came calling on his sister shouldn't interest him in the slightest, much less influence his decisions.

His nose prickled. There were more flowers here than at a state funeral. The butler had probably worn out a pair of shoes bringing them up as they arrived. The salver in the front hall was layers deep in cards, too. Polly had been a hit. Now he supposed he'd be tasked with screening her suitors. He sighed and absently rubbed his right hand along his left elbow. Though the wound was long healed, scarred over, it still sometimes tingled, as if at any moment it would burst into the agony of the fresh burns once more.

"Jamie!" Polly shot off the settee with unseemly haste and hugged Lady Jamesina as she came into the parlor. "Just look. Posies and nosegays, and Lord Tynewell sent an entire bouquet. Tell me, is it the same at your house?"

William turned and leaned against the windowsill, observing the new arrival, chiding himself for the light feeling in his chest. She wore pale pink, a color that complemented her dark hair and fair complexion. In spite of himself, he'd enjoyed their dinner together last night—and conversing with her on the terrace. Obviously, someone had erred in her formal education. Young girls today were told to cultivate a certain ennui, as if boredom were somehow attractive to a man. Who wanted a bored companion? How could a man be certain that a bored woman wouldn't make for a boring wife? But Lady Jamesina had been both interesting and entertaining, well-read and well-spoken. And she had treated him not just as if he were a normal man, but as if he were also interesting and entertaining. He'd quite forgotten himself.

Lady Jamesina laughed, returning Polly's hug. "My father teased me that he had to instruct the footmen to work in shifts, since they have been running upstairs with flowers, cards, and notes all morning. . .but I think he exaggerates." She drew her arm through Polly's and walked toward him.

At that moment William realized he should've sent flowers to her house. . .and to Polly. It was the brotherly thing to do, after all. He straightened, making a mental note to have his secretary see to the oversight, as Polly and Jamie came over to greet him.

"My lord, I wanted to thank you again for hosting my debut ball. I couldn't have asked for better. And for the flowers you sent. They are lovely. How did you know that pink roses are my favorite?"

Ah, so his secretary had come up trumps. He'd have to thank the man.

"You're most welcome." He bowed.

She lowered her voice. "And I wanted to thank you for your gallant rescue yesterday morning. I realize we were being very foolish by going out by ourselves, and I really don't know how we would've gotten home without starting a scandal. I'm most grateful." She curtsied, a flush riding her cheeks. . .which made her more becoming.

"You're welcome. I'm glad you suffered no ill effects."

Polly squeezed Jamie's arm. "Tell me who else sent flowers and who you danced with and what they said. Who took you in to supper? I was surrounded, and there were so many people, I lost track of you after the first set."

They put their heads together, turning to find a quiet corner. Jamie had come with her aunt, and that formidable woman was in conversation with his mother. They glanced his way a time or two, and William frowned. Breakfast had been an ordeal with his mother interrogating him about which ladies he had met last night, and did any strike his fancy? She had several in mind, and if he didn't exert himself, she was going to have to do something drastic.

Though what that would be, he didn't know. He was the titular head of this family, and she couldn't *force* him to marry.

But he would have to marry someone. He needed an heir. . .an heir who wasn't his cousin Cedric.

As if the thought of him had made him appear, Cedric strolled into the room, his dress impeccable, his hair slightly tousled, and with an arrogant sneer on his full lips. "Hello, Cousin." He flipped his fingers in a lazy gesture. "Thought I'd come see how the aftermath was shaping up." His eyes flicked from one face to another, sharpening when they lit on Lady Jamesina. "I have to say, last night was most diverting. The new crop of beauties holds some promise. The dancing was pleasurable, for once. Oh, sorry. You didn't dance, did you? Too bad." He never took his gaze away from Lady Jamesina.

William clamped his back teeth hard. Cedric loved to needle him about his war wounds, grinding on the fact that it made him less of a catch despite his title and wealth. Of course it did, but he didn't need Cedric emphasizing it at every turn.

"Yes," his cousin continued, "the new batch of debutantes is certainly fetching, but I think I'll forgo the usual flirtations. I've decided this is the year I pick one and settle down, and I've made my selection. I'm sure you'll approve, old chap. Though it really would increase my odds if you were to bump off sometime soon." He laughed, but a nasty gleam shot into his eyes. He often joked about his disappointment that William hadn't died from his injuries, but William always felt the thrust of truth in Cedric's statements. He lusted after the earldom, and only William stood in his way.

"To whom have you chosen to pay your addresses?" William asked through tight lips, though he had an inkling.

"That fetching little morsel there." Cedric jerked his chin toward Lady Jamesina. "She'll make an excellent countess someday." The leer in his eyes and the sneer on his lips made William's innards cringe.

"Is that so? Sorry I didn't oblige you by bumping off this mortal coil." His voice dripped with wryness.

"Time will cure that. After all, you are several years my senior, with no real hope of attracting a mate, nor from what I can tell, any desire to do so." Cedric laughed as if he had made some hilarious joke, drawing the attention of the ladies in the room. "Time to go begin my campaign." He clapped William on the shoulder and went over to Polly and Lady Jamesina.

William gripped his right fingers into a fist. The bounder. Bad enough they had to be related, but to have Cedric asserting his claim, not only on the earldom but on Lady Jamesina Everard, was too much. How he would love to show exceedingly bad manners and pitch Cedric out of the house.

Cedric bent over Lady Jamesina's hand, raising it almost to his lips. Polly frowned but merely greeted her cousin, who ignored her, focusing his attention on her friend. Would Lady Jamesina swoon at his feet as so many young ladies did?

Polly sent him an imploring look, and he was about to rouse himself to join their conversation when raucous barking came from the back of the house. Cedric stiffened, and a glimmer of an idea struck William. Would he dare? His lips twitched, and he quashed the idea as beneath him. It wasn't kind to play on a man's fears, after all.

"William, really." His mother flicked open her fan. "I wish you had left that animal at the estate. And when we have guests, too." She turned to apologize to Lady Araminta.

"Pardon me, Mother. I shall see to it." He gave a bow and headed for the door. He had barely opened it when a furry thump hit the oak panels and burst into the room, bringing to life William's quashed idea without him having to personally implement it.

"I'm sorry, my lord." Both Beckett and Percy, butler and bootboy, scrambled after William's hunting dog, Fergus. The black-and-tan setter bounced joyfully toward Polly, who was a favorite of his. Cedric froze, eyes wide, then backed away, actually putting Lady Jamesina between himself and the dog. He had the temerity to grip her upper arms from behind, using her as a shield.

"Get that beast out of here." Cedric's shout filled the room, his voice high-pitched and cracking.

Fergus halted, lowering his head and growling, the hairs on his neck rising, every muscle tensed. His lip curled, baring his white fangs. Fergus hated Cedric. . .something that had endeared him to William even more.

He started forward to corral his canine when Lady Jamesina shrugged away Cedric's grip, frowning and shaking her head. "Shhh, boy. There's no need to set up such a fuss."

William stopped, curious at her reaction, both to Cedric and the dog.

Fergus quieted, raising his head a bit, his stare moving from Cedric to Lady Jamesina. His tail swished as his body relaxed.

"That's a good boy. Aren't you a handsome fellow?" She held her hand out, fingers in, palm down, for Fergus to sniff.

"Don't do that. The animal is crazed," Cedric cautioned her.

"He doesn't look crazed." She kept her voice soft and conversational as Fergus stepped closer, smelling her hand before doing her the great honor of swiping her knuckles with his tongue. When she stroked his head, he wriggled with pleasure, plopped his rump onto the carpet, and leaned into her skirt.

"What a lovely dog." She knelt and cupped his face in her hands.

"Your pardon, miss." Percy, all of nine or ten years old, darted past William, pulled on his forelock, and grabbed Fergus's collar. "He got right away from me."

"Stupid boy. You should be whipped." Cedric smoothed his hair, glowering. "Allowing livestock into the parlor." He sniffed, shooting his cuffs and trying to cover the fact that he had squealed like a silly chit.

Percy's eyes grew round, and guilt drooped his shoulders.

Lady Jamesina put her hand on his shoulder, looking back and up at Cedric. "Mr. Crofton, please. I'm sure it wasn't intentional." She turned back to Percy. "No one is blaming you, young man. Dogs have a mind of their own sometimes, don't they?"

"Yes, ma'am."

William nodded to Beckett, indicating that the butler could take his leave. "Percy, you may leave the dog. I'll bring him to the kitchen shortly."

"Yes, sir. And I'm awful sorry." He bobbed a short bow and hustled out of the room, sending a glance of dislike toward Cedric.

Lady Jamesina took a place on a settee and Fergus followed, leaning against her knee, eyes adoring. She stroked his head as the dog's tail thumped the carpet. "I've never seen a dog with these markings."

"Fergus is a Castle Gordon Setter." William indicated the spot next to her, raising his eyebrows, and when she inclined her head, took the seat next to her. "The black-and-tan coloring is distinctive. It's a fairly new breed, bred, as you might expect, at Castle Gordon in Scotland."

"He's beautiful. And so friendly."

"Be careful," Polly laughed. "He's so friendly you'll have dog hairs all over your dress." She patted Fergus on the neck. "I should've known you'd work a dog or a horse into the conversation today, William, but I didn't expect the actual beast to show up."

"Neither did I." Cedric stalked across the room, and Fergus let out a growl as he passed by. "I'll be taking my leave."

Lady Jamesina caught William's eye and smothered a smile, cupping Fergus's head in her hands. "Such silky ears you have."

The dog blinked slowly, and William had a fleeting jab of envy. He shook his head.

Fergus was headstrong and loved people. Leaving him at the estate would've been the wiser choice, but William had felt the need to have his canine companion with him. Fergus didn't judge his infirmities, didn't pester him to get married, and above all, gave love and devotion unreservedly.

William wished he could find a wife whose companionship made him feel as contented as his dog's.

Lady Jamesina leaned her face close to the setter's. "You are a beautiful fellow, Fergus. And most attentive. The gentlemen of society could take a lesson or two from you with your soulful eyes and flattering attentions. How could anyone be afraid of you?"

"It's Cedric's own fault that he's afraid of dogs." Polly plopped into a chair in an unladylike move that drew a frown from Mother. "He's the one who tormented that sheepdog into biting him when we were children. If he hadn't been such a bully, he wouldn't have gotten bitten, and he wouldn't be afraid of dogs now. Fergus shows remarkable sense in distrusting him."

Lady Jamesina looked thoughtful, and her eyes met William's once more. The same feeling of being kicked in the chest that he'd experienced before hit him again.

Strange.

He only hoped she would have sense enough to deflect any of Cedric's advances.

⁕

William sat well back from the fireplace in the library. Ever since his injuries, he hated the sound of a crackling fire and the smell of smoke. No matter how cold the night, he refused to have a fire in his bedroom fireplace. He'd rather pile on more blankets than have a blaze stalking his sleep and causing nightmares. In the daytime he could suppress his fears, but at night, when he was sleeping, his terror of fire rose up and tortured him.

The door opened, and Polly peeked around the edge. "May I come in?"

Fergus raised his head from the rug, his tail thumping softly.

"Of course." Because it was only the two of them, William didn't bother to rise, merely shoved the ottoman out with his foot. Polly padded over in her nightgown and wrapper and sank onto the footstool. As she had when she was little, she tucked her feet up and wrapped her arms around her shins and rested her chin on her knees.

He leaned back in the chair, spreading the fingers of his right hand over his waistcoat. He regretted being unable to prop his elbows on the arms of the chair and lace his fingers together over his middle. It was odd the little things he missed since his injuries.

"I thought you'd gone to bed hours ago. Couldn't you sleep?"

She shook her head, her eyes troubled.

"I'm sorry about leaving the party early tonight." He'd almost dragged Polly from the soiree at Lady Carlton's, not offering an explanation, even though Polly had asked twice on the ride home what was bothering him.

"It's all right. I wasn't enjoying myself much anyway." She reached up and drew her braid over her shoulder, playing with the end. "William, are you going to marry, like Mama wants?"

"Is that what's keeping you awake?"

"Some of it. The rest is Cedric." She flipped her braid back over her shoulder. "Cedric is making a cake of himself, practically panting after Jamie. She thinks he's awful, but he won't leave her alone."

It pleased him to know Lady Jamesina wasn't falling into Cedric's arms. "Why is that keeping you from sleeping?"

"Because I overheard Cedric say at the opera last week that if Jamie kept avoiding his advances, he was going to find a way to put her into a compromising situation so she would be forced to marry him or cause a scandal. He would corner her at a party and be caught kissing her, or lure her into the garden, or even just put about a rumor that something improper had taken place. She'd have to marry him to keep her good name."

Anger lit in William's innards, and he fisted his hand on his thigh. "Have you spoken to Jamie about this?"

"I did, and she's concerned, but not as much as I think she ought to be. She doesn't know Cedric, and it doesn't seem like she's taking him seriously enough. If he did manage to compromise her reputation, I know her father would be honor-bound to force her to marry Cedric." Polly rocked, her arms tight about her legs, looking up to him for help.

"What is it that you want me to do about it?" He could have a word with Cedric, though what good that would do, he didn't know. Cedric despised William. He always had, hating him for standing between Cedric and the title he craved.

"I want you to offer for her. Marry her and save her from Cedric."

William sat upright, his boots slamming the floor. "What?"

"You heard me. It's the perfect solution." Polly unfolded and scooted off the ottoman, kneeling on the floor by his chair. "Mother's been after you to marry, and you know you need to, if for no other reason than to produce an heir to keep the earldom from going to Cedric." She gripped his knee. "Jamie needs a hero, and you're the best hero I know." Her big eyes pleaded with him.

Her naive faith humbled William. He reached across and brushed his right hand over her hair. He shook his head. "I'm no knight in shining armor, rescuing fair maidens from dragon-like suitors." And certainly not someone as fair as Lady Jamesina Everard. "I doubt she would consider it a rescue if I was part of the bargain."

His left hand resided in his pocket, out of sight if never off his mind. There was the crux of the matter as far as courting and marrying were concerned. To become engaged, he would have to find someone who wasn't repulsed by the ravages of war apparent to everyone. To marry and do his duty to produce an heir, he would have to find someone who would not run shrieking at the sight of the full damage the war had done him. His left hand was only part of the devastation. Red, shiny, puckered scars ran up the left side of his torso from waist to just below his jawline and from fingertips to shoulder blade.

How could he expose those ghastly wounds to the shocked eyes of a new bride? He'd overheard one young woman at the soiree tonight say that she wouldn't mind being a countess, but it would be too awful if his "claw" ever touched her. Why, she might faint or scream.

"That's nonsense. You judge Jamie unfairly. She wouldn't care about your wounds," Polly insisted.

"Ah, but I care."

He closed his eyes, frustrated with Polly's hopes. Offering for her friend was something which, if he was a whole man, he would do in a heartbeat. For the past six weeks—since Polly and Jamie's come-out ball—he had known he was in trouble. Actually, it went further back than that. He'd grown fond of Lady Jamesina Everard through Polly's letters telling of their friendship and exploits together at boarding school. . .and the brief postscripts she'd written on Polly's letters that he'd read over and over while stationed in Spain.

Lady Jamesina had been in and out of the house many times over the past several weeks, visiting Polly. Every time they crossed paths, whether here in this house or at some society function, Jamie—in his mind he'd taken to calling her Jamie rather than Lady Jamesina—was invariably polite. . .even warm toward him. Not shy, simpering, or suspicious as other young ladies tended to be when he was around.

"Please, William, will you at least consider it? I love Jamie like a sister, and I know if she was forced to marry Cedric, she'd be miserable." Polly's lip trembled, and her eyes grew bright.

He couldn't come right out and refuse, not with her staring up at him with so much hope. "I'll think about it," he promised. "But for tonight, you need to stop worrying and get to sleep. We can't have you dragging about here like a gorgon because you missed your beauty rest." He stood and held out his hand. Her smile broke over him, and she hopped to her feet.

"I love you, William."

"I love you, too, brat." He gave her a nudge toward the door. "I'm not promising anything, remember?"

When she'd closed the door, he dropped back into his chair, closing his eyes and for a moment, allowing himself to wonder what marriage to Jamie Everard would be like. . . was it even possible?

Jamie looked up from sorting invitations as Aunt Minty came into the breakfast room and went to the chafing dishes on the sideboard. "Good morning."

"Good morning to you, young lady. You're looking entirely too perky for this hour."

Aunt Minty selected some fruit and brought it to the place next to Jamie.

"Late night at the hospital?" Jamie poured a cup of coffee for her aunt, who preferred it to tea.

"Extremely. There was a crisis on one of the wards, and that quack Fitzgerald who calls himself a doctor was no help at all. I didn't get home until well after two." She sipped the coffee without even blowing on it. "I had hoped to have a lie-in, but with all the comings and goings in the house this morning, that proved impossible. Who knocks on the door at such an unseemly hour?"

Jamie smothered a smile. Aunt Minty was definitely not at her best before noon. "I don't know who it was. Someone for Father. They're still in the study. But it *is* after ten. That isn't an unseemly time for someone to call on business."

Aunt Minty looked at the clock. "Hmph."

Jamie placed an invitation to a Venetian breakfast into the "maybe" pile. None of the invites held particular appeal to her, and she knew why. It was the same reason she'd been unable to sleep well the past several nights.

Why did Cedric Crofton pursue her when she wanted nothing to do with him, while his cousin William showed no interest at all? Polly's warning about Cedric's plans had irritated her more than frightened her, but she didn't know how to stop him if he chose to put about rumors. She would have to be on her guard all the time.

The season stretched out like a bleak field strewn with caltrops, nothing like she had envisioned it would be.

It wasn't William's fault she had come into this season with such high hopes. Polly had told her that her mother was after William to marry and set up his nursery, and Jamie had secretly hoped that he would look her way. And it wasn't his fault that though she'd tried to kill her romantic feelings for him, those feelings had steadily grown until she could scarcely think or eat or behave normally.

Whenever she saw him she felt breathless and jittery. He was always polite, but remote, self-contained. She waited daily for word that he was paying special court to someone, but so far, she'd heard nothing. Hope and despair tangled within her constantly. If this was being in love, it was miserable, and she wondered how people survived the ordeal.

Her father appeared in the doorway. "Jamie, may I have a word with you?" He looked strained and uncomfortable.

Aunt Minty looked up from her coffee, eyes piercing, alerted as Jamie had been by something in his tone. "What's wrong?"

"Nothing's wrong. I just need to speak to Jamie in private." He stroked his sideburns and tucked his hands into his pockets, only to withdraw them and clasp them behind his back, shifting his weight and not looking directly at either of them.

Jamie rose and followed him down the hall, her heart fluttering. What had upset him? Her father was normally an optimistic, jovial, doting man who rarely showed agitation.

He led her into the morning room and stood with his back to the fireplace.

"Jamie, I've had a caller this morning. In fact, he's still here." He paused, looking at a point somewhere over her shoulder, as if searching for the right words on the wall behind her.

Worry skittered across her skin. "Just tell me what's wrong." Had Cedric made good on the intentions Polly had overheard?

"There has been an offer for your hand." His eyes were so clouded with worry, Jamie's stomach felt as if the bottom had dropped out of it.

"Before you meet with him, I want you to know that no matter what, the decision is totally up to you." Father drew his hands down his face. "I didn't think this would be so hard."

Jamie's hands grew cold. It must be bad, whatever Cedric was saying about her.

"This has to be what you want." But a hopeful light lit her father's eyes, and he rubbed his hands together. "It would be a brilliant match, but you're young yet. There will be other offers, I'm certain, after a while. People will talk, I'm sure, but you shouldn't let that affect your decision. Although I don't know that he would broadcast it about if you refused him, and we certainly wouldn't say anything. I wouldn't like this to damage our relationship with the Crofton family. . ."

Anger burst through her. How dare Cedric do such a dastardly thing? Well, he would leave here with no doubt as to her feelings for him. If he thought he could force her into marrying him by threatening a scandal, then he had another long think coming. She would rather marry. . .Fergus the Gordon Setter than Cedric Crofton.

"That's all I wanted to say. I know you'll do the right thing." Father all but bolted for the door.

Her mind raced with everything she wanted to say to Cedric, and she paced before the front window.

But it wasn't Cedric who entered.

William Crofton, the Earl of Beckenham, walked into the room, his face grave.

Jamie's knees turned to water. William? Had he come to speak on behalf of his cousin? Was Cedric so much of a coward he'd sent the head of his family instead? Bewilderment swirled in her mind. This was the worst kind of disaster. To have the man she loved here negotiating a betrothal on behalf of his odious cousin.

"You've spoken with your father?" he asked.

"Yes."

"Then you know why I am here?" He stood straight as a stair rod, his left hand in his pocket, his right fisted at his side.

"He told me there had been an offer for my hand." Her mouth felt dry as attic dust.

"You are amenable to the marriage?"

She shook her head, and his face went grim. "I am not. Why didn't he come himself? Is he too much of a coward? I'm not surprised." She gripped her elbows, feeling cold disdain. "I don't care what he's said about me, I wouldn't marry Cedric Crofton if he was hung from top to toe with diamonds."

His brows rose. "I'm glad to hear it." He paused and slipped his finger under his collar. "However, I'm not here in any capacity for my cousin. He doesn't know I'm calling on you. I'm here on my own hook, and I'm asking you to do me the honor of accepting my hand in marriage."

She put her fingertips to her chest, her mind feeling as if it had fallen off a cliff. "You? You want to marry me?" Anger bled away to be replaced by. . .she didn't know what. . .elation? Disbelief?

"There is no one else here. I realize this is coming rather out of the blue, but I've given it some thought. Our families are on good terms, I am of an age to contemplate marriage and setting up my nursery, and you are imminently suitable. I realize that I am no bargain, but I do come with a title and money enough to support you. Your father has consented to my paying address to you, and my mother and sister will certainly be pleased. Do you need time to consider the offer?"

Her mind darted off in a dozen directions, and her heart threatened to explode. It was her dream come true. . .after a fashion. It was the man she wanted, but the manner. . .he hadn't paid her particular attention, hadn't courted her, hadn't even seemed to notice she was around most of the time. And yet, here he was, asking her to marry him. . .in a cold, logical fashion that felt more like a business transaction than romance.

He ran his finger under his collar again, and suddenly, she knew. He was nervous! Of course he was. Asking for a woman's hand in marriage had to be an unsettling experience at the best of times. That must be why he seemed so. . .distant.

She hid a smile. She wanted to throw herself into his arms, dance about the room, shout down the hall. . .but that would embarrass him. Matching his demeanor might be the best way to help him through his discomfort. "I don't need more time. It is a brilliant match for me and will certainly please our families." She kept her voice calm, as if her most cherished dream wasn't coming true right before her eyes.

His face tightened. "Very well. I would prefer not to wait for the banns to be called. Procuring a special license will not be difficult. I propose that we marry three days hence. My mother will wish to hold a small celebratory wedding breakfast at Crofton House. Is that agreeable to you?"

"Three days?" She would be married to William in three days? Her mind whirled with a thousand thoughts, but she couldn't grasp even one.

"I know it is short notice, but I wish this to be done as quickly as possible." He pressed his lips together. "Are you willing?"

"Three days will be fine." Aunt Minty would have the vapors when she heard the news. A wedding in seventy-two hours?

"Then I shall see about procuring the special license." He bowed and turned toward the door.

That was it? He was leaving?

The entire encounter had caught her off guard, had taken mere minutes, and had all the romance of a mathematics lesson.

At the last moment, he turned, came to her, and lifted her limp hand in his. "I am sure my mother and sister will wish to call upon you later this afternoon. They will be delighted at the news." He pressed his lips to her knuckles briefly, something like life flickering in his eyes for a moment before he bowed and left.

And just like that, she was betrothed.

Chapter Four

O ver the next three days after meeting with Everard and proposing to Jamie, William operated on two planes. Outwardly he was polite, controlled, and organized, but inwardly, he battled fear.

Fear that everything Mirabelle Fordham had said to him right after he was invalided home and she learned the extent of his wounds was true. That no woman should be bound to someone who had suffered such devastation, that an earldom wasn't enough compensation for marrying someone with such hideous scars.

Fear that if he hadn't also insisted on offering her father money, there was no way Lady Jamesina Everard could've been coerced into becoming his wife. Waiting in the hall as Everard persuaded her had been torturous to his confidence.

His mother went about with a self-satisfied smile on her face, and Polly went into raptures, declaring him the best of brothers for making her dearest friend her sister, too, and saving her from Cedric. Polly, for all her naive ways, was certain he and Jamie would be happy together.

Happy. William shook his head. Happiness was something that happened to other people. This was a business arrangement, and he would be wise to keep his emotions out of it.

For some odd reason, Everard kept putting off meeting with William to transact the financial aspects of the agreement, but with all the wedding kerfuffle, perhaps he thought it best to wait. William had offered a sizeable settlement to encourage Everard to look past his shortcomings and make it plain to Jamie that she should accept the offer of marriage, even if he was disfigured.

Of Jamie, William had seen almost nothing. The engagement announcement appeared in the London papers, and he escorted her along with Polly to the theater one night and for a quick drive in Hyde Park one afternoon, but they were never alone. And when he was with her, he felt shy, awkward, very aware of his scars and maimed hand, and wishing he had never come to Town for the Season. His tongue lay like a plank in his mouth, unable to form a sensible phrase, and all the while he knew she would never have agreed to marry him if her father hadn't coerced her into it.

William waited every day for word that she'd come to her senses and wanted to beg off. She hadn't given him any indication of her feelings, beyond the fact that she studied him more closely, as if waiting for something from him, though he didn't know what.

Cedric was predictably furious. He'd stormed into William's office, face red, ready to fight.

"I should call you out. How dare you trade on your title and money to steal her away from me?" Cedric slammed his hands down on William's desk, eyes bloodshot. "You knew I wanted her. Why must you always stand in the way of what I want? I demand a duel. Hyde Park. Tomorrow morning." He glared and swayed. "I'll get the girl and the title in one schwell foop."

William rose slowly from his chair. "Don't be ridiculous."

"I demand shatishfacshun."

"You're drunk." The reek of alcohol emanated from Cedric's breath.

"What if I am? I'm heartbroken. You stole the woman I was going to marry."

"Go home, Cedric, and sleep it off. I'm not going to fight a dual with you. You don't love Lady Jamesina, and you know it. The only person I've ever known you to love is yourself."

Beckett hovered near the door, and William motioned him inside. "Show my cousin out."

The butler nodded, placing his hand on Cedric's arm. Cedric jerked away, his movement clumsy. "You can't get rid of me that eashee. . ." He glowered. "How much? How much money did you have to offer her father? It's the only way she'd marry someone like you—"

Beckett had heard enough. He grabbed Cedric by the collar and the waistband of his pants and frog-marched him from the room. Cedric's shouts of how he'd been cheated, how no woman would marry William if he wasn't a rich earl, how he was going to get his revenge, following him until William heard the front door close.

He sat down and rested his maimed left hand on the desktop, afraid that though Cedric was drunk and angry, he had spoken the truth.

And now the wedding day had arrived. William stood in the nave of St. George's Church in Hanover Square, under the massive chandelier, with blocks of colored light streaming through the stained-glass windows. In spite of his desire to have a quiet wedding, his mother had insisted upon St. George's, the fashionable choice for a society wedding.

His best man and former regiment mate, Paul Pargetter, Viscount Louddon, stood at William's elbow. "Are you sure you want to do this? It's not too late to run, you know?" His teasing tone belied his words, though William wondered if they were true. Was it too late to back out?

Every eye was on him, and he could feel the conjecture about his gloved, withered hand and emaciated left arm. He could hear the whispers in his mind about how Lady Jamesina Everard was marrying him for his title and money, the poor dear. A shame to be tied to a shell of a man with such an awful infirmity.

At least he had insisted upon a black suit, the better to camouflage his black glove. No pale silk knee breeches or satin coat for him. Why wouldn't people stop staring? He almost shook his head. Of course they were staring. He was standing in front of them, and he was the groom!

Then the organ music began the bridal march, and the guests were no longer looking at him.

Lady Jamesina Everard, on her father's arm, walked sedately up the aisle. She wore light blue, and a straw bonnet framed her face, but that was about as much as William could take in of her apparel. Her eyes drew all his attention. She gave him a trembling smile, face pale. She didn't exactly look overjoyed. She looked. . .scared? Perhaps sobered by the enormity of what they were about to do?

He swallowed. Was she regretting accepting his offer now that the moment was upon her? Not that she'd had a choice, really. Baron Everard was grinning broadly, looking like the proverbial cat with canary feathers on his whiskers.

Polly took her place at the front, Jamie's maid of honor, happiness on her smiling face.

When Baron Everard went to place Polly's hand in William's, William quickly substituted his right hand rather than his left, startling Everard into an awkward exchange. The baron reddened, cleared his throat, and stepped back.

Jamie squeezed William's hand, and he met her eyes with surprise as the cleric took his place and began the service. She surprised him further by loosening her fingers from his right hand and reaching for his left. The custom-made glove covered the mass of scar tissue that would never again resemble a hand, but Jamie didn't show any outward revulsion. She rested her fingers lightly on his claw and faced the cleric.

The service was over before he realized it. Had he spent the entire time looking into her eyes? Had he made a cake of himself repeating his vows? He couldn't remember. All he could remember was that she held his injured hand the entire time.

As they went into the small west transept to sign the wedding register, Jamie looked at her new wedding ring, speculation in her eyes. The plain gold band certainly wasn't anything to delight a young woman's heart. No jewels, no engraving, nothing. Just a gold circlet he had sent his valet out to procure the day before. He would remedy that once they were at Beckenham Hall.

She slipped her hand through his arm as they walked down the aisle toward the doors at the far end. The wedding guests were smiling, leaning toward one another, whispering behind their hands. Were they speculating on her motives? Were they feeling sorry for her? Was she already regretting her fate?

"Cripple." He flinched. Someone had whispered that word.

Jamie's chin came up, and she tightened her hold on his arm, her face serene, but it looked forced.

The church aisle seemed a hundred miles long, but finally they emerged into the sunshine.

His open landau stood at the foot of the stairs, and he assisted her into it. The coachman turned with a broad smile and handed William a pouch of coins. He nodded and set the bag in his lap. The drawstring was knotted tightly. He raised it to his lips to use his teeth to open the bag, but Jamie took it from him. "Let me help."

In a trice she had the string undone. Coldness invaded William at being treated like a child. He could have managed it himself.

Her brows raised. "My lord?"

He took the pouch, setting it on the seat and digging into it. Grabbing a fistful of coins, he tossed them over the side as the landau took off. The crowds gathered along the street pounced on the money. The scattering of coins, what was supposed to be a joyous, generous event, felt to William like one more mark of his failure.

Jamie buried her nose in the bouquet he'd had sent over to her house that morning. He'd done everything required of a bridegroom thus far—the ring, the flowers, the coins...if he was a normal man, he would put his arm around his new bride and kiss her, sealing the promises he'd just made.

But he wasn't a normal man.

Jamie listened to the toasts at the wedding breakfast and sampled the wedding cake, but she didn't really hear or taste. She was so befuddled. Here she was, married to the man she had been in love with for years, and yet, he seemed a virtual stranger. Aloof, even grim. She knew he didn't care for parties, but...it was his wedding. He acted as if he were seated in the dock and a death sentence had been handed down. If he hadn't wanted to marry her, why had he asked?

Crofton House looked even more elegant than it had for her and Polly's debut ball. Greenery festooned every column and railing, and huge urns of fresh flowers brightened every corner. The Countess of Beckenham. . .no, the now *Dowager* Countess of Beckenham had outdone herself, considering she had only seventy-two hours in which to accomplish so much. Polly said the place had been in an uproar from the moment William made his announcement.

The best man stood to make his toast.

"Ladies, and gentlemen, when I received word that William was finally getting himself spliced—" He paused as a ripple of laughter went around the room. "I couldn't wait to meet the lady who had nabbed him. He's been an elusive quarry for such a long time, I knew she must be someone special." He inclined his head to Jamie, and she smiled, heat warming her cheeks.

"I was not wrong. William, I believe you have found yourself a rare jewel indeed. Beautiful, kind, and a fitting countess for you. I wish you every happiness. It's long overdue and well-deserved." He raised his glass, but before putting it to his lips, he grinned. "But I believe this company will agree with me when I say that we have thus far been deprived."

"Deprived?" William's brows came down.

"Yes, deprived of a bridal kiss. If you don't kiss your bride soon, I shall have to take it upon myself to do the honors. Every bride deserves to be thoroughly kissed at her wedding breakfast."

Laughter rang out, and several guests began tapping their spoons on their glasses.

Jamie glanced at William, her heart hammering and warmth suffusing her cheeks. She raised her face toward his. There had been no kiss during the ceremony, nor had he kissed her as they drove away from the church. But now, though he was obviously shy, he would have to.

The muscles in his jaw tightened, and the scar just above his collar reddened. He leaned forward but at the last instant leaned to the side, giving her a peck on the cheek. She flinched, as if he had slapped her, sitting back abruptly. His lips flattened, and a chill went through her.

The guests clapped, but their response was as tepid as his kiss. Jamie bowed her head, staring at her hands in her lap.

When the wedding breakfast, which actually took half the afternoon, ended, Jamie thought the guests would take their leave, but she had underestimated her new mother-in-law. The dowager announced that the dancing would begin as soon as everyone assembled upstairs.

"Dancing, Mother?" William's low voice cut like a razor through the buzz of voices heading out of the formal dining room.

"You only get married once, Lord willing, and I won't have Jamie cheated out of the festivities." She flicked open her fan, her jaw set. "I weary of you blocking me at every turn."

"William?" Jamie put her hand on his arm, and when he jerked, she realized she'd touched his left arm. Did it still pain him? Was that the reason for his...reserve...today? He was in pain? Or had he heard the whispers in the church? Those whispers had made her angry, but she refused to let that ruin her day. People were ignorant if they couldn't look past his injuries or chose not to see them as the marks of valor that they were.

He took a deep breath and circled around her to offer his right arm. "We will at least go up to the ballroom, since it seems we have no other choice."

Jamie gathered her skirts and took his arm, wishing he sounded a bit more enthusiastic.

Her new mother-in-law had gone to great lengths in the ballroom, too. A string quintet played softly, and small tables had been set up around the perimeter of the vast space where guests could sit and visit. Along one wall, a buffet table laden with hors d'oeuvres and petit fours was flanked by liveried footmen.

Her father, resplendent in a new ensemble, strode to the dais, raised his hands to call for quiet, and proudly announced, "It is my honor to present to you the Earl and Countess of Beckenham." He beamed, pride shining from his face.

The quintet began the strains of a waltz, and the crowd clapped politely. Jamie moved to stand before William, waiting for him to take her into his arms for their first dance.

He blanched and leaned down. "Do you mean to shame me, forcing me to perform before everyone as a cripple?"

Anger burst in her chest. "Do you mean to shame me by refusing to dance with me at our wedding? You act as if you're on your way to your own execution. If I have to pretend to be enjoying myself, then you do too."

Without a word, he reached for her, taking her left hand in his right and placing his gloved left on the small of her back. Waiting a pause for the right beat, he swung her out onto the floor.

He danced well, leading her with confidence. Jamie glanced up at him, seeing his face from a different and much closer angle than ever before. Her heart jerked, flooding with love for him once more. Here she was, on her wedding day to the man she had loved for years, dancing their first waltz.

William looked down into her eyes for a moment, something vulnerable, hopeful, lurking in his. Her hand crept higher up his neck, just brushing his hairline, and he jerked. With a skillful pivot, he twirled her to a stop and stepped back, bowing to her though the music wasn't finished. He searched the onlookers until he found her father, beckoning him to come out.

"I know you're eager to dance with the bride."

It was the last she saw of the groom for several hours.

Chapter Five

Whatever Jamie had expected moments after the last guest left the wedding breakfast, being bundled into a carriage and headed to Kent had never occurred to her. William had ended their bridal waltz, bowed to her, and handed her over to her father for the next set. Then he'd disappeared. Jamie learned later that he had been giving instructions to the staff to pack his belongings, take hers that had only been sent over from her father's house that morning, and load the baggage cart.

She'd barely had time to hug a confused Polly and wave to Aunt Minty and her father before William was handing her up into the carriage and closing the door. He opted to travel on horseback, leaving her to ride alone. Fergus trotted at his stirrup. Her maid and William's valet traveled in the baggage cart at the rear of the procession.

The carriage was sumptuous and the weather fair, but her heart was heavy. What had happened to William? When he had been just Polly's older brother and escort, he had been cordial, kind, and even interested. The moment she agreed to become his wife, he'd withdrawn, becoming remote, grim, and cold.

Her overnight case sat on the seat beside her, and she reached into it to pull out a bundle of letters. Though they weren't love letters, and they weren't even written to her, she had tied them with a blue ribbon.

She pulled on the ribbon, selecting one of the envelopes and drawing out the folded paper. "Dear Polly..."

Letters from William to his little sister at boarding school. And because she and Polly were like sisters, and because Jamie had no siblings to write to her, Polly had shared them, letting Jamie have them when she was done reading them.

Jamie had treasured every one. She had thrilled to his accounts of battle...as much as he was willing to share with his fourteen-year-old sister. She had loved the stories of his fellow soldiers and his descriptions of the Spanish countryside. He was funny, tender, brotherly, engaging. Jamie saw him in her mind's eye as he had been the first time she had met him when she was a child. He had been tall and dashing in his military dress and polished boots, gold braid and gleaming sword. He was a hero and the repository of her girlish dreams.

She had wept when Polly received the news of his injury, waiting and agonizing with her for word from him that he would recover.

That first letter after he'd been invalided home...she drew it out now, touching the unsteady stack, her heart hurting for him as he told Polly he would never be a soldier again, that his life was over. . .wondering if it would have been better if he had died on the battlefield.

His next letter had been brusque, businesslike, asking after Polly's schooling, whether she was behaving herself, when she was coming home. He said nothing about his wounds or the despair of his previous missive. He asked Polly to write to him soon.

But Jamie had read between the lines. He was lonely, hurting, his life far different from how he thought it would be. And she had fallen deeper in love with him.

Somewhere inside her new husband, behind that mask of reserve and chill, hid the man who had written those letters, she was sure of it. How could she get past the walls he'd erected?

The carriage drew up to a posting inn, and she hurried to get the letters out of sight, unsure how he would feel about them if he knew she'd kept them.

William opened the door. "We'll stop here for the night."

He helped her down and ushered her into the building. The innkeeper bowed, accepted William's money, and showed them into a private sitting room. She'd never been received thusly at a posting inn, but then again, she'd never been a countess before.

When she approached the fireplace to warm her hands, William said, "Keep back."

She half turned, puzzled.

"You don't want your dress to catch fire. Stay well back. There should be a screen around that grate." He frowned and drew her a few paces from the hearth. "You can't be too careful around fire."

They ate dinner together, but beyond speaking of the decent weather and the excellent food, they seemed to have little to say. Jamie was nervous, this being her wedding night, but when it came time to retire, William showed her to her room where her maid waited to help her change.

"With an early start, we'll reach Beckenham Hall tomorrow evening. Rest well." He bowed slightly and left her, disappearing into the room next door, the dog following at his heels, leaving her gaping after her husband.

She didn't sleep well that night.

◦◦◦

William felt like a cad abandoning his bride on their wedding night, but as he had ridden beside the carriage on their wedding day, he had made up his mind.

She had been forced to marry him. Both to escape Cedric and because her father had pressured her. That he had a title made the decision more palatable, but didn't change the fact that he was an unsightly creature. She hadn't been able to hide her distaste when he'd leaned in to kiss her at the wedding breakfast. She'd flinched the instant his lips touched her skin.

Oh, she'd carried on well enough, even taking his scarred hand during the ceremony and not recoiling when he had held her during their bridal dance, but that was with a glove separating her from actually having to touch his skin.

The thought of a wedding night had been intolerable. The thought of continuing in London under the eyes of the ton and their families had been unbearable. He'd bolted. . .and he'd had to bring her with him.

She hadn't protested, but she had to be regretting having to bury herself in the country instead of enjoying the rest of her season as a newly-minted countess. Well, they all had to make sacrifices, didn't they? He'd gotten his mother off his back and kept Cedric from compromising Jamie; he'd lost his solitude and his freedom. He wasn't going to waste another minute in London.

By pressing hard, they reached his land late in the afternoon of the second day. Beckenham Hall stood square and stately, the sun mellowing the red brick, brightening the white trim, and reflecting off the many windows. Just looking at his ancestral home brought William the first peace he'd felt in weeks.

Fergus, who had alternated between trotting at his stirrup and riding in the carriage with Jamie, gave a bark and raced down the immaculate gravel drive. William almost smiled as the servants came out onto the steps and lined up. He had feared he might catch them off guard, but he should have known better. Galford and Crump, butler and housekeeper at Beckenham since he was a child, would never be caught off guard.

He swung out of the saddle, and a groom was there to take the reins. His carriage arrived a moment later, and before the coachman could climb down, William opened the door and set the step on the ground.

Jamie took his hand, alighting from the coach, and he was struck afresh at her beauty. He was finally bringing a new countess home to Beckenham Hall, something he had envisioned when he was a much younger man but hadn't allowed himself to think about in years. Jamie inhaled deeply, as if fortifying herself to meet the servants and assume her role as mistress of the estate.

He spoke to his staff. "This is my wife, her ladyship, Jamesina Crofton, Countess of Beckenham and your new mistress."

She carried herself like a princess, smiling softly, taking the time to greet each servant personally. What William had thought would take mere moments stretched out to more than half an hour, even though she must be tired after all the excitement of the wedding and two hard days of travel. Any staff might be expected to have reservations about a new mistress, but she left kindness in her wake.

Entering the large entry hall, she looked at the black-and-white marble floor; the oak paneled walls; and the high, coffered ceiling. Slowly, she pulled the ribbons on her bonnet, taking it off and smoothing her hair. "It's as lovely as I remember."

The butler took his cape and hat. Mrs. Crump, keys tinkling on the chatelaine at her waist, waited for orders.

"I'll see the countess to her rooms. Have a bath drawn for her." William winced against the ache in his bones. Was he really that out of shape after two months in London? Hours in the saddle had never bothered him before. He wiped his brow, surprised at the clammy sweat there. "Open a few windows. It's sweltering in here."

They mounted the stairs to the second floor, and William led Jamie to the north wing. "Our suite comprises the entire floor on this end." He opened the first door. "This is your room."

Pale-green rugs and bedclothes, pale-gold drapes at the windows, rich walnut furniture that gleamed with years of beeswax and polishing. "Your dressing room is here and mine beyond. My room is at the end of the corridor adjoining my dressing room."

She went to the window, drawing aside the curtain. "I can see the sea." Her face glowed in the late afternoon light streaming through the northwest windows, and her beauty stole his breath.

He remembered how she had said she loved the sea, and a spark of pleasure shot through his chest. "We'll go down there tomorrow. I'd like to show you over the property. Some of the cliffs are unstable, and I'd prefer to show you the safe areas myself." William reached out for the bedpost, dizziness catching him off guard. Perhaps he was just hungry. He hadn't eaten much over the past few days. A sweat broke out on his skin, and a feeling of clamminess swept over him.

"Are you all right?" she asked.

He straightened, shaking his head to clear it. "I'm fine. The footmen will bring your things up soon, and your maid can unpack. I'll be in the office checking with my bailiff, and we'll have dinner, if you're not too tired from the journey?"

"Of course."

"Jamie." He paused, feeling as if he owed her some explanation, but unable to bear broaching the truth. "This is your room. No one will bother you here, least of all me. You're safe here." Without giving her time to question him, he left.

◯◯◯

Safe.

Jamie shook her head as she brushed her hair, staring at her reflection in the dressing table mirror. She'd dismissed her maid for the night, and she was alone in the vast room.

William had sat through dinner, poking at his food but eating little. When she asked, he had shrugged.

"I'm a bit out of sorts, I suppose. Nothing a good night's sleep won't put right."

A good night's sleep. Wasn't that the last thing a bridegroom on his honeymoon was supposed to want?

He had led her to her room after their late supper, and her heart had raced in anticipation, but he'd left her at her door with nothing more than a "Goodnight, Jamie," before disappearing into his room at the end of the hall.

And just what was she to make of that?

She set the brush down and stared at her reflection. He'd said her room was a safe place and no one would disturb her. Did that mean he was waiting for her to come to his room?

Gathering up her dressing gown and sliding her feet into her slippers, she shored up her courage. If he was waiting for her, she didn't want to disappoint him or have him think she wasn't willing. If he wasn't waiting for her. . .she didn't want to contemplate her mortification if he wasn't.

She slipped into her dressing room and tried the handle of the door into his. If it was locked, she'd have her answer. The knob turned easily. Heart in her throat, she crossed the room, breathing in the smell of cedar and sandalwood. Pale moonlight streamed in the high window as she passed the drawers and shelves of his coats and boots and hats.

At the door into his bedroom, she paused. What would she do if he rejected her? What would she do if he didn't?

You can't stand here all night.

A low groan from the far side of the door made her jump.

She hovered at the door, indecision freezing her to the spot, until something crashed in his room. Jamie jerked the door open.

Overwhelming darkness.

The drapes were drawn, no candles were lit, and no fire, not even coals glowed in the fireplace.

"William?"

Another groan.

She crept across the room, straining to see by the light of a small gap in the drapes, until she reached the window. With a tug, she opened the curtains a few inches so she could see enough to find a candle and matches on the table beside the door.

Shielding the flickering flame with her hand, she approached the vast bed. Before she reached it, she stopped. Broken crockery lay on the carpet, a dark stain spreading across the rug.

Jamie skirted the mess and held the candle higher. "William?"

He lay sprawled facedown atop the covers, stripped to his breeches, as if he'd gotten that far in preparing for bed and couldn't finish. Candlelight flickered across his bare feet and calves, over his muscled legs, and the bare skin of his back.

Her fingers went to her lips. His entire left side was a mass of puckered, shiny, scarred skin, and his left arm, thrown out on the bedspread, was almost skeletal, ending not in a recognizable hand, but in a crumpled stump of red and white scars.

The poor man. How he must have suffered.

A fit of coughing seized him. A flush rode his cheek, and she climbed the steps beside the bed to touch the back of her hand to his forehead.

He was raging with fever. Setting the candle on the bedside table, she grabbed his dressing gown from the foot of the bed and spread it over him. He immediately flicked it onto the floor.

"Too hot." His voice rasped. "Go away."

"You're sick. You need help." She pulled the dressing gown away from the water on the floor and spread it over him again. "You'll catch a chill."

"Go away." He barely turned his head, his eyes struggling to focus, his voice raspy and weak.

"Nonsense." She hurried to the door, pattering down the hall and the main staircase, grateful for the vast windows that let in at least a little moonlight. Unfamiliar with the layout, Jamie had to search for the green baize door that led into the servants' part of the house.

Mr. Galford, the butler, met her in the servants' hall, his face ghostly in the light of the candle he carried. Keys dangled from his fingers. Locking up for the night. "My lady, what is it?"

She took a moment to gather herself and steady her breath. "His lordship is ill. Can you send his valet up with a bowl of cool water and some towels, and send a footman for a doctor?"

"The earl won't be pleased at the idea of a doctor, my lady."

"That is of no consequence. He needs a physician. His fever is alarmingly high." She tightened the belt on her dressing gown. "Now, hurry. I need to get back to him."

When Jamie returned to William's room, he had once again thrown off the covering. He lay on his back, his right arm thrown over his eyes. She noted that the scarring on his side and back extended around to the front from his hip in a jagged line up to his collarbone. She'd barely lit the candles in the wall sconces beside the bed before William's valet tapped on the door and entered.

"Evening, my lady." He carried a bowl of water, a stack of towels clamped under his arm. Going straight to the bed, he studied the earl. "Not feeling well, is he?"

"I'm sorry, I don't know your name." Jamie cleared a place on the bedside table and took the bowl.

"Ingram, ma'am." He bobbed a quick bow. "Been with his lordship since he first went to war. Was his sergeant. When he came home, I came, too." He rolled up his sleeves. "I can take care of him." His calmness helped calm Jamie. "You can go on to bed. His lordship won't be best pleased to know you were here."

So what else is new? He didn't seem pleased to have her anywhere in his life.

"I didn't even know he was sick." She smoothed the hair off his brow, anxious about the intensity of his fever. "He never said he was ailing."

"It's the malaria, my lady. He got it in the Peninsula, and it crops up from time to time. Comes on him quickly. You really should go back to your room, my lady." Ingram looked as if he wanted to scoop her off the bed and hustle her out of the room.

"I can't leave him, not like this. I sent for the doctor." Jamie climbed onto the bed, struggling with her dressing gown. Malaria was something she'd seen before, and she knew what to do about it. "Push that table close and light the fire. It's much too chilly in here."

"No fire, my lady. His lordship doesn't like a fire in the bedroom." Ingram brought the table near the edge of the bed and bent to gather the broken pitcher. "I'll see to this, my lady, and be right back."

Jamie dunked a towel into the tepid water, wrung it out, and began to bathe William's flushed cheeks and chest. "We've got to get you cooled down."

William growled and swiped at her hand. "Leave me to die in peace."

"You'll not make a widow of me before you've made me a wife." She pinned his right hand to the mattress and sponged his neck. "Lie still."

Ingram returned, and with his help, she was able to tug and pull and get William under the covers. He promptly trod them back.

Jamie sighed. She'd fought this battle many times at the naval hospital when she helped her Aunt Minty. "William Crofton, you'll keep these covers on or you'll force me to wrap you up like a Christmas present." She drew up the sheet and a single, light blanket.

He didn't respond.

"Go to the stillroom and brew a tisane of Jesuit's bark tea." Jamie glanced at the valet. "You do have Jesuit's bark on hand?"

"Yes, my lady. But he'll fight you. He hates the bitter taste. I always have to wrestle it into him." Ingram sent her a skeptical look.

"Leave him to me."

Through the long hours of the night, Jamie sponged William's face and chest, grateful for her nursing experience. She forced sips of tea down William's throat and kept a prayerful vigil. Ingram sat in a chair by the door, dozing, waking to bring fresh water, helping her turn William, helping hold his head when he wanted to refuse the bitter tea.

Fever gave way to chills that racked the earl's body. With the ban on a fire, Jamie had no choice but to crawl under the covers beside her husband and hold him, giving him the warmth of her body.

When the fever returned, she sponged him again, working tirelessly.

"I wonder if he knows what a fine wife he's found, my lady." Ingram stifled a yawn and scrubbed his eyes with his fists. "He never lets anyone close to him, hardly even me."

"We all need help sometimes." Her hands ached from wringing out the cloth, and her back screamed from being crouched over her husband for so long. "Even if we don't want it."

The doctor arrived with the dawn, apologetic and exhausted, fresh from delivering a baby. "Dr. Coyle, my lady." He set his bag on the table and put on a pair of glasses. "His lordship is ailing?"

"Malaria chills and fever, sir," Ingram supplied. "Her ladyship has been caring for him better than a surgeon, if I might say so."

The doctor examined William, his brow furrowed as he bent over his patient. Wisps of white hair hovered over his balding pate as he placed his ear on William's chest.

"We've given him Jesuit's bark tea for the fever." Jamie pushed a tendril of hair back over her ear, conscious of still being in her dressing gown and night clothes.

"Good, good." The doctor continued to fuss about, pursing his lips, his eyes seemingly unfocused. "I believe a little bloodletting is in order."

"No." Jamie shook her head.

"But, my lady, we must get the bad humors out of his system. I understand you being a bit squeamish, but it really is the prescribed treatment." The doctor removed a fleam from his bag and reached for the basin on the bedside table.

"No, sir. I forbid you to bleed my husband." Jamie had seen the ill-effects of bleeding too many times at the hospital. Aunt Minty had fought many a surgeon and physician over the practice, and Jamie agreed with her aunt. The practice was harmful, barbaric, and unnecessary. "Thank you for coming, doctor. I am sure Mr. Ingram will show you to the kitchen where the cook will prepare breakfast for you before you go."

Ingram sent her a look of respect as he escorted the blustering doctor out of the room.

She turned back to her husband, startled that he had his eyes open. "William?" She touched his skin, still too warm, but not as bad as before.

"You're back?" He frowned, blinking.

"I never left." Jamie brought the cup of tea to his lips. "Take a few sips."

The warm liquid touched his lips, and he grimaced.

"No, you don't. You need this," she said when he tried to turn away. "I'm tired, and I just had a fight with the doctor. I don't want to fight with you, too."

He swallowed the bitter tea, closing his eyes and resting his head on the pillow. Jamie studied his face for a moment, brushing the hair off his forehead, trailing her fingers over his temple, cheekbone, and neck, barely brushing the burn scars on his shoulder. Weariness seeped into her bones, and she crawled up onto the big bed once more, lying down beside him, resting her hand on his chest just over his heart.

She was almost asleep when his right hand came up and covered hers.

Chapter Six

William tried to behave as if nothing had happened. He recovered from his bout of malaria, slower than he would've liked, but steadily. He ignored the fact that his wife of such a short time, the wife he had decided would never be forced to encounter his damaged body, had seen the worst of his afflictions.

According to his valet, she had not only seen them, but touched them, sponging his body, moving him, treating him, even going so far as to hold him tight when the chills became too bad.

He did not know how to go forward from here.

Jamie refused to be categorized or safely kept on the perimeter of his life. Throughout his convalescence, she stayed close, fussing over him, reading to him, encouraging him to eat in order to regain his strength, bringing Fergus up to his room for a visit.

"He's pining away at the back door, sneaking inside whenever the housekeeper has her back turned." Jamie laughed when the dog leapt onto the bed and began licking William's face, his body a mass of furry wiggles and tail wags. "I had to smuggle him inside. Galford helped me get him past Mrs. Crump." She shrugged, looking like a naughty child. "When she looks at me, I feel like I used to when Polly and I got caught in some mischief at school."

"She's harmless." William restrained his setter, and Fergus plopped onto the coverlet, curling against his leg and resting his head in William's lap. "Don't forget, you're the Countess of Beckenham now. If you want something, don't ask. Tell her what you want done. You don't have to sneak around."

He made sure his stump of a hand was covered by the cuff of his dressing gown, running his right hand through Fergus's soft coat. Soft, but not as soft as Jamie's brown curls, which he had allowed himself to stroke when she'd fallen asleep atop the covers one night when he'd been seriously ill.

Odd how he missed her in the nights since his fever broke, since he had never wanted her to get that close in the first place.

She walked beside him now, toward the stables, on this first morning since coming home that he'd left the house. Fergus cavorted along the path, the picture of exuberance.

"I love that we can smell the sea from here." Jamie raised her face to the breeze, breathing deeply. "Are you sure you're up to going out today?"

"Why don't you wrap me in cotton wool and bung me into a Bath chair?" he teased. "I'm not made of glass, you know."

Her hand through his right arm tightened. "I know. But you will tell me if you tire?"

"I promise."

The stables, substantial, brick, with a clock tower in the center, spread out before them. "I have a little surprise for you."

"For me?" Her pleasure sent a kick to his chest. "What is it?"

"Wait and see." He led her through the main doors of the stable and into the south wing where the saddle horses were housed. Pausing at the first stall, he rubbed the nose of the tall gray. "This is my best hunter. I bought him as a colt for a song at Tattersall's almost ten years ago. Admiral was the first horse my father let me purchase."

They passed several more stalls, each housing a pedigreed hunter, glossy and well cared for. Since returning from the war, William had put considerable time and effort into turning the stables at Beckenham into the best in the country. The Prince Regent had purchased two yearlings from him last year, and as a result, his success as a breeder was made.

"Who is this fellow?" Jamie peeked into the next-to-last stall. William joined her, chuckling at the well-upholstered chestnut with the shaggy mane and feet like dinner plates. After a dozen of the country's best, the gelding looked completely out of place.

"That's Charger."

The old boy raised his head, blinked slowly, and ambled over. Age had whitened his muzzle, but he whickered softly, nudging William's shoulder. William reached up and fondled Charger's ears, and the chestnut leaned into him.

"He must have a story." Jamie let him smell her hand and then stroked his neck under his mane.

"He's an old war horse. When I first enlisted, he was part of my regiment, pulling one of the caissons. He was fearless in battle, nothing seemed to unsettle him. At the Battle of Vimeiro, all three of us—me; my valet, Ingram, who was my sergeant at the time; and Charger—were all wounded."

He paused, reliving for a moment the battle that had nearly cost all of them their lives. "Ingram had a saber gash across his upper back that should've killed him, and Charger took a rifle ball to his hip." William leaned to the side, looking at the scar in the chestnut's hide. "And I got too close to a cask of gunpowder that exploded." He raised his gloved stump. "A few days before the battle, I mentioned to Ingram that if Charger ever got the chance to retire, I wanted to purchase him and bring him home to Beckenham Hall for the rest of his days. I don't know how he did it. . .he still won't tell me. . .but Ingram managed to get Charger, me, and himself home to recover."

"So you're all war veterans. Ingram is devoted to you, wouldn't leave your side when you were ill."

Neither had she, if Ingram was to be believed. Did that mean she was devoted to him, too? Preposterous. No one who had been forced into marriage to a gargoyle like him would ever become devoted, especially not someone as fair as she.

"Your surprise is in the last stall." Gruffness invaded his voice.

She patted Charger once more and turned to the neighboring enclosure. "Oh, my." A dainty black mare with white stockings and a white blaze poked her head over the half door.

"She's for you. Her name's Fleet, but you can change it if you want. Broken to ride and to drive. So you can go into the township whenever you want." William waited, hoping he had pleased her.

"She's beautiful." Jamie turned quickly and put her arms around his neck, hugging him. "I couldn't ask for a better gift. I've never had a horse of my own." Her breath tickled his left ear and made his heart bump hard. Did she know what she was doing? Did she know her mouth was very close to touching the scars that showed just above his collar?

His arm had come around her waist to steady them both, and he quickly moved it, stepping back, swallowing. "I'm glad she pleases you."

"I can't wait to ride her along the beach. With you. When you're strong enough." She folded her hands at her waist, biting her lower lip.

"Why not now?"

The words were out before he realized. Though he rode nearly every day when he was at Beckenham Hall, it was always alone, without even a groom in attendance to stare at his one-handed efforts.

"I'll go and change into riding clothes. If you're sure it won't tax you too much?" She glanced over her shoulder, hurrying down the stable row as if afraid he would change his mind.

Which he should do...but then it was too late. She was gone.

⸎

The ride on the beach was something Jamie would treasure always. William, on Admiral, led the way down the path toward the water, and Jamie, following on Fleet, couldn't take her eyes off his erect carriage and easy way in the saddle. He held the reins in his right hand, his left resting on his thigh.

The sea breeze ruffled his hair, giving him a relaxed, youthful look, reminiscent of her first memories of him, a dashing young officer in red coat and gold braid, with a quick smile and heart-stopping good looks.

But he'd been more than the sum of his outward appearance then, even as he was now. He'd been kind to her, a gangly youth, the hoydenish friend to his little sister, going so far as to take a quick turn around the schoolroom with her when he'd come upon the girls having a dancing lesson.

Being swung around the room in his arms, she'd felt herself falling in love right then and there.

And she still loved him, though he seemed to neither want nor need her love. But if he hadn't, why had he married her?

The beach was a small strip of rough sand that butted up to the downs, dotted with clumps of sea grass. Waves pulsed in and out, as if in time to some giant, buried heart deep off the coast.

Fleet pawed the water, splashing and playing, tossing her dainty head. Jamie laughed and drew her away, patting the horse's neck, delighted with her new mare. Dog whelks and cockles lay in the wet sand, rolling gently with the push of the waves.

"I love hunting for seashells. I once found the most perfect pink scallop shell on this very beach. I still have it."

"Would you like to look for more?" William swung his leg forward over Admiral's neck and dropped to the ground. In two steps he was beside Fleet, reaching up to help her down, when he stopped, looked at his stump of a hand, and stepped back. "Never mind. I think we should be heading back now."

"William?"

"It's getting late, and the tide's on the turn. We'll come back another time." He scrambled ungracefully into his saddle and wheeled Admiral back toward the west and the path up the bank to the stables.

Jamie followed, her heart heavy. Every time it seemed they were making a bit of headway, he remembered his scars and withdrew.

"I'm expecting a delivery today or tomorrow." William looked up from his newspaper. "Something I hope you'll like."

Jamie set her fork on her plate and dabbed her lips with her napkin. She leaned back in her chair and pushed her breakfast plate aside. Galford entered the breakfast room with a tray piled with letters.

"You spoil me already. Are you going to tell me what it is?" She took the mail, nodding to Galford. Over the last several weeks, William had given her many gifts, big things like Fleet, her mare, and small things like a set of silver combs for her hair. It felt as if he were trying to somehow appease her, to make up for something, though she couldn't imagine what that might be. . .unless it was their separate bedrooms, a situation that continued in spite of the truce they had forged during the daytime. Yesterday William had presented her with the Beckenham jewels, opening the safe in his office to show her a diamond and emerald parure, a diamond and pearl tiara, and other lesser pieces.

"The parure is probably a little old for you yet. But you might like this." He removed a necklace from a velvet bag.

Jamie sucked in a breath. "That's beautiful." She fingered the knobby, iridescent beads. "What is it?"

"It's from the South Pacific, a necklace of paua shell. My father took it in trade from a sea captain who had transported prisoners to Botany Bay." He held it up and one-handedly slipped it over her head. "The colors remind me of the sea."

She wore the necklace now, touching the shell beads, rolling them between her fingers as she perused the morning post.

"Polly and Aunt Minty have sent letters. And there is one for you from Viscount Louddon." She handed him the envelope. Taking a hairpin from her hair, she slit the letter from Polly.

"She's certainly busy. An evening at Vauxhall, a literary party, boating on the Serpentine." Jamie laughed. "She says her craft proved seaworthy this time and there was no excitement beyond Lady Averill getting stung by a bee. She claims it's rather a let-down."

William laughed. "It would seem, then, that Polly's claims that it was always you who got her into scrapes is true? She's had a very sedate season since you left London."

"*Hmph*. She did her share of the troublemaking." Jamie scanned the rest of the letter. "It seems Cedric has left London and no one knows where he's gone. Polly hopes wherever it is, he stays away."

Barely glancing up from his letter from the viscount, William nodded. "Good. He was three sheets to the wind the last time I saw him. I don't like to think of him making a nuisance of himself around Crofton House."

"You don't think he would, do you?" Jamie frowned. "He didn't even come to our wedding. I know Polly was worried that he would cause trouble, but after our engagement, I never saw him again." She tucked Polly's letter into the envelope to reread later and opened Aunt Minty's thick missive.

"Oh, dear." Jamie raced through the first page.

"What does your aunt have to say?"

"She's feuding with the administrators of the veterans' hospital, which is nothing new, but it seems they've had enough. She's no longer welcome, not even as a volunteer." Jamie lowered the papers. "Poor Aunt Minty. What will she do? The hospital was her life."

"More to the point, what will the soldiers do? I spent some time in a military hospital, and the lady volunteers were the only bright spot to be had." William drummed his fingers on the tabletop. "Perhaps there is something we can do to help out, though I don't know what."

Affection for him, that he would care about her aunt and for soldiers in need, warmed through Jamie. "Aunt Minty used to take me along with her to help out. I felt as if I traveled in the wake of a hurricane. She would blow through a ward, all business and bluster, but the soul of kindness, too, making sure everyone was warm and clean and fed, bossing the orderlies and maids around. The soldiers called her a tartar, but they loved her. It was the administration that didn't like her. She has bold ideas about how injuries and sickness should be treated, and she wasn't shy about saying so. Aunt Minty isn't one to suffer fools gladly, and she seemed to think most doctors were fools."

"Men don't usually take kindly to being bossed by a woman not their wife." A smile twisted William's lips.

"Does that mean they take kindly to it as long as the woman *is* their wife?" Jamie teased. "That's good to know."

Galford came to the door and cleared his throat. "My lord, a delivery for you has arrived."

"From Scotland?" William rose.

"Yes, my lord. It's waiting out front."

William came around the table and pulled out Jamie's chair as she stood. "Come along." He held out his right elbow, tucking his left hand into his pocket. "Your gift has arrived."

"Something from Scotland? For me? What is it?"

"Come and see."

A rider in a blue-and-green tartan kilt on a tall bay horse waited on the gravel driveway. William led Jamie down the front steps.

"Any trouble?"

"Nay, sir." The rider reached into a bag hanging on the far side of the saddle and drew out a wriggling black and tan bundle. "I took it easy on the wee one all the way. Himself sends his greetings to you and your lady." His Scots burr was almost indecipherable.

William nodded to Jamie. "Go ahead. She's yours."

Jamie clapped her hands, laughing. "You remembered." She stepped forward and took the puppy into her arms, turning her head as the setter lapped at her face and scrabbled to get higher in her embrace.

"You said you always wanted a dog but could never have one. Now you can." William turned to the rider. "Stable your horse. The head groom will see to your lodgings for the night, and Galford here will see you fed." He reached into his pocket and withdrew his money purse, holding it against his waistcoat with his left forearm and digging out several gold coins. "Thank your governor for me."

The Scotsman tucked the coins into his sporran and turned his horse toward the stables.

Jamie set the puppy on the ground, delighted when she waddled toward the steps, nose down, tail wagging. "She's perfect."

"I was looking for a mate and companion for Fergus. I'd like to raise Gordon Setters myself. You'll have to think of a good name for her." William tucked both hands into his pockets, watching Jamie rather than the pup. "Beckenham is already known for its horses. Perhaps we can be known for our kennels, too. It will be quite a legacy."

But a legacy for whom? If they were never truly husband and wife, who would inherit Beckenham Hall and the earldom, the horses, the dogs, the beautiful coastline. . . ?

Perhaps she should approach him about it? But how did one say such a thing? She had no experience in these matters. For all her love of plain speaking, Aunt Minty had never talked with Jamie about her wifely duties other than to say her future husband would know about such matters. Of course, Aunt Minty was a spinster herself with no experience either. If only Jamie had someone she could talk to, someone to give her advice.

In the meantime, she had a sweet new puppy, yet another gift from her husband. He was generous with everything. . .except his heart, the one thing she truly wanted.

Chapter Seven

Wiliam fought his way up from sleep, sweat prickling his skin, his breath coming in gasps. He clawed aside the blankets, sitting up, searching the room. The fireplace grate lay dark and cold. His chest heaved as panic began to recede.

It was the same old nightmare. Fire everywhere, hemming him in, catching his clothes, tearing at him.

He swung his feet over the side of the bed, head hanging low.

Just a dream.

Fergus whined from the rug beside the bed, getting up and shaking himself from nose to tail, padding over to the window, and whining again.

An odd light glowed outside the window. Odd because it was nowhere near sunrise, and the window faced west. William lurched off the bed and drew aside the heavy drapes.

Fire. In the stables!

As quickly as he could, he dressed, stomped into his boots, railing against his useless left hand that slowed him down. He raced for the stairs, nearly colliding with Ingram, who was leaping up the steps to raise the alarm.

"My lord, the stables."

"I'm coming. Rouse the house." William passed him, running outside and down the gravel drive. Fergus shot ahead, circling back as if to hurry his master, barking and racing away again.

Fire.

William's worst fear, his deadliest enemy.

Smoke stung his eyes, and flames shot out of the windows in the south half of the stables. Dark figures ran through the billows of smoke, leading horses out of the blaze... his grooms and stable lads. Horses ran and squealed loose in the stable yard.

One by one, men plunged through the smoke-filled doorway, but William froze, unable to enter, unable to help them, paralyzed with fear. Heat gusted, flames crackled, horses screamed, and in an instant, he was back on the battlefield, burning, burning, burning...

Footsteps thudded behind William, and he whirled. The household staff, footmen, Galford, Ingram, even the scullery maids, all carrying buckets.

And with them, Jamie, her hair flying behind her, wrapped in a dressing gown. She halted her headlong flight when she saw him, relief pouring over her face. One of the stable lads emerged from the smoke leading Charger, who had his head up, eyes bright. The old war horse was unbothered by the fire and commotion, looking as if he were ready to dash into battle once more.

William knew he should go in there, knew it was his place to help save the horses, but his boots remained rooted to the cobblestones.

Men shouted, dozens of hands carried buckets, beat at flames with sacks and blankets, and plunged again and again into the fire, emerging with frightened horses. Ingram was everywhere, shouting orders. But William couldn't move.

Jamie clutched William's arm.

"Fleet! Where's Fleet?"

"There!" Ingram shouted.

The mare stood in the stable doorway, white ringing her eyes, fighting the groom hauling on her halter. She whinnied, half-reared, breaking free of her handler and disappearing back into the flames. The groom fell to the ground and scrambled back up, but before he could go after her, Jamie passed him, running after her horse.

"Jamie, no!" William's heart shot into his throat and then started a rapid descent. She disappeared into the smoke, and without thinking, William went after her, shrugging off Ingram's restraining grasp as he went by.

Flames raced up the walls and overhead, heat pressing in on all sides. Smoke seared his eyes and scorched his lungs. "Jamie!"

No answer. None that he could hear above the roaring of the flames and the thundering of his heart. He crouched, working his way along the row of stalls, sweeping his right hand in front of himself, hoping to feel her dressing gown or hair if she had collapsed.

A hand reached through the darkness and grabbed his shoulder.

Ingram.

"Go down that side," William shouted, pointing to the stalls on the left. "I'll take this one!"

Ahead of them, a horse screamed. Out of the smoke and eerie orange light, Fleet rose on her hind legs, thrashing the air. Jamie lay in a crumpled heap on the ground under the mare's feet.

"Get the horse!" William ducked the flailing hooves and grabbed Jamie's dressing gown. Awkwardly, he hauled her up, slung her over his shoulder, and started back the way he had come. All around him, flames hissed, popped, roared, and crackled. His left arm and side burned, ever-sensitive to heat. He could barely see for the tears scalding his eyes, and his chest begged for air.

Was she dead? Had she succumbed to the smoke, or had she been injured by one of Fleet's flailing hooves? His shoulder cracked against a post, sending him reeling. He barely managed to keep his feet.

Lord, help me find the door.

It was the first time he had prayed in a long time. The first time since praying that

God would let him die in the hospital in Spain.

Just when he thought he would collapse, strong hands reached out and hauled him through the doorway and out into the night air. Someone tried to take Jamie from him, but he wouldn't let go, staggering to the grass away from the fire and gently putting her on the ground. He cradled her against him, and when she began to gasp and cough, he buried his face in her hair.

Thank You, Lord. Thank You, Lord.

"Oh, Jamie, I thought I'd lost you." He kissed her face, brushing the hair back from her temple. "I'm so sorry. It's all my fault. Are you hurt? Tell me you aren't burned." He held her away to check her over and then crushed her to him once more. He forgot himself so much that he reached up with his scarred hand to wipe the tears from her cheek. "If something had happened to you, I don't know if I could've lived with myself." He kissed her forehead, her cheeks, her eyelids, unable to help himself.

For the first time in a long time, he felt like a whole man, capable of facing his fear of fire, capable of protecting his wife. Perhaps capable of letting himself care enough to be vulnerable. . .

He lowered his mouth to hers.

To his utter surprise, she didn't recoil from his touch. Her fingers tunneled into his hair, and she leaned into his embrace, kissing him back.

He forgot the stables, the horses, the fire, the staff looking on. . .everything but his beautiful wife, safe in his arms. . .both his arms.

Fergus bounded into them, lapping, whining, wriggling, trying to burrow between them. Jamie laughed, but shakily, not looking at William. She pushed Fergus back.

"I'm fine, silly boy. Settle down."

Someone cleared his throat. "My lord?"

Ingram.

"We saved all the horses, sir. Some are running loose, but we'll round them up in the morning."

"Is anyone hurt?" William's gaze went up to where flames now engulfed the clock tower and cupola on the stables. The roof would collapse soon.

"None of ours, my lord, but Jennings caught the culprit who set the fire. It's your cousin, Cedric, my lord. Jennings saw him sneaking out of the stables just before the fire broke out."

William forced himself up and drew Jamie with him. Cedric. Familiar with the stables from his many visits to Beckenham Hall. . .and furious with William for taking Jamie away from him.

Jennings, William's burly coachman, had Cedric by the nape of the neck. His cousin had a bloody nose and ripped clothing, and a generally put-upon air.

"Caught him red-handed, my lord. Boasted about it, he did. That's when I planted him a facer and roped him to the paddock fence while I went back for the horses." Jennings gave Cedric a shake.

"Send for the constable, Ingram."

"Serves you right, losing your stables. Too bad you weren't in them!" Cedric shouted. "You're a freak, a disgrace. You should've died in Spain. You had to bribe someone to even marry you!"

Jennings buried his fist in Cedric's midsection, doubling him over and silencing him. "Sorry about that, gov'nor. I'll take him away."

Mrs. Crump bustled over, her hair in a nightcap, a shawl around her shoulders. "My lady, come away to the house. You must be nearly overcome." She fussed, motherly and concerned, and Jamie's horrified shock at Cedric's words turned into a bemused look. Her expression seemed to say, "Is this the same housekeeper who intimidated me so recently?"

"Go ahead. There's nothing to be done here." Cedric's taunts sent icy shafts through William, stirring the ever-ready self-doubts to action.

She had kissed him. Was it just reaction to nearly dying? Was it duty?

He sighed and jammed his fingers through his hair. There was too much to do—the fire to put out, horses to round up, his cousin to deal with. He'd have to do something about Jamie, but it would have to wait.

Jamie stroked the puppy in her lap, staring out the window. She sat in the oriel window of the upstairs sitting room, looking out at the sea, but not really taking it in.

She no longer smelled of smoke, thanks to a bath and Mrs. Crump thoroughly scrubbing her hair. She'd been cosseted, fed, fussed over, and made much of until she could hardly stand it. The housekeeper wanted to relive every second of the fire, her anguish at seeing the master and missus disappear into the flames, and the agony of waiting for them to re-emerge.

Jamie had finally sent the woman to her room to rest.

The setter puppy—Jamie decided to name her Ailith, from the Gaelic for "ray of sunshine"—slept in a warm ball, tummy full and tired out from a run in the back garden with the bootboy.

William had returned to the house an hour ago.

He had saved her life. He had braved his biggest fear. He had kissed her senseless.

She touched her lips, remembering.

The door opened, and her husband, clean, freshly shaven, with hair still damp, came in. Jamie transferred Ailith to the seat cushion and stood.

"You are well?" he asked.

"Yes. And you?" She looked for any signs of ill effects from the fire.

"Fine. All the horses have been found, the fire is out, and the constable has come for Cedric. He'll be brought before the magistrate tomorrow. Jennings and I will testify. You won't have to see him again."

She nodded. Would William mention the kiss? He was so stiff and formal now, she could almost believe it had never happened.

"I owe you an apology." He tucked his left hand into his pocket and paced the rug in front of the settee.

He was apologizing for the kiss?

"Why?" If he was going to be so ridiculous as to apologize for kissing his wife, then he was going to have to say it out loud. She was tired of not speaking plainly. After almost losing her life and her husband last night, she had decided there would be no more shilly-shallying. She gripped her hands at her waist.

"I am sorry you were forced into marriage with me. If I hadn't pressured your father into pressuring you, you would have been safe in London last night, and you wouldn't be tied to the likes of me." He moved his left elbow.

Jamie's hands went limp at her sides. "You think I was coerced into marrying you? Is that what Cedric meant by saying you had to bribe someone to marry you?"

"Why else would you have consented?" His lips were stiff, and he didn't meet her eyes.

"Have you ever considered for a moment that I said yes to your proposal because I've been in love with you since I was a girl?"

His brows came down.

"It's true. My father didn't pressure me. He said the decision was totally up to me. Father would never force me to marry anyone; in fact, he wasn't in favor of me becoming engaged so quickly, when there were bound to be other offers before the end of the season." She crossed the rug and took him by the elbows. "Why would you think I had to be forced? If anything, my heart was breaking because you barely seemed to notice me."

She gave him a little shake, forcing him to look at her, knowing she had to convince him. "I don't know why you persist in thinking that you are somehow unlovable. William Crofton, you are kind and intelligent and witty. You're gentle and knowledgeable about your horses and dogs. You are generous to a fault, spoiling me with gifts every time I turn around. You're a wonderful leader and manager. Beckenham Estates runs beautifully, the staff adores you, and the man who knows you best, Ingram, can't say enough good things about you. Not to mention, you're the bravest man I ever met. A war hero, no less."

His jaw tightened as his eyes bored into hers. "What about. . . ?" He withdrew his left hand from his pocket.

"What about it?" She took the gloved stump into both her hands. "I'm not saying I don't wish you hadn't had to go through such pain, but William, these scars don't make me love you less. In fact, I think such marks of valor only make me love you more." She bent her head and kissed his hand.

"You really love me?" Wariness guarded his expression.

"I have for ages." Her heart beat hard in her chest. "If you only knew how I waited for your letters to Polly when we were girls, how I treasured every note of greeting you put in them for me. Polly let me keep the letters, and I've read them so many times, I am surprised there's any ink left at all. When you became engaged to Mirabelle Matins,

I thought my life was over. And when you were wounded. . .I cried and prayed for you every night."

When he said nothing, she boldly slipped her arms around him, resting her cheek on his chest. "William, you might think it a girlish fantasy, but it's not. I knew it the moment you pulled us out of the water in St. James' Park, and when we had supper together at my debut ball, and when I first met Fergus, and when we said our vows. . . . I'm not a child any longer, and I know my own mind. I married you of my own free will because I love you. I can only hope that someday you might come to love me."

He rested his chin on her hair, his right arm tight around her. "I guess that explains why your father has never taken the money I offered in exchange for his influence on you."

She pulled back to look up at him. "You didn't. I thought Cedric was lying."

He tucked her in tight against him again. "Jamie, I was a desperate man. I had been told by none less than my former fiancée that no woman would ever want to marry someone as disfigured as me. I had determined I would not ever marry, even though my mother was pushing hard, even though I was falling in love with you. Then Polly begged me to offer for you, to keep you safe from Cedric, and I thought I would be noble and see to it your reputation was unsullied."

"So you married me because you are chivalrous?" It made sense, but her heart lay like a stone.

"That's what I told myself. But it was a lie."

Again she pulled away to look at him. "You aren't chivalrous?"

He smiled. A real smile that reached his eyes and caused deep indentations beside his mouth. "I hope I am, but the reason I married you was that I was hopelessly in love with you. Every time you look at me, it's like a punch to my gut." He brushed back the curl at her temple. "You have the most beautiful eyes. But it's more than your face or form that I love, though that's true, too. It's you. You seem to shine brightly in any company, you're easy to talk to when I forget to be tongue-tied, and you like so many of the same things I do. . .dogs, horses, books. You rarely complain, you run this house with ease, and you fill my thoughts constantly. I'm miserable when we aren't together."

Dared she to hope? He really loved her?

He bent his head, his left arm coming around her waist and his right hand cupping the back of her head, bringing her lips to his. Melting against him, her knees turning to water and her head to a burst of fizzing fireworks, she kissed him back.

"William," she said when she could breathe, "I need you to know that I have never thought of you as less than a man, less than handsome. And when you kiss me. . .I never consider your injuries at all."

Which earned her another kiss.

Epilogue

Six months later

Y"ou're rather brilliant, you know that?" Jamie sank onto the settee beside William in the upstairs sitting room, glad to be off her feet at last. The crackling fire cast orange light over the room, and William stretched his legs out, resting them on the hearth. Fergus and Ailith lay in a furry heap on the rug, inseparable friends once Ailith stopped trying to use Fergus as a chew toy.

"I won't disagree with you," he teased. "But to what are you referring in this instance?"

She squeezed his arm, resting her head on his shoulder for a moment. "Turning a wing of Beckenham Hall into a convalescent hospital for wounded veterans. And bringing Aunt Minty in to run it. She's organizing and directing to her heart's content. We had four new arrivals today."

"That was easy. You were the one who pointed out how much space we had here going to waste." He put his arm around her and kissed the top of her head.

She yawned, covering her mouth and apologizing. She'd been so tired lately. Idly, she fingered the paua shell necklace around her throat. She loved it so much, she rarely took it off.

"Finding a surgeon with experience but open to new ideas and treatments."

"Aunt Minty had as much to do with that as I."

She smiled as he deflected her praise again.

"Designing the new stables so that doors can be managed one-handed?"

"Ingram's the driving force behind that one."

She sat up and jabbed him playfully in the ribs. "You're not taking me seriously."

He laughed, his face relaxed. "I can't. You're giving me too much credit."

"Well, there's one thing for which you alone must take the blame." She resisted when he tried to pull her back into his arms, wanting to see the look on his face.

His brows rose. "And what's that?"

"The fact that, in the spring, I will be a mother. Perhaps to the next Viscount Crofton, heir to the Earl of Beckenham." She pressed her lips together, waiting for his response.

He gripped her upper arm. "What?" His voice was so loud that the dogs both raised their heads. "You're sure?"

Jamie nodded. "The doctor confirmed it today, though I've suspected for a while."

A slow smile spread across William's face, and Jamie thought her heart would burst anew with love for her husband. He pulled her close, kissing her face, hugging her, his eyes bright. "A baby." He shook his head.

She took a deep breath. "I feel as if I'm in a fairy tale. You know, the ones that end, 'And they lived happily ever after'?"

He brought her back against him, resting his hand softly on her abdomen over the place where their child grew. "Except our tale hasn't ended. It's just begun. Jamie ever after." He brushed a kiss on her temple. "Now that has a nice ring to it."

Best-selling, award-winning author **Erica Vetsch** loves Jesus, history, romance, and sports. She's a transplanted Kansan now living in Minnesota, and she married her total opposite and soul mate! When she's not writing fiction, she's planning her next trip to a history museum and cheering on her Kansas Jayhawks and New Zealand All Blacks. You can connect with her on her website at www.ericavetsch.com where you can read about her books and sign up for her newsletter. You can also find her online at https://www.facebook.com/EricaVetschAuthor/ where she spends way too much time!

If You Liked This Book, You'll Also Like...

Seven Brides for Seven Texans Romance Collection

G. W. Hart is tired of waiting for his seven grown sons to marry, and now he may not live long enough to see grandchildren born. So he sets an ultimatum for each son to marry before the end of 1874 or be written out of his will. But can love form on a deadline?

Paperback / 978-1-63409-965-3 / $14.99

The Message in a Bottle Romance Collection

Follow the legacy of a bottle's message as it touches five heroines' lives. An Irish princess, a Scottish story weaver, a post-Colonial nurse, a cotton mill worker, and a maid with amnesia each receive a message from the bottle at just the time when they need their hope restored.

Paperback / 978-1-68322-091-6 / $14.99

The Secret Admirer Romance Collection

Key characters in this historical collection of nine stories are admired—even loved—from a distance. When can love be boldly expressed, and will it be received by love in return? Discover the journey hearts take in these nine romances set between 1865 and 1902.

Paperback / 978-1-68322-175-3 / $14.99

JOIN US ONLINE!

Christian Fiction for Women

Christian Fiction for Women is your online home for the latest in Christian fiction.

Check us out online for:

- Giveaways
- Recipes
- Info about Upcoming Releases
- Book Trailers
- News and More!

Find Christian Fiction for Women at Your Favorite Social Media Site:

 Search "Christian Fiction for Women"

 @fictionforwomen
